THE DARK

The Dark

CLAIRE MULLIGAN

Doubleday Canada

Doubleday Canada and colophon are registered trademarks of Random House of Canada Limited

Library and Archives Canada Cataloguing in Publication

Mulligan, Claire, 1964-
The dark / Claire Mulligan.
Issued also in electronic format.
ISBN 978-0-385-67177-4
I. Title.
PS8626.U443D37 2013   C813'.6   C2012-906561-7

This book is a work of fiction. Names, characters, places and incidents are products of the author's imagination or are used fictitiously. Any resemblance to actual events or locales or persons, living or dead, is entirely coincidental.

Cover and book design: Terri Nimmo
Cover images: Melanie Ezra/Millennium Images, UK; Moggara12/Dreamstime.com

Printed and bound in the United States of America

Published in Canada by Doubleday Canada,
a division of Random House of Canada Limited

www.randomhouse.ca

10 9 8 7 6 5 4 3 2 1

For Gibson, Marlow and Eleanor

PART ONE

"On Monday of this week the famous Fox house at Hydesville again furnished the people something to talk about. It will be remembered that in 1848 modern Spiritualism originated in this house while it was the home of the Fox sisters. At that time it was claimed by the Fox family that the spirit of a peddler who had been murdered and whose remains had been buried in the house wished to communicate to the world through the young Fox sisters, Maggie and Katie Fox. Persistent efforts to find any human bones failed, however, and that fact led many to discredit the demonstrations. Now, after a lapse of more than half a century, the old house has given up its dead."

ARCADIAN WEEKLY GAZETTE

"What is known is that by the winter of '92-'93 Maggie had become critically ill and lay bedridden in a Ninth Street Tenement house. There, a Mrs. Mellon, a non-spiritualist physician of the Medico Legal Society of New York, attended Maggie for several hours a day. 'Mrs. Fox Kane was unable to move a hand or foot,' the physician recalled. 'And yet the knocks were heard now through the wall, now through the ceiling, and again through the floor.'"

Nancy Rubin Stuart,
THE RELUCTANT SPIRITUALIST,
THE LIFE OF MAGGIE FOX

⸺ ⧖ ⸺

CHAPTER I

ROCHESTER DEMOCRAT & CHRONICLE
Wednesday, November 23, 1904

HUMAN BONES DISCOVERED

Children Find Body and Tin Peddler's Box In Collapsed
Cellar Wall of Fox "Spook" House at Hydesville. Find
Corroborates an Old Story. Was a Peddler Murdered?

⸺ ⧖ ⸺

Testimony of Mrs. Alvah June Mellon
of the Medico Society of New York,
December 1904

The bones have been found? Found at long last? I am not
amazed. My patient divined they would be, and by children
yet, bored and full of jack-mischief and playing where they
oughtn't. "Bored children are worse than hobgoblins" was what
she said, and as if she knew this better than anyone.

Bored those children may have been, but also brave to enter that
blighted little Hydesville house, so famed for its hauntings, so long
abandoned by all. Braver yet to continue on down down into the

dark of the cellar keep (or foolish, the line is needle-thin). As like those children wished they had turned back, and then it was too late.

Now, my statement of eleven years ago told only of the astonishing phenomenon that occurred just before my patient's death, of the knocks and patterings, that is, and how they sounded through the walls and ceilings and floor, though my patient, by that time, could move neither hand nor foot.

The brevity of this original statement was unavoidable. I was duty-bound to the Society at the time, as well as to a promise I had made my patient. And, too, I had my own griefs to manage. But now the story of the Fox family can fulfill its course. The bones of the "peddler" have been found, after all, and I am beyond the thick of things. I am, to be frank, an aged step from my own long home, by which I mean it is high time my gratitude were made manifest, for without doubt my patient, though bedridden and deathly-ill, saved my mortal life and my immortal soul, perhaps, to boot.

To begin: On the first day of February '93 I was sent to one of New York's 9th Street tenements from which reports had come of an indigent who, though set on dying, had no one to care for her, nor hear her last words, nor ready her for the last envisioning.

I arrived at the tenement in the fading light of later afternoon and trudged up a good many storeys until so high that even a brass band or a howling mob would become a muddled discord, and I found, at last, the garret. I stood in the vestibule, an Edison bulb crackling over my head, and from that vantage I saw a small woman in a small bed. She wore spectacles and a bedjacket of bishop's blue but no head cap, as if she thought herself impervious to malignant draughts. Her grey-palled hair was neatly braided in two, alike a child's; and her countenance, though drawn and pale, had a pleasing cast. You were once a very pretty creature, I thought then. I should add that she was reading, intently reading by candlelight.

"A reader! So that is what you are."

She looked up with considerable surprise, then regained what I soon learned was her considerable composure. "I *am* a reader, but not a dear one, I assure you," she said, and shut her book and set it hastily aside.

"I was only attempting a little jest," I said. "A little jest often breaks the ice with my indigents."

"And how many have fallen through and perished?" She gave a small and knowing smile, cornered with mischief (I would come to know that smile well).

I did not trouble with a retort, nor could I think of one. Instead I put on my professional airs and hefted my satchel and entered the garret to begin my duty. Now this garret was of the usual garret size and bleakness (though it did have three nicely linked windows) and within it raged the usual garret battle between the chugging heat of the basement furnace and the sweeping draughts of the outside world. For furnishings there was only a slat-back chair and a night table and that small bed, and in the scant light these appeared smudged and leaden, as if rendered with a penny pencil. There was, yes, a bible box on the nightstand, but no wardrobes, nor chests, by which I mean no hiding place for even the smallest mechanical to account for the otherworldly sounds that attended her final hour, and of which I will tell in good time.

"Ah, a whom-ever," she said as I approached.

"A what?"

"A whom-ever. Someone whom I don't wish to know. Or else someone whose name escapes me. But I suppose *you* must have a name or two."

Her manner was flat-out rude, and so I considered a nonce before giving my usual explanation: "I am Mrs. Alvah June Mellon. From the Medico Society. We care for the abandoned, the aged and the dying. And you, I must say, fit all three categories nicely." I took out my notebook and stylus. "To begin, I should need your name."

"But who sent you? How ever did you find me out?"

"The tenement landlord, duck. We're busy about these wretched tenements, as you might guess, and so the landlords know us well." I chanced, then, a look at the tome she had set aside on the bed-clothes. It was *Arctic Explorations in Search of Sir John Franklin 1853, '54, '55* by that Dr. Elisha Kent Kane. The book, though battered as if from constant reading, was beautifully bound and heavy with plates. "I recollect this. It was all the rage in its day. I can't claim I've read it, mind."

"I'd like you to leave now, Mrs. Whom-ever. Or vanish. I'm not particular."

I kept my temper in check, but only with effort. "I was just making a little small talk. A little small talk often helps ease into an acquaintance. Anywise, I've no interest in your silly book. Why must everyone search for the famous when *they're* lost, when *they've* died. It's not as if their lives are worth more. God sees even the fall of a sparrow. Surely He does. Everyone says so . . . everyone." I cleared my throat.

My patient studied me then in much the way a seamstress does when measuring one for a new fit-out. "If everyone says so, then, behold, it must be true."

"And all that searching for him, that Sir Franklin, why it was wasted effort. He and all his men were dead as hobnails by the time that glory-hunting Dr. Kane even started on his expedition. He had no hope of bringing Franklin back from those Arctic wastelands, nor any of Franklin's men."

"Indeed? Well, that 'glory-hunting' Dr. Kane was my husband, no matter what in tunket you've heard. And so if you require a name, then you may have *Mrs*. Kane and none other."

At which I realized just who I had in my care. "You're one of the Fox sisters! From the heyday of all that Spiritualism. The one, yes, the one the papers set up with Dr. Kane. You're a recognizable."

"A *celebrity*, that's the word. Or I was once." She reluctantly admitted herself then to be Margaret Fox Kane, the middle sister of the three. "Ever in the middle between Katie and Leah. And now I am the last."

"The last?" I said. And then I recalled how perhaps five years past there had been a lot of brouha among the Fox sisters three: public accusations and public confessions. Betrayals and recriminations. Reputations assaulted. Familial bonds rent asunder. That sort of thing. "Do not take offense, duck," I continued. "But I think your Spiritualism is all chalk and nonsense. The dead are dead, the living live. And I, for one, would no more ask the dead their opinion than knock on the door of a rich man's estate and demand to partake in his luncheon. Because, really, who can bear to know what the dead think of them?"

She studied me again, all kindness now. She had the most candid brown eyes and gave the sense that if the truth ever escaped her, it was only because she allowed it to do so. "Well, that proves it."

"Proves what?"

"That you're not the angel of death. Nor one of his minions. I was convinced you were when you appeared in the vestibule, all in your black garb and haloed by that sulphurous Edison bulb."

I was fleshy in those days, as I am now, and of good height, and I have this broad pink face from my Irish kin and a mass of crinkled hair, coppered at youth, silvered by then. And I wasn't wearing black. I was wearing my best fit-out of Bismarck brown, and over this I had tied my work apron, which was white as cloud and abulge with on-hand supplies: bromide pills and iodine ointment, bandage wads and catgut ligatures. As well, certainly, a stethoscope and pocket mirror for the gauging of life and breath. And two guides, one on the etiquette of mourning, the other on the etiquette of dying (people may call them whimsical, outmoded tomes all they like, but they do offer succour. I have them even yet), by which I mean I scarcely looked like the angel of death.

"Do I have a scythe?" I demanded. "Am I of the masculine persuasion? Am I gaunt? Boney? Do I have a grim leer?" I was peeved, to be frank, and so I added there were worse things that could visit.

"Oh, the good grief, like what?" my patient asked, and then she laughed. She had a delightful, chortling laugh. Infectious. *We are all part of a universal prank* was what that laugh suggested. I asked then if I might examine her. She said no. I said I would not leave until I did so. "I must. It is for the records," I explained. "The records are ever demanding."

"Are they? Dandy-fine. And then you'll leave me be?"

"Yes," I said. I fetched my medical lamp from its safe compartment in my satchel, lifted the chimney glass, trimmed the wick and lit it with my safety matches, then watched the ingenious mantle grow a steady white light, brighter and cleaner even than the light of day.

"Whatever else have you got in that satchel of yours? A gasolier?"

My satchel, though capacious, could scarcely fit a gasolier, and I told her this fact. I then took up her wrist. I discovered a wiry pulse—indicating ossification of the veins—which, along with her yellowed eyes and tender skin suggested a general failing of the organs due to a long dependence on stimulants and alcohol, exacerbated by a complete uninterest in living. After this brief examination I told her I would be visiting her every afternoon.

"But you said you'd let me be. No. This will not do."

"By which I meant let you be for *today*."

"But I want to be alone when my last comes."

"You can't die alone, duck. It's simply not done." I brought out my notebook again and the pencil and a square of Indian rubber. "Now, I will require names. People to contact for your funeral arrangements, that is. And people to hold vigil and record your last words. They can be the same souls, naturally."

"Ah, but there are no *souls* left to contact," she replied without the least hint of self-pity.

"Come, duck. You can't be all stark alone. Someone must be searching you out. Someone must be praying for you, worrying for you every moment. Someone must long to hear your last words. And as like they're going mad from trying to find you, as like they'll not ever recover from . . . and wish that . . ." I faltered and scrubbed a page with the Indian rubber, as if at some old unwanted wordings. (I own I was thinking of my son just then, and how I never found him on the battlefields of Bull Run, though I searched and searched.)

"Ah, hell and such," my patient muttered, then sighed as if all-resigned.

Surely she is accepting her fate, I thought. But she maintained there was no one. She was the last of the Fox sisters three, the last of the Fox family even, and she was determined, quite determined, to die alone. "And do not even consider seeking assistance from the Spiritualist Society," she added. "I am in bad standing with them. I do not want their interference, any more than I want yours."

I reminded her then (quite firmly, I allow) of that supreme solace: the good death. Of the importance of finding peace with your Maker. Of giving your last words to your loved ones. Of composing your mortal form for its last envisioning. "Oh, I know the good death is going from fashion, as if death *had* fashions like hats or hems, and that some folks wish to die in their sleep and so pass on without a single thought for others, but that is a dreadful habit, and selfish, to boot."

"Well, yes."

"And if there is truly no one, then I will be here for your last. I will record your last words if need be. Such is my duty."

She gave that resigned sigh again. "Dandy-fine. But you must promise not to go to the Spiritualist Society."

"Of course I promise. I cannot gainsay my patients' wishes, even if those wishes are chalk and nonsense. *My* Society is clear, quite clear on this."

"I've no doubt . . . Oh, and you must bring me some medicine, then—Rousseau's brand and a whacking lot of it. "

I took a bottle of Dr. Mongar's laudanum remedy out of my satchel. "Will this suffice?"

She eyed the bottle, all-cheered. "Proclaim the Medico Society sent you all you like. I say you're God-sent."

"Many do," I owned, and poured her a tumbler-full.

"But I should call you Mrs. Mellon."

"That is better than Mrs. Whom-ever."

She chuckled and agreed, then drank down the laudanum with practised ease and set the tumbler on the nightstand just aside her bible box. This bible box, I should mention, was clearly made for a large, family bible. On the lid was a pretty bas-relief carving of entwined lilies.

"That is a handsome item," I said, and indicated the box. "I could read a passage for you. Scriptures are ever a comfort."

"It doesn't hold a bible. I doubt it ever did. Only letters and accounts and clip-outs and other such ephemera." At which she hefted up the box's oddly thick and heavy lid. I had only a glimpse that day of the bible box's contents. (For the records, however, I should mention that she eventually bequeathed the bible box to me, and that I have the box and all its contents in my possession still.)

Now, many of the letters were penned by the immediate Fox family and their friends, such as those reformist-minded Quakers

Amy and Isaac Post, and that infamous newspaperman Horace Greeley. But there was also a pack of love-sopped, demanding letters written to my patient by that Dr. Elisha Kent Kane. These "love letters" of Kane's caused much brouha, more of which I will relate in good time. Also of note was the quantity of newspaper clip-outs, pamphlets, advertisements and endorsements pertaining to the Fox sisters, and a nearly equal quantity of such materials pertaining to one Reverend Chauncey Burr. He was the Fox sisters' very own nemesis, and of him, too, I will relate.

The most important and revelatory papers, I need mention, were those penned by my patient's father, John D. Fox, to his favoured daughter, Leah. These papers are an account of how he deserted his wife and first three children—Leah, David and Maria—and for ten long years. How he was a drunkard who gambled and blasphemed; how he was an all-about failure as a father and husband. How he, to be frank, hung his soul out for the Devil to snatch. And then how and why he returned to his family those ten years later, but as a tee-totalling, God-fearing Methodist (at which juncture he fathered my patient and her sister Katie). John's conversion was all-thanks to one Brother Able, and as I shall tell in good time, that story is the under-stitching of the one at hand.

To resume. My patient shut the bible box and I put it aside for her. The laudanum was grabbing hold and her face taking on a dreamy cast. I was not amazed when, soon enough, she was laying out the past like a bolt of fine, densely patterned cloth and that, like many who are peephole to eternity, the past seemed as the present, the present of no import. Not that I solicited her story. I surely did not, not at first. All of us at the Medico Society know better than to encourage tales of regret and woe. Such tales become a burden. They hamper one's duty and lead to melan-cholic thoughts. At the least they become entwined with one's own interpretations, filtered through one's own imaginings. With Mrs. Kane, however, my curiosity soon overcame these reserva-tions. To explain: My patients often speak of the past, but their purposes vary. Some seek absolution. Some a road to comprehen-sion. Some merely like to hear themselves prattle on. But Mrs.

Kane—or Maggie, as I called her by the end—had a more obscure purpose and this purpose, I came to think, had something to do with my own presence.

I should add that my patient spoke of her younger self as if she were some girl she had known intimately, but who had been a separate person withal. Such is what comes, I thought then, from taking on so many voices, and from making so many mistakes, mistakes that are incomprehensible to one's present self (to this latter fact I can well attest).

"I surely loathed Hydesville," she began. "My younger sister, Katie, and I both did. Hydesville was naught but a crossroads, a hamlet, the forlornest place in the world, we thought, and didn't we just surl like wet cats when our parents moved us there from the lit-up bustle of Rochester. We hated being away from our adored sister Leah, who taught music in Rochester, and from her daughter, Lizzie, who was near our age and ever up for jack-fun, at least at first. This move happened in, yes, the autumn of '47. David, our grown brother, lived in Arcadia, near to Hydesville, and he was doing dandy-fine cultivating peppermint. Our father, John Fox, hoped to do the same. He was a blacksmith by trade but failed-up at near everything he put his hand to."

She paused and reached for the laudanum. I considered, then gave her a measure more. "That Hydesville house," she continued. "It was one of those little saltbox affairs, all damp and dull and ever strewn with little clumps of dank dirt no matter how we cleaned our shoes, to our poor, fretting mother's dismay. It had no near-on neighbours and was quiet and dim as tomb within, even in the broad of day. And it was rumoured to be haunted by a murdered peddler. And here begins Spiritualism, Mrs. Mellon, the whole grand she-bang of it: those rumours of a haunting, two bored and mischievous sisters, an encounter, and a curse."

MAGGIE SHOULD STOP, turn back, but as always she clambers on past caution, clambers higher and higher up this tree that is older than reckoning. Past a hangbird's nest. Past branches sagged with apples of carmine and rose. She clambers as high as she can, up and up, into this azure and gold October day of 1847.

Her sister Katie peers up from below. "Get on down, Mag. You'll break your neck or something."

"But I can see the world from here," Maggie calls back. Maggie is fourteen. Katie is eleven. Their world is the hamlet of Hydesville, which is in the township of Arcadia, in the county of Wayne, in the state of New York. Their world is fields of peppermint, stands of woodlands, lines of drumlins, and the Ganargua River, muddy and mosquito-shrouded.

"Please, Mag! Let's get outta here. The tender's hound is real fierce and we're too far in. I can't see the road no more."

"That doesn't mean it ain't there, silly thing," Maggie calls, as she works her way down. It is a more fraught climb than up. She feels her cheeks flushing red, adding, no doubt, to that "healthful country prettiness" their mother insists she has. A prettiness, Maggie supposes, that must be better than none at all.

She drops to the green. Her pinafore, laden with thieved apples, bangs her knees.

Katie steadies her. And then the murderous barking statues them both. The sound is near, then far. Now everywhere at once.

"Run!" Maggie yells, and grips Katie's hand. Their brogans are slicked with rotting apple pulp and they slip once, stumble twice. Leaves flap at their braids. Quack grass lashes their knees. Brambles tear their stockings, which are already laddered with darning.

Maggie halts her sister in a copse of gnarled trees. For once Maggie is glad they are both smaller statured girls than average. Slips of things, as people say.

"Hold your breath, Kat. Listen."

No hound. Only the dread-quiet of something watching.

Then a peabody cries. A hare darts near.

"Damn-it-all, where's the fence?" Maggie whispers.

"Were it the other way?" Katie whispers back. Tears runnel her pale skin, her thin arched nose. Her eyes are grey or lavender depending on the light and are heavy-lidded, giving the impression of a sleepy nature, except when she is terrified, as now. Now they are as round as marbles.

"Here," Maggie says. "Up! Up! Get up the tree." She stirrups her fingers for Katie. Katie points, rigid. They see him: a teeth-bared, savage-eyed creature, big as a wolf. He is three trees distant and stalking onwards. Katie sobs. Maggie grabs her waist. "Get up. Up!" she yells.

Katie's pinafore is also weighted with apples, hindering her movements. "I can't!" she shouts. Maggie snatches up a fallen, jagged-edged branch and tears after her. They scream in unison as the hound breaks into a loping run. Katie stumbles and falls. Maggie stands over her sister, branch clenched like a spear. Katie prays face down in the grass.

"Damn it! Damn-it-all," Maggie incants. "I hate this place. I hate this place."

A distant whistle sounds. The hound halts. It is so close Maggie can smell its rank hair. Another whistle. The hound snarls and slinks off.

"He's gone, Kat. He's gone." Maggie helps her up. They walk quick, breathing hard, shriven with fear. Finally they reach the split-rail fence. They climb over it and into the dusty ruts of the public road. "We're safe now. Really," Maggie adds.

They keep walking, mind, putting the orchard at a distance. Overhead, geese call out warnings of winter. The woodlands are ablaze with dying leaves. The wind carries the smell of field burn, of something rotting, and now the faint smell of peppermint from the fields abutting the road. In August these fields are said to be oceaned with blossoms of pink. Maggie sniffs and thinks of peppermint sticks and peppermint tonics. The peppermint, she decides, is the one good thing about Hydesville.

From the verge Maggie spies their rented saltbox house, set there in its lonesome pocket of field, black shutters the only embellishment on its squat two storeys. She spies their father's smithy aside the road, the buttery, the necessary, a low stone wall, three balm o' Gileads in a row. A close grouping, small and plain as a doll set. No sign of the wagon or their old dun horse. Their parents must still be in Newark buying supplies for the long wintering-in.

Maggie's heart steadies. Already she is recalling the incident in the orchard as exciting rather than terrifying. Already she is angry at the tender for letting his hound chase them like that. She takes her sister's hand. Katie's face is pale. Her eyes have darkened to slate and her jaw is clenched. Her fingers? They tremble. Ah, no, Maggie thinks. One of Katie's peculiar little fits is coming on. They last only a few moments, these fits. Katie stands rigid, trembling, vacant-eyed; on three occasions she has fallen and drummed her heels. When she does return to herself, she can't recall a thing. "It's as if I plain ole vanish," she has told Maggie.

To distract her sister, to keep her in herself, Maggie stands with arms akimbo and pretends fussed perplexity, pretends, that is, to be their mother. "Now, girls. Girls!" she says in a raised, nervous voice. "What do you mean you hate it here? We'll get rich growing pepper-mint, won't we? Oh, and we've only been here in Hideawayville, I mean Hydesville, for two months. It's not so awfully dull. You've got me and your pa, don't you? And your dear brother, David, and a passel of kin are near enough. And your father is building us a place of our own, isn't he? And we couldn't stay with the Posts for-ever, could we? Oh, and Rochester was so rackety, wasn't it? All those carriages and, oh, all the night lamps made my poor old eyes ache. Here, folks respect the gloaming, don't they? They know it's God's signal to shutter themselves in nice and safe. And can't you just wait for winter. We can all go to bed at four o'clock so's not to waste the candles and rushies. Won't that be a lark!"

Katie's jaw unclenches. Her hand steadies. She giggles, as she always does when Maggie shows off her talent for mimicry. Katie's talent is for eavesdropping; she hears well beyond the ken of others, hears voices in far rooms, hushed conversations below stairs, foot-falls up paths.

"Someone's coming," she says now. The girls turn and see him. The peddler has a pronounced limp and uses a walking stick, and his rucksack bends him at the hips as if he is perpetually bowing. His wears a black cap, a frocked black coat, and grey trousers, and these garments are stiffed with grime and reek of onions and old sweat, damp leaves and dried shit. He is not much taller than Maggie and Katie.

When he reaches them he spits tobacco. Doffs his cap. "Good day to yous," he says.

"Well, yes. Good enough," Maggie answers.

His eyes are gold with a burst of green about the pupil. His face is sun-darkened to the mid of his forehead. Above this line is a pale dome. Maggie imagines it hinging open to show the worm-coils of his brain. Peddlers. Don't they disembowel cats? Thieve babies? Sell cure-alls that cure one of nothing except mortality? Didn't a peddler disappear in the Hydesville area some five or ten years past? Some say his throat was slit for his silver thimbles, others for his five hundred dollars, others for his secret sins upon children. All agree, however, that he is buried in the cellar of a house near on. Mayhap in our very own cellar, Maggie thinks, and nearly smiles. Wouldn't that be quaint. Wouldn't that just explain why the place gives me the willies. Why, I'd bolt in a shot given the half the darned chance.

"Something pretty for yous pretty girls?" this peddler now asks. "I's got perfume sachets and rose-essence. I's got broaches and pocket combs. I's got shaker's yarb and castor ile and bitters for the ague. I's got shadow puppets and baby's whistles. I's got delaine lengths and needle sheaves and I's got silk thread near invisible and strong as wire, I swear."

The girls shake their heads. The peddler wearily nods and trudges on past them. He is not a rod distant when Maggie looks at Katie. She wants to cheer her sister further, that's all, and so she composes a rhyme on the spot: "*Peddler man, Peddler man with all your wares. We'll give you a gaffe, if you don't beware. We'll salt you and pickle you and chop you up to keep. We'll throttle you and bottle you and put you in our cellar deep.*" Maggie smiles, proud of this quick contrive.

The peddler turns and sputters. He raises a fist. "Throttle me? I'll throttle you, you little bitches! Apologize, damn you."

He limps back towards them. The girls' shrieks are edged with laughter. They turn to run. He fumbles at his trousers. "Get on back here. I'll give you a gaffe and right in your nasty hinnies!"

"Don't you look, Kat," Maggie orders. She knows they should just run, but she is aburn with fury, abuzz with a curious elation. She hauls an apple out of her pinafore. "Horrid ole pig!"

The first shot lands square on his chest. He staggers, unbalanced by his rucksack.

Katie glances at Maggie. "Nasty, lousy man!" she yells, and hurls an apple of her own. It strikes his shoulder. He yelps and curses. Now the girls hurl apples fast as ever they can. One sends his cap flying clear off his head. The peddler tips backwards, his huge rucksack beneath him, his feet and arms waving in the air. He looks, in all, like a helpless beetle on its back.

Maggie advances on him; Katie yanks on her pinafore strings. "Don't keep on. We gotta go. Let the ole nasty be."

But Maggie is not finished. She thinks of their eldest sister Leah, and of the day she accompanied her to a Rochester bank and witnessed with awed delight as the clerk shrank under Leah's imperious gaze, then admitted that, yes, he must have been the one who miscounted, that he, certainly, was the sorry one. And that, by all means, he would never cheat a lady who had such a sickly daughter, at which Maggie had obligingly coughed and groaned.

Did Leah back down? Did Leah let it be?

Nope, Maggie thinks, and kneels beside the peddler.

"Apologize, damn you," the peddler says.

Maggie sees it then—his member, his prick, worming out of his pants.

"Never, never, never," Maggie chants, and picks up his fallen cap. Only now does she grab Katie's arm. They race down the verge towards their saltbox house, hardly imagining the peddler would limp-limp after them, following them as if determined to do so all his living days.

"You'll die alone and ranting for your lies, you hoyden bitches" is what he says a short time later, when he reaches the foreyard.

But the girls, all locked inside that little house, only laugh to beat the band.

CHAPTER 2.

"It was a curse, Mrs. Mellon, what that peddler said. A curse that's come to pass."

"What chalk and nonsense. Are you alone? Am I a figment? A patch of thought? And are you ranting? No, duck, you are completely yourself."

"Completely myself? That'd be a first since the beginning-of-it-all."

"I suppose you'll next be telling me what happened to that peddler, once he caught up with you."

"Why, we chopped him up and buried him in the cellar, just as we threatened. Why-ever not?"

"Oh, you are a one."

My patient agreed, then asked, "Do you believe in ghosts, Mrs. Mellon?"

"The hour! I am amazed. I'd not realized it was so late. I'll leave you the lamp. Turn it down here, the mantle-gauze lets it burn steady and for a good length of time."

"But my question. Spirits. Ghosts. The Invisibles. Do you believe?"

"I believe in draughts, which are likewise unseen, but which cause more grief than any ghost. And you with no head cap. Do you think yourself exempt from their influence? Do you wish to hasten your demise?"

She touched her bare braids. "No, not now."

"Then I'll be sure to bring you a proper cap next time as protection against them."

"That'd be sterling, thank you."

"Ah, and I'll bring spoon victuals as well. There's some measure of life left in you yet."

"Yards of it, I'm sure. But my question, again. Ghosts."

I was too busy with packing up my satchel to answer straight-aways. She was patient, however, this perplexing patient of mine.

"Do I have a choice, duck? At my age? In my occupation?"

"Your occupation? As a physician, you mean?"

"What else?" I asked, and snapped my satchel shut.

On my second visit to Mrs. Kane I brought spoon victuals and a nightcap, as promised. The cap was a simple one of white muslin that suited, I thought, her elegant bed jacket of bishop's blue.

She thanked me quite kindly, then swallowed down a good quantity of arrowroot pudding and of beef tea, to boot. (I had insisted she eat before taking her medicine.)

"You did not explain what happened to the peddler," I said at length.

"The good grief, didn't I?"

"No, duck."

"He would have been forgotten, understand. Katie and I would have been forgotten too. We would been ordinary girls who had once heard an ordinary ghost. We would have had run-of-the-mill, uncharted lives. But then Leah arrived from Rochester." She chortled. "Leah Fox Fish Brown Underhill. My eldest sister collected names the way a squirrel collects nuts. I was ever mired in ambivalence about her. Oh, but you should search out her memoir, Mrs. Mellon. She had it ghost-written, as it were, later in her life. *The Missing Link in Modern Spiritualism*, that's the title. If ever you read it, do so with a pot of salt, no, a bucket."

"Surely, but for now you might as well tell me what she discovered, your Leah," I said, not noticing then how my patient, the sly creature, had evaded my question about the peddler and his true fate.

⁂

LEAH FOX FISH—stately mannered, tragic eyed—holds fast as the hired buggy lurches in the ruts. The driver looks down at her. "Those are your people? At the spook house? I thought you was a gawker. Been naught but gawking and old-hen chatter about that peddler's ghost knocking about the saltbox, and how he got his throat slashed with a butcher knife, and how his ghost is claiming that he's buried in the cellar. The gossips are on and on about how that cellar's been dug up in spades, but naught a bone's turned up yet." He shakes his head, his tobacco spittle just missing Leah's cloak. "So those are your people," he says again. "Lord help ya."

I suspect the Lord is otherwise occupied, Leah thinks. Says for the driver, "Yes, *my* people, indeed."

"Some of those gossipers are even saying it's all an April Fool's joke, seeing as the ghost started knocking on the 31st of March. Close enough, wouldn't you bet, ma'am?"

"I do not bet, sir, nor gossip and, oh, my heavens, do mind your horses, if you please."

The driver obliges with a touch to his slouch hat, a crack to his whip. The two horses, piebald and ancient, do not change their pace, not even when a wolfish dog leaps across the road. Eleventh of April of 1848 and yet the drumlins are scrimmed with snow, the Hyde's orchard scrawled with bare limbs, the crocuses curled underground. Even the dark has not retreated. The sun seems the same pale smudge as in midwinter, the days just as short. The world is entirely out of tempo, Leah decides, and at this a raw wind snatches at a chestnut curl. She ties her bonnet tighter, her hands made clumsy by thick gloves. They must be cared for, her hands; she teaches piano to the children of Rochester's tony set. It is her sole means of survival since Bowman Fish, the charlatan, deserted her with a wailing babe and fifteen summers to her name.

A crow walks atop the buggy's hood. Mimics the rattle of the harness. The driver hacks and coughs as if to bring up a lung. Of a sudden Leah feels very much alone. Her dear friend Addy Granger was to accompany her to Hydesville, but she left off at Newark citing the vapours and the possibility of demons. And Leah's daughter, Lizzie, though she so wanted to come, would not have been a suitable companion. The girl is still prone to outbursts at age seventeen and Leah cannot have distractions if she is to deal with the strange events at hand. And thus Leah is on her own. As always. Never in all her thirty-two years has she begged help of anyone.

The carriage reaches the saltbox house under a fore-noon sky that is laddered with clouds, hung with birds. Leah half stands in the buggy. Clenches a fist to her heart. The house is abandoned, that much is evident even from this distance. The chimney is dead, the windows shuttered, the yard stilled of chickens and hogs.

"I wager the ghost ran 'em off with some new terror," the driver suggests.

Leah steps out, not waiting for his hand. The ground bears the impress of boots, patens, clogs. A barrow is upset. A portion of a rock wall is in rubble. There must have been a hasty departure, then, as if the inhabitants feared the coming of the plague and not just the visitation of a ghost.

"Will you attend me?" she asks the driver, keeping her voice low, melodious and warm. "Sure, sure, ma'am," the driver says, hefting out the feedbags. "Just got to tend the nags, they're particular. Yup, they are."

"When you're done, then," Leah says graciously, and wills up bravery and heads round the back of the house on her own. Her imagination reaches ahead, shows her mother, father, her two young sisters, mysteriously, horribly dead.

But no. Nothing. No bloodstains even. She hears a squirrel chattering on the roof of the buttery, the wind soughing in the three balm o' Gileads aside the road. And then a groan. Leah whirls just as the handle of the water pump shifts itself; it makes the same groaning—and yes, of course—mechanical sound. Water drip-drips onto the pebbles below.

From the side of the house she calls, "I cannot wait a moment longer, sir!"

At this the driver gestures helplessly to his horses as if, Leah thinks, they are holding him up in conversation. "My Lord, must I do everything my own self," she mutters, and hefts her skirts, then pats under her mother's collection of "curiosity" stones that serve as a border to the herb garden. The stones are of variant shapes and hues. Some bear the imprints of leaves, others of small and fragile bones. Leah tips over a particularly black and heavy stone. The key is there. She works it into the padlock of the buttery. Pokes the door open. Steps within. Claps her mouth to stay a shriek. The shed reeks of death. Ah, only a mouse, only a mouse; there, rotting in that basin. She berates her foolishness, walks in briskly, nearly slips on a trail of clumpy dirt. The dirt is a troubling sign: her mother would never willingly leave such a mess. She passes through the cramped scullery into the kitchen and checks inside the stove. The ash looks several days old.

Into the front room. There is not a lick of furniture. The walls show a few pale squares where the lithographs hung. The shutters are seamed with light, the window latches snagged with grey threads where, perhaps, her parents' old horsehair settee was dragged off. She turns in the room, once, twice. Without the furnishings the room looks smaller, not larger, as one might expect. She hurries out and up the narrow, creaking stair. The single upper room is empty. Her parents slept in that corner. Margaretta and Katherina there, on a trundle bed.

Leah shudders. The room is dark and cold and dim even at this early hour, but there is nothing of note.

The cellar. Leah cannot delay any longer. She must see for herself this peddler's grave.

She finds a candle stub in the kitchen. Pries the wick out of the stiffened wax and fires it with a pocket lucifer. The cellar door opens at a touch, as if she has been expected, invited.

"Keep on," she murmurs, and steps down. She trails her hand for purchase—there is no railing—and her gloves are soon dirtied and damp, her skirt flaked with stone. She descends the last stair into a space fit for troglodytes. The earthen walls bulge and curve, have stains the size of bears. The air is dank and loamy, the light a murky stain. Something snatches at her bonnet. She yelps, then swats at the wire hanging from the low, planked ceiling. She breathes heavily, then wills herself calm and sidles over to the hatchaway doors. Hefts them open. The pallid light shows a shelf empty of apples and preserves, a trough empty of brine barrels and lime pots. Shows the crumbling foundation at the cellar's far wall. And the deep dug holes. Six, no, seven in total. Two are planked over. The others are filled with muddied water. Aside one hole is a pile of animal bones, rabbit by the looks of them. Aside another are fragments of pottery. Leah has heard that if one digs deep enough something will always be found: bones of starved colonists, Indian graves, animals from Noah's flood. But not a murdered peddler, apparently. They have been reckless, she thinks. Anyone might have fallen in and drowned. Even I might have.

Footsteps sound overhead. Leah stills.

"Ma'am? You there?"

She hurries up. The driver is looking round the kitchen, committing everything to memory for later telling, no doubt. He stuffs a tobacco twist into his gums.

"Sir, you will not spit in here. That is, I surely hope you do not."

"No, 'course not. Everything tickety-tock? Anything happen? You find anything? That I can help with, I mean."

"Nothing, though I feared what I would find. Alone as I was. Ah, a moment . . . There," she says, and presses a hand to her chest.

The driver mutters an apology. Mentions a bad leg, his skittish horses.

"Never fret. However, I must carry on to the house of my brother, Mr. David Fox. He lives no more than three miles from here. That is where my people must have sought safety. That is, if they still live. Oh . . . another moment . . . There. Sir, I must ask. Need the price be more? I am stretched in the purse since all this fearful business began. Surely a man such as yourself . . ." She pauses and steps to the exact acceptable distance from him. She is not pretty, Leah knows this. Her features are not dainty-cut enough. She is arresting, however, when she smiles just so. When she shows the white teeth she need never hide behind a fan, the dimples like little scimitars. When she gazes at the beheld as if they are the world entire.

"'Course, 'course. No more particular payment necessary, ma'am, I'd be honoured to take you to your own kin or anywheres else."

Leah settles in the wagon. When she first heard tell of the haunt-ings of, yes, her own kin she had been in the midst of her music lesson to the daughters of a well-to-do printer, one Mr. William Little. She had been listening disenchanted as Mary . . . or was it Georgina? As one of them, anywise, plunked at the piano and sang "Rouse Thee, Child of Heaven" as if it were a happy song about picnics and maypoles and not a hymn about a child's lingering death. Just then Mr. Little rushed in with proofs for this very pamphlet, his face astounded. "Is your mother's name Margaret? Have you a brother David? And your father? He is Mr. John Fox, is he not?"

Leah can scarcely recall what she replied, what with seeing her family's name so emblazoned, what with Mr. Little reading aloud in a voice of rising incredulity, and then Mrs. Little joining them and voic-ing certainty that Leah would collapse in a nervous faint, what with the Littles' little girls hopping with delight at the drama, at being excused from their lessons, as any girl, rich or poor, might.

Leah now reaches under her cloak and opens her reticule and takes out this same pamphlet: *A Report of the Mysterious Noises Heard in the House of Mr. John D. Fox, in Hydesville, Arcadia, Wayne, Authenticated by the Certificates, and Confirmed by the Statements of the Citizens of That Place and Vicinity*, by E.E. Lewis. The pamphlet is forty pages long, as the citizens of Arcadia have much to tell. They recall that a murdered peddler has been knocking about for years in that saltbox house, even when it was inhabited by other families, the Bells, the Weekmans. Ghostly footsteps were heard in the buttery. A dog howled like rabid under a window. A child woke in terror night after night. A ghost, likely the peddler's, appeared before a horrified maid as a shadow-form. But the peddler was also seen alive, just before the hauntings. Mrs. Bell admired his fine thimbles and wares, so stated their day-girl, Lucretia Pulver. Not long after the peddler's visit Lucretia saw Mr. Bell carting dirt out of the cellar. "The place was infested with rats and moles" was what Mr. Bell said. The Bells moved soon after, their debts suspiciously cleared.

Leah tucks the pamphlet back into her reticule. The pamphlet reads, she thinks, like an elaborate game of whisper-down-the-lane. But why did none of Leah's family give a statement? And why did they not send word for her to come straightaway? Why did she need hear about these events from a public pamphlet? Surely her family knows she is the only one with the wherewithall to sort it all out.

Leah looks up. The wagon is trundling past the red schoolhouse her young sisters attend, though Margaretta, at near to fifteen, must be too old for schooling. She will be married off soon, poor creature. Leah closes her eyes. Never mind ghosts, she must warn Margaretta against the likes of Bowman Fish, who courted Leah with a talking bird and a mouthful of romantic prattle. Leah's mother muttered some opposition—Fish had a good twenty years on Leah—but hardly roused herself to stop the union. That should have been her father's task. John Fox, however, was in the middle of his decade-long vanishing act punctuated only with the occasional note to let his family know he was not boxed and planted. When he at last returned he offered Leah no explanation for his abandonment. No apology. He would only say he had been working on the canals and had found God and sobriety through hard aspects. Once, however, Leah had heard him mutter something most peculiar. He had been napping at the time. "I'll keep my promise to you, Brother Able, by God, I will" was what she heard, though her father refused to explain what this meant when he woke to Leah's prodding and questions.

Naturally, Leah had applauded her father's piety, whoever or whatever compelled it—as had her mother and her siblings David and Maria—who wouldn't? She had been astonished, however, at the arrival of her sisters Margaretta and Katherina. She had thought her parents past all that. Bowman was gone by the time her younger sisters were born, had shown his true colours just after Leah gave birth to Lizzie. He is now married to some woman in Illinois, having forgotten somehow that he is married already.

Leah hears the monotonous thud of a mill. Sees the Ganargua River glinting through a leafless tangle. A drowned little girl haunts that river. She wails and sobs, her face white as river stones. The crossroads of Hydesville are haunted also, as most crossroads are, by a suicide buried there. He makes the horses shy and bolt. And is there not an Indian who appears behind one in a looking glass? He augers misfortune. Or is it death? Well, the two, Leah supposes, are much the same.

The driver begins whistling a cheery tune. And in key. Ah, but then they *are* passing a graveyard, aside which is a small Methodist church, the one Leah's own family attends. Leah tips her head. Sees a rivet of amaranthus as the driver hits a high C. Only a few notes conjure colours for her now. B flat is a nacreous blue. D is lampblack. C this lovely amaranthus. F an egg-yolk yellow. When Leah was young, however, every note conjured a unique and dazzling colour, making each a snap to identify. It was her mother's parents, the Rutans, who recognized Leah's extraordinary musical talents—her perfect pitch, her gift for improvisation and elaboration, her mastery of timing and tone. "How extraordinary you are, Leah. Why you can sing any tune at all!" they often said (though Leah never told them, nor anyone about the colours). These compliments began when Leah, along with her mother and David and Maria, moved to the home of the Rutans in Consecon, Ontario. They had had no choice but to move—John Fox had left the family destitute—but the move proved advantageous for Leah. Her Rutan grandparents lavished music lessons upon her, after all, and convinced her that she could grace concert halls across North America, even Europe, if only she practised enough. And Leah might have had such an illustrious "career" if not for her wretched marriage, the too-soon arrival of Lizzie, after which the colours of the notes began to fade and become, she has realized, as they are for ordinary people.

On consideration Leah realizes it is hardly surprising this "ghost" has visited her family. Did not Grandma Rutan rise at night and follow premonitory funerals to the graveyard? Come morning, she would describe the procession in detail, often faulting the mourners' attire. And what of Leah's Aunt Beth? She dreamed the correct date of her death. Saw it carved on her tombstone and died to the day and year. Do I believe in such things? Leah wonders. Decides she does. After all, there is so much one must believe; another thing scarcely signifies.

Once the graveyard is behind them, the driver ceases whistling. He is a charming whistler, though Leah thinks it a pathetic superstition that a cheery tune would be enough to keep the dead at bay.

At last David's farmstead comes into view. It is a whitewashed, rambling place with three outbuildings and what looks to be stakings for a fourth. A giant oak is the only tree on the property. The fore-yard is crowded with wagons and buckalls, even a brougham, a landau. The buggy draws up. The ancient piebalds drop their heads. Leah sees three strangers, all men, tromp into the house. At a short distance, David's two boys and some others play at mumblety-peg. They laugh and yelp as the knife, balanced on a boy's fingertip, falls and nearly skewers their feet. Such is what passes for entertainment in the countryside, Leah thinks, this nearly losing a thumb or a toe, nearly gashing a thigh, the horrified delight of it all. They will take up gander-pulling next. As a child Leah played mumblety-peg too, of course, though she had always insisted on a few simple rules before she did so.

She alights from the buggy.

"I guess I could stay on, ma'am," the driver suggests. "Wouldn't mind staying on, in fact, out of naught but a practical curiosity, 'course."

"Why? To gawk? As if my family were an organ-grinder's dancing monkey?" She is more abrupt than she intends, and so she adds with her dimpled smile, "Forgive me, I am close to fainting in exhaustion. Many thanks for your assistance. I shall send for you if you are needed."

She lets herself into the back hall. Hangs her cloak and bonnet on the peg-rail. Doesn't halloo. There is nothing wrong with a quiet entrance. Anywise, with the low din emanating from the keeping room she would not be heard. She pauses in the shadows aside the entry. The keeping room is crammed with perhaps twenty souls, all speaking with contained excitement. For this occasion of uncertain etiquette some folk are sombrely dressed, as if for a wake; others are in their going-out clothes. At least Leah will not be out of place in her one good day-dress with its subdued stripes of butternut and madder red. The sleeves are slashed to show a clean white. Her collar starched and spotless.

The men clumped about the trestle-table with its jugs of cider and platters of food are concerned, as ever, Leah thinks, about their manly appetites. The women form a gaggle around Leah's mother, Margaret, who sits on the hearth stool and worries at the flaps of her old-style lappet cap. Mother is ashen-haired and pigeon-chested, that is to say, the very picture of a settled matron. She is voicing, at the moment, her sentiments on the ghostly horrors, and the alarming effect of it all on her health. "And I haven't slept a jot, have I? And, oh, how my old eyes ache and tear, as if filled with sand granules. I've used my eyestone thrice, haven't I, but still they ache so." She dabs her eyes with her handkerchief. Leah has ever been slightly disconcerted by her mother's eyes, they being of such a pale aqueous blue one can practically see her thoughts swimming by. Not that one need look for them; Mother will readily proclaim her thoughts to all who care to hear, and to many who do not.

Just behind Mother stands Leah's grown sister, Maria, nicknamed "the wall" by Leah's younger sisters, Margaretta and Katherina. It is a fitting nickname, Leah thinks, given Maria's brick-red complexion, her square figure and rigid posture. Maria's husband, Stephan, is also in attendance, as is their youngest child, Ella—a sweet-faced creature, all eyes and all of four. She is a favourite of Margaretta and Katherina, Leah recalls.

Leah now searches out her brother, David. Easily done. He towers over everyone. Looks alike a benevolent giant in a fairy book with his flaxen hair and heavy limbs, his genial face. His wife, Beth, bustles up to him with a mug. She is a bustler through and through, is plump and short with coppery curls and a cheery face. And why should she not be cheery? Her home is a fine one, even for the country. The chairs are upholstered, the floors laid with rugs, the walls papered, the candles all of beeswax. Davey must be profiting well from peppermint, Leah thinks, not for the first time. She adjusts her stance. Sees David conferring with the same three men she saw entering. They wear their coats still, their hats. The men look around, appraising, angered, then leave by the foredoor. The hazel nailed over the lintel trembles. Hazel, Leah recalls, is protection against evil spirits and must be her mother's idea. It is surely not her father's. And where is her father? She peers here and there, but he is nowhere in sight. Not that he ever has much to say to her or to anyone.

A calm, obliging expression is best, Leah decides, and forms her features accordingly before she steps into the keeping room.

CHAPTER 3

On my third visit, Mrs. Kane reached for the tumbler of laudanum even before I had finished pouring. "That is a scanty amount," she complained.

"It is sufficient. I have measured exactly for your size and level of habituation, which, I must say, is prodigiously high."

"Well, yes."

"I should add that you fell asleep whilst talking away."

"And did you watch over me while I slept? Is that part and parcel of your duty?"

"No, duck. I have better ways to apply my time." If her tone had held less challenge I might have told her the truth: that I *had* watched her, and for an hour or so, but only because she had a peaceful presence, unlike a good many of my patients, who tussle with fate until the last hours.

"Well, Katie and I were watching, but then we were watchful girls for all our giggling."

"Watching who? Whom?"

"Leah, of course, as she stood in the hallway of David's house and spied out the keeping room. We were contriving a game out of eavesdropping, and out of discerning words from lips alone. Katie was already very good at the former, and both of us became, in time, crackerjacks at the latter."

⟨⟩

"Leah's arrived," Maggie whispers to Katie. "But whatever is she doing? She's just standing there in the hall like some statuary."

The girls are peering through the balustrades on the second-floor landing. They are supposed to be resting. "All this excitement will flay your poor nerves," their mother warned Maggie. Maggie hadn't argued, for now she and Katie can sleep till noon if they choose. Now they have attention galore. The run of brother David's charming home.

"Is Lizzie with her, Mag? I don't see her."

Maggie cranes her neck but sees no sign of their niece. She shrugs.

"Fuss-it-all. I'll just die if I don't see Lizzie soon."

"I doubt you'll die of that."

"And what about Calvin? Is our Calvin here? I'm dying . . . oh, fine, not dying, I'm starving for his lemon drops."

"Nope, he's not with Leah either."

"Then he can't know about it all. He'd be here in a blink if he did."

Maggie agrees. Calvin Brown—aged twenty-three and gangly handsome as the dickens—is the orphaned son of a family friend. He stays with the Fox family so often on his holidays from military school that Maggie and Katie have come to think of him as a kind of brother. He is aiming to be a confectioner, of all things.

"I'm going on down to Leah," Katie announces. "She'll understand."

"Understand what? No, no. Wait. Best we listen first. We can't be willy nilly anymore. We agreed on that."

"Then what do we do? Pretend we're not here at all?"

"Well, yes."

"Fine. Wait, wait, but don't be late. You hear that, Miss Nettie?" Miss Nettie wags her wooden head from under Katie's arm. She has articulated limbs and a swivel neck and is their father's handiwork. He made a similar doll for Maggie, but she lost hers recently. Not that she cares, not really. She is too old for child's play.

Maggie and Katie peer on down at Leah as she hangs up her cloak, peels off her gloves, smoothes her chestnut hair, then enters the keeping room to a storm of greetings, explanations and tales, to myriad flourishments of the Lewis pamphlet. Leah flourishes her own copy.

"Did you know these are being sold in Rochester?" she exclaims. "And in the street. My heavens, to see my family's name so publicly writ. It did give me a turn. A moment . . . there." She presses her hand to her chest, says to Mother: "And why was I not informed straightways? Why did I need to find this out from a pamphlet? It was no small humiliation, I must say."

"But you're always so busy, aren't you? And your father, he . . . that is, he thought it best that we wait before making a fuss."

"Did he."

"Yes, but I am so very relieved you're here now, aren't I? And I am so sorry for not telling you sooner. Should we call on Calvin also? He is always ready to protect us, isn't he?"

"True. I counsel we wait, however. Too many opinions can obscure the right course."

"Then you'll sort this out? Laws, but it is such a perplexity."

"I will sort it, Mother. Yes."

"Have I told you about my humours? They are completely wayward. Dr. Hyde said he'd never seen such wayward humours. I've taken my grandmother's everlasting pill, but it hasn't worked at all, has it?"

Maggie nudges Katie, mimics their mother's voice again: "Laws! Isn't that a wayward humour now? Trundling down the public road? Catch it! Will you please?"

Katie stifles a giggle.

Below, Leah is asking for more information about the ghost, and in a fashion that suggests he is no more than a distant, unpleasant relation.

"But this ghost, Leah," Mother cries. "He knows more than peoples' ages, doesn't he? And much more than the whereabouts of lost keys."

The company agrees. Voices stack one upon the other. Questions have been asked of the Glory, of what lies beyond, of how the dead fare. The peddler's ghost seems to know everyone.

"But what fashion of spirit is this?" Leah asks, as if she is puzzling out the answer herself. Maggie catches her breath, strains to hear.

"That's what we're trying to fathom, isn't it?" Mother exclaims. This begets a heated discussion of will-o'-wisps, poltergeists, revenants, fetches and *giengangers*, the distinctions and subcategories. It seems impossible, however, to find a category for this ghost. He is heard, but never seen, and he comes in the broad of day, though he does prefer the night. And thus far he does not seem malevolent. No rattling of chains, no muttered prophecies, no pans hurled about.

"Why, he's a real polite sort," David puts in.

"Polite or no," Ruth Culver says, "in my opinion he's nothing but an interloper. Toss salt all about and clang every bell in creation, that should fix him. I've said this thrice or more, but does anyone notice?"

"Nope," Maggie says softly. Poor old Ruth. She is related by marriage somehow. Is ever about, ever poking at the fringes, her gaze as resentful and sorrowing as a sin-eater's. Maggie adopts Ruth's wheedling tone and whispers to Katie, "I've been dead myself for ten years. Here I am a half-rotted skeleton, but does anyone notice?"

Katie snickers; Leah's head tips towards the stairway. The girls hold their breath until David says to Leah, "Why, it's become our belief, dear sister, that we can choose not to be afraid."

Everyone agrees on this. Is being afraid a choice? Maggie wonders. She surely hopes so.

Mother says, "Laws, but that poor peddler had no choice, did he? He was murdered, and with a butcher knife, just like those rumours said. But we found no body, did we?"

"Murdered? You discovered all this through the knocks?" Leah asks.

"Why, yes, and more besides," David asserts.

"My word, such a clever ghost," Leah says, her voice raised.

"Clever. Ever. Never," Katie whispers.

"Quit that prattle," Maggie whispers back, and shifts to get a better vantage of Mother. She is gripping Leah's elbow. "Poppet, do you think the peddler wants us to avenge him? We're not the avenging sort of family, are we?"

Leah considers this. "No, we are not. And, no, I cannot believe he wants vengeance. As like he merely wants someone to attend his tune, someone to let him know he is of import. And at least he is not the Devil—that would be another matter entirely."

"No, no. Our Katie called him Mr. Split-Foot, but she was merely teasing, wasn't she?"

"I have no doubt of that," Leah says.

Maggie glances sideways at Katie.

"No, no, our ghost is not the Horned Gentleman in disguise," Mother continues. "We sorted that straightaways. But does it matter? The rumours are still flying thick as pigeons. The Reverend York has banned us from church, Leah. As if we're heretics."

"Truly? And what did Father say of this banning?"

"Nothing. Not a word. He just glared at the reverend, didn't he? And in that way he has, you recall it? Laws, but it did stop the reverend up short, mind."

Leah smiles. "Now, that I can believe." She looks about. "And where has Pa disappeared to this time?"

"Oh, your pa has not a jot of interest in all this, does he? The raps sound out when he's praying, but you'd think they were flies the way he ignores them. Anywise, he's all intent on building a house, isn't he?"

"A house?"

"Yes, poppet, so we can all be together."

"Why, just there," David adds, and gestures north. "Close on."

"Together?"

"Yes, together. You and Lizzie. Maria and her family. The girls. Gracious evers, it'll be wondrous-fine, won't it? At least if the ghost is gone?"

"Wondrous, yes," Leah agrees. "Just like a fairytale."

Katie whispers to Maggie. "Didn't Leah say she'd rather cut her own throat with a rusty ole fish-knife than live in Hydesville?"

"A butter-knife," Maggie corrects. Then adds, "Stay-down, Kat," as Mother pulls Leah into the hall.

"Poppet, I don't want the others to hear this, do I?" Mother says.

"My Lord, what is it?"

"How to say? How?"

"Slowly?" Leah suggests.

"It is just that the ghost. He *is* here and, yes, we all hear him, don't we? But, ah, there's more."

"I know there is, and you simply must tell me."

Katie shifts Miss Nettie, clanking the doll's wooden limbs together. The sound seems a gunshot. Maggie holds her breath, but neither Leah nor Mother seem to have heard.

"It is just that I . . . I suspect Margaret and Katherine, don't I? Yes. I suspect your sisters."

"Suspect them? In what fashion?"

"That the ghost has to do with them. And, oh, from the very beginning."

"Honestly, I do not understand."

Maggie's world shrinks to a pin-dot. She takes Katie's hand.

"Poppet, the ghost, he favours them entirely, doesn't he? It is . . ." Mother becomes resolute, as she does on inexplicable occasion. "Leah, it is they, your sisters, who are haunted."

"Haunted? Haunted as a house is haunted? My heavens! A moment . . . there." Leah drums her fingers on her collar. "And why would this be?"

"Their purity and innocence. Yes. That is it. It attracts him. Like a, a . . ."

"A light?"

"Yes, laws, but you're clever, aren't you?"

"I shouldn't say that exactly. By the by, Mother, where are the girls?"

Mother doesn't answer. More guests have arrived and she is hurrying off. Not that it matters, for Leah gives a secretive smile and looks straight up at Maggie and Katie, there on the second-floor landing.

A short time later, Leah herds Maggie and Katie above-stairs and into David and Beth's sun-bright bedchamber. Maggie twists her hands and contemplates the elaborate patchwork quilt so tidily laid there on the bed, decides she would rather be doing anything else at the moment, even sewing. Katie chews her braid and studies the polished floorboards as if longing to slip through the cracks.

Leah bolts the door. "We shall all three of us stay here until you show me this marvellous knockabout ghost of yours. Not to worry, sweetings, I know how to keep a secret locked tight."

The girls shift their feet. Look nervously at each other. And then Katie shows their sister. And then Maggie does. She is surprised at her tremendous relief. It is as if she has been carrying some spiked and heavy burden of which she was unaware.

"Honestly, the way you've improvised this all!" Leah exclaims. "The way you hit upon just the right composition. So many girls— even my own dear Elizabeth—can only see what is noted before them. Their imagination is stymied by convention. Improvisation is quite beyond them."

And then Leah asks if she may join in their delightful, harmless game.

That evening, a baker's dozen worth of folk cram into this same upstairs bedroom. Maggie huddles with Katie at Leah's feet. Mother sits on the bed with the neighbours. Ruth Culver stands by the window. A tallow dip is the only illuminate. "Too great a light makes our ghost go silent, doesn't it?" Mother says. "Now, Leah, two raps means *yes*. One rap means *no*. Silence suggests he doesn't know. Our peddler can't know everything. We can't expect him to, can we?"

Leah agrees this would be selfish. Unwise.

The tick of a pocket watch. Suspiration. Rustlings. A thin cough. Maggie recalls the piano recital she attended with Leah at one of Rochester's lovely churches. She recalls how the player sat and sat as if transfixed by woe, and how the audience grew restless, how some tapped their fingers to fill the silence. Others hummed. Waved fans. Then, just as the expectation became unbearable, the first note sounded.

A rap. Clear and sharp, followed by a collective gasp, as if the company have not expected this. A neighbour, Mrs. Redfield, asks the first question. "Our Agnes. Is she joyful in the beyond? Does she have a friend to play with? Please tell me."

Two raps. A pause. Two more. Agnes is joyful. Agnes is not alone.

Another woman asks, "My dear husband, he's been dead these two years. Lord, how I miss him, but I've always pondered, were it his true intent to leave me without a penny to my name?"

A single rap. *No*. The woman humphs in disbelief.

A man-shape asks if God is a Methodist.

Two raps. Then one.

"Yes and no?" Mother says. "How is that? I don't under—"

"The question is of poor tender," Leah cuts in. "I surmise, that is."

"I have one," Ruth Culver says. "A fella came to my door last month asking for refreshment. I swatted him with a broom. He was lousy in my opinion. But I query now if he weren't an angel come to test me, and how I'm to know the difference? An angel you'd want to give cakes and such. Those beggars got to be sent packing."

"That's too long of a question, isn't it?" Mother says.

Two loud raps in acknowledgement. Then a thud. Another.

A perplexed whisper runs through the crowd. "Fuss-it, that ain't the ghost," Katie says.

A heavy bang.

"Get back from that window!" Leah shouts to Ruth.

"We didn't mean . . . It was only—" Maggie cries, but she is silenced by the shouts from below: "Deceivers! Blasphemers! Witches!"

A whack on the window lite. The glass spiders, but holds. Maggie sees then the torchlight, fiery red, reaching up from below. She shrieks out a warning just as Leah presses her and Katie to the safety of the floor.

"AND THEN WHATEVER HAPPENED?" I asked, my curiosity having bested me.

"Oh, my brother, David, ever the peacekeeper, went on out to them and sent them off placated. But I should have told the truth then . . . yes, I should have." My patient fell into a study. There came the muffled noise of the street, the wail of a babe some floor down, the variant rattle-chug of the furnace heat.

"Alas and such," she continued at last. "It wouldn't have mattered if I had. Every time I tried to tell the truth I was gainsayed, interrupted, ignored. Or else some event would drown my voice, thwart my plan. Anywise, no one wanted to hear the truth excepting Leah, and then only on that occasion in the bedchamber. After that she, too, went on as if the ghosts were genuine. It scarcely helped that soon folks started hearing sounds that we had not made and saw ghosts and felt ghosts that we had not fashioned. And so Katie and I, but Katie in particular, began to wonder if the spirits weren't genuine after all. It was, dear Mrs. Mellon, as if the secret had an agenda of its own and we were powerless to stop it. As if we were only its agents."

She had an agitated air and so I poured her some laudanum, which she quickly drank. "We had meant only to terrify our mother," she continued. "It was all quite innocent. Our poor Ma, she was so gullible, and we were so full of jack-mischief. Ah, but then all children are resentful, plotting, molly-hawking creatures, and hold themselves superior to their parents."

I disagreed with the last, quite strongly to be frank. "Some children are not resentful in the least. Some would never cruelly tease. Some children are full-up with kindness. And this, too, can be a failing if not nurtured aright." I was thinking of my own son, I allow, and how he was lost in the war, but I did not ever mention his name, nor ever speak of him. I must be absolutely clear about this.

My patient was quick to recant. Quick to say that yes, certainly some children are sweet as a poem, kind as milk. "But does that matter where love is concerned?" my patient mused. "Our father, you see, I do think he loved Leah best, and she had more mischief in her than any. Not that I was jealous of the love he bore her. Men's love is ever conditional. I knew that at a tender age."

I twisted at my ring finger, as I did whenever the wretched Mr. Mellon came to mind. There was still a scar from when I had hacked off the ring with a coping saw. I had been in a fury, I should add, and the ring resistance to the usual offing. Conditional, I should also add, would be a generous way to describe Mr. Mellon's love for our son and my own self.

"Are your hands cold?" my patient asked, all-concerned. "Should you draw on some gloves?"

"I should surely not. What proper physician wears gloves? It is just, just that I am unaccustomed to having idle hands. I might bring my fancy work next time. Knitting. Yes. I will bring my knitting. Now, weren't you speaking of Leah and your father?"

"YOU WISHED TO SEE ME, FATHER?" Leah has found him in the oat field out back of David's house. He is praying on his knees, his broad hat in hand, his round glasses steamed white, a small man in a large field. He holds up his hand. Continues praying.

Leah counts out in compound meter—One *lee la* Two *lee la*—as this helps control her impatience when forced to wait. She is not the only one waiting. Margaretta and Katherina are sitting eager-eyed in the wagon for the ride to the canal dock in Newark. Mother is in complete agreement with Leah. The girls must return to Rochester with Leah. They cannot remain in Arcadia, with its superstitious louts, its threat of lynching by country mobs. If the ghost follows the girls then it will be proved: they are being signaled out, haunted in some novel fashion. This was decided two nights ago, when those twenty-odd men hurled rocks and dirt clods at David's house, then ranged menacingly in the foreyard, carrying torches, as if in a medieval pantomime. Leah's father oiled up his flintlock. "Why, that's scarcely necessary, Pa," David said, peering out the door. "I can't think they mean to harm us."

Leah caught her father's eye. She knew his thoughts. They were the same as her own. David was acting the fool. What else could these men mean but harm? She watched from the kitchen with the other women, the children, as David went outside, arms wide in a gesture of peace. Her father followed close behind him with his flintlock. Just then a woman, bleary-eyed and dishevelled, popped through the kitchen window. "Is this the house of the blasphemers?" she hollered.

Leah grabbed a poker. "No, nor is it the house of drunken sluts!" Her fury approached the operatic, but she did not skewer the woman. No. She stayed quite calm. Katherina and Margaretta looked at her with admiration. Her mother merely looked horrified. The woman yelped and crammed herself back out the window. Outside, the riff-raff was also leaving, their leader apologizing. He had recognized David as an upstanding member of the community. They would all come again, he promised, but in the daytime, like respectable folk.

"Father? Pa?" Leah asks now, his praying having lasted to the compound count of ten.

He stands. "I got something for you."

"You do?" She is oddly pleased, expectant. He made such ingenious toys for her once—a dog-cart, a string of fluttering birds, a mechanical tiger with teeth of iron nails. She recalls chasing David and Maria with that tiger; how they shrieked.

He leads her to his makeshift work-shed. It is chock with tools and barrels and planks. A house plan is unfurled on the sawbuck table. Leah notes the smudged lines where he has changed the drawings to allow for gingerbread scrollwork, a veranda, gables.

John follows her gaze. He taps the plans. "Don't trouble your head. It won't be any slipshod, balloon-framed house. Any mortal idiot can raise one of them." He tells her about mortise-and-tenon, his home-forged nails. He goes on, as he sometimes does, about his planned contrivances. Explains how his house will bring them all together again, shelter generations of the Fox family, hold against any vicissitude. "This house here, it'll have no history but our own."

"My word, how very interesting and—"

"And it'll be well-progressed by the time you and the girls get on back from Rochester. I know you'll want to decorate it up."

"Indeed, and what of this?" Leah says, and indicates a drawing that shows a system of levers and pulleys leading to a door.

"That's so if any dare enter they'll get their mortal daylights knocked out, though only by God's grace, 'course."

"Of course."

"You reckon your ma would favour a washing shed? Particular for washing clothes, I mean?"

"What woman wouldn't covet such a thing?"

He snorts in reply.

Leah gestures to his old flintlock. "I hope you are not expecting another mob."

"I saw a gawker at the field's edge." His shrug is a small movement of his boney shoulders. "A single man, if he's determined, can wreak as much mortal havoc as any mob."

"I suppose you would know." She studies the saws, the chisels. "By the by, what . . . that is, what do you make of the knocks?"

John considers before saying, "Ignore them. You'll get used to them in time. I told your ma that. Consider Job, him and his trials."

"But what of other folk? Those not our kin?"

"What of them? It's Our Lord above that matters. Him and his judgements."

"Yes . . . I see." He puts her at a loss for words, this man. When he first returned from his ten years gone Leah had called him an impostor. Naturally, she doesn't think of him as such any longer. Still, he is hardly the same man who made puppets out of chicken heads, who took her to see the fairs with their magicians and freaks and fortune tellers, who revealed to her the traveller birds in their glorious multitudes.

Leah rubs her forearms at this remembrance, feels the faint hatch-work of scars beneath the sleeve, the clawing of the birds themselves.

"Them wounds, they hurt you still?"

"My Lord, no, not at all."

"Don't say it like that."

"Say what?"

"*My* Lord. *My* heavens. *My* word. Mine and mine, like it all belongs to you, and not the *vice versa*, like them Latins say."

Leah sniffs at this. "Anywise, here I am. You said you have something for me?"

The box is perhaps a foot and a half wide and nearly as deep. It is made of plum mahogany and black walnut and smells of new varnish. The lid is carved with entwined lilies. "See them, Leah-Lou. Them are the lilies of the field, from the scriptures: Consider the lilies of the field they neither spin nor toil—"

"I know how it goes." Leah looks under the box. Opens the lid. Peers inside. "What does it do?"

"Do? It's a bible box. It holds your bible. I made it up large. For a family-sized bible, see. You got a bible, don't you?"

"Certainly. Perhaps I was thinking of the toys you contrived for me once. Remember that tiger? With the snapping jaws?"

"A dog, that was, not a tiger."

"A dog? My . . . word, perhaps it was. Anywise, you hurled it into the fire. Recall? When I chased Davey and Maria with it? It was deserved. They called me a liar, I believe, and said I was fit only for tending Hell's kitchen."

"You're the one who chucked that dog in the fire, not me. And it was because you broke it on David's head. You begged me to make it whole again. I couldn't. You sure did wail on about that."

"I did? Well, I do not wish to argue about it."

"Were we arguing?" John asks, and with no particular intonation.

Honestly, Leah thinks, did the Good Lord need take all his character away, along with the liquor and sin? Says, "I should haste. Will you come to Newark to see us off on the canal?"

He grimaces at the mention of the canal. Leah is not surprised. Her father avoids canal travel completely. Odd, she has ever thought, seeing as he had been a cannaller himself.

"No, no, I got work here. You go on. Just . . . like I said, don't you get anything in your head about them raps."

"Whyever would I?"

"Why? Confound you, girl," John says, and lists the grand schemes Leah had when she was young: the neighbour's privy she tore down to make a castle. The boy whose ear she near hacked off when playing Indians. The games of mumblety-peg that involved skinning knives and rules that only she could master. "Thing is, I was always fixing up behind you, placating the neighbours and the like. It got to be a real . . . *modus operandi* of mine. King Solomon didn't have a harder task, I tell you that."

Leah feels that faint throb in her temple, the one that heralds an ungovernable anger. "I suppose you wished I were more like Davey or Maria. I suppose you wished me placid and dull-witted as a cow."

"I wished nothing of the kind, Leah-Lou." He takes off his spectacles, then pinches the bridge of his nose, as he does when he is perplexed.

Her anger settles. "I often wished it," she murmurs. "I often wished to be someone else entirely."

In the foreyard her young sisters wait impatiently in David's wagon. John lashes down Leah's valise. At the last instance Leah kisses him on his cheek. "But the fault is not yours, Pa. Honestly, why ever would you think that?"

At this John falls back in astonishment, as if she'd slapped him, and not merely guessed his coursing thoughts.

CHAPTER 4.

"Thus it was Leah's?" I asked, and indicated my patient's bible box. "Then how did it come to be in your possession? And its contents, to boot? Your Leah, did she bequeath it to you? She *is* dead, is she not?"

"Last time I noticed, yes," she said, then glanced at the yarn skeins on my lap (I had brought my fancy work as I had said I would). "Do you plan to stay a while today?" She seemed desirous of my presence for the first time. Thus I did not press my questions.

"I need to keep my hands busy while you talk on, duck," I said, "by which I mean you seem set to linger a great deal longer than I had calculated."

"What will it become?"

I inspected the yarn, peeved by the colours. I have ever disliked aniline dyes, what with their false and lurid brightness (much like the electric bright of the night streets). The brown wool looked near to red, the red near to orange, and the yellow flat-out sulphurous. Years past I dyed my own wool with ox-gall and fustic. My son often helped me, as was his wont, and without a solitary complaint. When he was six I promised I would knit an article for his birthday (which fell on March the 5th), and that I would do so no matter his age or location. Mittens. Socks. Sweater-alls. He liked clay reds, earth browns, the blues of sea or sky. I should add that he was my only child.

"Mrs. Mellon? Mrs. Mellon!"

"Yes, I have ears. Do I look a statue?"

"Somewhat. And you didn't answer my question: what will it become?"

"I don't know. I merely follow its shape. Womanly arts require simple thoughts. Ruminations . . . ponderings . . . they only beget tangles and messes and . . . rat's nests."

"Well, yes."

I began with a cast-up stitch. The needles clacked in the garret's silence. "Shall we just get on with Rochester, duck," I said, and with my kindest manner to atone for my abruptness.

"Surely," she said, and described how Leah packed her new bible box in her battered old valise, then packed her young sisters off to Rochester. My patient owned that she did not know it at the time, but neither Hydesville nor Arcadia would ever be her home again.

IN ROCHESTER, Leah disembarks at Canal Street, her young sisters one step behind her. She tells a boat porter her address on Mechanics Square, raising her voice above the racket of tin horns, the calls of peanut vendors, the clatter of horses and commerce. The porter loads their luggage on a handcart, doffs his cap. No one else pays the three sisters much attention. Nor had they been noticed on the canal boat. A fine day for the glide, the mule and his hoggee plodding along the towpath, the sun aglint. "Astonishing," Leah said to her sisters. "How a lone mule can pull along a boatful of oblivious mortals."

Her sisters agreed and smiled and then pasted themselves on either side of her. The ghostly rappings began then, but were mistaken for the general workings of the boat. "And so the ghost *does* follow you, but for what reason?" Leah mused. "Surely he has a purpose. Everyone requires purpose."

"Come, lambs," Leah says now. "Lizzie will be awaiting us at home."

"Can we call on Amy and Isaac? At their apothecary?" Katie asks. "They're sure to give me a horehound, mayhap two of 'em."

"Of *them*, dear, and the Posts are still in Seneca at some women's suffrage conference."

"Well, I miss them. I really, really do," Katie says.

"Of that I have no doubt," Leah replies. Amy and Isaac Post are fast friends to the Foxes and have given shelter to the family during various financial crises. But then such is the way of Hicksite Quakers. They partonize good causes and treat all and sundry as equals, even children, hence Maggie's and Katie's affection.

"Thee. Thouest. Thine," Katie chants now, in mimicry of the Posts' antiquated Quaker speech. "It's such a cozy way to talk. Why can't we talk like that?"

"Because it would draw unwarranted attention, Katherina, and sound ridiculous."

Maggie asks, "Do you reckon Amy and Isaac will, I dunno, fancy our ghost, believe in him, that is?"

"They believe that women can achieve suffrage and that, Margaretta, is an equally fantastical notion."

"I recollect you saying women suffer all the time," Katie says, then scratches her nose, puzzled, when Leah laughs so hard she must cover her mouth with her gloved hands.

"Ah, but you are an amusing little thing. A moment . . . there. Well, come now, girls, do not lollygag," Leah says. She briskly steers her sisters through the thickening crowd, round ash barrels, carriage stoops, mounds of horse droppings. The girls cannot cease gawking. Rochester has changed since the girls were last here only nine months ago. Has grown presto-quick. Become even more the hub of commerce, thanks to the glorious canal. The wonders of American invention shall never cease, Leah decides.

"Honestly, if you walk any slower you will be going backwards," Leah says, but relents and slows her pace at Maggie's and Katie's beseechments. Everything is a marvel to her sisters: the gutted geese hanging in the butcher's window, the veiled bonnets at the milliner's, the fruit and vegetables heaped in stalls, even the proprietors themselves, who call out prices in pennies, shillings and reales. The girls now make a game of find-the-symbol. They count the helixed barber poles of the barbers, the trio of golden balls that mark the pawnshops, the show-globes of the apothecaries, the black lettered signs of the mourning supply shops. Six. Eight. Three. Four. What the girls like best, however, are the carved Indian figures of the tobacconists. They find five in all. "They are only facsimiles," Leah warns. "A true Indian may look nothing alike. They may, indeed, look much like anyone."

Leah leads her sisters on through the Four Corners with its banks and fine stores. Advertising banners hang hither and yon. A boy herds two cows past a bright-painted buggy. And on the centre rotunda a four-piece band plays, torching the air above with colours. Leah is the only one who sees these colours, of course. She thrills at their wondrous display, sighs in disappointment when the colours swiftly fade then vanish. Talents of perception are for the young, she thinks, and I am no longer.

Maggie is also watching the band. "And Calvin? Will we get to see Calvin? Please?"

"Why do you ask? Ah ... the band." Calvin, their ersatz brother, plays the fife in a military band. "Perhaps I shall write him. But first let us see how loud this ghost plays, shall we? And . . . Katherina!" Leah cries, and slaps at Katie's hand. "Do not point, dear. Honestly, there is nothing more rude, nor more noticeable than pointing."

"But look-it, Leah," Katie says. The coloured man plays a limber-jack, the wooden man's clackety limbs making the very music to which he dances. "Miss Nettie could never ever do that," Katie declares. She gave the doll to their niece Ella before they left. "I'm too old for dollies now" was what Katie said. "So you take care of our Ella, Miss Nettie, and don't go on with your rambly ole talk."

"Leah," Katie whispers now. "They do talk. See?"

Sure enough, the limber-jack is commenting on the fine June day. Next he sings, clear as a bell, his wooden mouth working open and shut. The coloured man's mouth, however, is set firm, and he looks at the limber-jack, there on his knee, with as much astonishment as anyone.

"How very clever," Leah says, and drops a coin in the pot at the man's feet. "Now where is your sister? Margaretta!"

Ah, there she is, standing agog afore a stall that is chock with almanacs and periodicals, books and newsprint. "Margaretta, you cannot leave my side without asking. You might be snatched off. Men, my dear, are not to be trusted."

The newspaper proprietor, as if in agreement, spits tobacco within an inch of Leah's hem, "Just the once, Leah?" Maggie implores. "Please?" She points to a dime novel, to the image of its whey-faced, hand-wringing heroine. "We'll share it, won't we, Kat?"

Katie shrugs, twists at her hair. Leah agrees after some calculation of her money. "But, once again, do not point, my dears, nor twist your hair. It is bad form. Walk briskly, double-time now, else you shall not get anywhere in this life."

Behind them the vendor calls out, "*Sir Franklin Lost in the Arctic Wastelands*! Read now!"

"Where's that?" Maggie asks.

"The Arctic? A place you shall never see. It is at the top of the world, apparently, or perhaps the bottom. Anywise, it is black as pitch and frozen over and has not a whit of life. Men like to to seek it out and tend, not surprisingly, to get lost forever there. This way, girls."

Leah hurries them over the long reach of the aqueduct. A funeral coterie plods by. The hearse wagon is drawn by a horse with a soot-blackened hide. The mourners look lightning-struck, the pine coffin ordinary and small. Leah and her sisters bow their heads, but only briefly before Leah indicates they must keep on. It would take a dog's age to get anywhere, Leah thinks, if one stopped stock for every funeral procession.

Beyond the aqueduct is the Third Ward, the finest neighbour-hood in all of Rochester. This is where most of Leah's young pupils dwell. Cats being boiled alive. Idiots banging on barrels. Such is what comes to Leah's mind when her students play, although she is ever kind, ever encouraging.

They step off the aqueduct path. This ward of Rochester boasts a plethora of tanneries, factories, mills. Leah's eyes tear up from the smoke and reeking fumes. Katie coughs, cries, "That's awful, awful. The ole nasty!"

"Grievous," Maggie adds.

Leah follows their gaze. Outside a livery, a boy is being whipped. He refuses to cry out, though the man wielding the belt shows no inclination to mercy.

"Uncle David would never ever do that to his boys," Katie says.

Leah shakes her head. "My heavens, no. But then most adults are cruel, I suppose you two have noticed that." She offers her sisters stories of suffering children. How they are banished to the country-side. Forced to toil. Left defenseless against the winter cold. Though sometimes, Leah reminds them, sometimes the resourceful ones, the clever ones, enact a small revenge.

"I'd really, really rather not be an adult," Katie says, as if she could forestall it.

At last: Leah's rented row-home on Mechanics Square Park. It is a narrow, cramped place, beset with draughts, the smell of the neighbours' cabbage stews and the dissonant symphony of other people's lives. There are only two upper rooms, a keeping room, and a kitchen in which Leah cannot swing a cat. Both the outside-scullery and the outhouse are shared with four other families. The park is large, at least, though it belongs to all of Rochester.

Lizzie clatters down the steep stairs, then hurls herself at the three of them. "Mama! You're here," she exclaims, and kisses Leah on both cheeks, as a foreigner might. "*Je suis si heureuse.*"

"I am here. Yes . . . Ah, Lizzie is taking French lessons," Leah explains to her sisters' puzzled faces. "I do so scrimp for them. And yet is it not astonishing what one can learn and so very quickly?"

"Well, yes," Maggie says with her little smile.

Lizzie shows her nieces her latest fancy-work sampler. "It's a milk, maid with a cow and a pail," she explains. This habit of Lizzie's—of explaining the obvious—does irk Leah, but she never chides her daughter for it, or at least, not often.

"You could stitch in a griffin, say, instead of a dull ole cow," Katie suggests.

"You can't milk a griffin," Lizzie replies tartly.

Leah claps her hands. "Go on, you three, take yourselves out to the park. Do not speak to any men. And Lizzie, I am sure your dear little aunts will tell you all that has happened."

Leah's sisters nod happily, then the three rush off, already whispering in each other's ears, and in that age-old way of children telling secrets.

Upstairs, Leah busies herself with unpacking. Her hand falls on her father's gift. She absently traces the lilies carved on the lid, then peers close. A wasp, hidden in the leaves. Clever Pa, she thinks, to tuck in a reminder that adversaries ever lurk.

The box is too large for the bible she has somewhere. Perhaps she will use it for letters. Her father always had a fondness for boxes, she recalls. There was a most delightful one he made for his cards. He showed it to her when she was a girl, just before his desertion. Within a secret compartment was the King. The Queen. The Jester with his pronged hat. Her father fanned the cards out, then plucked an ace from her hair, another from her sleeve. "Magic," he said, and waited for Leah's eyes to widen. "Don't never be fool enough to believe that, Leah-Lou."

Pointless advice, Leah thinks as she puts the box on her dressing table, then settles for her nap. "Don't marry Bowman Fish, the odious clod"—now, that would have been of use.

She takes a draft of sleeping remedy, closes her eyes. But she cannot find sleep, not with the girls so uncouth and noisy below. Yes, much about her younger sisters needs improvement: their manners, their grammar, their reveal-all countenances. And their voices! Maggie's has a country twang, like a banjo being plucked. Katie's is a tremulous falsetto. At least both girls look much younger than they are, being sweet of aspect and small for their ages. Maggie could take the part of a back-woods innocent, what with her plump cheeks and candid brown eyes. That little held-back smile is a worry, however. It is as if she is too ready to be amused. As for Katie, turn her sideways and she might vanish. Otherwise, Katie favours Father, has his narrow, arched nose and thin lips. Such features should render her homely. They do not. Instead they lend her a distinct, unsettling prettiness, as if a grown woman has been packaged up as a child. More unsettling is that vacancy that sometimes comes upon Katie, as if she is looking at some knowledge beyond the ken of others. And her eyes. Violet in some lights, grey in others. Who has such rare-coloured eyes but shape-shifters, witches? Such, Leah fears, is what some cretinous fools might say.

A bird smacks against the window. Another. Then a scrabbling. Leah starts up. Now the strangest sound: as if a pail of bonnyclabber is spilling on the floor below. She rushes outside. Sees the three girls hopscotching on the flagstones that lead to the foredoor.

"How pale you look, Leah. What's the matter?" the girls chorus.

That rage. No predicting its arrival. Leah's clenched hands grow hot. She breathes deep. "This ghost. He has been about for a time now. And I wonder. Truly. How does he intend to earn his keep?"

The girls laugh at this, though Leah is not jesting. She treads back upstairs, leaving the girls to their skipping rhyme.

"As I went up the apple tree
All the apples fell on me.
Bake a pudding. Bake a pie.
Would you ever tell a lie?"

A lie? No. The dead are not a lie. Leah hears them each time her fingers touch the organ keys. She hears them in the half-notes, which is, of course, where tragedy dwells. Indeed, when Leah sets aside her sheet music, when she plays without plan or intent, then the air near throbs with ghosts, their longings and regrets, their desire to speak. She wonders if, with some encouragement, the dead would do so, would actually speak aloud. At least the dead, unlike so many of the living, would surely know how to keep a tune.

That night cold fingers press Leah's cheeks. The raps sound all around her bed. She calls to the girls: "Are you safe?"

"We are. Are you? What's happening?"

"I cannot say. I . . ." Leah reaches for the matchbox to light the candle. The box tips away. The lucifer matches skitter off.

"*Quelle horreur!*" Lizzie shouts.

Thuds and bangs and more callings back and forth. Leah joins in until she wearies. The girls seem to have no need of early-night sleep. Did she at their age? Indeed she did. Sleep was an escape from household drudgery, from Bowman Fish and his grunting demands.

Leah wakes to a gauzy light. The girls are all heaped in Lizzie's bed, are sleeping as soundly on the worn horsehair mattress as if on a Queen's featherbed. Yes, it is for the best that I brought my sisters here, she assures herself. How, in truth, could I have left them so long with our aging parents? It is a wonder things have only now gone awry.

Leah fastens on her stays, then her underpetticoat, then five more petticoats over that. The stiff-cording on her petticoats is frayed. The seams on her stays so threadbare that the very boning prods her skin. The money from her music lessons is never enough, not for new clothes or new intimates, not for the smallest of nest eggs. Her future yaws before her. As does Lizzie's. And her sisters'. Those three cannot expect decent marriages without dowries. For that matter, just how will Leah manage into old age if she doesn't marry again? Marriage. The thought of it fills Leah's head with a hot, white noise. She rubs at the faint cross-hatch of scars on her forearms. The rubbing is mere habit now, a calming reflex of sorts, though as a child and filled with the usual superstitions, she had rubbed the scars for luck.

She is grinding the coffee, when the post boy comes with a letter from Arcadia. She searches out enough coins to pay him, then breaks the seal, unfolds the letter. The writing is upright and cramped—her father's. When has he ever written to her? Never, that is when. She reads, at first fearful of bad news, then in puzzlement.

15 June, 1848

Dear Leah-Lou,
I reckon you and the girls are settled in Rochester by now,
and I have been pondering over our conversation in the field
out back here of David's house. And I've been praying, too,
for God's guidance, but He has been quietude itself of late,
and so I am taking it upon my own self to steer you to a safe
and knowing course.

I need confess straightaways that I'd been indulging in whiskey that night of the hauntings, the first occasion in near to fifteen years. And that I was awoken by uncanny sounds before your mother and your sisters were, even though I'd been sleeping soundly, as the soused are like to do. And when the knocks started I knew straightaways unholy trouble was drawing nigh, though how much trouble I surely miscalculated. I knew it weren't the ghost of some peddler who'd gone and had his throat slashed, and that no mouldering corpse would be staggering out of that cellar, not even come the Last Trump, not even if we dug down to Hell's watchtower. Not to say the saltbox weren't a dour place. Straightaways on moving there your mother complained about the frowsy smell, and about those grey threads, thin as hairs, snagged round the spigots and latches. Straightaways she demanded I scrape my boots so as not to traipse in those rank clots of dirt she was ever finding on her new-cleaned floors. I scraped my boots. I surely did. Not that it mattered a holy whit. Your mother was determined to find that house haunted, just like all the places we'd lived in since I got back after those ten years gone. She had the Sense, she ever claimed. All the females in her family claimed the Sense. Your grandmother Rutan followed phantom funerals and the like, but there was, too, a great-aunt who could find any lost thing, and a midwife cousin who could make babies live just by scalding her hands in a cauldron. It were all blaspheming hogwash and I prayed constant for your mother's soul, and for mine, too, 'course. But our voices must be a clamouring riot to God's holy ears, and all a sinning man can do is hope the Lord attends one solitary word.

Anywise, recall, Leah-Lou, that this "peddler's" ghost arrived at the tail-end of the winter of '47-'48, the most God-forsaken winter the almanac's got on record. I blame my lapse in sobriety on that endless and frigid spell of darkness that seemed so deep you'd reckon it didn't stop at Heaven's gates, but went on *infinitum*, to use that Latinate word. Your mother saw portents falling thick on the world.

Woodland creatures were watching the house, she said, and were plotting, as if mayhap the cold had honed up their wits. Breath took on shapes, dragons and the like. Metals snapped like twigs. Then one forenoon your mother shrieked and pointed at the kitchen window. Sure enough, written out in hoarfrost were the words *Get gone*.

Get gone was surely what your sisters wanted for themselves. They were stir-crazed bored that winter and griped no end about having to go to bed so soon after supper as if they reckoned lantern oil and pine logs were God's free bounty. And how they did gab on about Rochester, the lit-up byways, the canals with their carnival show of boats, the ice-cream parlours, and all those stores crammed with whatnots we had no money to buy anywise. They surely gabbed about you and Lizzie both, my girl, and how they missed your singing and piano playing, and how you didn't come to visit near often enough, and that, 'course, was true as preaching. They teased your mother, too, and worked up some garbled language to confuse her thoughts.

Now, don't hold for an instance by the way I write of her that I don't love your mother. I surely do, but it's alike an old cat, one that keeps slinking off and then coming back, just when you thought it flat-dead. I know we make an odd pair to most eyes, her a vasty woman, all afret and ajostle and talking constant, me rake-thin and a good head shorter than my chosen wife, and skint with words besides. But Solomon's Song keeps a lively tune with us, as it should in any marriage. And don't hold that I don't love your sisters, for I surely do, but I had little time to attend their growing. I had peace to make with Our Lord, as I do even yet, and such peacemaking is a time-stealing occupation. I surely regret my neglect of those two now. They needed attending. Your mother reckoned herself old as the blessed Sarah when she bore them, and this has surely added to her superstitious bent regarding those two. But then they were queer babes, watchful as owls, even in their swaddling, and easy to mistake for those creatures of the old stories, those what choose a family for convenience but are only biding their time to wreak havoc. No, I scratch that. It's a blaspheming thought and uncharitable besides. I allowed your mother to be their only guiding rod. Their waywardness is my fault *in toto*, to use another Latinate phrase.

Leah-Lou, I was the one who heard those footsteps first. Not your sisters. First the footsteps, then a swish-drag. The night was dark as Egypt with not a fillet of moon, and the sounds were hard to situate. The keeping room? The hall? Outside our bedroom door? Anywise, those sounds surely made sleep a difficulty, and then they got loud enough to wake your mother, and so began it all. She shook me though I was already wide awake and silently cursing, too, the taste of whiskey in my mouth, the empty flask propped under our marriage bed.

"You hear that John?" your mother gasped. "Laws, where's the tinder? Where's the candle?" she said, and so on. I grumbled about it all, but I lit the candle stump obligingly enough and went to investigate. I found nothing, of course. The damp-reek had gotten worse over that long winter and it pervaded the house. I pushed aside a clump of dirt near the threshold and then stoked up the kitchen embers.

Your sisters were huddled up in bed with your mother when I got back. They'd lit all the candles and night shadows paraded on the walls.

"Rats," I said.

"Rats? Rats?" your mother near shouted. "Do rats wear boots? Do they?" She clutched your sisters into her well-endowments, one to either side.

"Boards," I tried. "In the wind."

"Is there a wind without? Is there? I hear none. John?"

I suggested next the neighbours were having a revel— a foolish grasp, I concede now.

"Are our neighbours giants? Are they?"

Those thump-knocks came again, and they were surely in the room with us. I noted the smell of apples then. Apples!

What follows next? I thought. Just then your mother and the girls shrieked in unison. You never heard such a godawful sound. Next the bedstead shook and the floor shuddered.

For frightened girls your sisters surely had some wherewithal. Katie called out, "Mr. Split-Foot, do as I do." She clapped her hands, and, lo, the knocks repeated the same. Now your mother has numerous names for the Devil. Mr. Split-Foot, the Horned Gentleman, Old Nick, Old Scratch, and the like. You'd think by her manner there were more than one devil, but there's only one, just as there's only one God, and he is a God of demanding nature. Anywise, Katie invoking the Devil only got your mother more lathered up. And then Maggie got the knocks to repeat her hand-claps, as well, and then Katie said it was April Fool's Day on the morrow, and that someone was playing a trick.

Your mother said, "But there's no one else in the house. Is there? John?"

I thought on that and said no, but I heard it again. That swish-drag. It was underneath the knocks, underneath all the foolishness. Your mother started asking questions of the "ghost" and so learned the ages of her children, even the age of the one who died in her swaddling. The Red Sea might have parted the way she carried on then, as if she didn't know the ages of her offspring already.

"Are you that peddler?" she asked. "Are you? That poor man who was murdered hereabouts for his five hundred dollars?"

I put in that no peddler carries five hundred dollars, and that it was only a gab-about tale, and that every village has its murdered peddler, or its self-murderer stalking the crossroads, or its ghostie children wailing like all-forsaken.

The ghost wasn't too sure of himself at that point, but your mother can be fixed as God's Heaven on occasion and the ghost wasn't going to get away with being anything but a murdered peddler who'd got his throat slashed and, lo, was buried there in our cellar. The girls acted mortal confused and skittish-scared when this was determined, but soon enough they settled into their routine of knock-and-answer as like this were something they were born to do.

It should have ended there, Leah-Lou. I should have stopped it all, but I kept my counsel for reasons of mine own. Quick as God's lightning the neighbours were flocking to the saltbox, and others rode in from near and far, and the cellar was dug up until it was pitted with holes, and some folk got riled and said our family was blaspheming to say the dead could speak.

Your mother was the one who insisted we go to David's house. She was thinking the ghost would stay behind and that, lo, we'd get safe away from the crowds and hullaballoo. I kept telling her that it was foolishness and that she should ignore the raps. "You'll get used to them in time," I said. "In time you'll scarce hear them at all." But on we went anywise to David's house, your mother having got that look against which a quarrel is useless prattle.

Your mother wanted to write and beg your presence. I said no to that, and she relented. My fear was that you'd make more of the raps than you should, that'd you court trouble somehow, or disaster mayhap, and when I gave you the bible box in the oat field just before your leaving that fear got even stronger and I could no longer ignore it. Hence this letter.

Ignore those raps, Leah-Lou. I say it again. They have naught to do with you or the girls. Causations are plenty in this world.

> Yours truly, your father,
> John D. Fox

P.S. The house is coming along a pace. I plan to paint the hall vermillion as I recall you liking that shade. And don't trouble yourself about my imbibing of liquor. It won't happen again, not ever. That night of the first "raps" was a mere foolish lapse. Nor will I abandon you again, I swear it, Leah-Lou.

Leah folds her father's letter back into its little rectangle. Considers, then pops it into the bible box. She takes a small bag of grain and goes out into the limpid spring morning, into Mechanics Square Park, and settles on the narrow bench far from the other park-goers. Sparrows, just returned from their winter vanishing, flick jewel-drops of water from a pedestal bath. The sparrows slumber underground some learned men say. Others speak more fantastically of the birds flying to Africa, which might as well be the moon, and that is a theory also.

Leah tosses some grain and more birds swoop to the flagstones. Oriole and warbler. Vesper sparrow and kingbird. Humility bird. Finch. She can identify many. Is happy as a treasure hunter when she spies a new variety. Oddly, she does not wish them stuffed and put in a curiosity cupboard to be viewed at her leisure, not even though the cross-hatch scars on her forearms were dealt her by birds, by, indeed, a multitudinous flock of the passenger pigeons. This incident— witnessed by her father only—is hazed by years, and engenders no terror or resentment, only a certainty she has been marked somehow, a certainty that grows when she hears, as now, the birds give voice to what must be God's music for God's enjoyment; for why else would He bid them sing? A pity that Leah lacks the daring to write music that warbles and trills, music that is an improvisation without clear pattern or end. Music bursting with colour. God would enjoy such music. And Leah surely would. But it would perplex all others.

She tosses the last of the grain. Pushes any thought of her father from her mind, any thought of his letter. She must rouse the girls. She will tell them "enough." This peddler's ghost must depart. He has no use among the living except to annoy the neighbours. Not the worst of uses . . . Still. Her father might be correct. She should not make too much of the raps. It might be courting trouble, disaster even.

Just then a cardinal, brilliant red, larger than all the others, hurtles to the flagstones. The other birds are no match for him. They scatter as he takes his due from what has been cast down.

A fortnight later, Leah writes a letter of her own. She addresses it to her mother only. The girls have been asking for their mother, and

Leah could certainly use her help with cooking and care-taking. And then there is the no small matter of Calvin Brown's arrival a week ago. Leah knows her reputation is solid as hewn oak. Still, her mother's presence will thwart any stray gossip about the gangle-limbed Calvin being too handsome and solicitous to be anyone's adopted brother.

30 June , 1848

Dearest Mother,

I have news of great and terrible import. You must come forthwith to Rochester. The girls and I so need your support and worthy presence. I suppose Father is too busy building that house of his and he has said the knocks need be ignored and are of no consequence anywise. I am in complete disagreement, as one might as well ignore a charging ox or a musical crescendo!

Now, the moment our dear Calvin heard of our travails he came bounding into Mechanics Square. How we needed his manly courage last night. My heavens. My word! Such terror and havoc. The wretched ghost must have stolen the candles, for none could be found in the dark and we were as blind as moles whilst the ghost heaved up our bed and tore off our bedclothes. The ghost was soon joined by others and the horrid things then pelted poor Calvin with carpet balls and struck him with a candlestick, bloodying his lip. That stopped the dramatics, I assure you. I played nurse as best I could. Calvin begged I dab his lip ever harder to staunch the dreadful bleeding, while Margaretta, Katherina and Elizabeth all watched in tears. And then Calvin seized my hand and swore that he would protect us or die in the attempt, that he would give up everything for me, for us, and so on. He drew up all manner of strategies and battle plans. You know how he is.

That, naturally, is not the terrible news of great import. No, it is this: multitudes of spirits are making themselves known now. It is as if a celestial door has opened between the worlds of the living and the blessed dead, who are, I must say, a veritable symphony of woe. As for that peddler, I have sent him packing back to his cellar grave. He is no longer needed as intermediary. The Fox sisters are the sole intermediaries of the spirits now.

Your ever-loving daughter,
Leah

She folds the letter and melts the wax for the seal. "Calvin? Calvin!" she calls. He promptly appears in her bedroom doorway. His lip is still swollen from the spirits' hi-jinks the night before, and he looks wearied, but becomes all smiles and cheer when she asks him to post the letter to Arcadia.

"I'll post it smart, Leah," Calvin says. His voice has a nasal tone and an uncertain timbre and is, Leah thinks, somewhat grating. He pushes a dark curl out of his eyes.

"Yes, is there more, dear?"

"No, except . . . except that I'd post anything for you, Leah. I'd march it my own self to the world's end."

Leah smiles. "Oh, I doubt we need ever take anything that far."

CHAPTER 5

O n the fifth day of our acquaintance my patient, out of the blue
yonder, declared that she would like some candy.

"Candy? What sort, madame? Gibraltars? Licorice? Chocolates
from Switzerland? Shall I steam over and buy you a passel forthwith? Do I seem a servant? A lackey of any stripe?"

She smiled. "No, and I am sorry, Mrs. Mellon." She explained she
had been thinking of the Posts and their apothecary. Thinking, too,
of Calvin, this "ersatz" brother. "The one I just spoke of? He ever
smelled of ginger-root and chocolate from the confections he made.
He aimed to have his own shop one day. Alas and such, he would
have, but he was swayed from his purpose."

"Young men are easily swayed. They just follow along, tra-la-la,
even if they know better, even if they're warned, strongly warned,
against rose-glassed ideals . . . and, oh, here is your medicine. Here."
I poured her laudanum into a tumbler, spilling a drop or two, I allow,
in my distraction. To explain: I had seen my son swayed by all the
rhetoric and brouha that preceded the abolition war. I agreed with
the grander cause, certainly, but not the method, by which I mean
the method of using young men as cannon fodder, and ditch filler,
and numberings on a damned general's tally sheet.

"Is there more?" my patient asked. She held the emptied tumbler
in both hands, like some pauper with a tin cup.

"No, no, that is sufficient for the now. But, if it is of such importance, then I suppose I can bring you some penny candy next visit." At which I hauled out my knitting (I had still not found its form). "I have time aplenty if you need to talk on, duck," I added.

A JULY DUSK THICK WITH RAIN, and inside the Posts' apothecary Maggie looks steadfast at the show-globe that illumines the window as might a green moon. Nearby the clerk tends to a pot of leeches. "They're God's creatures, same as any," this clerk says to Katie.

"Sure had me fooled," Katie replies. "I thought they were licorice . . . well, till they squirmed and all."

Maggie risks a glance at Amy and Isaac Post, who are conferring with Leah at the counter's far end. The Posts are angular, poke-edged people who fit together with ease, alike a child's wooden puzzle. Not that there is anything childlike about them, Maggie thinks. Amy wears her plainness with pride. Has a long face and slate-grey hair pulled taut; a forceful gaze. Isaac has the wisest eyes in the world. Usually he wears a beatific smile above his chin beard. Not this day. Indeed, Maggie cannot recall him ever looking so troubled and uncertain.

"I wish Ma were here," Katie says to Maggie. "Right *here*, I mean," she says, indicating the apothecary itself with its shelves laden with tinctures and powders and ointments, and all in clear jars and vials to show their true colours and nature.

"Me, too," Maggie says. Mother's unquestioning, supportive presence has become oddly comforting. She left Arcadia the moment she received Leah's letter detailing the growing manifestations and asking for her help and is now at Mechanics Square with Calvin and Lizzie, Leah having insisted those three stay to see if the ghosts would manifest during the daylit hours. After the ghosts hurled candlesticks and carpet balls at Calvin that night a week past, well, Leah said, anything is possible.

"It'll turn out all right, Kat," Maggie whispers.

"What will?" Katie asks, still surveying the apothecary's marvels.

"Everything." Yes, everything, Maggie thinks. Because after Leah tells the Posts of the events at Hydesville and Mechanics Square the Posts will nod in bemusement, surely. Then they will sit Maggie and Katie down and say in that comforting, old-timey talk of theirs: "Not to worry, loves. Thou may stop now. It is not too late. All is understandable. Thou art so young." Yes, that is what the Posts will say. They do not consider childhood an unavoidable malady, nor as a trial to be endured, but as a stage of blessed innocence. As such, they ever dote on children, their own as well as Maggie and Katie and any others in their purview. They do not whip, nor scold, but talk to children as if they have reason and sensible motivations. They certainly do not load children with chores and responsibilities. They have a maid for all that. Machteld. She waits on customers in the apothecary also, is wide-hipped and splotched-faced and eighteen or so.

Maggie chances another look to the counter's far end. Sees Amy shake her head. In disbelief? Disagreement? Admiration? The response will be an honest one, whichever it is. Amy Post is ever forthright. A champion, really, of all that is good. Of the truth. Maggie mulls over the word: *truth*. The Quakers give it a capital T and consider it the same as God, or something like that. And Jesus is the Light complete, but a man entire.

"Not God's son, then?" Maggie asked Amy once.

"Everyone is a child of God," Amy replied in her grave and kindly way.

At this Maggie realized nothing was as straightforward as she had thought. Things can be two, even three things at once.

Katie slips up beside Maggie. "You reckon they'll let us have some licorice? I've never tasted it. Never ever. I'll just die if I can't try it."

Maggie puts her finger to her lips. Machteld has turned and is watching them with a peculiar scrunched-up expression that Maggie cannot read.

"Fiddle and fuss, aren't you a worry-all," Katie says.

The threesome group of Amy and Isaac and Leah grows tighter. Hushed. The Posts glance over at Maggie and her sister with greater and greater astonishment.

"Kat, Kat, do you recollect the names of Amy and Isaac's two little ones, you know, the ones that died. When was that, six years ago? Think quick."

"Mildred? Nope, nope. Matilda and . . . Henry. And licorice." She grins. "That's not a name. I just really want some."

"For pity's sake, just ask the clerk . . . but make your best manners, now."

Katie does so and the clerk obliges with two ropes. Katie twists hers round her wrist and chews the end. "You a run-off slave, sir?"

"Kat, your manners," Maggie hisses.

The clerk chuckles. He is youngish and tall and crooked to one side. "No, miss, I'm a freed man. You want to scrutinize my papers? No? Pardon me, then."

He attends to a boy who has just entered the apothecary. The boy chants, "Coverton's cure-all. Bay rum hair tonic. A pint of castor oil. Another of worm syrup. A fold of chewing tobbaccy. A peppermint stick." He nods to show he is done and looks as proud as if he has named every angel in God's array. The Posts' apothecary often boasts a line of children. There is no need for haggling, that adult art. The Posts would no more overcharge than become highwaymen and wave about pistols. Instead they tag everything with an honest price. There is no coin nailed atop the counter to compare against dishonest tender, no pawned silver under it. Their apothecary is very successful because of this. Honesty, it seems, pays very well. At this thought Maggie's throat grows tight.

"You like it, this one?"

Maggie looks up. Sees Machteld, a lint-stuck peppermint in her open palm. Machteld's English is accented though she has lived with the Posts for several years. Her entire family died of ship fever on the way to America. The Posts are her family now.

"Thank you, but, no, Machteld. Peppermint reminds me of medicine, which I loathe."

Machteld closes her hand into a fist. She looks so stricken that Maggie nearly apologizes. But, Christ-in-all, why must Machteld ever ply her with unwanted gifts? Ever press Maggie to be her friend, when Maggie, clearly, doesn't even like the way she breathes?

"But what proof dost thou have? It is too remarkable," Amy says to Leah, and loud enough that Maggie can easily hear.

Katie chews her licorice rope in trepidation. Maggie understands her thoughts: Amy never ever raises her voice, and what this heralds is anyone's guess. "Amy and Isaac, they'll understand it all," she whispers to Katie. "Them of all people, they got to. And then it'll be like it was, Kat, I promise. Because things have gone too far. I mean, anyone can see that."

"I just want to go on back to Mechanics Square. Ma said she'd bake apple flummery. And lucky Lizzie got to help Calvin make chocolate, for drinking, I mean. "

Maggie sighs. Apple flummery. Chocolate. Childish pleasures.

"I think I miss the dull ole countryside," Katie adds, puzzled. "How can that be?"

"It was simple," Maggie replies, and pulls her licorice rope in twain.

Katie looks nervously at the two dangling strings. "Ma would say that's a bad omen. A really bad one."

"Don't be niddy-noddy, don't be . . ." Maggie trails off as Amy and Isaac hurry over, Leah close on behind them.

"Sit down, dear girls, sit down," Isaac says. He leads Maggie and Katie to a window bench, the one that is netted with the show-globe's green light. "Thy dear sister has told us all you have done."

Maggie stares at Leah. "She has?"

"Ah, loves," Amy says. "We have always suspected you art special in some fashion. Perchance the time has come."

"Special?" Maggie asks. "How?"

"What time?" Katie asks.

"The time for the arrival of the Universal Spirit, my dears," Amy says. "When the world is made whole and in Christ's design. The hungry fed. The naked clothed. Compassion reigning. Oh, I have told ye of it."

"Ah, that," Maggie says.

"I recollect it now," Katie says.

Amy kneels before Maggie, a strange look on her face, and says, "If it is . . . if it is a truth, and not, say, a phenomenon of the air or wind or some such, then we might speak with them again."

"With who? Or . . . whom?" Maggie asks, even though she knows.

"Why, with our children who have passed on. With darling Henry. And sweet Matilda."

"Henry. Matilda," Maggie says flatly. Yes, Kat had the names correct. Maggie comprehends Amy's expression now: hope run rampant. Isaac's expression is the exact same. He puts his hand on Amy's shoulder. "We pray for them, always, but that cannot compare to their dear presence."

Leah looks at Maggie, then Katie. "I was explaining, my dear girls, how we have spoken with not only the peddler, but also now with other spirits, and how it is the innocence of you girls that beckons them, and that if you two call on this spirit or that, they come, often as not, particularly if their beloved living are also present."

"Yes, them spirits like us a lot," Katie says.

"It is 'those' spirits, my sweeting," Leah reminds her.

Maggie works her mouth, but the words she wants to say are impossible to purge. She tries again, but just as the words take form, the apothecary door flies open.

Calvin. He is grave-faced and soaked from the rain. Lizzie, weeping, clutches his elbow.

Calvin gives the dire news. Their little niece Ella is racked with fever. It is doubtful she will live. Mother has already left for Arcadia. They all must follow on.

Maggie is hardly aware of Leah guiding them out the apothecary door, though she does hear Katie babbling, "It was all a real bad omen when Mag broke her licorice. I knew it."

"Get that out of your head, Katherina," Leah orders. "Causations are plenty in this world."

"DID I SAY THEY WERE HONEST? The Posts?" my patient asked.

"Yes, duck, champions of the truth, no less."

"Let me recant. They were not *entirely* honest."

"One is or isn't," I muttered (in those days I had little patience for straddle-acts of conscience).

"You see, one night when we were staying with the Posts in Rochester—this was before we moved to Hydesville, before the peddler came—anywise, one night I was awoken by the sound of scuffling and knocks and garbled voices. They came from above me, from the attic. I was terrified, and convinced that the ghosts of Matilda and Henry Post were up there playing Jacob's ladder or knuckle-bones or some such game. I was convinced they would creep down and throttle me with their cold little hands. None of the other children woke up, nor Katie, but I was owl-eyed the night through. Come morning I discovered the true source of the sounds."

She fell into a study.

"And?"

"Ah, they were escaped slaves, hidden in the attic. The Posts' house was part of the underground railroad. It was the first time I'd heard the phrase and ever after I imagined the underground rail as just that, as tunnelled beneath the regular streets and byways, existing as might a fairy world: the depots all tilted and coloured bright, the people so beautiful, and getting on and off the whispery trains with an joyous intent. I imagined glowing stones inset in the walls. Down there, the dark had no power, you see. And down there, a secret was sometimes good. Necessary. Righteous."

"Such a fanciful imagination you have, duck. You might have been a poetess. An advocate of good causes. A Samaritan sort."

She gave a bone-dry laugh as if she saw, just then, all the unplucked chances of her life. I cursed my wayward tongue. I am a straightforward person. I do not dissemble, nor varnish the truth of things, by which I mean I am often blunt, even tactless.

"Oh, but you're spot-on about the laws of men," I said. "They're not always good, nor just. And they're often at cross-hatch with the Higher Laws. Shameful." I spoke of how slavery was an evil of unchartable depths. I spoke of moral conscience and so forth. My patient, however, seemed to scarcely attend my philosophical chit-chat.

"Damn, but it's hot in here," she said, though the garret was cool that day. She shifted the bedclothes, then returned to the Posts, and without the least encouragement from me.

Still, I listened.

"CHRIST-IN-ALL, ARE WE DONE? Can we ever be done?" Maggie thinks. Luncheon at the Posts' is lasting an eternity this sweltering day in mid-July. Maggie, hot-pressed between Leah and Mother, visions herself melting into a sawdusted slab of ice, the ice-wagon drawing her off. She almost envies the Posts' four children for being sent back to school.

Think ice, she mouths to Katie, who is likewise in a cast-iron sweat. Katie shrugs and dabs at her eyes, which are ash-grey today and red-rimmed from crying.

Lizzie, seated at the table's end, prods the remains of her luncheon with her fork tines. Leah taps the table, slow and deliberate, as if hearing a dirge. Mother sniffs and worries at her sleeve. She wears mourning black, as does Maggie, as do Katie and Lizzie and Leah. Three weeks have passed since little Ella died.

"Dost thou think the spirits will grace us with their presence?" Amy asks Leah.

"They do prefer our home, but if we carry on as normal, then perhaps they shall grace us plenty."

So carry on they do, finishing their plates, making their conversations. Maggie attends all the chit-chat without seeming to, a fresh-honed habit of hers. It has become a habit of Katie's, too. At last the luncheon guests, fourteen in all, move to the keeping room, avoiding the squares of sunlight as if they are trap doors.

Maggie surveys the room. There are no tassells or fripperies, no wallpaper. No lamberquin on the windows. All is simple. Functional. Unadorned. The walls are linen-white. The rugs patterned only with lines. And yet the room has peculiar beauty, a soothing aspect. So why am I not soothed? she wonders. The heat, she decides, this damned perpetual heat. Yet it doesn't seem to trouble Abigail Bush. Abigail, plump and heavy-chinned, sits over her needlepoint, serene as a roosting hen. Her husband, Henry, round-headed and liverish, nonchalantly brushes crumbs from his whiskers. The Bushes are close friends of the Posts. Like the Posts they are Hicksite Quakers. Mr. Bush is in the stove business, Maggie recalls. And Abigail is a suffragette leader. She even presided over that women's convention in Seneca recently. Such a ruckus that caused, because who ever heard of a woman being chosen to preside over anything?

Maggie sits next to Katie on the settee. Katie sips her cider. She has been church-mouse quiet since Ella died, and has been all-worried, she admitted, about saying the wrong thing at the right time and the right thing at the wrong.

". . . and the buzzing wouldn't stop," Ruth Culver says to no one in particular. "It drove me near mad. It wanted to say something. Something of grand importance, in my opinion. You can ask my Norman here. Norman?"

"No Man? Noman?" Maggie undertones to Katie, using her cranky Ruth voice. Katie pokes her finger in her cider, doesn't smile.

Meanwhile "Noman" slides his thin self over to the melodeon, where Calvin is talking with George Willets. George is a cousin of the Posts. He has spindle limbs, carrot hair, freckles. He is about the same age as Calvin but not a jot as handsome. Maggie and Katie were quick to agree on this.

"No, no, Cal," George says loudly. "It wasn't Horace Greeley who advised 'Go West, young man,' but Soule of the *Terre Haute Express*."

"It seems a swell strategy, whoever said it," Calvin responds. "That'd be an adventure, wouldn't it? Marching off so far."

Norman Culver, eyeing his wife, Ruth, wholeheartedly agrees.

"And what of young women?" Maggie undertones to Katie again. "Why in tunket can't we run far off too?"

"We ain't—I mean *aren't* allowed," Katie says, as if Maggie had been serious.

Leah's voice rises over the general conversation. "The vote, Lemira? Do you truly believe we women shall have it soon? My Good Lord, I cannot believe that women have the fortitude for politics and other manly occupations." Leah is speaking to Mrs. Lemira Kedzie. Lemira is yet another Hicksite Quaker, and looks, Maggie thinks, like a wood-pecking bird what with her outdated topknot, her long thin nose and small black eyes, her manner of determined nodding.

"Whatever is Lemira doing here?" Maggie whispers to Katie, lips barely moving. "Or George. Or the Bushes even."

Katie's shrug is so faint it could be shudder.

Maggie continues, "I mean, spirit talking was to be just for kin and dear friends, that's what Leah said. Ah, the good grief, our elders are worse than six-year-olds the way they keep on telling and telling. If they don't heed caution, all of Rochester is going to know that the dead are tromping on back." She takes a long drink from Katie's cider. The cider is barely fermented, and tastes flat, almost sour.

Nearby, Leah, released from Lemira, tells Isaac, "We shall hear Ella in time. It was too soon, you see. Spirits need time to cross over, particularly spirit children, who tend to dawdle. Yes, I am only now discovering how it all works. Truly, it is like hearing the works of a daring new chamber ensemble." Leah is not trying to command attention, but her voice carries and all attend her.

Why always her? Maggie thinks, surprised at her own faint jealousy.

"Yes! Yes," Isaac cries. "That explains why our Matilda and Henry have not yet made their presence known. They were . . . are . . . of such tender years and might have lost their way back. Perhaps thou could guide them? Provide some signpost?"

"A signpost?" Leah says to Isaac, as if trying out the timbre of the word. "Mayhap."

Isaac gives his beatific smile.

"I'm all-empty," Katie tells Maggie. She indicates her mug, then rustles without another word over to the cider bowl on the sideboard. She looks, Maggie notes, like a wayward shadow in her overlarge mourning clothes. Maggie wishes her mourning clothes were overlarge, too. Her sleeves chafe her underarms, her stays cramp her breath. She yanks at her cuffs, sees her wrists black-ringed from the dye, sees Ella's small coffin being lowered into the ground.

"Your Ella is with us still," Leah told their sister Maria at the aftergathering. "She is happy now and forever. Who of us can say the same?" Leah tried to raise Ella's spirit then, but got only silence.

"Do you sense our dear Ella, Margaretta?" Leah asked.

"Nope," Maggie said. It was true. Among all these folk with their well-worn mourning clothes, Maggie sensed nothing but staggering grief.

Now something brushes against Maggie's skirts. She catches her breath, then chances a look down. No enormous-eyed face under the settee. No Miss Nettie doll clutched in Ella's arms. No, because Katie put Miss Nettie in the coffin with Ella. Nothing here. Only the feet of the living jostling for space.

Ruth sidles up to Maggie. "Our Katie's hooked an admirer. Well, that's my opinion."

Maggie glances over at Katie, who has found out the cider and is talking closely with Mr. John Robinson, a lawyer friend of them all. He is handsome for a man of years. Has all his teeth and all his hair and wears a natty silk waistcoat. "He's just being polite," Maggie tells Ruth, as anyone can see by his automaton nod. "Besides, he's ancient. Thirty at the least."

Ruth—well past thirty herself—sniffs and trundles off. Which is the better gift, Maggie ponders: a knack for raising the blessed of the dead? Or for avoiding the irksome of the quick?

"Come, Henry, John," Isaac says. "Thou must see my invention." He ushers Henry Bush and John Robinson past Maggie, then past Lizzie, who has posted herself by a window. She is watching the sundial in the garden. Has made a paper fan and is fanning herself like the Duchess-of-Where-ever. Since Ella's burial, Lizzie has been cool with Maggie and Katie, with Leah even. Has been reluctant to join in any kind of game. Would rather occupy herself with French books and sewing notions and with sketching. Still-lifes are what she favours—fruit bowls, flowers, doorways. Indeed, she has declared anything fanciful or fabricated a ridiculous waste of time, an idea Maggie can't wholly disabuse.

The grandfather clock strikes four. Isaac and Henry and John return from Isaac's study. Isaac carries a rectangular board the size of a serving tray. The top of the board is scripted with the alphabet; underneath are the numbers one through twenty; and underneath those are simple words: *and, thus, you, her, him, us, them* and so on.

"Invention may be too grand a term," Isaac tells the men, and with his usual modesty. "This board merely assists the spirits with communication, and allows them to speak for a lengthy time without strain or worry. They knock, you see, when the correct letter, word or number is pointed to. It is a far more expeditious than our previous method of spelling words by reciting the alphabet and waiting for a knock when each letter is attained."

"Can we expect greater clarity?" John Robinson asks. "Their wording is often vague."

"Oh, I am most hopeful the spirits will now give us a complete description of the after-life and of the nature of God and the Heavens," Isaac says.

"It is monumental, this dead returning business," Henry Bush puts in, his liverish face rapt. "A turn-point in history."

Listening to this conversation, Maggie's heart drops heavy as a plumb-bob. The air grows hotter yet. "Forfeits, anyone?" she asks. "Or, or lookabout?"

No one takes up Maggie's offer. Not her mother, who is always the first to spot the knick-knack in lookabout. Not Leah, who cannot be beat at forfeits.

"Charades?" Maggie asks, looking at Katie, because charades is Katie's favourite. Katie shrugs. Maggie suggests get-a-smile next, thinking of Ruth Culver, who generally wins, having never smiled in all her born days.

"Be patient, dear," Amy says in her kind, firm way. "A game may steal our minds from our purpose."

Machteld appears. "I pour tea now," she declares, and does so for everyone but Maggie.

When Machteld leaves, Maggie follows her to the pantry. She smiles. Machteld scowls in return.

"You're not going to . . . Are you?" Maggie hesitates.

Machteld smacks down the tea tin.

A week ago, Machteld had accompanied Amy and Isaac to a spirit-sitting at Leah's row-home in Mechanics Square. Maggie was in the keeping room below with Katie when Machteld appeared in the doorway.

Maggie lowered the broom she had raised over her head. "I was . . . we, I mean, the ceilings get *so* dirty. And I thought, thought you were above-stairs with Amy and Isaac and . . . and Leah."

Machteld clenched her pudgy hands and glared. "I was above-stairs, and the ghosts, they make knock sounds."

"It's what girls here do, that's all," Katie said desperately.

"She's right, Machy," Maggie quickly added. "We make a game out of the cleaning. Better than blindman's bluff. It's a lark. Here. Here!" She thrust the broom at Machteld.

Just then, Lizzie had traipsed in. She surveyed the situation, said archly, "Well, *tant mieux*. That is to say, so much the better."

No, it's not, Maggie thought. Not "better" in any language. She forced a smile, said, "Machy, we're going tomorrow to watch Calvin in the militia parade. We're going to make a banner and everything. Leah said we need to cheer ourselves up after Ella. Come with us. Amy will give you some time free. I know it."

Machteld considered this for a long moment, then took the broom from Maggie's hands. "Here, I show how you clean."

Now, in the Posts' pantry, Machteld says, "After the parade you say, tomorrow we go for a ride in canal boat, and so I come to the canal in my new dress. It is white. Never do I wear white dress. But that day I wear white because I go out with my 'friends.' Yes? But my friends not there. I wait at the dock and wait and wait. And the horns make racket. And then I leave."

"I confess, Machy, we plain forgot. I'm sorry, I surely am."

Machteld mutters something in Dutch and brushes past Maggie with a platter of teacakes. Maggie doesn't try to stop her.

Back in the Posts' keeping room, Maggie nibbles at an apple tart that tastes, of a sudden, like ash. Dandy-fine, she thinks, this will be the way it all ends. Her dread is entwined with relief, a curious dual feeling.

Behind Maggie, Amy exclaims to Leah, "I am in such joy to learn from the spirits that Hell does not exist. Oh, I had my doubts. Why would a just God damn innocent children merely because they are not baptized? How is this their fault? And why should pagans be tormented by eternal fire for ignorance of the Gospel? Why should the chance for redemption cease with the breath? Why should not the Glory await us, one and all?"

"Why not, indeed," Leah says. Then, "Should we try the parlour, dear Amy? The air is much cooler there. Perhaps the spirits shall find that more inviting."

"A sensible idea," Amy says. "Machy, dear, lemonade, please. Unless thou care to join us."

Machteld scowls at Maggie and shakes her head.

The parlour is indeed cooler, and more dim besides. The windows are draped with plain brown velveteen. The oval table is set with a simple candelabra.

The Bushes sit, followed by John Robinson. Katie takes a seat beside him. Lizzie mutters *"Merde"* and places herself opposite Katie. Ruth Culver orders her Norman to "sit," then sits herself. Maggie slides into place between Leah and George Willets. Now they are all around the table and holding hands. One of the Quakers must have suggested the hand-holding because it is becoming, Maggie realizes, like one of their queer services where they wait and wait until the Holy Spirit moves one to speak. Amy says a kind of prayer: ". . . or the world is God and the Glory is God and everything of flesh and everything of green and God is not one thing, but everything holds its portion."

Amen. Amen. Amen.

Machteld enters with the lemonade. Sets it down on a sideboard. Looks at Maggie. At Amy.

"Dost thou wish to join us, dear?" Amy asks. "Dost thou need to give voice? Please do so."

Damn you, Machteld, not now, Maggie thinks. No voicing. Not with everyone here. Please. Please. Maggie visions the looks of aghast disappointment, betrayal, hatred even, on the faces of these people she cares about. Why-ever had she thought she would know relief of any kind?

Machteld glances sidelong at Maggie, then tells Amy, "I know . . . I know I need go to market."

"Certainly, dearest," Amy says, perplexed.

"Spirits, please join us now," Leah says as Machteld leaves. They wait in silence until Maggie's hand—held fast by Leah on the one side, George Willets on the other—becomes hot as a flatiron. Finally, when Maggie can bear it no longer—the expectation and longing, the daggering eyes from Leah—the first faint knock comes and then a faint cheer from around the parlour table.

"It's the peddler in my opinion," Ruth says.

A strong, single knock. No.

"Is it someone we know?" Leah asks.

Two knocks. Yes.

"A child?"

Another two knocks. The Posts give joyous gasps.

Several other names are tried before the correct one is arrived upon: Matilda, the Posts' daughter. She is all of four, the same age as Ella. Matilda has been dead for three years, yet the Posts sob as if their hearts were freshly broken.

CHAPTER 6.

"After the first sitting at the Posts'," my patient said, "we began our Sunday strolls at the Mount Hope Cemetery. The place was ever chock full on Sundays with folks taking the air and picnicking and children playing leap-the-grave. You recall when cemeteries came into fashion?"

"Certainly, duck, do you wish to be buried in one? They are costly, but fine indeed." I smiled, pleased that I might get some direction in my duty towards her.

"Now, now, don't try to fish out my wants, Mrs. Mellon," she said. She was button-bright that day, I should add. Indeed, I was amazed at how she had improved since I began tending her six days past.

We spoke about cemeteries then, how blessed we were in America to have space aplenty, even for the dead. How there was no need to cram one's beloveds into a church graveyard where the headstones lean against each other like crooked teeth in an old man's head. How *cemetery* meant "sleeping place" in some foreign language, and how that made one think the dead were merely napping. How nice it would be to be buried in a place that looked the picture of Heaven, with sweeping views and winding paths, with scrolled benches and stately trees and with grass, lawned and tended all around.

I took up my knitting and began work on a decorative selvedge.

"Katie and I loved to play among the tombs and angel statues and obelisks," my patient said. "We'd challenge each other to memorize the most names and epithets and dates of death and such." As if to prove her stellar memory she quoted some of these names: *Jehu Phineas. Absolamon Good. Elijah Smithe. Robert. Frederick. James. Robert. William. Hank.* And so on. She quoted also the years of their births and deaths, even, yes, their epithets.

I tended to my knitting as she spoke, the needles clacking a steadfast rhythm. Then sighed. I gave my son a rare and lovely name. I should like to have seen it carved in marble.

"Have you decided what it will become?" my patient asked at length (she had finished with her recitation).

"A hat," I said after a moment. "And now you might as well tell me more. I have nothing better to occupy my time."

NO STROLL THIS SUNDAY. Outside Leah's Mechanics Square walk-up a late-autumn rain squalls. Inside, Maggie is bored, bored, bored. The dirty weather has kept away guests, denied invitations out. There is only Katie, Mother, Leah, Lizzie and Calvin to help fill the hours.

"Fiddle-it," Katie mutters.

"Fiddle what?" Maggie asks.

"Can't you sense it? It's all sour. A tiff. It's brew-brewing away."

"A tiff? My, that's spandy-new."

A fire draws in the grate. The mantel clock tocks to five. They have just finished guess-the-name. Maggie easily won, as she always does. Now each has retired to a separate occupation. At the organ, Leah puzzles out some sheet music. Mother sweeps the rug. Katie pokes at her sampler. Maggie reads *The Secret of the Vicar's Daughter*, and for the third time. She loves how the secret restores the girl's honour, and not the reverse.

Katie yawns, her mouth tiger-wide.

Mother stops sweeping. "Laws, Katherine! Cover your mouth. Do you want a Nasty Little getting in? Do you?"

"Gosh-it-all, Ma," Maggie says. "You surely don't believe that old-fashioned balderdash about your Nasty Littles."

"I might half believe it, what of it?"

"Which half do you believe?" Maggie asks, her face solemn. Katie tries not to smile.

"Oh, you young people don't know everything, do you? No, you don't." Mother swats at the drapes with her broom. Eyes the corners of the room. The Nasty Littles is her term for a variety of mischief-makers: Hobgoblins. Sprites. Mommarts. Bogarts. Bobs. Rumplegeists. They dwell wherever people do. They are not lost souls, nor invisible spirits, nor vaporous ghosts. Though only the size of teacups, they are of solid substance, with pliant bones and shadow-grey skin, all the better to hide in cupboards, drapery folds, dark doorways. One need look askance to spy them, and then the sighting lasts only for a clock-tick. And, ah, the stories Mother loves to tell about these dreaded Nasty Littles. How they steal small household items: buttons, stockings, pegs. How they shape-shift into mice and voles or curious stones if caught in the hand. And how they can reach into a child's yawning mouth and steal out a smidgen of their soul.

"Ghosts can't be the sole agents of all this ruckus, can they? No." Such was what Mother said to Maggie just yesterday. Some secondary mischief is clearly at work, she meant, and Maggie could only agree.

Maggie watches as Lizzie returns to the parlour. Calvin follows her. Apparently Lizzie needed him to get a notions box off a high shelf. Now she bids him sit in a wing chair and hold out his arms. He does so, doll-stiff, while Lizzie winds yarn skeins round his hands. Once done, Lizzie slides the yarn off and eyes Calvin through its oval. He is without a waistcoat and his shirt sleeves are rolled to his elbows. He picks up his cake plate, looking almost comical now. With those arms he could crush the plate as easily as he crushes his nut brittle. Maggie recalls how Calvin would play wedding with her and Katie when they were younger, how one of them would be the minister, the other the bride. They took equal turns. But when Lizzie joined them it wasn't as much fun. She always wanted to be Calvin's bride. Would close her eyes and look the silly goose when Calvin, chuckling, obliged her with a kiss.

Leah sits at the parlour organ with her sheet music. She plays a churchy chord, then stops. "My heavens, an F? A yellow? Here? What was Mr. Bach thinking?"

"Well, you know best," Lizzie says tartly.

Katie sighs and looks meaningfully at Maggie. Indeed. What *is* with Lizzie and Leah? They used to giggle together like intimate friends. Be of one accord. When Katie and Maggie groaned about their dithering and distracted mother, Lizzie would boast about her competent and gifted one. How Leah could have played piano for royalty if not for baby Lizzie (not that Leah ever minded, Lizzie insisted). Indeed, Maggie once wished Leah were her mother too. Not any longer. Now Maggie and Katie are quite happy with their own. Mother Margaret makes ketchup whenever they wish it, though it takes half the day. She sings to them lullabies when they cannot sleep for trepidation about the future. And she has purchased a lodestone, a small but costly item that she presses to their foreheads to draw out nightmares and any malignant forces that might be attracting the ghosts.

Lizzie tosses her wool to the floor. She looks at Calvin with exasperation. "Why don't I like the ghosts? Why?" She speaks loudly, as if intending Maggie and Katie to hear. "Crumb, because there's plenty of alive people to talk to, that's why."

"They don't always come when commanded, Liz," Calvin says. "You know that. They're not pets, or, or recruits. "

"Is that why you and Ma go walking in the cemetery and study gravestones? To help the spirits in case they forget when they up and died? Oh crumb, and, and *merde* too, it's a farce, is what."

"Everyone goes strolling in the cemetery," Calvin points out. "And, honour bright, the spirits, they don't forget, it's just—"

"It's courting damnation, that's what. I knew it when our Ella died."

"Elizabeth Fish!" Leah calls over. "Whatever are you arguing about?"

Lizzie gestures at Maggie and Katie. "My sweet little aunts. These two, it was all their idea and—"

Leah crashes the organ lid shut over keys. "That is enough! I cannot say I like your tone, Elizabeth Fish. No. I cannot."

Katie leaps up. "Play for us, Leah. Please. We all need cheering. It's such a bleak ole day. Let's dance a bit."

Leah eyes Lizzie, and then stretches her fingers. The tune begins simply enough. Katie's unbound hair capes her shoulders as she dances. She kicks off her slippers. Turns in her red stockings, faster and faster yet. Leah watches Katie instead of the music sheets. Her tune quickens to match Katie's dancing. Though, it is not really a tune, Maggie realizes, more like the rainstorm come within. Katie flails her arms and stomps and twirls and laughs and claps. Maggie can't stop herself. She stands and claps and sways.

Calvin follows suit. Mother looks up, worried. "Oh, but this is unseemly, isn't it?"

"Katie!" Lizzie shouts. "All of you. Stop this, for Christ's sake."

Leah ceases midway through a crashing chord. Calvin jolts as if stabbed. Katie stops dancing and breathes harshly into the sudden quiet. She draws her hair away from her face.

Lizzie hurls her sewing basket to the floor. "Listen. All of you. Listen. The spirits have to go away."

"The *spirits* will not be going anywhere," Leah says. "What is this, my girl? And how dare you curse. I did not raise you to speak so."

"Someone will be hurt. Katie will be, with these, these ghastly fits."

"I wasn't having a fit at all. I wasn't!"

"No? Then you're behaving like you're . . . like you're possessed. Don't any of you worry about damnation? Aren't you terrified about being called a fraud and having to live in utter disgrace?"

"Take care what you say," Leah says mildly. "You might well offend the spirits."

"Crumb, I'm not afraid of your stupid little ghosts. And I won't go to the Grangers' tomorrow for a stupid sitting-around-thing. I won't, is what!"

The Grangers, those Methodist friends of the Bushes and the Posts. Maggie had nearly managed to forget. A pain begins at the bottom of her skull. There is to be some kind of test. A skeptic will be in attendance, a Methodist minister yet.

"You shall come," Leah says. "And there shall not be another blasphemous word out of your mouth, in any language. Honestly, you are becoming so troublesome."

"Troublesome! What about Maggie and Katie? They're trouble incarnate. I'm just trying to save this family from ruin."

"Please, darling, I need you," Leah says, her voice gentling. "*We* need you. And this family shall never face ruin or disgrace if we stay as one." She embraces Lizzie, says into her hair, "You shall put on your best behaviour for the Grangers, then? Make your best manners?"

Lizzie sniffles. Says she will. After a moment of calm, adds, "*Séance.*"

"Oh, is that one of your French words, my dear?" Leah asks absently. "From your lessons?"

"Yes, and it's what you should call your tedious sittings." Lizzie talks about the Paris salons where ladies once held court, and about long sessions in French government. "And they're both called séances because they're about people sitting around and talking about nothing, over and over again."

How can Lizzie brave Leah so? Maggie wonders.

Leah raises her brows. "Séance? I should think *promiscuous circle* or *spirit circle* are better choices. They sound more American and thus more wholesome. And more . . . honest."

"LIZZIE, POOR GIRL," my patient said. "Alas and such. She only wanted to do the right thing. She was brave. Yes. And I was not. I couldn't fathom defying a hair on Leah's head. And I suppose I didn't wish to either. And by the time I did? Well, I was so too far in. What I regret is that Katie was swept along, perhaps more than any of us. Here is the question, Mrs. Mellon: If you believe in something strongly enough, does it then become the truth in some fashion?"

I unravelled a bobble; it would have looked ridiculous on the hat.

"No," I said. "That is all chalk and nonsense. And bullshit, to boot."

"Ah, but you are Practicality incarnate, dear Mrs. Mellon."

"An improvement on being Death incarnate, I suppose." My patient found this exchange most amusing, as did I on second thought— "Death incarnate" being what she called me when first we met.

"The Grangers', that was my chance, but I was too much the coward." She seemed agitated, even angry. I set aside my knitting and measured out her laudanum. More than yesterday; more than the day before. Her tolerance for laudanum, spirits, for stimulants of any kind exceeded, to be frank, any I had ever known.

"Now tell me of this Grangers sitting," I said, so as to distract her from distress.

THE REVEREND LEMUEL CLARKE is overlarge, with a glowering eye and a face like a boiled ham. He is a particular friend to Mr. Lyman Granger and he is affronted, he announces, by the mere suggestion of palavering ghosts. "Scandalized even," he adds, and studies Maggie as if she were a clockwork curio he'd like to disassemble and spread all over the petit point rug.

"How's your head? Nasty still?" Katie asks Maggie in a whisper.

"Dandy-fine. Sterling," Maggie replies. She did have a grievous head-pain, but thanks to a cocainated head remedy of Isaac's, the pain has transformed into a cool, tack-sharp light.

"I'm just real glad you're here, Mag," Katie says. "We got to stay together."

"Well, yes," Maggie agrees. How could she not come after Lizzie's strange behaviour? How could she allow Katie to stand alone between Lizzie and Leah and the havoc that is sure to follow? At this thought Maggie looks to where Lizzie waits separate from them all, arms crossed.

"Liz can't win over Leah. She really, really can't," Katie whispers to Maggie.

"Shhh, I know it. I'm considering."

"I sure wish I could disappear," Katie says, and closes her eyes as if expecting to do just that.

"Come, Leah, Abigail, girls," Adelaide says. "Watch the planks and nails. We're having a larder put in. It's so costly these days. Worse than robbery."

Maggie sighs. Adelaide Granger would tell a grocer her troubles, which are, in fact, considerable. She follows dutifully as Adelaide leads them to her daughter Harriet's bedroom. Adelaide holds the hand of her other daughter, Betty, a poke-faced creature of ten. Betty is the one who opens the door to Harriet's bedroom, who shows them the last daguerreotype of her older sister. In the image Harriet looks peaceful, even thoughtful, propped there in an armchair, eyes shut as if napping. Around this *momento mori* are candles of beeswax, jewellery made of Harriet's pale hair, her needlework sampler. Maggie peers at this last. *A* is for Amble. *B* is for Baton. Or balderdash, Maggie thinks, which is what I would choose.

Adelaide says to Leah, "I so long to speak with Harriet again. Will she manifest? Her very form? Is such a thing possible?"

"Manifest? No, our spirit friends are not called the Invisibles for nothing. It does no good to look for them. Listening with one's eyes shut is best. The raps are how our spirits make their presence known. Come, we should begin before the hour draws late. Katie, are you with us?"

Katie doesn't answer. She is peering at Harriet's death image. Maggie tugs her elbow. "I'm all here, don't be a worry-all," Katie says, though more to Harriet than to Maggie.

Back in the Grangers' parlour, Leah directs who should sit where around the large cherry table. First it is Adelaide and Lyman Granger and their one living daughter, then Katie and Lizzie and Maggie. Then Mother Margaret. Calvin Brown. Abigail Bush. Leah. The Reverend Lemuel Clarke.

Leah says to the reverend, "I must warn you, sir, the spirits are not interested in those who disrespect them. Indeed, they can be quite silent around those who profess disbelief."

"Is this true, Leah?" Mother asks. "I'd not thought so, did I? I'd thought—"

"It is true, Mother," Leah interrupts sharply. Mother falls silent.

"I shall show no disrespect, nor outrage," Reverend Clarke says. "But my powers of scrutiny are known to many and thus any devils I see may get a thrashing."

"You have my permission to thrash any devils you find," Leah says. "Come, let us begin our spirit circle." She emphasizes the word *circle* and glances at Lizzie.

"Not séance?" Lizzie mutters to Maggie. "*Merde*, she won't even give me a word."

"Shush, Liz," Maggie whispers. "Don't say anything at all and you'll be all right."

"Girls!" Leah calls.

The lamps are dimmed. Lyman Granger sets out the alphabet board, as expectant as a boy at Yuletide. Leah directs everyone to hold hands. "To optimize the spirit chain," she explains. "Now, we always commence with the Lord's Prayer. Would you be so kind, Reverend?"

Reverend Clarke agrees to be so kind, but his prayer is cut short by a thump that rattles the candelabra. He snorts. "I am insulted. Offended even."

"The peddler. He has returned," Leah says, as one does of an uninvited guest. "I know him by his crude, thumping sound."

Adelaide asks, "Is Harriet here also? Harriet? Darling?"

Light, womanly tappings now, so different from the peddler's great thumps.

Adelaide sobs with joy.

"I have a question," Reverend Clarke announces.

"Please ask," Leah says.

"Has God sent the spirits? Does he have some grand purpose in doing so?" His tone is accusatory yet hopeful. Hope. Maggie easily senses its presence now. As Katie does. As Lizzie must. And Leah, certainly. Hope; it is ever the Achilles' heel.

Raps. Loud and rapid. The alphabet board is brought forth. The reverend's question is found to be presumptuous. He must ask another.

All this takes a long while. Maggie is already getting tired, even with the head remedy working its quotidian magic. Katie, however, is keen and cheery. "It's like I'm all-threaded with energy when the spirits are about," she has confided to Maggie. "It's like I'm more my own self."

Reverend Clarke musters outrage. "This is a mockery. A travesty even! Turn up the lamps this instance."

"It may offend the spirits," Leah warns.

"Indeed? I ask again. Turn up the lamps. I must investigate."

No one stirs. The reverend is left to do it himself. He peers under the rug, the table. Opens the drapes to a salvo of daylight. Presses his ears against the panelling. Admits at last that he is puzzled.

Calvin, quiet until now, asks, "Would Reverend Clarke like to see the table move?"

"Move? Indeed, I should like to see an object *move* by spirit power alone. Yet first I must ask all to push their chairs away from the table. Excellent. Now raise your hands and now—" He stares at the table, which trundles towards him, past the seated party, the tea board, the organ. Leah snatches the candelabra as it tips. Maggie, Lizzie and Katie all shift their feet out of the table's path.

"Great heavens!" the reverend shouts. He sidesteps. The table halts. The reverend drops to his knees, peers again under the rug, then runs his hands over the curved table legs, apologizing to the ladies as he does so. The table nudges him. He stumbles back with a hoarse cry, swipes at his brow. "Never have I seen . . ." He trails off at the sound of sawing and hammering. "And what is that wretched noise? What?"

"Perhaps a spirit coffin is being made," Leah suggests.

Reverend Clarke shudders.

Lizzie whispers to Maggie, "Or perhaps it's just the men working on the larder. How obvious need it be?"

Maggie ignores her niece.

Leah says, "Yes, a spirit coffin, Reverend. The spirits, you see, are reminding us that we are mortal, that we could go to our Maker any moment. That disaster looms large for us all. One never knows when it may strike." She eyes Lizzie, adds, "Now, do ask another question, Reverend. Ah, but first let us link hands again. A moment . . . there, as I said, it does help the spirit chain."

"Spirit chain?" Lizzie mutters as Leah talks on. She shifts her foot along the floor. "There's your spirit chain."

"Liz. No," Katie whispers.

Yet why not? Maggie thinks. What is the worst that can happen? She poses the question, then realizes the answer: Ruination. Damnation. Just as Lizzie herself said back at Mechanics Square.

Leah raises her voice. "Linking our hands not only helps the spirit chain, it also lets disbelievers know that none dare work mischief in the dark."

Reverend Clarke looks chastised. He holds Adelaide Granger's hand on one side, Leah's on the other. He clears his throat. "Can God be known? That is to say, understood even? If one strives enough?"

Maggie thinks it a curious question for a reverend. He should know, if anyone does. Anywise, the answer will make a believer of him. He is at the tip-point. Maggie knows this. As Leah must. As Lizzie should.

Leah's turns her chin to the left.

Under the table, out of sight, Lizzie pinions Maggie's leg with her own. Atop the table she squeezes Maggie's hand in a claw grip. Maggie squirms furtively. Silence grows large in the room.

Don't, Lizzie, Maggie thinks. DON'T!

"Spirits?" Leah asks.

Nothing. The minutes stretch. Leah asks again. Then demands.

Leah looks at Maggie. Maggie hesitates, then dips her head towards Lizzie. Such a small movement for such a large betrayal.

Leah glares at Lizzie. And Lizzie? She meets her mother's eyes with pure rebellion.

Leah stands and points at her daughter. "You! Elizabeth Fish." And then . . . fury, the like of which Maggie has never seen. Not from Leah. Not from anyone. "You've done this. You! You wicked, wicked girl. You've grieved the spirits. You're the cause. The sole cause."

Lizzie is slack with shock. The entire party glares at her. Some stand. The Reverend Clarke looks on, appalled.

"Lizzie!" Calvin cries, and throws out his hand as if Lizzie were teetering on a precipice. Which she is—and the pit of ignominy for her entire family is beneath her, the desert of her own ignominy above. And if Maggie rescues her? The pit. The desert. They will be her and Katie's fate as well.

Lizzie claps her hands over her ears as accusations fall about her like stones.

"It's Lizzie's fault."

"All her fault they won't speak."

"Shall I never hear Harriet again? And because of you?"

"Cruel girl."

"Come now, people, have pity. Mercy even," Reverend Clarke says.

"Meanie, meanie, meanie!" shrills little Betty Granger.

"This has to do with her behaviour of yesterday," Leah cuts in, her voice above the other voices, above Lizzie's sobbing. "She must repent and beg forgiveness. And on her knees."

A slow rap-rap of agreement.

Lizzie buries her face in her hands.

"Will the spirits speak to us again if Lizzie begs forgiveness?" Leah asks. Nothing in her voice suggests she will relent, Maggie realizes.

"I can't help it," Lizzie says. "I just said what I thought and if I'm to blame I can't help it. I can't." She sobs a torrent. The Reverend Clarke offers a brief hand on her shoulder. Maggie doesn't dare offer comfort, not with Leah so near. Katie sits slumped like a rag doll.

Leah tells the sitters how yesterday Katie was overtaken by the spirits while harmlessly dancing. How Lizzie shouted she wanted the spirits to go away. How she blasphemed. "My daughter does not trust the spirits, dear people. She believes, actually believes, they would cause us injury. She believes they would allow us to be labelled frauds."

Frauds. The word stands giant and stark.

"Yes, Elizabeth Fish would have us labelled as frauds," Leah continues, softly now.

The reverend swipes at his brow again. Agrees a plea for forgiveness might be warranted. Maggie understands his thinking. For if she and her family *are* frauds, would they dare utter the word? Would they dare place that thought in any mind? No. Certainly not. Only the innocent would dare. Only the innocent have nothing to fear under eyes both mortal and divine.

More raps. They are are followed by bangs, thuds. The air in the room is thick and heady, like the air before a storm.

"Now, Lizzie. Now. Repent!" the company hollers. There is more name-calling: "wicked girl," "heartless thing," "unnatural creature." Maggie hears Katie call out, "Repent, you niddy-noddy!" At this, Maggie, to her own surprise, calls out, "Yes, now, Liz. Get it done with."

Maggie had meant to keep silent as a show of sympathy, but she has been swept along. I'm only fourteen, she thinks. And Katie is only eleven. It isn't fair.

Lizzie does not hold out long. She clutches her hair. Drops to her knees. Chokes back her sobs. "Forgive me, spirits. Oh, do so. Forgive me and, and, come back."

"And?" Leah asks.

Lizzie squints at her mother's face. Sniffs. "And I'll never doubt you again, spirits. Nor ask you to leave. Oh, crumb, but I promise. I promise. *Je promets.*"

"Spirits? Will that suffice?" Leah asks.

A heavy rapping. The company sighs. Maggie smiles with relief. Now things can go on as they have before. She will even get Lizzie to laugh about this incident once they are back at Mechanics Square. And then Maggie, with Katie's help, will cajole and jest and Lizzie will indulge her young aunts, as she did when she visited them in Hydesville, and help pass the dreary hours.

Lizzie meekly asks if she may leave; Leah says no, absolutely not. The Reverend Clarke wants to test the spirits with questions of his personal life and Leah does not want the spirit chain broken. Lizzie looks stricken. For pity's sake, Maggie thinks. Wouldn't it be a kindness to let her go?

The reverend asks the colour of his favourite pen-knife. When his mother died. If his son has passed his exams. The answers are all correct. "How can they know this?" he wonders aloud. "My dear friends might know all this, but no one else."

"Would the spirits like to hear the music?" Leah asks.

The spirits would; they are always in the mood for music.

Leah sits at the Grangers' fine organ. She scales on the reedy keys and then sings "Barbara Allen," her voice swelling out strong and toffee-warm. And without a single faltering note, Maggie realizes.

Reverend Clarke bows his head. "The visible and the invisible worlds have met together this day. I'm convinced even to the marrow."

Convinced, yes, and now suggesting that all and sundry should know of it.

Maggie presses a palm to her brow. Isaac's remedy must be wearing off, because her head-pain has returned, and in one telling shot.

CHAPTER 7.

The garret's ladderback chair creaked as I settled in. I spread my skirts to create a dish for my knitting. My patient smiled. "You look to be floating on air."

"Air?"

"Your skirts, they hide the legs of the chair so that you seem magicked, so that—"

"Not everyone is small as a mustard seed. Some of us need a tad more space to hang our hats." (I am, as I said, a fleshy woman and of decent height.)

"Do you live near to here, then?"

"Not so near, nor far."

"A walking distance?"

"At times."

"At times you need the omnibus?"

"At times I walk."

"You must have a very practical home."

"I move hither and yon, if you must know. To the precincts where I'm most needed. Such is my duty."

"I see. I moved a great deal also. No place seemed a home. I moved and moved. Was never quite here, nor there. As such, I don't wish to move again, is that clear, Mrs. Mellon?"

"As Heaven's bells," I said, and frowned over a lax cable stitch.

"Yet if I were ever to name my favourite place it would be the

Troup Street cottage." She paused, waiting for some response, but I was too intent on my task to give one, though I was thinking, certainly, of my New England cottage, of the whales slaughtered on the beach below, their bloody flesh laid out in strips long as roads, their illuminating oil filling barrels upon barrels. Of the scrimshaws that Mr. Mellon carved (his one and only talent). And of the sand carpets my son and I delighted in making for the keeping room. We changed the pattern each week. I should add that my son had an artist's keen eye, and these sand carpets were a marvel to all who saw them.

"Leah chose it, of course."

"Chose? Chose what?"

"Troup Street, the place I should like to return to, if ever I could. But I can't."

"No," I said. My patients are ever on about returning. But we are knit in our places and must make the best of it. I told her this fact, and she agreed. But she told me of Troup Street regardless, and when Leah first beheld it.

"WE ARE ARRIVED, MOTHER," Leah announces, and stops outside the cottage on Troup Street on this blustery March day of '49. The cottage is incongruously modest amid the mansions and stately homes of Rochester's Third Ward, but the path to the cheery red door has been cleared of any snow, the boxwood hedging is neatly trimmed, the lion's-head knocker fresh-oiled and agleam.

"It is the pitch-perfect residence for our spirits," Leah declares, as Mother huffs up beside her. Leah's sisters remain behind at the Mechanics Square walk-up. Their opinions on the new rental hardly matter. And they have been acting oddly—guarded, even surly— since Lizzie's departure, which was just before the Yuletide. But those two will sing a new tune, Leah thinks, once the merry times begin. For the Reverend Clarke has indeed been telling all and sundry about his meeting with the spirits. And these all and sundry have been clamouring to meet the spirits. And both sides, the visible and the invisible, need to be entertained in proper style. Leah finds it nearly impossible to believe that only a year has passed since the peddler's ghost started up, and then promptly knocked open the door to more worthy spirits. But only *nearly* impossible. Nothing is *wholly* impossible to believe. Not any longer.

The red door swings open at Leah's touch. No rattling. No difficulties. Ah, Elizabeth. Lizzie. The girl, granted, had been contrite after her abominable behaviour at the Grangers', but she still wants nothing to do with spirit sittings. And her reluctance will raise questions, questions that might weaken the spirit chain. Leah explained this to Lizzie no less than three times, and yet she remains obdurate; thus Leah had no choice but to send the girl to her father's in Illinois. Lizzie had been reluctant, true. She had wept and wailed. Likely because Leah has always talked about Bowman Fish as if he were pure evil. He is not, of course. Leah has met pure evil aplenty in her life, and Bowman is not of such mettle. No, Leah has lately understood that Bowman is a man much like any other. Prey to animal urges. Believing a woman the same.

Leah turns to her mother. She is plucking at a yew tree and muttering what might be a spell.

"My heavens, Mother, cease that, you will give the neighbours cause for gossip."

"But the yew . . . It takes its nourishment from the dead, doesn't it?"

"That is mere superstition. Besides, the owner assured me the place is not haunted. There have been no murders committed here. Nor has this house seen any deaths from strange maladies or from unexplained circumstances. No, it has known only the ordinary deaths, of infants and the aged and such. Now follow me."

Her mother does, though with cautious steps and darting, fearful eyes.

The vestibule is commodious, the hallway broad and painted a clear-day blue. The kitchen is tucked discreetly at the back of the cottage, along with the family keeping room. The parlour is set prominently in the front and is connected to the larder by a back stair. It has no furnishings except a sturdy organ, a chandelier hung on pulleys, and a nickle-plated parlour stove, nicely ornamented and surrounded by a wrought-iron guard.

"I suppose it is nice room," Mother says. "But parlours, well, they do seem wasteful, don't they? Being only for entertainment and for setting out the dead."

"No decent family can live without a parlour these days, Mother."

The mention of family must have brought Lizzie to Mother's mind, for now she is grousing on about sending for her. "It has been long enough, hasn't it? Yes? Now, poppet, I—"

"Ma . . . Mother. We have discussed this to bits. I shall send for Elizabeth the moment she regains her senses. Only, she must learn to govern her rage, a governance that I suspect shall take long and diligent practice."

Her mother sighs. "Well, you know best about all that. I suppose the organ is fine, isn't it?"

"In an antiquated fashion," Leah says, and taps the keys. Winces. "It requires tuning. And we shall need purchase sandwich lamps and a good-sized table for the sittings. An ovoid one, yes, to show the equality of all souls, and—"

"Shhh, Leah," Mother Margaret whispers, her eyes aswim with fright. Something, someone is in the room with them. Leah hears a suspiration. Her mother gasps. Leah slowly turns, then peers into the dimmest corner of the parlour, calls, "Hallo?"

He is of middling height and middling build. His skin has a greyish cast, as does his hair, his eyes, his clothes, his teeth. His expression is glum but not threatening. His voice when he bids them good day is flat-toned, unassuming. Leah doubts a more unnoticeable has ever lived. "Mr. Alvie Kincaid," she says in delight.

"Alfie, ma'am, not Alvie. Alfie Kincaid."

"Yes, that is it." She turns to her mother. "Oh, stop fretting, Mother, the landlord informed me he came with the place."

At Troup Street, once Mother and the girls are settled in, Leah arranges spirit circles for every weekday evening, and then for Saturday afternoons as well. The Posts, the Bushes, the Grangers, the Littles and the Willets; these are the regulars attendees, though Mrs. Lemira Kedzie visits often from Albany, and Ruth and Norman Culver come often from Arcadia. None of Leah's close family visits, however, not David, not Maria, and certainly not Leah's father, though Leah has asked him to do so many times in letters, as has her mother.

By mid-summer of '49 the regular attendees are bringing friends and relations. Some are respectfully curious. Others respectfully dubious. All leave offerings: baskets of delicacies, tins of beeswax candles, bottles of costly whale oil for the lamps, bottles of wine, champagne, brandy. Leah asks for no monetary payment. The Fox sisters are answering a call; they are doing a great service. Foremost they are ladies. And ladies do not have paid "jobs." However, if monetary gifts are obscured within the baskets and tins, Leah cannot object. Money is required, after all, to keep a good table, to pay the dressmaker (homespun is out of the question now), and to pay Alfie for his increasingly diverse services. Leah thinks him the ideal servant. Maggie and Katie do not. They think him nasty and unsettling. Those marl-coloured eyes. Those teeth.

One of Leah's regular callers to the Troup Street cottage is Mr. Eliab Capron. He is pin neat, his dark hair smooth as a cap. He is a Quaker. An abolitionist. A natural philosopher. A newspaper man. A doubter. "Foremost I am a man of science," he proclaims on this afternoon visit. "I cannot believe so readily in ghosts. Nor will I be swayed by what I wish to believe. Indeed, I am certain there is a scientific solution to the spirit phenomena. Consider the cholera that is wreaking such death and havoc in England and our own Southern states, even as I speak. Now, to the untrained eye it might appear that God has allowed one of his apocalyptic Horsemen out for a careless gallop, but on closer scrutiny the culprit is clearly only noxious, polluted air."

"My heavens," Leah says. "I must confess that all this science and philosophy is beyond our womanly ken. Do explain further, but slowly, if you please."

Leah, along with Maggie, Katie, Mother Margaret and Calvin, is receiving Eliab in the Troup Street parlour. They sit about the new ovoid table. Alfie has just brought in tea and a plate of Calvin's lemon drops. Katie pops a lemon drop in her mouth and smiles at Eliab. Maggie, however, is frowning into her teacup, as if seeing unwelcome answers in the soggy leaves.

"I will gladly explain," Eliab begins. "Do not hesitate to stop me if you cannot follow. You see, I believe Miss Katherine is the prime portal. I believe her bones conduct sounds from the earth's core. Perhaps the rumbles of earthquakes undetectable to human ears, or else the bangs of distant thunder." He turns to Mother. "Mrs. Fox, might I have your permission to take Miss Katherine to Auburn with me, the better to conduct experiments. All with the utmost discretion, by all means."

"Katie? What are your opinions?" Mother asks.

"You want my opinion? Mine?"

"Her opinion?" Leah puts in.

"Don't girls have opinions? I believe I did. Certainly you did, Leah. Gracious evers, did you have opinions. Well, Katherine?"

Katie takes another of Calvin's lemon drops. "I'll go hither and thither, but I won't slither."

Eliab smiles uneasily. "My wife and I will treat her as our own daughter."

"She may go. Yes, she should. I think so," Mother says.

"I must say that—" Leah begins.

"Poppet, if Mr. Capron can find an explanation to help end the hauntings, then who can argue? Who?"

"Not I," Calvin says.

"Not me neither . . . either?" Katie says.

Maggie sets her teacup aside with a clatter. "Nor me. Argue? Nope. But I wonder if Lizzie would? We could telegraph and inquire, but she's so really so far off now."

Maggie's tone is innocent, Leah notes, but her expression is grouty, devious. Honestly, Lizzie has been gone for nearly eight months now. You would think Maggie would have forgotten her by now. Leah sniffs. "Nor I, then. We cannot have discordance." She glances at Maggie. "From anyone."

"So, we are all agreed," Eliab declares, and rubs his hands together. He looks to Katie. "You are the most remarkable girl, Miss Katherine. Alike . . . yes, as you said, Miss Margaret, a telegraph machine—"

"I did?"

"Yes," Eliab says. "One that transmits betwixt the mortal and the immortal worlds and—"

Mother slaps the table. "No! I'll not have my daughter compared to a machine, will I? Not one that men touch and operate and . . . No, no. That is that."

"I agree, certainly, Mrs. Fox," Eliab says hastily. "Yet, then what of a . . . a conductor, a conductor of energy. Or more precisely, a 'spirit conductor.'"

"A conductor? As in a railway man?" Mother asks.

Eliab stands as if already at a lectern. "Yes. For is not the struggle for the dead to reach the living alike the struggle of those enslaved to reach freedom? Perhaps only now the dead are discovering the appropriate, yes, yes, conductors! Those who are pure of heart. Whose minds are free of the traps of intellect. The fetters of book-ish knowledge. Yes, you girls are conductresses on a railroad, one that is no more wrought of wood and iron than the so-named rail-road that takes slaves to freedom, but yet is of similar mettle, of similar God-given purpose."

Leah tsks. "My dear Eliab, *conductor* brings to mind a hulking man in cover-alls, yanking at a whistle. It is untoward. And comic."

Eliab taps his chin. "Comic? That won't do. This is a matter serious as . . . serious can be. Then what say of . . . of medium? Ah, in that you ladies are like the medium of water or ether through which the spirits flow." Eliab moves his hand as if writing some tome on the subject.

Katie pops another lemon drop into her mouth. "I like that. *Medium.* Um-um, mum. It reminds me of *hum.*"

"And dumb," Maggie mutters.

Leah says, "It is a splendid suggestion, pitch-perfect. *Medium* is neither hot nor cold. Neither this nor that. It is exactly in the middle, which is where we are—in the middle between the living and the dead. And be assured we appreciate greatly, dearest Eliab, how seri-ously all this is being taken."

"Laws, I don't know. I suppose it will suffice. I think so," Mother says.

Leah glances over at Maggie, then Katie. A rap sounds. Eliab looks up, astonished, eager. "Do they agree? The blessed spirits?"

He does not seem like a man of science now, Leah thinks. More like a boy at a country fair. "Yes, they do agree," she says. "For which, dear ones, I am most grateful and relieved."

CHAPTER 8.

"Tell me that is not a perfect gusset!"

"Do caps require gussets?" my patient asked. Saturday had come round again (it was a Saturday when I first arrived) and my patient and I were, by this time, all at ease with each other.

"No, duck, but mittens do."

"We have mittens now?"

"Yes."

She gave her mischiefed smile. "You have many skills, Mrs. Mellon. What of exorcism? Of demons and the like? Can you finagle that as well?"

I did not smile back. It was, to be frank, a question I am too often asked. "No, for that I call on a priest or rabbi sort. I don't hold with this do-it-your-own business. Why do you ask?"

"We became well-known in Rochester that summer and into the autumn of '49, you see. Talked about, noticed when we went out. Leah downplayed our notoriety, made light of it all, but then a preacher came and tried to exorcise the Troup Street cottage. Well, that's when even I knew we had crossed some murky threshold."

"Were you not afraid? Folks usually are."

"Of the preacher? No. I thought him a benighted addle-wit."

I had meant the demons, but did not quibble as she continued, "If the spirits had talked to a man, none would have questioned God's intent. But to a woman? Why, hadn't the Devil just tipped his hand, or so Leah said . . . But alas and such, perhaps that preacher was correct. Perhaps something squatted inside me, dark and wanting. I had ever disliked church, you see. The exhortations of preachers worked like some sleep charm. Many a whump did I get from the damned church stick. And those preachers, they were ever so certain about God's purpose. How could they be? How could anyone claim such certainty?"

"I surely don't," I allowed, and shifted in the ladderback. "Though some say His doings are alike those of a prankster."

"Ah, Some-say," she murmured. "Why does Some-say say that?"

"Why, in the fashion that He, God, sends us trials and privations and humiliations, but for such obscure purposes that it seems He might be playing a prank or a jape upon us, or even some manner of hoax or confidence trick, for we are let in upon neither the purpose, nor the truth of it."

"The good grief. I've had those thoughts precisely," my patient said, and with a satisfied air, as if we had agreed on new draperies.

THE PREACHER HAS A CHIN BOIL, a filch of black hair, a chalk in his chilblained fingers with which he marks crosses on the new-waxed floor.

Maggie counts out his followers on this chilled September morning. They are eight in all and are as dark-dressed, nasty-visaged and fearful as one would expect of people casting out demons. One follower even clutches an ancient copy of the *Malleus Maleficarum*. The cover image is of a witch being burned at the stake. How very quaint, Maggie thinks as she holds tight to Leah's hand.

These unwelcome visitors cram into the parlour of the Troup Street cottage. Maggie stands in the entry with Leah. Mother dithers about the interlopers. Calvin has gone off on a military drill. Alfie is at the butcher's. Katie is staying, as Mother insisted, at the Caprons' in Auburn. Eliab Capron's experiments are going badly—or well, depending on one's perspective. Anywise, he has written that he has found nothing yet to explain the spirits. Maggie had been worried about Katie being at the Caprons' on her own.

Now she is relieved Katie is not here at Troup Street, for if these superstitious niddy-noddies were to witness one of Kat's little fits it might well bring back the fashion for tarring and feathering.

A follower gasps at the white imprint of a hand on Mother's cheek.

Mother wipes her face with her apron. "But it's not . . . that is, I was just baking bread, wasn't I? Yes."

"Where is your reason, Mother?" Leah hisses. "Where? Why-ever did you let them into my house?" Leah's rage is barely contained. Maggie knows the signs: the drumming vein on her temple, the rising heat of Leah's hand, held fast to Maggie's.

"I had no choice, did I? He's a man of God."

Leah snorts. Maggie feels her sister's nail scratch twice in her palm: the signal for *wait*.

"Laws, but this is all because of the money. I told you not to charge, Leah, didn't I? I said folks would think it untoward, oh, and worse."

"Charge? Charge? We do not charge. We accept gifts, that is all. Because, truly, how am I to pay the rent? How? I cannot teach music any longer. The students keep away with all this spirit business, and the girls must have clothes suitable for society. It is not as if you sew up the latest fashion, Mother. And we must eat. And more and more people are asking us to help them. How can we help them if we have no money? How? The spirits know nothing of money. They do not need to eat or be presentable. They are invisible, which is lucky for them."

"Please don't be arguing," Maggie begs. "Not now."

"You are quite right, sister. We must be in strict harmony."

The preacher's followers kneel on the pretty hooked rugs. A mouse, or perhaps a beetle, skitters under the whatnot cabinet. Mother crosses her fingers.

"What are you doing, Mother?" Leah whispers. "Cease it. He might notice and think . . ."

But the preacher has already noticed. He approaches the trio as if they are feral dogs. Dips his chalky fingers in a bowl of water clutched by a woman plain, Maggie thinks, as all-sin. The preacher flicks the water about. "Begone! Begone. Draw back to your evil lair. Do not consort with these women."

Leah checks a laugh. "My heavens, sir, by your manner one would think the Devil has something to fear from us."

"Leah," Mother gasps. The preacher's followers chorus hallelujahs.

Hallelujah until you choke, Maggie thinks.

The preacher holds up his bible like a shield. "The Devil has gained your soul, Mrs. Fish. And the souls of your vixen sisters. You have gambled and—"

A thud. Another. The preacher calls out to Jesus. A third thud. The mantel clock shakes. And now rapid, smaller thuds, like hailstones falling. Or brimstone, Maggie supposes, and nearly smiles.

The preacher's followers stand.

Leah says, "It may be wise to leave, sir. This instance."

"I warn you, woman, this is the Devil's den."

Leah's gaze is so cold that the preacher, to Maggie's delight, shivers. "No," Leah declares. "This is *my* home."

The preacher and his followers sneer and hiss as they leave, like villains in a puppet show. Mother shuts the door firmly behind them, and studies her image in the vestibule looking glass. Her reflection, Maggie notes with surprise, is almost formidable.

The night after the preacher's visit, Maggie is jolted awake by angry voices. She pats desperately about for the candle and the lucifer matches. The lucifer flares on the third strike. Maggie slaps at the sparks as they fall on the bedclothes, holds her breath against the reeking fumes, lights her candle.

"My Lord! What do you think you are doing out here?"

Maggie tenses. But the voice is not in the room, nor even in the house; it is from outside: Leah's.

Maggie goes to the window and opens the sash, expecting to see some poor robber cowering from Leah's wrath. But it is not a robber, it is their mother. And Mother is neither cowering nor fretting, for a change. She stands opposite Leah over a smouldering pile. The moon is full and the garden has the metallic, sharp-edged aspect of a tin relief. Both women are in their nightdresses. Flakes of burning newsprint float around them. Even from her vantage Maggie can smell bitterroot, sage, burning hair. She rushes to her dressing table. Shakes out her hair jar, then Katie's. The hair, plucked from their brushes, kept for pillow stuffings and hairpieces, is gone, all of it.

Back at the window Maggie notices the bloodied linen wrap on her mother's wrist. "Is Ma ill? Injured?" she calls down.

"I'm all-manner of fine," Mother calls back. "That preacher had the wrong tack, didn't he? But now everything will be lovely, girls. I've sent the ghosts away. They'll not bother us any longer. Sometime the old ways are best, aren't they? Now, come, let's inside."

Maggie runs down to the vestibule and together she and Leah put their mother to bed. Mother plucks at her night wrap, her brief resolution gone. "It will be as it was, poppets, won't it?"

Maggie and Leah soothe her of one accord, then leave her to sleep. They make their way to the kitchen by silent agreement. They are often of such like mind these days. "I can't bear this," Maggie says. "Poor Ma. We should tell her and such. For certain we should."

Leah shushes her. Points to some crockery as if it might have ears. "Tell her? What? How you and Katherina got that peddler to haunt the old house? How you orchestrated it all? It would be seen as a crime, I tell you."

"A crime? That's balderdash, Leah, we—"

"And whatever will Amy and Isaac think? And all the others? Consider. If we cease now, just as we are preparing to show the wider world, then we shall be suspect."

The wider world? Maggie thinks, and visions the great maw of it before her. Because the preacher and his lot are not the only naysayers. The Rochester papers have taken note of the happenings at the Troup Street cottage. Some writers are calling the Fox sisters charlatans, gross opportunists, humbugs. Others are calling them gifted seers, divine diviners, illuminators of a new age. In short, the battle lines are being drawn between the believers and the doubters. And the spirits want the battle joined. Or so Leah insists. The regulars to their spirit circles are less certain, Maggie knows. Public humiliation is a worry. As is loss of business. Banishment from church. Mobs.

Leah grips her braid as if it were a cudgel, continues, "Indeed, if we turn aside now, Margaretta, our reputations shall be ruined. *Our* reputations, sister. Mine and yours and the reputation of this entire family. As for our honour, it is all bound together like so much rickwood for the fire. No, no, you simply cannot stop now, Margaretta. Even if that is what you truly wish, which I doubt. You have gone too far in. *We* have, that is—for you have taken me along, my lamb. Consider those men who swim. Do they turn back when crossing a body of water? No, they forge on. If they turn back, they shall surely drown in the dark depths. But the other side, ah, the other side. How lovely with its rich, green banks." She pours Maggie a cider. "No, we cannot for a moment shirk. Never mind the swimmers, we must be like soldiers who charge headlong into battle."

"And where'd you chance by that comparison? Calvin?"

"Hah, did you ever imagine he would be so enthusiastic about the spirits? After all the tricks they played upon him?" Leah's seriousness switches, as it often does, and her laugh—her genuine laugh—has a merry trill, unlike her parlour laugh, which is merely grating.

Maggie laughs also then, and says, "Still, it's got to stop one day. It's getting grievously dreary."

"And Hydesville isn't dreary? Imagine yourself there, all alone but for our dear parents, your life a quiet, endless interlude. Oh, there might be crickets cricketing and bats flapping and owls hooting, those sorts of sounds, but no happy evenings, no friends constantly calling. No spirits comforting the living. No new frocks or nice outings."

Maggie feels herself on a threshold. "Say it," she says, low-voiced. "Just once, Leah, tell what is really, truly happening."

"Dearest Margaretta, some things are best not uttered."

A silence as Maggie considers. She has the queer sense that her life's path is being decided, that her next step will lead her to some far-flung outpost, from which return is impossible.

"You said we could be quit of this anytime, Leah. You promised that, back in Hydesville when you made us show you."

"Indeed, I did say *we* could be quit of it. We. Us, together, not just you. This is not your decision alone. Do think of others, for once, Margaretta."

Maggie bites her lip to holds back desperate, pleading words. Such words are futile with Leah. She knows this much after seeing Lizzie banished. Instead she says, calmly, "I *am* thinking of others, Leah . . . of Ma, actually. I am thinking that mayhap her spell worked just dandy."

CHAPTER 9.

My patient said, "Mother's old magic did work for a time, of course, but perhaps she did not spill enough blood or burn enough hair because her spell was not enough to keep the spirits away forever."

"Surely you didn't believe in your mother's spells and charms," I said.

"No, by that time I had decided to believe in nothing but my own self. Indeed, after the preacher's visit I never attended church again, nor cracked a bible, nor prayed. Not, that is, until Elisha left me for the Arctic. I was stubborn then."

"You're just as stubborn now, duck," I assured her. "If not, you'd already be dead."

"Well, yes," my patient said, and fell into one of her brooding studies.

I put on my best cheery manner. "Well, this garret is certainly as chilled as your Elisha's Arctic realms. I'll bring an extra coverlet next time, duck, and a foot-stove, to boot. All right? Yes?" (I should mention it was now the 9th of February and a wet snow pasted the garret's three linked windows.) "And here is your medicine," I added.

She took the tumbler without a word and I dusted the garret, all-quiet, so as not to disturb her thoughts. I had hopes, I allow, that she was composing her last words, or debating on a hymn for her funeral. Working out, that is, all those details and considerations one should when nearing imminent demise.

I did try my heart's best to quit the spirits, Mrs. Mellon, Many times, alas and such. I ever tried. I ever failed." She set aside the empty tumbler.

I sighed. "Well, I am not amazed. Spirits are everywhere a body turns. They're sold in every dry goods and chophouse. Are ever a temptation. But they do keep the blue devils at bay." I picked up my needles, untangled some yarn skeins. "So I've been told."

"Hah, not those spirits. The ghost-talking, I meant. Mind, I did try to be quit of the liquid spirits many, many times as well."

"Not to worry about that, duck," I said. "We ever try."

To which my patient merely replied, "You work too hard." I should add that she stated this as an absolute fact, which was how she stated many things. She was, to be frank, very hard to contradict. Or doubt.

MAGGIE'S DAMP, unbound hair falls over the back of the sofa and nearly touches the coal brazier set on the rug. She holds her novel, *Tabitha's Dilemma*, away from the smoke. The parlour smells of benozine, of the lavender strewn in the coals. There is the ticking of the mantel clock. The faint snapping as Maggie turns the pages. Otherwise, quiet reigns in the Troup Street cottage. The spirits are silent. Not a thud. Not a rap. And for entire week now. Not even Katie's return from the Caprons' has inspired their presence.

But now there is a tap-tap on the cover of Maggie's novel.

Leah.

"Allow me to guess, little sister. A beanteous and gentle heroine raised in poverty is discovered to be the heiress to vast fortune. The impediments to her fine marriage are thrown aside and all ends joyfully."

Maggie puts the book aside and inspects her hair, which is now dry and pleasingly fragrant from the lavender smoke. "My, Leah, aren't you cynical."

"Cynical? What of you and your little comments?"

"I'm witty."

"But not wise."

"Why in tunket does a girl need wise anywise?"

"Nor imaginative."

"I can 'imaginative' you leaving me to read my book in peace."

Leah looks Maggie up and down. "And what of *imagining* your prospects if the spirits stay gone, Margaretta? With no dowry there's none will marry you except some ancient farmer, reeking of farm animals. What of *imagining* yourself banished to a kitchen, tending the heat-blasting monster that is the cookstove. You who have taken to an easeful life as sparrows do the blue air? And then the babes coming lickety-split. And if they don't murder you with their birthing, the likely deaths of these babies, one after the other, will render you aged before your time. Your witty comments will turn into arias of woe. God help you, since I shall not."

Maggie picks up the novel. Her throat is very dry—from the coal smoke, that is it. She opens a page at random. *Tabitha's heart split in twain at his mere glance.*

"And here is another *imagining*," Leah continues, as if she, too, has read the line. "You running off with some swain, your reputation in ruins. Scorned by all. A veritable slattern, and all because some spirits were acting childish."

Maggie flings the book to the rug. "Childish?"

"Yes. Childish. Brattish. Foolish. Running away without an explanation. Showing ingratitude." Leah heaves a breath. "Tell me, Margaretta, honestly now, what is required for the spirits to return?"

"I've not a glimmer. Mayhap you should go ask Ma. She's the one who spelled them off."

"And what of Katherina?" Leah says, as if to herself. She turns towards the kitchen. Maggie follows, grim-eyed.

Katie is at the kitchen table playing with jackstraws. She tumbles one off the edge. Picks it up. Shakes her head. "Now, really, it weren't as bad as all that. Buck-up . . . Oh, hallo, Leah."

Leah stands over her. "Truly, but I miss our invisible friends. Do you not, Katherina? These jackstraw men seem as poor substitutes."

Katie rolls her eyes up, as if to read her own thoughts. "Mag said we got each other and that should be enough."

"It is," Maggie says from behind Leah. Katie looks from one to the other.

"'Have' each other, my girl, not 'got,'" Leah says. "And what I meant to ask was: do you wish them to return?"

"I do really like them, I reckon, I mean, I suppose."

"As do I."

"Well, I don't," Maggie puts in. "I'm sick to the teeth of them."

Leah ignores her. "Just consider how nicely you are treated when the spirits are about, Katherina, how special you become."

Katie plucks forlorn at the jackstraws. "That's all-true, I guess."

"You're special anywise, Kat," Maggie says. "Don't listen to Leah."

"Katherina, would you care to visit with the Caprons in Auburn again? Stay for another nice interlude there? The spirits so enjoy Eliab's 'experiments.' They are rather like games, are they not? Indeed, our dear spirits might consider returning if you were there. And Eliab is such a respectful man, and so kind, and his wife keeps such a costly and gracious table."

"I got to . . . I mean I *should* ask Ma first," Katie says, near to tears. "When is she back from market? Is she back yet?"

"This is your decision, Katherina. You are hardly a child. Do you wish to go or not?"

"I dunno. I really, really don't. Why is it up to me?" Katie whacks at a jackstraw. It breaks into pieces. "Now what have I done? I didn't mean it. Poor thing. I'm sorry, sorry." She shuffles the pieces together.

"I am sure Mr. Jack has forgiven you," Leah says. "Ah, here comes Mother back from market."

Maggie follows Leah's gaze out the kitchen window to where their mother trundles up the back walk. She hefts a large package from which blood drips, an eye bulges.

"How savoury," Leah says to Maggie. "A calf's head . . . that brings to mind the bedtime tale. Of the Goose Girl? Wasn't it about a common serving girl who impersonated a princess. And wasn't there a calf's head that was hung from a gate?"

"A horse's head," Maggie mutters, feeling dizzy. "From an archway."

"No matter. The point is that the bleeding head gave her advice, but did she listen? No. And look what happened. The foolish girl was caught out for her lies. She was stripped and nailed in a coffin and dragged behind a coach until she was dead."

"That wasn't fair at all," Katie pipes in.

"Naturally, it wasn't fair, my dear, and—"

"And I never ever liked that story," Katie continues. "I didn't get the point of it all."

"The point, Katherina, Margaretta, is that once the serving girl began her charade, there was no backing down . . . ah, Mother," Leah says, because Mother has entered the kitchen and dropped the calf's head on the table.

"Have we a bag for the brains? Girls? Have we?" Mother asks.

"There," Leah says, and indicates the linen bag near to Maggie. "I do hope the butcher chalked that head, Mother, for our money is nearly gone. Soon we shall be as penniless as Mozart in his pauper's shroud. Soon we shall be dining on bread crusts and water alike prisoners or . . . inmates," Leah says, as if an idea has just come to mind.

"Dandy damn-fine by me," Maggie mutters.

"Is it," Leah muses, as if she hasn't noticed Maggie's cussing at all.

Thirteen days later, Maggie, Leah and Calvin alight from a hired coach. They are on the outskirts of Rochester. The building before them is stark and low-built and girded by a high, wrought-iron fence. It is late September and leaves skitter in a cool wind and cling to Maggie's pelisse coat.

"But what is this place?" Maggie asks, appalled. "I thought . . . thought we were going for pastries, and for a gander at the big falls."

"We are, after," Leah says. "Have courage, my dear, this is dear Amy and Isaac's latest concern. The mad and the wretched need somewhere to live, like anyone, apparently. Now come, we must support their Godly efforts."

"Support? How?" Maggie asks, her voice an unheard croak.

Calvin holds open the heavy door of the asylum. The gloomy corridor is rank with despair. Someone chants a child's rhyme. Someone else interrogates the furniture. There is a cackle of laughter. A shriek. Another.

God-in-all, I wish Ma were here, Maggie thinks, but their mother, upon Leah's urging, left a week ago for Arcadia. "The spirits are no longer tormenting us," Leah told her. "There is no need to stay." Mother asked Maggie to return to Arcadia with her, but Leah said, "Impossible. I cannot be alone here with just Alfie and Calvin. Consider the talk. Though if Margaretta truly wants to return to the quiet, distant countryside . . ."

Maggie did not. But with Katie staying once again with the Caprons in Auburn, the Troup Street cottage has become quieter yet. The news is out that the spirits have gone, and thus no longer do people leave their cards, begging a sitting. Close friends rarely stay long, having as they do their own businesses, families, lives. And Leah is gone most days, doing what Maggie can hardly guess, though often she is in the company of Calvin, who holds her arm with brotherly aplomb. Even Alfie is often away on personal business. Money. Well. Suddenly little is about. No more oranges and macadamias. No more shopping for reticules and point lace. Fewer outings altogether—thus Maggie's delight at Leah's suggestion for pastries and an outing to the Genesee falls.

"Afterwards, Margaretta, you may watch the water falling until you're mesmerized," Leah says now. "Afterwards, you may eat all the pastries you wish."

Maggie's voice fails her, as does her appetite. Really, she cannot imagine eating anything, not for a good while. Each cell has the semblance of a room—chairs and tables, beds and linens. But no lamps, no candles, nothing that might ignite. And nothing sharp-edged. She watches as a woman threatens an unseen mocker, as a man croons to a fly on his fist. A girl, near Maggie's own age, grins lasciviously at Calvin.

"The Posts and some of their Quaker brethren are advocating more humane treatment for these unfortunates—that is, no chains nor beatings and such," Leah says, looking around. "My heavens, but I do hope they can manage that."

Maggie can still say nothing. She trails behind Calvin and Leah as they enter a courtyard. The inmates here, all women, seem less afflicted. "Mild lunatics," the matron informs them. "They look normal. Then they get their fits or hear things talk. Sometimes they come at you. I teach 'em not to." She pats the strop at her waist. Just then Maggie sees a small, thin woman, standing alone by the sundial. A spare rains begins and this woman holds her palms up, weighing one drop, then the other, like some mad lady justice. Her black hair straggles over her face, hiding her features. "Kat?" Maggie whispers in horror. The woman pulls her hair back. Shows her lined and tragic face. Maggie's heart steadies. She is not Katie. No. Of course not.

"Well, should we head on before we get too chilled?" Leah asks.

Maggie huddles silently in the carriage seat for the seemingly endless ride back to Rochester. "Why-ever did you take me there, Leah? Why?" she demands once the aqueduct is in view.

"You know, dear."

Maggie doesn't answer.

"Margaretta. Attend me. Please. The world is cruel to women with any kind of talent, any kind of power. It must be guided aright or it is misunderstood. Consider that harridan with her strop just now, and that preacher who came dousing for devils, who hallelujahed to beat the band. His ilk must be guarded against even more. And I have been thinking, too, about those girls in Salem long ago. Honestly, I cannot get them out of my mind. Do you know of them?"

Maggie surely does. She has seen depictions aplenty. The Salem story is popular enough. The girls in their old-timey dresses writhing as if bewitched and bedevilled. The accused witches hanging from gallows. A four-year-old imprisoned. An old man crushed by stones. Appalling how it could have gone so far. That so many lost their reason.

Maggie manages the barest nod.

"Evil was done, Margaretta, when the wrong people, with the wrong understandings, took notice of those girls. The girls themselves were not evil, but they could not help themselves."

"I can," Maggie says sullenly.

"Perhaps, but Katherina cannot. That is why she needs our guidance so."

Back at Troup Street, Maggie re-reads Katie's latest letter from Auburn. Not an easy task given Katie's imaginative spelling, her joining hand that resembles a nailed fence.

27 September, 1849

Dearest Sis,

The Spirits came back, Mag. I'm sorry, I couldn't help it. It was like they wanted to have fun again. It was like they felt left aside or lonely or forgotten or something. The Caprons' parlour table didn't gallop. cross the room like at our Cottage, but it did tip and a teacup got shattered and it was Mrs. Capron's second best and the Sitters all accused each other of doing the tipping but everyone was real perplexed and supposed in the end it was the Invisibles. In one sitting a shadow on the wall looked just like a dog and someone said it was Cerberus and someone else asked, "Then why doesn't it have three heads?" And, Oh, Mag, I've met such a passel of admiring folk and all of Auburn is talking about the Spirits. And I've tried champagne and it's just the dandiest. Better than cider by leagues. It makes you feel real grown-up and cheery in a nonce. Oh, I had one little old fit, I guess, but I can't recollect it. Don't tell Ma or Leah about that, not that it matters anywise. Mr. Capron says I get the little fits because the Spirits like me so.

I sure miss you and I hope the spirits come back to Troup Street, too, because I really really don't like the quiet anymore.

Giant Love and Kisses,
Kat

Maggie folds the letter tighter, tighter. She wanders to the kitchen. Leah is nowhere in sight, though a pot simmers on the cookstove. Maggie peers in. Flesh floats off a bone. A cow's tongue turns in the broth. The cuts of meat are becoming cheaper and less appetizing by the day. Soon Maggie thinks, there'll be nothing to chew on but viscera and hung meats.

Into the parlour now. No Leah here either. No Alfie. We need more furnishings, Maggie decides. And the walls should be jammed with paintings and lithographs. Nothing bucolic, nothing with horizons or cows. Just scenes of bustling streets or crowded rooms. She would like the latest gasolier lanterns as well. Light and more light, until even the bleakest corners are illuminated. Katie. Kat. Maggie only now realizes how much she fears for her sister. And how fiercely she misses her. Is it possible I miss *them* also? Maggie wonders. Possible that I miss the spirits? That even the dead are better company than no company at all? Because it is only when Maggie is alone, as now, that she senses not the dead, that chorusing multitude—but death, which is the void, loneliness incarnate, the dark itself. Her mother warned her of it back in Hydesville, even before the peddler's ghost arrived. "The dark is at the approach," she told a bored Maggie at autumn's end, but Maggie didn't listen, because Maggie always listens too late.

A day later the Posts, the Grangers, the Bushes and young George Willets all arrive at the Troup Street cottage, and to a riot of knockings and raps. The alphabet board is dusted off.

Leah says, "Just as I suspected, the spirits left because they were angry. Angry that we would not proclaim them to the wider world. Is not that so, Margaretta?"

Maggie looks at Leah, then at Amy Post, at her long, plain face alight with expectation. "Yes, it can't be just about us anymore," Maggie says, and is astonished yet again at how Leah can turn a set-back to an advantage, amazed she had imagined she could best Leah in any fashion.

The spirits' first message is that Mother Margaret should return to Rochester forthwith. The second message is: *Hire Corinthian Hall.* The spirits then instruct Eliab Capron of Auburn to be their spokesman. George Willets to be their manager. The Posts to head a spirit committee.

"The spirits are so very correct," Leah says. "The best way to silence our challengers is to meet them head-on, as distasteful as that is. But the spirits shall lend us courage. They shall lead us to victory." She gives Calvin a dimpled smile. "We simply must, as this one says, rush headlong into battle without shirking."

Calvin looks up, awed; no other word suffices.

Maggie sits back, vastly relieved. She need only follow now. She need not think, nor wrangle with choices, nor make decisions. She will be safe as any prodigal.

PART TWO

"Now, of course, the adherents to the cult promulagated by the Fox sisters will claim that these are the bones of the peddler whose spirit cried out in vengeance away back in 1848. The skeptical will aver that these bones were placed in their hiding place by the Fox girls at the time of the excitement, with the expectation that they would be found by investigators, and their story thus corroborated. However that may be, the facts are as stated above, and the bones found in the old wall are in the possession of Mr. Hyde, the owner of the property. We are told that they have evidently been in their hiding place for at least 50 years judging from the appearance."

ARCADIAN WEEKLY GAZETTE,
NOVEMBER, 1904

"Charles Chauncey Burr was one of the most enigmatic and colorful characters of American magazine journalism. While today many of Burr's views seem outlandish and absurd, his apparent erudition, his dexterity with language and logic, and his fervent emotion will strike the reader of his publications as powerful and persuasive—even if it's hard to imagine Burr surviving without capital letters and exclamation points."

DICTIONARY OF LITERARY BIOGRAPHY

CHAPTER 10.

"This will warm you up nicely, duck," I said, and set up the foot-stove I had brought, as promised. This was on the tenth of February, the tenth day of our acquaintance. My patient was faring better, as my charges often do for a time before the Glory.

She reached out to the warmth from the fresh-raked coals. "You are Kindness itself, Mrs. Mellon."

"To that I must disagree. I've met paragons of the higher quali-ties, and I cannot say that I am of their ilk."

"I see, and what of the paragons of the lesser qualities? Have you met them?"

"Certainly. They are abundant in the world, and impossible to avoid."

"Then as like you will recognize my family's nemesis, Chauncey Burr. He was the paragon of Bluster. Of Grandiloquence."

"Was he, now," I said absently. I opened my satchel and hauled out my knitting.

"Yes, a veritable carnival of a man, all brass tacks and gall. Leah became quite fixed on him. It was as if she'd at last met a worthy adversary or rather, yes, someone of *her* own ilk. He surely enjoyed machinations as much as she ever did and, of course, he had his own facade to uphold."

She looked pleased, as one does at a decipherment, then took up her bible box and scattered onto the bedclothes the printed materials about this Chauncey Burr: the newspaper clip-outs and broadsheets and pamphlets, the pages that seemed ripped from his own rambling journal, with the writing aslant off the page and all-chock with untoward comments and observations and confessions.

I looked over these, quite closely, then took up my needles and yarn. The hour was already growing late, but I stayed while she talked. I must admit, however, to an apprehension that she had come to appreciate my presence too much; for it seemed she thought that as long as she held my interest, as long as I sat there, all-curious, knitting away, she would not pass-on. That is to say, as if she thought me the gatekeeper to Eternity and not a just member of the Medico Society as I so often proclaimed.

WHAT CHAUNCEY BURR wants is to be the apostle of a new and scientific mode of thought. *The Burrean revolution . . . It is a Burrish matter . . . Chaunceologists will meet at . . .* Oh, he has thought of all the permutations. He stoops to the looking glass and pats his stage makeup and practises expressions of dismay, joy, astonishment, all exaggerated for the benefit of distant viewers. He is thickly built, impressively tall. Has a dark beard cut to a slab, dark hair cut unfashionably close. He could be a labourer hurling rock instead of ideas and provocations, except he is light on his feet, as they say; except he moves with the confidence of one who has never been hungry, never unsheltered—though, of course, he's known both situations intimately.

He stuffs his pirate-head pipe. The pipe is of black meerschaum, the better to show its fire, and is mighty effective when pointed during discourse, a trick he learned when he was a lawyer bleeding dust.

Mr. Abelard Reynolds, the manager of Rochester's Corinthian Hall, appears in the doorway of the dressing room.

Chauncey directs his pipe: "Mr. Reynolds. What ho! I am a font of displeasure over these." He slaps a stack of pamphlets. Reads: *Mr. Chauncey Burr and Mr. Theophilus Fiske will commence their lectures at 7 ½ o'clock commencing Oct 15th Year of Our Lord 1849. After each lecture the most extraordinary, surprising, and amusing experiments will*

*be given in the newly discovered science of Electro-biology that have ever
been witnessed in the city.*

"Did I not insist, man, that it should read: 'The Reverend C. Burr,
renowned Editor, Lawyer and Scientist, shall give demonstrations
on Electro-Biology,' et cetera and so bloody forth. And then:
'Assisted by one Theophilus Fiske.' *Assisted.* I don't share a damnedo
sentence with the man, not neither a conjuncter. He's the assistant.
Note the 'ass' in the word, man. Hah! It comes before the mouth,
which is I."

"Scientist?"

"Yes, a scientist, Mr. Abelard Dabbalard—oh, where's thy
Heloise? It signifies a man devoted to the discipline of science, with
not even an edgo of philosophy or literature or natural what-bloody-
have-you. Are not you up with the fugging times, man."

"Apparently not," Reynolds says coldly.

"Or is it that you've no respect for science? Why else would you
have booked some ghost-talking ladies next moontide. A damnedo
insult to the very stage, that. Which is precisely why I demanded
new pamphlets. Must I do everything my own self? Science and
superstition spin in their separate spheres and—"

"There weren't no time for new pamphlets to be printed." This
from a man who twists round Abelard Reynolds and into the dressing room. Though young, he has a jolt of grey hair, spectacles,
a stoop.

"Fiske Fisko! Where the Hades you been hiding your mop-haired
brain? Stop for a dip in a Bordello's pool, did you? Follow a tart to
the very bakery? What of it, man?" Chauncey hurls a pot of grease
paint at Fiske, who expertly ducks. The paint spills on the floor.
"Bugger and slam," Chauncey mutters. "I thought it closed tight
as an unpaid . . . Apologies, Mr. Reynolds." Chauncey calls. But
Mr. Reynolds has already left the two to their own devices.

Fiske glares good-naturedly at Chauncey. Not easy, to glare
good-naturedly, Chauncey thinks, but Fiske Fisko has a knack for it.
And a knack for tolerating the Reverend Chauncey Burr. And why
not? The two of them have made a very comfortable living with
very little work.

"What have you discovered then, Fisko, by your sniffing and spying? Can't have the 'competition' getting the damnedo jump on us. What of it? Have you got a Hamletian ghost tucked into your odiferous armpit?"

Fiske folds himself into a chair. "No to that. Got some information, though."

"Spew it out, man! Quit masticating like a half-starved bovine."

"They're a lengthy affair, let me tell you, them so-called spirit circles or promiscuous circles or whatever you want to call 'em. Cost me an entire dollar. I'll expect that out of our takings this night, though."

"Oh, your dollar shall be returned to your seamy palm. Do not trouble your skull with minute calculations a mortal breath longer. What more?"

"Quite a show, it were. First you sit round a table in a half-dark parlour and hold hands to 'keep an energy chain.' The mother, she's not the key player. No. It's Leah Fish, the eldest sister, who's the keeper of the keys, and a Hun in petticoats, I tell you. Anyhow, she droned on for a good half-hour, with prayers mostly. Then there was some music playing. The music was just outside the room, but the 'sitters' all carried on like it was angels away at it. The little one, she's twelve if she's a day, and looks like she'd disappear in a puff of wind. And the other sister—Margaretta, Maggie? She's got up like she's the same age or so, but I reckon she's near plucking time, given her smirking ways. Dark-haired items the both of them. And I tell you, don't they look as pretty and sweet as ever you saw."

"Clever. Clever. They're working that modern bloody cant that children are sweet little innocents. But we know the truth of it, righto. Demon drink, like the medievalists would have it. No scruples. No nitpicking twixt right and wrong. Sly as cats. Fortunate you were never a child, Fisko, but hatched from some fu—"

"So by this time there's some sitters in a state and—"

"A state? What ho? State?"

"Much like our electro-biology experimentations, but the sitters are doing it on themselves. Suggest their dead pa is sitting there and they'd believe it. One old feller did in fact. A fat lot of weeping went on then, I tell you, though. Now the knocking—"

"Apparati? Accomplices?"

"Doubtful to that. I asked to investigate. 'Go on,' that Leah Fish woman said, 'if you dare to think us frauds.'" Fiske chuckles. "She's got bollocks, that one. Anyhows, I found nothing. No strings. No levers. No dwarves crouching under the table. Nothing."

"What ho, then, of the answering?"

"The 'spirits' dodge the hard questions. For the main they favour questions of the after-life. They sure go on, anyhow, about how lovely it is. Dead folk say they're doing swell and 'how are you?' That's the idea of it. They say: 'you'll be travelling'; 'you'll be happy.' The usual 'no' or 'yes' answers you'd expect from some Gypsy. Oh, but didn't the company think it marvellous, though. One woman started blathering in tongues and everyone looked to her in admiration like she were playing the harp or some such and not looking an idiot."

"The ghosties talked? Was that it? Aloud in some bloodyo soliloquy?"

"Yes to that, in a fashion. The ladies had a board with the alphabet and letters. The person asking the questions got to work it. They'd move the pointer over the letters and the spirit would rap when they got to the right one. A tedious business, I tell you, though. Another thing: they got a fella to write down several names on a paper, said the spirits would rap when the fella pointed to the one he was thinking of. Got it bang on."

"Watchful as damnedo vultures over a carcass, those Foxes, what ho?"

"Exactly. Anyone with a trained eye can read a countenance." Fiske steeples his fingers. "It's the knockings that were a stumper. They weren't all pretty little rat-tats. Some were loud as hammer strokes or . . . or like buckets being hurled at the walls. Some even made the chairs vibrate. They were, yes, a stumper like I told you."

Chauncey is undecided whether to reply, or hurl something, or both, when Reynolds beckons at them from the door. "Time for this final show of yours," he says.

Final, yes, and the Corinthian Hall is all-filled. Energy pulsates from the crowd and into Chauncey Burr. This is the sort of energy he would like to harness. One could set a city ablaze with it. It recalls his days as Universalist minister, a fine occupation that he misses still.

Chauncey and Fiske make their way up to the platform stage. It has no stage wings. No proscenium arch. But then, this is not a theatre for frothy plays, but a forum for serious lectures and the occasional concert.

Once onstage Chauncey thrusts his thumbs in the lapels of his frock coat that is black as coal, then paces ponderously before the audience, as if freighted with thought. Halts up. "Gentlemen. Ladies. I am no magician," Chauncey booms as if just realizing this for himself. "I am no illusionist. I offer no deception. I am merely a discoverer. We men of the science of electro-biology are set apart from superstitions. Effect without explainable cause? Effect is ever explainable. Mark me!"

And they do, and this because Chauncey talks to the rabble as if they are as learned as he. Reminds them of the Italian Signor Galvani as if they might have shared a grappa with the man himself. "Imagine the hot light of Italy, ladies and gentlemen, this same hot light that illumined the great Galileo as he probed the heavens. Signor Galvini is bent over a table dissecting a frog upon an electrified plate. And then, a twitch of the frog's legs. Another. The frog near springs from the table," Chauncey yells, startling the audience. "Apologies, people! That was Signor Galvani's shocked wife witnessing the vivified frog . . . She'd planned on frog's gizzards for supper."

The crowd laughs.

"But Signor Galvani was no medievalist, was he now?" Chauncey continues. "He did not imagine that frog resurrected, did he? What sort of a religion would that have spawned, eh?" The audience laughs again, there being nothing like a pinch of blasphemy to spice an entertainment. "No, good citizens of Rochester. The explanation is this: electricity had been vibrating through the plate upon which the frog lay. And thus we come around to an understanding of electro-biology. We understand that all living things are sparking with electricity. That is what animates us with life. A man trained in its particulars can control the electric fluids of another and thus direct his movements. Herr Franz Mesmer discovered this, true, but he believed movement was caused by moontides. We in these modern times, however, know that electricity is the cause."

Fiske says nothing. Stands stiff, acting as the faintly sinister assistant. Chauncey calls for gentleman volunteers. Up they come—some nervous, some amused—and sit as instructed, looking out to the crowd. Chauncey talks rapidly and softly to each in turn. "You shall be awake. You shall be in full control of your faculties. You shall not be humiliated. Concentrate only on my voice. Do not mind the din of the crowd. Here. Here. Only this. The world was splendid and all's swell that ends swell."

Fiske hands the first man a glass of milk. Chauncey tells him it is wormwood. The man frowns and spits. The crowd roars in laughter. Another man is told his leg is caught in a snare. In vain he pulls. Yet another is told he is drunk as a lord. He totters and stumbles and is herded about by Fiske to the claps and cheers of the audience.

The last man, when told to admire the charms of a goat, looks at Chauncey with disgust and strides off the stage.

"Some have less of the charge than others," Chauncey mocks, and yet he admires the man. Chauncey also cannot not be mesmerized and led about like an automaton. He is master of his own will.

Back in the dressing room Chauncey scrubs at his makeup. The applause should have been louder, longer lasting. The audience wanted more. But bloodyo what?

"Fiske Fisko, what is the date, exactly, of the ghost ladies' little demonstration?"

Fiske glances over the pamphlet. "November the 14th. Two bits gets you in. You thinking of getting on the committee?"

"What fugging committee?"

"The one the audience gets to choose. Five respectable types they're to be, though. And they're to do their own private investigations and then . . . look here, damn it, read for yourself for once."

Chauncey runs oil through his hair, then cracks his knuckles—a sinister and practised sound.

"Right to that," Fiske mutters. Reads: "'The committee is to report at the following evening's lecture whether there is collusion or deception in the knocks. COME AND INVESTIGATE.' That's in capitals."

Chauncey grabs the pamphlet from Fiske. "Capitals, is it!" He thwacks the dressing table instead, right aside Fiske.

Fiske jumps. "Hell, Chaunce, what you—"

"What? What Fiske Fisko? Didn't see it coming? Hah! Our petticoat competition won't see us coming neither. Make ready, man."

Close on a month later and Chauncey and Fiske spill out of the Corinthian Hall into the November evening. They halt outside the entrance and let the crowd roil round them. A woman slips on the wet and flashes her red petticoat, drawing hoots, a catcall. Horses and hacks clatter in the street. A newspaper boy hollers about the latest revolution in distant Europe. The ill-bred spit tobacco juice into the snow. And all this racket is as fuel for Chauncey's racketing thoughts. He hikes his muskrat collar, lights his pirate-head pipe, then rounds on Fiske, as if Fiske were responsible for the sideshow of superstition they just witnessed.

"Their promoter, that elf, that cheapjack magician Capron and his bloodyo jabber about a New Age. That'll never stand the test of time. The corporeal and the spiritual dwelling together? What a damnedo mishmash. When I was in the pulpit did I trumpet electric magnetism and mesmeric forces? No, I did fugging well not! It was all God and the Holy Ghost and lakes of hellfire. Science and religion should never meet. It insults them both. Faith and bended knee on the one; rigour and intellect on the other." Chauncey slaps his own knee, adds, "What ho? Mediums, that's what he called the females, eh? Making his own lingo already?"

"Sure to that, but some were mighty convinced, though," Fiske puts in. "'Course they as like used plants in the audience for the correct answering. But those knocks. I tell you, I'm still stumped as to them."

Yes, indeedo, those knocks, Chauncey thinks, they emanated, loud and sharp, from all areas of the hall. And all the while that Leah Fox Fish might have been on some high throne the way she held herself, the way she bestowed her benevolent, dimpled smile on the crowd. Chauncey barely noted the supporters flanking her onstage, barely noted her doll-sized sisters Margaret and Katherine. No, only Leah worthied his gaze. Her rounded figure, her hair agleam like a crown of copper in the kerosene light.

"What you thinking, Chaunce? You got that squint-eyed look."

"The crowd, they should have chosen me for the damnedo committee. I'd have investigated, what ho!"

Fiske kicks at the tobacco-pocked snow. "Mayhap you shouldn't have called the audience a lot of deluded dumbwits."

The competition for the audience's attention had been fierce, Chauncey allows. One idiot vowed to eat his hat if he couldn't uncover the Fox women's means of deception. Another vowed he'd hurl himself over the Genesee falls if he failed. "The truth is ever a painful item, Fiske Fisko."

"Could be that the doctors, the ones the audience picked for the committee, could be they were plants too, though."

Chauncey studies his pipe. The pirate's fierce eyes resemble Chauncey's own, he likes to think, as does the pirate's grin. "I suspect not. A doctor's pride knows no bounds. To agree to assist? Why? To what endo?"

"If the docs weren't plants, if they're not in on it, then they'll find the females out. Doctor sorts like that, they've got smarts galore."

"Hah, bloody, hah. They'll not find out a fugging thing, Fiske Fisko. To find out a charlatan you need be a . . . Fiske, an idea has just sprung to my brain."

"An idea? What sort?" Fiske asks, stepping back.

"An exposé sort. We'll hang it on the what-end of our lecture."

"Exposé?"

"Of the Fox knocks, you cotton-brain. We'll show how the ghosties are created by legerdemain, by the mesmeric forces of a person's own mind seeing and hearing what it chooses."

"But those knocks, you don't know how they're done? Do you, though?"

"I'll fathom them in good bloodyo time. See if I don't. What ho! We'll set it up like in Hamlet. When that lawyer goes knock-knocking at the Gates of Hell. Hah, what a comedic aside. But instead of a sniffling lawyer knocking it'll be the Fox women. And

I'll be the gatekeeper asking who's there, and they'll admit who they are at last, and on their knees: The Fugging Fox Frauds Three! That's who."

"I don't recollect a lawyer knocking. Mayhap a tailor and a farmer, though. And isn't that from Macbeth?"

"Who gives a ratter's arse which pommy bastard wrote it. Let's say we knock-knock the Fox females straight to ignominy!"

CHAPTER II

"Do you hold with bloodletting?" my patient asked.

"What is that? . . . Ah, this," I said, and held up the steel fleam I was using to prod alive the foot-stove's coals. "The letting does ease some people. Older folk for the main. The efficacy is mostly in their heads, but it can't hurt. We've all too much blood in us from what I've seen." At this I shut the little door and set the stove at the end of her bed.

"You are a fine physician, Mrs. Mellon. Has medicine always been an interest of yours?"

"I am not precisely a card-holding physician," I allowed. "I am a lay physician. Women were not allowed the doctoring profession in my day, not in any fashion."

"So you've had other occupations."

"Certainly. Women must earn money how they can. Money does not rain from clouds and . . . The fumes! Here," I said, and trudged to the garret's linked windows and hefted at the sash of one of the small side windows, grateful to have my back turned away from my patient. I felt an old shame, I allow. For just after the abolition war I engaged in an occupation I would rather not mention, although I daresay it is an older profession than doctoring.

The stubborn sash at last creaked open, but just a crack.

"Charcoal fumes," I continued. "They can create visions and fig-ments, I've heard. Indeed, all your ghosts might be naught but trapped, invisible vapours working havoc on the brain." I was still facing the window and was looking through to the smoke palled buildings across and below. I noticed my reflection in the glass just then, and I was amazed at how pale I was, how muzzy my features.

"Mayhap that is all they were, then," my patient murmured, as if to herself. "Fumes. Vapours. Reflected forms."

"Who? Your knocking spirits?"

"No, no, the Fates, the three old women who assisted the doctors at the 'investigation' that followed the Corinthian Hall display. They were cramped, sin-ugly creatures, all dark-garbed and fetched up from God-knows-where. I dubbed them the Fates because I forgot their names as soon as they were uttered. I was beginning to do that a great deal, choosing to forget names and, oh, many other things besides."

"To ensure you're not concealing any mechanicals beneath," the doctors explain as the Fates tie Maggie's skirt about her ankles, then tend to Leah's shirts. Amy Post and Machteld wait in a room down the corridor of these dusty, untenanted offices. No one else has been allowed to accompany Maggie and Leah.

The doctors number four in all. One of them presses Maggie's throat with his cold, blunt fingers, then slides a stethoscope over her chest. It is all Maggie can do not to slap him.

Another doctor—a short-necked, squat man—does the same to Leah; Leah reaches for Maggie's hand. "Toad," she says to Maggie, and in the barest whisper. Maggie nearly laughs aloud. Because who fears toads? Creatures of such serious mien, and yet such stupidity withal.

Maggie and Leah are now instructed to stand atop glass plates, which are in turn set atop two close aligned tables. "We are testing," this Dr. Toad explains, "to ascertain, I should say, test, whether the knocks are caused by what is known as electrical energy. And whether this energy is somehow vibrating between you two women. Do you understand what I am saying?"

"Well, yes," Maggie says tartly, and nearly asks if Dr. Toad believes them children or half-wits.

"We do understand, good sir," Leah says. Because you explain so very well."

"Spirits? Give us a knock if you please." This from Dr. Blunt-Fingers, as Maggie now thinks of him. Leah still holds Maggie's hand. She scratches Maggie's palm.

No knocks. Only faint taps, a good dozen of them.

Dr. Blunt-Fingers scowls. He turns to the Fates. "Escort them into the anteroom. There please disrobe them entirely."

Entirely? Maggie cannot recall ever being entirely naked, and certainly not in front of strangers. "I can't, Leah. I just can't. It's grievous. Awful."

"Just this once, dear sister," Leah says quietly. "We must pass this test. We must."

Maggie shakes her head, then wearily nods.

Once the two are in the anteroom, once they are disrobed by the black-garbed Fates, Leah's calm demeanour nearly cracks. Her lips are clenched as if she'd rather scream, and that vein at her temple is throbbing as if fit to burst. Maggie feels a knife-keen sympathy for Leah then. Leah's breasts swag to either side. Her belly is striated with purple. In comparison, Maggie's figure is as smooth and unmarked as a marble statue. Poor Leah, Maggie thinks, bearing a baby so young, bearing up for us all.

The Fates asks for the knocks, but the knocks, faint or otherwise, do not come. Maggie feels equal measures of relief and trepidation. Perhaps everything will end now. Just like that. Done.

And then? Knockings. Loud. Unmistakable. The Fates hop about as if the floor were afire. Somehow, I'm again rescued, Maggie thinks wearily. At this the door bursts open to show Amy Post.

"What have they done to thee!" Amy cries. "This is beyond all cavil. It has gone far enough."

No face is more formidable than Amy Post's when she is angered. The Fates look chastised. Embarrassed. As well they should. Amy is the fierce upholder of all that is true and just, everyone in Rochester knows this. Maggie reaches for her dress. At that moment she glimpses Machteld trotting briskly down the corridor with a broom, as if, being a maid, she likes to sweep wherever she finds herself.

It is the evening after the doctors' investigation and Maggie, nerve-shot and sleep-deprived, sits beside Leah on the Corinthian Hall's platform stage. It is the final night of their display and the hall is filled to a jam, the crowd an even rougher assortment than on the first night. Ranged about Maggie and Leah are Amy and Isaac Post, George Willets, Lyman Granger, Lemira Kedzie and the Reverend Lemuel Clarke, a firm believer now. Katie is not with them this night. She had one of her little fits and is resting up with Mother at Troup Street. Damned good thing, Maggie decides, because the mood of the crowd is decidedly unpleasant.

Eliab Capron takes the lectern. He looks smaller than usual. Polishes his spectacles and calls for attention. The crowd settles with difficulty. Money passes among four young swells with soap-locked hair. They spit tobacco. Laugh high. Are they betting? On what? Maggie has never been to a cockfight, of course, but surely this is how a cockpit smells—of onions and ale, of cheap cigars and cheap perfumes, of people steaming in their own woollens, of the desire for blood. Leah told her only the most respectable people would attend. Respectable? What of that burly man with the black-spade beard who, on that first night of their demonstrations, jumped up like a jack-in-the box and called the crowd a lot of deluded dumb-wits? What of the man who'd said he'd eat his hat if he couldn't find the means of their deception? And the one who said he'd throw himself over the Genesee falls if he didn't uncover all. "I so hope he can swim" was what Leah said before taking the stage tonight.

Maggie looks to Leah for counsel and support, but Leah is too busy smiling blithely at the crowd to notice her sister. The sympathy Maggie felt for Leah during the doctors' investigation abruptly vanishes. Indeed, Maggie longs to slap the dimples right off her face. She twists her hands instead, then looks down to the comforting sight of Calvin waiting just below the platform stage.

And Machteld.

Machteld looks up at Maggie and presses a finger to her dour lips, then bites it so hard Maggie expects to see a line of blood. "I not like you," Machteld told Maggie just before they entered the hall for this evening's demonstrations. "No. But I love Amy. I love Isaac. They save me. Understand?"

"Well, yes," Maggie replied. "Do I got a choice?"

Onstage Eliab is speechifying. The far audience demands he speak louder. Eliab polishes his spectacles again. Rustles his papers. Maggie thought he would be better at this. Hadn't he insisted she and Leah rehearse endlessly for the show?

Eliab finds his voice again. "Nothing could be proved. The committee found no means of deception. None! You've heard the good doctors' report. They have ruled out ventriloquism. They have ruled out electrical currents."

The crowd cheers loudly, or jeers; it is difficult to tell. There is the sound of boot stomping. Hooting. Maggie stares at her clenched hands. Amy and Isaac look out over the audience with expressions both distant and reproachful, a look Leah imitates well. "Leah, Leah," Maggie calls over hoarsely. "What in tunket have we done to deserve this? It was only—"

Maggie chokes back her words as a young swag leaps onto the stage, his top hat at a tilt. Josiah Bissell. His father, Maggie recalls, had been a hellfire preacher during the revivals of the '30s, and had lost a celebrated feud with the hard-drinking, Sabbath-breaking canal men, a feud that Maggie's own father once told her of, and with a curious pride. This elder Bissell is now one of the wealthiest men in Rochester. Thus it is no wonder his son, Josiah the Younger, looks down at Maggie now, and with the arrogance of God's favoured.

Maggie covers her face with her hands.

"Margaretta!" Leah orders. "Never show fear. They are alike wretched dogs. Stand fast and we shall not be hurt."

Josiah the Younger holds out his arms. "Hear me! I'll be the chairman then of the next committee. That of the True Doubters."

A rough in a cap and stained jacket scrambles up beside Josiah. Hollers, "they's got lead balls in their dresses!"

"Yous got in them your trousers, Packard!" someone hollers back, and this ribaldry encourages more of the same. Maggie hears a demand to have the women stripped. Hears calls for tar, feathers, faggots for a fire. The hecklers are laughing, as if in jest, but lines are being crossed, Maggie knows, lines of modesty, of chivalry, of common sense. Her head buzzes. Her hands tremble. So this is terror, she thinks.

"I'll see the proof, ladies!" Packard shouts. He lurches towards Leah as if to heft her skirts. Yelps as she kicks his shins. Everyone on the stage is standing and talking wildly now. Calvin is fighting his way through the audience towards them. Alfie and Machteld hang back. Onstage, spindly George Willets thrusts himself between Maggie and the riff-raff. "Off the damned stage, you and you! Get away from them. These women won't be lynched unless it's over my dead body."

"That's fine comfort, George!" Leah calls.

"Yes, don't thou give them any ideas," Isaac shouts.

Maggie screams, clutches George, then Amy. Reels back as a torpedo-cracker, tail flaming, bounces on the stage. It erupts in a reek of cordite and smoke. Maggie coughs and retches. Her eyes stream, burning tears. A man grips her shoulder. She wrenches away. "Leave me! Let go, damn you."

"Easy, miss, easy." She might be a skittish horse the way he says it. He declares himself the chief of police. "My men have been among the crowd all along." He gestures at three baton-carrying men in workaday clothes who are elbowing through to the front row. More torpedo-crackers explode on the stage. A woman faints. There is rabid laughing, flailing arms, wailing voices. Maggie huddles against the police chief. Or is he? He could be a confederate of the younger Bissell's come to take her hostage and compel the truth from her. He will put red-hot irons to her feet. Poke out an eye. Force her to confess about the peddler at last; though something will stop even that confession at the last instance. She chokes back a horrified laugh at this thought. Looks about and realizes she has been shuffled off the stage, down the aisle to the door. Ah, the door. Leah is behind her along with Calvin. Amy and Isaac are in front with Machteld. They all attain the street and the snow-wet November night and cram into the waiting hack. Eliab Capron leaps in at the last instance.

The driver cracks the whip. A small crowd makes chase, but swiftly gives up, laughing as if it were all a lark.

Maggie sits cramped between Calvin and Leah. She is numb with exhaustion. Eliab, however, taps his feet in excitement. "It might be called a success. Yes, it just might."

Amy stares at him. "A success?"

"What dost thou mean, Eliab, for God's sake?" Isaac demands.

"Yes, what precisely?" Leah asks.

"A riot," Eliab says. "It will appear in all the papers tomorrow. Yes, I have it! I will report how the mindless, bigoted mob was enraged when the spirits proved themselves genuine. Hah, if the spirits want to be known to the wider world, then the spirits shall have their wish." He rubs his hands, as he often does—against the cold, Maggie supposes, although it looks, unfortunately, as if he is anticipating money. He tells them of his pamphlet, half-written already. "It will do justice to our wondrous scientific age. But it will only be the precursor of the great tomes to come. For surely these communications from that other realm are all part of the natural world, all part of the grand scheme. The time is ripe as . . . ripe. We must act swiftly."

"My dear Eliab," Leah says, in admiration. "You would do Mr. Barnum himself proud."

At which Eliab smiles. At which Amy and Isaac look troubled. At which Maggie telegraphs her thoughts to Katie, as Katie asked her to do, for might not clairvoyance be possible?

Katie, Kat what have we done? Alas and such, we should have left our ghost in the cellar keep. In the dark and the quiet there.

CHAPTER 12

"And did you?"

"Did I what?" my patient asked.

"Transport your thoughts. I, too, have heard that such is a possibility."

"No, don't believe that, Mrs. Mellon. One can't hear another person's thoughts. Not a glimmer of them, no matter how closely linked two people are; no matter how much they love each other. I should know, for Katie and I tried. We even made a game of thought-guessing, just like we made a game of so many things. Often we were nearly correct. It helped when we were in the same room, of course, because then we could attend each other's every breath and twitch. One's body can speak buckets."

I vowed then to keep my own body alike a cipher. I did not wish to be read. I was, and am, a private person, and I did not need my past held up like a cheap bolt of cloth. "Clotho, Lachesis and Atropos," I said, to change the topic.

My patient looked bewildered. I took up my knitting and clipped at the stray skeins with my shears. The mittens were forming nicely. It seemed my creation might go on without another hitch. "The Fates," I continued. "From the doctors' experiments? You said you forgot their names. I searched them out for you. The first, Clotho, spins the threads of life, or the cloth, I suppose. The second, Lachesis, she measures it out, by which I mean how long you will live. And the last one, Atropos, she cuts the thread of one's life, with a knife or scissors, it depends."

"Atropos?"

"Yes." I set aside the knitting and tucked in her blankets, making concise triangle corners. "Even the highest gods fear her. She can't be bribed, nor tricked, nor turned aside, not like all those other Greek deities."

"Best to just accept her, then?" my patient asked, and with that mischiefed cornered smile.

"Yes. Best for everybody, to be frank."

APRIL OF 1850, and Maggie sits on the bed that she and Katie share and searches through a heap of tasselled reticules, kid gloves, jet beading, paisley shawls, jewellry of paste, collars of lace. Katie is on her knees by the bureau. "I'm done," Maggie announces, throwing up her hands. "Done like a dog's dinner, done-it-all, damn-it-all."

"Fuss, you can't give up now," Katie says.

"I can so. I swear on somebody-or-other's grave, I'm done searching and—"

"There you are. At last!" Katie interjects. "Naughty old thing, you've been hiding from me." She holds up her spanking-new May-month bonnet, the one she bought specifically for their outing today. The destination is a surprise for their mother, and a well-deserved treat for all. In the five months since the Corinthian Hall exhibition, the Troup Street cottage has been so thronged with spirit-seekers that Maggie barely has time to change from morning dress to tea dress to dinner dress. She is allowed floor-length dresses now. Katie too. And all of these dresses are tailored to Leah's precise specifications with wide-banded hems and discreet little pockets. Costly, yes, but there seems to be money aplenty now. Leah has even upped Katie's and Maggie's stipends; as well she should, for Maggie can cipher better than most girls and now that the rates are set at a dollar per head (shillings and reales accepted also), and with three sittings a day, and fifteen people at one sitting, and then private sittings at five a head that makes, well . . . a lot. And Leah, Maggie must admit, does keep a fine table. And she has curtailed their chores considerably. Laundry is sent out. A cook comes in. Candles and soap are bought. Anything can be bought, Maggie has realized.

Katie says, "I really hope Leah lets us stop at the arcade. I'll just die or something if I can't have a pearly broach or two. You're allowed jewellery now, why not me? Oh, fiddle-dee, but I've spent my stipend. I reckon that means I'll be in for a lecture about budget and prudence."

Maggie inspects her braid. "Budget and Prudence? I haven't seen those tiresome old spinsters for an age."

Katie giggles. Maggie smiles. Because she, too, now enjoys the prosperity the spirits have brought them. She, too, enjoys the "game," as Katie calls it. And besides, everyone is in on it: the grown, the aged, children. Everyone wants to play. And ambivalence is such an exhausting state, Maggie has found, like balancing on a fence post in a gale. Better to just jump and land in the muck of one side or the other. And Maggie has jumped, though she can't pinpoint when exactly she did so. Perhaps when she realized she could have all the pretty clothes she desired. Perhaps when she realized the game has become so easy and automatic that she is scarcely aware of the rappings' source; and then there are all the people, even judges and doctors, telling their mother she should be proud of her gifted, lovely daughters who offer such succour, and their mother replying that she *is* proud, and moreover that she is no longer afraid of the spirits, but considers them friends. And isn't the talent catching? Maggie thinks in wonderment. First silly Betty, the Grangers' daughter, announced that she, too, could hear spirit knockings. Then George Willets felt ghostly rustlings on his collar. Next Abigail Bush heard scratchings in her cupboard and Katie's adored John Robinson's fingers tingled for no reason. Even prune-faced Ruth Culver in Arcadia has written that the spirits rattled her husband Norman's cuspidor, and that, in her opinion, the spirits were at her house first.

Katie tips her head. "Hear that? Something's been delivered." She pulls Maggie out of their bedroom. Chants, " *'Will you walk into my parlour?' said the spider to the fly. 'Tis the prettiest little parlour that*

ever you did spy. The way into my parlour is up a winding stair, and I
have many curious things to show when you are there.'"

The parlour is dusted and shined and smelling of linseed oil and
empty of all souls. Maggie can scarcely believe she lives with such
finery. The parlour now boasts drapes of valerian red, blue glass
lamps fired with spermaceti oil, an ovoid mahogany table that sits up
to twenty, and Leah's pride: a sideboard chock with carvings of
slaughtered bucks and trussed birds and dead gaping fish. A newly
delivered gift basket, sure enough, sits on this sideboard. Katie
plucks out an orange, then a tin of sugared almonds, then a bottle of
champagne. "It's a really fancy one," she cries, and expertly pops
the cork and pours them both a glass. Maggie likes it as much as
Katie does now. They might never drink weak old cider again.

Leah's voice floats to them. "Girls! We must leave forthwith. We
are reserved."

"We're just getting refreshed," Katie calls back. She smiles at
Maggie. "Be nice to old sis, Mag. She's been trying really hard, you
know, to make it all less work for us. And her new technique works
just swell, don't you think?"

"Well, yes, but I still like the old way better," Maggie says, thinking how two weeks ago Leah halted playing the parlour organ in
mid-chord and fixed her gaze on the candelabra, its swimming little
flames. The sitters were astonished when the voice hauled up from
Leah's lungs was deep, sonorous, and not her own. A woman half-
fainted, then claimed the voice was that of her dead father. Since
then odd voices have bubbled out of Katie as well. Leah is calling it
magnetic somnambulism. Katie and Maggie are calling it trancing,
mostly because the word is easier to pronounce and spell and these
new, talky spirits get tongue-caught over long words. And like the
older, quieter spirits, they are terrible spellers all.

"There you are, girls," Leah says, coming into the parlour. "I
have sent Mother to wait outside. Now, do keep a secret for once."

The Four Corners is bustling as usual. The air is shot with the blat-
ting of tin horns, the rumble-turn of wheels, the clatter-clop of
horses, and the hollers and hammering of labourers as the canal and

aqueducts are readied for the spring and summer traffic. The secondary canals are already flooded with water, and as they pass one Maggie catches a whiff of that smell common to populated waterways, that is, the smell of offal and factory waste and chamber pots galore. Or, as Maggie considers it, the smell of spring.

She wends with Katie, Leah and their mother through the lattice of ash barrels, manure heaps and hawkers' stalls. Calvin is busy with his militia today, and so they behave as unchaperoned females must and keep their greetings brief, their gait brisk, and their gaze cast down, mostly, to the muck-caked boardwalks. None of which lessens Maggie's certainty that the four of them are being seen, noted, thought of. Attend! There they are, the spirit-raising females. But where is the father? What have they done with him? Save for this "brother" Calvin who comes and goes they have no guidance from any man. No protection. It is as if they have scant concern for their reputation, for their precarious toe-hold in society, that is to say, the world.

Yes, Maggie can easily guess what the watchers are thinking, whispering, it is evidenced in the secret language of glances and sighs, of tightened brows, crossed arms, of quickened breath and quick-changed topics, of drumming fingers and shifting eyes. It is nothing like the language she and Katie once fashioned up to fool their mother. No, this is the language of the unsaid and unwritten, a language she is comprehending better and better each day. Would Maggie prefer illiteracy of it all? No, she is quite certain not.

"A moment, my dears," Leah says, and stops, as she always does, at the bookstall on Exchange Street. Prominently displayed is the first tract ever written about their family, the one by E.E. Lewis. Maggie vaguely recalls the man, his fingers blued with ink, his goggly eyes. He had wanted to talk to her and Katie but their mother said no. She's a good ma, Maggie thinks, and knows by Katie's fond glance that Katie thinks the same. They hook their arms through their mother's on one accord.

"I suppose this is still a popular item?" Leah says to the bookseller, as if she has only vague interest in Eliab Capron's thick pamphlet: *Singular Revelations: Explanation and History of the Mysterious Communion with Spirits: Comprehending the Rise and Progress of the*

Mysterious Noises in Western New York, Generally Received as Spirit Communications.

"Still selling like griddle cakes, ma'am," the bookseller says. Indeed, upwards of six thousand copies have already sold, Maggie knows. Six thousand. It would take her an age to count that high. Many of the buyers must live beyond Rochester, beyond New York state even. And all are reading of her and her family. The thought unsettles her. It is one thing to be known around Rochester, another to be created in God-knows-whose mind miles and miles away.

Leah turns to Mother, says, "I do hope Eliab considers a shorter title for the next printing. Two lines, no more, lines that are like sharp, clear notes that catch the ear."

Mother frowns. "But then a body, I mean that is, one person, shouldn't know what were inside it? Would one?"

"Two might," Maggie murmurs to Katie. Katie smiles into her glove.

Leah glances at her sisters. "What is inside can be discovered. Well, I have left such details to Eliab. I cannot orchestrate every-thing. I must recall this. Come. We are almost arrived."

An ornate sign hangs outside a crown-glass window. Mother peers through. Maggie does likewise, though more discreetly. Sees fine-dressed people sitting at fine-draped tables, an aproned man bearing a domed and lidded platter.

"But we're not travelling or staying here, are we?" Mother asks, agog.

Katie cries, "Ma, it's not a tavern or a hotel. It's a restaurant! You can go any old time."

Once seated at a window table, Mother hefts the silverware, smooths out the stiff napkin, then grips it in near panic. "Laws, laws. Look! Diamond folds."

"For pity's sake," Maggie says. "That's not a diamond. It's a . . . a skewed triangle."

Leah and Katie agree, and their mother looks mollified. Maggie tries not to smile. And she doesn't bother asking what diamond folds portend, because it is surely death—her mother's own, or someone else's. Death if a curlew cries. If a dog howls under a window. If an owl is seen in daytime. If it rains on an open grave. If a bird flies into a window. If a picture falls. If one dreams of birth, or of death itself, certainly. Maggie does not wholly discount such auguries. Death does come for everyone, doesn't it?

Leah encourages Mother's attention back to the menu. Mother dithers, then decides on the bullock's heart with macaroni. "Remarkable, isn't it?" she sighs, as if in the presence of magic. Mayhap it *is* magic, Maggie thinks. Consider this waiter who bows and asks in a foreign voice what they wish for. And then supper appears, without visible preparation, visible fire. And no washing to be done later.

Now the coffee is being served on silver trays. Maggie inhales the coffee scent; it is rich as gravy, sweet as pie. From the waiter's trolley she, Leah, Katie and their mother share out fancy creams, eclairs and biscuits glacés. Now they chat and jest, all of them at their most congenial, their most content, that is until the commotion begins in the street.

They hear the newspaper boys calling. The call is taken up and passed on.

"But I knew it, didn't I?" Mother says, gripping her napkin again.

Maggie holds her fork upright as a spear, says nothing. Leah and Katie are also mute. The other diners murmur in agitation. Rise. Space themselves away from their neighbours.

The world stops. The cholera has come to Rochester.

"I'VE FORGOTTEN HOW IT ENDS," my patient said. "That old rhyme about the fly. The words, I mean."

I clacked my needles. I recalled the rhyme well and many others, to boot. My son ever felt badly for the foolish fly. Yet how could it end in any other fashion? "*'And I have many pretty things to show when you are there.' 'Oh no, no,' said the little fly, 'to ask me is in vain, for who goes up your winding stair can never come down again.'*"

"Yes, that is exactly it." She mentioned again the cholera. "It kills so many, even yet," she said, and eyed me as if I might disagree.

I did not. "Cholera. Typhoid. Consumption. They're like the rain and snow—they fall on all without regard. At least they're not a nameless visitation. At least the sick can be tended and have the benefit of the good death. That sort of thing." I sighed then, I allow, with wishing that my son, if he had to perish, could have done so in a sickbed and not, as I assumed then, as so much cannon fodder.

"Like me," my patient said.

"What is that? Yes, like you. You have time aplenty to ready yourself for the Glory, a thing for which you should be grateful."

"I'm grateful in bucket-loads, Mrs. Mellon. But at the time of the cholera announcement I was not interested in dying, in a good fashion or otherwise. The epidemic the year before took, what, four thousand in the Southern states? And mayhap ten thousand in England. No surprise, then, that we wished to be far from its reach, that we all fled to brother David's farmstead in Arcadia. Of course our father, John Fox, was there too. He was still building a house for our benefit and believed that now the family would stay together for good. He truly did believe that. It was as if he had no knowledge nor interest in his daughters' burgeoning fame, as if he cared not a whit about the ghosts we'd set loose upon the world.

NOTHING MOVES ON THE PUBLIC ROAD except John. He walks with a resolute pace, cradling his old flintlock. A few figures work cautiously in the fields. A meagre commerce stirs the crossroads a half-league off. Wagons and carriages crowd the quiet yards of the farmsteads. The visitors hunker within. Droves of such visitors have come to Arcadia from Rochester and New York. Cities are where the cholera somehow breeds and thrives. Perhaps in the miasma. Perhaps in the breath. The countryside offers sanctuary, that much is known.

He attains the Hyde's orchard and clambers over the split-rail fence. The apple trees are in full spring leaf, the afternoon warm and the breeze a balm, though it brings only pestilence. Or punishment? It might well be. Punishment for his daughters' sins, or mayhap for the general, unceasing sins of the world; his daughters are scarcely the only wrongdoers about. And of course, he's followed his daughters' "career." How could he not? What with folks talking behind their hands when he passes by, and children playing at ghost-talking on the dry goods stoop; what with his son, David, ever bringing home newspapers and pamphlets, ever shaking his head in aghast wonderment, as if the ghosts are the animalcule of some infecting plague, worse than any cholera.

John whistles loud, sharp. A hare trembles in the grass. A cloud crosses the sun. John calls out, "Here! Here!" then turns at the rumbled growl. He hefts the flintlock. Fires. The air plumes with gunsmoke, echoes with the crack. The tender's massive hound flips back. Yelps once in agony, then dies. John nudges him with his boot. Spits tobacco into the grass. He doubts anyone will come questioning. Shots are heard often. Raccoons are hunted. Squirrels. And the fear of the cholera is keeping everyone occupied. If anyone does ask, John will tell the truth: that he sought the hound out. As a Godly man he must only tell the truth, a rule he finds vexing still.

He walks homeward. Leah, Katie, Maggie and his wife are cloistered with David's family at the farmstead. Maggie felt poorly this morning. "Just ate too much slip-gut pudding," she said, "that's all, that's all." But the decision was quickly made to send Katie to Ruth Culver's on the morrow.

He passes their old saltbox house. Quack grass grows high in the foreyard, ivy runnels over the walls and a shutter hangs listless over a shattered window lite. No surprise the house cannot be rented, not to anyone, much to Carlos Hyde's annoyance. But who would rent a house in which a body is buried somewhere? In which a murdered man knocks about at all hours?

John's pace slows when he passes Hydesville's small white church. He stops and rests his musket against the church gate, then cuts off a twist of tobacco with a hunting knife. Just inside the gate the Reverend York bends wearily among the gravestones. He is wielding a yardstick, measuring for space. John supposes the plaguestruck will need to be buried one atop the other, as in the old countries of Europe, where the dead are said to be stacked a mile deep.

The reverend looks up. He is a tall, bull-shouldered man and yet he casts the slight-framed John Fox a fearful look before he hurries towards his church, the church from which he has banned John and his family for blasphemy. And yet perhaps even this expulsion is in God's plan. For when reverends expound on the evils of liquor, John ever wishes for the whisky burn on his tongue, and for the hard pews to become the hard benches of a grog house, the shuffle of the prayer books the shuffle of the playing cards, and the church windows those of a tavern through which a whore might be spied, skirts riding high. Indeed, the Reverend York gave an entire sermon about the sins of the drunkard on that March 31st of '48, and the longing for liquor thus lodged in John's brain in a way it had not in years, and then he found the flask of whiskey in the snow outside the church where another churchgoer had tossed it in righteous determination.

Hamartia, is that the word? It's akin to *Hubris*, John recalls and is Latinate or Greek mayhap, and anywise has to do with how small unthinking actions—alike his idiotic lapse in sobriety—can spawn titanic consequences.

The Reverend York vanishes through the church's banded door. John tips his hat. Just then, Brother Able comes to the fore of John's mind, as he often does. You, Reverend, could sure take some lessons from that stripling preacher, John thinks, there was some mortal keen tenacity, some courage. And best recall, all you high-handed reverends, that God gives his true will to the oddest figures, the oddest voices. Best recall that in the beginning of God's revelations there were no churches nor reverends, only the domed sky and bushes afire, only the expanse of desert and God in all things. John would have been more at home in those times; he is certain of it. He'd enjoy letting his beard grow apace with the wisdom of his years, or have his women mind him at least. He is the patriarch, is he not? Is father to five living children and one in the grave. It should signify. He imagines palm trees and camels and Margaret and the girls in old-timey dresses. They are bearing platters of dates and casting him looks of respect—gratitude even. They are listening to him say once again, "Ignore those raps. It just makes them worse. You'll get used to them. In good time you'll scarce hear them at all." Just then John recalls Abraham's Sarah and wonders if women have ever been as respectful as men would wish.

Dusk is coming on. John quickens his pace. He has not brought a carry lamp and does not wish to stumble about in the full-dark until he breaks a leg, or becomes lost, or encounters the malevolent night dwellers of which his wife ever warns.

Finally he reaches the rambled length of his son's farmstead. There is the welcome smell of fried lard and manured fields, the clear song of the vesper sparrows. He nears the oak where little Ella loved to sit and talk with her Miss Nettie doll, the doll Katie passed on to her, the one he made.

He glimpses a flit of braid. Overhears a little girl's make-believe prattle. He halts, his gut dropping. No, Ella had been much smaller. He comes closer. Sees only Katie, talking to herself alike a child of Ella's age. She looks up at his approach.

"You all packed for the morrow?" John asks.

"I am, but I don't want to go. Do I got to? Really? Truly?"

"I know Ruth can be sour, but she's got no children and space aplenty. You can't share the same bed with Maggie till her sickness is over. You know that."

"It's not the cholera, is it?" Katie clutches her old pinafore. She turned thirteen last week, but her voice is still reedy high, and her eyes have not settled on their colour, are showing a heather-grey in the fall of sun. A few nights past she woke up caterwauling. John hovered as his wife soothed her. Katie told them about the tender's hound. How she and Maggie were thieving apples and how the tender's hound chased them, and how she fell and how they would have been surely killed if the hound hadn't been whistled off. In her nightmare, however, the hound did catch them, then tore them to pieces. The bloody pieces struggled to return to some whole, but Katie's pieces and Maggie's were mangled together in the orchard grass and they couldn't sort themselves out. At that point Katie woke up screaming.

"I doubt it's cholera," John says now. "Maggie's got a belly-ache, is all. We can't take a chance, mind. David's boys are at Maria's and . . . well, leastaways, you won't have no more night-mares about that hound. I shot him dead. Don't tell no one."

"I won't, Pa. I won't. Cross my heart and hope to die. And thanks and all. Really."

John nods and spits tobacco. As usual he can think of nothing more to say, but then Katie and Maggie have ever stumped him for talk, even more than most people do.

That night John listens to his wife's soft snores. Pale moon at the window beyond him. Pale mound of Margaret before. He traces his fingers on her arm. In this matronly woman he still sees ghostings of the sixteen-year-old Margaret Rutan he met at the county fair. She was pink-cheeked, golden-haired, her fluttery eyes a drown-a-man blue. Her endowments? An almighty wonder. She giggled at something he said, which no one had ever done. Love had been scarce in his life and so love was, and is, a surprising and perplexing thing, complicated these days by his love of God, under which his worldly love has been subjugated. Of course Margaret appreciates his piety, what woman wouldn't? Yet things have been different between them ever since he returned from his ten years gone. To this day they argue blandly, without their former heat, as lawyers might. And they make love dutifully only once a month, as if they hadn't chosen each other completely.

John whispers her name. Dares a ribald endearment. Margaret mutters back what sounds like a charm. She has no hand in this spirit business. Of that John is certain. She considers doubt some exhausting task. John-Before had never needed to invent original or elaborate excuses as to where the tin-can money had gone, or where he himself had gone on an afternoon, a week. He counted himself lucky for this, though it vexed him also—gullibility in grown people has always vexed him. That was why he never felt guilty for cheating at the cards: the gullibility of the duped seemed more perverse than the cheating itself. Was that why he taught Leah the truth of things? Things a child should not have known? He can't recall. He supposes he must have been drunk: "You got to have an accomplice somewhere in the room. A child is best. Like you. No one suspects a child, Leah-Lou. You get a system of signals, see, like scratches or blinkings or a sniff or a head tip. Best make that accomplice guilty as you are. That way he won't betray you, not unless he wants to fall alongside." He told her such things, and more. And Leah, it's apparent, listened too well.

His wife shifts to her back. Her endowments rise up and up. John hefts one breast, then the other. Kisses her brow, her nose. She stirs.

Bolts upright and clutches her nightcap. "What is it? What now? Leave me in peace."

"Peggy, it's only me for . . . for crimmey's sake. Your husband. Hush."

"Oh, you. I thought it was a wretched spirit up to no good again, didn't I?"

John pats her back. He nearly tells her then about the past he hauls with him, about Brother Able and his sorry fate, about those first knocks at the Hydesville house and what they meant. Then he decides no, best she be kept in the dark. Best for us all.

The next morning John is mixing lime plaster in the foreground of his half-built house when Leah announces her presence with a stiff, rustling sound. Her dress of bronze-green is fronted with rigid pleats and agate buttons. Her day-dress of madder red, the one she wore for years, is long gone. She wears a different fit-out near daily now.

"You wished to speak with me, Father? Here I am."

John pushes up his spectacles and pinches the bridge of his nose. "You've got yourself in a perilous situation, Leah-Lou, and I want to be a help to you."

"Help? My Lord, but we could use another man's help. Calvin is kept far too busy. You shall come to Rochester, then? When the cholera passes? We shall be so very busy. Eliab is planning a grand tour. He has exhibitions booked for us in Auburn and Troy, and in many other towns besides. And then the city of New York itself! And Mr. Greeley himself has written Eliab and asked to be our champion. He and his dear wife are eager to meet us the moment we arrive in New York. They lost a son to the cholera, though that was in last year's round. Pickie? Yes, that was his name. Odd, but there it is."

"Who's this Greeley?" John says, exasperated, because lately Leah has taken to tossing down names with the same abandon she once tossed knives in mumblety-peg.

"Who? Father! Horace Greeley. The editor of the *New York Tribune*. His name is writ large on every issue of that publication. He is most recognizable."

"I don't hold with New York papers. They've nothing to do with us."

"With you, that is true. But what of P.T. Barnum? Surely he rings a note or bell in your head. Horace is keen to introduces us to that celebrated man—they are fast friends, apparently—and Mr. Barnum will surely be keen, in turn, to promote our blessed spirits." She gives her dimpled smile.

"Don't talk like they're real, them spirits of yours, or *quasi* real, or any kind of real."

Leah frowns, then masters herself in a way she never could when she was a child. "And I have assured Ma that New York is not a pit of snakes, but you know how she worries."

"Recall the commandment, my girl, *thou shall not bear false—*"

"I know how it goes. Who doesn't? And anywise, the spirits *are* real. As real and true as you or I. I have felt them course through me, speak through me even. An astounding thing. Many have witnessed it."

John waves this off. "I prayed to the Almighty all morning in the field so that I could see things clear."

"That must have been quite damp."

"You can't keep on." He stammers out his intent. He meant to be calm, convincing, meant to explain how he only wants his family together again under one roof, meant to employ phrases of sentiment: one true heart, the joy of family, the duties of women, and so forth. Says instead, "Order your spirits to leave. Order them." He laughs dryly. "I've got no doubt they'll obey you." He picks up a hammer and attends to the boards laid out on his sawhorse.

"Leave, Father? But I do not wish the spirits to leave, even if they did listen to 'orders' from me. I have grown quite accustomed to them—and must you hammer on like that? The board cannot go anywhere."

He pauses, the hammer in mid-strike.

"As I was saying, I have grown quite accustomed to them. They quell the loneliness I have always endured as a woman abandoned with a child, struggling to pay the rent, alone against the trials of the world and—"

"Sure, sure, I can understand all that, I can; but you're risking the damnation of your eternal soul, anyone can see that."

"Anyone? Perhaps we should leave the judgement of my soul to God. I have no doubt He will find it honourable."

John drops the hammer, and on his thumb. He clenches his teeth to cut off the oath. Abjuring foul, blasphemous words is no easy task; they had once constituted a good third of his vocabulary, after all. Yet an oath is the only thing to utter when you have bashed your thumb with a hammer, or when you must live on the charity of your son, or when your daughters are set on the road to damnation and ruin.

"Are you in pain, Father? Whatever is that sound?"

"Damnit, girl. Then what of your mortal flesh? Take your lesson from Jezebel. The woman was hurled out a tower for worshipping heathen gods. Got herself torn apart by dogs, nothing left of her but—"

"I know how it goes, Pa, but that was such a long time past."

"Then what of Joe Smith? Him and his false religion and false gods. Got jailed for his sins, but he weren't safe even behind bars. The mob shot him up and chucked him out the window, just like Jezebel. They finished him off with a firing squad and then tried to saw off his blaspheming head. That was naught five years ago."

Leah backs away. Eyes his hammer—as if he would ever strike her in wrath, or in any other fashion. "That Smith was a man. Honestly, none would treat a woman so."

John sighs and clenches his thumb to stay the blood leaking from the nail. At this Leah rubs her forearms as if recalling her own wounds. Have the scars have faded over the years since she was a girl? John wonders. Decides it unlikely. There were so many wounds at the time, he knew she would be marked for life.

"Besides, I have no fear of such things," Leah continues. "Crowds. Mobs. You of all people must know that. How could I fear any such thing after the birds lifted me in their multitudes?"

John doesn't waste his breath arguing this memory of hers. He takes off his spectacles again, wipes at his eyes. Leah is a blur, pink-red with blood. Last card, he thinks. He speaks of newspaper men. How eager they are to listen. He thrice mentions reputation.

John has seen Leah quake with fury, but never stilled with it, as she is now. "Newspaper men, Father? I am on intimate terms with many, not just the famed Mr. Greeley. And indeed they love to listen. They pick up on any innuendo and turn it into such tales. Already they have spoken of their suspicions that you devised levers, pulleys and such to make the noise of—"

"I'll take on the blame. I'll do that. I haven't steered you right."

He should have known that Leah would not retreat. Has he ever known her to do so?

"Many things are hidden in this world," she says softly. "Occurrences in the dark. I have heard of fathers so blinded with drink they attempt to treat their daughters as their wives, when alone with them, in a barn, say, and these daughters of such tender years. The daughters always run off, horrified, before the unspeakable happens. Still. They cannot ever forget it."

When he finally speaks it is with the voice of John-Before and with the rage of John-Before. "You, you dare suggest . . . how can you even brew-up such things? How? Damn you, you were a mean 'un as a girl. You're meaner than an old sow now."

Leah flinches, brushes at her eyes, then points to the joists of this house he is building for them all. "Cobwebs, Pa. They're settling in. They do that in empty places." She walks off, her dress of bronze-green rustling the fallen boards.

John calls to her, but she does not turn back. He can't help but notice, however, that she neglects to lift her skirt hem out of the dirt.

CHAPTER 13.

"Whatever are you doing?" I demanded. (My patient had flung off the bedclothes.) "You'll catch your death!"

"Catch my death? Oh, the good grief, I'd say I've caught that already." She yanked off her stockings then.

I was not amazed by the sad bloating of her legs—a prime symptom of her dipsomania—but her feet were another story. They were, to be frank, ghastly: all knobbed and muscled and the toes dreadfully overlarge.

She indicated the soles of her feet, then showed her palms. "Such was all that was left of Jezebel after she fell, after the dogs tore her apart as punishment for blasphemy. This: the palms of her hands, the soles of her feet."

"It was a harsh judgement on Jezebel," I allowed. "And peculiar how the dogs left only that. I objected, quite strongly."

"Objected? When?"

"When I heard the story, oh, so long ago it seems another age. Would a man be treated the same? No, he would not."

"And yet it made no difference," she said, and studied me for a moment, as if she had mistaken me for someone else.

☙

"You're as quiet as a church mouse, aren't you poppet? Are you feeling poorly? Do you need more brandied tonic?"

"I have had sufficient, Mother," Leah says. They are in David's keeping room. Leah sets the kettle over the smoldering hearth. Mother diligently polishes the table-tops. Above stairs her sisters play at games. It is the day after Leah's father refused to help her with the spirits and so, yes, Leah is quiet, and filled with that same distasteful sensation as when she hears a song played off-key. Just then John enters and drops a bundle of kindling into the wood bin. He leaves without a word or nod. Mother casts Leah a bewildered glance. Leah pretends nothing is amiss. "This fire is not drawing. Not at all," she proclaims and jabs at the fire with a poker.

Leah's sisters now tumble into the keeping room, all-agiggle. Maggie's belly-ache has passed and she has sworn off slip-gut pudding for life. Katie has recently returned from the Culvers' and she and Maggie are delighting in making sport of Ruth Culver once again.

"Old Ruthie wanted the spirits talking constant, Mag," Leah hears Katie say. "She reckons she's got medium qualities too. And she really tried. She even invited her wall-eyed cousin Orville over to hear her ghosts rapping away, but the dead can't abide her, not at all. No wonder, she's such an old nasty. She wanted to drown her poor old cat because it wasn't catching mice enough. She said it was to teach it a lesson, but if you're dead you can't learn much, can you?"

"Well, no. Not usually," Maggie replies, and adds that Ruth is so sour she could curdle milk with her eyeballs.

"She said she'd teach me a lesson, too," Katie continues. "Said I was a lazy skeezick and ungrateful, and just 'cus I didn't want to do her nasty old scullery work."

"A lesson?" Leah puts in. "What sort of lesson?"

"I dunno. You know how old Ruth gripes on."

"Come, lamb, that's unkind, isn't it?" Mother says.

"Gripes on? How, Katherina?" Leah insists.

"I dunno. I guess about it not being fair that she can't get the ghosts talking. Oh, but I hate, hate, hate her. I thought I'd just suffocate if I had to stay there any longer. The only thing that helped was this refreshment that Norman makes out of juniper berries. Mag, you got to try it."

Leah looks at her two young sisters. She sets down the poker, having forgotten she was even holding it, then turns to leave the room. My Lord and the spirits! she thinks. These two.

"Leah? Poppet? Where are you off to?"

"The veranda, Mother. The smoke in here. Honestly, how can you bear it?" She ignores her mother's warnings of the night air's noxious qualities, her brother David's offer for company, her sisters' questioning eyes.

She holds vigil on the verandah, watching as the last brindled light fades into the drumlins and the dusk overtakes the world. There is the smell of spring roses, the fairy blink of lightning bugs, the mutter of the Ganargua River.

She hums the *Moonlight Sonata*. Delights in the nacreous blue and green lines it evokes. Music rarely reveals its colours to her nowadays, thus the appearance of the colours is a sign of renewed prospects, surely.

She ceases humming. Gasps. Strains to comprehend what she is witnessing: a black tower rising out the woodlands some rods distant. The tower builds itself higher and higher yet as if to reach the sash of stars, the gibbous moon.

Leah is about to call her family to come bear witness, then decides, no, if *this* is her sign—and not the coloured music—then its agent might be questioned.

The tower begins to break apart into fragments, fragments that wing hither and yon across the ashen skies. Bats, Leah realizes with some relief. The tower is composed of thousands upon thousands of bats, creatures who have no need of light. Some consider them malignant—harbingers of misfortune and misrule. Leah has her doubts. Perhaps bats are merely fortunate to see in the darkling hours. Perhaps to them night is a transparency.

She hears her sisters' giddy laughter. Hears Mother scold them for their mollyhawking of all and sundry. Mother has her power, Leah knows, and likely more than all the Fox women parcelled up. She wonders now if some portion of Mother's frettings and questionings are a pretense. Not that Leah would judge her for that. Has there ever been a woman who has not fretted or trembled or uttered inanities at times, as befits her sex? Has there ever been a woman who has not once worn a cloak made of modesty and manners and piety? Soon the cloak hardens into a shell, which is quite useful, as it keeps one from screaming.

A hammer's staccato tat-tat. Leah looks over to her father's house. The windows are slabs of yellow light. Outside the house, the sawhorse stands like some skeletal creature at sentry. Inside the house, her father's shadow passes the open door. She cannot see the man himself.

Where-ever have you gone, Pa? Leah wonders. She recollects an evening back when she was seven or eight and they lived still in Rockport. She had hidden in the barn to watch her father with his sporting friends. The men wore their Coke hats tipped back. They rattled dice on tins. Drank whisky straight from bottles that glinted in the lamplight. She was hiding because her father had already sent her back to bed twice, and she always wanted to be near him in those days.

The men spoke of quims and snatches. Of where in Gotham to find the cherry whores. They spoke of cock-chafers and sodomites. Of men who went at their own daughters. At that, John, who had been silent through it all, said, "That's enough of that damn talk." His eyes never rose from the cards, but his words held pure menace. The other men fell quiet.

Young Leah had never heard such talk, and yet she knew it was vile. She felt something splinter inside. Her innocence, she supposes now. Of course Pa . . . her father never touched her. Not that way. But then why, yesterday, did she suggest he had? Perhaps as a small retaliation, she decides, for being given the unwanted knowledge of such depravities. Anywise, both of them understood she would never accuse him to the newspaper men, nor to anyone. Both of them knew she was bluffing. Had he not taught her that very term?

From within David's house comes singing and then the sounds of a mouth harp as Leah's family makes a celebration out of the cholera's swift passing. Presently, she will go in and take her place at the organ. In a few days she and her sisters will return to Rochester and begin preparations for their tour.

She looks over the yard once again. Nothing forms out of the gloaming. No torches wielded by men featureless as paper cut-outs. No preachers shouting "blasphemy." Leah and her family have been warned that some are blaming the Foxes for the pestilence. Medieval dolts, Leah thinks. She knows, however, that as long as she is watchful no harm will come to those she loves. And love them she does. No matter if they ever think otherwise.

The hammer tat-tatting on the new house ceases. Her father will cross the foreyard soon. Leah tenses and waits. Best to make amends now, she thinks. As like he will call her a Jezebel again, but she can hold herself above such discourtesies.

She waits and waits on the veranda, counting out to a compound meter of twenty, then twenty-five, but still her father, stubborn man, does not appear.

"Leah," Mother calls from the doorway. "You'll get the catarrh, won't you? Come in this instance."

David looms behind Mother, puts in, "Why, our music cannot succeed without your voice, sister."

"As ever," Leah mutters, and turns into the house.

"MY, BUT YOUR LEAH NURSED A GRUDGE," I said, and sliced at a bread loaf.

"Yes, she did, and better, I'd wager, than you have nursed the most grevious-ill patient."

"Oh, you are a one, but should she not have gone to your father? Made amends before it became too late and . . . damnation!" I cried, the bread-knife having slipped and gashed my finger.

My patient sat upright. "Ah . . . you're bleeding. Are you in pain?"

"Pain? Do I seem a spleeny sort? A cosset? The sort to make a brouha out a nick?"

"Apparently not . . . How bad is it?"

"It's not to the bone, duck, and that is the important matter," I said, and wrapped my finger up snap-quick in a bandage.

She indicated the laudanum on the nighttable "Would you care for measure or two?"

It was a generous offering, I thought then, knowing how possessed she was of her medicine. I eyed the bottle. Thought, too, of gin, and how that perilous drink was surely the "juniper refreshment" that Katie tasted at the Culvers', and how this did not bode well for her, gin being gin and of such easy imbibing.

"Go on, Mrs. Mellon, I would not think you are a, what was it . . . a spleeny, nor a cosset, nor a—"

"Your father," I said abruptly. "You must have thought him dead when he vanished for those ten years. You must have given up hope. Waited till doomsday for some letter or note."

She settled back, and did not offer the laudanum again, for which I was grateful. "I wasn't born at the time he abandoned the family, recall? But it was peculiar, my father's conversion. I wonder, Mrs. Mellon, do you think a grown man can be a changeling?"

"No, that is a ridiculous superstition," I said, and gave her a bowl of milk-sopped bread, keeping my bloodied finger off the rim. "People change, certainly, they take on this profession or that. Alter appearances, character even, but they still have a human soul and heart. A true changeling has neither, being, of course, a hobgoblin in disguise."

"Yes, I suppose that's true. Yet a changeling returning home would be better than nothing—returning, that is."

To this fact I agreed. Or perhaps I kept my counsel. I can't recall. To explain: The conversation had brought my son to mind and in those days any thought of my son was often accompanied by a harsh white emptiness, a nothing, as it were. I do recall that my patient asked if my finger still hurt, and if the pain had grown worse, and that she ate a small portion of the bread-sopping, then asked for her medicine, and then her bible box, and then her father's letters.

WHEN JOHN SEES LEAH on the veranda, silhouetted as if on a ship's unreachable prow, a certainty comes upon him, the sort God grants him on rare occasion. He waits until she returns to David's house, then rummages out an inkwell, blotter and pen nib, and then hefts out the quire of paper he had intended for expense calculations, for sketches of porticos and gables. He draws the lamp closer and pinches his nose so hard the bone aches. He might reach her yet. His first letter, written just after the knocking began, had made no inroads. Had likely only been tinder firing her plans. He need take a different tack now.

2 May, 1850

Dearest Leah,

I give you here an account of my ten years gone. I never thought I'd see the mortal day I'd tell of it, but I want mightily to save your soul from Hell's everlasting flames and torments and the like, and this account might bring you reason. Understand, Our Lord can be insistent and peculiar in His demands and He sees all, and has ways to bring round even the most determined and ingenious sinner, which I was—as you are, my girl.

Thing is, Leah-Lou, you're made from my own stamp and I'm sorry for that. It must be hard tender for a woman to have a man's pride and ferocity and a man's stubborn will. And because of your nature you've held an almighty grudge against me for my leaving, which I did, if you recall, on a spring morning of April something of '23. The sky in Rockland County was the shade of good whisky because everything under God's sky spoke of whisky in those days. I told your ma I was going to town for seed. She muttered and sighed like always, then cast some hair strands in the hearth, and those hairs had the look of mine. I was thinking, 'course, how your Grandmother Rutan followed ghost funerals and of all the stories of your female kin that go back to the Old World. She was working a spell, your ma, and I now know she wanted me gone. I hand her no blame. My drinking had become an all-consuming vice and she had cause for complaints aplenty.

So I left. I walked right out of town and it were like my feet were taking me and I had no say in the matter. All I had were my hip flask and my thin coat and my broad hat. I sent a letter. I didn't leave without a word. I explained I'd be working on Clinton's Big Ditch and that I'd send money home soon as I could. But I didn't send a dime, Leah-Lou, and I know you and the family suffered for my lack. Mayhap that was when you started thinking the world owed you a passel . . .

1823, two years before the canal was complete and there was still work aplenty. Already boats were being drawn between Utica and Seneca, already the freight charges were dropping like pigeons under the gun.

"The canal shall traverse there!" announced some pockmarked engineer.

The men, John among them, scoffed at this prophecy. The tree trunks spanned ten feet or more, the underbrush was a mesh of stinging nettles. The rare natural clearing was but a swamp with malarial fumes and mosquito clouds, snakes and water rats.

John watched the targetman confer with this engineer. They discussed where a lock should go, calmly, as if it were like putting in a gate. The engineer . . . ah, but Pock-Face was *not* an engineer, as John soon discovered. Indeed, not one true engineer was to be found on this American marvel—the Grand Canal, the Erie Canal. The planners were instead inspired amateurs who had invented, among other things, a monstrous stump puller with wheels sixteen feet high, and a cement of crushed limestone that hardened under water. The latter seemed an impossibility. But then the whole canal seemed an impossibility. The plan was to build more than four hundred miles of this watery road, from the Hudson River at Albany to Lake Erie at Buffalo. Off this route, feeder-canals would link to lesser places. Some surmised that in time canals would be cut from New York to Florida, and even across the great plains to the far West. As grand an undertaking as any, and John was mortal proud to be part of it all, though he resented that he, a home-born Yankee, must labour alongside a multitude of Germans, and an even greater multitude of Irish. At least the foreigners' scarce English excused him from chit-chat, and from joining in the pointless songs of the grievances they'd left behind.

John first worked with a crew that bulwarked the canal with manure and hay and hand-cut stones. Other crews built up the berm on one side, the towpath on the other. John spied the sketches and heard talk of bascule bridges and swing bridges, and then of aqueducts, eighteen in all. The largest was to be in Rochester itself. John liked the ring of that Latinate word: *aqueduct*. He'd heard some of old Rome and its wonders. Thought: But we'll do better than them fucking, dress-wearing dagos yet.

John rolls the blotter over the page. Considers well before dipping his pen again.

Hubris. Sure you've heard that word, Leah-Lou. It's Latinate, same as *aqueduct*. I heard it plenty from those who called the canal a doom-struck monstrosity, or a tax-sucking parasite, or just plain Clinton's Folly, seeing as Governor Dewill Clinton was the one who urged its creation. Other folks were more commending and would lob us bottles of whisky to lubricate our efforts. My point is that I know what it is to be part of some grand undertaking that's mocked by some and lauded by others. I know this hubris comes easy to the American character because novelty holds no terror for us and we've yet to learn any sharp lessons and we've mastered our own course without Kings and Bishops. But hubris is hubris all the same and it's always punished in the end, as mine was, as yours will be if you continue bringing the dead back to the living world. God and God alone brings back the dead, and only on some rare occasions, and you are heading down damnation alley, Leah-Lou, by your mimicking of God's powers. Resurrection business is the Lord's business, His alone and for His purposes, as you'll soon see.

By summer's verge John's hands were gloved with calluses, his muscles knotted like cordwood. He had no pocket watch. Like most of the crew, he marked his time by the whens of liquor. Before the whistle blew for lunch a boy was already running to a grocer or candy store for buckets of ale. Sundown was the time for black-strap corn-juice and whisky, after which the men were often working again by lantern light. On a Sunday, he and a gang-up of men would bet on the nags racing at the local ovals. He was called Grim John for his lack of happy chat, but was admired for his trove of cusses, his steady hand at the cards, his ability to pour into his small frame quantities of liquor that would topple the strongman at a fair.

John worked hard for all his imbibing, put to use his blacksmithing talents, his talents with mechanisms and levers. That autumn of '23 he was assigned to the Niagara Escarpment, at a settlement soon to be called Lockport after the extravagant terrace of five locks designed to drop boats down seventy feet. The locks reminded him of the clever traps he once made to catch rabbits for the stewpot. Leah would help skin them, eager for their pelts. She was collecting them, she said, to make a fine lady's coat.

He laboured through that winter of '23–'24 in a boat-building yard, the boats taking shape under a heated shed. He sent home not a nickel. The wages didn't hold to his fingers, which were the fingers of a free man. Far too long, his view had been the ass-end of a plow mule. For too long he'd been hidebound to his parents, then to a family of his own. Once the canal was done he had no intention of returning to Rockland County, to his wife, Margaret, to his children: Leah and Maria and David. He could have been a lock-tender, mind, for such an employ was offered after his tenure at Lockport. He could have sent for his family, had a neat little house, a garden, some sly commerce of his own. Or he could have been a towpath-tender and slaughtered muskrats that dug into the canal walls. In winter he could have helped restore the prism of the drained canal. Likewise, his family could have been near to hand. Yet even on contemplation of such employ, John's throat tightened as if in a stranglehold. He plumbed the gold depths of his whisky glass and saw himself as a canaller, nothing else.

———

. . . and it seemed a thing I was always meant for, Leah-Lou, though mayhap that was the Devil talking, or mayhap my own prodigious pride. And I see that you, too, think you're meant for grander purposes, but there's no grander purpose than humility, and this is a lesson I hope you learn without suffering a passel, though on consideration I doubt that's any kind of possible.

Your father, John Fox

John stretches his fingers, then turns down the lamp's wheel, then half-cups the chimney glass, then blows out the flame in one expert breath. He has never shattered a chimney from wayward spittle, nor burned his palms, nor caused undue soot to sully the glass.

He walks out into the foreyard, the moon casting a tarnished but sufficient light. Now notices that David's house is already dark. His women haven't even called him in to bed. No matter. He is surprised, even pleased that he, a taciturn man by nature, could give so many words to a page. Surprised, too, that his mind feels lighter, his thoughts more clear. Prayer has never produced such an effect, he realizes a short time later, as he kneels aside his blessed marriage bed.

CHAPTER 14.

"You are rallying some, duck. This should settle," I said, and unfolded a newspaper to show my patient the soft-fried oysters. "And these," I added, and indicated the sweet-dates. "The hawker proclaimed them 'an exotic little treat from a land afar,' and offered two-for-one on the deal. We have fourteen of them to mark the fourteen days of your biding. Few of my patients have such time before they're called to—"

"To the Glory, yes, I know," my patient said, her tone all-huffy. She peered at the sweet-dates, then poked at the grease-soaked newspaper, which was an old copy of the *New York Times*.

"Is the *Tribune* no longer printing?"

"Printing what?"

"Itself."

"I wouldn't know. Should I know everything? Am I a genius? A polymath?"

She smiled. "They do come in many guises, though when it comes to common sense you are surely a genius, and common sense is of more use in life than dead languages or algebra."

To this fact I wholly agreed.

"I only ask about the *Tribune*," she continued, "because Horace Greeley became a great friend to me and my family, though he favoured Katie most. We fell out with him, or rather I did, then found a way back to some mutual regard."

"Did you now, duck?" I kept my voice level, but only with difficulty.

"Yes. Could you manage to bring a copy, I—"

"No! I cannot 'manage' that. I don't hold with the *Tribune*, that damned rag. I won't read a column of it. It's not fit for wrapping cow brains. It scarcely figures if Greeley is dead. It's his paper through and through, and I cannot forgive his meddling exhortations during the war. So if you want a copy you'd best bestir yourself forthwith and buy your damned own."

She waited until I dumped the oysters into two bowls, then said, "He was often plagued with melancholy, you know. Horace. He took his responsibilities hard. He was a good man."

"Good is as good does."

"Now there's a catchy slogan, fit for P.T. Barnum himself. Should I tell you of when we met him?"

"Barnum? You met him? The man himself? In truth?"

"Yes, Horace introduced us, just as he offered to in his letters. Though first we Fox sisters had a, yes, a 'triumphant' tour of New York state. Albany. Troy. We held private sittings with all the local worthies, gave displays in local halls and lyceums, became very public creatures indeed. Eliab, you see, wanted to make certain we were prepared for New York. That city of cities, he warned, would either shower us with fortune and fame, or break us into bits and bobs."

"That is, yes, New York in a nutshell. And when did you meet that Greeley?" I said, and frowned and set aside a dubious oyster.

"Direct upon arrival, yes, in the early summer of 1850. He came to us at Barnum's Hotel. It was not owned by P.T., incidentally, but by a cousin of his who no doubt liked the association with his more celebrated kin. And then a week after our first meeting Horace took us to P.T.'s famed American Museum, the first incarnations of it. Did you ever visit it, Mrs. Mellon?"

"No. That one had already gone up in flames by the time I arrived here . . . the poor animals."

"Should I tell you of it? The meeting? The museum?"

"If you wish to, I won't quibble," I said. To hide my curiosity I set out the remainder of the oysters, the dates, the laudanum. "We have, after all, our dining to do."

MAGGIE, HEAT-FLAGGED AND ANXIOUS, watches as the piebald boy studies Horace Greeley, who studies Phineas Theodore Barnum, who studies with a sweeping gaze his small empire of the hideous and the strange. "Damned vexing. And you can't figure the how of it?" she hears Barnum asks Horace. Barnum's gaze now passes over Leah and Mother to fix on Maggie and Katie, who are feigning listening to a giantess tell the joys of giant life.

Maggie tips her head towards Barnum. "He's nothing to worry on, Kat," she whispers. "It'll turn out right."

"Tragic, just tragic," Katie answers, her eyes still on the Giantess, whose heavy face is sheened with sweat, whose breath is working like bellows in the early July heat. "I mean that Calvin and George have got errands." Katie adds. "They'll just die when they find out we got to visit Barnum's . . . These poor old ghastlies, though. Do you reckon Mr. Barnum ever lets them out to have fun or anything?"

At this Maggie chances another look at Barnum himself. He is a solid man with a blunt face and wiry hair in two queer protrusions on either side of his head, as if covering small horns. In his presence the human curiosities are performing their best. Yan Zoo the Chinese juggler. Zip the Pinhead. The Mammoth Highland Boys, fat as barrels in their kilts. Mr. Diwali the Snake Charmer. A Circassian Beauty caped in her wild black hair.

If the Devil were come to earth . . . No, no, Barnum's only a man, Maggie reminds herself. And you're too old for foolish thoughts. Didn't Horace say he first met Barnum at the Universalist church? And don't the Universalists preach salvation for all and hellfire for none? Such is not Mr. Split-Foot's cant. And Mr. Barnum is an abolitionist and a temperance man, just like Horace. The Devil would be neither.

Maggie watches Yan Zoo juggle what appears to be shrunken heads and ponders what it is she finds so distressing about Barnum's American Museum; it is, after all, one of the finest and most edifying establishments in New York. Everyone says so. Besides this hall of human curiosities there is an ornate lecture theatre and then the

Great Hall, where the eye can barely take in all the displays—suits of armour, skeletons, mechanical dolls, stuffed creatures from every corner of the globe and wax figures of the famous dead that seem more alive than some people Maggie could name. In another room are scale models of cities: Paris by moonlit, Dublin on St. Patrick's Day and Moscow in flames. In yet another are aquaria aswim with fantastical fish. And in the largest is a menagerie of animals whose squawks and growls pervade the museum, and whose simulacra are nailed to the museum's outside facade.

Leah nudges Maggie, then Katie. "Edge closer. The both of you. This is of such importance."

"Isn't every old thing," Katie mutters. Maggie nods in agreement with Katie But they both edge closer to Barnum and Horace, as told. Maggie concentrates on shutting out the marvelling comments of the other museum attendees, the rustling of their museum guide books, the snickering children. Near on Mother watches enthralled as Mr. Nellis the Armless loads a pistol with his toes. She is, as usual, no help at all.

"The how?" Maggie hears Horace say. "Phineas, I can't imagine there is a 'how' at all. They're country girls and little educated. Miss Katie, the one in the lilac affair, she's just on thirteen. Miss Maggie, the doe-eyed one there, in the green, she's sixteen, I believe. And Mrs. Fish, she is, what, twenty-five? Or passes for that at least. My point is that I can't imagine any of them duping a baby out of his rattle, let alone duping the worthy men who've tested them."

Barnum snorts. "Two correct questions out of ten. That's what their spirits average, Horace. That's what you told me. And if the spirits ain't infallible, I might ask, what deuced good are they?"

"Solace?"

"Not a bad commodity, that," Barnum concedes, and eyes Horace with what might be pity.

Just then the piebald boy points at Horace. "He gonna be one of ours?"

Barnum roars with laughter. Horace *is* odd in appearance, Maggie allows. Like one of our spirits made visible, she had thought with faint alarm when he first called upon the Fox sisters last week at their hotel.

He is wraith pale. Has the flaxen-white hair seen only in children. Is rarely without his droopy white hat, round spectacles and white linen duster, the pockets of which are always stuffed with notes and newspaper. His face owns scarcely a wrinkle and his voice is high-pitched, grating really, especially compared to Mr. Barnum's rumbly one. Maggie finds it hard to believe that Horace Greeley is the most powerful newspaperman in New York. Leah said that Horace is a "genius," a "polymath," an opinion swayer, a president maker. She said that when he started writing his personal opinions for the front page of his newspaper, every other editor followed suit. He has no fear of the powerful, nor of controversy. He writes scathingly about slavery. And he supports the causes of the weaker sex. Has even hired a woman to write for him. Miss Fuller? Yes, that is her name. Miss Margaret Fuller. She corresponds from Europe at the moment. Apparently all kinds of revolutions and wars and government experiments are going on over there.

Barnum's laughter sputters off. "What do you say, Horace? Half ghost! Half man! You could lug about a coffin, one foot in, one foot out, that kind of thing."

Horace smiles. "I should hope I make a better journalist than a freak."

"You're a deuced better journalist than ever I was. Let's say we display you as the Amazing Incorruptible Man. The rags wouldn't dare cry *you* down."

Horace and Barnum smile and nod in unison at this, and in the way, Maggie notes, of old trusted friends. She edges even closer, Katie keeping step.

"I look forward to Miss Fuller's return to America." Horace continues. "She should be on board the ship even now. Yes, I should very much like her opinions on the spirit rappings. It could be seen as a revolution and she is my chief expert on those."

"She is damned remarkable. All the beauty of the female. All the brains and ambitions of the male. She'd draw mightily if she'd lecture here."

Horace's voice grows higher yet. "She has taken up with, that is, has succumbed to the attentions of, a petty Italian noble, a would-be revolutionary, a good few years younger. I admit some feelings of betrayal. Not, no, not in that manner, Phineas. It is just that she was as a second mother to Pickie when she lived with Mary and me, and now she has this son of her own." Horace sighs and roots about in his duster. Pulls out a sweet and gives it to the piebald boy. Manages a smile. "How old are you, my boy?"

"I be seven and a half."

"I bought him in the Carolinas," Barnum says. "He's free to bugger off, of course. He's got his papers. But it's a far kinder life here than in the streets. And Clarissa there has taken him under her wing, as it were."

Maggie looks to where Barnum points. Clarissa the Fat Lady does indeed have a wing: a dewlap of fat that sways as she nibbles a turkey leg.

"Seven and a half," Horace says. "Pickie is the same age."

"Is?"

"Yes." Horace adjusts his spectacles.

Barnum stares at his friend. "Jumping Jesus! Don't tell me he spoke to you."

"No, no. They don't speak. He, ah, that is, he rapped. The raps are the loudest about Miss Katie." Horace grows animated. "He said he was happy and that he was with his brothers and sisters. They grow up in Heaven, apparently. Well, the ladies call it Spirit Land, and vow that everyone is at their best age there, whether they had to grow to such a state or return to it."

"Spirit Land, eh? So are there heavenly nurseries? Angels for governesses? Don't tell me we must carry on working above."

"I know it sounds ridiculous. But, truly, the young ladies were as perplexed as any in the room."

Barnum wags his head. "Caution, old friend. Heaven is the show of all shows. I ain't doubting that. And I ain't doubting we're all happy as the larks when we're with the Good Lord. But for now we're in the waking world. Stick with corruption. Stick with unmasking human wretchedness in all its shapes and guises. That's where you hold sway."

"You think them charlatans?" There is no challenge in Horace's tone. Only curiosity. He adds, "You of all people would know, Phineas."

"Oh, the good grief," Maggie mutters as her view of Horace and Barnum is blocked by a party of what must be factory-men, given their ill-fitting jackets and caps, given that one man wears an eye-patch, another is missing three fingers and a third has an ear burned away.

"What is it, Maggie? Katie?" Mother calls. "Is it the Rubber Man? He is just wondrously dreadful, isn't he?"

The girls ignore their mother and circle round the factory-men to pick up the conversation.

". . . so, in truth, Horace, I rather think they're geniuses. I'd pilfer their show, that I would, but for the matter of a conscience.

Maggie shams interest in the antics of the Rubber Man as Horace and Barnum approach. Katie does likewise. The hall of human curiosities near empties of spectators, as if Barnum has given some silent command. He approaches and makes the slightest of bows. "Ladies, I am intrigued. And Horace here makes a swell case for you."

Leah smiles, her dimples on full display. "We shall need your lecture hall, of course. This sort of general display is not seemly for our dear girls."

"Gracious evers. Not at all!" Mother puts in.

"The cost of entrance can be divided and . . ." Leah pauses as Maggie taps frantically at her throat, a signal for quiet.

"I don't recall talking up an agreement," Barnum says.

Leah frowns. "But Horace has assured us that you were a man of perception and—"

Barnum holds up a hand. "My friend vouches for you, no falsity there. But to work upon grief? To presume Heaven? I do no harm with my humbuggery. But you, ladies, well, you risk giving charlatans a bad reputation."

"If you are attempting humour, you are failing, sir. Utterly," Leah says. "The most reputable people in New York are eager for our acquaintance. We are highly spoken of and in the . . . highest circles and . . . grandest places." Leah is as imperious as ever, but Barnum has unsettled her. Maggie can tell by that hitch in her voice, that throb in her temple.

Barnum chuckles. "No doubt. But I needn't pilfer my Madame Forer's crystal ball to scry your coming infamy, nor to know that a contract will never share the names of Barnum and Fox."

"You are too forward, sir. Entirely," Leah says, and in her coldest voice.

"Hah! Better than backward, ma'am. Now, do excuse me, ladies . . . Horace. I've business to attend to. Oh, and ladies, I hear you've booked into my cousin's hotel. Do bid him capital day for me if you espy him about. He's doing a bang-up business, but then ain't every self-promoter and showman keen-set on taking rooms at a Barnum's Hotel."

Horace gives Leah a helpless shrug. Leah, chin raised, takes a step towards Barnum. Maggie grips her elbow. "We thank you so much for your time, Mr. Barnum," she says hastily.

"Yes, we really, really do," Katie adds.

Mother echoes this. Leah inhales, gathers herself, says, "Yes, our thanks. And I agree: it is best we work in separate spheres."

And best we not make an enemy of Phineas T. Barnum, Maggie thinks. Why in tunket can she see this, but not Leah? A surprising idea comes to her: Perhaps Leah is not as all-knowing as she seems. Perhaps she needs Maggie to keep her steady, just as Maggie needs Leah for all manner of things. Perhaps Leah needs Katie and Mother too. Somehow, this comforts Maggie.

"I'm near starved to death," Katie says. "Can we lunch at Delmonico's again? Can we, Leah?"

"Certainly. Delmonico's is a finer establishment than this by far. Horace, will you join us?"

Horace will. "Follow me, dear ladies," he says solicitously, and leads the way out of Barnum's museum. They are soon lost. The crowds have become too thick. The corridors and rooms and distractions too many. A dead end here. Confusing signage there.

They stop short. Maggie looks about in astonishment. They are in the hall of curiosities. Again. The piebald boy hollers, "You're back!"

Zip the Pinhead nods his tiny head. The giantess has, improbably, vanished.

"Stay a while," suggests Mr. Nellis the Armless.

"Stay forever," adds Mr. Diwali the Snake Charmer.

"It's like a dreadful maze," Maggie says to her mother and sisters, to Horace. "That's what's wrong with this place. That's what so blamed distressing about it all."

"Do you believe in signs, Mrs. Mellon?"

"As in, from Providence?"

"Well, yes."

I considered this, then said, "I suppose that like anyone I believe in signs. And portents, yes, and auguries and omens, but only when they suit my purposes."

My patient gestured to the garret's three linked windows. "They are why I chose this garret, Mrs. Mellon, I took them as a sign." She did not say more about this. One did not need to be an oracle sort, however, to see how they might have represented to her the Fox sisters three, the two outer windows being small and squared and discreet, at least compared to the centre window, which was fat and arched and seemed in command of the garret's variant light.

"Did you want some air?" I asked. "The centre window is fixed as the firmament, but those outer ones should crack open with some encouragement."

She chuckled at this and then talked again of Chauncey Burr.

"It's closer than a bloodyo tomb in here," Chauncey declares to his brother Heman, and hauls up the boarding-house windows in defiance of the landlady's orders to keep them shut fast. He thrusts his head out and "takes the air," as they say, this air that is shot with August heat, with manure dust and coal smoke, with gnats and blue-bottles, and with that high din of banging, rattling and shouting that is so particular to New York and that reminds Chauncey of a desperate, enraged leviathan shaking loose its shackles.

He pulls his head back into the room. "I say again, Heman: Gotham is a cesspool of the ignorant and the arrogant. Mark you the cousined soundings of the words."

Heman chews a plumbago stick. Does not look up from the heaps of papers and periodicals, likely because Chauncey is using his stage voice, the one that discourages a two-way conversation.

"A 'spirit sitting' packed with a baker's dozen of blue blood hotty snot literati? Oh, oh, it must be ghosties since we fucko geniuses of the age can't figure the why of it. Did that Cooper's romantic blather about doomed Indians gives him a tinker's worth of credibility? And what ho the grand historian, Bancroft? Surely he knows that any pea-brain can get intelligence about the high-up dead. Isn't their every mutter and fart inked on broadsheets and chiselled on their damnedo crypts? Phineas T. was bang-bang and righto! There's a sucker born every minute, and not one of them ever dies."

"That wasn't Barnum that said so," Heman ventures. "He'd never insult his paying public. Nope. Besides, he couldn't figure how the Fox women were doing it neither. I heard it pissed him off to China. That's why he wouldn't contract them for the museum. He couldn't figure it. Nope."

Chauncey studies his brother. He's got the eyes of a porker, he thinks. And look how he wallows in his clothes. Look at his pig-piggy nose. The bristles sprouting. God's holy slippers, but why won't he cut them? Surely he's seen his visage in a looking glass. Not for the first time, Chauncey thanks Christ and all his cronies that he doesn't resemble Heman in the least. He sighs. He misses Theophilus Fiske. Fiske understood the moods of Chauncey Burr, the firecracker nature of this thoughts. And he could take a ribbing, unlike Heman, who scowls at the least jest at his intelligence. Ah, but Fiske Fisko is dead as a dodo, of cholera that killed him so quickly it was as if the disease couldn't be bothered to make his carcass suffer. And as Chauncey's older brother, Edwin—the sharp, sporting one—died over a decade ago, there is only his younger brother, Heman—the slovenly, bacon-brained one—to assist Chauncey with his mesmeric electro-biology demonstrations. But people are not attending such demonstrations as they once did. The enthusiasm for science lost ground along with the shutdown of the theatres and lecture halls during the last cholera epidemic. No enthusiasm was lost for the ghost-talking, mind. The papers groused on about it, even before the Fox sisters arrived in New York in the summer. Reported every exhibition and "lecture" in Auburn and Troy and the lesser towns. Worse, this idiotic superstition is being further wrapped up in scientific cant—Chauncey's cant.

"What ho, Hemano! Spirit telegraphs? Spirit vibrations? Invisible forces? The four laws of spirit attraction? Next they'll be reeling up that fish-eyed Newton from the damnedo River Styx to explain old wives' tales in fugging equations and—"

"Great God!" Heman cuts in. "They've made a conquest of Horace Greeley himself. And convinced him. Yup." He shakes his head and circles a column in the *Tribune*.

Chauncey snatches the paper from Heman. Reads aloud, his voice rising with incredulity:

"Their conduct and bearing were as unlike that of deceivers as possible, and we think no one acquainted with them could believe them at all capable of engaging in so daring, impious, and shameful a juggle as this would be if they caused the sounds. And it was not possible that such a juggle should have been so long perpetrated in public, yet escape detection. A juggler performs one feat quickly and hurries on to another. He does not devote week after week to the same thing in view of hundreds. A deceiver naturally avoids conversation on the subject of his knavery, but these ladies converse freely and fully with regard to the origin of the rappings in their dwelling years ago, the sensations they caused, the neighborhood excitement created and what they have seen, heard, and experienced from first to last . . ."

Chauncey hurls the paper to the floor.

Heman gives a telling smile. "They're hiding in plain sight. That's what. Plain sight. And in the open. Yup."

Chauncey stuffs his pirate-head pipe. Half listens as Heman suggests rethinking their lecture. At Chauncey's insistence, the Fox Sisters'

Fallacy (as he has dubbed that segment of his demonstration devoted to this growing preoccupation) has gone from being a comedic aside to a lengthy warning about the raising of the dead in general and the Fox sisters' spirit sittings in particular. A warning of how the "ghosts" are created by legerdemain and by mesmeric forces—the person's own mind, that is, hearing and sensing what it chooses. Chauncey can prove that part. His whole lecture is proof. The science of electro-biology is proof. But, yes, as Heman is harping: "If we had a true expose, folks would come in spades, sure, Chaunce. In spades and aces. But it can't be an expose if we don't know the trick. Nope. Then it's just a rant. A canard. And we'll be accused of envy and the like—like, jealousy."

"Envy? Hah!" Chauncey laughs, but has to admit his brother is righto for the once. Yes, and Chauncey *is* touched by envy. A new religion is not as easy to fashion up as one would think. Takes a confidence that gives even Chauncey pause. And she has played it so damnedo well, that Leah Fox Fish, that conductress of it all. No set doctrine. No new text daring to supplant the holy book. No single person claiming Godly powers. Because all can channel the dead, apparently, with a cup or two of practice, a dash of faith, a fat lot of dim light. Spread the damnation around. That's the trick. Never give the mob a set thing in which to sink its fangs.

He surveys his brother, his saggy linen shirt that would better suit a labourer, a sailor. "Give me that damnedo rag off your back, Hemano. I've a plan."

Heman pretends absorption in the *Tribune* and the predominant sketch of a ship being smashed by monstrous waves, the shore in sight, the passengers waving all-forlon from the listing deck. "They never did find the body of that learned lady . . . that Miss Fuller, that's it, nope, nor her husband, just the babe's corpse washed up. Sure was some spectacular wreck. There's got to be some lesson in it all, or something like it, like a warning or a sign."

Chauncey snap-snaps his fingers in front of Heman's nose. Heman swats them away. "Give it up, is what I mean, Chaunce. Better men than us have tried to find those females out. Yup, they have. "

"Better fucko men than you. Not 'us.'" Chauncey now snaps his fingers against Heman's periodical. The sound is a cracker shot.

"Stop it. Just . . . stop! Goddamn it and God help you, or I'll—"
Heman's shout dies away as Chauncey cracks his knuckles. Such a
tremendous loud sound for such a small action. Heman eyes
Chauncey's balled fists. Slinks back.

Chauncey hauls his brother up by his lapels. He towers over the
younger Heman. Has since they were both boys. A great benefit in
their situation. "God helps those who helps themselves, brother
mineo. So says the scriptures, and so says I."

Heman, released from his brother's grip, rubs his neck, says
warily, "Wasn't that Benjamin Franklin? I heard that, anywise."

"Not God? Well, Benji was a damnedo American, wasn't he?
And that's the next best thing."

CHAPTER 15.

"Again you hit the mark," I cried, as if my patient were five years of age and not (as she had confessed) a year shy of sixty. We were spitting cherry pits into a tin bowl—a good exercise for weakened lungs. My patient spat out another blood-red stone. I thought of my son just then. I should have insisted, I realized. Insisted he practise his marksmanship. But he had no desire to shoot birds out of the blue air, raccoons out of green branches. "What a ninny-man he'll be," Mr. Mellon sneered. "What a lily-liver." But my son wasn't lily-livered. He was kind.

"Mrs. Mellon? It's your go."

"We've played enough, duck. No more," I said hastily. I brought out her medicine then, as well as some blancmange and white-cake. I should add that she was feeling particularly fine this day. Had even stood up just before we began our cherry-spitting game and, with my help, walked one turn about the garret.

Now, back in the safe confines of her little bed, she said, "Come, let's pretend we're at a charming hotel. New York is at our feet." She chuckled. "Yes, our very feet, and the moment is full of happy talk and harmony, the future full of triumphs."

I did not generally advise false optimism, but there seemed no harm in it that day. And the sun, as if in agreement with our fantasy, buttered those three linked windows and nearly encompassed us in its fleeting warmth.

LEAH TAPS STACCATO BEATS on the table. "Now did any of you attend That Man? The one with a spade beard? He came to the afternoon sitting. He asked not a single question. He merely smirked. I have seen him before. I am certain, but who is he?"

The girls shrug and laugh. Maggie reaches for the champagne. "I've not a glimmer, I was too busy dancing attendance with Madame Hippopotamus. Dash-it, but my toes still ache . . . from her tromping." This elicits much laughter, then Katie says, "But all Madame Hippo wanted to know was if spirits get to eat anything."

"And do they?" Mother asks, her question suggesting honest bafflement, as usual.

"Surely! Chocolate eclairs and sherry trifle," Maggie says.

"With water-ice and quince preserves," Katie adds, and both girls chortle.

Leah gently admonishes, "The spirits were being naughty. A good spirit would have declared the love of Our Lord sweeter than any food."

Church bells strike the tenth hour of this August evening. The last of the sitters have only recently left the sisters' suite at Barnum's Hotel. Really, Leah thinks, there should be a sign explaining this is not P.T.'s establishment but his more worthy cousin's. Indeed, Leah is glad she decided against working with the churlish P.T. himself. She is busy enough without his cheap-john promotions.

Leah turns at a swishing sound. Her mother has begun sweeping the peanut husks from the carpets. At the sideboard Calvin is arranging the offerings from all the gift baskets. Oranges and grapes. Brandy and champagne. Tins of biscuits and chocolate. In the anteroom, Alfie is taking account of the ledgers. And how much account does he take of our conversations? Leah wonders, and looks at him sidelong.

"Capital, don't you judge, Leah?" Calvin asks, and indicates the pyramid he has made of the oranges.

"Very clever. And pretty. But, my spirits, how precarious," Leah says, and thinks again of That Man. He wore a linen shirt with the collar open in sailor fashion, wore his trousers tucked into his knee-high hessian boots, and no waistcoat under his Albert coat; and yet his black spade beard was immaculately cut, and his movements had a surety, even a grace for one so tall and heavy-built. Several times he pretended to fumble and drop items—a pirate-head pipe, a key, a copper token—items that he then bent to pick up, looking all about the floor as he did so. He apologized gallantly each time, and the *tessatura* of his voice was a rich baritone verging on the bass, the like of which Leah had never heard. She kept discreet watch on him as he rose to leave. A good idea, for just before That Man exited he gave a triumphant smile, as if confirming a suspicion.

"You look fit to gasp your last, Leah," Katie says.

Leah presses her temple. "My head-pain. It is starting up again."

"Here, let me get you some tonic." Katie jumps up, jostling a candelabra. The flames hiss as wax sloshes onto the table. The candles themselves have been lit so long they have melted into a menagerie of grotesque little shapes.

"What? Ah, yes, but only a half-glass for now," Leah says as Katie proffers a bottle of *Bertucci's Finest Cinnamon Laudanum*, a gift from an admirer. "There, that is sufficient, Katherina. Now, who was the lady who asked about a dog?"

"That was Slick-Wig," Maggie puts in. "She asked if dogs had souls. And if she'd see her dachschund in Spirit Land."

Katie says, "But the spirits just gave out that they sure hoped so. Then they pattered off."

"And she was content with that?" Leah asks.

Katie shrugs. "The Whomevers aren't particular."

"I have always thought it would be grand to have a dog," Leah muses. "Excepting it would have to be fed and watered and such."

"I'd feed the dog for you," Calvin offers. "Honour bright, I would." He is on his knees, adjusting the wobble-legged table. His zeal irks Leah, though why she isn't certain. Perhaps, she thinks, it is not his zeal but his voice, which is still nasal-toned and still of an uncertain timbre, though the boy must be what? Twenty-five?

"Then it would be your dog, Calvin. And do stop passing notes to Katherina during the sittings."

"Fiddle-de-dum, it's just funny old rhymes and nonsense," Katie says.

"Of course it is," Leah says, "but people might imagine something untoward."

"But I get bored to death. Fuss-it, but I wish John were here. He always makes me laugh."

"Which is peculiar, as *Mr.* Robinson has never been celebrated for his repartee."

Katie makes a face at Leah and reaches for Calvin's glass of toddy. He snatches it away. Grins.

"Oh, here, Kat, steal my champagne, if you must," Maggie says. Like Katie, she is evincing a worldliness that goes beyond Leah's tutelage. Perhaps it is best that their sojourn in Manhattan will soon be over, Leah thinks. It has been a great success, of course, the grand finale of their tour that played first through Albany and Troy and a host of other towns. But success has also brought the envious out from under their rocks. Leah has been accused of profiting from grief, of overstepping God, and so forth. That is to be expected. But more recently some have accused her of having an amalgamist agenda, even an anti-Christian agenda, and this because she encourages clients of any colour and religion to patronize the dead. All that she requires of her clients is that they be upstanding and of good society. Leah considers, as she often does, whether she should assist Amy and Isaac Post in their abolitionist struggles. But, no, no, she cannot court more controversy. Poor slaves, mind. Leah knows she would make a shoddy one. To be held captive? Forced to constant toil and constant deference? To be forced, even, to fornicate with the man of the house? It is likely worse than marriage.

Men. That Man. Leah's hands ache for the keys, as they do when she is troubled. She goes over and sits at the suite's fine parlour organ. The brass wall lamps are still aburn and give off that sweet and tenuous odour of spermaceti oil. She touches the foot bellows, then a chord. Sings the most popular song on Broadway these days, *The Rochester Knockings at Barnum's Hotel.*

The girls call out, "Not again!"

A knock at the door; they fall quiet.

Alfie answers the knock, doorman being one of his many tasks these days. The door opens on George Willets, gusting with excitement, his ginger hair dark with perspiration. He heaves a bulging carry-all onto the centre table.

Mother takes his arm. "George, we were getting worried. Weren't we? You've been gone all the day." She and the girls crowd around him, cooing with excitement. Leah slips the cover over the organ keys. Alfie retreats to his ledgers.

"Now did you ever think? Did you?" Mother cries as she pulls a handkerchief from the carry-all. The handkerchief is bannered with the words: *The Strange Rochester Knockings* and is imaged with the dead pushing open doors to the living world, the living beckoning them on.

Leah saunters over. Picks out an earthen mug. On it a ghost hovers over a table of sitters who stare, not at the ghost, but at a girl with dark braids. She is saucer-eyed, woefully thin. Katie peers at it also. Giggles. "You reckon that's me, Leah? I look ghastly! I look fit for a coffin myself."

Mother says, over and over, "Did you ever think? Did you ever imagine?" She pulls out one souvenir after another. The pie plate makes Leah laugh outright. The plate is engraved so that each slice of a pie will reveal more of the story. In this slice a man is dying, now he is coffined, now buried, now he rises as a ghost alongside the Fox sisters three while his wife gapes in either joy or vexation at his return; it is difficult to tell, the engravings being so crude.

Calvin sets the mug and pie plate and handkerchief aside the souvenirs already on the sideboard: a plaque, a pin cushion, and Leah's favourite—a small book that when flipped through shows the events at Hydesville as if the figures are moving inside the covers: first a shadowed figure slashes the peddler's throat with a butcher's knife, next this same shadowed figure buries him in the cellar floor, now the little Fox girls are hearing the peddler's tap-tapping on a gloomy night. The book is a small marvel. Static pictures made animate. Yet, realizes Leah, Maggie and Katie looked at it but once, then proclaimed it cheap dross.

These souvenirs will be added to the gifts for their kin back in Arcadia. These gifts include: a gold-embossed bible for their father, a French linen apron for Maria, embroidered red suspenders for David and a filigreed apple-press for his wife, Beth. For Lizzie in distant Illinois Leah has personally bought a sketching folio; in a recent letter Lizzie revealed she has taken to sketching and that her subjects, as she stressed, are rendered exactly as they appear.

"George?" Leah calls. "Tell me you purchased a shawl for Ruth?"

In answer George hangs a paisley shawl round his head, to general merriment. Even Alfie, helping himself to the punch, gives his lipless smile.

"But it's so costly? Isn't it?" Mother asks.

"Consider it a consolation gift," Leah says. "You know how it irks Ruth that she has no talent for mediumship, the green-eyed sourpuss."

"That's because she gives even dead people the willies," Maggie says. She is hunting through the newspapers. "Now, wherever did I put it . . . Ah, here it is. Here! The poem. Not precisely Byronish, but . . ."

Katie reads over Maggie's shoulder. Chimes into the recitation:

"When Leah Fox Fish
Became talked of like this
And compared to the famed Witch of Endor
I thought 'twould be best
To apply the old test
And to fagott and fire to send her

Tis no wonder her spell
Should on everyone tell
And worm out our secrets by scores
Her eye's such a piercer,
I never saw fiercer;
It made me leak out through my pores!"

Maggie and Katie curtsy at Leah.

"I think it pitch-perfect. It rhymes very nicely," Leah says, and watches Alfie place the takings into a padlocked box. She reflects on how Horace Greeley was dismayed at the price she charges, how he advised her to charge five dollars a head to keep the rabble away. But Leah insisted that a dollar a head was sufficient. The spirits commanded the price, she told him. She would trust in them and trust in Providence, though privately she reasoned that in New York a dollar was spent with a shrug. But five? People would expect the saints themselves for that.

Alfie pockets the padlock key, then trudges back to his desk. Even without seeing the ledger Leah knows the final tally of the takings on this day, August 28th, 1850: ninety-eight clients at a dollar per head. Ten private clients at fifteen dollars a head. Total: two-hundred and forty-eight dollars. An astounding sum that will be just as astoundingly spent on dresses and fripperies, on outings, on the hotel. Her young sisters, in particular, spend money like regular heiresses. Margaretta cannot get enough of the Bowery theatres. Katherina of embroidered anything. And everyone must have their share: Alfie and Calvin, and young George Willets when he is about, and her mother (though, granted, her needs are few). And some money must be sent to David for the support of their father, who is still hammering on his house in Arcadia and who does not know, of course, that the money is from Leah. Thus, the busy schedule: sittings for thirty people, sometimes more, are held at 10 a.m., 5 p.m., and 8 p.m. The private sittings happen between those times and late in the evenings. It astonishes Leah how they can all stay upright, laughing and talking into the advanced hours. Calvin, in fact, is laughing so hard at the moment at some witticism of Maggie's that he doubles over with a spluttery cough and needs to wipe his lips on a souvenir handkerchief.

Leah says, "Horace has asked again that we visit with him, and soon. He has a particular fondness for Katherine." She puts her hand on Katie's arm. "He has asked you to stay for the autumn and has even offered to pay for your education. And so you must do your best by him and Mary, my dear. They have five or six dead babes—I forget—but their boy Pickie is the one they would most like to contact, he being the only one old enough to chat, I presume."

"Wouldn't he want to talk to Miss Fuller too?" Maggie asks, her face scrunched in worry. "She'd be grievous hard for Kat to raise. I mean, that lady knew things . . . about everything."

"I know things!"

"Girls!" Leah calls to head off the bickering. "No spirit can be raised who does not wish to be, not even from Neptune's depths, where that poor Miss Fuller now resides. Margaretta you know this. Now, Katherina, what do you say to abiding with the Greeleys?"

"Can Mag come?"

"For a time, yes, until you are at ease there."

"Why is it always me, me and me again?" Katie grumbles.

"Because you're the best, aren't you, lamb?" Mother says.

"Indeed," Leah agrees. "And Horace is a man of great influence and power. He believes in us, and is not blinded by snobbery like some other editors. He is on our side. We must do what we can to keep him there. Think of others, for once, Katherina."

"All I ever do is think of others," Katie sighs.

"Pish, Leah," Maggie says. "You only like him because he said that you were a lady of twenty-five."

"An easy enough mistake," Calvin says. Leah smiles in agreement. She feels a tug on her sleeve, looks down. A boy porter has slipped into their suite. He holds a bouquet near the size of himself. "From an admirer, Mrs. Fish," he says gravely.

Leah frowns and studies the bouquet. The daffodils and bellflowers signify regard, yes, but the thorn-apple blossom? That signifies disguise. The begonia, beware. The clematis both artifice and ingenuity. Thus it is a puzzling, contradictory message. But clearly some kind of warning. Even a threat. Leah snaps off the begonia and drops it in the wastebasket. Then gathers herself. "My heavenly word, that porter was so charming in his little uniform. Calvin, did you tip him well?"

Calvin claims he did.

"Honestly, there are so many funny children in this city," Leah continues. "The bootblacks with their cigars, oh, they look so comic. And that parade of orphans we saw. All so neat and clean and wistful. I do so love children because—"

"They're so obedient," Calvin interrupts, looking proud to know her mind.

"No, no, it is because—"

"They're so . . . callow, that's the word," Maggie puts in, with that sly smile of hers.

"No, it is because—"

"Ah, because they're innocents who so need our patience and protection, don't they?" This from Mother, and in all seriousness.

"I know," Katie says. "It's because they're so dainty and sweet that folks just want to eat them up." She frowns, adds, "Poor things, I'd hate to be eaten."

"Allow me to finish," Leah says in her strongest, attend-me voice. She has decided to enjoy this teasing exchange; it does take her mind from the threats around every corner, from That Man, who no doubt sent Those Flowers. She says loudly, "I love children because they are small."

"Small?" Katie echoes, and grins and makes an inch-size with her fingers.

"Not that small, my lamb, small like General Tom Thumb. How I should love to steal him from his cruel taskmaster, that Phineas T. Bunkum. Just pop him in my carpet bag. And off!"

Laughter and giggles. And something else. A sandy rattle. Leah turns around. "What is it, Alfie? Are the books not squaring?"

"They're good. Tallied and squared, yes. I thought . . . I'm retiring, is all."

"Good night, then," Leah says, puzzled. It is almost as if he wished to join them. "Alfie!" she calls.

He turns. "Yes?"

"Are you going straight off?"

"No, no. I can stay up a time and—"

"How grand. Then do double-check the takings-box, there's a dear."

"So that is the trick of it. I am amazed!" I exclaimed.

"The trick of what? What do you mean?"

"The kinetoscope. The moving daguerreotype? You pay a nickel, and there you are, peering into a box, the past illumined and all amove. Now don't look a puzzle-wit. You mentioned the souvenir book. Flip it and the pictures become animate. It is the selfsame trick as the kinetoscope, that is all."

"Not magic?" my patient asked, wide-eyed, mimicking an innocent.

"Oh, you are a one. No, not magic. As well you know."

"But still astounding. Still intriguing."

"Yes, very," I agreed.

My patient tapped her fingers together for a nonce, then mused, "That makes me wonder: Did Chauncey disbelieve in magic? Or did he merely think it a paltry second cousin to human ingenuity? If so, then is that why he so wanted to find us out—to uncover and comprehend our ingenuity? Our downfall would result, but perhaps he didn't see that as the worst thing that could happen to us, and perhaps he was right."

"I don't know about all that, duck," I said, and gathered out my knitting (she seemed all-set to talk). "But I suppose I will."

CHAUNCEY RAISES HIS FISTS as the bowling pins topple with an almighty clatter. Five pins. Eight. The pin-boy rushes to set them up. Chauncey takes up another ball, big as a cannon ball, white as a skull. Behind him is a phalanx of gilded mirrors, above are chandeliers the size of sea-skiffs, and all about are brass cuspidors that rattle away as men spit tobacco and try to best one another with turns of wit, tales of valour, boasts of seduction. The sound of this talk is as restful to Chauncey's mind as seaside waves. Unlike the sound of Heman's voice.

"I dunno, Chaunce. Like I said. I dunno and I'm not convinced besides. Why not restart the mesmeric shows? Got folks laughing. I heard them. Give up on those women, they're getting us nowhere. And we're broke besides."

"Bloodyo laughed, did they!" Chauncey declares, and studies the bowling ball in his hand. Heman backs up. Chauncey, however, is not considering bashing in his brother's scarce brains. He is considering the "spirit" sitting he attended at Barnum's Hotel several weeks past. He went incognito, as a labouring-sailor sort. None recognized him, although Leah Fox Fish slid him suspicious glances, spying out a doubter, no doubt.

What ho did that minx of a Fox Fish made of my bouquet? Chauncey wonders. He sent it to her at Barnum's Hotel just after that sitting. Spent an age choosing the flowers and deciding on a message. Surely Leah gleaned that, although she must beware, he, the disguised sender, had the highest regard for her ingenuity, her beguiling person, her glints of passion—but then, Chauncey well knows that the passions of women can equal those of men, if only fired aright.

Chauncey hurls the ball down the polished alley. It thuds into the gutter. Nearby a three-piece ensemble starts up. The players are all coloured men: a fiddler, a banjo-player, a grey-bearded man with a tambourine. The grey-beard has a club foot, and his one shoe is engineered to conceal the deficiency. Chauncey watches him for a nonce.

"Their music sounds fair and the like," Heman says. "Like good. Didn't I always say you should pick up a banjo or a . . . trumpet."

"What for, Hemano, to stuff in your fucko trap? Best keep it shut."

Heman obliges and Chauncey considers again this "séance" he attended. *Séance*, that's what Leah Fox Fish called it, as if the Frenchifying gave it credibility. Certainly there were vibrations, Chauncey allows. Certainly there were knocks that sounded as if on the ceiling and floor. And certainly there were thrilled expressions from those chosen from the crowd. All eyes were on these chosen as they shone in momentary fame. The spirits guessed at the past, gave solace, offered a smattering of advice. Inane, all of it. Not a word or idea a man could sink his teeth into. And how he wanted to sink his teeth into Leah Fox Fish. She was better rounded than when he had first beheld her at the Corinthian Hall. More imperious than ever. And her art was more refined. Indeed, the woman could write the damnedo manual. First: Put hand solicitously on client's arm. Second: Gaze as if no one else exists. Third: Nod as if you have unbounded sympathy for their quotidian tragedies. Fourth: Speak in a low-toned trill. Last, and most importantly: Tell your clients only what they want to hear. Repeat with each client until your coffers are the envy of King Midas.

Chauncey asked not a single question. Said not a word. No easy task, but he prevailed. He forced his attention only on the sounds. Rat-a-tat. Thud. Not from the hands. No. The sisters were not snapping their fingers as he had supposed. How could they when they are forever gripping the sweaty palms of whoever was seated next to them? Chauncey dropped his pipe and then a key, a copper token, as if unable to contain his astonishment. A quick peering under the table. No clacking devices were in view. The sisters' skirts swept to the ground, even when they were seated.

Chauncey comes out of his thoughts as the three-piece ensemble starts on an allegro tune. All three players tap their feet, although the tambourine player has only to shift his club foot a short space to give out a resonate thud.

At the sitting Chauncey had noticed the youngest sister, Katherina, as Leah Fox Fish called her, shake out her skirts, as young women so delightfully do when first donning long dresses. He had glimpsed her shoes: graceless, heavy shanked things, a tad overlarge.

The *toes*. Not the fingers. They're snapping their damnedo toes!

Chauncey hurls the bowling ball. It glides alongside the gutter and knocks over near every pin. He raises his fists. "Eureka, eh, Hemano! So says Archimedes and so say I."

CHAPTER 16

"And Chauncey was right?" I asked my patient, though I had guessed the answer.

"Oh, yes. Eureka," she said, at which there came a loud tap-rap. It seemed to come from beneath the bed, the bedclothes even. She looked at the three linked windows of the garret, and I did also, and the raps sounded again, though now they seemed to emanate from there.

"A genial magic," I said, and wondered how anyone could have thought it otherworldly, or anything more than the rattle-clack of one's skeleton in a room. "However did you keep it up?"

"We didn't 'keep it up,'" she answered, all-tetchy. "The secret became its own creation. I've said that. Have I not? It took on its own life, as golems do, after the right incantations are said. Or that monster out of Mrs. Shelley's novel, after the right amount of electricity was applied."

I asked her then if it was not a dreary thing to be ever surrounded by ghosts, monsters, golems, call them ever what you will, if it did not give her pause? She did not answer exactly, but began to talk about the Greeleys' house, or "Castle Doleful," and what she came to understand while visiting there.

MAGGIE PEERS OUT the carriage window as they draw up to the Greeleys' home on Turtle Bay. The house is not far outside of New York, but might as well be in the western regions of the country, Maggie thinks, what with the autumn-fired woods all about, the bay aglitter and empty of boats. The house is good-sized but plain in its lines and as sparsely ornamented as any factory or school.

"I'm real glad you can stay a while, Mag," Katie whispers as Horace Greeley steps out of the carriage to hand them both down. "I don't like fetching up spirits on my lonesome."

"I know," Maggie sighs. Leah has allowed her to accompany Katie to the Greeleys' but she can only stay for two weeks. Then she must be back in Rochester to assist Leah at the sittings there.

"You'd think Leah doesn't want us being alone together," Katie said before they left. "As if we'll think up our own plans or something."

"That's not the case," Maggie replied, but thought, Of course, that's it exactly.

"Miss Maggie? Miss Katie?" Horace peers into the carriage. "Come, please. Mary waits for us." As she does, and on the veranda.

"About laggardly time you arrived" is what Mary Greeley says straight after the introductions. She wears a creased mourning fit-out of dullest bombast, and a nightcap though it is midday. Her skin is sallow, her hair tattered from overwashing, and her nose spidered with lines. Unhappiness wafts off her, along with the smells of camphor and lanolin. Maggie has met her sort aplenty by now. People who wear their misery like a badge, who make mourning a full-time occupation. Still, Maggie suspects this woman will take the biscuit.

"Is my Pickie here?" Mary cries. "Is he? Horace, you said these girls can talk to him. You said that."

Horace gives a resigned shrug.

Maggie says, "He needs . . . needs time to feel at ease with us, ma'am. Spirits can't be hurried so much."

"Oh, that's it, is it?" Mary's eyes dart suspiciously over Maggie's head, and then Katie's, as if they are the forerunners of an ambush. She says, "Horace! Talk to the cook. She scalded the beans. I can't abide scalded beans. You know I can't."

Horace nods and moves off gratefully.

"Come, don't dilly-dally, you two," Mary says. "I'll show you Pickie's favourite places. You need pay rapt attention."

Maggie assures her they will.

Mary shows them the tree where Pickie loved to play smash-the-ants, the stair where he carved his name five times and which Mary cannot allow to be sanded over, not ever. Now she leads them through the wide hall. "And he dismantled this all on his own." She points to a grandfather clock, plain as a pauper's coffin, with a smashed casing and broken pendulum. "He was so curious. He could have been an engineer and made proper monuments. He wasn't going to scribble for the rabble like his father does. I was going to send him to school. I was. Don't let Horace tell you different. But I wanted to wait. Such influences at schools. Children of farmers and hack drivers and blacksmiths and, oh, other incorrigible sorts."

"Blacksmiths?" Maggie says, thinking of her father at his forge. She smiles quick at Katie. "My, but their children are the most grievous incorrigibles."

"Ghastly," Katie agrees.

Mary shows them round every nook and cranny of her house. Pickie this. Pickie that. Mentions Ida, her toddling daughter, who is living with kin until she is a more manageable age. She halts up. "Will Ida outlive me? Can you know that? Her at least?"

Katie casts Maggie a nervous glance.

"We're sorry," Maggie says. "We don't know anything about what's to come. That's for Gypsy sorts."

Mary humphs, pushes open a door. "And this is Pickie's bedroom."

The bed is rumpled as if he had just risen. His few toys are still set on a shelf. His few clothes still hang on a peg-rail. Poor boy, Maggie thinks, and feels the dread tug of pity. Imagine being stuck here all day with this horrid woman, in this horrid house. For Pickie's room, though plain, is the most adorned room in the Greeley house, has striped wallpaper, some soft white linens, a red rocking horse. Elsewhere the linens are a coarse brown, the furniture of plain workmanship. Maggie counts only three cushions, four simple pictures, a single braided rug. In all there is a sense of bankruptcy, as if everything lovely and unnecessary for life has been sold. But the Greeleys aren't bankrupt. They aren't even poor. Horace makes buckets of money. Maggie is sure of it.

"We're Grahamites," Mary explains, as they sit down to black bread, raw vegetables and boiled, tepid water.

Maggie looks at her meal. You're lunatics, she thinks.

"We met at Mr. Graham's boarding house," Horace explains. "Mary and I." He tells how this Mr. Sylvester Graham sees health as a category of science. Vigorous exercise. No stimulants or alcohol. Plain food. No fripperies about the house to distract the mind.

"You'll get accustomed to it," Mary adds.

Maggie, sawing at her bread, doubts that very much.

Horace turns to Katie, "The academy we've selected for you is not far off and it is most reputable. You will learn the ladies' arts—dancing, French, composition and so forth. You might become a writer like our dear Miss Fuller."

Mary says, "And you'll come back here right after school. No dilly-dallying or talking to the other girls. Pass the water, Horace."

"We shall, of course, have to give you another name, Miss Katie. You're too celebrated now. Have you thought of a name?"

"A different name. Like in a play?" Maggie puts in. She lifts a carrot. Is she to chomp on it like a horse might? She is already yearning for some blood pudding, tripe with ketchup, a glass of claret or champagne, or a toddy. Katie drinks her water, looking all-perplexed. She surely longs for a proper refreshment, too, Maggie knows. I mean, who ever drinks water?

"Yes, exactly, like a play, Miss Maggie," Horace says patiently.

Katie frowns. "It just seems really devious, doesn't it? I don't know if I could carry it off. I'd have to pay attention all the time or something."

"Oh, fush," Mary said. "It wouldn't do if everyone knew you were here. We'd be mobbed by unprogressives. Think of other people, not just yourself, girl."

"All I ever do is think about other people," Katie says with a sniffle. It has become her new refrain, Maggie realizes.

Horace puts his hand over Katie's. "What of Sarah? That was our dear Margaret Fuller's true, given name." He looks at Maggie. "Margaret wouldn't do, as that is your name."

Maggie agrees it is.

Mary says, "That would suffice, I suppose. I do miss our Margaret, even if she was often so difficult and so masculine in her intellect. Well, you shall take her place, Katherine Fox."

"Me?" Katie says.

"Katie?" Maggie says.

Horace puts down his fork. "No one can take the place of Margaret Fuller. No one. It is a tribute, merely. Does Sarah suit, then? Miss Katie?"

"I reckon so. I mean, yes,"

Why does Katie have to be someone else? Maggie wonders. And then straightaway regrets the thought. She'd heard how bereft Horace was after the death of this Margaret Fuller, heard how the ship ran aground in a storm, in view of American shores, in view of the salvagers who watched the ship list and crack. None helped. Miss Fuller, her dashing Italian husband, their babe. Gone. Gone. Gone. The papers were chock full with the woeful story. Maggie found it dreadfully romantic, and even more so when she read Miss Fuller and her "husband" had not been properly married. Indeed, Maggie thinks now, the tale is as romantic and tragic and drama-filled as any in a novel.

Of a sudden Mary fixes her lunatic eyes on her husband. "You're slopping, Horace, you incorrigible slob. Is he here yet? Pickie? Pickie? . . . Horace, you said these girls talked to him. You promised so!" Mary holds her knife as if to plunge it into Horace's heart.

Poor Horace, Maggie thinks, just as knocks patter along the table.

With one accord Horace and Mary drop their cutlery and cry out with joy.

In the days that follow Maggie and Katie bring forth Pickie again and again. He is not a difficult spirit to have about. His observations of the world beyond are uncomplicated, given his age of eight. His demands are all reasonable: some cider in the house, some cooked food, some rest for everyone.

Mary Greeley is insatiable, however. Pickie must be about every minute. Often Mary weeps and begs Pickie's forgiveness for a whipping on this occasion or that. Pickie always gives it, because Pickie,

Maggie knows, only wants his crack-brained mother to leave him be. Once, when Pickie is reluctant to talk, Mary screams at Horace, "He won't manifest because of you. You berated him when he came into your study. You told him to get out. As if your endless scribblings matter at all."

Horace looks near to tears at this. Then Pickie arrives. Three raps. "It's a call for the alphabet," Maggie says. She and Katie draw one up on scrap paper.

"I didn't mind, Ma" is what Pickie says. "Father is a busy man with really important things to do."

"Humph," Mary replies. "You're taking your father's side just for spite. You always did."

It is just past ten o'clock on the last evening of Maggie's stay at the Greeleys' and she wanders into the keeping room, unable to sleep, even with the rum toddy finally allowed her by wretched Mary Greeley. Maggie would rather not leave Katie here, but what choice does she have? *Our talents are much in demand*, Leah wrote. *You are needed here in Rochester.* Anywise Katie will soon be off at school. And this house, well, it is hardly a place one would want to kick around in for long. Horace's dear Miss Fuller apparently dubbed it Castle Doleful, and Maggie can't imagine a more fitting title.

I sure wish I could speak with Miss Fuller, Maggie thinks. They would be great friends, she is sure. Sometimes Maggie catches a whiff of Miss Fuller's perfume, hears a rustle of her expensive silks, an echo of her knowing laugh, but that is all.

A whispering: "Miss Maggie. Miss Maggie."

She whips round.

"Apologies," Horace says. "I did not mean to startle you."

"You're home from work so early tonight," she says, because Horace does often not arrive home until past the midnight hour.

"I felt unwell. How fares Mary?"

"I've not seen her today. She's still abed, I believe." Maggie smiles her helpful smile. "We gave her some of that new medicine, though, just as you asked."

"And it eased her? The new concoction?"

"Yes, I believe it did." A stronger draught of laudanum was all it was, Maggie thinks.

Horace fidgets with the papers in his pocket. "You must know that Molly—Mary—was not always like this. When we met she was a teacher. She had such a love of books and learning. Her students adored her. She was exacting, yes, but gay. And for a woman she had such interesting opinions on worldly matters. And then the babes . . . and so we thought here in the country she would be refreshed with all the unsullied air and trees and birdsong. There's a fellow, Thoreau, who has a theory about nature, that it is a tonic for both mind and soul."

Maggie hears the sagging wind. Sees the dark at the Greeleys' undraped windows. Recalls Hydesville. That's flat-out addled, she thinks, people need people, not birds and trees. They need illuminated things and shops and ice-creameries and theatres. Nature's not a refreshing tonic. Nature's boring. And doesn't Maggie just know how boredom can cause all kinds of trouble? She feels a sudden, nebulous sympathy for Mary-Mary-Quite-Contrary who is going mad from loneliness and isolation, her thoughts spin-topping in the quiet.

"It was the second one," Horace says, sadly. "You hardly expect the first to live, but we had hopes for the second. He came early, that one. And Mary was injured. She might well have recovered but I, well, the wrong doctor was sent for. He operated but made a botch of things. She was never the same. And then the next ones died. Mary Inez was the one before Pickie. She was nearly four. The other three were babes of some months. It's not unusual, I know, but for someone like Mary, who thought, well, that she had some guidance over things, it unhinged her, you see. We have Ida, I know, but Mary can't even bear to see her until she's at a safer age. That is why she's staying with relations. And it's just . . . I was hoping, I suppose, that you could, could . . . well, not only give her solace about Pickie and the others, but bring her back, Mary, as she was."

"I'm sorry, Mr. Greeley—Horace. Gosh but I am," Maggie says, near to tears. "I can't do much for the living. I can only bring back the dead."

"Of course. I know. I shouldn't have spoken so to you. It's not seemly." His voice breaks and he brushes at his eyes. "I'll leave you now."

Maggie listens to the creaking of the stairs as Horace ascends to his private bed chamber. She hears the sough of the wind, the shush of the waves in the bay below. Maggie thought Horace spent his days away because he could not abide Mary, not because he couldn't bear to see what she had become. Maggie imagines them as newly-wed and all the world a possibility. How can I hate her? When she is loved? Is loved even now?

Maggie makes her way along the hall passage, a candle-hold the only light. She passes the grandfather clock, the one Pickie broke and that is now suspended at ten past eight, on a day when Pickie lived. She climbs the stairs and then into bed beside Katie. Her sister stirs awake and they talk for a while, as they always do before they sleep. And what Maggie confides to Katie is that after her conversation with Horace she came to the abrupt understanding that any succour they offer is short-lived. "Gone in a nonce, Kat, like some vaporous cloud."

"That's true, all right. What I'll just never ever understand is how our elders get so fussed and grieved about their children, seeing as when the children are alive they're just plain old mean to them, or they ignore them, or tell them to be seen and not heard, or just consider them generally vexing."

"That, now, is a conundrum I guess we can only sleep on," Maggie says, and douses the candle.

"So that is what you came to understand at the Greeleys'? That your succour is only a stop-gap? Surely you knew this before. Surely you didn't think you could patch up the Greeleys' household so neatly and so quick. Their griefs were beyond your childish management, duck." I allow I said this not only out of sympathy for Mary Greeley, but also out of sympathy for Horace, and that this sympathy was unexpected and oddly welcome.

"Their guests were beyond anyone's management," my patient said, all peevish.

I took my knitting from out of my satchel. "And it is not a conundrum, not at all, what your sister said about her elders. She would understand this if she had her own babes."

"But she did have her own babes. Years on. Two boys. And then, yes, she understood the fuss and grief all too well, particularly when Leah dared involve the boys in our drama."

"Boys," I said, and laid out the yarn skeins.

"Yes, and I helped Katie name her boys. Such a list we considered, names galore: Matthew. James. Paul. John. Robert . . ."

I purled and knitted smoothly while my patient ruminated on names (if she had said "Rumplestiltskin" I would not have been amazed, so obviously was she trying out names that might be of import to me). ". . . Michael, Isambard, Alonsis, Cole, Morris and . . . Your mittens, Mrs. Mellon. They're conjoined. And big enough for a giant."

I held up my handiwork. "Mittens? No. This is to be a scarf, a very long one I should think, for winding. And what were their names? Her sons?"

"Ferdinand and Henry. As for me, I never had children."

"I'm aware of that. Would I not have found them out otherwise? Would not they be here at your side and not me? Kinfolk. No one else can be counted on for help when one is in distress."

"That certainly is the fiction," she allowed, then asked me to turn down the medical lamp and fire the candle. Her eyes ached these days, she said, and she had come to appreciate a mellowed light.

LETTER CLUTCHED, Maggie wanders around the Troup Street cottage. It is four o'clock and already downright stygian outside. The sittings are finished until after supper. And then there will be yet another go round the parlour table. How she misses New York. Such a success the Fox sisters were there. Such a nice passel of citizens they met, so modern, admiring, polite. In New York night is a merry time, the avenues lined with gas lamps, the theatres lit with a limey glow, the oyster cellars with their painted lamps casting painted shadows on the sidewalks. And, ah, the Drummond beam atop Barnum's museum.

Such a creation: a man-made sun revolving and illumining both the heavens and all of Broadway, even at night's darkest hours, at which time the streets are still peopled and noisy. Little wonder Maggie is melancholy now that they've returned to provincial Rochester. To make matters worse, Katie is still at Castle Doleful being educated to be a lady. Mother, laden with city gifts, is in Arcadia visiting Father and assorted kin. And Calvin is off on some month-long military drill. All of which means that Maggie has only Leah for company. Not even Alfie is about. Leah terminated his employ back in New York and left the man behind at Barnum's Hotel. He was stealing from the takings-box, Leah insisted. His tallies were not any kind of square.

Maggie breathes deep, then enters the reading room.

"Have a seed, my cheery dearie, my sweeting," Leah coos to Vivace, an Amizonian parrot of emerald green. She bought him in New York along with a wicker cage shaped like an Ottoman temple.

"I'm-so-sweet. I'm-so-sweet," Vivace caws back.

"I've been invited to Troy," Maggie says, holding up the letter. "By the Boultons."

Leah pats at a flounce. Her dress today is a primrose concoction all figured with lace and hung with galoon. You'd think she was expecting the Queen-of-Where-ever, Maggie thinks.

"The Boultons? Of Troy? Ah, yes, they were such a help with the tour. A most respectable family. And they had that lovely large home, nearly a mansion . . . Well, do you plan to go?" Leah asks this as if she has no say in the matter.

"I do plan to. Yes, yes, I do. If I can't go back to New York, then I'd like to be in a new place. They've asked me to stay for a fortnight or more, for as long as I please, in fact. "

Leah shrieks, and Maggie starts back.

"Bad Vivace, biting me like that! No fly-about for you today." Leah wags her nipped finger at the cage, says to Maggie, "Indeed, you could get some practice raising the spirits by yourself. The Boultons are known in society and have a wide circle of prosperous, upstanding friends. And that sister-in-law of Mr. Boulton, she took a shine to you. I suppose you require a friend, what with Katherina at the Greeleys. And a change is always good, I say."

Maggie thinks, And I could get some respite from you, sister-of-mine.

Leah looks troubled, as if she has heard Maggie's thoughts. "Dear Margaretta, I know you find me difficult at intervals, but since all this began I have come to love you, not just as a sister, but as another daughter, in particular since Lizzie refuses to come home and hardly even writes, wretched girl. And, honestly, I do loathe it when we are discordant. We must stay as one mind, my girl, we simply must."

"One mind, of course," Maggie says. For what choice does she have when their thoughts collide like so many blinded birds?

"And so, yes, do go and stay the fortnight," Leah says. "And be charming to all and sundry. And do secure as many cards as possible, though without seeming forward. And certainly do not allow people to place their monetary gifts directly in your hands or, spirits forbid, aside your bed. Allowing them to slip notes into your reticule is best. And do not worry on how I shall fare without you and Katie. Our sitters have come to love my trancing as much as your knocks. And I will ask Amy or Adelaide to stay with me now that Alfie has left our employ, the thieving ingrate."

Worry about Leah? Maggie thinks. Gosh, that'd be a first. "I'll try my heart's best not lose sleep over your situation, Leah," Maggie says, and as if she is perfectly sincere.

Leah contemplates her, then shrouds Vivace's cage with white sheeting. "But do be careful when alone there," she says. "I recall now that some of Troy women, those who were not associated with the Boultons, were awful and common and of jealous aspect. Indeed, I must say, Margaretta, that whole town gave me something of turn."

A few days later, the Boultons' brougham rattles through the town of Troy, then down, down a frost-heaved road. The brougham has Moroccan seats and glazed windows. November dusk, and the glassed-in world shifts by in greys and blacks. No ice. No snow. No moon. No whiteness at all, except that of Maggie's face reflected in the scene.

Alice Boulton holds Maggie's gloved hand in hers. She is newly wed to Mr. Boulton's brother and she giggles and whispers like the schoolgirl she so recently was. Mr. Boulton, Dundreary-whiskered, in a frock-coat of checks, orders caution of the driver. "We want not a speck of harm to come to our guest."

Finally the Boultons' home. It is on the far imaginings of town, but so inviting, what with its gables and columned portico, its colour scheme of lilac and olive and jonquille yellow. It is homey and grand at the same instance, Maggie decides. But what of that lumberyard alongside? What of the stacks of shorn trees that form a giant's labyrinth? And that close-on wood with its dense brambles?

"We shall have a gay time!" Mr. Boulton proclaims with manly certainty.

And they do. For three days exactly. Fine meals and brisk walks. Singing and music-making. Charades and draughts and reading aloud. The Boultons and their friends do not demand much of the spirits, are grateful and delighted with any answer to any question. They promise not to tell what is transpiring at the Boultons' home and press fingers to lips like children promising inconsequentials. Not tell? Maggie thinks. Who does not tell of ghosts? The tell is the key to unlocking the dead, to releasing them from their every nook and crypt.

A party in East Troy? Certainly! Maggie would love to attend. Would love to wear her latest gown. It has pagoda sleeves and cartridge pleats and is sewn from a green satin that shimmers like an insect wing. "What an exotic you are!" Alice exclaims. Maggie smiles, delighting in the idea of being an exotic—that is, a someone else from somewhere else.

At the party Maggie dances with a handsome son of the house, eats up Madeira ham and sweetbreads, tastes a ginsling, a martinez. Practises breathing in sips. Her new corset cinches her waist into a doll-like circumference and makes her feel the perfectly grown-up seventeen that she is.

"Come, ladies. We've stayed too late. We must get home before night gathers," proclaims Mr. Boulton, and he gives Maggie his arm. They wait in the brougham while the driver fires the dash lanterns, then snaps the reins over the two Clevelands. Maggie cozies with Alice under a furred robe. Across from them, Mr. and

Mrs. Boulton smile benevolently. Maggie has not felt such contentment for the longest time. She is far from Leah, who is demanding more and more of her. Far from her fussing mother. She misses Katie, true, but Katie needs oversight, protection, and this scarcely generates relaxation. Thus reserve is shedding from Maggie hour by hour. If I remain here, she thinks, I'll become another kind of girl entirely. She can't imagine what kind exactly; but she is curious, hopeful, as if in expectation of a gift.

"How pretty you look when you smile so," Alice says. "Are you thinking of a beau?"

Maggie is about to give a witty reply, something to do with bureaus and borrows, when they jerk to a halt. They wait.

"Winter is truly with us," Alice sighs.

Before them is the Hudson River—very wide, very deep. Behind is nothing. No other carriages or conveyances. No visible houses.

Mrs. Boulton calls to her husband, "Where's the ferryboat, dear? Should not the boat be here?"

The men must have been there all along, just outside the cast of the dash lights. Five. Six. Heavy coated. Hats worn low. Not gentleman. Nothing of the kind. They range around the brougham and slouch against the doors. One scrapes at the window with his fingernails. Another strokes the horses with exaggerated tenderness. The driver stands up, his whip held ready. "Sir?" he calls nervously.

Laughter. Spitting.

"Drunkards. Louts. That's all. That's all," Mr. Boulton assures the women. He steps out, letting in tendrils of cold. "Who are you? Name yourselves. And where's the ferryman. I demand—"

"You can't put your faith in the ferryman, see?" says one.

"Best go round by the Long Troy Bridge," says another.

"Sure, and we'll take you there," offers a third.

"Or maybe that witch inside will float you over!"

"Maybe Miss Consort will open her legs and let the Devil out. He'll help ya."

A whip cracks. The Clevelands snort and hie. The driver shouts, "Get back!"

Mr. Boulton grabs for the brougham door. Hands grip his collar. He smacks at them. Lurches inside. Yells at the driver, "Get on! Make haste!"

Maggie, Alice and Mrs. Boulton scream in tandem. One of them—not Maggie—begins to pray.

The horses haul the brougham around so fast it nearly tips. Mr. Boulton shouts through the call-slot, "Not the bridge! The way by town. We'll be murdered if we go by the bridge." Turns to the ladies. "Not murdered. I meant . . . well, bully."

The horses are at a near gallop, dangerous in the dark, but preferable to being chopped up and tossed into the frigid river. The louts race after them in a flat-wagon drawn by a lone horse that, lashed by whips, somehow keeps chase. Maggie, Alice and the Boultons are tossed about like dice in a jar. The women sob. Mr. Boulton utters apologies and assurances until a jounce makes him bite his tongue. Blood trickles down his fine whiskers. Maggie feels like to faint. Open her legs? Witch? Devil's consort?

"It's not my fault," Maggie cries when the Boulton house is finally attained. The pursuing wagon is nowhere in sight.

"Of course it's not," Mrs. Boulton says shakily. "Come, dear. It's over now."

But it isn't over. Strange, how Maggie has spoken so much of death in these last two years, has encountered death by disease and accident and murder and old age and suicide, and thought it all ordinary. At times romantic. But it is neither. Dying is an extraordinary thing; and the terror of it far eclipses any joy of living.

Finally to bed. Finally a half-calm, thanks to opiated wine and Alice's soothing presence. Then the drapes billow in and the windows shatter and glass skids over the floor. Gunshots. Yelling and pounding feet. Alice and Maggie hide under the quilt, as if this will keep them safe. From outside comes shouting: "Bring out the witch!" "Show us Satan's whore!" And worse.

The girls scream as the door bursts open. Mr. Boulton and another man shout for them. They take Maggie to a room that is as small as a closet. "You'll be safe here," Boulton declares, and locks the door behind him. He has forgotten to leave a lantern or even a candle.

Maggie huddles on the narrow bed, crying and shaking, even praying. Forces herself quiet at the limping, dragging noise in the corridor beyond. The sound is slow. Relentless. The peddler? God help her, has he returned? "I'm really sorry," she sobs. "We're sorry. We didn't mean it. Damn, double damn. Go away! I'm not going to die alone and ranting like you said. I won't!"

The dragging-limping sound ebbs. It is only someone hauling a mattress for the barricades. Surely. Maggie, exhausted beyond measure, buries her head in the coarse, stiff sheets.

Maggie is in that closet-room four days. Is let out only to use the privy, and to eat. The Boultons give her an argand lamp, books, and occasionally someone or other for company. All this is of little comfort. Outside the house a small mob continually mills, threatening and cursing anyone who comes and goes.

Men from East Troy arrive for their defense. That same night, Maggie hears splintering wood. More smashing glass. A horrendous commotion. The house—it has been breached. She presses against the wall as if to seep into it. Become a mere stain.

The house quiets at last. "We sent them off for now," Mr. Boulton tells Maggie. "They don't mean to kill anyone, we're . . . well, bully, we're hoping not." Mr. Boulton eyes are dark-rimmed. His cravat and checked coat are gone and he wears a wide belt thrust through with a pistol. In all, he looks more a pirate than a gentleman, and is oddly more handsome for it. He assures Maggie they have procured means for their defense, that he would give his life to defend her, as would the other men. "We are a fortress here," he adds.

"But where's the sheriff? Where?" Maggie asks. "Or the police? Anyone?"

"An excellent question," Mr. Boulton says. "I've sent word to town." He looks at her helplessly. "Police are only found in cities, I'm afraid."

Maggie attempts a smile. "A fine guest I am . . . Have you telegraphed Leah again? Have you?"

Mr. Boulton assures Maggie he has. He has found means to telegraph her three times now.

Leah arrives on the evening of the fifth day and fills Maggie's closet-room with her presence. "Well, there you were!" she exclaims as if Maggie has been playing hide-and-go-seek.

Maggie falls into her sister's arms. "They want to kill me!"

"And me," Leah replies, easing Maggie off with a shudder. "On the train a most disreputable man sat near me and asked me questions that proved he had heard of my journeying here." She takes off her gloves. "It seems he thought I would be much older in appearance. Anywise, I promptly told the conductor that I—a woman alone on his train—was being harassed by a low character and the conductor escorted the man firmly elsewhere. When I arrived, there was Mr. Boulton. He said he knew me because I was just as pretty as you. The flatterer! He had a pistol. Well, you know that. And sitting in the lovely brougham was yet another man with a pistol. Pistols! My heavenly spirits, I have never seen so many. I can hardly speak. A moment . . . there. Indeed, a mob is in the yard just now. Did you know that? Or have you been in here the whole time? They might have had at me, too, sister, but those brave men lifted me out of the carriage and bore me inside. I did warn you, did I not, about Troy? Well, now it shall be right as rain." She looks about the room. "Honestly, but you cannot stay in here forever."

Maggie finds Leah's insouciance irritating, but encouraging, also, as if it is a small matter to be mobbed and threatened. Still, it takes much coaxing about having a nice glass of claret to get Maggie out of her closet-room.

"Not now!" Mr. Boulton exclaims when Leah and Maggie enter the kitchen. He waves them back. Glass litters the floor. The doors and broken windows are barricaded. Men sit against the walls and crouch behind the settees and chairs. They grip rifles, pistols, even Bowie knives should the fighting come hand to hand.

On the table is the cooked carcass of a chicken. Mr. Boulton brandishes a half-eaten drumstick as he gives orders to the men. Even the besieged get hungry, Maggie thinks, and this thought somehow wearies her more than anything. She risks crossing the kitchen for the bottle of claret over on a far, high shelf. She takes it to her closet-room, leaving Leah to plot and plan with Mr. Boulton.

A day more and at last the mob disperses. At last they can safely leave.

Once home at the Troup Street cottage, Maggie stays abed for a week. At night giant men rape her on a woodpile. They burn her alive while a hooded priest offers chicken and Methodist prayers. A mob transforms into a tentacled monstrosity and swallows her whole. She vomits and cries and in general carries on, her nerves reverberating like piano wire. She piles high the quilts. Barely eats. Subsists mostly on toddies and mulled wine.

Leah offers advice on recovery: "Put it behind you." "Our good friends would never let us come to harm." "Stay with me." "Follow my advice." "I only ever have your best interests at heart." And so forth.

Calvin, once back from his military exercises, is more understanding. "I'll protect you all, honour bright," he says, and takes her hand. He has lost weight, Maggie notices. He coughs and shakes his head when she voices concern, then stands and draws back the bedroom drapes to show the vault of sky, the potent light of afternoon. "Perhaps we both need more the sun. The bright rays. Look!" At this he gestures outwards like a magician tired of his own tricks.

The following afternoon Maggie forces herself out of bed and down to the reading room. She huddles in a wingback chair near a smoking fire. Vivace trills wistfully from his Ottoman cage.

Leah paces the small room. "I have the horrid sense, Margaretta, that it was Josiah Bissell, that delinquent lout, who was behind the Troy attacks. He was the ringleader of the Corinthian Hall attack, so why-ever not?" She gasps. "Or else his father. My father . . . ours, once said the elder Bissell was a devil who used God's words." She pokes a finger into Vivace's cage, strokes his feathers. "I saw some men, no doubt in Bissell's hire, lurking about last night. Thank the spirits for Calvin. I sent him out to scatter the miscreants."

Didn't those "miscreants" just turn out to be the night-soil men? Maggie thinks, vaguely troubled. It is as if Leah has forgotten that Maggie witnessed last night's affair. More troubling is that Leah's unpredictable displays of courage, such as Maggie witnessed in Troy, are becoming offset with unpredictable displays of paranoia.

First she became convinced, back in New York, that Alfie skimmed from the takings, and now she sees these imaginary adversaries from Troy. Oddly, however, Leah is not troubled about the Reverend Chauncey Burr. She surely should be, Maggie thinks. Burr has begun a full "exposé" of them in New York. Leah has been receiving daily telegrams and newspaper reports about it from friends. In response she is nonchalant, even proud.

Maggie reaches out of her huddle and picks up a copy of the *Tribune*, the one that shows a caricature of the nemesis, Burr, himself. He stands on one foot. His other, gigantic and bare, sticks straight at a sparse, nose-holding audience.

"Leah, do any believe Burr?" Maggie asks from the comfort of her wingback chair, her voice a croak, then wonders, why-ever do I ask? I know the answer. This Burr could write the answers on the sky and none would heed him. The secret has become a monstrous thing that stops ears, blinds eyes, thieves all reason.

"No. None believe him. None!" Leah cries with triumph. "His claims are ludicrous, as is the man himself. He came to one of our sittings in New York. That man. I suspected him straightaways. He acted the gentleman, oh, but he had a ruffian's smile, and a voice that was as deep and dark as, as . . . his nefarious plans."

"I'm wondering, Leah, wondering if this next tour, the Buffalo tour, is a such a swell idea."

Leah doesn't answer. She looks, instead, so intently at Vivace it as if they are in a silent communion.

"Leah? Leah!"

"Pardon? Ah, Buffalo? What was your drift, my dear?"

"Mr. Burr and the, the toe business. I know none believe him. But I dunno. Mayhap we should take it as a warning or a sign."

Leah gives Vivace his birdseed. "Now, no biting, else I'll have you roasted for dinner, naughty bird." She slides the caricature sketch of Burr into the bottom of Vivace's Ottoman cage. Chuckles. "Poppycock. There is your warning, Margaretta. Your sign."

Maggie watches Leah, round-eyed. Later, once Leah is elsewhere, she takes the few shaky steps over to the secretary desk and writes to Katie.

20 November, 1850

Dearest Kat,
I don't think Leah is afraid of anything. I sure do wish I had
her courage because any small store I had was ruined after
Troy. How are you faring at the Castle Doleful?

The letter Maggie receives back is folded lengthwise and sealed
with wax. Katie's writing is even more difficult to read than usual.

28 November, 1850

Dearest Mag,
I'm writing with a quill! A quill for darn old sake. Mary doesn't
hold with steel nibs nor even envelopes. Oh, how I wish you
weren't going on tour to Buffalo and the like. I hate hate hate
Mary Greeley. I really do. She cries on about her gone ones but
I don't think she liked them much when they were alive anyways.
And I miss Mother. Oh, I'm sick at heart and wish you'd come
and comfort me. Why hasn't Leah answered any of my letters?
I asked her to fetch me away and she would if she knew how
miserable I am. Mr. Robinson won't answer my letters neither
and my head-pains are coming back and I cry a night in my
horrid room that's got the comforts of a hat box. Mary talks on
and on about being cleansed and such as if a person were a
washbasin with a drain or something and she makes us go
walking in the yard because it's "good" for the body. We go
quick quick, round and round, like we're in a hurry, but we get
nowhere. We only get all huffy and perspire like nasty and I can't
think how that's healthful at all. I hope you recover soon from
that awfulness in Troy and I miss you like anything and wish I
could take your sadness away. I even wish Miss Nettie were here.
She could be irksome with her chatter, but she gave good advice
sometimes, and, oh, how I hate hate hate mean old Mary Greeley.
                          With love always & always,
                          Your sister, Katie

Maggie folds up the letter. She ponders that phrase: *with love*. Maggie knows love. She has a bemused love for her parents. A difficult love for Leah. A depthless protecting love for Katie. Such loves are like furniture—necessary but unnoticed after a while. But hatred? The kind that Katie has for Mary Greeley? The kind that Maggie faced in Troy? That Burr is fomenting against them all? Well. Such hatred has no gradations. No ambiguities. It is an absoluteness. Little wonder, she thinks, that hatred leads people to grievous action in a way that love does not.

Of a sudden Maggie is wind-blasted with fear. She drops Katie's letter. For in reviewing this villain cast of hatred she has understood for the first time how much their reputations, their very lives, are as a string before a blade.

CHAPTER 17

"Are you chilled, Mrs. Mellon?" my patient asked. "You're shivering like a half-drowned cat. Here, draw close, and take the coverlet, for your knees. I'd hate myself if you caught fever on my account."

"I'm all-fine, duck, not cold. No." And indeed the garret pipes were giving out the usual furnace heat—though that day the warmth had an oppressive quality, alike damp flannel wrapping tight. "I was only visioning your trials in Troy," I added. "The mob, and how all that brouha must have unravelled your poor nerves."

"Well, yes. Afterwards my nerves were as unravelled as your yarn skeins, and tangled, and frayed, the whole yardage."

"Mobs," I sighed, and this time kept back the shudder. I should mention that, during the draft riots I'd had my own experience with mobs, and knew well their pitiless fury, the misery left in their wake. I should also mention that I became a physician because of those experiences, and that those experiences changed me utterly; indeed, they rendered me into such a different entity that I might not have recognized the previous Alvah June Mellon if she'd knocked on my door and tried to sell me pudding sticks.

"A mob, yes. The first. And surely not the last," my patient said. She told me then about the tour she and Leah made of Buffalo and all the brouha that transpired there. "A Dr. Foote came to our hotel door. Foote, hah, that was his true name. Anywise, he warned

Leah and me to escape the city at the once or face a mob. I nearly dropped to the floor in a faint, as if yes, those nerves holding me upright had been snipped easy as any yarn skein or thread. I'd really had enough of mobs. But Leah? She just slammed the door in his face, then summoned up the hotel proprietor and told how this Dr. Foote had dared come to her door in her private hours, and without first sending his card; how he had threatened, insulted and terrorized her, a woman alone—two women alone. I remember how the proprietor gravely assured our safety as he left. And sure enough, there was no mob, not that time. We did not escape the latest investigation, however. Now these Buffalo doctors had unearthed a Mrs. Patcheon, a befuddled old whom-ever. She could make a cracking sound with her knees. This is it! I thought, once and twice and three times again. But nope. Leah, why didn't she just convince Mrs. Patcheon that she and Leah were old school friends. Soon enough, Mrs. Patcheon was saying that Leah would never ever commit a deception, that her sounds were nothing like ours, and that she hoped and prayed we would raise the spirits of her three sons. They had died from, oh, this and that—I forget."

"Three sons?" I said. "Poor woman, I am amazed she had even a measure of sanity left. And though you might have forgotten the mode of her sons' demise, I am stone-sure she did not."

"No, no . . . of course not," my patient said, abashed, as if I had just exposed some failing of hers. "But the doctors had the right tack. As did Chauncey."

"As one cracks the fingers!" Chauncey exclaims to the sparse audience at New York's Hope Chapel this frigid night late in the month of January '51, the last night of his expose. Chauncey sheds his boots, unbuttons his garters, peels off his socks. Heman reluctantly does the same; he had tried begging off this night, and practically on his knees.

The audience does not gasp in realization, nor astonishment. No. A man sniggers. Another heckles Chauncey and Heman on their caterpillar appendages. A woman flounces out, as if the naked feet of Chauncey and Heman were any more risqué than her ankles, on show there under her rick-racked hem.

"To enhance the sound, a good conductor is all that is needed. And a loose shoe of special design, and a stalwart toe. A warm toe . . ." Chauncey snaps his toe but the sound is faint in the hall. Heman follows suit, his snap even fainter. The cold is at fault, Chauncey exhorts, when a hiss comes from the audience. The evening goes from this to worse. The audience is unimpressed even when Chauncey explains all of the Fox women's tricks. How the Fox women use "leading questions." How they watch the questioner's countenance when formulating answers. Use plants in the audience. Use mechanical devices. And the worst, pay spies to ferret out information on the dead.

Chauncey hauls his boots back on, stands at his lectern. "Some of us give away so much without realizing it," he expounds. "Some of us are as transparent as glass. Even I can claim a measure of gullibility for I was, during some little time, pained by a kind of half-hope that my sainted elder brother, Edwin, who, in his lifetime, was a young man of the finest taste and of high poetical genius, would so far forgo the natural dignity and delicacy of his character as to come back to commune with me by making the most vulgar noises, rattling about under chairs and tables and kicking over light-stands and bureaus in the dark, to excite my wonder and horror."

In truth, Chauncey thinks, kicking over light-stands and making vulgar noises is exactly what Edwin would do if he could return. Chauncey looks over the chapel. Over at Heman, who is morose as a neutered mule. Now Edwin, he had appreciated a laugh, had appreciated life's joys to the very hilt. He was the one who led the young Chauncey to his first grog hole, his first brothel. Handsome, golden-haired Edwin so afire with his rebellious ideals. How well he had taught Chauncey to act. How proud he would have been to see Chauncey onstage, applauded and attended to. On consideration, however, Chauncey is grateful that Edwin, being dead, cannot bear witness, as the few attendees seem almost bored by the lecture's end. They hike their collars and trickle out to the next entertain-ment. Bowling. Billiards. Grog shops. As if these are all a piece with Chauncey's display of erudition and insight.

"Guess our time is up and the like. Like over," Heman says.

"We waited too damnedo long, Heman." As they had. The Rochester Knockers were all the rage in New York during the summer and early fall of '50. There were souvenirs and songs and newspaper articles galore, and other mediums and ghost-chatters sprouting up in the Fox sisters' path like mushrooms under a good layer of horseshit. It was a vast misfortune that the Fox sisters left New York nearly five months ago now. Chauncey should have put on an expose the moment he realized the truth. But it has taken much time and practice to become proficient enough at toe snapping to convince an audience. Even now Chauncey's toes ache from the effort. No, it isn't as easy as snapping fingers, cracking knuckles. But the sound, who can deny it? And haven't most of the news-paper reporters lauded his effort? Excepting, of course, the Fox sisters' cheapjack promoter Eliab Capron, who has called Chauncey and Heman "knaves" and "mountebanks" and "capital puffs." Excepting the *Tribune*, which published that unjust caricature of Chauncey, his toes the size of pug dogs. And excepting Horace Greeley, who has reported that Chauncey Burr's soundings are as different from the Fox women's soundings "as the sounds of a flute and a trumpet."

Flute? Trumpet? Chauncey takes his showman's stance and faces the empty chapel. "We are the 'instruments' of our own demise, good people, and the Fox sisters? Their knocking is the sound of their own requiems. They are fiddling their own . . . fiddles, etcet-era, while their reputations burn. Hah! How is that, Heman? A neat twist on the bible quote, righto?"

"That's not from the bible, that's from, damnit, I dunno."

Chauncey folds up his lectern. Takes out his pirate-head pipe.

"And smoking's disallowed, Chaunce," Heman adds. He points up to a sign that proclaims just that.

Chauncey does not grace the sign, nor Heman, with a glance. He strikes a lucifer, the resulting flame approximating the size of a gambling chip. He lights his pipe, singeing his fingers, as always. And as always, he does not wince, nor give any indication of pain.

"Make ready, Hemano. We're not defeated yet!"

Five weeks later, Chauncey, hessian booted, tromps the New York sidewalks. He kicks at a mound of snow; out volcanoes mouldy cabbage, slops, excrement. "God's a Yankee but I detest March," Chauncey mutters. "Freezes a man's arse one moment then blasts him with sun the next. Beware the Tides of March. Bloody betraying month, trust it not. Or is it Ides?" He supposes Heman would know, as would Chauncey if he'd had the benefit of his clod-headed brother's education.

He stands aside for a covey of women. Taps his forehead in lieu of tapping his top hat, which has vanished in the bachelor disarray of his boarding room. The women glance at him with . . . What? Curiosity. Suspicion? Admiration? Because what kind of man goes out wihtout a hat? Does he trust that no slops or night water will be chucked onto his head? Why, yes, he trusts no one would dare. Does he think everyone needs to see his close-cropped head? Why, yes, he does. He strides faster, the cape of his Albert coat flaring over his broad shoulders, his steel-tipped cane thumping the sidewalk.

He notes a cut-rate oyster stall. "Get street oysters" was what Heman said as Chauncey left. "We're near broke. Penniless too. And all because you're spending a pack of bills on this latest angle and—"

"Righto, brother dearest," Chauncey interrupted. "I'll scavenge up a whole slime heap of them."

He doesn't. He passes the oyster stall, sweeping aside the strewn wrappers with his cane. He can't comprehend the craze for the sea-stinking innards' purses. But then he can't comprehend a fat lot of things these days, the blinkered faith in ghosties for one, his continued association with Heman another.

He marches abruptly across the street, caught up in his own loud thoughts. Damn and blast to ruin those Fox women! People continue to believe them over him, a scientist. A "commanding man," as one paper so rightly said, "whose jet-black beard and obsidian eyes bring to mind a fearsome hunter of yore."

But that is not the worst of it. No. The worst is that his expose has been stolen. And by those pill-rolling quacks known as doctors. Chauncey's blood roils. All this competition. What's a nemesis to do?

He arrives on Broadway. Finds the usual jammed chaos of cabs, wagons, carriages. Whips and traces entwine in a giant cat's cradle. Horses whinny in panic. Drivers bellow curses with a Gotham fluency and a Gotham ingenuity. An omnibus, misshapen by clinging riders, shunts by and splatters Chauncey's trousers with mud and horseshit. In response, Chauncey stomps on a crocus growing in an edging of dirt. He would like better to stomp on those Buffalo doctors. Knee-knocking, not toe-cracking, was their explanation for the Fox sisters' raps, as if relocating the expose up the leg could hide their blasted plagiarism. As proof, the doctors had one Mrs. Patcheon who could dislocate her knee at will and thus make the exact knocking sound the sisters do. The Fox women agreed to an "investigation." The doctors' report described how they grasped the knees and ankles of the females to detect any vibrations. How they would have bandaged the females' limbs but this was deemed unseemly.

Unseemly? The newspaper report was dust-dry in tone, and yet Chauncey recalls every word. Again he imagines Leah scantily clad and then the doctors—no, him—gently prying open her knees until . . . Stay off, you debauched damnedo thoughts, Chauncey orders himself, and return to the quandary at hand.

The doctors said no knocks were heard when the knees were held.

"The spirits are affronted by such intrusiveness" was Leah Fox Fish's retort. The final blow came when this Mrs. Patcheon admitted that she was astounded and mystified at the Fox rappings, that hers were nothing like theirs. Hers were faint and raspy and done only with great effort.

Was Madame Patcheon paid off? Chauncey wonders. Or is Leah merely possessed of the luck of the bold? Likely the latter. For Leah rivals Chauncey himself in boldness and luck. Perhaps that is why he has become so determined. Obsessed even. He is like a famed hunter after a wily she-wolf—or fox, rather.

Of course the Fox women were thronged with spirit-seekers after that latest investigation. Publicity. Publicity. Now they've got the spirits ringing bells. Now the spirits are writing messages through the slender fingers of the sisters, a damnedo sight easier, no doubt, than that toilsome alphabet board and "yes" or "no" knock-knockings. Easier even than trancing. Improvise. Improvise. Yes, Chauncey admires the Fox sisters three. He truly does, even as he is determined to expose their chicanery. Their reputations might suffer, but they will rally, find some other means of survival, just as he always has, for they are of the same ilk. This he has never doubted.

Chauncey halts and looks about. He has made a wrong turn. Barnum's Hotel is on Maiden Street. "Well, shit, shit, shito," he mutters, and strides off again, unbuttoning his coat in response to the sun prodding round the buildings. He passes two poor-shod girls who are hawking hot corn. Near on, another girl holds out wilted posies. Yes, Chauncey can follow Leah's reasoning: females have few ways to earn substantial coinage. Who could begrudge them a niche or two?

A newspaper boy spits a tobacco stream with elderly aplomb. Holds his paper high. "Citizens now obliged to help capture slaves! Jail and a one-thousand-dollar fine for any who help them! Lawmen to give ten dollars for every slave caught! Owners promise bounties in the hundreds for their own runaways. You'll get their descriptions! Right here, sir, right here!"

The boy waves the paper in Chauncey's face; Chauncey flips him a coin. He thumbs through the paper. Much on the wayward Sir Franklin and the latest expeditions that are being sent to find him in the Arctic Wastes, but nothing more about the Foxes, though there are advertisements galore touting phrenologists and bibliomancers. Advertisements, too, for palmistry, crystallomancy, and various kinds of sortilege. And yes, indeedo, a plethora of advertisements for mediums, spirit sittings, séances.

Chauncey tears the newspaper to pieces and tosses the bits in the gutter. A fire cart tears by, bells clanging, startling a small cat. No, not a cat, Chauncey realizes, as the rat scuttles into an alley where four pigs nose at a refuse pile. The pigs must have wandered in from the shanties. Where's the hog reeve? Pigs are not allowed any longer in the uptown of the metropolis.

The pigs knock over a stack of crates. The racket startles them and they trot off down the alley.

"Just my damnedo day," Chauncey says to himself. Behind the fallen crates three men are fixed in a momentary tableaux. Two are lank-haired white men in oiled greatcoats. The third is a young black man, his face purpled with bruises. He is hand-tied and gagged. Chauncey's stance is official. His eye appraising.

The slave-hunters look over. "We's found him first," says the one, and shows his scarce teeth.

"Yes, sir. We've been hunting this one a while," says the other. His face is constellated with pustules, his breath fearsome even at five paces.

"It must be bloodyo satisfying to capture the wily rascal, then, eh?" Chauncey is close. Closer. The alley narrows and he nearly blocks it with this bulk.

Pustule-Face adds, "Yessir, but he's a fighter for all that he's scrawny."

Chauncey taps his steel-tipped cane to his boot. "The scrawny ones are the most obdurate, I've noted."

Scarce-Teeth nods. "And stubborn, too. This one's got a bounty of two hundred dollars on him. Ain't that something?"

Pustule-Face whacks his companion. Says to Chauncey, "Ignore him. He's an idiot. No, sir, the fee is just the usual ten dollars from the law."

Chauncey dips his free hand in his pocket. "Allow me to assist you." He looks down at the young man, who glares up at the lot of them.

"Appreciate your good citizenry, sir," Pustule-Face replies. "But . . . fuck the devil. What?"

Chauncey levels his pistol at Scarce-Teeth, his stell-tipped cane at Pustule-Face. Pustule-Face reaches into his belt. Chauncey stabs him in the throat with his cane. He drops gasping beside his quarry, Chauncey's boot on his neck.

"Untie him," Chauncey orders Scarce-Teeth, and cocks the pistol. "Or I'll blow out your idiot brains and let the fucko pigs lap them up for breakfast."

Scarce-Teeth slobbers out an insult but obeys. And then Chauncey beats him and Pustule-Face senseless with the butt of his pistol, his fist and, for good measure, his hessian boots.

The young black man spits out the rag. Rubs his wrists. Eyes Chauncey, who tells him, "You're a bloodyo idiot yourself, getting caught. Canada's naught but a boat ride off. I advise you getting your carcass there forthwith."

The young man stammers out his thanks.

"Oh, I'm merely making my sainted mother proud, as would any man. Here." He hands the man two dollars. "Now bugger off."

The man does so and Chauncey pockets his pistol and wonders how much money he has lost playing the valiant these days. Seems these damnedo escaped slaves are around every corner. And he can ill afford it. Ah, but his sainted mother *would* be proud—his mother who was not, of course, the same mother as Heman's, nor Edwin's. No, Chauncey's mother was the cook, Hester. Chauncey's father freed her after she birthed Chauncey, but she stayed on, brave woman. Endured Mrs. Burr's hatred for it, though Mr. Burr senior treated Chauncey like his own son, which, of course, he was.

Chauncey leaves the slave-hunters moaning in pig shit and continues on his path. Yes, he knows exactly what the Fox women are about. He, too, hides in plain sight, as Heman likes to remind him. It is the best place to hide and certainly beats acting the happy, servile nitwit like his whip-smart mother had done, so as to keep her employ and her son. As for the Fox sisters, they are only acting the part allotted them: empty-headed women, innoncents incapable of subterfuge or calculation or any kind of guile.

At last: Barnum's Hotel. It is five storeys with a pillared entrance and little balconies on every window. It would be a marvel in some village, but here, in this city of astounding edifices, it is of average wonderment. In the lobby Chauncey flings off his coat, and sets aside his cane so as to look less imposing, less Chauncey Burr-ish. Near on, a boy porter kicks surreptitiously at a heavy trunks. A maid scrubs the marble floor. Chauncey stands out of the arc of her suds and rummages up his smoothest persona: "Madame, would you chance to know if the remarkable Fox women are still about?"

The maid shakes her head. "They're gone."

Chauncey lowers his voice, asks if, when cleaning their room, she overheard any comments about toes.

"Toes?" the maid whispers back. "If it's toes you're wanting, my aunt runs a place." She winks, and Chauncey thanks her and hastens on to other game. The boy porter only says that the Fox ladies were kind and merry and tipped handsome. Chauncey turns on his heel. Ah. There: A man who is like a statue vivified by some pagan god. Though truly, what god would bother giving such a countenance life? It has no significance whatsoever. The man waters a fern as if he has done so all his days, though Chauncey knows he hasn't, no indeedo.

"Alfie, is it? Forgive me, I'm ignorant of your family name."

Alfie stares up. "It's Kincaid. How you got my acquaintance?"

"I witnessed you at the Fox ladies' 'séance' in August. I heard Mrs. Fish call to you. She seemed to rely most heavily upon your presence. Forgive me, I am the Reverend Chauncey Burr."

Alfie considers him, then takes the proffered hand.

He doesn't even have an odour, Chauncey notes. No smell of hair grease or rot-mouth or sweat or musty wool. The perfect accomplice. I'd cherish a tenfold of him my bloodyo self, he thinks.

"May I treat you to luncheon, Mr. Kincaid? There is a well-spoken-of establishment a block from here."

Alfie agrees to meet him there in an hour. Chauncey nearly skips out the door. *Leah, Leah, you are not the only one adored by Lady Lucko!* For the situation is obvious. An argument, a misunderstanding, and Alfie given the heave-ho, resentment like cement in his veins. Hadn't Alfie barely considered whether to meet him? He must be burning to spill the beans.

"Oh, March," Chauncey says to the skies. "You lovely, traitorous month."

Chauncey is correct and righto. Alfie gives up the goods, but only after pondering the menu a quarter-hour. His job, he informs Chauncey, was to take care of the books, count the takings and hand them to Leah, who then doled out the money to the others. "Tight-fisted, that one. Said she worries about how the girls spend, but I think she likes a short leash on 'em, is all."

"Yes, I imagine she does, Mr. Kincaid, I imagine it well." Chauncey orders more wine, more dreaded oysters. He is sparing no expense and does not hurry Alfie Kincaid. Looks him straight in the eyes and says his name at every turn, taking a page from the manual of Leah Fox Fish herself. It is enough. Alfie becomes more animated, garrulous. It isn't the wine, the pullet, the costly *fricandeau* of veal. It is the attention given a lonely man who cannot even comprehend that he *is* lonely, so accustomed is he to the state. I might be of the minor pantheon myself, Chauncey thinks, as Alfie's cheeks flush, as he emits a rattle sound that might be a chuckle.

Chauncey speaks of Mrs. Fox Fish with respect, even admiration.

"Sure, sure. But she'll cut you down, that one," Alfie says, and extracts a morsel from his teeth. "I did everything for them. I was their dog's-body. Loyal as a knave. And here Mrs. Fish accuses me of skimming. She were bug-eyed on a laudanum brew then. They get lie-down-and-cry headaches, all three of them."

"Do they? I am aggrieved to hear of it. But it must be difficult for such honourable women to be so . . . on display. And difficult for you, as well, Mr. Kincaid, to cope with their feminine ways and overwrought demands."

"She'll ask me back. Heed me on that score."

"I heed you. More wine?"

"I offered myself to Barnum's Hotel when she tossed me to the midden heap. Not that I like it any . . . To the top now." He indicates his glass. Chauncey keeps pouring. Alfie keeps talking. "The job takes no braining at all. Water this plant. Haul that up." Alfie has not yet shown any curiosity as to Chauncey's purpose, Chauncey's profession. Still, he must understand that more pointed questions will come with the cream cakes, the brandy, the cigars.

Chauncey says, "The doctors in Buffalo unearthed a Mrs. Patcheon who could make a knocking sound with her knee joints by slipping them in and out."

"But you're betting it's the toes."

Chauncey sits back in surprise.

Alfie slurps the wine and rattles out another chuckle. "I know what you're about. I've seen your show. 'Imagination, Ghost-seeing and the Temperament of Genius,' was it? Weren't the worst show ever."

"I see, righto. My lectures, you mean." Chauncey leans forward. "Tell me more, Mr. Kincaid. I am abrim with curiosity."

"They don't let me in on the all of it. And I've never caught them in any kind of . . . indelicate doings."

Chauncey contemplates him. It is not a lie. Chauncey, having to lie constantly himself, can spot one a league off. "What of other, ah, employed persons? Those who have, alike you, offered their services, their loyalty, their skills to the Fox sisters, or their associates?"

"Associates? Like the Posts. Their maid Machteld? Wouldn't know. Would I?"

"No, I suppose not," Chauncey says, barely containing his glee.

"Too bad she'd hang by her neck, that Machteld, before she'd gift anyone with conversation—anyone sides those Posts, I mean."

"I see. Mr. Kincaid . . . Alfred. You've been about the family aplenty. Surely there's someone who might know. Who might wish to reveal . . . who has seen with their own eyes . . . You understand, Alfred, that taking money from the bereaved is neither right, nor moral?"

"Right and moral has got sweet all to do with it."

"Yes, of course," Chauncey says hastily. He has put a step wrong. Morality? Righteousness? These things hardly mattered to one such as Alfie Kincaid. Getting even is his tipple. Sure enough, he evades Chauncey's questions about what else he did for the Fox women besides organize their accounts. A dull man but not a stupid one, Chauncey realizes. For Alfie's spying—and Chauncey is certain now that Alfie spied out information on the dead to pass along to the sisters—might be a matter for the law. It thus takes all of Chauncey's resources and several costly brandies and several promises not to utter Alfie Kincaid's own name, to pry out the name of the one Fox kinfolk who might be of any use.

"'Course, you'd have to go to Arcadia," Alfie adds, and licks the cream out of a puffed shell.

CHAPTER 18

"And were you betrayed?" I asked my patient. "By whom? What kin would do so?"

"Guess."

"I don't like to guessing games. I've told you that . . . It wasn't your father, was it?"

"The good grief, no!"

"Katie? Was she in Arcadia then?"

"No. She was at the Greeleys' home in Turtle Bay when the tell-all appeared in the *Times*. Mother and I were there, too, on a short visit from Rochester. And how could Katie have betrayed us? She loved us, not to mention that she believed in her own magic by that time, lock and stock. Indeed, I recall her denying the tell-all so strongly to the Greeleys she nearly had me convinced of her version of things."

"And did the Greeleys send you packing anyways? I would have. And in a Saratoga trunk, to boot."

She smiled. "No, Mary Greeley was a stalwart supporter of us by then, and of Katie certainly, though she still couldn't abide the woman. Horace continued to be supportive, too, though I suspected he was having doubts about the wisdom of his connection with us."

"Then perchance he had sense after all."

She smiled at this, said, "The tell-all sent Leah into a fury, of course. I wasn't near as bothered. Our little prank had grown into a juggernaut, and it would not be swatted aside so easily, not by jealous kin, not by the likes of Burr. Not by proof, really, of any shape or size."

"NO, AMY, DON'T STRIKE THE TINDER," Leah orders. She regrets her vexed tone straightaways, but assures herself that Amy Post, being a Quaker, would never judge nor condemn Leah for mere ill-temper. Nor for anything at all, surely.

Leah sits up. Lets Amy plump the pillows. Sundown and Leah is only now coming awake. She has become a night creature since returning from Buffalo. Her veins bleed fire. Light hammers her brain. Dizziness assaults her. And her poor soul. Last night it detached itself and floated over her bed and observed the woman there—the abundant chestnut hair with its glimmers of silver, the brow etched with worry, the shoulders weary from carrying her family pigback. And yet a most handsome woman even so, the soul observed. One would never guess her at thirty-six years. Leah has not told anyone of this event, not even Amy—the better to forget it. The idea of her soul taking a practice walk is terrifying. She does not wish to contemplate her own demise. She has to contemplate everyone else's. Surely that is enough.

Amy measures out several drams of elixir and hands it Leah. Leah tastes hellebore, as well as tolu—dear Isaac is always tinkering with his remedies. Leah offers her gratitude to Amy. "And to your Isaac as well. You have both stood fast through these trying days." Unlike Margaretta and Mother, Leah nearly adds. They have left her to join Katie at "Castle Doleful." And all because Katie has threatened to drown herself in the shining waters of Turtle Bay should she be left alone a moment longer with Mary Greeley. "Ignore Katherina's letters," Leah counselled. "She is merely being her usual dramatic self. And I do need you here." Maggie and Mother left regardless. Granted, they left before the betrayal, before Leah fell ill with shock. Still, Leah cannot but feel abandoned.

"As well you should," said Lemira Kedzie, Amy's trusted friend, and now Leah's, apparently. She kindly offered to lead Leah's sittings while Leah recovers. An offer that Leah just as kindly refused. As for Calvin, well, he would be at her side every minute if she allowed it, but Leah prefers he does not see her thus. Anywise, Calvin seems to need rest of his own these days, as if he weren't blessed with manly strength and youthful energy.

Alfie slips into the room and places a sweet roll and a sheaf of newspapers on the table beside Amy. He hands Leah a folded telegram. Dear Alfie. Leah never fully realized his usefulness until he was absent.

"Thank you kindly," Leah calls, though Alfie has already gone. Three weeks ago she wrote and asked for his forgiveness. He gave it, though she cannot recall his exact reply. Something, likely, about her accusation being an understandable mistake, seeing that she has so many adversaries, seeing that jealousy and treachery abound. She has upped his pay, of course, has even offered him the money she accused him of stealing back in New York and that she much later found in her reticule, just where she then recalled she had put it for safekeeping.

Amy brings a lamp close and looks through the newspapers. Are Ruth's lies printed among them? Leah wonders. That hoyden. That damned bitch. Yes, Ruth Culver is so far beyond the pale she has forced Leah to think in curses.

Leah dares not ask Amy if she has confronted Machteld, who is clearly the "Dutch servant girl" mentioned in Ruth's self-serving attack on her own kin. Nor does she show Amy the telegram Alfie just handed her. It is from New York. From Maggie.

Not Kat's Fault, it reads, nothing more.

"Is that from our Horace?" Amy asks.

"No, though I am certain he will write or telegram forthwith. He is a very busy man, dear Amy."

Amy gives Leah a strange look—not an exasperated one, surely.

"Yes, soon, very soon," Leah continues. "Horace will give his rebuttal to this latest slander. The girls and Mother are at his country house. They are the mediums for his son, Pickie, that importunate little spirit. And the consolers of his wife, Mary, that . . . Mary. He cannot continue to stand upon neutral ground."

"I grant thee: it *is* difficult ground to stand upon," Amy says dryly.

Leah nibbles on the sweet roll, sips Isaac's elixir. Nothing eases her. "A pen, Amy, the inkpot. Now that you have put Horace in my mind it seems I must . . . ah, thank you," Leah says as Amy, without another word, hands her the writing tray and implements.

Amy takes up her needlework while Leah writes.

5 April, 1851

Dearest Horace,

I am writing to tell you that Ruth Culver is obscure and talentless and resents to Heaven and the Spirits the growing fame and remarkable abilities of me and my sweet sisters, and that she is green-appled with jealousy at how the papers describe us as "divinely countenanced" and "lovely seeresses" and so on, because Ruth Culver, it must be said, has a face like a ripped bun, and anyone can see that the so-called-Reverend Chauncey Burr is behind all this and surely fed Ruth lies as one feeds a wallowing old sow slops left over from a table . . .

Leah lifts her pen. The ink drips and blossoms black on the page. Yes. Chauncey damned Burr. Ruth Culver must have contacted him somehow after his failed, so-called expose in New York. Surely none of their intimate group would have directed Chauncey to Ruth. And here Leah purchased that fancy shawl to keep sour-faced Ruth from jealousy's beck, as if she had known somehow that Ruth had a traitor's soul. Leah presses her hands to temples. I must take some blame for this disaster, yes, she thinks. I should never have allowed Katie to spend time with Ruth during the cholera fright last year. But Ruth had insisted, and Margaretta had been ill and my nerves on screeching edge and . . . damn Ruth to hell.

Leah re-reads her letter to Horace. Tears it in half. The wording is too frank, yes, too frank and honest by far. Amy glances up from her needlework, but she doesn't admonish Leah for the flagrant wasting of paper.

"I will purchase a quire more, Amy, don't look at me so."

"It is just, just that I must go now," Amy says. "Lemira and I have a meeting for the women's cause."

"My spirits, another meeting?"

"Yes, dearest. Women will never win the battle for suffrage without meetings. Now, don't thou sigh."

"But Amy, Amy, a battle rages here also. Nasty forces are aligning against the spirit world. But you are much occupied. I understand that."

Amy sits beside Leah on the bed. "Dearest, perhaps each world should be attended to in its time. The spirits live in a world of justice and love, but we, well . . ." She takes Leah's hands. "Come with me and Lemira when thou art feeling better. Thou would be such an asset to the women's cause. Is it not galling to thee how we women are treated as if we are simple children incapable of an original thought or action? As if we are frail and silly, weak of will, bereft of any true intelligence?"

Leah considers this. "It *is* galling to be so discounted and . . . underestimated because of one's sex, certainly. And if ever the spirits desert me, I promise I shall march with you wherever you ask. But of course I have my sisters to consider. They do need me every moment."

"They do, yes," Amy says, and shuffles the newspapers again, leaving the *New York Express* atop the pile, folded there at Ruth's damned lies.

Why-ever would Amy do that? Leah wonders. Ah, Amy does not wish me to relent, that is it.

Amy leaves, suggesting rest, sleep. No, courage is what I require, Leah decides. She thinks of the Corinthian Hall investigations, of the mob at Troy, of Buffalo and the naysayers there. Mulls over all the difficulties she has overcome ever since she was a girl and her father left, and then Mr. Fish demanded marriage, and then Lizzie came squalling into the world, and then, well . . . and so on and so forth.

Leah drinks down more elixir. The headache is receding. Another day, perhaps two, and she will be herself again. Know thine enemy, Leah thinks, and reaches for the newspaper and reads again the traitorous lines:

I was getting suspicious of the spirits' origins and so when Katie was sent to me during the cholera I asked if I could help in the manifestations—we had other kin staying—and Katie said yes. She said that when my cousin

Orville consulted the spirit, I must sit next to her, and touch her arm when the right letter was called.

Leah reads how Katie then told Ruth the knocks were made by the toes—shades of Burr, who could not see it? Apparently Leah's own daughter, Lizzie, was in on the discovery that one could make loud raps by cracking toes against a headboard or, indeed, any conducting surface—floors, table legs, doors.

Leah licks a plumbago lead and writes in the margins, *When? In Rochester when Mrs. Fish brought Lizzie and Katie there? Lizzie is known to be a mischief maker. And it hardly explains the initial hauntings in Hydesville.*

Lead poised, Leah now reads Ruth's in-depth instructions on this fine art of "toe cracking": how one must warm the feet first and then practise many hours. How it is best to begin when one's toes are young and pliable. How one should vary the pitch and loudness of the sounds, and look earnestly here and there so the knocks seem to come from the ceilings and walls, from farther off or closer. *And Katie said that I had better have a child at the table with me, and make folks believe that the child was the medium, for they would not suspect a youngster of any trick.*

Leah's plumbago lead nearly drills through the newspaper as she writes, *And what of the trances? What of the tables moving? Of the sounds of coffins being made? Bells ringing? What of spirits writing through the hands of others? What of the known fact that women are incapable of deception and guile, being so frail, silly and weak, and bereft of true intelligence?*

Next comes the foolery about how to read a countenance. The worst, however, is the accusation of accomplices, such as the Posts' "Dutch servant girl" who had, apparently, often made knocks with a broom.

And what of Katherina pledging on a bible that Ruth is telling lies? That she recalls nothing of what Ruth claims? Leah writes. The bible is a nice touch, she decides. And likely Katie *would* pledge on one, if Leah asked.

She puts aside the plumbago, then carefully tears the story from the newspaper, folds it smaller and smaller still. She studies her handiwork. Here are Ruth's lies rendered small and inconsequential, the size, really, of a medicine tablet.

She wonders, even as she opens her mouth, if some mysterious force is guiding her own, is directing her to swallow that folded newsprint and wash it down with the entire bottle of Isaac's elixir. She wonders if, indeed, she has stumbled upon some rare and peculiar magic. And then she doesn't wonder at all. She is intent only on struggling through a webbing that is warm and viscous. When she breaks through she is a young girl again, afire with projects, belted with emotions. She is in a field that is dark-edged with forest, and she is staring, pole-axed with astonishment, as the forest undulates as if in readiment to break free. She is running towards the forest when her father appears. Her true father, John-Before. He tips back his Coke hat and grins. "Don't you polka-dance with the Devil like I did, Leah-Lou. Best you stop now, you hear."

Leah wakes, hours later, to a bell-clear mind. I shall stop, Pa, she thinks, and vows to God and the spirits to never again overindulge in stimulants, alcohol, or soporifics of any kind. She will henceforth drink only tea and coffee and the occasional glass of watered wine. She will order her sisters to also cease overindulging. Surely with some firm encouragement they will be happy to do so.

That night, Leah sleeps well for the first time in days. Come early morning she finds Calvin in the dining room. "Leah! You've rallied. I'm so glad of it," he says after much throat clearing.

"My pardon? Ah, yes, I am a grand sight better. Tip and top of the scales, thank the spirits."

She is layering her sweet roll with butter and quince jam when Isaac rushes in. He brandishes a telegram. Tells her in breathless detail of Chauncey Burr's latest nefarious attack.

"He is slandering you directly now. He calls thee, forgive me, a woman of notoriously bad character. I have telegrammed Cleveland. It is too dangerous to keep your engagement. And Ruth and her . . ." Isaac's voice trails off, his gentle face terrained with worry.

"It might well be dangerous. Indeed, I might expire under all the gross scrutiny but, dear Isaac, you know that I must confront this horrid Burr, and now."

"But our friends there have put him under bonds in your name and—"

"And that is why I must go. Our friends cannot face him alone."

Calvin starts to say something, wisely changes his words to a cough.

"And Isaac, do fetch one of your lovely tonics for our Calvin. Honestly, I can barely hear him talk these days."

Four days later Leah steps onto the Cleveland docks. Fine-bonneted ladies jostle each other to take her hands in greeting. Whiskered gentlemen bow. Behind Leah, Calvin waits along with Leah's sister Maria and Maria's son, Charlie, who is all of three and has the disposition of a badly trained terrier. Leah insisted Maria accompany her, having come to realize that Calvin is not a suitable sole escort, not given the way he presses her shawl about her, or gazes at her, or utters her name at every turn like some incantatory charm.

While Calvin unloads their baggage, Leah surveys the countenances before her. She senses not a whit of disrepute. Still, something is amiss. She shrugs off her concern, however, once the greeters thank her for opening the portals to the spirit world, once they express horror over Reverend Burr's slander, his mountebank shows. They say nothing of Ruth Culver's accusations.

One lady cries, "You're calm as a clock. Why, I'd be having hysterics if I was you!"

Another declares she'd have her husband challenge Burr to a duel.

A third, the finest dressed, says, "Violence solves little. You must publish a rebuttal against this Mr. Burr. Destroy him with pen and ink."

Leah holds up her gloved hand. "If you ladies had passed through one half the abuse I have, you would not wonder that I am personally quite indifferent to all my enemies may say against me." At this, a gust of wind peels wide Leah's bonnet, making a comic flower of her face. She swats the brim back in place. "Shall we make haste? The weather is refusing its co-operation."

The group leads her to the waiting coach. Maria and Charlie follow close behind. Calvin stays at the dock's edge to grapple with their luggage. A valise tips and Calvin lunges to save it from the waters, then vanishes from Leah's view. She gasps with relief when she sees his silhouette standing victorious, valise in hand.

"You looked so worried when I fell," Calvin says later, and chuckles hoarsely. They are in their Dunham house rooms, refreshing themselves before the first callers arrive. Maria and Charlie are napping despite the wagons and coaches rattling below, despite the muffled hubbub in the tavern alongside. The storm has retreated and the spring day has turned clement.

Leah looks up from the secretary. She has just finished a letter and is searching out a blotter. "The lily box, dear Calvin, honestly, it might well have plummeted into the depths. What would we have done then?"

"But I was guarding it closely, Leah, like always," Calvin says, his voice tetchy, and more nasal than usual.

"All I meant, my dear, was that if the box is lost, then we are lost."

Calvin sighs and pushes a curl out his eye. Leah supposes he is handsome, even as his older self ghosts itself upon his young man's features. In twenty years his generous mouth will be a slash, his square jaw pouched with fat. Think of him thus, Leah tells herself as she straightens the complicated ruffling on her gown of teal and peach, as Calvin presses himself up with both hands to answer the ringing of the caller-bell.

The caller, their first in Cleveland, is Mr. Joel Tiffany. He is a lawyer, a spirit believer, an abolitionist. Has a pompadour of dark hair and a profile chiseled to a wedge. He is shortly joined by Mr. John Gray, the editor of the *Cleveland Plain Dealer*. Except for a white shirt and collar, Mr. Gray's suit is entirely of black, as if life were fit only for mourning. These singular shaded "ditto" suits are the latest fashion, and a dull one of which Leah does not approve at all.

She pours the tea. Tells Mr. Tiffany and Mr. Gray how Katherina and Margaretta will be arriving in Cleveland soon. Tells of all the remarkable manifestations, and how baffling they are. "And I have been assured," she stresses, "that neither of you gentlemen are the sort who attend gossip and lies, nor the jealousies of distant kinfolk such as that Ruth Culver, who is not truly kin, but related by marriage."

Mr. Gray and Mr. Tiffany shift nervously at the mention of Ruth, begin their platitudes. Leah holds up her hand. "I appreciate your concerns, and I apologize, but the matter needed to be spoken of. I do so hate when the unsaid lingers in the room like so much cheap cigar smoke."

The learned men agree to this. Express admiration for her candour, her expressive turns of phrase. Leah gives her dimpled smile, then asks if the learned gentlemen have any opinions on the matter of the spirits.

The learned Mr. Tiffany surmises that the spirits have been awaiting this epoch of discovery and invention. "For the human mind is at its zenith and is as capable of understanding complex phenomena as it shall ever be."

The learned man Mr. Gray surmises that the spirits use the forms of the Fox women as a catalyst.

Leah looks abashed.

Mr. Gray apologizes, red-faced. "Use, that is, their inner forms. Their superior feeling . . . or something similar."

Mr. Tiffany clears his throat. "I regret to report that some are being infected by Burr's slander and by the, ah, report of this Ruth Culver, which—"

"Ruth Culver is clearly in Burr's clutches, and his wallet," Leah interjects. "I surely cannot guess what other method he might have used to seduce her . . . mind."

Mr. Gray says in a rush, "Burr has posed the risible idea that you and your sisters have a machinery concealed about . . . about your person, that is, your apparel. He has said it must be a great convenience to wear such, ah, concealing skirts."

Mr. Tiffany lifts his hands in resignation at Mr. Gray's untoward talk.

Leah smiles graciously. "Then he should don skirts and petticoats and know the delight of such womanly apparel for himself."

Mr. Tiffany chuckles. Mr. Gray, emboldened, continues. "He suggested, or else someone did, that this machinery has an intelligence to properly answer the questions, be they posed orally, or solely with the mind."

"What a silly suggestion. A computing machine such as that would be so large it wouldn't fit under a teepee, never mind our skirts."

Mr. Tiffany smiles in wonder. "Mrs. Fish, you are indeed tremendously intelligent. Just as everyone says."

"In truth, I have never thought of myself that way," Leah says. She is not feigning modesty. She has, indeed, never considered herself as intelligent, tremendously or otherwise. It is just that Leah has found, to her surprise, that most people are quite stupid. "Though I must say, dear Joel . . . may I call you Joel? You see, I have been among the Godly Quakers so much that I have taken on their ways."

Mr. Tiffany says he would be delighted if she called him Joel. It seems then as if they've known each other for years.

"To continue, I must say that your support puts you in the company of many gracious people of the highest standing . . . Calvin?"

On cue Calvin, who has been sitting apart from them, fetches the lily box and opens it to show a thick sheaf of letters. He reads aloud excerpts from this admirable gentleman and that exceptional lady.

". . . without doubt the raps were not made by any human form."

"My life was changed. I am filled with joy at Eternity's proof . . ."

"The Fox ladies have the highest most reputable characters."

"Never have I met a woman of such noble intent as Mrs. Fish . . ."

Calvin now reads out a letter from Mrs. Patcheon of the cracking knees. Says how she is eager to hear the spirits her own self. How the Fox sisters' raps are nothing like the slight and obvious sounds that she can make. Next come the engraved medals. Calvin hands them round. People ascend heavenly ladders. Spirits comfort the living. Children, a good many, are grouped in clouds, touched by rays. They are smiling. Laughing. The medals bear inscriptions thanking Leah and her sisters for all they have done. Last read is a letter from "anonymous" confirming that Mrs. Ruth Culver was paid by Reverend Burr for her lies, most likely with thirty silvered coins.

Calvin tucks everything back in the box, his hands lingering on the carving of the entwined lilies.

"Impressive," Mr. Gray says.

"Such testimonies will stand in any court," Mr. Tiffany adds.

A good hour later Calvin reads aloud the letters again, this time to an audience of some twenty callers, callers who have been arriving in a constant stream and now fill every corner of the Dunham suite. They murmur approval when Calvin finishes reading. Some even clap.

Leah stirs a fourth sugar chip into her coffee. Without her young sisters to counsel, she can pay close attention to her callers, closer than usual. The callers are nothing remarkable. Are similar, even exact, to so many other clients she has lately met. Leah puts down her spoon. That is it. The sameness. That is what troubled her on the dock. Oh, the names change and the countenances and the clothing. But not greatly. Rather as if the same actors are tricked out to play many characters at a boardwalk show. She seeks out Calvin's face. He is not an automaton with a nodding head and stock phrases of agreeable sentiments. He is real. Actual. She reminds herself to chide him for reading the letters as if by rote. To add more verve and steel. Reminds herself to never be alone with him in any intimate space.

The next evening, Leah walks through the Cleveland streets alone. She wears a borrowed shawl of Mrs. Dunham's so as to appear as a woman so ordinary she does not require an evening escort. Calvin feels poorly, as does Maria's little Charlie, which means Maria also has an excuse not to be useful. Leah stops at the entrance to the Melodeon Hall. The "Reverend" Burr is drawn overlarge, his thick arms held wide. Three women, all with dark hair and stupid expressions, cower from him. Their Fox tails stick out from under their skirts. The name *is* unfortunate, Leah has to admit, and is tempted to kick the placard to Kingdom Come.

She checks her pocket watch. The show will carry on for another hour yet. She walks down the street to the hotel where this Burr and his brother are staying. The lobby smells of cigars and carbolic and camphene. Timing in life, as in music, is everything, she reminds herself, and so she waits and observes until she marks out a likely

candidate: The head waiter. He is an older man with a jaded countenance, a weary stoop. Leah watches as he cautiously navigates the
stairs down from the guest rooms, a dome-covered tray in his gloved
hands. He has been in the suites of the Burr brothers at least once a
day, he tells her when she asks after these celebrated men. He carries
meals up to them after their lecture-demonstrations.

"The lectures that seek to discredit the Fox sisters? What gentleman would speak in a public forum against a genteel widow and two
innocent girls?" Leah muses. "The ladies cannot engage him in the
public arena. They cannot call him to satisfaction. He is taking
supreme advantage."

The head waiter agrees. In his day, Burr would have been called
out to duel for his impertinence. "Mr. Burr, he does tip, mind . . . Ah,
but not as handsome as you, ma'am," he says, and tucks away the
folded bill Leah has pressed upon him.

The next morning, promptly after breakfast, Leah offers the head
waiter's report to Mr. Gray at the offices of the *Cleveland Plain
Dealer*. She next calls upon Mr. Tiffany the lawyer. Tells him that
since no gentleman has yet challenged Burr to a duel (to quote the
head waiter) it appears the law is left to defend her honour.

An editor and a lawyer. What a perfect duo to have onside, Leah
thinks, and cannot recall ever being so satisfied.

CHAPTER 19.

"Thank you for this," my patient said as she took the pot of *Mrs. Howe's Neroli and Rose Miracle Hand Cream*. "But what-ever is the occasion?"

"No occasion, duck. It's just a little gift. A little gift, I've found, often cheers my indigents in their last days. And besides, one should look one's best when meeting one's Maker."

"Well, yes." She peered at the lid, then indicated *Doctor Noble's Tonic For All Female Complaints* (which was the only laudanum brew I could find that day). "Why, there she is, and there again."

The images on the hand-cream lid and the tonic label were indeed much alike, were of tall and broad-shouldered young women with plumped-high hair, buxom hour-glass figures and narrow skirts raised to the ankles. We chatted for a time about this new, distinctly American female, by which I mean modern, the sort who goes to college and picks out her own husband and plays tennis and rides those bicycles and determines her own fate.

My patient said, "Nor would she think it the least romantic if a suitor took her to a cemetery to view her own potential grave."

"I suppose not, but it *is* a practical idea and does prove the suitor is considering the longer draw. Did your Elisha—"

"He will present when I want," she said, like a surly child of a sudden. "Not a moment sooner."

THEY SLIP INTO THE DUNHAM HOUSE unannounced and unexpected: Maggie, Katie and Mrs. Lemira Kedzie, their newest confidante. Lemira is thinner than when the girls first met her at Amy and Isaac's house three years ago. She still wears her black hair in a high topknot, however. And she still reminds Maggie of a woodpecking bird, what with her considerable nose, her constant nodding. They are all three still in their travelling clothes: sturdy shoes, cottage cloaks and half-veiled bonnets, the better to remain unnoticed, for the moment, among the nearly thirty callers who crowd the Dunham suite.

"Won't this be a smacking surprise?" Lemira whispers to Maggie.

"Well, yes, I'd say so," Maggie whispers back, and gathers her defiance, squelches her fear. Fear of what? She is near grown, can make her own decisions. Hasn't Lemira said so? Hasn't Lemira said women are as capable as some men?

"Dear people," Leah calls out, from where she holds court on the settee. "Before the spirits come forth I would like my dear associate Calvin Brown to read the latest edition of our learned Mr. Gray's illustrious newspaper, the *Cleveland Plain Dealer*."

Maggie shifts for a better view of Calvin as he stands and clears his throat and holds up the newspaper. Reads:

"A source employed at the hotel where the Messr Burrs are residing has told us that Burr and his brother use copious poultices and salt baths for their swollen, bloodied toes, and that they oft speak with bewilderment over how the Fox sisters could make loud raps and knocks so continuously and with no apparent effort. This is of no surprise to we who have witnessed the skirmishing between Mr. Burr and the gracious Mrs. Fish, the eldest of the spirit rapping trio, for notwithstanding the burlesques of the Burrs, and the scoffs of the prejudiced and ignorant of our town against the Fox sisters' rappings, the spirit cause is gaining ground on every side. One month ago, there were not fifty believers in the city; now there are hundreds, including some of the best minds."

Calvin finishes reading to claps, faint cheers. Only now does Leah begin her séance, shutting her eyes and tap-tapping her fingers, as if to heavenly music. The drapes are drawn, the lamps and candles doused.

Rap. Knock. The sounds are faint. Even pitiful. Leah's cheek twitches. She grimaces. Maggie grimaces herself, albeit inwardly. Fortunately no one else in the murky room has Maggie's high standards for knocks. Instead the callers listen with awed concentration while Calvin works the alphabet board. Seems the spirit holding forth is Benjamin Franklin, that old standby.

Calvin calls out the letters and words. As he does, a man dressed all in black, like some ambulant obelisk, copies them onto a slate.

"Did you get that, Mr. Gray?" Calvin asks.

"I have, blessed be the spirits," Mr. Gray replies, then reads from the slate: *"Ruth. Lies. Led by Burr."*

"By Spirit Land!" Leah cries. "Does Mr. Franklin have more to say?"

The taps laboriously spell out: *Burr. Fraud. Court. Sander.*

"Sander? Who is—" Leah asks.

"Perhaps Mr. Franklin meant 'slander'?" Calvin suggests, and pats his mouth with a handkerchief. "As in, he is slandering Leah and should pay for it."

Katie pinches Maggie's wrist. Maggie stifles her giggle. They are both excellent nowadays at stifling and so the giggle is the barest sound, alike the rustle of a crinoline.

Leah's head swivels. "Girls? Margaretta? Katherina? Is that you, dear children?"

Lemira ushers them forth. Someone draws the drapes and the afternoon spills into the room. The sitters make a commotion.

"Here are the famous little girls themselves!"

"Now the spiritual battery will be boosted."

"Greetings, sweet girls."

Sweet girls? *Little* girls? Katie, though close on fifteen, might still be called a girl. But Maggie? She is nearly eighteen. Beaus will soon be dropping at her feet like so many apples. In fact, she and Katie talk of little else but beaus these days.

"And you, Lemira, what a pleasant surprise," Leah declares, though it is not surprise at all that registers in her voice. "And where is my dearest mother?"

Lemira says, "Mrs. Fox was utterly exhausted after her sojourn at the Greeleys' and so we, that is Amy and Isaac and I, thought it the very best if she rested in Rochester for a time, and that I accompany the girls instead."

"*You* thought? My spirits, how considerate of you all."

Once the sitters have left, Leah, in a sparking fury, paces round and round. A card holder catches her sleeve and tumbles to the rug. Calvin gathers up the calling cards. Offers a nervous smile that Leah ignores. Maggie holds tight to Katie's hand. Maria and little Charlie hasten out with the sitters. Calvin now excuses himself, claiming exhaustion. And Lemira? She nods and nods as if Leah is being entirely reasonable and not shouting:.

"Bringing the girls to Cincinnati, Lemira? You alone? Honest to . . . I cannot believe that you would do this, a friend. Are you not a friend?"

"I am. I am a most excellent friend, Leah. That's not the point—"

"It *is* the point. It is! I am betrayed." Leah stands in front of Maggie and Katie. "By you, Margaretta, but mostly by you, Katherina."

"I didn't tell old Ruth. I didn't! I'd remember!" Katie shouts. "How many times have I got to say that?"

Leah wrings her hands at Maggie and Katie—not pathetically, Maggie notes, but as if to hold back from swatting them both.

"I shall telegraph Mother." Leah declares. " Yes. I shall. You two left without her permission and with this, this woman!"

"Lemira," Lemira reminds her.

Leah scowls at Katie and Maggie. "Mother shall come and put you to rights."

"Ma will?" Maggie asks.

Leah takes several deep breaths, then forces out a smile. "Oh, you two do these things and then throw it all on my shoulders. Come now, this woman cannot 'manage' the two of you. Not in any sense of the word. She does not know you as I do."

Maggie looks over at Katie. The understanding floats between them that perhaps this was not such a swell idea after all. Lemira called on them in Rochester shortly after they arrived there from the Greeleys'. She offered to be their new manager and explained how she had easily gleaned that the spirits often needed a helping hand or two; that they could not always manifest on their own. "But why should clients be disappointed because of that?"

Why indeed? Maggie thought. And why argue with Lemira? She is woman known for piety, devotion, honesty. Is a determined abolitionist and suffragette, just like their beloved Amy Post. And Lemira has none of Leah's temper. She has even promised that the money will be more equitably divided. Promised them the freedom to attend dances and parties, drink champagne for breakfast if they like, a habit that Leah has been quick to criticize. "And not to worry," Lemira said. "I'll wholly convince your sister."

But she hasn't. Not yet. The two of them, Leah and Lemira, have been at it hammer and tongs for a good half-hour now. They ignore the girls. What in tunket do they take us for? Maggie wonders, as she and Katie perch on the settee. Part of the upholstery pattern? Pretty, flat-drawn flowers for everyone to sit upon? Good grieving Christ, but she could use a refreshment. The only thing about, however, is a mug of leftover brandied coffee. It is tepid, but better than nothing. She and Katie pass it silently between them.

A few moments later Leah stands over them, Lemira close behind. "Lemira and I have agreed to hear your opinions in this matter."

"Our opinions?" Maggie and Katie query in unison.

"Yes. Lemira says that you are eager to tour Cincinnati with her. She says that you have no compunctions about leaving me as the solo force against our greatest, most diabolical enemy, that addle-wit Chauncey Burr."

"I didn't say that, I—" Lemira begins.

"You are both welcome to go with her, of course. I have no other claim on you except sisterly love and devoted affection. And in all truth, Cincinnati will be a great triumph. It is already chock with followers and boasts more mediums of its own than any other city. They will welcome the famous Fox sisters—well, the two of them." Leah looks now to Maggie. "But recall that where many believers reside, an equal number of enemies also reside, those who would like to see us tarred and feathered, or trussed up like a Yuletide goose for slow roasting. And Cincinnati is poorly stocked with police and famous for its mobs. And Margaretta, you know you cannot abide a mob, not after I rescued you from that business in Troy."

Maggie sips the brandied coffee that is really quite cold, really quite awful.

"I am sorry, Margaretta," Leah continues. "My spirits, I am. I should not have mentioned a mob. It is just that bad luck follows us when we are discordant. Have you not noted this?"

Eventually it is decided. Katie, who is the most accustomed to giving spirit sittings on her own, will go with Lemira to Cincinnati. Maria and Charlie will accompany them. Maggie will remain in Cleveland with Calvin and Leah, who, as Maggie discovers over the following week, is more interested in consultations with the lawyer Joel Tiffany than in consultations with any ghost.

"What do you say, Margaretta," Leah asks one sunny afternoon. "Does ten thousand dollars sound a sufficient amount to demand as compensation for Burr's disgraceful attacks upon our honour? That is the amount dear Joel has suggested."

Maggie nearly spits out her claret. "Sufficient? Leah, that's a staggering lot. A fortune. How can you even conjure up that much?"

"In a snap."

"Or, or, well, spend it?"

Leah now gives her rare, genuine laugh. "That shall be even easier, I need not consult anyone or anything on that score."

Maggie is mulling over the possibility that, yes, she, too, might easily spend that money on clothes, shoes and lace, when the telegram arrives from Cincinnati. Her hopes for riches are quickly forgotten. Little Charlie has fallen deathly ill.

At this news, Leah takes to her bed. Maggie finds her muttering and groaning, Calvin hovering near.

"Fetch cold water, Cal, a cloth," Maggie orders. She pats Leah's shoulder. "Poor sis. You were right. Bad luck happens when we're at odds. I'm sorry."

Leah's eyes spring open. "Charlie must return here. The spirits have said so."

"Leah, it's me, Maggie. Margaretta."

"The spirits cannot be ignored."

"But that'd be perilous. He can't travel when he's grievous sick. It's not—"

Leah throws off the bedclothes and stands. "Only I can save him."

Katie, Lemira and Maria rush Charlie back from Cincinnati as Leah orders. Leah bundles Charlie into bed, sends for Cleveland's finest doctors. "Death is imminent," these doctors pronounce. Maggie watches aghast as placid, pious Maria tears her hair and screams, "Not again! No! God's got my Ella. Damn him. Ain't He satisfied? Leah, don't you let this happen."

Let? Maggie thinks, as Leah vows again that she will save little Charlie. She plies the boy with some willow bark concoction sent by Isaac, refuses to allow even the forlorn hope of bloodletting and hot-cupping. "Benjamin Franklin advises against such antiquated means," Leah tells Maria. "He considers them poppycock. Mortals require their life fluids. It is something he has discovered in the other realm. Do you not agree, Margaretta? Katherina?"

Maggie dumbly nods, as does Katie.

Days pass and Charlie, to everyone's astonishment, recovers and becomes his hale little self again.

Leah refuses credit. She tells her family that it was only the spirits working through her. "I am a woman of modest background and little educated. I do not have tremendous intelligence. But the spirits *have* granted me tremendous gifts, and I promise I shall use these gifts only for the greater good."

What a peculiar thing to say to her intimates, Maggie thinks. It's as if we're just another audience, as if we don't know her at all.

"Charlie lived, then?" I asked.

"Indeed, yes. He lives even yet, though far out West."

"I am amazed. And gladdened," I said, and in some surprise. For I *was* glad and amazed, and delighted, to boot. For not long past I had only known jealousy at stories of children who survive terrible odds. Not jealousy, perhaps. No. But resentment, I suppose. Why should theirs survive and not mine?

"I am, yes, very glad," I repeated, but my patient had eased to sleep.

I knitted on for a time. Presently, there came a thud—soft but definite. I suspended my knitting (my patient was still sleeping fast) and rose and looked about until I saw the tiny, cinder-coloured creature on the ledge outside the centre window. The bird was stunned and looked astonished, too, that he could not merely fly on through empty space. That window was the centre fixed one, as I have said, and so I tapped the panes hoping he would rouse himself before a hawk swooped down.

I thought then of my son. When he was five he found a hatchling in the switchgrass. The hatchling was of hideous aspect, bulge-eyed and skinned-looking, as they ever are, and yet my son lifted it up and warmed it by the stove and fed it crushed worms and prayed for its recovery and loved it, in all, as if it were a thing of beauty. When the bird vanished, Mr. Mellon boasted he had eaten it. He made ogre faces and laughed until I threw his supper in his face. A beef dodger, if I recall.

I tapped at the window again. At last the bird shuffled off the ledge and dropped away. I turned at a rustling and saw that my patient was quite awake.

"I'm sorry if I woke you, duck."

"The hawks are worrisome," she said, as if I had spoken my thoughts.

PART THREE

"The midnight sun came out over the northern crest of the great berg, kindling varioulsy coloured fires on every part of its surface, and making the ice around us one great resplendency of gemwork, blazing carbuncles, and rubes ad molten gold . . . In this we beat backward and forward, like China fish seeking an outlet from a glass jar, till the fog caught us again; and so the day ended."

Elisha Kent Kane,
ARCTIC EXPLORATIONS IN SEARCH OF SIR JOHN FRANKLIN

"A brawl between rival crews that began at the basin and spilled into the Four Corners in 1829 was certainly seen if not heard by the citizens of South Fitzburgh. So were the transgressions of one Erastus Bearcup, a steersman arrested for shouting obscenities at ladies on a passing boat."

Paul E. Johnson,
A SHOPKEEPER'S MILLENNIUM:
SOCIETY AND REVIVALS IN ROCHESTER,
NEW YORK, 1825-1837

CHAPTER 20.

"Why-ever so disgruntled, Mrs. Mellon?" my patient asked the instant I arrived this day.

I did not think my moods were so well-writ on my countenance, and told her this fact.

"They are. Now, where-ever have you been?"

"Why do you ask? Am I a dawdler? A laggard? A johnny-come-lately?"

She replied no, I was as punctual as ever (a queer thing to say considering she had no timepiece). "But your hem, Mrs. Mellon, it's sopped with wet, and you have a tired gait, thus you must have been walking longer than usual, and you look, as I said, disgruntled, as one does when an errand is thwarted or goes awry."

I reminded myself to compose my features better before arrival. "I'm not disgruntled. I'm rag and bone tired. I have trooped up and up these tenement stairs twenty-odd times now. And I am amazed, to be frank, that I have not yet keeled over from exhaustion. And if you must know, I've been to the Spiritualist Society."

"The Spiritualist Society? Why in tunket did you do that, you busy-bird? I asked you not to. I did!" She thumped her fists as she was wont to do when in a temper.

"Oh, don't get all-afret, they refused to lend any help. Not a name. Not a nickel for your funeral, not even advice on the rites of you Spiritualist sorts." I should add that I usually abide closely by my patients' requests, but her tellings had given me a scattered sense, an uncertainty even, of the specifics of my duty. And then I could not get that sorry bird of yesterday out of my head. Indeed I had slept not a jot from hearing over and over (in my imaginings) the soft thud as the little creature hit the window, and from visioning the benumbed and helpless fashion the bird hunched on the ledge over vasty space.

She looked over, her expression rueful, even contrite. "I'm not terribly surprised they refused to help, given all my confessions and accusations and all my tell-alls. And then, of course, there was the recanting, which confused all and sundry even further. And so, what did the Society's gatekeepers have to say of me?"

I busied myself with portioning her medicine. "This, that and the other."

"Come now, I am past concerns, tell me 'the other,' at the least."

I banged down her medicine bottle. "Ah, so now you want to hear from me, the busy-bird?"

"Yes, and I apologize, I do, for calling you that."

"Then, then, if you must know, they said that you lie. They warned me not to believe a syllable you utter. A beet-faced man, he called you a sot and said you would do anything for a drop of laudanum. What gentleman would say such a thing? Then this woman, oh, she was homely as a stone fence, she sneered that you were vengeful and that 'dear' Leah had only been trying to help her wretched sisters. And this woman, she insisted, too, that your marriage to Dr. Kane was ever in question and that you only wanted to wallow in his grand fame and be celebrated alike to him."

"Damn-it-all, my marriage to Elisha was true and legal. We were——"

"And I said it was a nonsense religion, your Spiritualism. All-up superstition. One may as well believe in fairies or hobgoblins."

"I see and——"

"And then I said good-day cool as an icebox, and told them that *Mrs. Elisha Kent Kane* and I would manage cracking-fine on our own."

My patient looked past me to the garret vestibule, at the Edison bulb crackling there. "Elisha," she said, as if the man himself had strolled in, and at an expected hour.

From Mrs. Leah Fox Fish
78th West 26th, New York

To Miss Margaretta Fox
Webb Union Hotel, Philadelphia

14 October, 1852

Dearest Margaretta,

How are the spirits and their beloved mortals—that is to say,
our clients—faring in Philadelphia? I am sorry for the
disagreement we had just before your departure. You were
quite right to take Mother and embark on a personal tour in
response to the requests from the many upstanding believers
in that gracious city. I merely hope that you and mother are
keeping up with all requests and scheduling and the arduous
business of it all.

Now, if I may be so bold: Do remember to keep the
disrespectful and disbelieving away from your door. And do
not neglect to take your morning breaks for study—you may
need secondary skills one day should your spirit powers falter.
And, most importantly, do not allow any young bachelor sorts
to patronize your sittings more than twice. Such men are not
interested in amorphous spirits. They only feign interest so
that they may ogle your more corporeal charms, as I am sure
you realize now you have turned the mature age of nineteen
and are, as you said so clearly before you left "able to manage
my own d_____ self without harping from you, or from that
busy-bird Lemira Kedzie, or from anyone at all." I agree
completely. When we sent Lemira packing out of Cleveland,
I feared that in her disgruntlement she might peck our eyes
out with that sharp, lengthy nose of hers.

Another item: Do not worry on how Katie and I are faring
in New York. We have Calvin and Alfie to help us and I am

considering taking on a personal maid. It must be said that moving here, as we all agreed together this summer past, has been best for our entire family. The sit-for-raps, as the New Yorkers have so jargoned them, are all the rage and our brownstone boasts lines of clients each and every day, and these clients are often of the wealthiest and most upstanding circles. Indeed Mr. Partridge, the match magnate, is chanced to become one of our most faithful clients, but only, I suspect, if Katherina can see fit to bar the spirits of his workers, whose constant complaints about the phossy jaw are becoming alike a tedious song. Might you join me, Margaretta, in convincing our sister that West 26th is our private home, not a Union Hall? She seems particularly concerned about the spirit of a young boy who died in a factory mishap, an explosion, I believe. He reminds her, she says, of our little nephew Charlie, though I cannot see how, as little Charlie is quite alive thanks to me.

Do write me as promptly as you are able. I look forward to your return. Though your affection is an every-changing tune, *my* affection is a constant one, as is my desire that we stay in harmony of purpose and mind, even when apart.

I am sealing this now for Calvin to post. My clients are arriving and they are asking I play *The Vale Of Our Own Genesee*, a lovely, melancholy song that does remind me of Rochester and the unforgettable times we all of us had there, together.

> All love and kisses to Mother
> Your faithful sister, Leah

Maggie sets aside Leah's letter on the tortoiseshell tray. The owner of the Webb hotel, a gimlet-eyed man with slick-curled hair, brought this tray up to Maggie himself, along with a breakfast of devilled eggs and champagne and an invitation to a Philadelphian soiree that Maggie turned down with the aloof politeness she has honed over the last year in response to all manner of male impertinence.

Maggie takes a drink of champagne, says to the letter, "Now, Leah, as for that Mr. Partridge, I can only hope Kat *does* pry an apology out of him." After all, Maggie thinks, Leah was the one who went on about the "greater good" in Cleveland. And this, along with a recent influx of aggrieved spirits has made both Maggie and Katie realize that the needs of the living and dead do not always match up like a pair of store-bought shoes. The living most often want succour, yes. But the dead? They often want justice these days, or at least contrition from the living, an apology or two. And, really, Maggie wonders, why can't Mr. Partridge just apologize to that burned-up boy, even if he wasn't to blame for the boy's death? An apology would show that the man has heart, that he is capable of insight and humility, that he is more than just a moneyed prat. And then, who knows? That poor little ghost might just leave him be.

She finishes her champagne and her devilled oysters, then rises and looks about the table for a napkin; none are in sight, and so she discreetly wipes her fingers on the tablecloth instead. She would have used Leah's letter for the task, but her sister's writing paper is too heavy and thick for wiping. Maggie smiles ruefully at this thought, then opens up her book of German verbs. Her first clients are not due until the afternoon, and thus she can enjoy some peace and quiet here at this elegant suite, the bridal suite, as it happens. "Not that a lady need be a bride, with a groom or husband or, well, I mean. Ah, your key!" Such is what the hotel owner stuttered when Maggie and her mother booked in two weeks ago. He roved his gimlet-eyes about Maggie's person, slicked down his already slick hair. He clearly had no idea where to slot Maggie in his understanding of women. She socializes with upstanding citizens, but she is not a member of high society. She "works" and earns money, but she is not a lowly governess or factory girl. She is celebrated and applauded, but she is not a brazen actress or chorus girl. Oh, Maggie could see him silently puzzling out the conundrum. She didn't care, not much anywise. She is accustomed to dwelling, as the spirits do, in some nebulous, unnamed stratum.

Maggie looks up as Mother, accompanied by several whomevers, bustles into the suite. "They've just come on a social call, Margaret dear. They know we're not taking clients until after one o'clock, don't they?"

They do, and are happy to wait so that they are the first in line to question their dead relations.

"I'll ring that nice owner and ask him to bring us up some more oysters and tea cakes," Mother tells Maggie. "Yes, and you continue studying your French."

"Not French, I gave up on French," Maggie reminds her, and opens her book and shivers in her dress, an out-of-season white muslin trimmed with illusion (she had meant to wear her brown sateen, but it had been soiled by a claret spill).

"And no more champagne, Maggie Fox. Leah says it wreaks havoc on your constitution, doesn't she?"

"All the time," Maggie grumbles, and takes up the book and sits by the suite's one arched window, in the nimbus of its October light. Warmed now, she peels the undersleeves of her white dress off the pale length of her forearms, then forces her attention to her German verbs, determined to find a pattern within their shifting, unpredictable rules for the past, present and future tenses. *Werde sein. Wirst sein. Wird sein.*

The air thins.

She does not look up. Spies him, instead, out of her eye's corner. He stands in the doorway as if pole-axed—a slight, handsome man with startlingly blue eyes and extravagant whiskers, and dark hair that hangs to his collar in bohemian fashion. He is obviously of high station, given his fine, all-black suit. And he is obviously staring at her. Maggie often endures such blatant masculine stares; thus she has taken to considering her "self" as dwelling in a private room. She will exit this room when she chooses, no sooner. But this man's stare is a battering ram. Maggie looks out the arched window to the Philadelphian street, its squeezed-high houses, the red-gold palette of its few trees. The sky is an impossible cerulean blue; the same shade, she realizes, as the eyes of this presumptuous man.

The man apologizes to Maggie's mother. Claims he has made a mistake. He is looking for the spirit raisers.

"You've found them, haven't you?" Mother says. "We are they. Or is it 'them'? Anywise, we're not taking anyone till after one. And who are you, if I may ask, sir?"

"Forgive me," he says, and utters his name. Maggie still refuses him attention. She turns back to her book of German verbs. The sun warms her neck, her spine. Meanwhile, the whom-evers in the room exclaim and gather closer to this man, this Dr. Elisha Kent Kane. He has no need to boast. The whom-evers do it for him.

"His father is Judge Kane, and wasn't his mother a famous beauty in her time?" asks a woman with a blithe, high voice.

"She was Miss Jane Leiper. Lafayette escorted her to a dress ball when he toured here. She went as Mary Queen of Scots. Everyone knows this," says the usual know-all man found in every congregate of souls.

"Wasn't the doctor in the Mexican war? I heard he was sent on a secret mission of some kind to get rid of General Pot, or was it Scots?"

"Scots. And it's hardly secret if everyone knows of it," says Know-All.

"And hasn't he explored the seven continents?" continues Blithe Voice. "And didn't he climb a Chinese volcano of some sort and meet, too, the heathen King of Dahomey? And wasn't he the one who cured the Sultan of Whampoa, or was it Goa? And, yes, that was it, he nearly died in a fall when he was trying to scale a statue in Karnack."

"It was the fall out of the barge on the Nile that nearly killed him," Know-All declares. "And it was not a Chinese volcano, it was in Talel. Is no one listening to me?"

"And isn't he returning to the Arctic to find Sir Franklin, this time with his own ship under his own command?" Blithe-Voice asks, clearly not listening at all.

"My, my, but that Arctic!" puts in an elderly female voice. "Such a terrible place! Imagine an ice-wagon the size of a continent!"

"Not his own ship—Grinnell's ship, the *Advance*," Know-All says, exasperated. "Henry Grinnell is sponsoring the second expedition, just as he did the first. The papers are full of it. One only has to read them."

"My, my, but is there anything the man cannot discover?" Elderly-Voice wonders.

Maggie lays a red ribbon in the pages. Closes the book with a sigh.

Mother says to the whom-evers, "My daughter doesn't read those vulgar newspapers, does she? I don't allow it. She has her studies to attend to." She turns to Dr. Kane. "We can't make exceptions. You understand, don't you?"

"Forgive me, of course," he says. Then presses and cajoles, and soon enough, Maggie finds herself seated at the table with this Dr. Elisha Kent Kane. Mother and several whom-evers are seated with them. Maggie promptly forgets about their presence, her attention caught up with this celebrated man.

"I wish to know of my brother," Elisha says, though in a bored manner, as if he doesn't wish to in the least.

"Do we need the alphabet board, Maggie? Do we?" Mother asks.

"No, no, " she replies, at which the knocks sound on the table, then the walls. Maggie cants her head towards Elisha, "He is in Heaven, your dear Willie."

"You know his name? Impressive."

"*I* do not know it."

"Thus he is in Heaven. Capital to have the intelligence. And how old is he, in Eternity?"

"Fifteen. He hopes you are proud of his death. He tried for a good death, a brave one, so that your mother would not be so grieved."

Elisha studies his cuffs.

Knocks sound along the floor, an interior rain. "And he says he's forgiven you completely," Maggie adds.

"But I did not, that is, I did not apologize."

"There's no need now, really, it's clear you're sorry."

"Miss Fox. I came here to merely, merely to . . . no matter. Now I must—"

"He loves you. Willie. He knows you did all you could to save him."

Elisha pinions her with his blue gaze. "You are a riddle of a girl, Miss Fox. Yet this much is also obvious: this is no life for you."

Elisha comes again, this time with his colleagues—men of learning and high standing—bearded and amused, professional discoverers all. They don't worry Maggie. But Elisha? It is as if he has already discovered her.

He says to his colleagues, "She may help us find Sir Franklin. Then we needn't brave towers of ice and days of endless night. We

need merely sail the *Advance* to the spot and bid him a capital day."
Elisha says this seriously, yet he gives Maggie the slightest smile.
Maggie gives the slightest smile back. Feels a grand relief. He is not
pursuing her, then, not in that fashion.

And the sum of the spirits' knowledge about Sir Franklin? He
may be alive. Or. He may be dead.

"Much like any of us," Elisha muses. During a break for tea he
passes Maggie a note: *Were you ever in love?*

Ask the spirits, she writes back, suppressing a laugh.

Is this him? The one she has imagined so often of late? He is
thirty to her nineteen, true. But he *is* handsome and though not
overly tall he gusts with energy and confidence. And he is heroic,
though not, it must be said, a true hero yet. That will come when he
finds Sir Franklin. When he conquers the Arctic for America.
Maggie knows this because she *does* read the newspapers, though
always once Mother is asleep. Mostly she reads the obituaries, but
also the Society Page, and the news both local and foreign, there
being much to keep up with in these hectic times.

Maggie's outings with Elisha throughout November involve numerous carriage rides about Philadelphia and its environs. For chaper-
ones they have Maggie's mother and Elisha's valet, William Morton,
a ruddy Irish youth with pea-green eyes.

Elisha tells Maggie of the fever that nearly killed him at sixteen.
"The physician said that with my injured heart I should never reach
thirty and so my father advised me that if I must die young, I should
die in the harness. I couldn't agree with a sentiment more." Elisha
strokes his jaw. "But God, I despise being ill. I want to leap out of
my skin, to not waste a day, and this because each day has been given
me for some greater purpose. I feel that as a certainty, Miss Maggie.
Did you know that I am a veritable connoisseur of fever? I've survived rice fever, Nile fever, rheumatoid fever, septic fever even,
after the lance wound in Mexico. Sometimes I think of Death as a sly
uncle. Pocket watch in hand. Tapping with his cane. 'Get on with it,
boy! No time to waste. Get yourself a name!' Any second he'll snap
his watch shut, and . . . it's not fair. I've more to do than most men.

I do. It's why I carry on with five, six projects at once. I feel like one of those Indian deities with their many arms whirling about and brandishing tools and weapons and, ah, forgive me, death is a tiresome topic, let us speak of life."

And he does talk Life, henceforth. Talks of what he will do, not of what has been. Doesn't boast overly, as Maggie presumed he would, of his adventures abroad. And when she talks, he attends her every word. And every day he writes her letters, even on the days when they meet.

On this particular day he writes: *You are a strange mixture of child and woman, of simplicity and cunning, of passionate impulse and extreme self control.*

Maggie peers into a looking glass. He sees me thus, but am I thus? It is an odd, disjointed feeling to be seen so differently from one's own perceptions. Cunning? With passionate impulses? He makes her sound so intriguing. She has a modest wit, a decent penmanship, a face prettier than some. She knows that. But she does not have Leah's musical gifts, nor Katie's ethereal beauty. And besides talking to the dead, she can't claim supernatural talents either, unlike Leah, who sees thoughts captioned over people's heads. Unlike Katie, who seems to hear the utterances of insensate objects. Unlike Mother even, with her knowledge of the old magic, its spells and remedies.

Maggie puts down the looking glass. Leastways Elisha sees her as something more than a nervous battery, a blank conduit to the Other Side. A witch. In time, he might see her as a nice, ordinary girl, caught up in extraordinary circumstances, which is how she sees herself.

At the beginning of December, Elisha departs for New York for several days, on exploring business, he explains. Maggie now has time to write to Katie of this admirer, of their outings, of his presents—white camellias, white handkerchiefs, a white ermine stole so well dressed the creature seems to breath at her neck. All this white because of the white dress she wore when he first beheld her sitting by the arched window of the Webb hotel. "And you were haloed by golden light, alike the spirit of light herself," he told her. "And so raptly attentive to your book of French poetry."

"Oh, it was a German one, a manual, on verbs."

"An irrelevance."

5 December, 1852

Dear Kat,
. . . and Elisha is so interesting! And such fun. He can do impersonations even better than you or me. He did one of a fussy old lady that had me in stitches. You'll just adore him!

Maggie writes his name slowly, twice dipping her pen to ensure the name is dark and bold and lavish. *Elisha Kent Kane*. Before she can post the letter, however, she receives one from Katie. It is much more coherent than usual, but then Katie, like Maggie, has so improved her speech and deportment and mature habitudes that it could never be guessed that their father is an out-of-work black-smith, their place of origin a back-country hamlet where the domin-ion of night is still respected and feared.

11 December, 1852

Dearest Old Mag,
A very pleasant gentleman named Dr. Kane called on Leah and me. He said he met you and Ma in Philadelphia, and he has offered to escort me from the railway to the Camden steamboat and then all the way back to Philadelphia to see you. Oh, I can barely wait! I want every detail!

How has Elisha managed it? Maggie wonders. As if he can be every-where at once. As if he is one boot step in front of her.

Four days later, and Morton, Elisha's valet, opens the carriage door for Maggie, Mother and Elisha, and they rattle-tattle out of Philadelphia along the newly laid macadam. Elisha has not yet told them where they are bound, only that it is a place near to his heart's heart. The mid-December sun is glaucous and unseasonably warm. The tattered snow shows its under-green.

Elisha wraps his overcoat over Maggie's shoulders. "Your deli-cate form! Such wintry air!"

Maggie decides against telling him that as children she and Katie used frosted windows for writing slates; that they were quite accustomed to wintry air, both inside and out. *Get Gone* was what they scratched on the kitchen panes one frigid Hydesville morning a few weeks before the peddler came to them. Their mother gasped in terror at sight of the ghostly script, and this was of keen amusement to both Maggie and Katie. Recalling this and other past collusions, Maggie wishes again that Katie could have joined them today, but her sister was exhausted from her journey to Philadelphia by steamboat and rail and wanted only to curl up with a toddy and then a mulled wine. "Just give me all the hoary old details," she told Maggie.

"There shall be a small ramble," Elisha announces as the hired carriage passes the gatehouse of the Laurel Hill Cemetery. The main of the cemetery is carved out of a vertiginous hill that overlooks the broad and abiding calm of the Schuylkill River. They walk down and down, and then along a cat-scratch path. Statuary blends into the ashen sky. Neat rows of evergreens alternate with wild groves. A crow caws and a woman in mourning black kneels at a plot of four small graves.

The tombs and cenotaphs are of modest size and are over-clasped with hawthorn and ivy. Elisha explains to Maggie how there is room aplenty for many more dead, of any religious persuasion. For this cemetery, unlike the old-fashioned churchyards, welcomes all and sundry.

Maggie replies, "How interesting," and "How modern." She is sincere. Because it *does* sound as new information when Elisha tells of it. She certainly doesn't mention how she spends time aplenty in cemeteries and graveyards studying the epitaphs scripted on gravestones and the like, and has done so ever since Leah took her and Katie to Rochester's Hope Cemetery and bid them make a game of recalling dates, names, beloved remembrances.

Elisha halts them up before a tomb that boasts Grecian columns, a cartouche of flying doves, a statue of a woebegone cherub. "Of what are these monuments made?" Elisha asks.

Maggie taps the cherub's stunted wings. "Granite?"

"Forgive me, I didn't mean what material of the gross earth, my pet, but rather what ideals."

"Of course. I see. It's just that I remember my pa talking about granite. Where he came from in Rockland County there was such a bucket-lot of it. I recollect him saying that if you dug anywhere you'd ring into it straightaways. He said Rockland was a fine-all place for a gravestone carver to live, but no one else."

Elisha chuckles. Was what she said so humorous? With Elisha, when she attempts wit he looks displeased. When she attempts gravity, he laughs.

"A monument crumbles to dust, Tuttie. And when it does, all that remains are the remembrances of a man's valiant deeds. Valour, mind, is not enough in these modern times. A man must invent, discover, reveal! A man must leave a legacy to be immortal. These stones—which are marble, actually—are naught but dreams made manifest."

Maggie looks again at the cherub. He is grey and coarse-grained, but, ah, Elisha must be correct. Marble he must be. But would Mother think so? She does know her rocks, Maggie recalls, and even had a collection of "curiosity" stones lining her herb garden back in Hydesville. At this thought, Maggie looks down to where Mother, escorted by Morton, pauses to rest on a grave slab some distance behind. Elisha follows Maggie's gaze and then makes a complicated gesture that would not be amiss in charades. Morton nods and sits aside his charge and directs her attention to where a barge endeavours to ford the distant river.

Elisha whispers into Maggie's hair, "Close your eyes, my pet. Open them only when I give word." Maggie obliges, and then allows him to steer her over the path. She hears the seep-seep of a winter bird, the rustling of Elisha's trousers, the squeak of his boots, the creak of her corset, the thud of her heart, and another thud-thudding—an inconstant, palpitate sound. The heart of Elisha? It must be so. Her attenuation to this sounding world happens in a nonce. And if she waits, and if she strives, she can become as one blinded at birth. Listen: the funeral monuments are slowly crumbling; the worms are moistly chewing; the wind is sawing at branches, and that, in the far-off, is the ring of the gravedigger's shovel finding stone, frozen ground. Maggie squeezes her eyes shut even tighter. Surely below these soundings are murmurs, whispers, sighs.

"Open your lovely orbs."

She does and the soundings cease, as does the sense of solid ground. She looks down. Gasps. Her shoes are halfway over the edge of a small ravine. She gives a little shriek and clutches onto Elisha.

"I was holding your skirt, my dove, I'd not ever let you fall. Now, look there."

Across the ravine a small vault protrudes from the hillside. The roof is thick with brambles, the sides heaped with cut stones. "It is yet in the process of creation," Elisha explains.

"What a handsome thing," she says. Because it is: inventive and elegant and welcoming in its copse of trees.

"That is our family crypt. That is where my beloved brother Willie rests. I should be resting there instead of him, so our mother said. She was quite correct. I'm the one who was prophesied to die young, after all, and thus she had expected my death. Indeed, she was quite prepared for my death, but not for his, no. God, but her grief was terrible to see! She blamed me, of course, for not saving him. And Willie was brave, just as you envisioned, Maggie-pet. He wanted to know if he bore the sick-pains as well as I had my own wounds. He even managed to compose his own funeral music. He was a talented musician for his fifteen years. My mother loves music, too, you see, but this exploring and discovery business . . . well, she considers it a ridiculous occupation for a grown man."

Elisha falls quiet, and studies her face. Maggie regards him back, her expression grave, unflappable, and deeply interested—the same expression she uses to entice her clients to speak further. This time, however, she *is* deeply interested.

"I tried every remedy I knew," Elisha continues. "But at times it seems these physician's hands aren't even mine, but those of a puppet who is being worked by some other agent."

"I know the sense of that," Maggie says, and leans her head on his shoulder as he likes her to do.

Elisha gathers himself. "Ah, but mothers always love one child more than another."

Do they? Maggie has seen no evidence of this with her own mother. Her father clearly loves Leah best, but that hardly signifies:

men's hearts are known to be conditional. Of a sudden Maggie appreciates her own mother very much.

"I didn't mean to speak of all that," Elisha adds. "But then you make me talk, a talent needed I should think in your, hmm, profession. But I brought you here, Miss Maggie Fox, not to grouse on about mothers, but to tell you . . . to ask you, rather, if this might be your final resting place. Do you take my drift?"

Maggie, dizzied with joy, says she does.

"Capital! Splendid! But first you must devote herself to an education, so as to fit an entirely different sphere."

"Sphere?"

"Yes, my dove, a sphere, a round . . . Anyways, after you are educated, then I shall be proud to make you my heart's eternal keeper."

"But I'm educated, I read. And I—"

"And you must resolve to leave all that surrounds you, to forget the past, and think only how you can become worthy of one whose existence shall be devoted to you." He speaks of Maggie's need to sacrifice and strive as he does. Looks for once uncertain. "I need tell you of a slight difficulty. My mother has threatened . . . that is, has chosen an Intended for me already."

"An Intended?" Maggie's breath draws tight. "But are *we* not now—"

"Hush. Yes. We are. And I shall forthwith inform my mother that my heart is bound with another's."

"But when do we—"

Elisha hushes her again, then indicates Mother and Morton, who have just hoved up.

Mother, ignoring Morton's gentle protests, says, "But I didn't want to sit on that bench all the square day, did I? Oh, is this where we're to picnic? What a lovely crypt over that ravine. Don't you think, Maggie-lamb?" She taps a nearby statue of a weeping angel. "Oh, and I do so like all the lovely granite."

CHAPTER 21.

"Kat was soon calling Elisha 'Mr. Intrigue,' and not without cause." At that my patient put down a ten of clubs (we were playing cards, but a game of our own invention, with our own rules). "He ever wanted to avoid talk" she continued, "and so he used Morton, his valet, for an intermediary. I had to fold my letters this way or that according to our agreed upon meanings. I had to recall the blinking light codes he, or more often Morton, made with a carry lantern at night outside my window. Two blinks meant he was arriving soon. Three blinks meant he was feeling poorly. He often did, poor Lish, a result I suppose of all those exotic fevers he suffered when discovering abroad."

"I'm sure," I said, and put down the King, which was a wild card, as we had agreed. "Your go, duck."

"Oh, and I had to learn little code words. And I had to pretend, oft-times, that we were minor acquaintances." My patient finally looked at the fan of cards in her own hand. "You've won again!"

"Well, I do play often. Many of my indigents like to play. It helps pass the time before, that is, the final time."

"Of course."

"I would not otherwise play cards."

"Well, no."

"Although I cannot imagine why it's considered unladylike; it's merely a game, and enjoyable, to be frank, when one wins."

"Hah! You sound like Leah. She played cards like a regular black-leg. Few people knew that. Chauncey never did, unfortunately for him . . . ah, might you hand me the box, Mrs Mellon?" My patient shuffled her cards back into the deck as she said this (and without ever showing me her hand I should add).

"Careful with the weight, now," I warned, and handed her the box as requested. Presently the bedclothes were strewn with the many clip-outs and pamphlets and dense-worded legal documents concerning this Chauncey Burr, all of which were in that bible box—or rather the lily box—that once was Leah's, and now was hers.

"Peculiar," she murmured as she shuffled through the papers.

"I don't see how. Lawyer documents may be complex and tedious. But never 'peculiar.'"

"Not the papers themselves, but that Leah collected them at all. Or any of these letters and ephemera. What card, as it were, was she playing? I had presumed it was all for pride, as a way to gloat even, over Chauncey's humiliation."

I picked up my knitting and resumed the macking. Her perception, I realized then, was not always as tack-sharp as she might think. "Tell me, duck, what is more peculiar than the heart?"

MARCH OF 1853 AND LEAH gives last-minute advice to her sisters before embarking on her journey to Columbus, Ohio. Her sisters are to remain in New York with Mother. Someone must gratify the clients when she is gone. Still, upon departure Leah cannot deny her anxiety. It is not over the impending court case—she will see Chauncey Burr chewed up and spat out on the judicial floor, of that Leah has no doubt. Chauncey Burr with his bluster and theatrics is an adversary to be met head-on. No, it is this damn Dr. Kane who troubles her. He is another category of nemesis entirely. Has not sought out Leah, as Chauncey has, but Margaretta, the tremulous undertone of the Fox sisters three. Maggie with her doubts, her mooning over poetry and romantic novels, her diminutive size, which makes even a small man like Kane feel large as a cannon.

And Burr could not convince a starving man to eat soup. Elisha Kent Kane has convinced an entire nation that he—a mere physician with no command experience, a man with a heart as unstable as a grenade, a man plagued by fevers and ill health and an overwhelming sense of his own worth—should be the one to lead the expedition to the Arctic and find that Sir Franklin basking on the warm shores of this fabled Open Polar Sea. No, against Kane, Margaretta hasn't a fiddler's chance in Hell.

Leah wills herself calm. Kane is departing in a mere three months, she reminds herself. Likely he will die of starvation up there in the Arctic, or freeze into an effigy of himself, or be strung up by the natives in the nearest tree. Leah chides herself for this last thought. There are no trees in the Arctic, as everyone knows.

Leah's sister Maria huffs up to her. She is busy chasing after little Charlie, who is long back to health and jack-mischief since Leah's intervention in Cleveland. Maria and Charlie are again being useful as escorts, at keeping minds from sliding into idle gossip. For here is Calvin, hoisting Charlie onto his broad shoulders. Calvin came to Leah just before they left for Columbus. He reminded her of the confection shop he would have one day, once this spirit business is concluded and all their battles won. "What I mean to say is that I intend to earn a decent income. Lizzie can return and we can regroup and be together. I can make you happy, honour bright I can. What I mean, dear Leah, is I—"

"There are other things in life besides happiness," Leah interrupted, but kindly.

Happiness, Leah muses now. Never has an ambition seemed more paltry. She makes her stately way around the crowded boat. Is serenaded by the hock-splat of chewing tobacco hitting the water, the chatter of passengers and sky birds. The day is fine and many people have staked out deck chairs. She spots a rotund woman of mature years. The woman's sleeved cloak is of richest indigo, her sober bonnet touched with sable. A doctor's wife, Leah quickly learns. They discuss the weather and the unfortunate presence of riff-raff on board. Leah voice is as serene as the passing waters and agreeable to anything the woman has to say.

The doctor himself joins them. He is as sheeny and plump as an oyster. He proclaims himself Mrs. Fish's servant and prods an old-fashioned monocle onto his eye. "Look there, ladies! Aside the berm." He points to an ordinary, white-flowered shrub. "*Rhododendron oblongifolium* in all its glory."

Leah turns to the doctor's wife. "My heavens, but your husband is a remarkable naturalist."

The doctor flushes with pride and scrutinizes the dull shrub until it passes from sight. In every congregate of human souls, Leah discovers people who are respectable, upstanding, reputable. Such people might not wear the latest fashions; they might not be well known in society, nor even speak with much eloquence. Still, Leah recognizes them. She feels safe when they are near, as if their reputations are a fortress. Leah has never yet unwittingly made the acquaintance an adulterer, a liar, an embezzler, a drunkard, a gambler, a charlatan or quack.

Leah thanks the doctor and his wife and excuses herself. She beckons to Maria, who is helping Charlie dangle a makeshift fishing line over the low rail, and then to Calvin, who is promptly at her side. "This air, ah!" he proclaims. "It's like a good slap in the face. Or a dawn revel. Leah, would you object if I volunteered my assistance at the approaching locks? The captain is short of hands and—"

"No need to shout, Calvin, and if you must go jumping about you need eat more. Honestly, you're thin as a beanpole." She offers to cook him lunch on their portable stove. He looks at her in admiration, as if offering lunch were a great talent. Dear, loyal Calvin. He is the only one of their intimate group who is helping her to face Chauncey Burr. She puts her hand on his gangly arm. He covers her hand with his own.

"Darling Leah, I—"

She pulls her hand out from under his. Cocks her head, looks at the sky. "Shhh. Listen."

"I don't hear . . . ah, yes!"

Excitement shifts down the boat. A crewman demands quiet. Another calls out that there is some time yet. He is ignored. Men search their rucksacks and valises. The ruffian sorts merely reach under their coats. Soon the boat bristles with pistols and rifles, and hums with talk of strategy.

"Damn, I've nothing to fire," Calvin says.

Leah gasps.

"I shouldn't have cussed. Forgive me for it, but gosh!"

Leah's doctor friend appears at her elbow. He has an extra Colt.

"An actual Colt," Calvin whoops, and proclaims he now has a sporting chance.

Maria tries to quiet little Charlie, who hops about with expectation. The crew primes lanterns and hangs them in readiment. Children gather at the prow. On the canal all boating traffic slows. On the berm the hoggees tether the mules. On the road aside the berm, all conveyances halt. And in the fields the farmers wait, inert as scarecrows, armed to the teeth.

The lamps are lit.

The children yell and point to the south. A tattered blackness ridges the half-world. The muffled sound becomes a deafening cacophony.

"Ready your fire!" shouts a crew member.

"*Ectopistes migratorius*!" shouts the doctor. "In all their glory!"

The pigeons are overhead now, are as dense as a thundercloud. The sun is eclipsed and a weird grey light falls. The birds have come on faster than any horse could run or any train could steam. Millions upon millions. Their droppings fall like a rank snow. Their wings create a whirling, agitated wind. Skirts sashay. Hats tumble off heads. The air shakes with gunshots, thickens with gun-smoke. The flock splits into immense, conjoined coils, becomes a writhing hydra, glinting purple and green. The children scream in delighted terror. The shot birds rain into the water and trees and fields. Many plunge onto the deck, where the children crush the birds' skulls with their little heels. One bird falls stunned near Leah. She kneels to pick it up, holds it gently. A male. Red feet. Red eyes. He stabs vainly at her with his slender black beak. No other pigeons are so large, nor so beautiful. His belly is rose and white. His throat and neck an iridescence of purple and bronze and green.

Leah tosses the bird over the side. Prays he escapes to the trees. He does not. A shot and he plummets into the canal waters. Leah snorts in anger and yanks on Maria's arm and then on Charlie's. "Below! We must below. This is no place for us."

They come reluctantly, but Calvin stays for the sport, slip-sliding in blood and bird droppings.

Leah stretches in her bed slot. Charlie pouts and counts out his fingers. Maria lights their portable stove, making tea at Leah's behest. No soporifics. Leah must remember that, because her head-pain is returning with the retort of the pistols and rifles and the reek of gun-smoke. She wads her ears with cotton batting. She has a strange and fierce affection for birds in general, but for the passenger pigeons in particular. So many shooting at them, so few to protect them. Their passing is not as it was; will only take a day and not three, as it had when Leah was a girl and she waited for their arrival with greater anticipation than her siblings awaited Christmastide.

"Come, Leah-Lou," her father said when Leah was a child of nine. "We'll get us some pigeons." They took the flat-wagon to the edge of the forest. She recalls how she gaped at the sight before her, how the vast cylinder rolled over the forest and reached to the horizon's bounds. "A fifty-miler," her father said with satisfaction. He spat tobacco, poured powder into his flintlock.

First, young Leah smelled the reek that obliterated all other odours. Then heard the tumult of coos that was like the ringing of every bell in God's heaven, then witnessed the massive branches of the oaks and elms breaking under the weight of the nesting birds. Five hundred, even a thousand to each tree and their droppings were a fantastical white quilt. The forest would be devastated in their wake.

Her father caught a pigeon and sewed shut its eyes, the rivulets of blood like copious tears. He tied a small stool to its legs, then tossed the bird into the field where the farmers stood at the ready with nets and with pots that spewed out poisonous sulphur. The stool pigeon flew low and erratic with the weight, crying piteously. Leah ran from her father's side to the forest's edge and held fast to a stump. Her father was talking with the farmers and did not see her until she was too distant.

"Come back, you damned idjit!" he yelled. Too late. The guns had fired to startle the birds and make them notice their companion and so follow him low in his distress. And then it was as if the soul of the forest had lifted out. Leah was immersed, not in darkness, but in a dazzle of copper, green and white as the sunlight struck the feathers. Wings beat at her with the power and swiftness of angels' wings and she screamed out in horror and wonder as the birds lifted her in flight. She woke earthbound and in the same spot. She was badly bruised and her forearms were cross-hatched with deep wounds, the scars of which she bears even yet.

Her father wrapped her in his greatcoat and carried her back to the flat-wagon. She remembers how he shook, how his coat smelled of tobacco and ale. They came home with enough for a year of smoked-pigeon pies. Leah was sent to bed. She slept until Maria appeared, her black, button eyes staring. "Here, Pa told me to bring you supper . . . Oh, and *now* why are you crying on?"

"How could he have betrayed them all? That bird. Even if I had my eyes sewn shut I wouldn't betray mine own."

"Sakes alive, Leah, if your eyes were sewn shut you, you wouldn't know what you were doing, would you?"

Now Leah sips her tea. The gunfire on the deck has slowed, either from boredom or from lack of ammunition. Though the farmers and village dwellers will continue to fire as long as the flock is in sight. The majority of the carcasses will be sold to the Southern plantations for slave food. The birds captured alive will be sold to the firing ranges.

"Maria, do you recall when I was caught up in the pigeon's flight?"

Maria looks at her. Her eyes still remind Leah of black buttons. "Surely. I recall you convalescing like a princess and I had to do your chores for a good week."

Leah sniffs and calls Charlie over for an embrace. Thinks: No wonder I was not afraid of the mob at Troy like Maggie was. No wonder I am not terrified of human mobs at all. Who would be after such an experience? Who wouldn't feel protected by the multitude by some uncanny luck?

MULTITUDES, I THOUGHT, as my patient spoke of Leah and the passenger pigeons; it is a handy word to employ when numbering loses meaning. Consider the "multitudes" lost in the abolition war. Oh, there was some attempt at tallying the dead. Thus one can read that approximately twenty-three thousand fell at Shiloh. Twenty-six thousand at Antietam; fifty thousand at Gettysburg. Approximations. Souls rounded up or down. Where was their luck, uncanny or otherwise? Their guarding angels? Their watching gods?

I considered the scarf in my lap. Why had I not knitted the lines tighter? Even a paltry rain would come through. "Rot and nonsense. It won't be any kind of useful."

"What do you mean? Mrs. Mellon. Ah, your scarf. Well, let it become something else, then."

I didn't answer straightaway. They were looking askance, I thought, the gods, the angels, the lucky this and that. They were tending oblivion. Worse, they were, and are, imagined only. We, the dominion of souls, are unguided. A multitude alike the passenger pigeons, winging hither and yon and without true understanding or intent.

"A cover-all," I said at last. "Or blanket. That is what it will be. They are ever needed."

My patient agreed.

"So, who won?" I asked, and sighed, and began again with a cast-up stitch. "You have them set to join each other in Columbus," I reminded her. "Your Leah. Her Chauncey.

"BALLS, THAT'S WHAT," Chauncey tells Heman as they lurch in the Concord towards Columbus, Ohio. "She's got them the size of a bloodyo mule. Ten thousand dollars! I'll give her ten thousand thwacks on her fine arse, what ho."

Heman says, "I did mention that calling her a woman of notoriously bad character weren't wise. Not clever neither. There's a line, Chauncey, and if—"

"I'll set fire to everything we own before she sees a damnedo nickel of it. Won't I? Won't I?"

"Everything *we* own?" Heman echoes. He looks with longing at the Concord door.

"I'll see her ruined. I'll see her reputation strung up in the nearest tree, won't I, Hemano? She'll not make a jackass of Chauncey Burr. Not neither a fox-ass, hah."

"Jimmeny Jesus," Heman mutters. "Why'd I leave the dry goods business? Why?"

"Because it was a fucko bore."

At this remark the stout lady across from Chauncey nearly asphyxiates from shock.

"My apologies, madame," Chauncey says, all amiable of a sudden. "I've been unjustly accused. My dander is up. My ire aroused."

The stout lady clutches her carpet bag like a shield. A man in a bang-up coat glowers. Let him call me out for a duel, Chauncey thinks. I'd rather have a fucko hole drilled in my skull than suffer a court dock.

Heman whispers, "It's thanks kindly to your mouth that we're in this rotten pickle. Yup, it is. You're a reverend, recall that? Start acting the part. You were fair good at it once. And convincing besides."

Chauncey agrees with his brother for once. He *had* made a damn fine reverend. He conjures up the high vaulted tent, the sea of people within, and never has a metaphor been more apt. He visions the revivalists arrayed in storm-greys, their hair straggled as seaweed, their faces are whitecaps; their undulate movements a wave's movements; their voices like wind roaring, water crashing, and Chauncey high in his makeshift pulpit, more alike to Neptune than a preacher of the Christian world.

The revivals would tumult into dawn, men and women collapsing and shaking with the spirit. Even yet Chauncey can hear the hallelujahs, the rousing hymns, his own bellowing exhortations. He became an expert at the head-smack that sent a participant into ecstasy. The power of suggestion, that was all. But there'd been no need for such a trick on the baker's wife. She came to him—splendid woman—fearless and broad-beamed. He left before a scandal broke. Before, in fact, she could follow him with her baker's dozen worth of children. Chauncey smiles in nostalgia of those glorious days. Still, is it not better to be a scientist? Is it not better to dine with men who are so learned it takes them half an hour to make one damnedo point? Unlikely the learned men would dine with him now, and all because of those Fox females.

Chauncey sighs and rolls up the window flap and surveys the open countryside. It has been unusually warm for March and the main of the snow is gone. Flowers are thrusting up hither and yon. Birds are making their usual racket. Chauncey squints in disbelief. The entire horizon is heaving and undulating as if to detach from the earth. Ah. The passenger pigeons. He wonders if he should point them out to the others in the Concord. Decides, no. He will take credit for the sighting only if the birds fly overhead. They do not. The line sinks away and Chauncey's eye falls now on an itinerant knife grinder. The grinder ignores the Concord even as it overtakes him. He walks head-down with poverty's defeated gait, which is the gait of itinerants and peddlers the world over, no doubt.

Chauncey swats at a foot dangling from the stage roof. Maggie and Katie Fox said a peddler had been murdered for his money, and that made sense. Who gives a ratter's ass about peddlers, or for itinerants of any stripe? Who marks where they go, or why? Their names are unknown. They have no set residence. And they might as well have *Blame Me* scripted on their backs, so often are they scapegoated. Indeed, if Chauncey were a miscreant, he would choose such men as victims, as had the Fox girls, those cunning little demons. No, society does not respect itinerants, not even itinerant preachers.

Chauncey recalls now a stuttering young circuit rider he'd met— in '32, was it? At the height, anyhow, of all that bullshit and ballyhoo about temperance. The young man, scrawny as a plucked rooster, was just commencing his mission and was yet agog with optimism. Said he was not going to accept donations. "No, s-sir!"

That'll bloodyo change, Chauncey had thought. His advice? "Be God's bulldog. Never accept a reluctant convert. Sinners must be brought to the fold! Or else you fail in God's design." Such blather, but it had seemed the fitting thing to say.

"Th-thank you, s-sir. I'll t-treasure your a-a-advice," he replied, clasping his hands as if he were holding actual words and not just vacant air.

"Oh, and hey-ho there, boyo, get yourself a horse if you aspire to be a circuit rider. Hard to seem above it all when you're squelching in the mud with the downtrodden."

The young man stuttered that he didn't know how to ride. That he couldn't afford a horse anyway. "It's j-just my m-ma and m-me now. And we're a p-poor family, p-poor as Job's t-turkey," he said, as if that explained everything.

Chauncey heard rumours later that the young man was having an exceedingly trying time as a preacher. Well, indeedo. Listening to him stutter out a sermon must have required more patience than Job ever had, never mind his turkey. And then Chauncey heard no more about him. Likely he became a bookbinder or a tailor. Likely he realized, as Chauncey did, that a wanderer had no respect.

Recalling all this Chauncey decides that whether he wins or loses this court battle, he will settle down and marry a good woman of ample charms. Become a professor of something or other. Botany, he decides as the Concord rolls on past an endless wood of what might be chestnut trees or elms. Chauncey sees polecats and deer and bears, now a field of horned cows, now a marsh crammed with ducks. At the edge of this marsh a horse, shod with clogs, balks at crossing while a child beats him with a stick. Chauncey sympathizes with the horse and the boy in equal measure. But then he has a knack for holding contradictory emotions. Particularly for Leah Fox Fish, whom he'd like to ruin and ravish and at the same instance.

"Great damn it!" shouts Heman. A woman screams. The Concord has rounded a curve too fast and now lists precariously on two wheels.

"Now, people!" Chauncey orders. In one practised go, the passengers heap to the high side of the Concord, forcing it back down to four wheels. The passengers then pop back to their own seats, as neatly as corks in a toy gun. The Concord has only tipped over once this trip, the driver seeming more sober than most.

The excitement past, Chauncey stretches out his legs and taps his feet, to the annoyance of the other passengers. He thinks on the brothel in New York, the one recommended by the maid at Barnum's Hotel, the one that specialized in feet. The madame, the maid's aunt, showed him a collection of footwear that made Chauncey appreciate man's ingenuity anew. Research, he told himself. And indeedo, those ladies had some tricks with their toes the Fox females could never imagine. But truly, how did the Fox women manage the constant cracking and snapping? Chauncey's feet were always swollen after his exposes, became so sore and knobbed that at times they barely made a sound. He'd kept the sorry state of his feet secret, of course. But then that Leah had found him out. She or a confederate must have visited his hotel in Cleveland last spring and paid off a porter or waiter. How else could the *Cleveland Plain Dealer* have known of the wretched state of his feet after every demonstration? Why else would the writer have compared his grimaces and scowls when toe-cracking to the Fox ladies'—ah, yes—*placid, blameless countenances when attended by what are indisputably spirit noises given how effortlessly they emit from any room in which the Ladies are sitting*.

Blameless. Blamed. Blasted. Bullshit.

"We shan't lose. Righto, Hemano!"

"'Course," Heman mutters.

Chauncey sighs. It had all been going so well. Mrs. Ruth Culver had been his *coup de grace*. For her name he had to thank that animate clockwork Alfie Kincaid. Chauncey arrived at Ruthie's door on a day of spitting rain. He was accompanied by reputable men—a doctor, a lawyer, a possible minister. The face of Ruth Culver was a map of disappointments, her house the dwelling place of bitterness. It had a smell, bitterness did: vinegar, lye, rapeseed-oil lamps, musty carpets, burned biscuits, rancid butter. She sat bolt upright by a hissing fire. No need to coax a story out of her, no need to offer money, either, though Chauncey gave her three silver dollars. Maggie and Katie, she said, were experts at mimicry. They'd imitate their old mother most cruelly, and their schoolmaster, and their saintly old father. They were far better at repartee than farm girls should have been. And they had a strange language between them.

"What manner of language?" the lawyer asked sharply.

"Couldn't say, but it were strange in my opinion," Ruth Culver replied. "A jumble. It were like something you thought you could recognize but couldn't. Or like to some language you'd forgotten. Not foreign, so much is what I mean. But old."

The possible minister frowned. The doctor looked uneasy. The lawyer scribbled something down. Chauncey steered the conversation away from weird languages and mimicry. What next? Talk of spells? The riding of brooms?

Ruth Culver's every word was scribed down. Was only altered a small bit here, added to there.

"Katie disappointed me, I'll say it again," Ruth said. "Never could get the spirits to locate my ivory comb nor Norman's boot jack. Oh, she helped some with the milking, but she wouldn't raise a tiny hand to help with the cooking. She had the worst case of blanket fever you ever saw."

"Blanket fever?" asked the doctor with a professional air.

"Like none you've ever seen! She'd laze in bed past dawn unless you hollered at her five times. A good whipping would have cured her, in my opinion, but I don't reckon her pa ever whipped that little skeezick once. And those barn cats. She wouldn't let me drown them. Threw an unholy fit. After that, those cats followed her around near everyplace."

"Cats?" echoed the lawyer, the doctor, the possible minister.

"Fortunate I'm not superstitious or I'd nail juniper over my door," the lawyer said as they left the Culvers' yard.

"Horseshoes work just as well," said the possible minister, then quickly added that he was jesting, of course.

The Concord arrives at last in Columbus. Chauncey and Heman search out the courthouse on foot. Get lost twice before finding it on the outskirts. A small crowd specks the steps.

"They've come to see a 'scientist' and a sorceress before a judge of the land!" Chauncey says to Heman. "An honour, isn't it, brother mineo?"

"I suppose," Heman mutters. "Not really, though."

"You hungry? Damn, but I am." And Chauncey's gut is indeed light and hollow. He buys some early-ripe apples from a stall. Nearby, a wainwright kicks at a mangy dog. The dog yelps then slinks off.

"We wait until the last chiming second, righto?" Chauncey continues. "The females aren't the only ones who can make a damnedo entrance, eh?"

The beaten dog has returned. He slinks up to his master, all acringe. The wainwright tosses the dog some gristle, then boot-kicks him again.

Heman watches this, shakes his head. "I'm just hoping we can make an exit."

CHAPTER 22.

"And what of the helpless dog? You mentioned him yesterday. The one outside the courthouse?"

My patient smiled. "What would you like to know?" Her tone, I should add, was all-inviting, alike an open door to a some sun-struck garden.

I understood her tack then, clear as glass. She was luring me to question, as was her lifelong habit. She was fishing for truths beneath. Questions reveal as much as answers, she had said that herself. Or perhaps this Chauncey had. "Nothing. Forget I asked." I said.

She made no reply. She was fast asleep.

I had only asked about the dog because my son had so hated to see dogs beaten or even chained. Consider this: when he was six he padlocked himself to the dog post and let Queenie, our yellow hunter, roam free. My son was weed-thin and tall for his age. He was no great scholar. Not one who promised fine looks. But he was fierce in his idealism even then. He wanted to know, he told me, how it felt for poor Queenie. He'd tossed the key, he confessed, into the shell road aside our cottage. Dark clouds boiled while I searched through those whitened fragments. It began to rain and thunder.

I begged help of Mr. Mellon, but he only laughed and said the larky fool could get lightning struck and wouldn't that teach him a lesson.

"He's not a fool. He's full of good!" I yelled.

"Hah, hah. Much the same," Mr. Mellon said. I could have killed him then, but my hand had alighted on the key, there among the crushed shells and bones of sea-creatures, and I was intent on rushing back to the post and padlock.

I took the half-worked cover-all out of my satchel and studied my patient. Her eyes were fast shut, but I knew she was awake. I could tell by the cadence of her breath, the tension in her hands, the sense withal. Maggie Kane was not the only one who could read a sign or two.

"Are you sleeping, duck?"

She opened her eyes, tugged at her braid. "I should like the lily box," she said abruptly. "I was just thinking about my father. He met the same young man, this Brother Able, the one that Chauncey met, surely. Is not that fated? A meaningful thing. It must be."

"Coincidence," I said, and saw in this another tack of hers: the fixing together of rags and shards to make a tidy sense.

A MID-MARCH IN ARCADIA and the weather is at last allowing John to labour constant on his house. His latest additions are a side pantry and buttery. Next he plans to add a water-closet. It will be inside the house itself and wide enough for this fashion of ever-widening petticoats. And all these plans have a cord-taut urgency. His wife, Leah, Lizzie, Maggie, Katie. It has been five years since the cholera, since his prodigal women spent any notable time at home. But that will soon change.

"This was at the post for you, Pa." The letter is like a playing card in David's massive hand.

John Fox cracks the seal in puzzlement. Adjusts his spectacles. Peers close. Leah. She reports that they have moved into a Manhattan brownstone on a street where the *majority of the ambulatory could find them*. She writes that her court case against the dreaded Reverend Chauncey Burr has been won. She is ten thousand dollars richer; though of course the money cannot repay the grief his slander cost her. And she with all her expenses . . .

His eye skips down. *The flock.*

On the canal, Pa, while I as en-route to the Columbus courthouse. They were returning very early in the season from
where-ever it is they disappear to, and this I could not help
but think is a propitious sign. It was not a unending flock like
those when we lived in Ontario, but still a goodly sized one.
Do you recall when I was lifted up to the heavens? Surely you
do. You were the only living person who witnessed what must
have been a sight wondrous beyond description. I suppose it
will not happen again as I am too grown. And by the by I do
still cherish the bible box you gave me, the one so finely
carved with the lilies entwined. It has been of great use.

Your loving daughter,
Leah

John reads it three times over. Lifted up? To the heavens yet? When the
flock passed over he found her crumpled by the stump where he had
seen her last. She was bloody and senseless and he'd thought her certain
to die. He had nearly begun a wailing when she stirred and smiled.

John folds up the letter, wonders if mayhap she *had* been borne
aloft. The flock had obscured her. It was possible. Anything seems
possible where Leah is concerned.

I should have carved a swarm of pigeons on the lid of her bible
box, he thinks, and visions Leah standing at the canal-boat prow, the
flock a black and tattered cape stretching from her shoulders and
over half the world.

The canals. John lives far from them and now eschews canal
travel completely. Still, even now, if God's grace would allow it, he
would be of the watered world. He walks back into his house. Steps
over the planks and tools and sits at his makeshift desk. He considers
for a while, but a direct response to Leah's letter fails him. Instead,
he takes the scribed papers out of their keeping. Fires the new-hung
betty lamps. Dips a nib.

. . . Year of Our Lord 1825 and you've never seen a
Celebration the like of what marked the opening of the
Canal. Some hundred cannons were booming along its length

entire and there were brass bands playing on the berms, and roman wheels exploding overhead, and flotillas of boats in the harbor of New York, and one of these boats was festooned up like Noah's Ark, complete with stuffed pairs of exotic animals and a pair of bona fide Indian children shivering in their loincloths . . .

Five days later at an Utica barbershop, John met one Erastus Bearcup, captain and owner of the *Morning Star*, a bullheaded boat that hauled flour from Rochester's mills as far as Buffalo in the west and Albany in the east. Erastus wore his mat of dark hair long and pulled back with twine. His beard, stained with tobacco juice, was a shade lighter, and spanned his wide chest and obscured his mouth and crawled up to his cheekbones, above which were eyes of bottle green. For all that, he was a style-setter in this canaller world. Wore red suspenders and red garters over a smocked shirt. Wore a black sack coat, a straw hat banded with paisley, and gummed boots toed with steel.

John had heard of the man, his boat. No scolding wife hanging petticoats out like frilled flags. No thumb-sucking, nappy-shitters tied to the rail so as not to plop overboard. Just a crew of five, men of free ways all.

Erastus finished his whisky and took his place at the barber chair. The barber tossed back his own whisky, then sharpened his razor on a strop.

John spoke in his usual clipped tones. "I can fix near anything. Worked on the locks. Worked in the building yard. I'm a blacksmith by trade. Looking for work as a bowsman now."

Erastus said to the looking glass, "We could use a bowsman. Ours just up and died of some fucking ailment of the heart."

"He damn well drowned." This from a man with a bulbous nose that ill-fit his gaunt face. He returned his attention to a periodical, said, "Keeled off a bridge after a Saturday spree. Not easy to drown in four feet of water, but he always was determined. *Veni, vidi, vici.*"

"That there's the cook, Jeb O'Doul from the Carolinas, he's a swell at the Latin," Erastus explained. "Attend and you might start jawing like a learned man same as him."

"He won't," Jeb said, eyeing John.

"Or I might."

"Why, just for *exempli gratia?*"

"That's it," John said.

"And by the by," Erastus warned. "There's not a fuck-all thing Jeb won't contradict or argue on about."

"There shore is," Jeb said. He stabbed at the periodical and nodded at some outrage. Such was the way of the man, John soon learned. Convincing him of anything through conversation was nearly impossible. He held only with what was in print. Scorned using his fingers to guide his reading, an odd thing to see, though often, as now, he licked a stubby lead to underline this important fact or that.

Erastus snorted and ordered the barber to trim his ear hair, said to John, "You're a little shit of a thing. What's your tipple?"

"I'd drink the Holy Spirit itself if it had any bite, but I've never slept past the bell. I've never slipped up."

Erastus eyed him appraisingly. He stumped out of the barber chair, adjusted his suspenders, then heaved his fist at John's head. John ducked, sprang up and kicked at Erastus's knees, dealing him a glance-blow to his throat at the same time. Erastus staggered into a shelf of hair tonic and oils. The bottles rattled but held.

Erastus grimaced. "Fuck-lucky for you I were holding back."

"Fuck-lucky for you I were too."

Erastus straightened. Jed flipped a page with a wetted thumb.

"Well, that satisfies," Erastus said.

The *Morning Star* was seventy-eight feet long and ten feet wide. She was flat-bottomed and squat like all canal boats so as to fit under the bridges and aqueducts. Had a long, covered hold for the cargo, stacked bed-slots for the crew, and an oak stable for the resting mules. Her paint was a ravishment of vermillion, blue and panoma green. Her rails were nickel-plated and polished to a gleam. "A flesh woman couldn't be more beautiful," Erastus said, and his crew chorused agreement.

Ambrose York was the steersman, a heavy-framed man near to forty who lacked most of his hair and one of his front teeth. He contended he lost this tooth when he was held captive during the Indian wars. "They pulled it out to torture me. Some squaw is wearing it round her neck even now, such are their adornments, I'll have you know it." He told this with a genial snort, as if recalling a fatherly beating. Ambrose, John soon realized, was one of those who lived in the sun-shaft of nostalgia. By afternoon he was missing the morning. By evening he was missing the afternoon. As for his tales of his life as a boy, his life as an Indian captive, John was to hear them relentlessly.

Clement Kinsworth was the mule hoggee, and was near big as a mule himself though not yet eighteen. His strength was legendary. Once a gangplank slipped when Clement was tailing on a mule; mule and hoggee should have crashed into the canal but Clement kept hold of the mule's tail and hauled it back to the towpath as easy, it was said, as if he were hauling up a baby. Erastus depended upon Clement, not just to rescue his mules, but to do his ledgers as well, for the boy could cipher in a blink. Still, he was often taken for an idiot given his toad-wide mouth, his swivel eye and lumbering gait. Or else a constant drunkard, which he wasn't. "Christ's truth is that the boy don't drink a thing except ale," Erastus said with faint disdain.

He had no such disdain for John's drinking abilities. "Never seen your like. Liquor must pour out your damned fingers for all it marks you."

John was set to earn ten silver dollars a month with his board an inclusion. His unit of monetary value was whisky gallons. At twenty cents a gallon, that meant ten dollars a month was fifty gallons. A decent wage, then. Not even he could drink that amount.

Erastus. Jeb. Ambrose. Clement. John. These five stopped each night at taverns or lock stations, even toll stations, anywhere the mules could be bought clean stabling and decent feed. There the five men of the *Morning Star* met with the crews of other boats, drank to oblivion, participated in foot races and wrestling matches and fist-fighting bouts until the acreage around was trampled. John worked from 4 a.m. to 10 p.m. like all canallers. Sleep was a snatched luxury during idle hours.

. . . I'm telling of these men for a purpose, Leah-Lou. In the first instance you need know how one can get comfortable with others who sin *in situ* as you, how it seems then not a sin at all but just the way of it, and I know how the Lord gets distant when we find power in the company of the like-minded instead of prayer . . .

John's first battle came one morning after his hiring. They'd been held up at the Cohoes Lock, a waste weir having broken through. Already they were running a half-day late for arrival in Buffalo. "A half-day less fucking profit!" Erastus roared. He called to Clement to kick the mule up a pace. Called to John to ready the tow line. John was confounded by this, then saw the boat, specking the distance. As the loaded boat the *Morning Star* should give the right of way and press to the berm side so that the lighter boat, coming unloaded from Buffalo, could pass over the lowered tow line. This was canal etiquette, such as it was.

Erastus looked through his telescope. "It's the *Sweet Eleanor G.* That's Severen's boat. I've sworn to never give way to that son-of-a-whore."

Childish. All of it. John-After can see that. But not John-Before. Already whisky-eyed he balled his fists. Erastus called to Clement to hitch up the mule and wade on over. Jeb folded up his cook's apron and hefted a fry pan. Ambrose hauled out a length of chain.

The *Sweet Eleanor G* drew near. Looked to have a five-man crew as well. An equal match, then. Demands were leavened, and then insults hurled, and then they were poling over to the *Sweet Eleanor G* while the other crew cursed them on and the *Morning Star* men cursed back, gleeful as boys. The battle raged across both boats. John took on a man wearing begrimed cover-alls. They grappled, then fell into the prow. John's head rang from a glancing blow and his nose dripped blood and then he gripped the man's arm and wrenched it backwards. The man screamed out his surrender. John accepted and kicked the man into the shallow waters.

The *Morning Star* won the day easily. The right of way was theirs. It was not won without pain, however. Erastus had split and swollen knuckles. One of Jeb's eyes was a flower of violet and black. John's head had a lump the size of a ball of yarn, and Ambrose was missing half his remaining front tooth. Only Clement was unscathed. Had taken on Captain Severen as if he were a boy in short pants.

They stopped at the nearest canal tavern to doctor themselves and have a celebratory draft. Other canallers crowded round to hear the livid details of the battle. Erastus didn't care that now they would be behind schedule. Erastus didn't care that now they would surely be behind schedule. Severen and his crew had been the toughest on the canal. No longer. That honour now belonged to the crew of the *Morning Star*, and that honour was often challenged. They had to often fight for the right-of-way—a spectacle so common that children came running as soon as the shouting started. And there were arguments to settle at taverns and grog shops. But soon they wallowed in respect. They allowed the hurry-up boats to pass on to their tasks of repair and rescue, but they catcalled to the packet boats, those passenger-haulers with their velvet dining rooms and deck chairs of teak. The packet boat captains ignored the canallers as if they were calling out in Gaelic or Chinese. The female passengers shielded their faces with parasols. The male passengers shook their heads in disgust.

A year slid by and then another. In winter the *Morning Star* was mud-larked and the crew worked on caulking the seams with oakum. John could have visited his family during these months when the canal was drained. Instead he found work repairing locks and drinking, ever drinking. He missed his wife only in the rare evenings when he was vaguely sober. Had, for compensation, the paid attentions of a widowed seamstress whose breasts, though near the size of Margaret's, lacked the musky scent, the moon whiteness.

> . . . I missed your ma sorely, Leah-Lou, and I missed you near worse, but I knew I were *persona non gratis* with my family unless I ceased imbibing. And I know, too, that God had his plans for me. I reckon you'd call this Fate because I've heard you toss that word about like a child's ball, but I warn you, Fate is only God plotting hard lessons . . .

In the months of navigable weather John came to know every ingenious thing and every wondrous sight along the length of the canal—the weigh-locks with their front pillars sunk into the water like some ruins of old, the swing bridges and bascule bridges, the towns that were said to be alike to Venice, with water-streets lapping at the boardwalks and towpaths and house fronts, the aqueducts fenestrated with arches. He knew the towering rocks of the Niagara Escarpment, the green hills of the Mohawk Valley. He knew all the businesses crowding the canal's edge—the provisionists and gin mills, the doggeries where a drink could be had for a twelve-pence, the boarding houses, barbershops and smithies, and the shops farther down watery alleys, too, where a man could tie a skiff, enter an unmarked door and have a go at the faro, the whores.

Erastus had a fondness for the shanty boat people, for their children swarming in the brown water and for the women, certainly, who in the limpid heat went without petticoats and wore only a single calico skirt that showed the outline of their legs. The crew bought whisky and vegetables from these folk whose skiffs nuzzled alongside the *Morning Star*. Not for these people the same patch of immobile earth; they moved every few months as they were forced. John could have lived among them, but not his wife, Margaret. She would never love this liquid world as he did. Here a man's worth was measured by how well he fought and how hard he worked. But most of all, by how much he drank.

> . . . and so you must see it, my girl, that my worth were sky
> high . . .

Five months later, on a transparent August day, John and the *Morning Star* crew listened all-humoured as Jeb read from a pamphlet: "*. . . and so give your workers a bible and cold water and they shalt respect you as a wise father.*"

Erastus laughed. Clement and Ambrose joined in; even John-Before gave his dry chuckle.

Erastus said, "Fucking what? Hah! Imagine the look on your pug-ugly faces if I gave yous all a bible and cold damned water as reward for your labour."

Even Jeb—who usually held with the written—had to agree it was an idiotic proposition.

The *Morning Star* was awaiting loading at the docks on Rochester's Warehouse Row. It was the third boat in line, but Erastus did not press the right of way as top boat of the Erie Canal, proving the truth of his near-daily remark that he had a magnanimous streak.

A wagon loaded with milled flour clattered up Warehouse Street. The wagon came from downriver where the mills and factories sheathed the cliffs aside the falls like battlements and the race chutes beckoned children and often drowned them. Even from the dock John could hear the rumble of the Grand Falls. He'd been told it was ninety-six feet high and two hundred wide and that farther north the Lower Falls were higher yet and torrented through a gorge. John-Before had never trudged the few miles to see these lower falls, which were said to be so awe-inspiring they could flush a man clean of sinning thoughts. But it'd take more than some damn waterfall, John thought, to clean me out of sinning thoughts.

He looked over to see that some well got-up gentlemen had made a table out of barrels. Another unfurled a rolled-up plan for what looked to be yet another factory. A flat-boat captain offered a bottle of whisky and the gentlemen passed it round. Erastus added to the bounty from his own formidable stash and the wagoners were invited down. More bottles appeared. Only in America would there be such an egalitarian sight, thought John, and he was glad again he was not born into some foreign country.

Workers filed out of a tannery, some half-grown children among them. The owner was said to be generous; he allowed the child workers a frolic outside each day, allowed a crock of ale for the oldest ones, and reasonable compensation for the family when a child now and then got yanked into the machinery and mangled.

John watched these children as they shifted on the rock paths. One plucked at the sooty leaves of a shrub. Another dragged a finger through the green slick of the canal. It was as if they had forgotten the rituals of play. Or mayhap they were lingering over each clock-tick of freedom. He wondered if tannery work was worse than school.

. . . Then I clenched the boat rail so hard my hand ached, and this because I spied a girl exact to you, Leah-Lou. The world was small for all its waterways and I'd heard rumours that you and your ma and siblings had returned from your grandparents' place in Ontario and were living in Rochester with Margaret's sister, that is to say on plain sufferance, and so I wasn't surprised overmuch but felt wretched all the same to think of you toiling in a factory. Then I realized that girl was mayhap seven, which was about your age when I left, and by then you'd be fifteen and a woman near grown . . .

Ambrose and Clement poled the *Morning Star* up the line for loading. Clement and John readied the lines. Erastus led the crew in singing dirty ditties. The got-up gentlemen were laughing now, their mood lightened by the passed-round bottles. One of them sent a boy for some buckets of ale. "Help yourselves, ye men at toil!" this gentleman called, and the toiling men did, the shining on the amber drops of ale.

That was the last occasion of such camaraderie. The last, and John had not known it. None of them had. When they returned some ten days later the warehouse manager was at the dock, pacing before the line of canal boats. The manager was a grave-faced man, lately graver yet. His black stovepipe was centred exact on his wagging head. "There shall be no more liquor at my docks!" he proclaimed, and handed Erastus a paper bill that said so. "We men of God are sick of witnessing fingers crushed under barrels. Of hearing crude drunken ditties. Of smelling the demon-reek of whisky. Of seeing men squander their God-given time in debauchery and carousing. And we are sickened unto very death of men who destroy their families with the bottle. Temperance has come to Rochester, and thus to America!"

Temperance. At first John thought this was the name of some meddling woman. Jeb put him to rights, and the crew of the *Morning Star* stood as silent and aggrieved as if a strong friend had dropped dead without warning.

"A passing fucking fancy," Erastus assured. "How can it hold?"

But Temperance not only held, it grew in strength and reach as the year went on. Rochester was the hub; from there it radiated along the canal and into the surrounding towns and counties. Committees of men, many once proud imbibers themselves, demanded a closing of the theatres, the circuses, the ninepin alleys, the billiard rooms, anyplace a working man might find distraction and a dram. And no longer could a working man make a decent side-living selling liquor from his shoe store, candy store, livery—from anywhere he chose, that was. Licences were required, and licences were costly and were meted out from the miserly fists of men raised on three square meals a day.

When in Rochester the crew of the *Morning Star* had to forage farther and farther from the canal to find liquor. After the gentle tilting of the *Morning Star's* deck, John found the macadam and brick hard and unyielding. One Sunday of April 1830 he ventured up Exchange Street, down Main. He was disheartened. Signs over shops proclaimed that no liquor would be sold. There was quietude even in the Four Corners. Everywhere, everyone was alarmingly sober. That morning he had seen two merchants roll a barrel of whisky to the canal's edge, and then, to the disbelieving eyes of the canallers, stab a hole in its side and let the whisky drain into the water. The merchants had called out their vows to temperance, though they could hardly make themselves heard for the catcalls and swearing.

John was stewing over this when he saw Leah not a carriage length away.

> . . . You were coming out of a chandler's with a basket over your arm and a blue shawl draping. I'd have known you anywheres, even if you were ten feet tall. Your walk hadn't changed nor your springy curls and you were pretty as a daisy in your yellow walking-out dress. Then you turned and I saw that you were near confinement or past it even. 'Course I saw that Bowman Fish loping aside you and holding your elbow and trying to steer you, and 'course I saw that he was plenty older and greying in his hair, but that he had a tooth of gold, tasselled boots and cravat of all-silk. He looked bewildered as a snared stoat and I might well have pitied him if it weren't my Beloved Daughter he'd got with child . . .

———

Leah stopped and looked in this direction and that, and then in John's.

John-Before drew into a shadow. Heard the man beside his daughter saying, "Now Leah, now angel. I'm your husband, I know what's best . . ." The man's voice trailed off as they rounded a corner.

Husband. At least they're married, then. But Christ in a fucking handcart, why had Margaret allowed it? Leah was barely a woman. John decided to demand an explanation from his wife. This time for certain he would knock on her sister's door . . . and then? He was the wayward husband. The drunken father. What authority did he have? He wandered the streets of Rochester for the better part of that day, his mind steeped black.

When he returned to the *Morning Star*, John was a changed man. Purpose was in his step, determination in his hawkish face.

"Where the buggered devil you been?" Erastus asked, without much interest. He was morose these days. Had threatened to sell the boat and go west. Become a buffalo hunter, a fur trader.

"We gotta take those fucking Temperancers on."

"What are you gabbing about?"

"The Temperancers. The Sabbatarians. The what-you-call-'ems, fucking Evangelicals. Buck-up, Erastus. You got goddamned raisins for balls?"

"That ain't a manner to be talking to your captain," Erastus said with a sigh.

By way of answer John handed him a bottle the size of his hand. The label was dainty and pink.

"Fucking Christ, what's this? Jeb, get your half-rotted carcass over here and read this!"

Jeb obliged. Held the diminutive bottle into the sun. "Says here: *Doctor Gibson's Finest Brandied Infant Sleeping Draught.*"

"It were all I could find on a Sunday," John explained. "That's how fucking far it's gone: infant's draughts."

Erastus shook his head at this outrage. He fumed for a time, then stood on the prow of the *Morning Star*. He looked bedraggled and weakened, but the green fire was back in his eyes. "Clement!

Ambrose! Move your fucking lazy arses. We's got planning to do."

The target was to be the Pioneer Line, a mix of packet and freight boats owned by one Josiah Bissell, Elder of the Third Church.

. . .Who didn't know of him and his filthy rich kin in Rochester town? He originated that pious rag the *Rochester Observer* and a more righteous man never sucked air. You know the kind, they'd have you think our Jesus loved the rich and scorned the poor and was joyous to see suffering instead of healing all and sundry as He did. I reckon in another time Old Bissell would have led Crusades to the Holy Lands and butchered Saracens for their lack of Christian feeling, but in our time he had only the Working Men to hate so. His Pioneer Line hired only men who had forsworn all spirits—even coffee was considered a kind of sin—and these men did not work on Sundays, not ever. Fine and dandy for them, but Old Bissell demanded that all boating traffic cease on Sundays, that all horns and bugles be silenced, that all liquor be banished. Everywhere. And not just on Sundays, but for the rest of God's Time, and as you might imagine that didn't sit well with us canallers. We found him out one morning leading a bannered march over Calamity Bridge and on down the steps to his lead packet boat. Jeb hollered out what the banner said and I recall it ever yet—*There is a Special Place for Drunkards. It is not the Tavern. It is Hell's Hottest Circle.* We laughed, thinking it horse___, but I came to understand that Bissell's thoughts on drunkards were smack on, though the man himself had the wrong tack on religion—unlike Brother Able, who was God's True Emissary though he could barely utter a thing, and I'll get to him presently. Anywise, aside Bissell was a boy of six or so, and he, too, was as pious as a barn rat. That was Bissell's son, also named Josiah, and he was the one who led the torpedo attack on you and your sisters at the Corinthian Hall. He was the very lout who tried to get you mobbed and even murdered, and he was the one who called you blasphemers and witches and such, and I admit I felt a stir of the old pride when I heard how the Young Bissell's attempt to rout you did naught but bring you sympathy and attention from all quarters . . .

That spring and summer of 1830, the *Morning Star* led the other canal boats in the battle against the Sabbatarians. With a common enemy, fighting plummeted among the canallers. Handbills touting the Pioneer Line were torn from posts and walls. John himself cut the tow line to Pioneer packet boats on four occasions. Soon boats of the Pioneer Line could not get a half-mile before their tow lines were cut by one canaller or another. The sight of Pioneer Line hoggees dodging back from the whipping lines, cursing in a way most intemperate, became a common entertainment for Rochester's children.

The battle intensified. Canaller boats formed barricades when one of Bissell's boats wanted through an aqueduct. They cut in at the locks. Prodded mules into the canal to flounder afore the Pioneer boats. Used flotillas of logs to block narrower passages. Pried up the planks on the towpaths when a Pioneer boat was behind them. They levelled abuse at Bissell when they spied him. Laughed when he begged God to smite them.

And the Pioneer Line suffered mightily. Their boats took twice as long to attain their destination as boats with imbibing captains. The ladies aboard were scandalized by catcalls. The men infuriated by the waits. The children, however, enjoyed the mayhem no end.

Soon enough the Pioneer Line was bankrupt. The canallers celebrated with as much whisky and rum as they could find. The celebration spilled off the boats and into the Four Corners, where Erastus Bearcup was arrested and thrown in jail for an evening for shouting obscenities at the ladies.

The victory celebrations went on for days. How was John to know it was only a battle won, not the war? That the Elder Josiah Bissell had published a letter addressed to the Reverend Charles Grandison Finney, the greatest preacher ever known, in his stronghold of Adams, New York.

. . . I recollect the letter even yet because it was published in a newspaper and we laughed it up buckets and made a mockery of Bissell and Finney both. Bissell wrote about "the specimens of the large budget of evils rolling through our land and among us. The Devil was a water serpent that rises from the canal and infests Rochester with its spawn." He weren't far wrong. It was Finney who sent emissaries out to the canallers as a forerunner to his own coming . . .

John pauses in his writing. Mops his forehead even though his room has grown cold with the dying fire. He writes in a tired scrawl. *Brother Able was one of these emissaries.*

The beginning of the end—an October forenoon of 1830. The *Morning Star* glided up the main street of Syracuse, crossed under the Salina Street Bridge, then passed the Coffin Block Building wedged at the fork in the canal. It passed the ornate edifice of the *Syracuse Daily Star*, passed warehouses, men fishing, children diving. Outside a tailor's shop, an incongruous potted tree shimmered crimson and orange. The sky was the blue of a baby's eyes. The rancid heat of summer was gone and the air was flannel-warm and smelled of new-pressed apples, of bayberries simmering for candles. John-Before hummed the ditty *Mad Sally the Slut* and mended a hemp rope, as happy as he'd ever been. Jeb read his almanac and scoured a cook pan. Ambrose was at the wheel whistling past his broken teeth. Erastus stroked his massive beard and drank his rum and coffee and spat tobacco over the side and waved to the passing ladies. Clement hulked amiably with the mule along the towpath. The towpath functioned as a sidewalk alongside the water roads, and here in town pedestrians stepped round the mule and over the tow line with nary a glance.

The crew tied up the *Morning Star* in line at the Syracuse weigh-lock. Half of the weigh-lock rested on dry land, the other half reached over the canal where the front pillars joined a cement slab and formed a square tunnel. A canal boat was being slung in the harness. The gates closed and the waters drained, then rose again. All in a mere fifteen minutes. Aren't we Americans just fucking inge-nious, John thought, not for the first time.

While they waited, Ambrose told again the story of how the Indians had held him captive. John paid only half a mind. The one constant about the tale was how it changed at every telling.

"They said this-here tooth of mine would be good for Injun magic. So they yanked it. And there was an old hag. She ordered me to give her a spawn else she'd go at my prick with hot tongs . . ."

John told Ambrose to shut up, then nudged Erastus and pointed. "What's that mother-screwing stripling want, you reckon?"

The stripling was standing on the towpath gawking at the *Morning Star*. He had hair of dun-brown, lips red as a girl's, and an expres-sion like a kicked hound's. He wore a black bang-up coat and a grey vest, both of homespun, both too large for his skinny limbs, unlike his hat, which was small-brimmed and also black and better suited to a child.

He cleared his throat and his bulging Adam's apple jounced up and down. "G-Gentleman of the c-canal. I b-bring you, good news. Chr-Chr . . . Jesus is among us!"

"Go fuck your grandmother sideways," Erastus called out genially, and had the satisfaction of beholding the young man's pop-eyed astonishment. The young man gathered himself and started again. He stammered out something about salvation being open to all who choose it. At that, he got on his knees.

"Has he lost some fuck-what thing?" Erastus asked.

Jeb stuffed the almanac into his cook's apron. "He's lost nothing excepting his wits."

"Ah, could be the poor mite's gone and hurt his little toe," Ambrose put in.

Clement hopped aboard. His toady face showed amazement. His swivel eye scrolled inward. "Gosh-damned. He's praying,"

It was a prayer, sure enough, a droning stammer that seemed more a pitiful begging.

"I'll be buggered," John said. "They're worse than water rats, these fucking preachers." Like his crewmates he'd never seen anyone on their knees at prayer excepting saints in pictures. And like his crewmates he found it unseemly, like shitting in the open, say, instead of finding the quiet side of a building.

"Stand up, you sorry arse, for fuck-what's sake!" Erastus called.

The young man did so. "I should l-like, p-permission to sh-share with y-you the g-good news of our L-Lord."

Erastus laughed. "Look here, Mister Preacher, whoever-you-were, we've trounced the fucking lot of you. Ain't you heard?"

"My n-name is Br-Brother Able," he said, a species of pride crossing his face each time he stammered out a word.

"Abel?" Jeb called. "I know that name. I suggest you watch your damned back if you got a brother named Cain!"

The crew laughed; even they knew that old bible story.

"N-No, my-my b-brother's n-name was W-Willing. A-And my n-name is spelled *le*."

"Able?" John said. "Sure it ain't your sister who's Willing, then?"

Erastus backslapped him for this witticism.

Brother Able's pale cheeks turned scarlet. "N-No. S-See our ma r-reckoned it had a g-goodly r-ring. We d-did get s-some r-ribbed for it in the sch-schoolyard." He sighed and turned to go, head down, carryall dragging, his incongruous little hat making him even more pitiful.

Later, each man said Able recalled to them their own mother's insensate cruelties. Erastus recalled being sent in short pants to school when he was a good year past the time for it. Jeb recalled his mother citing the tortures of Hell that awaited him if he did not finish his prunes. Ambrose recalled his mother making him count change for her clients while she whored in the room above. Clement recalled his mother dying and in delirium asking that he not be near, for the sight of him terrified her, and terrified the good angels come to get her. John-Before recalled nothing of his mother, she being dead soon after he was born.

"Ah, fuck-a-whore," Erastus said. "Get back, then. You got yourself until we're weigh-locked. Fifteen minutes, no more."

Able nodded in wordless gratitude.

The crew argued against it. John was the most vehement.

Erastus said, "Shut it, I'm the captain, and truth be told I'm sick of listening to your fucking jawing. A change is damn-dandy, I always say."

"Huh, I ain't never heard you say that," Ambrose said.

Erastus winked, then whispered, "'Sides, one's got to knows one's fucking enemies, eh? Circle round the boy. Let's see if Able is able."

Good man, John thought, and glared past his hawk nose at Able as the boy scrambled on board. Ambrose and Erastus spat tobacco over the hull. Jeb tested the blade of a gutting knife. Clement smiled, an honest act, which only made his ugly face more fearful. Able stumbled over a rope.

Erastus proffered a bottle of whisky. "Seeing as you're our guest."

Brother Able's eyes looked about to pop out of his head with nervousness. "I-I don't d-drink. S-Soberness is n-next to G-Godliness."

"I thought it were cleanliness," said Ambrose, who was neither.

"T-That t-too."

Erastus eyed the sun. "Now you got yourself only nine minutes left."

Able said, "If y-you p-pray, w-with people and humbly, on your kn-knees, then th-the light c-comes. W-We're not all d-damned. It's a ch-choice. You can save your-yourselves, you c-c . . ." He fell silent, looked as if about to weep.

The weigh-master called out to bring in the *Morning Star* and Erastus clapped Able on the back, nearly teetering him into the fetid canal waters. "Able-y done, Brother Able. Now bugger yourself off. Find some greener pastures to spread your horseshit."

. . . And so we made a pact after Brother Able's leaving to never again waste our time listening to some preacher's cant and that by Job's blood we'd never become knee-kneeling God beggars. Two months later, Christmastide not a week off, and only me and Ambrose were left unconverted. What I mean here, Leah-Lou, is that all your certainties can collapse swift as the walls of Jericho.

CHAPTER 23.

I heard the coughing even before I reached the final stairway. I hurried, my satchel banging. The poor soul was doubled over, her barking a harsh sound. I slapped her back, all-brisk, all-business, then readied a poultice of black mustard and calomel and applied it in a nonce. Next I gathered up the letters scattered on her bedclothes and put them back in the bible box. Now for the laudanum. Her coughing eased.

A time later my patient asked, "Have you not a glimmer of fear for your own health, Mrs. Mellon?"

"Do I look a nervous nelly, a worry wart?"

"Not at all."

"Exactly. I could scarcely carry on my duty if I feared for my own self." (I presume she meant did I trouble myself about germs, those invisible infectors so talked about these days.)

"One day doctors will cure all manner of ailments and disease," she pronounced. "It won't be just luck and guesswork and that not-so-common sense that Leah put to use when playing nurse."

"What chalk and nonsense. If everyone should be cured, whatever would *my* purpose be?" I smiled then, at which she gave me a startled look, as if she did not recognize me.

"I was making a little jest," I added hastily. "Indeed, I'd rather be far less busy in my duties."

LEAH HUMS AS SHE TAKES UP her appointment ledger. Since she moved to this genteel New York 26th Street brownstone last summer she has been engrossed with building a roster of reputable clients. Now, in this early April of '53, her days are chock with sittings and consultations. Never has she been busier; never has she been happier. Burr's ten thousand is going towards decorating and furnishings (as well as to some prudent investment) and soon the brownstone will be a haven of colour and tasteful comforts, even luxuries. Mother lives here also, as does Calvin, and faithful, useful Alfie. And Leah's sisters, of course, though Katie has many private clients of her own and is often out at their homes, giving séances and conjuring up children, her speciality. And Maggie is often out with that Dr. Kane, with Mother or Elisha's valet serving as chaperone. Lately, however, the doctor—being so occupied with organizing his Arctic expedition—has not been calling on Maggie as often as he was (to Leah's relief), and because of this Maggie's moods have been snapping back and forth like hung laundry in a gale, and she is often too much in a sulk to be of use at the sittings. Not that Leah needs either her or Katie as she once did. She can fetch up the spirits nicely on her own, though her spirits are mostly older sorts who cannot rap quickly, nor for a lengthy time. Trancing and automatic writing are what these spirits favour.

She sweeps down the hall, list in hand, calling for Alfie.

Stops short. Screams.

Calvin. He crawls down the hall in a slick of blood. His fingers are webbed with mucus. "Which door? Which is it?" he gasps, as Leah sinks beside him. "I'm done for, though a doctor, a doctor might not be amiss."

The doctor proclaims he has never seen such a quantity of blood hemorrhaged.

"My spirits, and yet we had no idea!" Leah exclaims.

"The afflicted often conceal their illness," the doctor says. He is a diminutive man, his reddish hair slick with macassar oil. "Though I can't comprehend how you missed it. This, ma'am, is the most hopeless case of consumption I've ever seen. Nothing can be done."

"Poppycock. I shall care for him. *We* shall."

Her mother and sisters agree. They sob and wring their hands and look to her for guidance, as always.

Calvin coughs up more blood. He is paper pale. His eyes bruised pits.

Katie says, "You just have to stay with us, Cal, please. I'm so sorry the ghosts teased you so, back when you first came to help us. The carpet balls and that candlestick that made your lip bleed so. We're sorry. Really. Truly."

"Kat's right," Maggie says. "We should never have let it go so far."

"Oh, he's forgiven you girls," Leah says. "Have you not forgiven them, Calvin? Just nod . . . Good. Now, Mother, you fetch the linens and poultices. And a bucket, yes, and I shall telegraph straightaway to Isaac for medicine and advice. We shall triumph as ever. Did I not save little Charlie from Death's clutches? Did I not defeat our dread nemesis, that prattling poseur, that Chauncey Burr?"

Her mother and her sisters agree again. Even look cheered. Calvin murmurs, "I should have duelled Burr. I would have if—"

"Hush. Rest," Leah orders. Thinks: Yes, it might have come to a duel if poor Calvin hasn't been overtaken by a fit of coughing. God and the Spirits, how could I not have known that this one was in such peril?

Leah recalls Burr striding into the Columbus courtroom. He was a head taller than any other man and he bit on an apple to show his contempt for the proceedings. As the case went on, Burr fixed on Leah as if they were alone in the room, as if no one else was of any import. And when the verdict came down against him? He actually laughed, and continued to do so even when the raps sounded loud in agreement.

Leah looks down at the man in the bed. Ah, Calvin.

The hours spin into days. The days grow warmer. Calvin coughs ever harder. Grows ever thinner. Leah learns resignation. She cannot always conquer Death it seems. She sings him *Over the Hills and Far Away,* his favourite song. The notes do not reveal their colours, not even faintly. An ominous sign.

Calvin consoles her, consoles them all. He is determined to have a good death for their sakes. Has already selected a minister, a grave plot, has already proclaimed his sins, such as they are. Has composed his last words, made suggestions for a eulogy. He has left the music selections all to Leah.

Bach? Mozart? Leah cannot decide. She is in the parlour sifting through her music books. Perhaps a gladsome song to prove that death is but a beginning. Or perhaps a military march. Poor Calvin. He has missed his chance at battle. There will be no more wars on American soil. "We may expect peace for a thousand years," or so the spirit of General Washington assured at a recent sitting.

Leah comes upon her father's last missive. Here she had merely asked her father if he recalled the passenger pigeons lifting her up and he had gone on for pages about his own self. Her father had never been one to "paper the walls with his talk," as the saying goes, yet his letters could paper a small parlour. She reads this particular letter twice through to the end. *What I mean here, Leah-Lou, is that all your certainties can collapse swift as the walls of Jericho.*

Jericho? Did not its citizens deserve to be crushed by divine will or some such? And how is it, exactly, that her father became a knee-kneeling man of God? He has not yet said. It is as if he is too stubborn to do so.

She folds his letter and tucks it in the lily box, but far beneath those other letters of commendation and gratitude, and just atop the clip-outs she has collected on Chauncey Burr. She does not collect them merely to relive her victory over the man, but as a reminder, yes, that she must be ever on her guard against . . . well, many things.

A touch at Leah's shoulder. Mother. "Leah, our Calvin has asked for you."

"My spirits, is it time already?"

Mother dabs at her red-rimmed eyes. "I believe so, yes, but he wishes to ask something of you first, doesn't he?"

Leah finds Calvin propped up with feather bolsters. He has combed his hair and wrestled on a boiled shirt, a starched collar. Has coughed his lungs clean of blood and phlegm. He takes Leah's hand on one side. Mother Margaret's on the other. Maggie and Katie stand distraught at the foot of his bed.

Leah does not give her answer for several days, and then she does. They marry on the 10th of September. Calvin says his vows while tucked in his deathbed. Leah says hers while arrayed in silver taffeta. Maggie and Katie weep into their champagne glasses. Mother Margaret throws rose petals on the couple as the minister intones the marriage rites. And then Alfie brings up the cake Leah has ordered from Weins and Rice, the best bakers in all of New York.

Calvin gestures to Katie and Maggie, who are occupied in mixing rum flips. He whispers hoarsely to Leah, "I fear for them, my darling wife. They are of an age now. And this Dr. Kane. I must tell you, Leah, tell you that Kane's intentions with Maggie are suspect. That his intentions may even be . . . dishonourable. God, I wish I could protect her! And Katie! Watch them closely, beloved."

Leah promises she will, as she has always done. Promises to keep a vigilant watch on Dr. Kane, as she has also been doing, by the by, since the cad entered the scene.

"At least you will have the shield of my name now, dear heart. Now you will be a proper widow and I may go to my grave knowing slander cannot assault you."

"You should not think of me at this hour, you should—"

"You are all I've ever thought of, Leah. You and this family. You took me in and loved me when I lost my own family and—" He sobs.

Leah pats his shoulder, slightly aghast. Need a deathbed scene be so overwrought with emotion?

Calvin gathers himself. "Know that even once I am dead I will do my best to protect you and your name. Call upon me during the sittings. I will arrive without delay."

Leah's sisters look over at this, perplexed.

"Do compose yourself, Calvin," Leah says. "For soon—"

"Listen, Leah. My mortal remains mean nothing to me. I am yours in death as in life. If ever I am needed to—"

"You need to rest, Calvin."

"Mrs. Brown. How I like the sound of that." Calvin sits up and gauges the wedding cake on the sideboard. "They should have used gum paste for the scrollwork. But it looks passable. Do hand me a slice, my darling."

Leah does, and looks on with astonishment as he eats not only that slice, but three more.

———

12th April, 1853

Dearest Lizzie,
I am charmed and delighted that you are to join Calvin and
me in New York at last. Our brownstone is on the most
reputable of streets and we have all the latest fixtures and keep
the finest table possible and I do miss you. Your assistance is
most strongly needed. And in answer to your question, yes, he
has been asking for you, and in a manner most forceful.

Now, Katherina is abiding with the Partridges for a time
and Margaretta and Mother are in Philadelphia again at the
behest of the thousands of believers there. Thus, it shall just
be the two of us for a little while, and just as it ever was.

Your Most loving Mother

"And hardly any can claim *these*!" Leah tells Lizzie and twists a valve
near the hallstand. A sconce hisses, then fires yellow. "You shall get
accustomed to that gaseous odour, as we all have."

"One can get accustomed to anything, Mother," Lizzie says, and
unpins her fashionable little man-hat, then smoothes the jacket
bodice of her three-piece fit-out, which is all of duff silk and is also
mannish, also most fashionable. Though, God and the Spirits, Leah
thinks, why would any woman want to emulate a man?

"You do look wondrous fine, Elizabeth. I scarcely recognized
you. You look so progressive."

"Why, thank you. And what a colourful dress *you* have today. Is that
orange? What does one slaughter to get that shade? And the embellishments, so very many, one can scarcely fathom the amount of fabrication required." Lizzie looks impatiently upwards as she says this.

Apparently Lizzie left Bowman's place in Illinois the moment she
received Leah's request. Leah is grateful, of course. Still, have all her
former requests for Lizzie's return not signified? Leah squashes this
thought and does her best to impress her daughter. She shows her the
ovoid mahogany table that seats up to twenty, the Belter suite of

furnishing that is upholstered all in matching red brocade, the étagère, the whatnot cabinet, the piano. "Not a Chittering grand like the Littles had, sweeting. But a true piano! Just as we always wanted!"

From outside the brownstone comes the rattle-clop of swank carriages. From inside comes a racket of birds. In the parlour three new cages hang by the window and house two budgerigars, two finches, a firebird, a thrush. Alone in his Ottoman temple, Vivace—Leah's cherished Amazonian parrot—preens his green feathers and cackles as if crazed.

"Chatting to dead folks pays very well, then?" Lizzie asks, looking arch.

Leah swallows a sharp comment, a momentary fear. No, Lizzie would never slander them as damned Ruth Culver did. Ruth was a relation by marriage only. Lizzie is Leah's only flesh and blood. Surely the girl would not have another outburst as she did at the sitting with Reverend Clarke those five years ago. In any case, Lizzie's help at spirit sittings is not the help that Leah requires.

Leah hastens them to the reading room. Shows Lizzie the stacks of spiritualist journals: *Shekinah, The Spirit Messenger, The Banner of Light, The Spiritual Telegraph.* "Our dear Horace was the first to use the terms *Spiritualism* and *Spiritualist*. He's come round since all that silliness with Ruth and with our dread enemy, that bray-mouthed Burr. Anywise, I like the terms very well. Foxist or Foxism would have been absurd. I must admit that."

Lizzie agrees completely. She shows slightly more interest in Isaac's book: *Voices From the Spirit World; Being Communication From Many Spirits*, by the Hand of Isaac Post, Medium. "Pity for Isaac. Was there not some criticism of this?"

"*Pity* for Isaac? Why do you say that? Imagine having a book published with your very name on the cover."

"My imagination cannot stretch that far, Mother, as I'm sure you know. As for why I pity Isaac, well, because the critics weren't terribly gracious, were they? Did they not say that the, hmm, famous dead, sounded all a piece? You know—Quakerish. And didn't one reviewer remark it peculiar that Thomas Jefferson, that great speechifyer, would sound so wooden and so—what is the word?—*trite?*"

"So, Elizabeth Fish, you *have* been attending the writings about your loving family."

"At times, Ma, at times." Lizzy browses the shelves, exclaims in ill-concealed mockery: "Dear spirits, such authors! Let us see. Benjamin Franklin, Jefferson, Plato, Swedenborg, Andrew J. Davis. Have you read *all* these?"

Leah sniffs. "I think it only respectful to have their writings. Many of these fellows communicate during our circles, or I should say séances."

Lizzie nearly drops Thomas Paine in surprise.

Leah tries a beseeching smile. "The French does have a nice ring. And the fashionable people do like foreign things. I always say how it was you, my beloved daughter, who minted the term. Oh, Lizzie, I am so grateful you have returned home! It shall be as it was, I know it." Leah reaches to embrace her daughter, but her arms fall awkwardly short, Lizzie having turned away at the sound of a bell.

"Tell him I shall be up shortly," Leah calls as Lizzie hurries off to see Calvin, who has miraculously transformed from a man stepping through death's door to Leah's invalid husband on the second floor.

"I suppose he must be sleeping now," Leah says when Lizzie finally rejoins her in the parlour. "I shall visit him later."

"He would like that," Lizzie says flatly.

The two women settle on opposing chairs. Between them a fire burns low in its marbled keep. The birds sleep in their covered cages. Alfie serves tea, then fades off to bed. Lizzie hums while she works on an embroidery round. Was she always a hummer? Leah wonders. Honestly, the girl cannot carry a tune in a basket.

Leah says, "Our Katherina might be coming home sooner than expected from the Partridges'. The spirit of a yet another little boy keeps pushing on through, you see. Apparently he worked at the Partridge match factory when in the quick and now he is complaining incessantly about the conditions there."

"He would complain, wouldn't he, if the conditions killed him."

Leah has to agree. Tries a new tack. "Tell me of Illinois, dear."

Lizzie speaks as if reading a list. "The weather is lovely in spring and summer. There are many wildflowers about the main house. Pa's wife Charlotte does beautiful paintings of them. She taught me every-thing she knows about art. She can make anything look exactly real."

"Wife? Do you not mean housekeeper?"

"They're married," Lizzie says firmly. "And Charlotte is very kind."

"Kind? You honestly think her kind?"

"She *is* kind. Thinking has nothing to do with it."

"I suppose your father often spoke of me."

Lizzie bites off a thread. "I shouldn't say often."

"I suppose he said that I was such a foolish young thing when we married, barely more than a child, and that I had not an iota of sense, nor an iota of my, my duties."

Lizzie humphs. "The only thing he ever said was that you terri-fied the living bejesus out of him."

Leah can think of no rejoinder, is, in fact, oddly flattered. She watches her daughter stitch-stitching away, calm as a cat with a milk bowl. And here she had been such a wriggly infant, peevish at the breast. And then as a toddling child always pasted to Leah's skirt as if Leah might be blown away by wind and circumstance. Does she recall how Leah doted on her? How she scrimped for her French lessons? Allowed her to listen in on Leah's music lessons?

Like any modest woman, Leah has never mentioned the horrors of childbirth. Has certainly never mentioned to Lizzie that she came too soon, too quick. That Bowman ran for the midwife too late. Leah cut the cord herself with a fish-knife, then wrapped the squall-ing babe in a quilt. She had been told she would forget the pain of it all, the terror. What a load of poppycock that was. "No point in crying, my girl," she said those years ago to baby Lizzie. "We're alone and that is the way of it."

Leah hefts a poker and prods the fire. She is not one to be still as a houseplant. Sparks fly over the low grating and onto Lizzie's embroidery round.

"No! No! *Mon Dieu!* All that work!"

"Oh, here," Leah says, and dabs the round with her hands, but the damage is done. The embroidered scene is of a royal court at Versailles and the Queen, old and stout, looks only the more ridicu-lous now that her ear has been burned away. About her the courtiers and handmaidens look as mocking and resigned as courtiers the world over surely do, once the eyes of the monarch are askance.

Leah thrusts the embroidery back at Lizzie. "At least you could always earn your keep with a needle, my dear, if you don't marry."

Lizzie gathers her sewing basket and coldly says good-night. Leah longs to call her back. Why is it so easy to be gracious to clients and acquaintances, but to those she loves she is snappish, even unkind? Her father is to blame, Leah decides. He allowed her an impertinence that would have earned most children a proper whipping.

Now Calvin, on the other hand, never gets in a huff. He understands Leah's burden of caring for them all. And he is happy to see her any time at all.

Calvin's room is lit only by a banked fire. A greyness stirs near the window. It is man-sized but not a man: a form in slow flux. Leah starts back and stumbles on the rug. Whispers, "Calvin?"

No reply. Only creaking. Only a susurration that is not a human breathing, not a fire dying.

She is about to rush for Alfie, when the movement takes on sense: the velveteen drapery. It billows in front of the window, which is open, a young physician having advised that Calvin breathe outside air. Ridiculous advice in New York, but Calvin agreed it worth the try.

Leah hurries to close the sash. Calvin jolts awake. He is propped up so that his lungs can drain. The bucket on the floor shows little blood. His breathing is less hoarse than usual.

"Mrs. Brown!"

"Yes, I am arrived. I am here, Calvin."

"Ah, you must be so pleased to see our Lizzie again. I've missed her these years. But you, you I miss every moment you are gone."

"And I miss you." She *has* missed him, the helpful young man ever at her side. She turns up the gas valve, brightening the room, then busies herself with the plumping of pillows, the emptying of the ashcan. The young physician also prescribed medicinal cigars and Calvin smokes three daily. It makes more work for Leah, but she does not complain.

She drops in a wing chair and lets escape a small sob.

"Why the tears, my heart?"

"I have not, not appreciated you. Nor Lizzie. I am a wretch of a mother. A terrible wife."

Calvin chuckles. "And what sort of a husband am I, then, who is bedridden and needs such cosseting . . . but look!" He throws back the bedclothes.

"Calvin!"

"Leah. We're married. It's not improper." He swings his thin legs onto the floor. Walks five steps to the window. Five steps back. "This is the second time today I've walked so. I am regrouping. My strength is returning. Those cigars are working like the a magic charm."

"But this cannot do. Come back to bed. Here. Allow me . . ." She reaches out and Calvin pulls her into his arms. She cries his name. He cries out hers in answer, then attempts to kiss her, and on the lips.

She pushes him away to arm's length. "Calvin! You are too weak for such, such things and it would drain you further. And . . . I thought, surmised, that this marriage was only to protect me, my name, that is."

"Leah, you know I adore you!"

Leah becomes all briskness. Takes his thin hand and leads him back to bed, ignoring his spleeny looks. All this effort has cost him and he hacks blood into the bucket. She pats his back and bids him good-night and turns down the gas lights.

"One kiss?" he beseeches, fingers to his lips. "Only one, honour bright."

"You need think of your recovery. Only that."

He coughs into a handkerchief. "Bully, then, it's not like it would kill you."

Leah treads wearily down the hall. If Calvin recovers he will certainly force his husbandly rights. She thinks of Bowman Fish and his coffin-lid weight. She kept Bowman at bay for some time before he became forceful, though he was always contrite and sorrowing in the aftermath.

In her private room she undresses layer by layer until she is down to her chemise and pantalettes. She cannot abide being fully naked and barely tolerates her weekly bath. She recalls the Corinthian

Hall investigations when she and Maggie were stripped and stood before strangers. She hid her terror and humiliation then for Maggie's sake alone.

She burrows under the quilts and wonders how other women endure sexual congress. Perhaps they become blasé and study the ceiling rose. Oh, she has heard there is some comfort, even pleasure, in such physical closeness. But there is precious little comfort in dying in childbirth, or in putting child after child in the grave. She must remind Maggie and Katie of this. Lizzie as well.

I will make a far better widow than a wife, she thinks before sleep takes her.

CHAPTER 24.

"Where have you been?" my patient asked this day. She had just stirred awake.

"Where? Why, right here, duck, I've been here forever. You were elsewhere, mind, dreaming on about some other place."

"I don't dream."

"Don't dream? That's chalk and nonsense. Everyone dreams. And you were tossing about like a skiff at sea, duck, and amutter besides. If that is not evidence of dreaming, my name isn't Alvah June Mellon."

"Fine to that, but I only see fragments. My dreams don't unfold like a story, not even a muddled one. They're alike fragments, or a tableau, though they *do* move a jot . . . thus perhaps more alike a cosmorama, a fancy one that shifts when you view it through a keyhole."

"I've never been one for entertainments nor—"

"And dreams don't mean anything. Interpreting them is alike pulling hankies from the air, like an illusionist does." She plucked at her bed jacket, her little hands looking very pale against the fabric's deep bishop's blue. "I muttered? About what?"

I smoothed out my cover-all. I was pleased with its design of stars and rays. "You muttered about Elisha. And thus you may as well tell me more about him, and this grand romance you shared."

THE BEGINNING OF MAY and Maggie has just returned from her short spirit-rapping tour to Philadelphia with Mother. She is determined, despite Leah's dark looks, to spend her every available moment with Elisha before his early June departure for the Arctic, and before her own mid-May departure to Washington with Katie. It is a tour she would love to cancel, but cannot, apparently, not without bringing disgrace upon them all, or so Leah has asserted. Leah. Thank Christ, Maggie thinks, that at least here in New York Leah is too preoccupied with Lizzie and Calvin and her clients to make much fuss over Maggie and Elisha's many outings.

On this balmy afternoon Elisha escorts Maggie to New York's Lyceum of Natural History, where he is set to lecture and raise last-minute funds for his expedition supplies. The *Advance*, Elisha has informed Maggie, must be stocked with several years' worth of foodstuffs and sundries in the off-chance she becomes trapped in the polar ice.

"Which is nothing, nothing alike to this," Elisha explains as he shows her the enfilades of saw-cut bergs, the walls of glacial ice and the wooden shores painted with birds. "And, ah, behold, my pet, the *aurora borealis*!"

Maggie looks up at the dangling bits of coloured glass. "How pretty they are!"

"Pretty? They are tawdry, a far-fetched illusion, an artifice. The sublimity of the Arctic can only be painted with words. I have informed the manager of this, but that cretin hardly cares."

"He should attend you," Maggie says gravely, and wonders how she could have misjudged his tone. She vows to do better, to attend every shift in his voice, every nuance of his expressions.

"Yes, he should. Ah, Tuttie, the Arctic is such a clean, white place, even when assaulted with endless dark. The dawn when it comes is a purpled blue, alike a bruise or, no, alike a raven's wing in angled light."

"Bishop's blue," Maggie offers, and thinks: Not blue, not purple, but both at once. A lovely shade. I'll have a dress made forthwith.

"Bishops have no place in the arctic, pet," he says wryly. "It is a queer, immutable world. Deathless and yet the landscape of death itself." Elisha shakes his head. "I do so despise this vulgar business of raising funds. I'd rather raise the dead as you do . . . I jest. But little wonder my mother—that is, my parents—begged off attending my lecture." He faces her. "Did you know I'm being called a celebrity?"

"A what?"

"A celebrity, as if I were something to celebrate, a party of a man, if you will. Something to enjoy and then forget the next day. It is an insult, nothing less."

Maggie frowns, shocked, though she can think of worse things to be called. Has been called worse things aplenty. "I do believe I'm becoming one of them . . . of those celebrities too."

"Dreadful enough in a man, pet. Anywise, it's hardly the same, your celebrity and mine. Mine is chanced to become something greater." He gives an intricate wave to Morton, who is busy pointing out the lime-lights to Maggie's mother. Morton nods, then ushers Mother out the back door, as if to show her something more delightful beyond.

Elisha cups Maggie's elbow. "Have you told your family? Of our plans? Have you told that tigress of a sister?"

"Should I? That is, should I now? Calvin is so sick, it might seem selfish."

Elisha nods. "Selfish, yes. You're correct. To be wholly quit of your profession, timing is of paramount import. I will tell you when to cease. When you return from Washington perhaps. Yes, that will be your last tour before you are stashed away for tutoring. How different you will be when I return. As will I."

Maggie, gusted with faintness, puts her hand on a glacial wall. She half expects to feel a coldness, so real does it look, feels instead the sticky wetness of fresh paint. "Why is that bird by himself?" she asks of a sudden. The bird is glossy-black in the well-lit hall and is shaped like a large, fat urn. It has white patches about its eyes and a witless look.

"Himself? No. That is the female of the species. A Great Auk." Elisha explains how, on his first expedition to the Arctic, he and two companions found her on the barrows, how the bird cocked her head as if trying to recognize their faces, then waddle-climbed up the hummock, her stubby wings used as a propellant. Elisha's companion shot the bird and she slid down to where her green-hued egg was sitting on open ground.

"We were delighted at the time. We had bagged, you see, what was certainly the last Great Auk in existence. The captain and I decided to have her stuffed for the ship's library."

Elisha strokes his jaw. "I told the stage painter to put her there because I admit it nagged at me, the shooting of that beast. Though, why so greatly? Why at all? Consider my little brother. He was the last of William Kane, never the like to be seen again. Every death is the same and yet unique and comes to all without favour. Thus what could it possibly signify, the death of one dumb animal on an Arctic plain?"

"I don't know. I don't know these things at all, Lish," Maggie says softly, desperately. "And that's why, why I need tell you the how of it all." She looks to where her feet might be if they were not encircled by layers of skirting and petticoats.

"Ah, God. Stay alike that, my love," Elisha says, his voice catching queerly. "I see an image of you. You are looking down, your countenance pensive just as now. But your body erect, yes, also just as now, as if you are determined for something. You are dressed as an enchantress, as Circe. A white sheath but no . . . corset. Your hair is loose. An ambrotype. I must have one made. Only glass could do such an image justice." He trails off into his own imaginings. Maggie makes bold and reaches for his hand. She slides her fingers between his. His fingers tremble, then tighten. She would give her soul, or some portion of it, to remain fixed with him on this stage, amid these painted shores and bergs, beneath these sparkling bits of cut glass. She makes to speak again. To tell. To make things plain and honest between them.

"You're so wondrously mysterious, Tuttie, promise you will always stay so," Elisha says, at which Maggie blinks and finds herself as mute and witless as any Great Auk.

Three nights later Maggie sits in the audience with Katie and their mother. Katie wears her favourite gown of cream and fawn, Maggie a new-sewn gown of bishop's blue. Mother, at Maggie's insistence, wears a brown silk gown instead of her usual fit-out of brown woollens, and a band of faux flowers instead of her usual fussy lappet cap. Leah has not come, to Maggie's relief. A new doctor is examining Calvin, and as his wife she is apparently required.

I am in love, Maggie decides. She must be. The feeling—giddy and sapped and anxious—is alike that described in the novels she reads. And how can she not be in love with Elisha Kent Kane, given his station, his handsome countenance, his erudition, his renown and reputation, even his "celebrity," as he so mockingly called it?

Elisha takes the stage to polite applause. He invites the audience to play "detective" and discover, as he had on his first expedition, the remains of Sir John Franklin's encampment, the abandoned sledges and heaps of discarded food tins. And then, the stone-heaped graves of three members of Franklin's party. Elisha asks why no written record was found, no brave notes as is usual when all is lost. The audience confers.

"The Open Polar Sea, dear listeners!" Elisha exclaims. "The evidence for its existence is overwhelming: The warming currents as one travels upwards. The birds that have been seen to migrate north. The perpetual rays of summer that could not allow for an icy cap on our world. No, no, good people, at the top of our world are warm shores bounded by vivid trees and strange grasses. Food is abundant there—fishes the colour of the *auroras*, sea-hogs that can feed a man for months, and creatures unnamed and strange beyond telling with jellied limbs and a multitude of eyes to see during the six months of utter dark. Sir Franklin and his men are there! Surviving in that undiscovered realm. Awaiting, nay, praying for rescue. I have volunteered to lead the next Grinnell expedition. And I give you my heart's vow that I will not rest until Sir Franklin is found, until we, the Americans, succeed in this noble search."

The audience claps. Some listeners huzzah. Many reach for their pocketbooks.

After the lecture, after the applause, Maggie, Katie and their mother wend through the milling audience towards Elisha. He is still onstage, tight-grouped now by admirers. Closer and Maggie realizes these "admirers" have the proprietary air of close kin. She steadies her breath. His family has come after all. The older man, upright as a post and all distinction, is no doubt Judge Kane, Elisha's father. The youngish man, who looks a better-fed version of Elisha, must be his brother Tom-the-lawyer. And the woman? She is taller than any of the men, her beauty astounding though she must be past sixty. Her features are delicate and pale, as if cut for a cameo. Her hair a vivid gold, her slender figure arrayed in forest green. Maggie finds it hard to believe she has borne seven children, of which Elisha is the youngest.

Maggie readies a demure smile, adjusts her gloves. Decides she is glad to meet his parents at last. They are always out of town when she asks to meet them, or moving house, or indisposed.

Mrs. Kane sweeps something minute from Elisha's collar, then swivels her lovely neck an almost imperceptible degree. She might not be seeing Maggie at all.

Maggie whispers to Mother and Katie, and the three move forward as one. Just then Morton appears. "Miss Fox, I'll be honoured to see you home."

Maggie looks in dismay at Elisha. He is nodding to his mother. His face has a strange, tight expression. Embarrassment? Surely not. He darts Maggie a pleading glance. She understands then. Understands completely. His expression is not embarrassment but that of a little boy about to cry. Volcanoes. Wars. Fevers. Foreign heat. The endless Arctic ice and dark. He fears none of these. Fears only his mother. Yearns for her. Resents her. A suffocating quilt of emotion, perhaps alike what Maggie feels for Leah.

She lets Morton shepherd them away, ignoring her mother's queries, Katie's disgruntlement, her own frustration, and all because the pity has allowed a revelation: Maggie loves Elisha with all her heart. Loves *him*, not his "celebrity" and station and all that. And I will love him, she decides, for everlasting more.

"BUT DID HE HAVE IT MADE? The ambrotype?"

"Oh, yes."

I knitted a line or two. "I've heard said your sort can hold a picture, an image, and then scry what happened to the person, or some such. That is superstition, of course."

"Of course."

"Do you have it still, the ambrotype?"

"It met a bad end. Then again, it *was* made of glass. Why?"

"No reason. Such images are pleasant to have, is all."

"Has anyone taken an image of you, Mrs. Mellon?"

"No," I said. This was not entirely untrue. The image I had—a tin-type clasped in a velveteen case—was not of me alone, but of me and my son. He was fifteen at the time. We looked out all stoic and grim (as does everyone in such images, to be frank), but we had been laughing the moment before.

"I am sorry for that," my patient said, and in such a way that she might have heard me screaming at Mr. Mellon as he threw the tin-type on the hearth, where the flames blackened and bent it, and erased it of any image. Not even a silhouette remained.

"It ain't natural," Mr. Mellon had sneered, "for a woman to love her son more than her husband and sit with the milk-sop for images, alike they are a married set."

I took up the cover-all, my needles. "If I were the gambling sort, I would bet that your Elisha was prone to ludicrous jealousies—for anything or anyone. I would bet that he wanted your attention and regard only for himself."

"Well, yes. He wished to plant his flag, as it were, on my person. But I can't say I was devoid of the green demons either. This I learned when in Washington in the mid of May of '53, not long before Elisha was set to sail for the Arctic, where he hoped to rescue Franklin and set his flag on the shores of that chimera, the Open Polar Sea."

"MAG! GET ON BACK! Lish was just playing. Really! You'll catch your death out there."

Maggie ignores Katie's frantic calling, hastens up the street, round a corner, through a small square; hastens far from Mrs. Sullivan's Washington boarding house.

By the time Maggie spies the small shopping arcade her house-shoes are sopping from the puddles left from the recent rain, her face sopping with ongoing tears. The arcade is an austere place with no fountain, no potted plants and only a few customers at this hour of late morning. She passes a small daguerreotypist's studio. It is a beswagged, cramped space, stacked with false backdrops—Italian castles, flowered fields, shaded rivers. An advertisement in the windoe touts the Gabriella pose, whatever that may be. A clerk arranges the props, books and chairs and pens, his movements a portrait in bore- dom. Before they left for Washington, Maggie and Katie had, on a whim, visited a New York studio similar to this one. Katie wore a capped-sleeve dress of white muslin, Maggie a gown of bottle-green that showed charcoal in the finished image. The effect was a chiar- oscuro: Katie-the-light and Maggie-the-dark. And their expressions differed also. Maggie was looking off to the left with her held-back smile, as if she had spied something amusing out of the corner of her eye. Katie was looking directly at the camera. A rimming of kohl enhanced the translucence of her eyes. She had her hand on Maggie's shoulder, as if to bring her to attention, or to keep her there.

The studio clerk gestures Maggie in, his smile too encouraging by far. Maggie pats at her tears, composes her face, then escapes away into a haberdashery, where she snatches up a pair of white kid gloves. Elisha will approve of these, she thinks. He likes white stuff. And he loves me. I know he does.

The clerk packages up the kid gloves, and then a white lace collar that Maggie adds at the last instance. She does not ask the price of either. What lady expresses an interest in money? What gentleman would cheat her? The clerk eyes her with a bemused curiosity, at which Maggie realizes that many in the arcade are eyeing her in the same fashion. Her cheeks tingle. Her breath grows short. She feels indelicate, coarse, noted. She rarely goes out alone and she certainly never goes shopping alone. She always has her mother as chaperone, or Leah, or Amy. Or Katie at the least. Someone.

As it happens, the gloves and lace cost nearly all the money in her reticule. Maggie did not intend to spend so much; she never does. The brief satisfaction from her purchases vanishes completely once she is outside again. The leaden skies threaten more rain and for protection she has only a crocheted shawl, a cap decked with silk flowers, and her useless house-shoes. Not pattens. No bonnet. No cloak. And why is she wearing this dress? Yellow with black stripes? Double damn-it-all, she thinks, I look a fat bee. I look mawkish and old. Why can't I ever make a right decision?

Get yourself on back to Mrs. Sullivan's, she orders herself, and keeps her eyes down and walks with resolve, as if she knows where she is going; but there are few signposts and soon Maggie is lost in this half-built city amid the marshes. Wasn't Washington burned down by the Canadians and British some forty years past? For what reason, though? She resolves to ask Elisha, even though he has said that ladies shouldn't trouble their heads with politics.

Elisha.

What matters if he writes to Kat and says he's going to buy her a set of Honiton lace, too? Maggie thinks. He can buy her a pasteboard crown for her little head, for all I care. What matters if Kat won't show me his latest letter? He loves me, not her.

She halts, bewildered. The street ends abruptly: no path, no outbuildings, and nothing but a marsh ahead. The brick buildings are vacant. The street adjacent peters to nothing. Just another marshy field, a distant forest, though here at least is a sign for a dry goods, another for a barber-dentist.

A man peers suspiciously at her from out a doorway. A woman hangs a red rug over a balcony and flails at it, as if punishing it for some ruggish crime. Maggie can hear wheels rattling somewhere close, but nothing moving in this particular street. Where are the children running aside their hoops? The dogs? The pigs? The beggars and shoe-shines and hawkers of half-rotten vegetables? Where are the dustbins? The horse manure? The area does not seem deserted, exactly. Rather, it's as if it has never been inhabited. Is more like a theatre prop of a town, but without play actors, without an audience, or imagination even. The streets are named for letters: H Street, E Street, and so forth. The crosswise streets are numbered. Such planning should make finding one's way an easy task. Instead it is alike some puzzle designed to strengthen the brain. Or a card game where one must keep count. Maggie has never done well at card games nor puzzles, though Leah always has.

She stops. Tries to orient herself. Elisha warned her about Washington. God, but she should have attended him better! "You will be lucky to find a true gentleman in all the place" was what he said. Warned her of senators and their vulgarity, told her of one senator who had killed his favourite hound with a shovel. Penwit? Fenworth? She often has trouble recalling details when she is in Elisha's whirlwind.

Just as Maggie turns up C Street, a black dog lunges for her. She shrieks and runs towards a larger cross street, her skirts lifted with both hands like some washerwoman. Stumbles over a carriage block. She is sobbing and furious. At herself mostly: Here she saunters to the Underworld and back nearly every day, yet in this backwater town she is totally lost. And where in damnation is the Maggie who braved that hell-hound at the Hydesville orchard only six years past? That Maggie wouldn't have been afraid of some mongrel.

Behind her the dog twists and yelps at the end of his chain. He is knee-high. Riddled with sores.

An old woman detaches herself from a wall and limps over to Maggie. She wears a coal-scuttle bonnet and a dress of faded calico and carries an overlarge basket. She must work under fierce suns, for her skin is scoured and browned. "Poor miss, you look as if you've lost your way."

"I have! Thank you. Do you know the way to Mrs. Sullivan's boarding house? I seem to have misplaced it." Maggie smiles.

The old lady smiles back. Her eyes are a clouded green.

"Sure, but you can wander these streets till time's end. I'll be a help, then." Her voice hints of some foreign place. Ireland? England? An old place, surely; she has that sort of gravitas. She grips Maggie's forearm as if to find the bone beneath. Guides her now down this street, now that. Walks fast for an old woman with a limp. Her basket bump-bumps her thigh. She smells of onion, tilled earth, peppermint.

Here is Mrs. Sullivan's at last. On F Street, as it happens. Maggie vows to attend to addresses better in the future.

"Will you be all right, then?" the old woman asks. One green eye roams over Maggie's face, the other stares down the street.

"Most certainly. You're kind, very kind," Maggie says, and looks askance.

The woman taps her pupil with her fingernail. "It's glass."

"My, but it looks real. Completely." Maggie thanks her and hurries into the boarding house, certain the one eye is fixed on her.

"Maggie Fox! Where have you been?" Mother Margaret exclaims over the manly din emanating from the parlour. "We were so worried, weren't we? General Hamilton is here and a passel of senators and you've kept us all waiting, haven't you? Did you forget? Did you?"

"As if it matters," Maggie mutters. "There's no end to the parade."

"What parade? I don't hear it, do I?"

"Nope." Maggie tucks her package out of view behind the hall-stand. Her mother dislikes her spending overmuch, which means spending at all.

"Laws, then . . . Come now. Come, will you?" Mother Margaret takes Maggie's arm and Maggie enters again into the parade of the curious and the grieved; and on this day, as it happens, the presumptuous and the rude.

"Ah, the vision of Miss Maggie herself!" exclaims one General Hamilton, looking her over, hem to collar. Around Hamilton soldiers stand resplendent in their gold-buttoned coats, in their sky-blue breeches sided with dress swords that whack the bric-a-brac. "I designed the uniforms myself," General Hamilton tells Maggie. His face is craggy and genial, his epaulets the size of small wings.

Maggie sips her hot brandy. Blinks back tears. Katie casts her a beseeching glance. She looks a picture in her pearly gown. Maggie wishes again that she had worn something besides her yellow and black striped dress. I look old and stupid, she thinks, and not a bit like Kat.

"What could be troubling your pretty mind, Miss Maggie?" General Hamilton inquires.

"I lost my way. I don't like Washington at all. It's a horrid city altogether. Like, like the labyrinth in that Greek story."

"Now, now, Washington is as easy to navigate as a draught's board." General Hamilton drops his voice. "Unless, that is, one is having an *affaire de coeur* and is off on a secret rendezvous, and not with a bull-headed man, of course, but a man of more modern structure."

The brandy pools on Maggie's tongue.

General Hamilton leans in conspiratorially. "I heard you've stolen away the heart of our brave Dr. Kane. Indeed, it is all the talk."

"Indeed?"

"Yes, 'indeed,' and I've heard further talk that you are to be married before he leaves for the Arctic." The general crosses his legs with surprising delicacy given they are thick as trees. "I hear so many things. I'm a confidant, you know, in this gossipy town. I've heard, for example, that our first lady, Mrs. Pierce, will be coming to you, most privately, of course. She is inconsolable and our president-in-waiting hasn't been sober for weeks. That Benjamin was their last child left. Did you know there shan't be an inaugural ball! Imagine that? Well, it was most untimely, and most unfortunate the Pierces were witness. Train wrecks are never short of terrible. Indeed, the iron horse is best avoided when a trusty carriage can be found . . . Ah, are these cookies?" He takes one from Mrs. Sullivan's offered plate. Mrs. Sullivan simpers at the famously unmarried general.

A man, thin and dandified, eyes Maggie. "Miss Fox, were you not at the ball of Mrs. Bachard's? I've a bet that you were there."

"I was not. I do not attend balls, sir." She looks to the general for assistance with this impertinent man, but the general seems fascinated by the brocade on the man's breeches.

Dandy-Man sniffs. "If it was not yourself, then it was certainly your, uh, what is the word?"

Maggie stands up, upsetting the general's plate of cookies. She ignores their chuckling, helps herself to a cup of punch at the sideboard. Above the sideboard hangs a collection of silhouette portraits. Some of the portraits look recently done. Where do you find a silhouette-cutter these days? Maggie wonders, what with ambrotypes and daguerreotypes being all the rage. And why would anyone want themselves rendered as a mere outline? As a dark, blank space?

Katie comes up next to her. Maggie ignores her.

"I could just kill myself to get away from these awful fellows. I mean, really, couldn't you? . . . Is that punch any good?"

"Good enough," Maggie mutters. Katie ladles herself a cupful. Looks up at the silhouettes. "I hate those. They don't tell you a thing about a person, and I'm sorry, Mag. I am. Elisha wrote me just to, to, uh, fiddle-it, I don't know. He said you were fickle. *You* fickle? Hah! Here." She gives the letter to Maggie, whose eyes fasten on this passage, then that:

Katie, the older you grow the more difficult it will be to liberate your-self from this thing . . . Maggie esteemed me too lightly . . . I shall not call, for I am a person of strong will.

"Now, don't be a worry-all," Katie continues. "Your Mr. Intrigue will call on you. You've made a total conquest of him."

Maggie folds the letter away into her reticule. "Sorry, Kat, sorry for rushing off. I . . ." She pauses, then tells Katie of the old woman who guided her back to Mrs. Sullivan's, of her glass eye, the click-click of her nail on the pupil. "She reminded me of . . . of him, that old peddler."

Katie frowns at her empty punch glass. "Pish, I don't see how."

"She had a limp, like I said, and she carried that basket like it was everything in the world. And she smelled like he did."

"I don't remember how he smelled."

"You must remember how he smelled. You talked about it for days after. I had to stuff your pillow with lavender to stop you complaining."

"You were lots older than me then. I was a child and children forget things."

"What are you jawing about? Much older 'then.' The difference in years between us hasn't changed."

"Fiddle and damn! I haven't forgotten. There. But I'd like to, and you're not helping with your talk of that smelly old peddler. He was so mean. He deserved to be turned into a ghost, he did. You're the one who said so."

"Hush," Maggie whispers as the soldiers and senators look over.

"I'm sorry, Mag, I am. I mean, what were we thinking? But it's not as if we can change it. What's done is done and here we are, and it's not so bad."

"I suppose."

"And that old lady who got you back here, why she was just some old fuss-budget, not some, some—what's the word?"

"*Doppelganger*, it's German," Maggie says, thinking how Dandy-Man hadn't been able to wrestle the word up either. "A *fetch* is what Ma would call it, I'd guess."

"That's it. Well, those doppelganger-fetch things, they don't always mean disaster, do they?"

"You'll have to ask Ma," Maggie says, half in earnest.

Mrs. Sullivan enters with a tray of Johnny Appleseed cake. Apples. Apples. There is no getting away from them. The peddler certainly couldn't, not on the public road, nor at the Hydesville house once he caught up with Maggie and Katie there.

"Come, girls, will you?" their mother calls. "The gentlemen are ready for you. And this is Senator Penworth."

Penworth. That was the one Elisha talked about.

Gentlemen, hah! Maggie soon thinks as they sit round Mrs. Sullivan's table with an assortment of senators and higher military sorts. Senator Penworth stares at Katie's bodice and proclaims, "This is all a humbug but it is worth a dollar to sit in the sunlight of Miss Kate's eyes!"

Guffawing and knee-slaps. Mother Margaret croaks a protest that no one attends. Why would they? Maggie wonders. She looks like a harried scullery maid in her brown-stuff gown, her hands twisting in her apron.

Dandy-Man pounds a minstrel tune on the parlour organ. Maggie sits cross-armed and sullen-faced at the table. She pushes up the rug with her foot as General Hamilton saunters to his seat. He stumbles. Looks mystified. Mother, beleaguered, tries again. "Sirs! You've come to ask questions of the spirits, haven't you? Compose yourselves, will you? And behave as gentlemen. Please?"

Poor Ma, Maggie thinks, a few years back she would never have spoken forcibly to those above her station, which means nearly everyone.

The men smirk and dally and finally settle. One asks if ghosts are wanting the vote. Women were, why not ghosts? There is much laughing at this.

A soldier whom-ever says, "I hear you ladies can manifest up ghosties that look like nymphs or pagan princesses. I hear you can see through their getups. That, I'd pay mightily to see! How about it?"

The spirits do not dignify this with an answer, nor the next question from Dandy-Man: "Can these spirits be trained to come when called, like dogs? Because all this is taking a deuced long time."

Senator Penworth rattles the cuspidor with a well-aimed spit. "Hah, that brings to mind my favourite bitch what died not long ago. Call her up, will you please, ladies?"

"Dogs have no souls, Penworth!" a young senator asserts.

"This one did. She was smarter than most people, and I loved her like my own daughter." Penworth pretends an aggrieved tone. "I move that we not support any Paradise that disallows dogs."

Cheers of "hear, hear" and such. More laughter. And then a sound alike a hammer blow, followed by five more blows. The table shudders and the glassware trembles. The room quiets. The men look at each other in astonishment.

Maggie glowers at Senator Penworth. "That's for every time you hit poor Clementine with a shovel. She's furious you killed her and she's coming back to haunt you snap-quick. She'll rip you to bloody pieces while you sleep, just see if she doesn't!"

"I'll be damned," Penworth says. "And now how'd you know her name, you pretty minx?"

"The spirits told her, who else?" Katie puts in.

Penworth looks about. His friends are shrugging, half smiling. "Now, now," he says. "I'd not meant to thwack Clementine so hard."

Maggie rises in a huff from the table. The men stand also, at least those who still can. Katie sits back and drinks her brandied coffee. Mother looks, of course, bewildered.

"What say we take a roam about the White House, gentlemen," General Hamilton suggests. "Damn fine claret to be found in the Blue Room."

Maggie sweeps by Hamilton, and then Penworth.

"And damned pretty maids to be found in the White House hall," she hears Penworth say, to more laughter.

In the vestibule Maggie grabs her package. She will try on the new kid gloves and lace collar above-stairs. She wishes now she had bought more accessories at the arcade—a chatelaine perhaps, or some gimping, some zigzag ricing. Nothing puts her mind at ease more quickly than shopping, except, of course, trying the latest cocktail.

She makes to rush above-stairs, nearly careers into Mrs. Sullivan.

"This came for you, Miss Fox."

"What? When?"

"Just now. My stars, but I just can't say what I make of you and your sister."

"You're in swell company, then." His fingers tremble as she takes the intricately folded handkerchief and finds, inside, an intricately folded note.

After all the "gentlemen" leave, Maggie and Katie help their mother tidy the parlour of glasses and bottles.

Katie says, "If Leah had been here they wouldn't have dared insult us. Oh, fiddle-dee, but I need a clean glass. My lips won't touch anything those nasty men have touched. Ma, where are the clean glasses? My nerves are all in shreds!"

"Here, now settle yourself, will you? But only a half-glass, poppet . . . that is enough . . . Leah said you're not to overindulge even if it's for your constitution."

Katie drops into a chair. "But I hate it here. I wish I were dead. I wish I were lying in a cold, cold grave."

"Never say such things, Katherine. It tempts Fate, doesn't it?"

"Can even Fate be tempted?" Maggie muses. She is looking out the window, smiling away.

"That is not what I mean—oh, never mind."

"Fine and damn-dandy, then." Katie's face is flushed, her words overloud. "I don't wish I were dead, but I wish I were poor as a church mouse then. Yes, I'd rather live on a crust of bread and old water than endure this life."

"You wouldn't last a day on bread crusts, would you? Come, lamb, the spirits have honoured you. They've chosen you. Don't forget that. It scarcely matters if some louts make sport, does it? I promise, I'll let no more wretched senators or soldiers come to our sittings, no matter what honeyed words they offer. I'll be as vigilant as that dog, won't I?"

Katie looks up bewildered. "Clementine? Mr. Penworth's dog?"

"No, she was hardly vigilant, was she? Otherwise she wouldn't have got herself thwacked by a shovel. No, the one with the three heads. Down in Hades, is it?"

"Cerberus?" Maggie puts in, trying not to laugh. She presses the handkerchief to her lips. It is of the whitest linen and squared with Belgian lace and smells of Elisha's hair pomade.

"Cerberus, that's it, now . . . Laws, Maggie . . . where did you get that handkerchief?"

"This one? Well, Elisha, Dr. Kane . . . he brought it because . . . well."

"Brought it? What do you mean, 'brought it'? Is he here? In Washington? Here now? Why isn't he in New York preparing for the Arctic? And where is he staying? And why hasn't he announced his presence to me? I'm the mother, aren't I?"

"It's just that . . . the truth is, he needed to come for some last-minute fund-garnering and legal maneuverings. He's with his brother Tom-the-lawyer and—"

"Margaretta Fox. Tell me. Tell me this instance. Where is he staying?" Mother's voice has that tone that beggars argument, and so Maggie points slowly upwards.

"Here? God help us! Here? Has Dr. Kane no concern at all for your reputation?"

"There was nowhere else! All the hotels were full-up."

"He's the one who's full-up, isn't he? Yes."

A short time later they are all huddled in the boarding-house vestibule: Maggie, Katie, their mother, and Elisha himself. His brother Tom stands at a tactful distance.

Maggie is relieved that Mother's indignation does not last; but then her indignation never does. Elisha takes Mother's hand. Repeats his honourable intentions. Insists that he would never endanger Maggie's reputation. Insists that, indeed, all the hotels are full.

"Now, Maggie," Elisha says. "You must never knock at a gentleman's private parlour, nor ever call upon them in any manner. You must wait for them to call upon you."

"Oh, I know that. Everybody does."

"Them?" Mother Margaret puts in. "What do you mean, them? Will there be many? That won't do, not at all, not at all. Will it? I am quite perplexed, sir."

"No, no," Elisha says. "There is only one *them*, which is *I*. It is a matter of speech, and of no . . . matter. I assure you, my dearest Mrs. Fox, I will be so engrossed in this dreaded business of raising funds that you shall scarcely notice my presence."

Maggie doubts that, but is glad Mother seems mollified for now. Maggie and Katie truss on their bonnets. Elisha and Tom assist with the wraps. The four of them are off to tour the sights of Washington.

Their mother is nearly asleep at a writing desk by the time Maggie and Katie noisily return, cheeks red from an unexpectedly brisk May wind. Elisha and Tom bid them elaborate good-nights and ascend to the gentlemen's chambers.

"We saw that Capitol thing they're building," Maggie announces to Mother. "I told Elisha it looked queer with all that scaffolding, like a cracked-open egg with nothing inside but air. He said that was just the place for politicians." She covers her mouth to laugh.

"And we saw the Potomac," Katie puts in. "It looked really glorious in the sunset. All wine-coloured. And, oh, the aqueduct. It isn't as nice as Rochester's, but I didn't say. Elisha's going to take us to the cosmoramas soon as we're back in New York. Fiddle-it, but my fingers are chilled. What say we have a toddy or two."

Over the next week Elisha, promises forgotten, makes no secret of his ardour for Maggie. Nor of his disdain for the spirits. He interrupts sittings, demands her attentions, admonishes her for attending too many dinner parties. On the tenth day of his presence, a letter arrives from Leah. Friends have informed her of the drunken, debauched sittings in Washington. Of Elisha's arrival. Mother and the girls are to return to New York forthwith: *And do not neglect to pack your reputations, dear girls.*

That is, if you can find those priceless items amid the mess you have made.

Maggie, Katie, and Mother pass the letter hand to hand in silence. Leah's words are tight-knit and ink-splattered; Maggie can almost see her writing in one of her rousing furies. Katie sighs and asks Mrs. Sullivan for a spruce beer. Mother Margaret insists they pack that very instant. "Our Leah's right, isn't she? Gracious evers, but I miss your father sometimes. And Arcadia. And those quiet, ordinary days. Don't you, girls?"

The girls don't answer.

"Well, laws, but I do. I'd even prefer that peddler's ghost to all this, wouldn't I?'

Katie brightens. "I nearly forgot. Mag wanted to ask you about dopplegangers. Or you know, fetches? Do they always warn of disaster or death or something really bad? Maggie reckons she saw one."

"Kat? What are you—"

"Saw one. Where? When?"

Maggie reassures Mother. Katie misunderstood her story of the old lady with the basket. Katie pouts at this. Sips her spruce beer.

"That's how stories become something else," Maggie adds. "People change them up. They grow them, one word at time, until they're no longer a little inconsequential story, but something else entirely. Something everyone thinks is important, but wasn't at the outset, not at all." She is babbling, she knows, and Mother and Katie are giving her the puzzle-eye. And so she falls quiet, says nothing more. And nothing, she thinks, is exactly what she and Katie should have done when Mother woke up in alarm that night in Hydesville five years past and shook awake their father. He did not wake straightaway. He had about him an unfamiliar smell that Maggie understands now was that of whisky. Mother was often making a fuss out of night noises—the scratching of branches, the pattering of rats, the sound of wood collapsing in the stove—and so neither Maggie nor Katie believed her when she proclaimed she had heard footsteps. Instead they smirked and then colluded. The loud and inexplicable raps sounded shortly after. Mother decided then and there, that the sounds were made by the peddler rumoured to be buried in their very own cellar. There was no convincing her otherwise.

CHAPTER 25

"Come, Mrs. Mellon. Try," my patient said this day, and propped Dr. Kane's tome open on her lap. "Katie and I, we had such a lark doing this."

"That's all chalk and nonsense," I said. Many of my older patients practised sortilege (albeit with the bible) but I did not hold with such superstition, and I told her this fact. "It's no more possible than divining from a tin-type, as you said."

"Oh, I agree, it's a mere amusement. Before I met Elisha we did this with Byron's books." She smiled. "The passage I fell on would ever indicate I would love a doomed, adventuring poet sort. Imagine that. Now, here."

"Very well." I put down my knitting and hefted *Arctic Explorations* from her lap and decided not to remind her that Byron was known for other doings besides being adventurous and doomed: fornicating with his half-sister, for example, and with any other woman who fell to his eye.

"You must close your eyes for the magic to work."

"Of course. And my mind, to boot." At which I fast-shut my eyes, then opened Kane's book at random and traced my finger round and round and then stopped and read what I had settled on: "*Refraction with all its magic is back upon us; the Delectable Mountains appear again; and, as the sun has now worked his way to the margin of the north-western horizon, we can see the blaze stealing out from the black portals of these uplifted hills, as if there was truly beyond it a celestial gate."*

I stopped then. Perhaps that is all my son saw—a refraction. To explain: I had been thinking about dopplegangers and fetches since she mentioned them the day before, thinking on how, when my son was twelve, he spied me standing on the rocky shore. As he waved from the hummock above, I walked straight into the sea and vanished. He raced on home, all in tears, and there I was, making lobster pie, not drowned in the least. Nonetheless, as one might expect, he looked at me askance for a good few weeks after.

"A vision is often a natural occurence, nothing more. That is what this means," I said.

"Why, that is exact to what I might have said."

I handed her the book. "Your turn, Mrs. Kane."

She closed her eyes and let her fingers hover before finding their place. Read: "*Hans has not returned. I give him two days more before I fall in with the opinion that Godfrey has been waylaid or seized upon his sledge. This wretched man has been the very bane of the cruise. My conscience tells me that almost any measure against him would be justified.*"

She mused for a short time. "I have it. One should not see enemies where none exist. That is what this indicates."

"Or that we make enemies of ourselves."

"Yes. You might have been a star in my profession, Mrs. Mellon. We might have worked together as a perfect team."

I was oddly pleased at this, and so listened all-attentive while she brought out Chauncey for his last bow.

CHAUNCEY BURR SPOTS HER in a crowded New York omnibus. Lady Leah Lucko herself. He thrusts past the coated obstacles. She is seated. On her head is a brimless bonnet, its fat ribbon tied under her dimpled cheek. Even Chauncey can tell it is costly. On her lap is a parcel wrapped in parchment. Just the fucko size, Chauncey thinks, of some poor bastard's head. Likely she plans to make it bloodyo sing or tell a prophecy or two.

Leah sits between two dozing women. Their three skirts take up the space of six men, men who must then stand in the aisle and study the advertisements plastered on the omnibus roof. Ah, but Leah Lucko is clearly not acquainted with these women, not given her scornful expression at their bobbing heads. She is unescorted, then. Fortunate for Chauncey Burr that an unescorted woman is allowable in this modern city, for ever since the court case in Columbus, those months ago, he has longed to speak with Leah face to face, without her phalanxes of supporters, and here she is on a shining May day, wedged and alone. Quite unlike how she sat in the courtroom, a chilly sun firing her russet silks, some jackanapes perched on her lap. What a picture of innocent womanhood she was! Was he the only one who noted how she kept stuffing the boy—Charlie, was it?— with sweets to keep him genial?

He pushes himself past two scrivener sorts. They mutter but allow the indignity. Though Chauncey Burr is sporting an unkempt look—his beard straggled, his Albert coat stained, his hessian boots unpolished—this suggestion of disrepute only makes him a more formidable presence than usual.

"Good day, Mrs. Fish, or should I say, Mrs. Brown? Or might it be Mrs. Brown Fishy Fox, or Browno Foxy Fish."

Her glittery eyes fix on him.

"What ho! You look as if you've seen a ghostie, a real and factual one. Ah, do not be afeared. It is only I, the Reverend Chauncey Burr, at your service." He gives a mock bow, no easy trick in the jolting omnibus.

Never has Chauncey Burr seen such a purled lip, such splendidly contemptuous eyes.

"You."

"Me, indeedo. My proverbial hat is off to you, madame." Yes, my hat, he thinks, as would my vest and trousers at half a chance. Damno, but she is a fine figure of a woman.

Leah gasps then, as if his thoughts are a signboard. Yanks the hanging bell-pull and forces past him. The horses halt.

Should Chauncey seize this moment to tell the truth? The truth being that he alone understands that Leah—and her sisters also—are no vapour-headed ladies, as most would have it, as they themselves like to promote, that he alone sees through their guise completely, and that he has a true respect for them, their ingenuity and intelligence and sheer verve. Perchance he'll don some skirts along with an aura of purity and innocence. Gnaw his knuckles in nervousness. Be a spiritual battery, empty and at the ready for energy to suffuse his form. Become a medium! Yes, indeedo! Become a "Spiritualist" and believe in modern "Spiritualism"—for it is now an official movement, a "something" beyond the Fox women and their imitators. It is now heading for the history books and dictionaries. But not the word "Chauncelogist." Not the movement "Burrism."

Leah Lucko steps into the street. Chauncey considers for a half-block, then jumps off the moving omnibus. Follows her up 23rd. Once the pedestrians have thinned, he quickens his stride, blocks her passage. His expression is one of contrition, even regret. "I was attempting an honest compliment, Mrs. Brown. Indeedo, I've never seen your like in the female department. Such is the truth of it."

Leah's look is indignant, but she does not flounce off. Seems interested in what he has to say. Is at least not behaving as the quavering heroine in distress.

"I am a plain and ordinary soul, Mr. Burr, surrounded by people of the highest standing, true, but I myself am plain."

"I think not. No, indeedo. You've outwitted Chauncey Burr and that's something neither ordinary nor plain. Made a pauper of me. Ten thousand dollars, does that ring a bell?"

"Oh, it is practically a tintinnabulation, sir. But then lies cost. Slander costs."

"They do, they do. Righto, then! Have you settled yourself here in our grand metropolis? I have no doubt you can well afford it now." His mild tone might indicate that he does not care that his money lines her frothy reticule.

"My friends encouraged me to move. I am needed where the most can find me."

What a damnedo voice, Chauncey thinks, so melodious it could convince birds to shit golden droplets. "Find? But not find *out*, what ho! Your trick, and I've only just understood it, is that you've convinced *yourself*, have you not? You've stood so long amid your own bullshit you can't smell it at all! How else can you keep it up and up, eh?"

Her lips twitch, though whether to smile or snarl Chauncey can't gauge. "Good day, sir. I advise you turn and leave now before I cry for a policeman."

He doesn't leave. She doesn't cry. They face each other, neither willing to be the one to turn away. The crowds flow round them. Hawkers proclaim their wares from storefronts and handcarts. A team of greys stand square in the traces of a Phaeton. Three pigeons skim over Leah's bonnet. She does not flinch.

"I shall good day awayo," Chauncey says at last. "But allow me to add that we would make a fine team: Burr and Fox. Take your pick of phenomenon. None could challenge us."

There, he has unnerved her. She grips her package. Meets his gaze for the span of a breath. Two. Tips her head with a taut and desperate expression, as if trying to catch a prompter's voice from the stage wings. "A team? You have lost your senses! If I were a horse I would not stand in the same harness with you."

"Haho! But you stood in the harness with that besotted wide-eyed—Calvin, was it? Hardly a matching pair, the two of you."

"How dare you . . . you despicable, wretched man. And how dare you attempt to besmirch the reputation of a defenseless woman. I am delighted to have ruined you, for you well deserve your fate."

"Indeedo. As for my fate? It is the same as any mortal's—to become bones and dust and food for the crawling things." He gestures to the pedestrians about. "All these others see Heaven in the clouds, God in the details and the Devil in the dark. But the flesh is all we have, Leah, and you know this as well as I."

"All I know is that I am going home!"

"Good day, then, but I shall keep atrack of you, and your ascension in this damnedo life. What poor chap you marry next is anyone's guess." He bows and turns. Resists looking back, though she is watching him stride off, surely.

⨎

"D<small>ID</small> L<small>EAH SEE</small> C<small>HAUNCEY AGAIN</small>? Did any of you?" I asked.

"No. Though I heard he reinvented himself once again, as a biographer and then as a Unitarian of all things. And that he became, too, a great friend of that Mr. Poe."

"The one who wrote those dreadful stories?"

"Yes, in which the mysteries are always solved." At that my patient asked for her bible box and searched through until she found a small advertising card. She put the card atop the box and closed the lid. "This is for you to keep when I pass," she said. *Pettifew's Ingenuities,* it read, but nothing more, no hint of what these ingenuities might be. It was a mysterious little card.

"Thank you," I said all-polite. "I'll cherish it."

She chuckled. "I meant this, the bible box, the lily box, and all its contents—the letters, the pamphlets, the lot. They may wend into the world when you see fit. It won't matter a jot to me once I'm gone past the so-called celestial gate."

I said I would be honoured to inherit her bible box. (I should add that some weeks later, once the box was in my possession, I noticed that, on flip side of Pettifew's card, was an address. It was written in pen-ink and was for a less-than-savoury part of Manahattan. The letters "RM" were also written there.) "I'll guard it as if my life depended upon it," I added.

She said she hoped my life would depend upon other things besides that, and then recalled us back to Leah.

"W<small>ELL</small>, I, <small>SIR</small>, shall not be keeping 'atrack' of you!" Leah proclaims to Chauncey's receding back. "You pass from history as of this moment!"

And yet she watches until the steam arising out of a grate half vanishes him, until the jostling crowd vanishes him entirely. Only then does she walk on, slow and cautious, the package held firm. My spirits, she thinks, why did Alfie have to get afflicted with the catarrh? This should have been his task. But the errand could not wait, she knows; the séance two days hence will be the most important of her career. Everything must be ready for Leah's illustrious guest. She must not put a single step wrong.

Leah catches her breath and leans against the stair-post of a brownstone that is the spit-image of her own. She wishes she could sit on the stoop, but that would look common. She presses her hand to her forehead. A pain chews away there, as it often does of late, often tempting her to take up soporifics again. One evening with her overindulging sisters, however, is enough to shoot that notion to penny-bits.

A couple stroll by, arm in arm, talking with close confidence. The gentleman tips his hat at her. Leah smiles benignly back, thinks: How dare that Chauncey, that so-called reverend, that Burr stuck in my side, how dare he suggest we would make a "team"? She considers how his buttons were askew, his fur collar bedraggled, his dark beard growing this way and that. He looked, in all, like the hard-used plaything of some giant child. A grand team! What damnable poppycock.

She shifts the package in her arms. The store was almost impossible to find. The advertising card Alfie gave her bore only the address and name. No directions at all. When she found the store at last, it was down an alley and up several outside stairs. The sign, "Pettifew's Ingenuities," was barely noticeable, the store not much larger than a horse stall. Only a few items were on display—thick canes, brass piping, women's fans of unusual size, quires of waxy paper, spools of thread, jars of inks. And not a label to be seen. A man, Mr. Pettifew himself, as Leah rightly supposed, put aside his periodical. He greeted her without rising from his high stool. He had thick, stooped shoulders and a narrow-cut beard. A visor banded his near-hairless skull. The place was poorly lit by its one cheap gas fixture, but Leah could tell an ugly man in any light.

"I am Mrs. Miller. I have come for a package. I do hope it is ready. I have no time to tarry."

"No one ever does," Pettifew said, with what may have been a snicker. He brought out a package with great care. Gave her instructions and warnings along with her change. He eyed her as he did so, as if they were acquainted, as if he knew what she was about. "You care to take a gander at my other offerings? I've got the best and rarest, and since you're . . . well. Let's just say I'm honoured, Mrs.

Miller." He cleared his throat. "There's something I'm working on. It's a secret listing for those of your ilk." He showed her a book then; it was big as a ledger cheaply bound and blue."

"I'm going to call it the Blue Book."

"How very original."

"You could add to it. It'd be a rare honour if you did. I want it to be the best, see, the finest."

"I think not."

"Consider on it, for the next time we see each other."

The next time? Leah thinks now as she steps away from the stairpost of the brownstone. I cannot imagine there will be a next time. Her thoughts of Pettifew and even Burr have made her heedless and she stumbles on a protruding brick. The package lolls in her arms. She gasps and clutches it, sensing every dread ounce. Steady. Steady, she warns herself

At last she attains 26th Street and her lovely brownstone. "Thanks be the Spirits," she murmurs. A chestnut tree arches over the stoop. Well-dressed people are dotted here and there. There is a lessening of refuse. A plentitude of gas lamps and decent paving. *I have already ascended in this damnedo life, Mr. Burr, as you can see.* Yes, such is what Leah will say to that Chauncey, if he dares come call upon her.

Once inside, Leah eases the package onto the hallstand, then takes her bonnet off with both hands, as if the bonnet were a helmet. She studies the woman in the looking glass. The face is not much lined for her thirty-eight years, provided she does not scowl. The hair is not much greyed, provided she is vigilant with the hennaed oil. The thickening of her features is something only Leah would note . . . and God and the Spirits why would she care how Chauncey Burr visions her?

She takes up the package and makes her way to the front parlour. The girls are out at a sitting, she recalls. She dearly hopes they will not "encounter" that odious Dr. Kane on their way home. Honestly, she cannot comprehend Maggie's attraction to him, given the way he patronizes her and winds her up like a top. He will never accept Maggie for what she is.

In the front parlour, Leah's birds racket welcome. Warblers, finches, wrens, even several exotic parrots flit in a cage that is man-high and fashioned alike a Chinese pagoda; about this cage range five or six smaller cages aflutter with budgeriear, chats, and tangiers. An indigo bunting fixes on her, his look quizzical and wide-of-eye, as if in miminry of some of Leah's clients.

"Good afternoon, my darlings," she says.

"Good afternoon, you're looking well, dear Leah."

Leah peers at the birdcages, then at Horace Greeley as he walks in from the back parlour. Mother trails behind him. "Leah! Poppet! Wherever were you? Have you been shopping? What do you have there?"

"Nothing, Mother, nothing. No, don't touch. Must you always touch . . ." She slides the package onto a side table. "Horace, this is a surprise."

Horace apologizes. He was in the neighbourhood and came to offer advice on this connection between Margaretta and Elisha, since advice was what Leah asked of him in her last letter.

Leah owns that she had asked for his advice, albeit a time back, but no matter, here he is, better late than never and all that. She sits Horace down in their best gentleman's chair. Mother brings in the tea and Horace's favourite oatcakes, then sits quietly.

Horace begins. "Now in regards to this incessant reportage of Maggie and Dr. Kane, I have to apologize, in that—"

"No need, any small advice from a worthy man such as yourself is greatly appreciated."

"What I should say is that I have only thoughts at the moment."

"Thoughts? Ah. What sort?"

"Most disagreeable and perplexing ones. The attention paid to Maggie and Elisha, to their every last movement and utterance is, I've realized, part and parcel of this newfangled rage for trivial personages, this 'celebrity,' a word, I can assure you, that was not minted by my pen."

Mother pinches Horace's sleeve. "I cannot bear to see my angel's name appearing in print this way. One fellow . . . a reporter? Is that what they're called? Anywise, he asked me such questions, and in the street! 'Are they engaged?' 'Are they not?' 'What do you, the mother, think of this?' Such a perplexity. One might think there is nothing else of import happening in the world, mightn't one?"

"I agree completely," Horace says mournfully. "The world is shifting, ladies. The trivial holds sway. Gossip is taken as conversation. Here Kansas is bleeding, the slavery question is becoming a battle cry and all the papers can write about is where Miss Fox and Dr. Kane are dining and what she is wearing to the theatre. Will they marry? Won't they? I can't fathom it. They're not royalty. It is not as if their marriage will herald some transfer of power. Furthermore, love should be private; it cannot withstand such searing light." He nibbles at an oatcake. "But few attend me any longer."

Leah feeds her own oatcake to Vivace the parrot. "I assure you, dear Horace, you are attended. And your name will last down through the ages, unlike your friend Barnum, the prattling huckster." She says this last kindly, and with her best dimpled smile.

Mother puts in, "Our Maggie said Elisha gave her a lock of his dead brother's hair—Willie, was it? Also a ring, one that he found in the Arctic on that first expedition. Doesn't that indicate . . . something? But then he insists she call him 'brother.' I had a brother, but I certainly never carried on with him thataway, did I?"

"What is your opinion, Horace?" Leah asks. "Are there rings in the Arctic, growing amid the summer mosses?"

"I suspect he embellishes," Horace sighs.

"He is a man obsessed with secrets," Leah says. "How I despise secrets. We must . . . what is the term in vulgar card games? Ah, we must *force his hand*. He must either marry Margaretta or renounce her. I have some intelligence about our Dr. Kane, dear Horace. There have been other girls who—"

"Other girls? Other?" Mother cries.

Horace presses his hands over his ears. "I must return to the office. I must."

Leah raises her eyebrows at her mother. Her mother twists at her lappet string on her fusty old cap. Wisely keeps her counsel.

Horace uncovers his ears, says firmly, "I shall write that the papers have perverted their columns to the gratification of an impertinent curiosity and so forth, but I cannot publish rumours and innuendo. I wish I could help you more, but in these times I feel a great ineffectiveness, as if all my words have been for naught."

"I have learned that if you wish something to be done, you must do it yourself," Leah says. "Seek public office, Horace, that is my advice. Even the presidency. Why-ever not? Then you would not have to cajole and convince and wear out your fingers writing. You could merely give orders like a maestro. Snap, and it would be done. Imagine how grand that would be."

Mother looks startled. "Have the spirits said our Horace should seek office, Leah? Have they?"

"God and the Spirits, Mother, my advice is surely just as useful as that of any dead person."

Once Horace is seen out, his droopy white hat in hand, and once her mother is bustling elsewhere, Leah takes up her package and wends through the front parlour to the back parlour. This back parlour is closed off by a green baize door and is where the main of their séances are held. It is well-appointed with candelabras and lamps, as well as the new-installed gas lighting, a gleaming ovoid table and hooked rugs so thick that Leah's footfalls are deadened to silence. She walks to darkest corner of the room, where, concealed by a sliding panel, there is another door. This one leads down to the kitchen. Leah ordered it put in because, really, who needs to see how servants come and go?

Alfie is huddled aside the stove in the downstairs kitchen. "You found the place, then?" he asks, his voice a rasp.

"I did, obviously. Though it was a trial. There was not a cab to be found. And on the return I had to take a horrid omnibus. On my own! And who should cross my path? Oh, never mind. Here it is."

Alfie shuffles over. He unwraps the parcel with his accustomed care. The cotton wadding falls away. The glass canister is wax-sealed and water-filled. Leah peers at the whitish pebbles within. "My spirits, but they do not look special."

"They'll sure be special if they hit the air. This amount here would set the whole house afire."

Leah eyes the pebbles again. Tries to imagine herself blown to pieces. "The flesh is all we have" was what Chauncey had said. She wills that palpate sense to cease. "That Mr. Pettifew person recommended lard on the hands, and gloves as well when handling even the smallest of fragments."

Alfie wipes his nose with his sleeve. "Sure. You can't be too careful with phosphorous."

CHAPTER 26

"Elisha suspected that the creatures of the deep, to light their way, used a kind of phosphorous too," my patient said. "He said the Arctic waters were often all aglow, and with the faintest blue. Alike the resting place of stars, my pet."

I had slept poorly the night before, hence my peevish tone when I replied. "Since when are stars blue? What rot. What nonsense. Is your Elisha a naturalist? An astrologist? The resting place of the stars? Hah. More likely the resting place of the blue devils. They are as unnumbered as the stars. As elusive, to boot."

"I agree, there is no end to the blue devils and the melancholies they cause, the nagging torments," she said. Or perhaps I did.

"He decided then, my Elisha, that he would light his own way, make firm decisions and not ever be swayed. He told me that such was the way of all great men."

"And did you believe the cad?"

"Ah, alas and such, I had to believe in something. Some*one*."

"Elisha came here? When I was out? That can't be true, Kat. It just can't."

"But it is. I mean, we don't ever lie to each other. We swore on our own graves, remember?"

"I guess I do," Maggie says, though she doesn't, which is odd. She is generally excellent, as is Katie, at recalling the minutia of conversations.

Muffled rattle-bangs. Maggie glances out the window. A carriage-in-four clops leisurely down their street. A coalman upends a sack into the coal bunker of their brownstone. He wears his coating of soot and black dust as nonchalantly as a gentleman wears a frock coat. A post boy runs past him. He is carrying the message that Maggie just gave him. Katie had peered over her shoulder as she wrote it. *Yes, come for me, Lish* was what it said.

And now the wrenching sounds of Calvin coughing his life's blood away, just down the hall. Maggie still cannot think of Calvin as Leah's husband. He has always been too much of a brother to them all. And Lizzie certainly does not think of him as a stepfather. She is the one who cares for him most days. Maggie's and Katie's company, however, she avoids like the plague. But then, Lizzie loves Calvin, Maggie knows; the fact is stamped on Lizzie's face as clearly as the signs of grief and woe on the faces of her clients. Nonetheless, Lizzie has stepped out again with one George Blauvet, a suitor of suitable standing, according to Leah, though Calvin doesn't like him. He has come to appreciate Lizzie too late. Yes, too late, Maggie thinks, and it occurs to her again that some invincible prankster is at work in their lives.

Mother is busy in the kitchen preparing a selection of delicacies. Maggie and Katie are to be preparing themselves. A whom-ever of the highest order is arriving later this afternoon. "It will be the greatest triumph yet, my girls. All must be pitch-perfect." Leah told Maggie and Katie, no less than four times.

"No, we don't lie to each other, Kat," Maggie says, "but it still can't be true. And why would Elisha talk to Leah? He calls her the Tigress. He can't abide her."

"I don't know. I don't know everything. Fush-it, just because you can't believe it doesn't mean it isn't true. We say that all the time, don't we? And where are you, key? Stop hiding. We've not much time." Katie fumbles around on their bureau past the faux pearls, the diamonds of paste, looks behind the daguerreotype of herself and

Maggie, the one they had made before just before their Washington tour. They chose a thick gilded frame for the image. A fronting of thick glass. Katie-the-light. Maggie-the-dark. Together as can be.

Maggie slumps on the bed they share. It has a rosewood headboard, a mattress stuffed with the finest wool, the softest feathers, and yet for the last few nights Maggie has barely slept, not even with the help of her usual rum toddies.

"... and your Dr. Kane is nothing but a deceptive cadence of a man," Leah said yesterday and all out-of-the-blue. She and Maggie had been bickering, yes, but over something-else-not-Elisha. Expenditures? Imbibing?

"A what?"

"A deceptive cadence, a musical chord that leads you to believe it shall resolve itself. But it does not. And never ever shall."

"And what am I, then?" Maggie asked, in her voice a challenge.

"Hmm, I am afraid, Margaretta, that you are the common-room organ that is being well and truly played."

Why in the bloody tunket did I ask? Maggie wonders now. She twists at Elisha's ring of onyx and silver. Looks to the daguerreotype again, at the selfsame ring there on her imaged hand. He said he found the ring on his first expedition to the Arctic. Found it? Where? Damn, but nothing makes sense.

"There you are, you rusty old thing." Katie holds up the key, then kneels to the trunk at the end of their bed. She twists the key, lifts the lid, reaches in for a brass horn, a glass-domed bell, a spool of silk thread, a spool of catgut, a sheaf of waxy paper, shoes, a stylus. Makes a ditty as she sets these items on the bed: *"Thanks to Pettifew, though our needs are ever-few. Would that our lustrous guest would—"*

"Illustrious," Maggie says dully.

"Sure, and, oh . . . look, Mags." Katie tosses out a sash, a long wind of white muslin, a brass diadem, feathers. "You wore all this for your Mr. Intrigue's ambrotype. Why, you looked just like a pagan princess or something with your hair all tumble-down."

Maggie has to agree with the "or something." All Elisha's behest she had worn no corset under the tight-pinned sheath. He watched —too intently—while the ambrotypist arranged the props and lanterns. An impropriety was at work, Maggie knew, but decided she didn't care.

"You heard not a drop of the conversation, then? Between Leah and Elisha? You're certain of that?"

Katie sits back on her heels, hand on the trunk rim. "Oh, fine and all. Look, I was coming on back from Calvin's room. We'd been sharing that French cognac and some cigars—you know, the ones that help his breathing—but we ran out of the cognac. And so I went to get more from the front parlour, but stopped at the top of the stairs . . . Oh, remember way back at David's house when the ghost first started rapping, and when Leah arrived from Rochester, and we were listening from above-stairs and—"

"Kat. What happened between Leah and Elisha?"

"I really just wanted more cognac or a rum flip and—"

"And?"

"I didn't hear the whole conversation. I swear on my cold, dead body."

"All right."

"So, Leah said she knew about Elisha's 'exploits' and 'conquests' abroad. She said he had to cease toying with your affections and all that. But what she really, really wanted was to know if you'd told Elisha anything about our, you know, sometimes-tricks, the ones we have to use when the spirits are being old fuss-budgets."

"I haven't told him a damned thing!"

"And Elisha said he knew the all. The *all*, Mag. He said he's not gullible, but that he doesn't care. Alfie slithered up just then, so I went on back to our room."

"Hell. What . . . conquests? Did she say?" Her heart sinks. Mountains. Rivers. Pyramids. That is what was meant by conquests. Yes.

"No, they talked then about reputation and all that, and whose was more important, Leah's or Elisha's. Elisha's or Leah's. It seemed a draw, more or less." Katie closes the trunk lid. Locks it. Surveys the objects on the bed, then leafs through the newspaper clippings and obituaries for the president's son. Maggie has already read the material dutifully. Train wrecks, as General Hamilton opined back in Washington, really are never short of terrible.

"Fuss-it-all, you'd think the Queen was coming, the way Leah's going on, and not just about the First Lady. Come, Mag, let's go visit Calvin before she arrives. He's had some more of that cognac delivered."

At two o'clock Lizzie returns. She heads straight up to Calvin, does not even wish Maggie and Katie a bonnychance, or whatever the word is in Lizzie's beloved French.

At three o'clock Katie decides to have a last lie-down before the Big Occasion, and so it is Maggie who must wait with Leah in the vestibule. And wait she does, her throat dry, her hands atremble. Her nervousness has nothing to do with their imminent guests, but with Elisha's plans for her, which will be coming to fruition any moment now. And it doesn't matter a bit what Katie heard, she tells herself. Elisha's heart is true.

Leah cracks open the entry door for the third time. No fine carriage as yet. Leah is arrayed in a day-gown of green and yellow tartan. The skirt yaws across the entire hall and is scalloped with bows the size of small cats. "Please be to God and the Spirits, you did not lunch on cider or toddies, did you, Margaretta?"

"No. And no again. Is that a new timepiece?" Maggie abruptly asks, having just noticed the thick chain that loops over Leah's pleated bodice down to a fat watch at her waist. It looks, Maggie realizes, like a medieval flail. The thought hardly eases her mind.

"No, I have owned it for a good month now. It keeps perfect time, and now do cease looking down like a sullen housemaid. And what message were you giving to that post boy? And Katie? Where is Katie?"

"She's having a fortifying rest."

"She is fortified plenty, I am sure. And Lizzie?"

"Dosing up Calvin, just like you asked."

"Ah, yes. A moment . . . there. I am near to fainting with nerves. I do hope the medicine is sufficient. We cannot have our Calvin coughing in such a horrid fashion, not while our guest is here."

"No," Maggie says, and feels alike some doll-form, emptied of substance.

Mother brushes past Leah with a platter of chutney and sweet pickles. "Laws, but I can't imagine she would actually favour these, can I?"

"What you imagine does not signify, Mother. A trusted source told me of Mrs. Pierce's favourite edibles. Now, leave the platters in the front parlour sideboard, if you please. Here, let me help. And Margaretta, do lend us a hand."

Maggie nods, and all three of them go to the front parlour, where the birdcages are already shrouded in white cloth, the thick drapes drawn, the lamps primed, and the lily box in full view on the marble-slabbed sideboard. Maggie lifts the lid. "Have courage," Elisha told her.

"Close that, Margaretta."

"Dandy-fine, but I won't be the one who reads the letters out like Calvin used to. I won't, Leah."

"Did I ask you to?" Leah is breezing about the parlour, checking the table, the rugs. "Oh, I know you think the lily box trite, but a president's wife will want assurances she is consulting ladies of the most stellar reputation, ladies who are highly thought of by the most moral people, that she is consulting the originals and not their imitators like Cora Hatch, that mincing coquette, with her cow-eyed trances, or that Daniel Home with his sideshow levitations. Heavenly spirits, why are men taking on mediumships? They have enough occupations of their own, and their manifestations are only theatre. They cannot manage a jot of the divine."

Maggie says nothing. What to say? Leah owns the floor, the house, Maggie's fate.

"Surely the First Lady will write a recommendation letter of her own," Leah goes on. "It will be the pride of the lily box, a seal on our reputation. None will ever dare say again that our acceptance of currency is in any way untoward, or unladylike, or that our ghosts are in any way reluctant."

From upstairs comes hacking and a hoarse call for Leah.

"Calvin wants you," Maggie says.

"Obviously."

"Do go up, will you, poppet?" Mother says.

Leah checks her fat watch. "There is no time." She hurries into the hall and calls up the stairs, "Lizzie, dear, shut his door. We must have quiet. Give him an extra measure of sleeping draught if you must."

Lizzie's reply is muffled. But a door closes. The coughing quiets. Poor Calvin, Maggie thinks. How can any man linger so long? She studies her reflection in the hallstand mirror. The reflection is of a petite young woman, eyes wide and brown and long of lash. She is fetching, even pretty. She is also nervous, but resolute. She faces the door.

"The carriage will be most elegant, but discreetly ornamented so as not to attract attention. Do you not think so, Margaretta?"

"Well, yes."

Leah loops her arm through Maggie's. "Dearest, I know we have had our little squabbles, what with that Dr. Kane of yours, but this marks a point of turning. Ah, I hear it. I hear it! No, do not look out. Katherina! Mother! Alfie!"

The others rush in. Katie wears a delicate duff-coloured gown. She gives Maggie a questioning glance. Practises a curtsy. Alfie practises a faint bow. Mother worries at her lace-trimmed sleeves. No apron today; Leah has abolished it.

Alfie opens the door before the bell is pulled. Stands aside.

Leah is all dimpled smiles, until, that is, she recognizes the ruddy-cheeked young man. "You! You're Morton!" She rounds on Maggie.

Katie looks surprised. Though why? She saw Maggie write the note replying, *Yes, come for me, Lish.* Did she think Maggie would lose courage just because of some overheard gossip?

"Don't look at me so!" Maggie cries. "Any of you! Elisha asked me not to rap for Mrs. Pierce. I thought hard on it. I did. And then I promised him I wouldn't. I couldn't refuse him. And Elisha's not feeling well. All those fevers he had, they nag him sometimes . . . And he needs me."

"*He* needs you? Margaretta Fox! We must appear in harmony. I, that is, *we* need you for the spiritual battery to be at its strongest. We cannot turn Mrs. Pierce away. It would be the gravest insult. She is the First Lady of our land. And she needs to speak to her poor dead son. To hear about the train wreck. How can she understand such a horror if . . . Sister! Do not leave. If you leave now . . . if you step out this door . . . Where is your damn head?"

"Exactly here!" Maggie says as she pins her little hat onto her head, which is clearly on her shoulders. Morton takes her arm.

They are nearly out the door to the brougham where Elisha awaits when Lizzie rushes down the stairs, calling for them all. Her bodice jacket is mapped red with blood.

CHAPTER 27.

"Poor soul," I said. "To pass away amid all that brouha. You should have been with him."

My patient sighed and owned that was true, at which I felt badly. I was becoming far too familiar with her.

"And I had the selfish thought, Mrs. Mellon, that Calvin's last was part of some larger plan to thwart me, even punish me."

"Chalk and nonsense. It had naught to do with you."

"No. Nothing?"

"No," I said, surprised at my own firmness. To explain: I had often had similar "selfish" thoughts. For I viewed my son's death as God's way of teaching me a lesson for my pride, as if the Deity were merely the cruellest of schoolmasters. Thus, when I said "no" to my patient just then it became apparent that my mind had altered on this score, though when and how I couldn't say.

"No," I said again. "We are none of us of such importance."

At this there came the lightest tap-tapping. Only the rain on the garret's three linked windows, I realized; yet the tapping seemed as if in agreement with my words, and was comforting withal.

"AND SO IT WAS FOR THE BEST, wasn't it. John? That the séance was cancelled?"

It is nearly June. John and his wife are taking the warming air on the near-completed veranda of his house. His wife's weeds are rust-shaded at the elbows, the skirt spotted from rain. She can afford new mourning attire but her old weeds give her comfort. She peers through the crepe streamers on her black cap, her pale blue eyes aflutter, her round face anxious. It is a face John finds lovely even still.

"You should have come to the funeral, John, oh, but you should have. You could at least have met us in Rochester for the interment. The coffin was so heavy with ice that—"

John interrupts his wife to explain he'd had some employ at the village forge. An imperative, lucrative job. His wife resumes talking. Maggie is still living at the New York brownstone, yes, but she and Leah are cold as ice tongs with each other. And Maggie will not speak of her plans, not to any of them. And she is certainly no longer giving sittings or raising any spirits, what- or whom-soever.

As John listens to his wife talk on, he measures the alcohol and turpentine for the lamps. Cautiously, mind. He is no fool. But this combination, though highly combustible, burns far cleaner and brighter than lard or rapeseed oil, and is far cheaper than whale oil or even this newfangled kerosene.

The parlour behind them is crowded with tools and debris— sawdust and planks and wallpaper lengths. His women have shown no interest in decorating their home and so it has fallen to him. Thus far he has chosen some pictures of the British being cut down by the ragtag Americans at Bunker Hill, a brass cuspidor for male guests, a conversation chair, and some flocked paper for the keeping room, where the family will sit of an evening round the hearth, the women chatting and sewing while he reads scriptures. His pleasure in choosing patterns and furnishings has surprised him, as has the reasonable price of it all. Mechanicals have made things once available only to the tony set available for all. True, the woods are veneered, not solid; the pictures are lithographs, not oils; the wallpaper roller-printed, not painted by hand; and the ceiling roses are of papier mâché, not plaster. But who are his women to quibble about verisimilitude?

". . . and the eulogies were lovely, weren't they? And given by important sorts, though our Lizzie was so distraught you'd think Calvin's death had been unexpected."

Over at his son's house, Leah's silhouette, plump and stately, frames itself in a window. Above the house a gibbous moon rises. John prays for Calvin, certainly. He loved Calvin, this sort-of son. And thus he grieves, but it is an interior grieving. He cannot abide the theatre of lamenting and handkerchief crushing that has been going on since his women arrived.

". . . and here is the curious thing, John. When the main had left and it was just the family and the closest of friends, Dr. Kane stared into poor Calvin's face, then ordered Maggie and everyone else to gather round the coffin. He said, 'I have something to say, and it must be said in front of all who love truth,' or some such. Anywise, he gripped Maggie's hand overtop Calvin and toppled a candle as he did, too, didn't he? And it fell on poor Calvin's breast. Katie thought quick and tossed her cup, but it just made the flames worse—I can't imagine what she was drinking—and Calvin's waistcoat was singed. After all that, Dr. Kane asked our Maggie if she'd marry him when he returned from the Arctic. He declared he'd be true to his Maggie until he was as dead as the corpse before them. It was a definite promise this time and couldn't be mistaken, could it?"

John pours the mixture into the lamps' reservoirs, his nostrils searing with the reek. "Young people are mortal romantic these days. They entertain gratuitous talk."

Margaret huffs. "I shouldn't say Dr. Kane is so young. And I didn't find it all that romantic, did I? Gracious evers, it was over a corpse . . . Oh, and then the doctor insisted this great secret of the engagement not leave the room. Oh, it was all very hush-hush, wasn't it? I almost thought he'd want us to write out the promise in blood."

"Need it be so difficult? If he loves her, he should marry her. Be done with it. It were that way between us."

His wife pokes at the spindles on the work table between them. He is making rockers so that when she returns for good they can sit out here on a warm night and contemplate the stars in God's sky. She has become less fearful of night, perhaps from living in an illuminated city where night and day differ little.

"I suppose it was that way with us, John. Yes, it was. Did I say how pale our Maggie was? And how her smile was set as if she were a waxen figure of her own self? And our Leah simply gushed tears, didn't she? And she kept claiming that life went on. And I kept asking if it were official then, and Katie kept asking where was that champagne because a toast was needed. And everyone was congratulatory, weren't they? But I was in a perplexity, wasn't I, John, because, really, shouldn't engagements and funerals be kept to their separate occasions? Doesn't this somehow bode ill?"

John says it would be superstition to think so. That his wife should pray for some answers. It all comes out more abruptly than he intends, and his wife frowns in exasperation. "I suppose I must fetch up some food. Join us, won't you? The night air is coming on, it's bad for your lumbago. And, gracious evers, why are your fingers stained? Is that ink? Whatever are you using ink for?"

John curls his fingers into his palm. "I was attempting it as preservative for . . . wood stuff."

"Humph, you're always experimenting and concocting, aren't you? That's the man in you. Now, do come. You might lead us in prayer. Leah is up to singing again now—though only a hymn, of course."

"I'll join at a later hour."

"Laws, John, you're like a child." She leaves him to his work, skirts swishing at the sawdust.

A child? he thinks. Children, his children, are the ones who sawed up this family, who have created these blasphemous ideas that are reaching to all corners of the world. And it is John Fox, a man long grown, who has been left to right it all.

He waits until his wife has crossed the yard, then sweeps aside the woodblocks and shavings on his desk. He takes out the ink pot that he keeps hidden from sight, the feeling much like when he stashed bottles of whisky, flasks of rum. He had ended his last letter with the story of the day when only he and Ambrose were left unconverted. Telling further is a difficulty, and he dips his pen several times before he starts at last.

Dear Leah:

Erastus didn't bestir himself to dry-dock the *Morning Star*.
He just left her in a feeder canal on the outways of Rochester.
He didn't care if she mudlarked. Leastaways he allowed me
and Ambrose to live aboard her for the Winter of '31, but
come Spring he was sure to sell her, his canalling days *fait
accompli*. I hated the change in him. It seemed a betrayal and
so I know how you felt about me, Leah-Lou, when I came
back after my ten years gone, but I could no more have
changed back then than a bird could have crawled back into
his cracked-apart shell . . .

John and Ambrose warmed themselves over the hatch-stove.
Above them was the stink of the tanneries, the pall of coal smoke,
the low din of the high falls. They listlessly debated going to town
and decided against it. Work was near impossible to find for men
who had not forsworn the bottle and embraced God's grace. And
neither of them could stomach the sights that greeted them in
Rochester. Seeing both men and women on their knees was com-
monplace now. They clustered like pigeons around fountains and
in squares, their prayers heard by all who passed. The theatres
were closed clam tight, as were the ninepin alleys, the dramshops
the billiard halls. The dry-wagon rattling through town was a
common sight, the preacher aboard bull-horning for all to jump
on. The pledge-seekers were declaring mere temperance was not
enough. Called on men to mark a "T" beside their name to show a
total abstinence. Erastus Bearcup had become one of these tee-
totallers. Proudly *T*'d his name, and in public view at that. All talk
was of Reverend Grandison Finney. The churches couldn't hold
all the faithful and many knotted outside the doors, straining to
hear, oblivious to the cold. Revivals lasted for days. All over the
country the pattern was repeating.

Years later it would be called the "Great Awakening," but to John
it was the Great Sleep, a time of interminable boredom. He had only
Ambrose for company now and had no choice but to listen to his
nostalgic jabber, mostly about the Indians whom he had warred

against and for whom Ambrose was becoming strangely sentimental. "I was their captive, see."

John poured out a ration of whisky for himself and then Ambrose. Finding any liquor at all took an ironclad determination and John and Ambrose were subsisting on the lone stash of whisky that Erastus had not found and fouled with salt. "I know it," John said. "You tell of it damn near constant. Them and their torturing, tearing out your tooth and poisoning you, hot somethings on your prick, the old hag wanting your baby and how you clocked her and escaped. Got it fucking covered, haven't I?"

Ambrose's stroked his unkempt beard. "I reckon I lived three months with them. I saw things you wouldn't believe. This here Reverend Finney couldn't work anything finer. I seen those Indians call up spirits by looking into smoke. I seen them walk over fire. Jesus could only manage water, couldn't he? I seen them turn a dead man to life. That's what I witnessed, I swear."

"Thought you were trussed like a hog in one of them fucking wigwams."

Ambrose stared out the small window at the moon-shining waters of the canal. "My tooth was festering and they yanked it out and buried it so it couldn't come back to pain me. I got lost, see, when I was hunting away from the farm."

"You weren't a soldier?" John asked flatly, his capacity for surprise long diminished.

"I were just a stupid weedy boy, worse than that Brother Able we met, recall? Back in Syracuse? Anywise, I was out hunting and I stumbled and speared myself in the bowels and those Indians found me and took me to their camp and fed me some of their medicine, which was foul as shit, sure, but it healed me up, and there was a woman and she had hair shining like black water and she'd put moss on my wound, and every time I saw her it felt like hot tongs on my prick, just like I said, I swear. And then I healed up and they trusted me and I even learned to talk some like them. And then one day I find that woman alone and I . . . and I run afterwards, run east to here."

Where has the loyalty gone? John thought. Ambrose lying; Clement, Jeb, and Erastus fallen to the Church.

Ambrose poked at the failing coals. "You reckon there's any left?"

John studied the bottle. "Half or so."

"I meant Indians. You reckon there's any left hiding in the woods and that? Not just living in them museums?"

"How in Christ's shithouse should I know?"

The next morning John found a note on a whisky label: *I shud nevr hav left them. They was more famly than my family and I just got to find them and beg forgivnes from her, thats all, I swer. Good luk to you, Ambrose York.*

John crumpled the note and fed it to the fire. Hoped the Indians would do the same to Ambrose.

Wasn't there a child's rhyme? About sparrows or crows and how they fell off the branch one by one until only a solitary one was left? John felt alike that last one. Alone and unrhymed.

Jeb O'Doul had been the first to fall. Returned to the *Morning Star* hefting a bible. "They're giving them out free of payment. *Gratis,*" he said, astounded.

"That's right, all theys want is your ever-loving soul in return," Erastus said.

"That's not the case, that's not it at all. Besides, a real man of learning knows his bible as well as his almanac and his Latin." Jeb explained that he'd been raised a Catholic and the Catholics didn't hold with the ordinary man reading the holy text. "Not that my kin could read anyhow. And I'd go to church and there'd be the priest reading out bible passages in Latin. You can see how it wouldn't hold a boy's interest. But this . . ." He smoothed his hand over the black cover and settled on his stool by the prow.

"Don't open it," John warned, but it was too late. Jeb was already reading, was already muttering and arguing with the book, as if it were any other. John was not surprised when Jeb attended a Reverend Finney sermon later that week.

"Finney, he talks a blue streak, but he has no true poetics in him, not like the King James did," Jeb reported, his bible tucked under his arm.

Two weeks later John and Erastus spied Jeb in a chophouse with some dark-dressed tradesmen. He was in an ardent discussion over a point in Leviticus. He didn't see them and they made no attempt to lure him back to the *Morning Star*. They'd both seen the fanatic's cast to his eyes. He was done and gone.

Clement fell next. A clucky aunt of his arrived at the boat armed with currant cakes. "Come with me to a sermon, Clemmy, I need your strong hand to guide me. Ah, but we've missed you."

"You have?" Clement asked. Four days later and he was packing up. "I don't feel lonely when I'm with all those people praying, that's all. And I felt like God don't care about this hideous face I got. It was like an invitation to a party, but a party with lemonade and tea only. And butter cookies. And currant cakes."

"Lonely!" Erastus yelled. "Sweet screwed Mary! Lonely!"

Then Thomas told Erastus and John that plodding all day with a mule for company and then listening to the same drunken rants was, yes, lonely. He was tired of counting stones and multiplying them by the number of boot steps it took to walk a mile. His aunt was going to pay his way to college, he said, so long as he kept to the righteous path. She thought he might be good at algebra, or even the ministry.

Erastus grumbled over that for days, then suggested that, to rouse their spirits, they visit a grocer that sold liquor on the sly. Erastus, Ambrose and John had their boots up on the back table, a dram before each heel, when the two women walked in. The one woman was overtall, with a pinched look. The other wore a fur-trimmed cloak, a velvety plum gown with a matching bonnet. Underneath the bonnet were curls so perfectly spiralled they might have been carved from gold. Erastus gaped and stood. John and Ambrose followed suit. Plum-Girl fiddled shyly with her gloves. Her pinch-faced companion said that they were going door to door to spread the Gospel and would have a word with the lady of the establishment.

Erastus pressed back a greasy strand of hair. "Door to door? Now there's a da—a real catchy phrase."

The grocer reported that the "lady" of the establishment was at market. To which the pinch-faced lady said, "Then we shall return on the morrow. Good day, gentlemen."

"Hold up there, please," Erastus said. "We can listen well as anyone, can't we, boys?" He turned to John and Ambrose with what was likely a fool's grin under his mass of beard.

"We're not allowed, obviously, to preach to canal men," said the pinched-faced lady.

"But I can pray for you if you tell me your name," Plum-Girl put in shyly.

"Pray for me? You? You'd use my name? I'd like that, I surely would," Erastus said, and gave her his name, though he might as well have torn his heart out and handed it over.

The next morning Ambrose and John walked a funereal pace behind Erastus back to the grocer. Erastus had gone to the barber directly after the encounter and got far more than his ear hairs trimmed. The beard that had spanned his chest and crawled up his cheekbones was entirely gone, as was the long hair and its wrappings of twine. Revealed was a jaw that a level couldn't have made as square. He'd traded his sack coat for a frocked one and his straw hat for a top hat of beaver. His hair was pompadoured out of his eyes, and these eyes shone like emeralds. He was a damned handsome man, even John could see that. The owner of the grocery stared at this transformation.

Erastus opened the door for the women when he saw them approach. Gave a clumsy bow. Plum-Girl stared in puzzlement, then blushed when Erastus said her praying must have worked its wonders.

"Ah, I would not have recognized you," she said. "Not for all the world."

. . . I wouldn't have thought mortal love had such power, Leah-Lou. But it did. And it seems God uses mortal love to direct us. Now that I'm thinking on it, it were Brother Able who told me this fact . . .

February of 1831. John was balled up in the niche-bed below the decks of the *Morning Star* with only a banked fire and horsehair blanket for warmth. He couldn't tell if it was morning or afternoon, not from that muzzy light at the top of the hatchway stairs. His teeth were loosening in his aching gums, his hair littered his pillow, and his eyes were often so itchy he wanted to claw them out of his head. Likewise his skin so itched he longed to shrug it off entirely, as if he were some grimey moth inside a tattered chrysalid.

He scrabbled for the bottle. Only two finger-measures of medicinal brandy left. This he promptly and despairingly swallowed. It was the last of his stash. John would have to forage in Rochester. But how? His legs shook when he stood. He cursed Erastus and his children to be. Shivered. Prodded at the coal fire. Only a few coals were left in the box. He supposed heat might be as important to his survival over the winter as liquor. He'd have to forage for both.

Boot steps above his head.

"Thank shivering Jesus," John muttered, thinking it was Ambrose come back from a failed mission to find the Indians. John lurched out of the hold and onto the tilted deck.

Brother Able staggered back with a cry. He wore the same overlarge homespun coat along now with mittens the size of paddles. Wore the same too-small black hat, the same pop-eyed look of astonishment. He had a scribble of beard and matted hair and red-rimmed eyes. Looked, in all, as if he were faring even worse than John.

"Son of a poxed whore! What the hell you doing here?"

"I—I, that was, M-Mr. Bearcup, he s-said, y-you were s-still here. Th-that y-you are s-still r-renouncing G-God."

"Not 'renouncing' any fucking thing. Want nothing to goddamned do with it."

Brother Able's Adam's apple bobbed up and down. "I—I h-have a p-proposition, M-Mr. F-Fox."

It took some time for Able to make himself clear. Seemed he wanted John to come with him to one of Finney's sermons so that John could pray with those who were with the holy spirit. Seemed that Brother Able was taking John on as a personal cause. "C-Come with me. N-No man can l-listen to R-Reverend F-Finney and n-not be c-convinced."

"And how damn many you converted? I mean, you personally?" John asked slyly.

Able shifted his feet. A tannery stink wafted in on an iced wind. February sleet splattered on the deck. "N-Not a one."

"Hah, that's 'cus you don't offer any enticements." John scratched at his cheek. "Here, I'll make you a deal. I'll go with you to this here fucking sermon and if I ain't convinced, you got to buy me a gallon, no, two gallons of whisky. I'm damn clean out of money, see."

Able stammered a protest.

"If you're so cunt-certain no one can resist this Finney, what were you fussing about? Mayhap he's not all he's damned lathered up to be." John enjoyed watching Able flinch after each foul and blasphemous word. But wasn't expecting him to stammer out, "A-All right."

"All right? That what you said?"

"Y-Yes."

"And?"

"A-And?"

"You got to drink the whisky with me. Don't fancy this damned drinking alone. Even your sorry company might suffice. Not that you'll have to. I'm gonna see the light, ain't I?"

Brother Able swallowed. "A-And y-you'll pray w-with us?"

"On my fucking knees, as is the fashion."

Able stammered out that they could make it to the sermon by ten if they walked briskly.

John-Before studied the grey-lit sky. "Ten? I'll be buggered. Is it morning?"

Central Presbyterian on Plymouth Avenue was crammed to its naves. Able guided John into a back pew and sat aside him as if to stop him bolting. John was a filthy, stinking wretch and the congregation cast the two men grouty looks. And not just for the stink, John knew, but for his stubborn, cross-armed slouch, his disdainful glances at the cross above the pulpit. The Reverend Finney wanted only those who were on the cusp of conversion. His was not a Broadway show that one attended out of curiosity or for a lark, but a revelation of God's will. So John had heard, and so John couldn't give a rotter's arse.

John yawned and closed his eyes as Able stood and was greeted by those Rochesterians who had seen him attempting stump preaching. On the walk over Able confided how he preached every day, no matter the weather, but that it was hard to hold a crowd, what with his impediment—at least, John supposed this is what he'd said. John's mind had been too pre-occupied by thoughts of whisky, by the certainty that Finney could not possibly move him to contemplate his own navel, never mind God's grace.

The church fair steamed with expectation. A hush fell as Reverend Finney strode in.

... You couldn't imagine a form more fit for the Pulpit than this Finney, Leah-Lou. He towered over all men and had eyes like blue torches that burned sinners at the far reaches of the crowd. He preached without text and used common talk, but then there was his lawyer mind and lawyer training and those allowed him logical explanations of Hell and Heaven and of the ways of Redemption that were open to all and sundry. He preached on how Salvation was a free choice and how a body could not be forced to it by rule and dominations, only by constant prayer with true believers, often for days upon end, and with women praying freely with the men, and I tell you these new ways were some scandalous to the conservative-minded. And how those old-style Preachers despised that phrase—*Born Again.* They snided that Finney must reckon himself a midwife or a nursemaid. I suspect they were trepidatious, was all.

Curious, isn't it? How religions and revivals flame through this upper corner of the Union and one idea rises fertile from the ashes of the other, and I suppose that's one reason folk aren't wary of this so-called Spiritualism of yours, my girl, and why you had the gumption to fashion it from a prank, no less. And yet if Finney's converts and yours were lined up side to side, I reckon your line would be far longer, and this thought gives me pride—a sin, sure, but then I am a sinning man even yet ...

In short order Finney was hurling up his arms as if to raise a whirlwind and dropping his finger down, down to show the descent to Hell, at which the congregation gasped. He spoke softly, persuasively, then thundered out the message: constant prayer would cause a change of heart. It would cause you to be saved, for you were the agent, the genesis. Man was not passive afore a vengeful, capricious God. There was no elect, as the Calvinists would have it. Even that word *elect* reeked of brimstone.

The congregation sniffed in terror as if smelling brimstone for themselves. John roused himself awake and picked his teeth with an overlong thumbnail.

God's intentions were clear, Finney insisted. He loved every soul. And even the most recalcitrant soul could be pried open to God's mercy. In America any man or woman, no matter their past, no matter how poor, could lift themselves up and be saved.

"It was a fair show," John admitted when Finney was done. He and Able were waiting in an alleyway that was troughed with cold. The back door to a warehouse stood ajar.

Able was a sad huddle within his large coat. John was nearly cheerful. "My, my, all the shakings and hallelujahs. And that 'anxious bench' was a nice touch. Even the naming of it. Gets people all, all, well, damned anxious, don't it? My knees, mind, are damned sore from all the kneeling. Worse was my throat." John rubs it theatrically. "All that praying. Sure need some damned lubrication, that I do. Ah, here's the good man now. Milk containers? Swell idea. That way we won't be attacked by the God-fearing. Pay the man, will ya, Able?"

Able did so, complaining weakly that it was all the money he had.

"God will provide, Able my boy, just see if He fucking don't."

Back at the *Morning Star*, John-Before grubbed up two glasses. Able perched on the stool beside the stove. The last of the coal was burning hot, but Able still clutched his great coat about him. "I—I've n-never imbibed a-anything s-stronger than a-ale. And that j-just once."

"Horseshit. Musta drank cider like any child. Musta had some brandy. Who ain't had that for sickness?"

"My m-ma didn't h-hold with e-even weak spirits. We d-drank water."

Water? John admitted that women could be peculiar. He poured a full glass for both of them. Felt elated. He had nearly begun to shake in the church—not from the Holy Spirit; only from the lack of more familiar spirits. Finney's words had coursed round him like midges, annoying but hardly lasting. He was immune to it all. Inoculated by stubbornness, he supposed.

"D-Do you n-not worry about y-your soul in H-Hell?" Able asked. He sipped his whisky. Spluttered and made a face.

"Those are tales to scare children into behaving," John said, though in truth his imagination never stretched up to Heaven nor down to Hell. It only reached to the bottom of an empty bottle, which was hell enough for him.

"Toss it back now. Like so. It'll make the burn less. That sipping will be naught but a sister-fucking torment."

Able sighed, then nodded with an abrupt determination. Drained his glass. He coughed, eyes streaming. John couldn't recall enjoying himself more. Convert John Fox? The whippersnapper would find his own self converted for his impertinence, and to the worship of Libation.

Able shook his head like a dog shaking off water. Chuckled. "My brother, Willing, he used to pull chairs out from under me. Bam! Down I'd go howling like a banshee. Never learned. Think I woulda . . . Well, gosh darn, eh?"

They were both stunned to silence. Able ogled his glass. Cautiously opened his mouth again. "I've never spoken clean like that. Like now!" He thrust the glass at John, who obligingly filled it.

Able drained his second glass, then a third, a fourth. Stood and swayed, his head knocking on the low roof. "I can talk! I can talk!" And talk he did. In a torrent. Told John of his father and how when drunk he'd beat his children, but was in general a kind man, and that he'd lost all he owned to drink and left his wife and children penniless and they had to live above a butcher shop and his mother had to work as a maid, though she was not born to such work, and she died only a year ago from labouring so hard. "So when Mr. Bearcup saw me and told me you were a wayward, drunken husband and father, I thought of mine own pa, and I knew I had to keep on trying to save your mortal soul as mine were saved, and that started with my brother Willing's death a while back. See, his dying turned our ma near lunatic with grief, but I wasn't troubled. No sir! I even knew some relief and, my wordy word, but I felt terrible for that. That's about when I started turning to God. I'm gonna tell you a secret. Mustn't tell a soul, promise like an honest Injun? I didn't start praying 'cus I felt sorrow, it was 'cus I *didn't* and I was sure my soul would roast in Hell's fire because of that. Willing would make fun of my talk, see, be right mean about it. He always called me Bother Able, and I thought he was saying Brother, but he wasn't. Bother. Bother. That's what I was. But I liked Brother Able, that's why I kept it, not 'cus I'm a monk or damned papist. Oh, Willing! If you could hear me now! Listen. Hear me talk like anyone else!"

Able was shouting by now, and cutting a shuffling jig in the confined space. John made no move to shush or stop him. There was no one close by these cold days to hear, not that he gave a tinker's damn if others were irked by drunken ranting.

Able wagged his finger at John. "You're a good man, Mr. Fox, yes, you are. Here I thought you were the worst kind of bastard, 'scuse me. Here I thought you were even some kind of evil man who'd blanked out God," Able whispered. "I even considered you might be the Devil himself, or a minion of him. No real man could be so stubborn, could he? But I was wrong, wrong, wrong, wasn't I? 'Cus you've cured me!"

Able dropped back on his stool. Held out his glass. John eyed him warily. He'd never seen anyone get so drunk so quickly, but then it was new to the boy. He filled Able's glass only halfway, but Able jiggled it angrily, so he filled it to the brim. Able tossed back the liquor as if he'd been drinking all his born days.

"Now I can preach! Hah, I'll find me the highest soap box! Nobody's gonna stare at their pocket watches because I'm looking like a fish caught on a hook. You know, I spent three months on the canal byways talking and preaching, but your crew was the only one who even let me aboard. But I didn't convert even a one of yous. It were other auspices, as they say. I haven't converted a single soul. But I will now. Hah! I'm gonna be alike to Finney himself with words flowing out like the river of Babylon!"

"Babylon, sure, sure," John said. He'd begun to wonder at the soundness of his plan. Drinking alone was hardly that bad. And the stripling was drinking more than John wanted to spare. He was considering on how to get Able off the boat, when Able grabbed the water bucket, his cheeks bulging. Eyes frantic.

"Christ and all his fucking cronies!"

"Sorry, sorry," Able said, over this bucket of his own vomit.

"Get up! You're needing the air. Me too. Fuck, what a reek!" He grabbed Able under the armpits and after some stumbling and falling, got him up the ladderway and onto the deck. He went back for the bucket and hurled the stinking contents into the canal. It was later afternoon now. The wind and sleet had stopped; it was warm enough. "You need to be walking. It'll clear your head some. And try being quiet, will you? Enough babbling about fucking devils and minions."

Able nodded dreamily. John used his sleeve to wipe the vomit off Able's chin. It was a gentle gesture, but then he supposed he should take some responsibility for Able's tottering condition.

He decided against leading him along the towpath, though that would have been easiest. He'd had enough of a lark getting the boy sheeted, and even John wasn't heartless enough to allow Able to be spied by gossiping bible lovers and reap humiliation. Nor did John wish to be harped upon for Able's state. And so he took Able in the opposite direction, over a frozen, rutted field, grasses aright as flat-nails. In the near distance was a small wood. Beyond, under a reddening sky, were the jagged outlines of Rochester's warehouses and factories.

Able sagged against John, mumbling incoherently, and it took all of John's wiry strength to keep him upright. The boy was not stuttering, though. Still not stuttering. Of a sudden he scrabbled at John's arm and shouted, "Willing!" then veered away, staggering in the ruts.

John cursed and ran after him. Caught hold of his flapping coat. Hauled him up from where he'd fallen. Able's face was bluish and sheened with sweat. His breath puffed out in clouds.

"Here, take it slow. We'll get to those trees, then rest, then walk on back. You'll sleep it off. Hell, you can sleep aboard the boat. Doubt anyone will miss you wherever you're fucking holed up. And I could use the company, I suppose. We'll get you on your feet tomorrow." John affected the sort of heartiness he had heard Erastus use to cajole drunken acquaintants, but his teeth were clenched in worry and annoyance. Able's feet dragged heavy. His head flopped on his scrawny neck and his little black hat fell off and sat in the midst of the field like a hunched crow.

Then Able stared at John with rolled-up eyes as blank and white as a statuary's.

John slapped him. Once and then again, much harder. Able's tongue slid out of his mouth and he puddled to the ground. They were but twenty yards from the shelter of the woods. Cursing and pleading, John dragged Able to the base of a giant oak and propped him against the gnarled trunk. "Fuck. Fuck. You'll be right now. You'll be right. Just take a breather. Take a rest. Guess it were a lot for you. Next time we'll take her slow, all right?"

Able retched out curdled whisky onto his vest. He moaned and his arms flopped up as if worked by some disinterested puppeteer.

"Guess your belly ain't full. Should have seen to that, before the whisky. I've heard drink doesn't go down well for some if they ain't recently dined."

Able sobbed. Tears fat as grapeshot slid out of his eyes, which had unrolled enough for John to see they were a green-brown. "I—I th-thought you were a g-good man. B-But it w-were a cruel t-trick."

"A trick? Then I'd be damn well laughing. But I ain't, am I?" John said, though he was smiling a bit to hear Able speak, and with a stutter, which meant he must be sobering. Able then stuttered out something about Willing being cruel as well. Stuttered out that he would never, not *ever* forgive him—though whether he meant Willing wasn't clear. And then Able convulsed. And then he died.

. . . So you, see, Leah-Lou, how mischief can go awry and cause damnation, and so I tell again, cease it all afore you and your sisters are trailed by the ever-lasting dead for true.

CHAPTER 28.

"It was a cruel trick of your father's, making the boy drink like that. Drink can destroy a body as everyone knows."

"One can die in many fashions," my patient said, her voice half-raised in question as if I might disagree to this most obvious statement.

"He was stubborn, and foolish, to boot," I said. "But he only wanted to do good. What kind of man would he have been if he had grown older? Would he have gained any prudence?"

"Brother Able?"

"Yes, of whom else would I be speaking?"

"I've not a glimmer."

"Well, what happened next? Your father didn't leave the poor boy there, did he? Without proper rites or burial?"

"You have to wait to know. Wait. Wait. As I did. And where is my medicine? Mrs. Mellon?"

EARLY JUNE, and it is Maggie's final visit to the studio of the painter Joseph Fagnani. She must leave the New York brownstone this very afternoon for Crooksville, eighteen miles east of Philadelphia, and there wait Elisha's return while undergoing her own metamorphosis—though into what, exactly, is hazed, mysterious. Her tutor will be a

Miss Turner, an old family friend of Elisha's. Leah has thrown up her hands. "Your fate and reputation are yours to toss in the midden heap, if you like," Leah said. "I merely hope you do not toss ours away at the same instance." Katie is more supportive and has vowed to visit if she can slip away from her busy schedule of sittings and dinners and outings with clients.

Maggie takes her customary place by Fangani's window. Elisha wishes her to be just as when he first beheld her—caught in a nimbus, framed by a window's arch, dressed in white. He has confessed that he fell utterly in love at that instance. Would he have felt the same if she had been chewing at her oysters? Wearing her old brown sateen? Maggie can't but wonder.

"But then, shouldn't I be reading a book, Lish? One about German verbs?"

"Tuttie. Attend. I said I wish you 'to be' as I first saw you."

"Ah, to be. To be?"

"To be the essence of you. The appearance is of secondary import. That's why this photography science with its tiresome emphasis on exactitude has not a chance of surviving against a good painter and his kindly workings of the brush."

Fagnani agrees. He paints Maggie stroke by leisurely stroke—meanwhile she must be as a living statue, a tableau of her own self. A wistful expression is not easy to hold for hours, but she must. Such is how Elisha remembers first seeing her. How can she quibble that no one looks so when they are studying German? That likely her brow was furrowed. That likely she squinted in the light and her expression hung between exasperated and bored.

The finished portrait shows a girl's face from her sloping shoulders up. A high white collar circles her thin white neck. Her face is delicate, her hair in flaps over her ears, as if to keep out harsh words. Her eyes are wistful and dark as Indian ink.

"So ethereal," Elisha murmurs, "as if a wind might lift you aloft."

Maggie is proud of her small waist. But ethereal? That is Katie's attribute. Maggie looks at the portrait again. Recognizes herself and yet does not. No matter what Elisha says of photographic science, the daguerreotype of her and Katie is still her favourite image. She recognizes herself completely in it. Is the daguerreotype still with Katie? It must be.

"It is exact!" Elisha says, and kisses the painted surface. "Know that if I become weakened or despondent during my journey I shall only need gaze upon you here in the palm of my hand and then utter your name: *Maggie, Maggie, Maggie*. I promise you, this portrait shall never leave my keeping, in all the years that I am gone."

Years?

"Ich warte. Ich wartete. Ich werde warten," Maggie chants. "Does that suffice?" It has been over a month now since Elisha's ship the *Advance* set sail out of New York harbour to fanfare galore. July is underway and the torpid heat only aggravates Maggie's already spleeny mood.

"It is satisfactory," Miss Turner answers. She is the eldest daughter of the Turner house and, as Elisha warned, she is ugly as all-sin, her face like a cellar potato. She seems to know quite a bit about quite a lot, however, and thus Maggie has resigned herself to Miss Turner's constant company. Has resigned herself to the Turner home as well. And why not? A prettier country dwelling cannot be imagined. There is a fence of white pickets, a bower of honeysuckle and roses, and the clarion chimes of the village church clock with which to mark every solitary hour.

In late July a letter finally arrives from Elisha from a place called Upernavik.

Dear Tuttie,
I think of you under the shade of some drooping chestnut,
startling the birds, your play fellows, with dreamy tokens
from the spirit world. Imagine me there by your side, and that
I am answering all your questions . . . Cherish this letter! You
may not hear from me again for a year. And promise me,
swear it, that you will never sleep again within the house of
your Tigress of a sister . . .

"I promise, Lish," Maggie says. "I'd rather swallow coal than live with Leah again."

She re-reads the letter. She is, yes, sitting on a garden chair under a chestnut tree. She cannot imagine, however, what a "dreamy token" might be. And she certainly cannot imagine Elisha by her side with Miss Turner grousing on. "Do you understand, Miss Fox, that the genitive attribute may be seen as merely another nominal phrase in the genitive case, which may hang off another nominal phrase?"

"Well, yes."

"Excellent. Now form a sentence with two variant conjugations of *wait*."

Maggie considers. "*Ich warte auf meinen freund. Sie wartete und wartete.*"

Miss Turner frowns. "You pronounce German as might a frog. It is not a language of croaks. It trips along thus: *Übung macht den Meister, aber geduld macht gute.* Hear the difference, Miss Fox."

Maggie manages a studious smile. Wonders where it was that Miss Turner heard a frog speak any language, never mind German. Wonders if the language has a word for this sense of suspension, of dread and boredom mingling. German contains words for all manner of rarified sensations and phenomena—*torschlusspanik, schadenfreude, weltschmerz, doppelganger*—which is why she wished to study the language; that, and Elisha's confessing that he knew nothing of German and wished her to be ahead of him in something other than beauty and spirit trances.

She looks up into the chestnut leaves. Hopes to see a flit of yellow. Elisha bought her a canary before he left, but it escaped as soon as Maggie opened the cage door. How does Leah manage to keep her birds contained? She has never lost a one.

"Miss Fox, repeat if you please: *Glücklich was die heimat, wo die kinder das lachen ringe.* Please now, I do not have the patience of a saint."

"The patience of a saint? A saint?" Maggie looks over the fence to the public road, her hand at her throat. The road is empty. No stunted, limping figure approaching. No laden silhouette.

"You act so strangely, Miss Fox. You are a perplexing student. Terribly so. Attend—we must work now on the *accusativus cum infinitivo.*"

Once the lesson is thank-godfully over Maggie collapses in her bed. Her quiet little room has floral wallpaper, quaint bric-a-brac, a chamber set of china blue and, really, if she has to stay here all autumn and winter she might drown herself in the rose-covered privy in the yard. What was she thinking? Why-ever had she agreed to this? She is safest in city spaces amid the soothing clamour, the endless entertainments, the surround of supporters. What is to stop a mob from finding her out here, as it did in Troy those years ago? And then there is Miss Potato Face and her patience-of-a-saint comment, which made Maggie think of the nasty peddler. Though, really, the peddler has been limping into her mind unbidden all too often ever since Washington. Ever since that limping old lady guided her back to Sullivan's boarding house, then tap-tapped her hoary fingernail on her green glass eye.

Maggie punches at the decorative pillow on her bed. Written on it in florid embroidery are the words: *Least Said Soonst Mended*.

Why-ever did I do that to the old peddler? Maggie wonders. For after she and Katie pelted the peddler with apples, Maggie grabbed his cap that had fallen in the ruts. And why-ever did he follow them? For there he was, limping behind at some distance, across the little bridge, then into the foreyard of the saltbox house. Surely he noticed how isolated the house was, how desperately plain it was. How there was not a neighbour in sight.

The girls who were Maggie and Katie heard him banging the door. They ran above-stairs as he shouted, "Give me back my cap, you hellions! Give it! I's got the patience of a saint. I can wait till the Resurrection."

Maggie and Katie lifted the sash. Their dark braids dangled as they leaned out the window.

"Oh, take it! And git!" Maggie yelled, and hurled the cap down. She hadn't meant for it to land in the pig trough.

The peddler picked it up between two fingers. "Damn you. It's ruined, ain't it? Ruined! Where's your ma, you two? Where's your pa? Or were you whelped by wolves? Don't matter. I'm gonna tell them about them apples you chucked at me. I will, damn me if I don't!"

"Mag, we can't let him tell," Katie said. "Ma warned that if we got up to any more silly mischief she won't take us to the Rochester fair. Remember? We ain't gonna see Amy, then. We ain't gonna get roasted peanuts or ice-creams."

"We'll go. We'll get there. Shhh. I'm considering."

They looked down into the foreyard. The peddler was still here. "An apology ain't enough now. It ain't! I want you two to have a hiding. I'll cut the switch myself!"

A tear dripped down Katie's nose. "Why don't he just git?"

Maggie gnawed at a fingernail. They did not have much time. Their mother was at a neighbour's birthing. Their father was at the village forge. He was always home before full-dark.

The peddler limped back and forth under their window. They had given him back his cap. He should be accustomed to taunting. To things hurled. Such was the way of the world for one such as he.

Maggie ran down to the cellar. Returned with an arsenal of turnips and potatoes and apples. "Look, Kat, it's like we're in one of them besieged castles."

"Oh, are we like them princesses, then?"

"That's it! And he's the evil sorcerer. If we can get him gone, everything'll change."

"Lovely clothes. Pretty rings."

Down below in the foreyard the peddler dodged their turnips and apples, hopping about in a queer fashion that nearly made the girls laugh. He yelled again: "You'll die alone and ranting, you hoyden bitches!"

Just then Maggie found the rock amongst the potatoes. Mother must have collected it to add to her "curiousity" rocks bordering her herb garden. It was the shape of a man's fist and bore the imprint of a fantastical whorled shell that was not, Maggie understood, of this place or time.

Maggie took careful aim.

"Mag, you got him!" Katie whispered, thunderstruck.

The peddler yowled and hopped, and pressed a hand to his bloodied face. Maggie feared she had taken out his eye, that the law would now be coming for her. A rhyme rang in her head: *Lock her in the cellar with only turnips for food.* Put her on a chain gang building schools. She gave a quick and horrified laugh.

"I'll up and die now, see if I don't! And you'll swing for it, you two."

"I didn't mean to!" Maggie called down.

"Me neither!" Katie added.

The peddler staunched his bloodied forehead with his sleeve. His eye was intact, Maggie saw with vast relief.

"I think yous killed me!" he yelled, then limped out of the fore-yard, out of their dull and ordinary lives.

Katie sniffled. "Leastaways, *he'll* never come on back again."

Maggie jumps at the knock on her door. It is only Miss Turner, asking if Maggie requires anything. Her tone is apologetic. She reminds Maggie somewhat of Machteld, Amy Post's maid, who so wanted Maggie's and Katie's friendship. Would it have killed Maggie to give it?

"I'm just sterling," Maggie calls. "Should we have tea in the garden?" Miss Turner replies that would be *gut*, and also nice.

Maggie presses her face to the pillow. *Katie, Kat, Katherina.* Maggie misses her even more than she misses Elisha. Hell, then, is not a fiery well crammed with sinners. Hell is a black, cold place, barren of anyone. For what fire and torment can compare to the self left alone?

Over the next year Maggie, as Elisha warned, does not receive any news of the expedition. Nor does anyone. *The* Advance *is beyond civilization's beck and call, though Dr. Kane is surely quite safe, and surely having quite an adventure*—such is what the expedition's sponsor, Mr. Henry Grinnell, writes to assure her.

The months spin by and though Maggie tries hard to be a good student of Miss Turner's, a good guest, the lights of New York beckon her on, as if she were a small-brained insect. The Turners object to Maggie's toing and froing, but they cannot deny her right to visit her family. Maggie feels badly for going against Elisha's wishes, yes, but at least she keeps the promise she made Elisha to never sleep again within Leah's house. Not that Maggie has a need to stay with Leah now. Mother and Katie have moved into an apartment on 10th Street and she stays with them whenever she is in New York.

I want to be my own Mistress, too! Katie wrote to Maggie when she first moved to Tenth Street. *So much that I could scream. And Leah is such a bossy-bird. "Don't drink that, my dearest dear! Another glass? Don't talk so loud!" Well, you know how she can go on. When I called her a battle-axe she said she'd battle-axe my cabinet of spirits. "But everybody wants spirits with their spirits," I said. Wasn't that a clever quip? And then I reminded Leah that she was the one who wanted me to have a spirit cabinet. She turned near purple at that—because of course she meant one of those people-sized cabinets for our séances, the ones she gets from that Pettifew.*

"But please, please, Mag, it's no fun on my own," Katie pleads this autumn day of '54. Maggie is staying with her and Mother again at the 10th Street apartment.

"No. I swore to Lish that I'd never rap again. Ah, don't stay cross, Kat. It's still me. I'm still here."

"Gosh-it-all. You haven't forgotten about Mr. Intrigue yet?"

"No, no, of course not." Maggie hasn't forgotten him, just the hollow and giddy way she felt when with him. Just the exact way he looked and sounded.

Katie does not stay cross at Maggie for long; she never does. And she is earning plenty on her own, without Maggie's help. Mr. Partridge, the match magnate, has hired Katie to give séances to the public, all for the improvement of mankind and for the betterment of the world order, or something like that. Twelve hundred per annum. Imagine a young woman of seventeen earning so much, Maggie wryly thinks. Imagine being able to shop for whatever lovely clothes and pretty rings you wish. Maggie swallows her envy. She lives on the modest funds that Elisha set up before he left and that are administered through Mr. Grinnell. How quickly that money vanishes, however And how sour Grinnell's letters are becoming in reply to her polite pleas for more funds. He does not understand that she must continue her studies of German and sketching and speech and deportment if she is to be worthy of the Elisha-who-returns. And Maggie has to be dressed in some semblance of the latest style.

17 October, 1854

Dear Miss Fox,
We have no tidings yet of the Doctor. If he is not heard from
by November, we must assume he intends to remain another
winter in the Arctic regions.

> Your Servant,
> Henry Grinnell

Intends? Maggie thinks.

Winter of '54 55 passes, and then the spring of '55, and Maggie is
even less at her lessons, less in Crooksville and ever more out enjoying New York's entertainments. She wonders if she should return to
rapping. She does miss the fun of it at times, as well the challenge,
the gratitude of the clients, the money-all-her-own. Some days she
does not think of Elisha at all, that is until someone reminds her what
a grand hero he is, how esteemed and intelligent and really quite
handsome, and how easy it must be to love such a man.

CHAPTER 29.

"Do you mind reading today, Mrs. Mellon? My eyes ache and blur so." (My patient had just quaffed down her medicine. We had long dispensed with measurements.)

"Certainly, duck." I reached into my satchel. "Here. I have the almanac . . . the *Times,* an issue of *Godey's Lady's Book.* Not current, but does that signify?"

"None of those. This." Mrs. Kane shoved Elisha's book across the bedclothes.

"Sortilege? Another go? I suppose we could . . . Not that I hold with it."

"No. Not that. Not today. You must read out all the names you find. Perhaps you can see what I cannot, because I've searched it over and over again. Searched it to see if I'm mentioned. If my name is writ there—if, that is, Elisha thought of me at all when he was gone. Oh, I know his book is all about men and their adventuring, but still why won't he tell of me? It's as if I don't exist. Not at all. And yet when I was with him, I felt as if I existed as much as I ever would." She stared at her thin little hands then as if they were disappearing (they were not). Those brown eyes of hers took on a lost and wild cast. But then she was ever at a loss with this shilly-shally man.

"Settle yourself, duck. I'd be happy to read now—"

"Begin with the crew, please." She found the page. "There."

I did as bid, then soon wished I had never touched her damned book. "Henry Brooks, first officer; Isaac Hayes, surgeon and officer; John Wilson, sailing master: August . . ." I cleared my throat and squinted. "The light. It's far too bright." I shifted the ladderback away from the slant of sun.

She waited, said nothing.

"August Sonntag, astronomer and officer; James McGeary, executive officer: Amos Bosnall, photographer and naturalist." And so on. I read the others without even hearing them, the name of August rang so loud.

August was my son's name. I called him thus, not because he was born in August (he was born in March, as I have said) but because it is a tradition in my family to name children after the months, which is why I am called June. March would have been a ridiculous name for my son; August, however, suited him like a kid-glove, his manner being as warm and genial as a New England's summer day.

I could read no more and told her this fact.

"Perhaps it's a riddle," she muttered, and took the book from my hands.

THURSDAY, OCTOBER 11, 1855, 1:10 p.m. and the steam-ship *Release* arrives in New York Harbor with Elisha and his surviving crew aboard. Maggie hears the news of his return, of the loss of Elisha's ship the *Advance* to the Arctic ice. She hears the boom of cannons in the harbour, the cheers of the throngs at Battery Landing. The *Advance* left New York Harbor in June of '53. This means, Maggie calculates, that two years, four months, ten days, and five hours have passed since she last beheld Elisha. Now that she will soon see him again, her feelings for him have returned in a shot.

"Come, lamb, you'll wear a gutter in our new rug," Mother says. "Sit. Will you?"

"I can't! I can't! Where is he?"

Five o'clock and Elisha has still not called at the 10th Street townhome Maggie, having given up on the Turners altogether, now shares with Mother and Katie. Maggie has her own private parlour, very small, but all her own. She insisted on that.

"He's detained, that's it," Katie offers. "Or, or he's ill. You know he's ill a lot."

"I'll go to him! I will. I should have gone to see the rescue ship arrive! Why did you stop me, Ma? Why in tunket do you keep me trussed to your damned apron strings!"

"That is enough. Enough! Sit down, Maggie Fox. Ladies wait. They do not seek out men as might, as might . . . oh, never mind. And they do not ever speak to their mothers so. Nor do they cuss."

Maggie apologizes. Sniffles. Resumes pacing.

They wait. And wait. The clock chimes midnight.

Katie hands Maggie a glass of spiced rum. "For her nerves, Ma," she says at their mother's sharp glance. Katie is arrayed in fawn and amber, but it is Maggie who looks the heiress in a gown of changeable blue silk. It is trimmed with figured lace and tiny crystal drops and fits her every curve. The cost was exorbitant. Enough, as Mother groused, to keep plain wholesome food on a table for a year.

Maggie finally permits Mother and Katie to coax her to bed. They unfasten her buttons and hooks and ties. Loosen her corset. She refuses to take the dress off entirely. She wakes at first light, shivers at each hour-dong of the clock as if it were a death knell. At just past eight, the newspapers are delivered. Elisha's name is emblazoned everywhere, the front pages columned with his exploits. Maggie snatches the papers up and reads them over once, twice. The first account describes in detail how the *Advance* was trapped in ice for two years, how the intrepid Dr. Kane gave orders to abandon ship and then led his stalwart men south on foot, a harrowing eighty-three-day journey to the whaling post of Upernavik. Only two of his crew died in this epic adventure.

The next account tells much the same but adds how, though Kane sought hard for more clues to Sir Franklin's demise, he sought in vain, and this because in April of '54 one Sir John Rae, a Scot, found evidence that the Franklin expedition had made it as far as the Boothia Peninsula, which was a thousand miles away from where the *Advance* had searched. And then the Esquimaux in those parts had reported seeing mad, hideous white men gnawing on their dead comrades. Not that this, the account stresses, could be considered anything more than primitive fancy. At least the Grinnell expedition sighted the Open Polar Sea and Dr. Kane can now present firm evidence for its existence at last.

The final account gives much the same story, though it adds hints of desertion, a near mutiny, a near murder or two, and the news that Dr. Kane will soon be marrying Miss Margaret Fox.

Maggie stares at these lines. *Marrying?* Their engagement had to remain secret, or else be placed in jeopardy. Elisha had assured her of this several times. And who gave the rumour to the paper? Leah? Could she have done so? She had certainly been afume ever since Maggie refused to help with séances. "You might as well marry Dr. Kane," Leah said. "That is, Margaretta, if he doesn't return a cadaver, and even if he does, for all I care. Secret engagements. What poppycock. At least if you marry, people will cease calling you his mistress, his wh—his what-have-you."

Thinking on this, Maggie pats at her gown. It is too snug-fit. Too aglitter.

Katie reads out from her paper: "*Dr. Kane is much improved in physical appearance. He has a bronzed face, a long and heavy black beard, a stouter body and a hand with a hearty grip.*"

"He's not ill? Not at all?" Maggie asks.

"Well, I mean, he could be underneath . . . Here, let me get you a soother." Katie opens her cabinet of spirits. "There you are, my pretties." The bottles are arrayed on the insides of the doors as well as on the shelves: champagne and whisky. Gin and brandy. All are of fine vintage, the bottles of every colour. The crystal glasses of every size and shape. And every one is of crystal.

Katie mixes Maggie a martinez, and then one for herself. Mother sighs.

By six p.m., Maggie is at last ready to take off her blue silk gown, which looks, she allows, rumpled and desperate in the failing light.

"The door! He's at the door!" Katie cries. "You didn't hear the knocks?"

Maggie rushes to the looking glass. Fusses with her hair, pinches colour into her cheeks. "Open the door, Ma. Open it! But without showing your agitation! Please!"

Mother does not show agitation, only astonishment. "Mr. Morton?"

Morton takes up the offer of tea. There are awkward pleasantries and strained small chat, then Morton says, "Righty, then. The letters, you see. His love letters, that is, to you, Miss Fox. He wishes, that is, he pleads with you . . . pleads that I should retrieve them. His mother, you see, has also read the reportages and these, uh, rumours about an impending marriage." Morton attempts a laugh. "Gossip and all, but . . ."

Maggie clenches her teacup. Katie frowns. Mother shakes her head. All of them, Morton included, sit on the edge of their brocaded chairs, stiff as effigies.

When Maggie finally speaks, she is surprised at her own becalmed voice. "The letters are mine. Mine. Why is he not here? He should be here if he wishes such a . . . such a thing."

"He's indisposed and unwell."

"The papers said he's hearty as a walrus!" Katie blurts out. Mother nods. Maggie stands, giving Morton no choice but to stand also. "Mr. Morton. Tell your master to never come here. And to never contact me again, in any way. "

Elisha arrives the next afternoon. He is indeed bronzed and hearty looking, and is dressed in full naval regalia—braids and epaulets and gold buttons and such. His expression when he sees Maggie atop the stairs is astounded, intent, alike those of the new-convinced at a séance. Maggie's resplendent blue dress is crumpled, her cheeks a burning red, her hair a yanked-at mess. She looks her worst. And she hardly cares.

"Get gone!" she yells.

At this Elisha dashes up the stairs and catches Maggie as she turns to flee. He kisses her brow, her lips even, proclaims, "By God, what a vision you are. God, but I love you. I adore you!" He attempts to kneel but it seems the breeches of his uniform are too tight. "Keep the letters, dear heart. Morton misunderstood entirely. We shall be married. I give you my word. And my heart."

He guides her down to the parlour, continues more sedately, "I have walked these streets the night through, pondering our course, and then seeing you draped in light . . . well, my mind is set. Attend closely, my pet, I have been promised a great deal of money for my account of the expedition. It will be unlike anything yet written. And then I, you, we, shall be free to do as we please. God, but I wish I were not born to status. It is an enchainment. The reputation of my family rests upon me. And my mother . . . my mother has been distraught about our, our, connection, and she will cut me off from all funds if she believes we are engaged. I've not a cent to my own name, Tuttie, thus . . ."

He draws an official-looking paper out of his inner pocket, and then a handy travel pen with its own little inkwell. It is part of the grander plan, he tells Maggie. She need only sign here, where Elisha is said to be her concerned patron, his interest in her brotherly, nothing more. "Do it for me, Tuttie. You shall never suffer. It is for my mother."

"Don't, Mag!" Katie warns.

"She's right, lamb. It's abominable. Isn't it?" Mother adds.

But Maggie has already taken up Elisha's little pen. She sobs as she signs her name, then looks aghast at her own signature. What in bloody tunket is she thinking? "But you have sworn to marry me, Elisha Kane." She snatches at the document, just as Elisha tucks it away.

"You're a coward, that's what. Not a hero at all!" Katie shouts.

"A cad!" Maggie shouts.

"Get out!" Mother demands.

All three of them thrust him out the door, skewing his epaulets, ignoring his please and protests.

Elisha is back promptly the next morning. "Damn my mother and her demands," he tells Maggie. He is still in his Navy regalia, though the braids are squashed, a gold button hanging. "I didn't sleep a jot last night. I roamed the streets once again, espying you at every corner." He hands Maggie the document. "Destroy it, my love. I will defy my family, my mother, the world entire for your love and regard."

In a nonce paper fragments are spinning out from Maggie's wrenching hands.

Elisha watches her raptly. "Tear it, Tuttie! Oh, do. That's it, don't stop. Allow me to help!"

Folding and tearing. Tearing and folding. Until both she and Elisha are exhausted, exhilarated, the paper fragments like snow at their feet.

"Gracious damned evers," Mother grumbles. "You two should be a theatre act."

Two weeks later and Maggie and Elisha are shuttered-up in her private parlour. It is a pink-hued space with silken shadows, a nacreous light. "Alike a seashell." Elisha says. "And we curled up inside safe from all eyes."

They have just returned from mass at St. Ann's Church. Elisha assured Maggie she would be awed by the sublime arch of the dome, the stained glass windows, the organ, the theatricality, in all, of the papist religion, and Maggie was indeed awed. The soaring cathedral was so unlike the workaday churches of her girlhood, the Latin liturgy—mysterious and rhythmic—so unlike the exhorting, condemning services of the Methodists, and the kindly old Father Quinn so unlike the severe ministers she has known. And then there was the exotic scent of the smoke wafting from the censers, the gleaming chalices, the turning to the strangers aside her: *Peace be with you, and also with you.* What affected Maggie the most, however, was the little candle-lit shrine she found tucked into a side alcove, the five crowned, elegant ladies set there. They were made of wood and no more than two feet high, and their articulated arms were held out as if in supplication. Three of the ladies bore expressions both wistful and mysterious, the fourth looked as dolorous as could be, the last was faintly smiling, as if privy to some delicious, long-held secret. What was most arresting, however, even unsettling, was that they had only skirt-shaped cages for their lower halves. These cage were empty of limbs, but not empty. No. Inside were hung objects of devotion: papers writ with prayers, crosses of silver, rosary beads of clay and stone, and hearts of reddened glass.

"Ah, you've discovered the Santos dolls," Elisha said when he saw her puzzling over these figures. "Lovely, queer females, are they not? They were once used to convert the heathens, but are now banished to the distant fringes of belief, they having misfortune to be considered graven images, idols. Many of them were burned during less encompassing times." Elisha then added that the one lady, there, the faintly smiling one, resembled Maggie, his tuttie, and to perfection. At this put Elisha delved his hand inside the lady's cage and gently touched the heart hanging there.

Now Elisha edges closer to Maggie on the settee. Gone is his hearty-walrus health. He is gaunt and pale from writing day and night. He has admitted his journals are a bit . . . raw, given the circumstances, and need to be entirely re-worked, made more tally-ho and all together.

An organ grinder's music drifts up to them. A street-monger calls out his wares. No sounds stir below-stairs. Mother and Katie are out. Mother has, to Maggie's astonishment, allowed her and Elisha unchaperoned time. She has, indeed, withdrawn objections altogether, as has Leah. Not that Maggie sees Leah much anymore, for which she is glad, though she does, on occasion, miss Leah's decisiveness, her praise, her rare and genuine laugh.

Elisha strokes the blue veins on the underside of Maggie's wrist. "Brother Tom came to see me today. God, but he rides on my coattails. He gave me quite the lecture and said that I must let the nation make a pet of me. That I should practise sham modesty, be more respectful of the newspaper men, and praise my colleagues, by which I suppose he means I should not admit to wishing I'd murdered that William Godfrey. He said that my tack will be 'the official scientific'—science, with the brevet of sword, spunk and gentlemanly *savoir faire*."

"Your tack?"

"Yes, the image that will spring to mind when my name is mentioned in any region of this country." Elisha chuckles. "There ought to be a name for someone who manages the . . . what? The reflection of another. The image?"

"There should be, you are so right."

"At least one day I shall be sung of by school children. They'll gnash their little teeth over having to read my epic when they'd rather play skin-the-eel. That's immortality enough for me, an epic with my name, like Achilles or Odysseus. You, my pet, can have my soul if you wish. Decorate your parlour with it. Or let it seep into your lucent skin, as you please."

"You sound like an, an atheist."

He chuckles into her neck. "What a dread thought. Oh, I don't doubt the existence of God's Paradise any more than I doubt the existence of the Open Polar Sea. What I doubt is whether I'll enjoy myself there. It's unchanging by all accounts and my soul is like a leaping fish, my mind aswim with my ideas, projects, ambitions. Pity I can't have a thousand lives, all conjoined perhaps, like bubbles in a tin tub. Imagine: in this life my heart is strong as a metronome and I'm a designer of grand edifices. In the next I command an army. In another I find Franklin and his men, safe and alive. In yet another life we grow old together, you and I, my pet; I write amusing little books for a living and we sit by the hearth of an evening and have our passions still."

He shakes his head. His dark hair is arrowed with grey, his pale eyes fierce with intensity. "I'm delighted you enjoyed the mass and all the gold and embellishments. You could do worse than to be a Catholic, Maggie-love, for they are not allowed to raise the dead."

The dead are distant these days, she tells him. And she does not miss them. Not at all.

"Then perhaps we should both become Catholics. They're given to visions and I had visions in the Arctic that would have made a pope proud. You recall the cosmoramas? Ah, no, you failed to meet me there. Well, my visions are alike to those. Imagine, Tuttie, peering into a scene of such veracity you swear it can be touched: the Temple of Karnack, the Hanging Gardens of Babylon, the Colosseum of Rome. And yet something is awry. The proportions? The shadows? It is as if you are the false vision. Does that make sense?"

Maggie says it does, certainly.

"My first vision was of my family. They were feasting at Christmastide. The vision was so real that I could smell the roasted pheasant. My family was laughing and talking, having a merry time. My mother looked terribly beautiful. She said she wished that I were with them, but she said it in such a manner that I leaped up and cried out that I was here. Here! And then they vanished, and I was alone again in the ship's hold, and it was dark as pitch but for the blubber lamps. And my men were groaning like spectres in their frozen sacks, and the ice was slowly crushing the ship, like a giant crushing the ribs of a choice victim, and then there was that sense of betrayal, the stench of it even. Ah, but I'm rattling on like some near-naked mystic."

"You must have been so hungry, poor Lish."

"Yes . . . Just thank God for roast rat. It's not so bad with a touch of salt. I shall cook some for you."

"How awful!" Maggie declares, and laughs with him. This could be our tomb, she thinks. It's even nicer than the Kane tomb at the Laurel Hill Cemetery. It has windows at least.

"Tuttie, listen, you must promise me something."

"Anything."

"Do not read William Godfrey's account. It is all lies."

"Why in tunket would I? He's a Judas to you and a deserter. I despise him."

"Good. Stopper your ears when he is mentioned. Listen to none but me. Swear it?"

"Of course I do."

"That's my sweet girl." He kisses her hand. Says, "Now I must tell you of my second vision. It was of you. You came as an undine— Undine, the water nymph. She is—"

"Oh, yes, Undine. That's a Germanic story. I know it from Miss Turrner."

"Ah, yes, your Teutonic studies, I'd forgotten. Well, let me continue. I was hunting for seal. There I was, crouched before a round of water in the ice. I was in my furs and must have looked like a bear halfway to being man. My gun was poised. And then the green water rippled and you climbed over the rim. You were so graceful, as if you could swim in air as well as water. Your hair was unbound and tumbled wetly to your knees. A pale dress clung to your form. You did not shiver. You did not seem cold at all. Your skin had the sheen and cleanness of ice. Your lips were the red of the reddest carnelian and you were not . . . not wearing a shift, nor a corset."

"Those undines don't have souls. Now I remember."

"Ah, yes, dear heart. Until they marry a mortal man and then they, too, are mortal and know all the sorrows and pains of mortal life." He kisses her hand. "As we are married."

"We are?"

"Consider the Quakers. They have no need for intermediaries to sanctify their marriages, only declarations of love, devotion." He kisses her neck, her collarbone. "I take you as my wife, Maggie Fox. Now say you'll take me. Say that I am your husband."

She does so.

"Now stand fast." He unhooks her gown and unties her five petticoats, sliding each one down her legs, all while she is obediently stilled, scarcely breathing. He studies her standing there in the pool of her fallen garments. Maggie shivers. The room has become cooler, larger.

He unpins her hair. It is oil dark in the lamplight. He arranges it over her shoulders. His fingertips continue down her spine to the lacing of her corset. It hinges open at his deft tugging. She wears only her white chemise now, her white pantaloons, her black stockings that are tied just over her knees.

He steps back. "Am I your captain?"

He is, absolutely.

"Do you obey me out of love? Only love?"

She does. She does.

"Then you are now Mrs. Elisha Kent Kane."

"I am. I do."

"And I am yours, yours."

Now he orders gently, firmly that she take off her pantaloons, her stockings. She does. Her face burns, but she does not look away from the pale regions of Elisha's eyes. He shrugs off his vest, his shirt. His body is thin and ribbed, but he does not look weak. His hands and neck and face are dark against the white of his torso. It is an odd figuring.

"Recline there on the settee. Good . . . how delicious you are. And now I must tell you of my voyage and how it began. How up and up Smith Sound I went." He runs his hand under her chemise, over her knee and thigh. "I wanted to go farther than any man had gone. And there I found a safe harbour and there I stayed locked within."

Maggie can barely breathe. His fingers find her furrows, her untrammelled interior. Is this pleasure? It must be, for she wants him to continue his exploration to wherever such things lead.

He kisses her throat, her lips. He eases the chemise away from her breasts. "Ah, such a discovery. So lovely, so . . ." He strokes them, presses briefly so hard that his thumbs leave an impress. Presses her hands aside as he suckles, like a babe might. Maggie bites her lips at the quick, gorgeous pain. Is this a natural thing? Is this what is done between men and women in darkened rooms across the city? The world?

He wears his trousers still. Now he takes her hands and presses them between his legs. Why is he whispering of envelopes, and that he has none? Why is he thinking of letters at this time?

He groans and says she has achieved him. They lie in silence for a time, until his fingers walk up her arm, her shoulder, to rest in the dip at her throat. "You would not betray me, my love, my darling, would you?"

"Never. Never. How could I?"

"You'd not desert me? My men . . . some did so."

Again she swears no.

"There can be no secrets between us now."

"No, Lishy, no. None," she agrees. Yet he still does not ask how it is the dead can speak. It is beneath him to ask. She understands that.

So she tells him at last. Shows him. Her legs and feet are bared; it is a simple matter. He takes each of her toes. Makes the child's rhyme of piggies and markets and crying home. Says he knew. She is not as clever as she had thought. "It's just that I wished that you would tell me, willingly and without guile, and now you have."

Maggie's mouth is dry. Her feet cold. She tells him more. Of how the haunting of the Hydesville house came to be. Of the peddler. And why his corpse was not found in the cellar floor.

"I thought mayhap he died from the wound I gave him." Maggie confesses. "I did hit him square in the head."

"A capital shot from the window. Remind me not to cross you, my pet."

"And then I worried that he'd get the law after us. And then I worried about the curse. Now I don't worry at all. Not when you're with me."

"I've killed men," Elisha murmurs, and kisses her.

CHAPTER 30

"Whatever are you fixing on?" I asked my patient. She had ceased her tellings (which had become more intimate that I needed hear, to be frank) and was now staring on the Edison bulb there in the vestibule. The bulb crackled and faltered, but held its sallow radiance.

"Perhaps it is possible," she said. "Perhaps I've been mistaken all these years."

"About what? The peddler?"

"Because I did see Elisha once after he died. And I've been hoping all these years that he would appear again, and that the vision of him would not be figment of my brain, nor of opiates, and that he would speak. He had answers to all things." She smiled wryly.

"No one has those," I said, but she continued as if I weren't there at all.

If it did appear, Elisha's ghostly self, apparently, would be as young as when they first met, there at the Webb hotel in Philadelphia. This time, however, he would be the one framed in the arched window, caught in a nimbus. He would be pale, his hair glossy-dark, his eyes even more blue than when he was alive, as if the Arctic waters had settled in. Not a large man, but a handsome man, and a famed one, for a time.

"What will he say?" I asked, trying to hide my interest.

She was quiet for the span of three breaths. Her face lost all expression. "Do you not pity those who come to you in grief, Tuttie? You give them false hope. You make a parlour game of their loss. And surely we, the dead, do not wish to be hauled back to the living world with its stinks and melancholies, its misfortunes scattered random as buckshot. Listen, my sweet, touch me here, this is all we have."

I should mention that her voice changed when she spoke this. Became deep and cultured and manly. And the garret had become, I swear, as chilled as a springhouse.

"And did then you see him again? Did you?"

"I'll get to that," my patient said, entirely her own perplexing self again.

⁓

ELEVEN DAYS AFTER THEIR PARLOUR TRYST, Maggie and Elisha clutch each other on the stoop of the Tenth Street town-home, oblivious, nearly, to the passing stares.

Elisha beseeches, "Command me to stay. Give me one word."

"Stay."

"But, pet, I cannot! Duty calls to me."

"I thought it was Lady Franklin."

Elisha frowns.

Maggie could slap herself. She knows her attempts at wit distress him. And now that they are married she must attend the right cues, say the proper lines. She simply must.

"Tell me you will dream of me."

She reminds him that she doesn't dream. Or that she can't recall the dreams. Adds hastily that she will try.

"Try very hard. For I intend to come to you while you sleep in your sweet bed. I shall enter your dreams, your . . ." He stops. Clears his throat. Gives her a stack of envelopes lined with muslin. "These are addressed to my London lodgings. I want no prying eyes to view our correspondence. And these ones are to signal an emergency. If you send the one with the three little stars—see there, in the corner— then I will return to you immediately."

She vows to write each day, asks, "You have the lock of my hair? My letters?"

He presses her hand under his travelling coat to the lump in his inner pocket. "They are close to my heart, as always. And Morton has packed Mr. Fagnani's portrait of you as well as my cherished ambrotype." He clasps her. "I can calmly part from all the rest, even from my mother; it's parting with you, Maggie, that kills me."

Then why go? Maggie would like to ask, but does not. He has his work. He must meet with eminent natural philosophers and fellow explorers, must accept accolades, give lectures, must listen to Lady Franklin's ludicrous insistence that the search for her husband continue.

Morton, waiting beside the carriage, gives one of his odd little waves.

"I'm being told to make haste. Listen. I tell you again: If I should perish I've left a legacy for you, my dear wife, in my will. The legacy is in the trust of my brother Thomas, who loves you as a sister. Look to him. Thomas shall care for you. But you must renounce the vulgar spirit rappings. Promise me again."

"I promise. I promise."

"Now wait, wait there in the doorway so that I might see you until the last instance."

The carriage draws away. Grows smaller and smaller yet, but Maggie doesn't move, not even when an omnibus obscures the carriage entirely. But Maggie is not worried. She will see him again. Hasn't Elisha, for all his talk of his own death, survived two Arctic winters, near starvation, a brutal trek? And no matter how wretched British food and British weather are reported to be, it seems unlikely that they, of all things, will be his undoing.

———

28 December, 1856

Dear Tuttie: I am quite sick, and have left London for Havana on doctor's orders. I have received no letters from you; but write at once to E.K. Kane care of the American Consul, Havana.

———

Over two months later, in March of 1857, William Morton, Elisha's faithful valet, stands before Maggie. He is hatless and dishevelled and unshaven, is drunk as a lord or a pauper; nothing in between. He tells Maggie every detail of Elisha's last days, and in doing so he breaches all propriety, all common sense.

He begins with himself and Elisha striding with Yankee confidence through London, that antiquated city with its musty aristocracy, its fetid river. Perhaps it was the brumous fog, the lingering sea-sickness from the three-week steamer journey, but Elisha was shivering, coughing. "A severe chest cold, no more," said the good doctor Holland.

"You shall stay at my estate," declared Mr. Edward Sabine, a fellow Arctic explorer, a geologist and so forth.

"But you must get well. You must return to find him!" cried Lady Franklin, bending to Elisha's sickbed, snatching the medicine from Lady Sabine to feed Elisha herself.

"Franklin's dead as a fucking door, you stupid crone!" Elisha yelled. "Cannibalized, that's what, and by his own men. I'll wager they gnawed on his stringy thighs and popped his eyeballs down their thankless fucking gullets!"

Lady Sabine reeled back in shock. Lady Franklin gripped the spoon as if to gouge out Elisha's own eyeballs. Morton soothed and assured them both that Dr. Kane was raving. That he was not in his right mind, not at all. Days passed before Elisha regained any semblance of his mind, right or otherwise.

"William Damned Godfrey, he's planning to publish, isn't he now?" Morton continues to Maggie, his brogue thickening by the minute. "As like he'll say it were Elisha's fault those miscreants betrayed him and struck off on their own. Bloody Godfrey, he'll be spouting that Elisha acted the tyrant. But he didn't, now. Is a father at his wits' end with his misbehaving children a tyrant? Oh, there'll come nasty rumours. It'll be said Elisha tried to murder him. Murder! Godfrey would have deserved it so. Godfrey, that mutinous prick. And sure, but that damned Wilson and Bonsall and Hickey have told treasonous accounts. Sure, Miss Fox, but Elisha's book will outlast them all, won't it now."

Miss Fox? Maggie nearly stops crying.

Morton takes the liberty to pour them both a sherry. The glasses slosh overfull. "We didn't find old Franklin. But sure we discovered the Open Polar Sea. Sure, but I spied it my own self. That is, Hans and me did. He was the Esquimau boy Elisha hired because he was handy with the spear. And what thanks did Elisha get? Hans deserted, too, and for good. He found himself some Esquimau girl and stayed with her up there, though wasn't her home the bitterest place on this earth? Who'd give up that much for a girl?"

Morton drains his glass. Maggie does likewise.

"Anyhow, surely what we saw weren't just a stretch of open water. Things can't be two ways at the once." He talks then about how, even though Elisha hated the hot places of the earth, he was sent to Havana for his "health." How he suffered on that voyage from England. Heart. Stroke. Apoplexy. Elisha uttered these words like an apology, Morton said, and the words hung by themselves. His limbs refused him obedience. His speech become as thick as an Esquimau's speech. At one point Morton swore Elisha sang the same dirge as did a young Esquimau man they locked in the hold of the *Advance* for thievery. The Esquimau escaped. Elisha was glad he escaped. Morton was also glad. His emotions were in tandem with Elisha's; they were of one mind.

Morton holds up a finger before Maggie's face as he says this. Studies the finger and then pockets it, his expression strange.

Elisha's mother arrived in Havana as soon as she could. She was escorted by her husband and Elisha's brother Thomas, but it was to his mother Jane that Elisha looked, and as might a sweet boy who so wanted to please.

Jane Kane pressed her hands to Elisha's chest. "Be still," she said kindly, and Elisha's eyes leaked tears.

"Not because he was afraid like, not at all." Morton explains. "He thought of death as like some impatient silly aunt tap-tapping her knitting needles. Those were joyful tears for his Mam's simple kindness."

"An uncle," Maggie sobs into her handkerchief. "With a cane. That was his Death, not a wretched aunt. No."

"Sure, but I knew his mind. Better than anyone." It is as if Morton hasn't heard her. As if he has forgotten she is Elisha's wife. Is that why Morton didn't telegraph her and bid her come to Havana? Because he doubted their marriage?

"Only the Mrs. Kane was there, there for Elisha's last words," Morton slurs out. "His father, his brother, out they'd stepped for a nonce. It was only her and me, and I'd been told to stand apart, as if Elisha and me hadn't been alike one soul, as if we hadn't been through all kinds of Hell together."

Morton tells Maggie, he was certain he heard Elisha's final words, the truest words a man could speak. They were nothing profound nor original nor quotable for the ages. No, they were the ordinary sentimental ones of a son's love for his mother. But Jane Kane did not hear, perhaps because she was looking so intently at her bible, her nail gliding along a passage.

"But now I see that she didn't love him," Morton continues. "She scorned him, like. And you could see the loss of her love were like a black pit under his feet. Sure, but love's end is as mysterious as its beginning. It's why Elisha tried so hard at all things, to regain her regard. And can you fashion a thing crueller? To not attend his last words?"

Maggie cannot. She manages to ask if her name was uttered. If Elisha gave any message to Morton. For her.

"No, ah, he barely spoke, miss."

"Mrs . . . it is *Mrs.* Kane."

"What happened next, mind, is the reason I came to call. And that is to warn you about his mother. You need watch your back with her, she's a Gorgon bitch in a fine lady's hat is what."

"Tell me the rest of it," Maggie says, astonished at her own composure.

The second stroke came on the 10th of February 1857. For five days Elisha gaped and gasped, his limbs fixed as if caught in a net, and then he died. He said not one more intelligible word. It was Jane Kane who closed the lids over the blue wonder of his eyes, and in the gentle way mothers do to coax their little ones to sleep.

Then came the crowding and wailing about the deathbed. A good ten people were in the room at this point. As such, Morton didn't notice when Mrs. Kane left. When at last he did notice, he sought her out immediately. She might be doing herself harm was what he thought. He found her on a filigreed balcony of the hotel. She was on her knees, her skirts like a moat about her. She held a lucifer. Morton gaped at the pile of blackened, smoking papers.

"Hello, Morton," she said. "My, but these letters are hard to burn. They smoulder, see. But what else would they do? That Fox creature dared write of the sordid things she and Elisha have done together, oh, but in such veiled little words. She's even signed herself 'his wife' when she's naught but a dashed adventuress. She shan't see a penny, of course."

"Where did you—"

"The letters? Stashed close to Elisha's heart, but you knew that. Perhaps their oiliness was what caused his poor heart to combust."

She stood and brushed ash from her hands. It was then Morton saw the glass at her feet, the shards of the ambrotype clinging to her hem. Saw Maggie's face in fragments.

"Did you ever see such an image, Morton? The girl was got up like a Greek slattern. Now fetch me that little round portrait, the Fagnani. I know you have it."

Morton, aghast, shook his head.

"Well, Morton," Jane said calmly. "Damn you to hell." And then she plucked a glass shard from one elegant finger, and sucked it to stay the leaking blood.

"I did have it, 'course," Morton explains to Maggie now. "Sure but I kept the Fagnani safe all through the whole two winters we were trapped in the arctic 'cepting when Elisha took it into his sleep sack, as a comfort, like. And don't you know that it started to have a kind of life. You could have sworn to its warmth. Mayhap that's why it disappeared once. William Damned Godfrey, it was with him. I saw him sneak it back to Elisha's hand. What'd he been using it for . . . oh, a lady needn't know, 'cepting it's a long two years and some can't stand having only men for company."

Morton stops, shamefaced. Reaches into his vest pocket and pulls out the Fagnani portrait of Maggie, and dangles it before her on its blackened chain.

PART FOUR

"It was no small irony that, by turning night into day, modern technology also helped obscure our oldest path to the human psyche. No longer did most sleepers experience an interval of wakefulness in which to ponder visions in the dead of night. That, very likely, has been the greatest loss. To paraphrase an early poet, we have been 'disannulled of our first sleep, and cheated of our dreams and fantasies.'"

A. Roger Ekirch,
AT DAY'S CLOSE: NIGHT IN TIMES PAST

"The concept of the Good Death was central to mid-nineteenth century America. Dying was an art, and the tradition of 'ars moriendi' had provided rules of conduct for the moribund and their attendants since at least the fifteenth century: how to give up one's soul 'gladfully and willfully'; how to meet the devil's temptations of unbelief, despair, impatience, and worldly attachment; how to pattern one's dying on that of Christ's; how to pray."

Drew Gilpin Faust,
THIS REPUBLIC OF SUFFERING:
DEATH AND THE AMERICAN CIVIL WAR

CHAPTER 31.

"Reading, reading again, are you? A reader, that's what you are. Didn't I say that when we first met? And, ah, this damned bulb!" I was proclaiming this from the vestibule where the Edison bulb was crackling as was its wont. "Come and go. Wax and wane. No damned reason. No cause."

I swatted the bulb with my satchel. The bulk shattered and shards rained on my cloak. I marched into the room and swept off my hat, but the pins caught in my hair and I lost a few strands from the consequent wrenching.

I made to sit on the ladderback, but it moved, the damned thing. I kicked at the chair from where I sat on the plank floor. "No matter. Not a trouble. Floor's as good as any."

My patient looked at me as indulgently, as one does a child.

"I own I've partaken of some refreshments. Yes, yes," I continued. "Ah, and what of your shilly-shally cad man today?" I said this because she had Elisha's tome astride her lap.

"They have eaten the puppies. Next will be the rats. Some of his men have deserted. He is having a harsh time of it and sees plots everywhere. Godfrey plagues him."

"Godfrey. That was your Elisha's nemesis. Everybody needs one. You had your Chauncey, he had this . . . Did you ever read his version? Godfrey's? One man's truth is another man's lies."

"No, I never read it. I swore I would not. I stoppered my ears if anyone spoke of it. Come, Mrs. Mellon, sit here, next to me."

I thanked her, from what I can recall, then pitched her medicine in her lap before rummaging out my own bottle and stretching out aside her on her little bed. I own that I was drunk. Sotted. Five sheets to a howling wind. I had not been so for, oh, many years. And, ah, oblivion's beck was as inviting as it had ever been.

"Read on. Read on, then, my little reader," I said.

And so she did. Read one of the passages about the Dark, because it is ever Dark up there, in Elisha's Arctic. And then it is ever Light. *"We have lost the last vestiges of our midday twilight. We cannot see print, and hardly paper. Noonday and midnight are alike and, except for a vague glimmer on the sky that seems to define the hill outlines to the south, we have nothing to tell us that this Arctic world of ours has a sun. In one week more we shall reach the midnight of the year."*

My patient may have read more. I cannot say, for I had fallen asleep, and when I awoke it was an uncertain time and I was con-fused, to be frank, as to where I was. Then I saw the three linked windows, saw my patient. She had covered me with a good portion of the bedclothes, and my half-worked cover-all, to boot.

"I took it out of your satchel. I thought it might warm you best."

I apologized, of course, for the lapse in professionalism and said I hoped I had not made a brouha, nor snored, nor taken the lion's share of the bed. She assured me I had been quiet as a mouse and that we'd had a genial chat before I fell asleep. We said no more about it, but it was after that our friendship deepened and we began to use our Christian names with each other. She no longer called me Mrs. Mellon, but Alvah or Alvah June. And I no longer called her Mrs. Kane, but Maggie. And I supposed she now understood that I did not attend her out of pity, nor charity, but out of an understanding that comes from stumbling about in the selfsame shoes.

She took out her bible box a time late, and spread the letters all over the bedclothes. "It all comes on down to Pa, you see."

JOHN HALTS THE BUCKBOARD in the foreyard of the Hydesville house. Hobbles the dun horse and sets him to graze in the blighted peppermint fields. Was it always so quiet around here? As if the birds keep away. As if the very wind does.

He will not go to New York and join his wife and daughters, as Leah continually suggests. They will return to him once he finishes their new house. Once they witness how handsome it is, rising out of the Arcadian fields in sight of their Brother David's house. Once Leah comes to her senses.

He squelches through the mud towards the saltbox house, past the three balm o' Gileads with their round, spring leaves. The Gileads have grown fast and tall and sure. The saltbox, however, seems determined to fall to quick ruin. Spring vines runnel over the listing shingles. Brambles cover what was once the garden. The pig trough has become the nest of some uncertain creature. All this disheartens John. A man might labour half a lifetime to build a home and yet the creeping forces of the earth can reclaim it in a nonce.

He is loading dressed stone from the buttery wall—he will be using it for his latest project, a springhouse—when a shift of light causes him to look up to the upper windows. He loads a few stones more. Looks again. "You're a fool," he mutters, then adds, "darn you, anyhow." He mops his brow. Takes off his coat. The air is steamy-warm for late April. He sits on the buckboard and swallows water from his canteen. Sniffs hard. Catches nothing frowsy, only the usual smells of spring flowers and spring rot. John can hardly fathom it all began here, in this ordinary saltbox house, with his ordinary family. Advertisements for these séances appear in all the papers. The Spiritualists are said to number over a million strong, and that does not include the newest converts in Canada, England, and Europe. Mere rapping is long past. Trumpets play suspended in the air. Writing pops up on forearms in red welts. Spirit lights float, blue and sparking. Mediums are bound and gagged and stuffed into spirit cabinets, structures the size of privies out of which waft mist and eerie voices. Trances and channelling is being done by all and sundry. Most ludicrous, a petition has been sent to Congress asking for a scientific investigation into the spirit invasion, which is worse, some claim, than the continuing invasion of famished Irish.

John crowbars a heavy stone out of the mortar, then hauls the stone to the buckboard. Slaps it down. Looks back. He hefts his crowbar again and approaches the house. He hesitates for a long moment outside the barred and padlocked door. Then pries off the plank and padlock in one hard go.

He crosses the threshold. The floorboards creak. The hidey-hole door shifts open as he treads above-stairs. The second storey. This is where the four of them were sleeping that March of '48. The latest versions of the story have the girls in separate chambers, as if they had been some family of the middling class and not near to scrabbling poverty. And in the latest versions the girls are younger than they were. Twelve for Maggie. Nine for Katie. But they were two years older than that when it all happened. Old enough.

The small room is scattered with rat droppings, dust, the dank clotted dirt his wife always complained about. "How did it get in? How?" she would ask, and demand John scrape his boots again.

John complied, though it made no difference. Not then. Not now.

He runs his nail over the window moulding, feels a long thread beneath where he so diligently painted. He starts back. Something, or someone, moves in the yard below. He berates his chariness. Rattles the stiff sash and hauls it up. Nothing. No one. It is a figuring of the mouth-blown glass. Such glass gives everything a rippled, gauzy aspect. His new home will have only plate glass, he decides. It is costly, but clear as still waters. He turns and his boot nudges something soft and small. A doll, one of those he made for Maggie and Katie years ago. The dress is in dirty tatters, the wooden limbs scraped and disjointed, the mouth only a single stitch now above a single button eye. This one must be Maggie's doll. Katie gave hers to Ella, his granddaughter, their niece. Sorrow rushes him at the thought of little Ella. He smoothes the doll's woollen hair. Recalls something strange about Katie. Other little girls would give audible voices to their dolls. Katie always listened as if to a silent voice, and then replied, and often as not to disagree with the unvoiced comment. Miss Nettie was what she called her doll.

He puts the doll back by the window in a lozenge of sun, alone in that room as any offering.

The gloaming has begun by the time John returns to work on the new house. He funnels his home-brewed burning liquid into the peg-lamp's reservoir, taking his usual care, then wipes the chimney glass clean with newspaper, checking it first for those black-bordered eulogies and landations to Dr. Kane that leave markings on the glass. But it seems the nation is at last done with remembering Kane. His funeral was reported to have been the grandest the nation has yet seen. The man died in Havana, which meant his remains had to be transported to Philadelphia. But first: New Orleans. Louisville. Pittsburgh. Baltimore. By boat, rail and steamer. Each city paraded Kane's coffin with pomp and glory. Such a hero. Such an American hero. Kane's book *Arctic Explorations in Search of Sir John Franklin* is apparently outselling the Blessed Bible. In Philadelphia, Kane's body lay in state at Independence Hall, a rare honour. All the public offices were ordered shut. The city's church bells tolled for five straight hours. It took four pages in the obituary to list the divisions, orders, committees, regiments, societies and clubs that followed the funeral cortège. Even the Ancient Order of Druids was represented, apparently, there at the tail end. By the time Dr. Elisha Kent Kane was interred at the Kane family tomb in Laurel Hill Cemetery he had been a month dead.

Lamp in hand John navigates about the sawed-off boards and wood curls, newspapers and wallpaper sheaths. I'll commence the clean-out tomorrow, he decides. David has been grumbling of late that his father's projects will never end. But they have. Nearly.

He twists the peg-lamp firmly into its wall socket and by its steady burn reads his wife's letter, pausing often to decipher her accordioned writing.

22 April, 1857

Dear husband:
I'm terribly worried about our Maggie, aren't I? The poor
child is broken and lost like a raggedy doll and she is constantly

vowing that she and Dr. Kane were married and that she was named in his will, but Dr. Kane's brother is being difficult about all that and doesn't agree at all that she should have a legacy. At least our Maggie has agreed to abide with me here at the Greeleys' town-home. Isn't this a better arrangement than leaving her with Leah and Katie at the brownstone? Leah has no patience for Maggie and her tears, does she? But then I suppose she had little patience for Dr. Kane either. And now I can make certain our Maggie rests and eats—she is getting so thin, poor lamb.

Now John, is there any chance or hope that you will come to New York at last? The Greeleys' town-home is nicely appointed and of goodly size, and Horace is not allowing us to stay out of charity as you might think. He and Mary are most often at Turtle Bay house and Horace has been con- cerned about the management of the gas lights and general upkeep of the place. I am, you see, a kind of caretaker. But I could surely use your help in this regard, couldn't I?

Your loving wife, Peggy

John digs through his desk for paper and writing implements. Jabs his pen in the inkwell.

26 April, 1857

Dear Wife,
Your house is near finished. I put gingerbread on the gables and veranda and added a cupola. I have painted and wallpapered but I'll give over the bedrooms for you women to decorate. There is the springhouse to finish but that will be shortly done.

John writes of the indoor privy. The new cookstove. The stone sink in the scullery. He does not apologize for the impossibility of gas lights. Such false lights are for the godless crowds of New York. Lamps and candles will suffice. And a crackling fire of pine. He plans to burn sage to rid the house of the odours of turpentine and milk-paint. He has no intention of going to New York, not ever, but this he does not write. He has made that all clear enough to his women. His role is to care for them. How is he to do so if they are scattered hither and yon? They must come here, to the family house that he has toiled to provide.

He considers for some long moments, then takes out his letter to Leah. Each time he thinks it done, he writes further.

I know, Leah-girl, that you're busy raising the dead each and every day and it starts with hymns and sweet music, then come the floating lights and rat-tats and tales of isn't-it-lovely-beyond. It's all entertaining and prettified, but I tell you that when the dead return for *bona fide* there's naught a thing pretty about it. . .

"Fuck Christ," said John. Brother Able was a slumped-over thing with staring, open eyes. John looked to the field, then to the feeder canal in the middle distance. Not a soul. Only three feral dogs. He could leave Able right here under his giant oak, in this small wood. Leave him as crow-feed, rat fodder. But, no, a stinking corpse would bring questions and Able might have told any number of people of his mission to save John's whisky-sotted soul.

He propped Able up so he looked to be relaxing in the scant warmth. Loped to the *Morning Star,* stooping to pick up Able's little black hat from the rutted field, found a coal shovel and a crowbar— the very one he'd used to pry up towpaths and so sabotage the Sabbatarians, back when the world was fine. At the last instance he grabbed the grey horsehair blanket, then drank down the remainder of the first whisky jug. The second jug was still stoppered. It could wait for his return. The digging wouldn't take long, he figured. But it did. The earth was rocky and half frozen and John-Before decided he wanted the requisite six feet down so the feral dogs wouldn't dig up Able's corpse for curious eyes.

He dug in a small clearing some ten feet from the roots of the oak. Every sound was intensified—the hammering of a woodpecker, the witnessing chatter of squirrels, the bells tolling in a town church. He searched Able's pockets for money and valuables and found nothing save a cracked-paint miniature of a pretty young woman in an old-timey high-waisted dress. John supposed the miniature was of Able's dead mother and this filial affection of Able's was a further annoyance. John couldn't imagine carrying about a portrait of his mother, even if she had ever been young or pretty.

John was sweating and breathing noisily from the digging. Soon enough, I'll be fuck-all sotted and asleep, he thought. He fixed Able's hat on Able's head, then rolled Able into the grey horsehair blanket. John could have made use of that blanket, but even he didn't fancy shovelling dirt into the open eyes of the dead.

He tamped down the final patch of earth. Covered the grave with brambles and limp winter leaves. At the last moment he lugged over a grey-white rock and dropped it at the grave's head. The rock could be considered a slab, a marker of a sort. He did not say a prayer. He did not even bow his head.

By the time John walked back to the boat the field was silvered by a full, high moon. *Moonshine!* John thought. *Hah. Give me a fuck-all sky full. Give me whisky, grog, corn liquor, black-strap.* For though exhausted and filthy and sorry for it all, John felt triumphant. None would ever attempt to convert him again. If nothing else, Able's sad death was surely an inoculation against piety, bibles, preachers.

John climbed down into the chilled hold of the *Morning Star*, his fortress. First a drink and then he would attend to the fire. He balled his hands into fists. Could barely comprehend what he was seeing. The second jug had been stoppered. And he'd left it upright. He was not careless about such things.

"Son-of-whore-mongering bastard . . ." The jug lolled on its side. The whisky had soaked the patch of rag carpet and seeped through the floorboard cracks. Not a drop was left.

John fell to his knees. Licked the boards until his tongue was raw and bleeding. Squeezed the rag rug into a tumbler. The whisky, swirling with filth and hair, rose inch by inch. Was just enough to slake his thirst. He collapsed into his niche-bed. Hauled the blanket to his chin. The night turned cold. Why had he given that second blanket to Able? It wasn't as if he'd need it.

"Damn your rotting eyes," John said. Blood from his tongue splattered his beard. He calmed himself with assurances. Come first light he'd go in search of liquor. Since he was penniless he supposed he'd have to turn to crime, but that hardly signified.

He woke up, with bile in his throat and a tongue so swollen it barely fit between his teeth. He tried to rise, only to collapse shivering on the floor. He hauled himself back to the bunk in a fevered agony. All that day he thrashed and groaned. He pushed his swollen tongue into the tumbler, then hurled the tumbler against the wall. The hold reeked from the spilled whisky. A reek, however, could not sustain a man.

The shakes came first and then the spasms. The horrors would be next. He'd seen men in the screaming grips of a rum fit, but never had he let himself go so far.

Let the fucking giant rats and spiders come, thought John-Before. How real can they seem?

But it was not giant rats and spiders who came in the end, it was Brother Able, and he was mighty real indeed.

The rank-sweet stench of rotting flesh was what told John-Before he was no longer alone. He half sat up in the bed and pressed himself against the wall. He hup-hupped in terror. Clutched the blanket as if it might be a shield.

Able sat cross-legged on a barrel. There was moist dirt clumped on his clothes and John-Before's grey blanket at his feet. Able had only been buried a day, yet already he was the very picture of decay. His face was half skull, half raw flesh. One eye hung limply on a flayed cheekbone; the other looked calmly at John. A worm curled past his rotting gums. Death must have sobered him, because he was stuttering as he berated John for giving him the whisky, for the sorry burial. He did thank him, however, for the blanket. "I-I s-suppose that w-were the b-best you c-could do."

John worked his mouth. No scream. Just a silent rush of air.

Able continued. Told John about his mother again. Her fine house and the loss of it to drink. "My f-father b-beat her. D-did I m-mention that?"

John twisted his head to one side. Did Able realize he was dead? The thought of telling him he was made John even more terrified, if that were possible.

"He d-did. D-Darn him. I c-could hear him y-yelling and her c-crying." That was another reason Able had become a preacher, John learned; he wanted to have some purpose. He wanted to change the hearts of people, but through kindness and persuasion.

He stood and walked agitated about the cramped hold, dirt and skin dropping from him. "B-But now I w-won't b-be able to ch-change anyone. I'm d-dead." He sobbed. It was a dry, rattling sound. No tears. His eyes were too decomposed for that. At least he knows he's dead, John thought.

Hours passed. Able-the-dead spoke on and on. Lamented the failure of his ambitions and hopes. Relayed the minutia of his ordinary upbringing, his quotidian sufferings. Told constant of his poor mother, how she longed to be with him in his endeavours. "B-But I told her, n-no, that I wanted to be a-alone." And that was a lie. It was the burden of her love that Able didn't want. And now? Now she was dead. Now he longed for such mortal love. For human company.

Able-the-dead pushed his rotting face close to John's aghast one. John gagged from the stench. Twisted his head aside. Able squelched his hanging eye back into its socket; pus dripped onto John's hands as he did so. Now Able could stare properly at John. Stuttered out that love between mortals was as necessary for salvation as a love for God. "It's an ex-extension of D-Divine love, is all." One cannot exist without the other. And this was where Able had failed. He had not loved his brother, Willing. Nor his mother, not in the way he should have. "W-We should have b-been together. S-She needed me. L-Love is hollow unless y-you show it."

By this time the swelling in John's tongue had abated enough for him to croak out, "Go away, please. I'm begging you."

Able's rotting lips curled up in a smile. He promised that he would leave. But John had to promise something in return. John had to cease drinking spirits. John had to become a man of God. And John had to return to his family and provide them with his love and unceasing protection. If not, Able would walk with him wherever he went. He would never cease talking, and he would never cease rotting, and the stench would follow John, and John would be a pariah among even the most wretched of the living.

"Fucking dandy, then. I'll do it. Just leave me be, damn you."

"Sh-Shake on it?" Able stretched out a rotting hand and John took it. Felt Able's exposed knuckle bones, the veins looping out of his palm. John-Before squeezed shut his eyes.

When he opened them, Able was gone but for a lingering stench, but for some dank clots of earth from his grave. Some mouldy grey threads from his blanket shroud.

... And he haunts me still, Leah-Lou, though I've not seen him manifest again in a rotted state or otherwise. I know he's about, mind, because he's ever leaving those threads from his blanket shroud and those dank clots of his grave dirt, though I'm doing my mortal best to fulfill my sworn promise to take care of my family, and love my family, and serve my family, and at the selfsame time as I love and serve God. Take what you will from what I tell you, but know that it's my fault, this haunting business. That was Able's ghost tromping about the Hydesville house that first night, before those "raps" of your sisters started up. He came back that night because I gave in to the temptation of whisky, and for the first time since I made that promise to him to not ever drink again. Let's hope and pray, for your sake and mine, that Able will atain peace in due time, and that he'll stay quiet in his grave under that great oak near Wayne.

John sets aside the pen, stretches his stiffened legs. Takes his spectacles off and pinches the arched bridge of his nose. He cleans the lenses with a rag, breathing on them first, the round mist showing like a second eye. He folds up his narrative—for that, he supposes, is what it has become.

A clatter. Then a shattering.

He whirls. The peg lamp has fallen. He stuffs his narrative in his pocket. He yells. Flails his rag. Too late. Flames tear along the spilled burning liquid. Ignite the newspapers, the wood curls. In a blink the flames are shooting up to the ceiling and hurtling out sparks. The Currier and Ives prints vanish into a fiery maw. The wallpaper blackens and disintegrates. John stamps and swats. Curses as he has not done in years. Coughs and gasps, his lungs hot as forge-irons.

David pounds at the smoke-whirled window. "Pa! Get out. Leave that."

John staggers out, the flames grasping at his legs, David grasping at his arms. A small explosion tosses them both down the fresh-painted stairs. John hears glass breaking. A ferocious crackling. He lies stunned on the cool grass, his limbs flung wide as if he were afloat in a pond. Above him stars tunnel the sky, their multitude a humbling thing.

"Pa?" David's broad face wanes into his view. John stands with David's help. David's sons and two farmhands rush by with buckets of water.

"That's a waste of decent water," John says. "Attend to the other buildings. Forget this one. There's no saving it."

A farmhand tosses his bucket of water at the porch. It might as well be a thimble-full. The porch collapses in flames.

David's wife, Beth, runs up, skirts clenched in her hands. "Lord, how'd it happen?"

The flames tower up and up. The smoke thickens to a pall. John could say it was his carelessness with the peg-lamp, the burning liquid, but that is a falsity. He puts his hand in his pocket; his fingers rustle against the pages of his narrative, then touch something else—a thread that has the unmistakably coarse feel of horsehair.

"Don't claim to know, Beth," he says at last, "but I'm guessing the Good Lord has his reasons. I'm gonna pray now. We all should."

———

Dear Wife,
. . . And so there's naught left excepting some burned slabs. I'll come assist you women then since you're needing it. I'll attain New York Wednesday or so and then I'll hire one of those cabs to the Greeleys' town-home, so as you don't have to trouble yourself.

Your husband,
John

CHAPTER 32.

The walk-up was hard going this day, and I so stopped on the tenth-floor landing to catch my breath. I steadied myself against the wall, felt the cracks, the peeling plaster, the grave-damp of poverty. The tenement reeked, as always, of sewage pipes, onions, cabbages, piss. I heard a child crying, a dog yapping, and a muted argument cycling through accusations of betrayal and want.

I sat down on the step and set the gin bottle aside me. It was near empty.

To explain: I had not uttered my son's name—August—for many years. And uttering it—that is, reading the same name aloud from Kane's book, well, it had brought him back utterly.

"We're on the side of justice," was what my August said before he left to join the Union Army. By that time my August owned eighteen years. He was strung-tall and rackety-limbed and homely in parts (I admit) and he blinked too often, as if in constant aghastment at the cruelties in the world. Still, he had an arresting grace.

I had a hundred discouragements to him joining. They made no difference. He was stone-wall stubborn, as the truly good often are. I refused him my blessing. I was that mad. I just watched, arms akimbo, as the green horizon folded him up. When I came to my senses and ran after him he was gone, gone, gone.

Mr. Mellon rolled his mean, piggy eyes. "Ah, let the weepy fool go save them darkies," he said. He would have said more but something in my glance stopped him, murder to be frank.

I waited and waited for a letter to tell me where he was. And one arrived, yes, but that Mr. Mellon kept it from me until it was too late. When I found the letter I was so enraged I thwacked Mr. Mellon with a hot pan (I was cooking eel stifle at the time). He dropped and did not move, not even when I shook him. I left that very hour for Bull Run. No sign of Mr. Mellon dead or alive when I returned to the cottage some weeks later, nor have I seen him since.

The letter Mr. Mellon hid from me, out of jealousy and spite, is tucked into a side pocket of my satchel. I keep it with me always, like a talisman. And like any talisman I hold it often, though I surely know it off of heart.

"Gather yourself, Alvah June. Look presentable. Look brisk," I said, and stood and then huffed up the last storeys.

My patient began her narrative straightaway upon my entering, as if I had not even left.

MAGGIE LATCHES THE DOOR softly behind her. When the Greeleys lived here the room had been the nursery for their five (or was it six?) dead babes. It has been shut up for years. No one enters anymore except Maggie. Not even the maid, a sturdy Nantucket girl. She wouldn't, even if Maggie allowed it.

"That thing in there!" this maid exclaims. Excessive, is the general opinion; shudders and perplexity, the general reaction. A closet shrine to the dead is one thing; a whole room quite another. Leah would nag constantly about this, which is another reason Maggie has chosen not to stay at her sister's brownstone. Leah has no sympathy for Maggie's determined grieving, unlike their father, who has been nothing *but* helpful since he moved here to the Greeleys' town-home. No one could fault his attention to the gas lights and candle-trimming; and when Thomas Kane came to bribe Maggie out of Elisha's love letters, and with a puny insult of a sum, what did Maggie's father do? He shoved Thomas out the door as if Thomas were a petty bill collector, a sight that almost made Maggie laugh again.

Maggie shuts the black bombast drapes against a slip of light. She has sold the more frivolous of her jewellry to buy not only these drapes, but also the black candelabra that sits on the black-draped table. Displayed on this table are Elisha's "white gifts"—the lace handkerchiefs, the Honiton-lace undersleeves, the fox stole, the silk cape, and the white diamond bracelet from Tiffany's coiled there in a velvet-lined box. Also displayed are newspaper clippings detailing his exploits, maps of his journeys, copies of elegies, and two black-framed daguerreotypes of Elisha-when-alive. One shows him in his explorer's furs, rifle in hand; another as a beardless man of twenty. But, alas and such, no daguerreotype of the Elisha-when-dead, not one of him in his coffin nor propped in an armchair. Maggie does not even have a death mask of her beloved. No *memento mori* at all. But at least Father Quinn, her confessor, has helped her to purchase something close.

She strikes a lucifer and lights the candles. Blinks to stop the flames from dancing so oddly. She drank perhaps more of good Dr. Bayard's laudanum medicine than she should have. She often does.

I will cease it all soon, she vows, and kneels on her black stool, her widow's weeds stiff and heavy in the spring warmth. She feels alike a black bauble suspended on a heavy chain, unable to swing this way or that. Is she a true widow or not? She and Elisha had indeed vowed themselves to each other. But no minister blessed their marriage ceremony. No papers recorded it. And what to make of their peculiar, bloodless consummation? For love to be consummated there had to be blood. Didn't there? Consummated? Or is the word "consumed"? She conjures Elisha. He stands over her, his torso candle pale, his trousers buttoned fast. He presses her hands there. From behind Elisha, the peddler leers. He is as ugly as Elisha is handsome. He shows his member. He curses her again: "You'll die alone and ranting for your lies, you hoyden bitch."

Maggie presses her fists to her forehead. The image thankfully recedes.

Does Elisha wander Purgatory? she wonders now. That grey place between Heaven's light and Perdition's dark? Such is the place for questioning souls. And if Elisha should attain Heaven, will he be happy there? He joked he wouldn't be. All that stasis, all that dull perfection. He said he would prefer that his soul seep into her skin.

Maggie wills her breath quiet. Elisha will speak to her if she is quiet. Patient. Still. He will send her a message from the beyond or wherever, and in one of his clever little codes. She must simply attend. And then he will utter her name. Then he will make a clear declaration to his family, the world. Come soon, she thinks, else I'll vanish inside these weeds, leave only a black puddle of crepe and tears for the maid to scrub off the damned floor.

Maggie looks to the side wall, up and up, the dreadful image there giving her comfort and a sense of substance, as always. Now she rearranges the objects on the table, polishes a frame with her sleeve, polishes harder and harder in her frustration. She has again been denied a way out, again her inentions have been thwarted and denied. She was set to leave behind the spirit sittings, the ghost talk-ings. Become a wife and mother. She would have been happy with an honest life. Katie would have come to live with her and Elisha, would have found a husband and another life as well.

She approaches the far wall. The tortured Christ looks down at her from his cross. The rendering is macabre even by papist stan-dards. Blood sheets his face and body; thick nails split his palms and feet; heavy thorns gouge his head and brow. And such an expression on his gaunt handsome face: of agony and resignation. The wood carving is twice the height of Elisha, but the resemblance, well, it is undeniable.

"Do forgive me," she pleads. "I will find a way to make it all right. I promise."

CHAPTER 33.

"Was it not terribly remarkable, Alvah? That we invented this religion, if you could call it that, and in such an accidental fashion withal. The séances, the spirit boards, the spirit writing and spirit cabinets, the hundreds of Spiritualist Societies, the uncounted mediums and charlatans, the endless hope and yearning, and all invented out of that little lonesome house after a long dull winter, and by children, playing as they oughtn't, the hobgoblins."

"Inventions? Discoveries? Well, what about Bell's telephone? It's trustier than any old medium. And what of that special paper, nice and soft, and only for the wiping of one's ass. And tabulators, and zipper-thingos. Now a lady can undress herself, snap-quick." I hefted my tumbler of gin. She hefted hers of laudanum.

I added. "And let's not forget the damned Gatling guns and how-itzers. Such swell new inventions." I picked up my gin bottle from the nightstand and in doing so knocked over her pot of handcream, the one I had brought for her a time back: *Mrs. Howe's Neroli and Rose Miracle Hand Cream*. Miracle? Now there was a thrown-about word. Anywise, she had yet to use the cream by what I could tell. I set it back on the night table.

"What were we chatting about then, Maggie, dear?"

"Inventions unbounded."

LEAH'S NEW-HIRED MAID, Susie, fastens Leah's underpetticoat, then fastens six more petticoats atop that. Leah still prefers petticoats to give her skirts volume. She will never take-up these new-fangled crinolines of whale-bone and metal. What reputable woman would have her legs dangling inside a hooped-out skirt like the tongue of a bell?

Susie sets one of Leah's séance gowns on a dress pole, then climbs the stepladder. Leah holds her arms up stiff and straight. These séance gowns are of shadow-grey, ash-grey, cloud-grey—all the better to fade into dim-lit rooms. And though drab, these dresses are beautifully tailored, the pockets invisible, the hems of perfect length.

She surveys herself in a looking glass, or a "mirror" as they are called now; it is a costly one, with no warping or mist. "Susie, dear, would you say I appear younger than forty-three years?"

"Oh, yes, ma'am, years younger."

Leah sighs. Sometimes it seems a curse that she can always spot a lie.

She dismisses Susie and opens her supply chest and takes out her jar of lard, her special-made gloves. Now why did Alfie have to up and die? She never had to worry about dealing with her supplies before. Leah was the one who found Alfie in the outside privy, his trousers around his ankles—a most unfortunate discovery that. A watercloset had been installed inside the brownstone, but Alfie considered voiding inside a house unwholesome. He was slumped in the privy all through Sunday, his day off, and most of Monday; it was only then anyone noticed his absence.

Now Leah must do everything her own self. She must even deal with that sin-ugly Mr. Pettifew on her own. Generally Pettifew supplies her by post, but at times she cannot avoid patronizing his shop, which has moved several times, growing larger and more difficult to find on each occasion.

She reaches deeper in the supply chest and eases out the stoppered canister of phosphorous, her hands all larded and gloved—she does not wish to glow green like those "phossies" who make make matches for a living. And what had Alfie said about phosphorous igniting? She should have written it down. And, honestly, why had she agreed to go out for this sitting? The spirits are always more co-operative in her own home. Ah, but George Willets and his wife are of this circle and Leah is still grateful to him for standing fast with her against the rioters at Corinthian Hall those ten years ago. And this circle pays very well, and Leah, like everyone, always has need of money.

A few hours later, and Mrs. Simeon, the hostess for this evening's sitting, is introducing Leah to Mr. Daniel Underhill, a thickset man with a quantity of light brown hair, a quantity of good teeth and a stick pin of diamonds and gold.

"He is the president of the New York Fire Insurance Company, Leah, the city's largest, and he has long followed your career. It seems his sister is also a medium and can speak in tongues. And his mother can move tables merely by placing her hands upon them. Which must be so useful when rearranging the furniture."

Mrs. Simeon moves off. Daniel says, "I must apologize. I am mortified beyond calculation."

Leah smiles bravely, says in her trilling low-toned voice, "I hope the sitters do not expect great manifestations this night. The spirits so often refuse to co-operate for the disrespecting. Worse, they often get up to mischief." She presses a hand to her chest. "A moment . . . There."

Daniel offers Leah his arm. "I am your servant, Mrs. Brown. Indeed, I count myself among your greatest admirers."

"My thanks, Mr. Underhill. No doubt the spirits will favour a gentleman such as yourself." And so they proceed to the parlour, where the servants are already turning down the lamp wheels.

"WHATEVER ARE YOU DRINKING?" my patient asked.

"Absinthe, Maggie-duckling. I was once a faithful adherent to the green hour, which was five at any respectable tavern. How I loved pouring over the sugar-laden spoon. Ah, but little rituals do give credibility and justification, as you should know from your séances. Well, the green hour is gone now. Gone out of fashion, like bonnets. Like the good death. Like la-la, the rest."

"Absinthe makes the heart grow fonder."

"Hah! But of someone else. That's the last part of the poem—oh, everyone forgets the last parts, and damn it . . ." The bottle nearly slipped from my grasp. "No escaping me!"

To explain: the blue devils were swarming (Blue devils; how we love to colour our fears) and I had ever found that absinthe was a river they could not cross. Yet now they were crossing, and in miserable little boats.

"Nope, no escaping me at all," I repeated once the absinthe was safe again in my hands.

"I am quite aware of that," Mrs. Kane said, then asked if I could give her the hand cream. I did so, the neroli and rose scent wafting out as I unscrewed the lid.

"Put that down, it's toile porcelain, a *bona fide* French one," John tells Leah.

They are in the Greeleys' parlour and Leah has snatched up the vase as if to smash it, her expression one of rage and woe, the self-same expression she wore as a girl whenever a grand scheme went awry. The expression, John allows, is less charming now.

"Bona fide?" She glances sharp at him, as if he had just spoken Greek and not plain Latin.

"I bought one alike it for the Arcadia house. It's naught but a melted lump now, 'course."

Leah thunks the vase down. "I had a bad sense. A terrible sense. I should have heeded it. Ever since God and the spirits took Alfie I have known that a mischievous spirit would one day throw approbation upon me." She speaks as softly as she is able, which is not soft at all.

The Simeons' parlour was too crowded, she explains, the people jostling and talking and making jest, and so the spirits rapped that the party must split in two, that Leah should take a group of the most sensible and best-prepared into an adjoining bathroom. "The spirit lights had just appeared when my hands began to burn. Honestly,

I have never felt such pain, Father. Just look." She holds out her red and blistered palms. "I nearly fainted."

"Did you now . . . and then what?"

"I plunged my hands under a faucet of water and—"

"Inside a house?"

"Yes, inside a house. They have such things in the city. They have all sorts of marvels here. My spirits, you are worse than Alfie . . . Anywise, the water was not enough to quell the terrible pain, and so I rushed outside to the garden and plunged my hands into the dirt. And what came out? Tendrils of smoke and luminous spirit glows. None had ever seen the like."

"Spirit glows, was it."

"Yes, did I not just say so? It was Mr. Underhill who helped me to my feet, gallant man. But the next day Mrs. Simeon declared she had found granules of phosphorous in the dirt, just where I had plunged my hands, the lying old buffle-head."

"Hmm, and what do you reckon happened?"

"I cannot say for certain excepting . . . excepting that it is well known that the human brain is a reservoir of phosphorous. Likely the spirits draw it out in some complex manner."

"Out of the brain? Why, that's mortal interesting."

"Yes, the brain. Do not look at me so. I have had suspicious looks aplenty since this misunderstanding. Oh, indeed. And letters. From the Willets. From the Posts even. They are all asking me to explain what happened. They do not suggest . . . oh, but they do. They are. One scarcely needs a magnification glass to read between the lines. But I cannot explain what happened. It is beyond my ken. Only Mr. Underhill has been steadfast beside me. But then we Spiritualists are being assailed on all sides these days. We are like those poor early Christians. If there were lions in America our enemies would feed us to them, and just because of some dashed frauds. What of it? Of course some would hold false séances for monetary gain, the greedy pigs. And there's some would use gadgetry. Oh, and then the Blue Book, such a fantasy, as if there were a regular under-ground correspondence among mediums, as if we lived in some secret, contrary world."

John chuckles.

"This is amusing?"

"You've been feeding yourself this cant year after year and now you're swallowing it whole, Leah-Lou. Now you're choking on it." He does not say this as an accusation. Who is he to accuse? For after years of prayer he now believes wholeheartedly in God the Father, and God the Son, and in the Holy Spirit infusing all things. Believes in salvation and the resurrection and in winged angels. And in the Devil, surely.

"Will you speak plain, Father? No, no, do not bother." She rubs her forearms, mutters, "My Good Lord and all that, you sound just like damned Chauncey."

"What's that?"

"Nothing. No one. No one of importance. Now attend me, please. I am speaking about my reputation, about the dolts-heads who are challenging it. How could they doubt me?"

"God sees inside our hearts. Our heads too. Even the ones stuffed with phosphorous. Reputation is a thing of the world and the flesh. It won't be a help to you in Paradise. It don't matter what other people think of you is what I'm saying," John finishes, exasperated, for Leah is looking at him as if he were explaining algebra.

"Poppycock, you're a man. You don't require reputation as we women do. Reputation is what I survived on when you left me to fend for myself for ten long years."

This again. "It were just . . . I couldn't find you, that's all."

"Hah! You knew perfectly well that I was living in Rochester. I saw you that day when I was incommoded with child and that Bowman Fish was hauling me along."

"Confound you, girl. You got eyes in back of your head? And he weren't hauling you, if I recall. It were the other way, and—"

"And you didn't come and speak to me. That is what matters. You cringed back into the shadows. Oh, I am sorry for my . . . suggestion that time in Arcadia. I would never hurt your reputation with accusations, false or not. It was only so you would not harm mine. Just imagine if your reputation were endangered. You would feel as I do, as if you could stab yourself through the heart."

John looks at her fondly. Thinks how she would be the last person to stab herself through the heart, even if she could find it.

Tears runnel Leah's cheeks. "It may not be figured like some, but I do have a heart, Papa. I do!"

John starts. He hadn't spoken aloud. He is sure of it.

Leah continues, "I just . . . I cannot help who I am. I wish I could. I wish I were someone else entirely at times."

"So you say and say again. But you, my girl, become someone else 'entirely' each time you take on a dead person's voice with your so-called trancing and channelling."

"Need you be so dramatic, Father?" she asks, cool of a sudden.

"Ecclesiastes says, *Let thy words be few and—*"

"I know how it goes."

"Then say why you're here, Leah." He smiles grimly. "Your words, they've been few enough to me since I arrived in New York. Now you're telling me all this about phosphorous and doubters. Why?"

Leah paces, this way then that. "Do you recall that little box you made for your playing cards? You showed it to me when I was a girl. There was a secret place within it and inside that was the King and Queen, and the Jester, of course. Ah, but you made such ingenious things once."

"That I did. I made a whole ingenious house for you women. Noah never laboured harder at his ark. Lot of mortal good it did me."

"It is just . . . just that I need an ingenious thing—a box, an *ingenious* box, to prove my innocence. I need your help, Papa."

She kneels at his feet. Takes his roughened hands in her burned and blistered ones. She winces. At the pain? he wonders. Or the humiliation? What does it matter? His Leah needs him. Perhaps the house he laboured over all those years was not the safe haven he had imagined. Perhaps the haven was himself, all along.

He considers, then says, "You still got the bible box I made you?"

"The lily box? Why, yes. My spirits, I surely do."

CHAPTER 34

"Here, Alvah, attend."

My patient lifted the lid of the bible box. It was a very thick lid, I noticed then. She ran her little fingers along the lilies on the topside and pressured it just so. Just then a little hatch slid open on the underside.

"Oh, how clever, clever." I drank a nip of gin, and she drank a nip of laudanum.

"What is the hour?" she asked. "Is it night?"

I looked at my bracelet watch. It was a delicate gold creation that another patient, a French lady, had bequeathed to me. It had stopped at 2 p.m.—the time I usually arrived at the garret—and I told Maggie Kane this fact.

"But is it night? Day? I cannot tell the difference any longer."

"That's a common thing. It's the body preparing for Eternity. Night and day are indistinguishable there, from what I've heard. "

"Ah, like the Arctic."

"I don't see how."

"*Noonday and midnight are alike, and except a vague glimmer on the sky we have nothing to tell us that this Arctic world has a sun* . . . That's from Elisha's book and—"

"No need to show off your memory, duck."

"Dandy-fine, then . . . Perhaps you should wind it, your watch."

"I can't. The bit is too small—or my hands too large."

"Here, let me have a try," she said.

I shrugged and handed her the watch. Her little hands trembled faintly but were still deft enough to wind the stem. Afterwards my watch smelled of the neroli and rose oil hand cream I had brought her and I was pleased, to be frank, as one is when a gift is at last being used.

DANIEL NUDGES ASIDE the silk rose at Leah's ear, whispers moistly, "How is your tally of joy, my dovey?"

"Do not trouble your mind, Mr. Underhill. I am gifted with joy. I simply overfloweth with it," Leah says, and looks over the crowded parlour of the Greeleys' town-home. The scene *is* boding well: the Willets are not casting suspicious eyes her way. Amy and Isaac Post are not casting disapproving eyes at the lavish food, the masses of flowers, the oceans of punch, perhaps because a number of Daniel's family are fellow Hicksite Quakers, and with their own mountains of good causes. The Greeleys—who have come from their Turtle Bay home with daughter Ida and baby Gabriella—are not bickering for once. Certainly Leah's mother and father are as congenial together as Leah has ever seen. Lately they have taken to holding hands, of all things, and at this instance her father is helping her mother arrange the punch glasses, as if he were a servant, or a wife himself. As for Maggie and Katie, they seem to be attending out of affection, not just duty. Are perhaps even sober. Indeed, the years might be wound back on the Fox family and their intimates, so convivial, co-operative and optimistic is the scene. The only thing missing is her daughter, Lizzie, but she is now Mrs. George Blauvet and is abroad at the moment, though exactly where "abroad" Lizzie has neglected to tell her.

Daniel now whispers to Leah's cheek, "Are they all here and accounted for, our guests?"

"Yes, the guests are all here, all the invited ones."

"Are there other varieties?" He is not being sarcastic. She has yet to see that in him. Thus she does not enlighten him that, of course, there are always uninvited guests. People who take umbrage at their exclusion. People like Mr. Pettifew, whose note she tore up as soon as she read it: *And I heard it will be an affair of small grandeur. I admit I thought an invitation would not be unwarranted as we have been acquainted these many year and our Fates are knit up.*

Such a distressing little man, Leah thinks, what with his distinct ugliness, that twist to his back so that he must look up, up at one with a pained expression, as if he prefers the dirt at his boots. And what is that blather: *Fates knit up?* Is her fate knit up with her butcher's? Her dressmaker's?

Amy Post passes Leah's view. Even for a joyous wedding Amy wears her usual austere garb. Wears, too, her usual look of restrained concern, which, at the moment, is be directed at Maggie. Understandable given Maggie's fixed smile, her gaunt frame, her intent eyes, which are darker than before, as if the pupils, like ink blots, have stained the irises. And whatever does Amy make of Maggie's dress of light-sucking black bombast? Of her fingers twisting round her crucifix like blind worms? Leah, for one, still cannot believe that Maggie converted to Catholicism and all because of Elisha-the-dead. The baptism was officiated by that Father Quinn. Katie was the only member of their family who attended.

And where is Katherina? Leah wonders. She spies her out easily as Katie's gown is a startling aniline yellow. Leah approves—and highly—of these new aniline dyes: mauvine, magenta, fuchine, methyl violet. These inverted colours are much alike the colours that music once revealed to her, and does no longer. Perhaps the anilines are in compensation. Perhaps the brighter and brighter man-made lights are as well. Certainly gas lights are nothing remarkable now inside city houses, and the night streets are so lit that the stars and moon are no longer required as guidance. As for rushies and candles? They and their meek light will soon be found only in the countryside, which is where the dark belongs.

". . . but I do believe in justice and truth and all that, really," Katie says to Amy, her voice twanging loud, as it still unfortunately does when she is rattled.

"An easy utterance, dear, but can thou fathom how ill-paid seam-stresses are? How as like they go blind for our vanity?" She indicates the shirring and embroidery on Katie's sleeve.

Our vanity? Leah doubts that Amy, being plain as a hobnail, has ever been afflicted with vanity. Would I have been better off plain? Leah wonders. Is plainness one of those blessings in disguise? It is a consideration. For if one has never possessed beauty, how can one mourn its loss? Perhaps Pettifew *should* arrive, like that malignant fairy in the old story, the uninvited one who cursed the castle and sent all into the deepest slumber for a century. Leah would not mind being stilled in her autumn beauty, at this promising moment of security, even happiness. Oh, she knows "Her Fatness" is Maggie's and Katie's latest nickname for her. Likely they have snickered that her well-embellished gown would better suit a younger woman. But Leah's attractions are still considerable. Has not Daniel insisted so? Has not he insisted he was smitten the instant he beheld her on her knees, her wounded hands held up, there in the Simeons' rain-wet garden, the earth tendrilling smoke, her expression beseeching yet bold. She reminded him of some heroine, he said, possibly a Greek one.

Amy takes her leave from Maggie and Katie. Likely she feels as Leah often does in their company—as if toe-clutching the edge of a precipice.

"Pa's playing scout, Mag," Katie says, as their father hoves by with a tray. He hawk-eyes the three of them. The tumblers in Maggie's and Katie's hands vanish. Once their father shifts off the tumblers reappear, as if the girls have plucked them from the ether.

"Girls," Leah says. "You should respect our father."

Maggie says, "Oh, the good grief, Leah, he treats us like we're children still. As you do. I mean, we're hardly 'girls.'" She looks archly at the pink roseates on Leah's hem, then drifts off with Katie in tow, both all-agiggle.

So they are still gigglers, Leah thinks. Not something I have ever been.

"Come, dovey," Daniel says. "We must arrange ourselves for the ceremony."

He helps Leah to rise, escorts her past several of his relations— relations who listen with satisfying attention to George Willets: "... and it was a bible box, pretty carved with lilies of the valley, but otherwise simple as they come. We packed it with earth then bid our Leah plunge in her hands. After she withdrew them we found granules of phosphorous, burning hot. Just as Leah predicted. Don't the spirits act in the most mysterious ways?"

The spirits surely do, on this the relations agree. Daniel squeezes Leah's elbow. He, too, witnessed Leah's "proving" ceremony. Witnessed Leah's honesty with his own eyes.

They continue their way through their guests. Maggie, to Leah's dismay, is berating Horace Greeley: "And why should I give Elisha's love letters to his conniving brother? Why, Horace? Why? Do you reckon I'll publish them? It's not your business anywise. Why in tunket do you meddle so? I saw your letter to Thomas. You wrote he may direct you in the matter of Maggie Fox as he sees fit."

"Saw it?" Horace cried. "You more than saw it. You scrawled all over it. My private papers. Like a child of three might do. I've been gracious in allowing you to stay at my home and—"

"Stop this!" Mary Greeley cries. "It distresses little Gabrielle. Our little baby Mumpkee." She nuzzles the baby's cheek. The baby, a toddler really, yanks Mary's hair and chortles. Thin-faced Ida Greeley looks on with childish jealousy. Leah guesses she is, what? Ten? Katherina, Leah realizes with a shock, was not much older when the spirits first arrived.

Now there is singing and announcements. Now the bride and bridegroom take their places before the flower-decked window and the black-garbed minister. After the ceremony, which everyone agrees was short and charming, the company seat themselves in the dining room for a feast. Men servants brings in separate arranged plates of duck comfit and fiddleheads, the portions exactly the same for each guest. No more platters on sideboards as country folk might do. Champagne bottles pop. The talk grows louder, almost masks the rap at the door. Leah stiffens in her corset. Strains to hear Susie-the-maid's muffled talk. She is about to excuse herself when Susie brings in a blue-wrapped parcel. Leah takes the proffered card, reads: *Greatest Felicitations on your joyful day. I look forward to our continuing friendship and association. For your wedding, I'm gifting you a copy of the Blue Book. Come by and add to the original anytime at your convenience. Yours truly best, Mr. L. Pettifew.*

"Leave the package there in my sight, Susie," Leah whispers, and indicates the sideboard.

Daniel is about to make an announcement, when the new Mrs. Underhill puts her hand on his arm. He sits with a genial nod. Leah stands and thanks the assembled for their presence.

"Some have said that I must continue to be the guiding light of Spiritualism, that I and my sisters have been gifted by God and that it is our duty. However, I also now have a duty to my beloved husband, and it is my foremost duty."

She glances at her sisters, who seem to be counting the fork tines, at her father who is watching her. Glances, lastly, at the blue-wrapped package on the sideboard. She clears her throat. "Dear people, I shall hold no more public séances. My career as a medium is finished."

There are exclamations of surprise, even from Daniel. It is not really surprising to Leah, though it came to her mind just then. She rarely surprises herself anymore, though she used to, heaven knows. As do the spirits.

CHAPTER 35.

I tripped outside the garret vestibule and fell down square on the squalid floor. I should dust and clean, I thought as the vestibule's damned Edison bulb waned. The landlord, I realized, must have promptly replaced the bulb I broke during my first lapse. My, what alacrity. What dutiful attention. But really—does he assume we can no longer find our way without such contrived light? Does he think us childish in our fears? Craven in our souls?

I rose to my feet with the assist of the wall, then patted the side pocket of my satchel where August's letter was safely tucked. I took the letter out, even though I knew it off by heart.

Dearest Mother,
I hope this letter reaches you in good health. I have a haver-sack and forage cap and dandy blue jacket with buttons of brass. We've been drilling every day and I can now stick a bayonet and load a rifled gun in a clap. When I talked to you of joining you recalled to me that I could never even stick a pig nor break a hen's neck, but I suspect I only balked because they were innocent creatures. Now I can't help but wonder if the Rebs have a portion of innocence, too, and mayhap there's a better way to convince them of slavery's evils than the cannon and the gun. I allow I'm amazed how there's so many who joined up for the excitement and the four squares

and not from any loathing of injustice and cruelty. And I admit I'm afraid of killing a man. Do you believe it's true that compassion takes the greatest courage? If so, I'll need all the courage I ever had. I must go now. We're set to march. We join with the Rebs at Bull Run tomorrow.

Your loving son, August

I gathered myself and went in to do my duty.

"You look as if you've lost something," Maggie Kane said, to which I had no reply.

WINTER OF '62 AND MAGGIE STOMPS up the stairs of her Barclay Street let. She kicks the risers, loosening the snow on her over-shoes and shawl. She rubs her bare hands warm. *What! Lost your mittens, you naughty kittens? Then you shall have no . . . pie* was it? Not wine, surely.

Maggie moved to this let from the Greeleys' town-home just after Leah's wedding. She had no choise, given her rift with Horace over her court case against the Kanes. Given Mother's fretting over any refreshment Maggie takes. And this let is reasonably close to St. Anne's church, where Maggie often goes to confess to Father Quinn; and reasonably distant from the resplendent home on 37th that Leah and Daniel moved to after their marriage, and where Mrs. Leah Fox Fish Brown Underhill now holds court.

Maggie attains the upper landing, then halts. Her door is ajar. She must have neglected to lock it, leaving as she did in such a frantic rush.

She slides inside, feels the wall for the stop-cock, then flips the toggle for the gas light. The wall sconce flares blue, then burns steady. The science of such instantaneous light never fails to amaze her. "Magic," she murmurs, "why it just pales in comparison." She tosses her shawl on a horsehair chair. Her let is crammed with disparate furniture in nubby upholstery, the worn rugs strewn with calling cards and hairpins and newspapers. The War of Secession is, of course, the only news of note.

She hurries to the bedroom, intent on viewing her shrine to Elisha. The shrine takes up the north wall and is the only tidy area in the let. Six years since Elisha's death and his white gifts—the Honiton-lace undersleeves, the white handkerchief he gave her in Washington, the white fox stole—are yellowing, but Elisha is exact as he was, glassed into his frame.

Maggie halts in the doorway. A cloaked thief pokes at the Tiffany bracelet.

"Leave that!" Maggie screams.

The figure whirls, drops its cloak hood.

"Christ-in-all, Kat!"

"Sorry, sorry, the door was open and I—"

"I thought you were a thief after Elisha's love letters and sent by damn Tom Kane. Well, I've hidden them. He won't never find them. What are you doing here, anywise?"

Katie takes Maggie's arm. Steers her back into the front room. "I was giving a sitting at Mr. Livermore's and I saw the storm coming on. I was really worried. You nearly froze to death the last time."

"I was . . . down the hall. There's a woman whose baby died."

"There always is." Katie sighs. "Leastaways they're easy to roust up. Babies don't have much to say, seeing as they didn't talk much in life."

"Well, yes."

"I'm glad you weren't out in the storm, then, Mag. I don't know why you think you'll spy Lish when there's a storm raging. I've never seen a spirit out in ugly weather. They like nice warm parlours."

"And how is the nice warm parlour of your Mr. Livermore?" Maggie asks, changing the subject. "Or should I say your Charles?"

"Handsome and gladsome and rich as ever," Katie replies. Katie's reputation is such that she no longer has to offer sittings for the general public. Instead she lives comfortably thanks to a few select clients. And Charles Livermore is one of these. His wife, the lovely Estelle, died in 1860. Two years on, and Maggie would bet that Katie has raised Estelle perhaps a hundred times.

Katie pours them both a claret. "The trouble with Charles is that he's always wanting more and more again."

"More will always be required," Maggie says. This being something she realized a long, long time back.

"That's the thing. More and more for Mr. Livermore. He's tired of the simple old rappings, and even of mirror writing and trancing talk and sparking lights. Hell, I even manifested up a glimpse of Estelle's face in a luminous orb. But, no, he wants her full form to materialize. I warned him that's unlikely. They're not called the Invisibles for nothing, I said."

"That's what Leah always says."

"So she does. Here's to that." Katie raises her glass.

"And here's to Her Fatness. And so, are you going to give it to him? The full-form?"

Katie bites her palm, an odd habit she has taken up of late. "I'd like to. I think it can be done. I just have to write to Pettifew. He'll send advice and all the magic tools."

"Have you ever met him? Pettifew? You know, in-the-flesh met him?"

"What's that? No. I'd have told you. But he does send me round the Blue Book from time to time. Handy item that . . . Did she know it, I wonder?"

"Who?"

"Estelle."

"About the Blue Book?"

"No, silly. How fortunate she was to be loved so much after death and forever. Not that . . . oh, give me another."

Maggie pours Katie's glass full. They discuss love, or rather other people's experiences of it: Leah and Daniel with their separate sleeping chambers, their chummy habits.. Amy and Isaac with their shared love of good causes, their austere affection. Their own parents, who have become embarrassingly intimate.

Poor Kat, Maggie thinks now. Her sister often wants to talk about love these days, but though she is still slender and lovely and still possessed, of course, of those curious eyes—heavy lidded, violet-grey— her clients only ever look upon her as a device, nothing more.

Katie is talking now about her other select clients: Dr. George Taylor and his wife, Sarah. Katie raises their two dead children,

Leila and Frankie, nearly every week. In return Katie makes use not only of their grand house, but also of Dr. Taylor's Swedish Movement Cure Hospital. He specializes in the female complaints, this Dr. Taylor. His hospital boasts hydrotherapy baths, a back massager and a former wrestler who can realign bones. It is the pelvic table Katie likes best, however.

"He calls it the 'vibratory cure.' You've got to try it, Mag. You lie face down, and then there's this steam-powered sphere and then . . . Anywise, afterwards you feel like a straw doll. It's even better, maybe, than a rum flip. I mean, for a time."

"They don't want my acquaintance, you know that. Not the Taylors. Not your Charles Livermore. They think I'm a terrible influence on you. And *I* don't want to meet them. Why would I? Christ-in-all, they treat you like a house pet."

Katie shrugs, and peers out the window. "The storm is abating."

Maggie looks over Katie's shoulder. Barclay Street is sheathed in white. The wrought-iron fences turned to lace. The single gas lamp jaunty-capped. The pedestrians who push through the snow are mostly women but for an old man or two, a few boys. The young men are piling up in fields, their last words unheard, their graves often unmarked. Maggie could be busy at sittings every hour of every day. But a promise is a promise is a promise, Maggie reminds herself. And she promised Elisha she would relinquish her rapping career. Thus Maggie lives on the pitiful annuity Elisha's brother Thomas Kane has finally granted her, as well as on money that Katie surreptitiously leaves behind when she visits. And though Leah also attempts to give Maggie money from time to time, Maggie always refuses, seeing the marionette strings behind Leah's every offer.

Maggie opens another bottle and she and Katie pass it back and forth in companionable silence. By the advanced hours of the night, they are singing and dancing, are tipping tables, lamps, are speaking in that garbled nonsense language they invented ages ago to perplex their mother.

Maggie drops in a chair. She admits that she lied. She was not out consoling some neighbour lady about her dead babe when Katie arrived. No. She had, indeed, been roaming the New York streets, calling for Elisha, just as Katie feared. "Where else would he be found, Kat, but in such Arctic weather, in a such an adventurously, icy storm?"

Katie chants, "And did you find him? Or something akin?"

"Nope. No. Nothing." Although Maggie had seen something "akin"—a small, ageless man with a limping gait. He wore a tophat and swank Chesterfield coat. Still, Maggie knew him. Would have known him anywhere—the peddler, surely, come to make good his curse. She glimpsed a manicured beard over a twisted mouth before the snowy night obscured him.

Katie rummages up yet another bottle, and presently Maggie and Katie are giggling as if they are children again and afraid of nothing in each others' company.

CHAPTER 36

"I'm off," I said, and shoved my knitting, the vestiges of lunch, the clanking bottles, all of it, into my satchel.

"Where-ever to, Alvah?" Maggie Kane asked, all concerned.

"I have a duty towards my other patients, if you must know. Are there no other dying ones in all creation? Are you the only person who is giving up the ghost?"

"Some days it seems so."

I needed more to drink, I admit, what with this talk of apparitions, of the war. And yet even as I walked out of the garret I thought of the defeat at Bull Run, the moment I heard of it, the moment I knocked Mr. Mellon flat with the cook pan for withholding August's letter.

As an impediment, Mr. Mellon was of no consequence. The quartermaster was a different matter. He thought me a looter. (I was as bedraggled as one by then.) Mass graves had been dug, but with a combined dead of near a thousand, well, it wasn't a sight one would soon forget. God sees even the fall of a sparrow, as I've said, but not, apparently, the fall of a thousand boys in a green field. It was hot, too, the late July heat of Virginia.

"Leave off here," the quartermaster ordered.

I told him my story and he shrugged and suggested I search for my August in Washington, which was where the wounded had all been carted. "And a good thousand had been taken prisoner, ma'am. You could be searching till doomsday, not to discourage you."

No amount of hand wringing and begging would convince him to let me look among the battlefield. So I returned at dawn and scuttled past the sentries. Light edged the world and silhouetted the unburied, their stiffening arms reaching up. I searched, too, all the hospitals near to Washington and far. I set out notices on storefronts, in newspapers (there were thousands of similar notices). My sole hope was that August *had* been taken prisoner and that he would survive the war in one of the horrid Confederate jails. The only thing I could do, then, was to wait for the war to end, wait for him to return, which of course he never did.

"Stay, Alvah. Please," Maggie said, for I stood transfixed in the vestibule still. She shook her laudanum bottle. "Share this with me."

MAGGIE PEERS UNDER HER SOFA. She smiles in relief. A half-full bottle lolls there. The frigid winter of '62 has melted into the sweatshop summer of '63 and the air in Maggie's latest let is so moribund, the sitting room so small, that she might as well be stuffed in a bottle herself. There is no separate bedroom. No true kitchen. Barely space for Elisha's shrine. But the address is still good. True, she is even farther from St. Anne's than before, but arriving in time for mass or confession has become impossible anywise, what with her mantel clock stilled at two from a fall to the tiles one evening. And what more can she confess? How many Hail Marys can a body utter in one day?

She fans herself. Searches for her reticule under the pillows and oyster wrappers. Counts out the coins. The tally is enough for a small supply of brandy or a large supply of wine. Tomorrow she might tidy, even though Katie is her only visitor these days and Katie hardly cares.

In the street Maggie stands baffled. Two people rush by in their usual New York haste, but there are few horses, fewer carriages, and no hawkers at all. She notes then the distant, muted noise. A newly operating factory, she supposes. She presses her handkerchief to her face, steps over an open sewer, then round a heap of waist-high rubbish. *Christ-in-all, but we need rain*, she thinks. It would arrest the summer stenches, batten the dust, drown the flies, rub clean the distant sky.

She passes a man who is cursing his broken crate of duck eggs, two scabby dogs who are rutting and howling, and a lone begging child to whom she gives a half-dime. She comes onto 43rd. Only now does Maggie realize that something is awry. That muted noise? It is no factory, new or otherwise. It has become a roaring fronted by the shatter-sounds of glass, the crack-thud of gunshots. Maggie shrieks and hikes her skirts and tears down the street, the mob surging just behind, but she cannot outrun it, not ever. Her scream is buried alive. The mob will see her tarred and feathered. Will see her burn atop a pyre.

But I swore off rapping, she thinks bewildered, terrified. Yells out, "But I'm done!"

The mob engulfs her . . . then carries her along. It has not come for her. Not her. She stumbles along in the press of it. A high reek of alcohol and sweat. A confusion of limbs. Hide in plain sight, she thinks desperately, and makes no attempt to detach. Then, after a time, she doesn't think at all. She is swept up into a vast and savage joy. She is destruction and power and is now looking up at the *Tribune* building in Printing House Square. Her mob has joined another and the singing is at least a thousand strong: "*So, hang Horace Greeley from a sour apple tree. We'll hang him high! We'll flail his hide!*"

A howitzer angles from an upper window. An oily liquid hurtles down from another. Ink, Maggie realizes as a crying woman staggers past, her hair dripping black. Musket shots plume. The shots are joined. Just then she sees the militia outside the building. The soldiers are all grizzled antiques except for a few boys. Some are poised with rifles. The old soldiers are frantically barricading the lobby doors with desks and newspapers. To no avail. The mob overwhelms the barricades. The lobby is breached.

Maggie weeps and wails, then rushes from Printing House Square, paying no mind to her direction. *Horace! Poor Horace! God-of-all!* The mob is after him, she realizes, because he supported Lincoln and therefore the draft. It's after him, too, because of Bull Run. But that debacle wasn't his fault. He only encouraged through his paper that the Union should meet the Rebels there, a bad decision, yes, but not his. He is no general. No politician.

Her eyes sting hot from the smoke. Smoke? She has come onto 44th near to the Colored Orphan Asylum. Flames lick out a window. Mattresses, clocks, furniture and dry goods are being hurled to the mob below.

"Stop this! Stop!" Maggie calls out. "Children aren't to blame, not for this." She tugs at a man's arm. He thrusts her off. Near on the asylum's matrons—white women all—are trying to shepherd the more than two hundred children away from the jeers and taunts of a splinter mob.

Maggie is about to offer her help when a man steps out from the mob's edges and does just that. Cries, "If there's a man among you, with a heart within him, come and help these poor children." He is a handsome man with an Irish lilt and a jaunty cap on his pale hair.

The mob pauses as if realizing the truth of his words. Ceases taunting the children. Turns away from them. The Irish man smiles in triumph and relief. Maggie does also. Then watches in horror as the mob seizes the one person who dared speak reason. Maggie witnesses an instant of pale skin as his shirt is torn away. Sees his arms reach out, and then the mob takes him.

A paint-red sunset and Maggie is now lost. At least this region of Manhattan is calm. At a looted apothecary she steps round the slugs from a shattered urn. The slugs are sliming their way to certain death past scattered bottles of cocainated teething syrup and brandied elixir.

Maggie is leaning against a lamppost, drinking away, when the cab hies up. The horses snort and dance. "Smelling nasty old evil, are you?" she hollers.

A man in a top hat and black coat leaps down. "Maggie? What the devil? Come with me, dear girl. Quick now. They may return." The man steers her towards the cab. Maggie struggles and kicks at him. The driver shouts for them to make haste. The mob is returning, apparently. It is not done yet.

"Get your maggot hands off, you damned—"

"Maggie Fox. It's Horace. Horace Greeley!"

She repeats his name. Peers at his round spectacles, his pale fluff of whiskers. But where is the white linen duster? The floppy hat?

He smiles ruefully, guessing her thoughts. "The staffers told me I'd be lynched if I walked about in my usual getup. They said I'm as recognizable as Lincoln these days and about as popular."

"But I saw your building! The mob. Alas and such, but it was a horrid sight—"

"The mob was thwarted. Not to worry. No squalling Confederate sympathizers shall stop the *Tribune* from publishing. We've vowed to not miss a day."

"I was worried 'bout you, Horace, not your wretched old paper."

"That is good to hear." He hands her into the cab. "Don't look out the window," he orders as they move on. It is an order Maggie ignores.

They cut through Broadway past Barnum's American Museum. The place is as barricaded and fortified as the *Tribune* building— Barnum being a Lincoln-lover and an anti-slavery man just like Horace. Three men in shirt sleeves dash towards the cab. The driver cracks the whip. The horses veer. The men fall back. A squealing pig trips over its own entrails. A bloodied figure collapses against a looted storefront. A building roils out smoke.

Horace scribbles in his notebook. "Taking my impressions," he explains. The cab clatters sharply round a corner.

"But this is 19th! It's not the way to my let."

"I'm taking you to my town-home. You should be with your parents at this hour. Not alone."

"I don't want to see them. I want to go to *my* home."

"You're in no condition, young lady. Your nerves."

"Don't you see," she babbles. "It took him. The poor man. It hurled him up. Oh, it's so damn-it-all tragic. I'm sorry for what we did. It's enough, isn't it? Being sorry? We're cursed, though. That's it! That's why it don't matter what I say or do."

"Of whom are you speaking? Of what . . . never mind, hush."

"I gotta tell, somehow, find a way. Then Elisha will come back to me. Damn, but he will. Then he'll say my name. Maggie! Margaret! Margaretta!" She makes to jump out the door. Horace yanks her back. She falls against him, begins to sing: "*When I fell off the apple tree. All the apples fell on me. Bake a pudding. Bake a pie. Would you ever tell a . . . oh, no no, not you, Horace!*" She giggles and plucks the looted apothecary bottles out of her waist pocket.

Horace looks at her, then at the bottles. An understanding crosses his face. "My God, poor child, how could this have happened?"

She can't answer. She is too far away.

At Greeley's town-home, her parents take her in hand with shop-worn patience. Maggie, coming to some semblance of herself, hears them admit to Horace that they have known for years about Maggie's dipsomania. She hears Horace's astonished protests and she wonders again how people can believe in the most magical things while the mundane, the predictable stumps them all to hell.

Night claps fast to morning. Mother's voice insists, "Come, lamb, Dr. Bayard's orders now. He delivered a new medicine for you, didn't he?"

Maggie opens her eyes a slice. She sees a looming spoon. Smells the tar and alum, the damned peppermint. Visions the peppermint fields of Hydesville, the blossoms absurdly fat, obscenely pink. She thrusts the spoon aside and the medicine spills onto her chemise. Her chemise? Ma must have undressed me, she thinks, as if I were a help-less babe, though not a sweet one, certainly.

Her mother dabs at Maggie with a handkerchief. The medicine is a dark stain. "Oh, here, here, what have you done? No matter. It will come out, with, with ox-gall or salt, won't it?"

"That's likely . . . look, I'm sorry. But I don't want any of that medicine right now. It muddles my head and I need it clear and, and clean. Tell me about the people, in the streets. The mob. What have you learned? Are the riots raging still?"

"Never mind about that. We don't want you getting as upset and frightened again."

"Oh, the good grief, Ma. How much more frightened and upset can I get?"

Her mother relents after further pestering. Tells Maggie that two army regiments arrived from Gettysburg to help quell the violence. The day is Friday and the city, though ransacked and pillaged, has settled at last. And the orphans are safe, yes, but not so the many others. Over the next four days Maggie learns of mutilations, stomp-ings, drownings. Of the beatings meted to street vendors, hack drivers, sailors, to amalgamist women married to black men, to abolitionists of all kinds. Of the uncounted murders by lynching.

"Terrible, isn't it?" Mother opines. "How folks simply don't know when to stop."

Three days later, Mother folds the shutters open to the splendid sunshine. "Today you must get up, mustn't you?" Maggie doesn't answer. She sees no need to leave her bed.

Mother talks of Dr. Bayard. It seems he believes that both Maggie and Katie are cursed with the intemperate habits of their father. "And he's recommended a place alike a fine hotel but with all manners of cures and regimes. A sanitarium? Yes, that is what it's called."

"And who, pray tell, would be funding our respite in this sanitarium?"

"Laws, why-ever does it matter? Here, have some more tea. Toast? You need toast and drippings, don't you?"

Leah. Her meddling hand is ever present. Well, Maggie will not go. Cures? Regimes? Absence from Elisha's shrine? Leah finding satisfaction in pulling strings? No, Maggie would rather face a mob again. Fine. Perhaps not a mob. But certainly she would rather face the ignominy of a drunken encounter with Horace or with some other person who once thought well of her. "I won't go, Ma. I'm sorry. There's no point insisting."

Her mother gapes at her, then wrings her hands. "This is all my fault. I knew it. Oh, I knew how your father loved his drink. But I didn't think a woman could be that way. It's my fault. I'm a poor mother, aren't I?"

"It's not your fault. Not at all. And you've ever been a help. My indulgences are my fault. And so's all this spirit nonsense. Katie's not to blame I'm the elder, I should have seen how we were being led astray, and so caused harm, just like all those rioters. They lost themselves, you see, when they became a mob."

Her mother wipes her nose with her sleeve. "What do you mean, your fault? What do you mean spirit nonsense? Mobs? Gracious evers, I—"

"Attend closely, Ma, for once. It was a prank. And then it got away on us and went beyond our control. It couldn't be stopped. It didn't want to be stopped neither. That was the trouble, you see."

"What are you talking about? A prank? I don't understand, do I?"

Mother looks elderly and tired, but full of stubborn love. Does the entire story bear telling? Maggie wonders. Then says firmly, "Call in Pa. He must hear this also. The peddler's ghost is of no consequence. Indeed, he never existed at all."

THE LAUDANUM BOTTLE sat on my patient's night table. I admit I had helped myself, and now I felt a curious tingling, a warmth, a sense of time being created anew.

"You were in Printing House Square?" I asked.

"Well, yes."

"And Greeley, he helped you?"

"Yes. He was a good man and judged himself too harshly. The Bull Run debacle. His disastrous presidency campaign. They were his undoing, I'm sure of it."

"Good is as good does."

"Were *you* here for the riots, Alvah?"

"Here. There. I'm in all places. I grow black wings. I take whom I choose without regard. I am Havoc. I am Vastation." I chuckled at this. "No, no. Alike your peddler's ghost, I am of no consequence."

"You are consequence incarnate, dear Alvah."

I thought then of how, after I failed to find August, I came to New York, this city of nameless throngs and mindless work. When I could no longer hold scullery work, I laid down for whatever pittance or bottle a man cared to offer. This went on for a good while. The only joy I had was in spitting outside the *Tribune* building where that Horace Greeley worked his poisonous pen. I blamed him for the rout at Bull Run, as I have said. He had meddled. What did he know of warring things?

I know August would have counselled forgiveness. Not that the boy had any experience with forgiveness, having never held a grudge in his life. And at times I was afflicted with rage at August too. For, indeed, what divided the actions of fools from the actions of the good? Was it Mr. Mellon who said this? It must have been.

And to answer my patient's question. Yes, I was in New York during the draft riots. And it was then I had the sea change. I'd been caught up in a mob near Battery Landing when I stumbled. I looked down.

He was a man of middle years. Likely a shopkeep, given his apron and arm bands. His eyes were very blue, I recall, and they looked at me in hopes of a remedy for his condition, which, to be frank, was dire. He had been trampled. Or beaten. I could not tell. I did my best to save him. I could not. My healing skills were scarce, and there was such a lot of blood, poor man. After the riots I ceased imbibing and presented myself at the Medico Society for training, and in this care and comfort of the dying (of which we all number) I found the strength to keep myself sober. Until now.

My throat was dry. I took up my patient's laudanum bottle. It was empty. Surely I did not drink it all. "I'm sorry I've been so quiet, duck. You must think me a mute. A tongue-tied."

"What do you mean 'quiet'?" she asked, her voice sleepy.

"What do I mean? Quiet, as in silent, as in . . . Was I talking, just now? Was I? Damn, this medicine of yours. I won't touch another drop." I looked at the garret windows. "The gloaming!" I cried, amazed. Hours had passed and I had not noticed.

"The gloaming," my patient murmured. "I've not heard that for a time."

My patient slept then. When she woke she was keen to chat, and about her father and his final hours.

THE BED ROPES CREAK as John's wife wakens from her first sleep. She ever does about the midnight hour. She will potter about or mend for an hour or two, then take her lighter, second sleep until dawn. John, however, prefers to sleep through, as is the modern custom. Their daughters are sleep-throughers as well, as are most city people. In the city noone shuts themselves in after the supper-hour. No one fears the gloaming. Owl-let. Grosping. Cock-shut. Candle-lighting house. Indeed, there had once been many words for twilight and its gradations. People once attended the sky and feared the coming of the dark. No longer. Why should they, John thinks, with the abundance of gas lights and lamps, with new illuminations being invented by the week.

He feigns the breath of deep slumber and watches his wife through half-closed eyes. She strikes a lucifer. The match glimmers blue and eerie before it winks out. She lights another, studies the effect, sighs. She fires the candle wick and the light puddles about her hand. She slides on her house-shoes and night robe. John shuttles back his disappointment. She will not be demanding his attentions, then. A mortal pity. They have been regaining a measure of their old passions in these New York nights, though they are both in their seventieth decade, and both afflicted with ailments and aches. And in the New York days they take the air together, even shop arm in arm for trinkets and crockery, linens and lampshades. His wife is ever astonished at his patience for such excursions, his considered taste in gimcracks and baubles. She is ever astonished, too, on how he attends her every worry, he who has always been scornful of her fears. "Only rats. Only neighbours dancing" was what he told her that first night of the hauntings back in Hydesville. And now that the girls have confessed to contriving the knocks, she seems to have forgotten the rank smell that pervaded the corners of the Hydesville house, the little clumps of moist earth, the grey threads twisting round latches and buttons.

Nearly three months have passed since Maggie, and then Katie, confessed. For the first week his wife had been distraught. "But what of my mother and her phantom funerals?" she asked John. "Were they only night carriages? Only tinkers fleeing mischief?" This thought of explainable phenomena distressed her more, John noticed, than the thought of ghosts ever did.

John consoled her as best he could. Reminded her how the girls were at least no longer indulging in liquor. Katie has been improving mightily, thanks to her stay at the sanitarium. As for Maggie, she has sworn to abstain and seems to be making good that vow. Certainly she seems much more like the wry and watchful girl she once was. Is no longer addled. No longer prone to outbursts. Her court suit against the Kanes is proceeding much better because of this. She might get her money yet. John and Margaret, Dr. Bayard, Horace Greeley, the Taylors, Leah, they are all in agreement that Elisha Kent Kane is to blame for Maggie's dyspepsia and melancholy.

Damned Dr. Kane, John thinks, would that I had got off my knees and thrashed the shot-eyed prick. Would that I had thrashed the whole damned Kane clan. He says a hasty prayer for his blaspheming. He hears his wife, padding down the hall, and recalls her querying Maggie on her confession. "But what of the footsteps I heard?" she asked. "Before the raps began that night? They weren't your apples on strings. They weren't any bodily crack, were they?"

And Maggie said she didn't know.

His wife returns to their bed. Her hands smell of rose-water from the privy's wash basin. When he arrived in New York seven years ago, his Arcadian house still a smoking ruin, his wife admitted she had been making him pay by not returning. He abandoned her; she was determined to do the same. But such stubbornness seems ridiculous, she owned, now that they are both close-waltzing to the grave.

She slides in aside him and he throws his arm over her, as if she were a raft and he adrift in deep water.

The next morning John goes to the library, and sits at Horace's oaken roll-top desk. He uncorks a pot of new-mixed ink. Takes out a blotter. A sheet of fine, thick paper. He practises a flowery hand then writes the letter. Then he slides it into an envelope with a gummed seal; as an afterthought he adds an old-style wax seal. He addresses the envelope to *Mr. Thomas Kane, Lawyer*, then sets it out for the post. The letter may not be much, but it is all he can do for Maggie now.

John now digs out his narrative for Leah. He rereads his cramped, square hand. The canals. Brother Able. It seems mortal distant now. He folds the papers and slides them into another envelope, one more workaday. On this envelope he writes, *For Leah Fox. Your Father, John*

Fox. He does not write, *Mrs. Underhill née Fish née Brown*. The names she has acquired do not signify. She is his daughter most of all. And she will understand him now, and forgive him for his wrong-doings and neglect.

He settles into his rocking chair. The chair is the one thing he salvaged from the fire, the one thing of his own in the house lent on sufferance. Yet even the idea of sufferance no longer troubles him. Indeed, John often sits for hours in this rocking chair, in front of these bay windows, inwardly praying, entirely happy. Best is when he can hear his wife pottering about, querying the day-maid, humming lullabies. He does not long for whisky. He never thinks of whisky now. The thirst is finally gone, the dropping away so incremental he has barely noticed its vanishing.

John creaks forward. Back. The front parlour smells enticingly of linseed polish, of damp hanging ferns. His worn bible rests unopened on his lap. He has no interest in reading it. Not today. Perhaps because today, at least, John understands that his God is merciful. That He would forgive John's determination to keep his women safe.

John chills at a sudden thought. His breath grows short. His fingers tingle.

What if Maggie tells the public what she has told her parents?

No, he assures himself, she won't. She would lose her reputation, which, for a woman, is akin to losing her soul. He shifts in the rocker. There is only one instant each morning when the sun infiltrates the towering labyrinth of the city and shines through the bay windows of the parlour. It is then as if John is on a veranda, on a hilltop, with the green stretching all about. But even though he is expectant, even though he is ready, when the light of this particular day comes it is so fierce and so bright that John Fox gasps aloud.

CHAPTER 37.

"Not long after Pa died I had a meeting with Elisha's brother Thomas, and with their mother, the Mrs. Jane Kane. She must have suffered a syncope, because she did not make entire sense. And she saw threats and conspiracies where there were none."

"*Paranoid*, that's the parlance these days, Maggie-duck. The learned doctors are saying the brain can be afflicted like any other organ. Hah, and that the lust for liquor is an affliction too. To which I will drink." And I did.

"Well, I would not wish that paranoia on anyone. The Kanes received an anonymous letter, you see. They showed it to me at the meeting: *"Is not this withholding of money from Margaret Kane a robbery? I have read the letters and solemnly assure you that their publication will bring a cloud of reproach upon the memory of your illustrious son. As for the pittance, it was offered in such a way that Mrs. Kane could be wronged out of it."*

I set down my bottle of gin. "You recall the whole letter, duck, word for word, after hearing it the once."

"Is that so remarkable? There are men who've got all the scriptures scribed in their brains. And surely there are things you can recite even now."

I thought of August's letter, and touched the side pocket of my satchel where it was kept, then changed tack. "I should hope you gave up onog my satchal all that wrangling about Elisha's desires and intentions. At times it is best to give up, duck. I've had to tell many of my patients just that."

"Oh, I did. For there was Jane Kane declaring away that Elisha chose 'this creature,' meaning me, just to humiliate the family. She demanded my annuity be cut off. The way she said it, you might have thought she wanted my head cut off. I said I'd have Elisha's love letters published. Mrs. Kane burned my letters to Elisha, if you recall, so any love-letter book would seem a one-sided affair. Not that I cared at that juncture. Thomas Kane and I looked at each other over his desk, just like two petulant children over a teeter-totter. I stood up abruptly. 'Elisha's letters will be published,' I announced. And damned if Thomas didn't look nearly relieved, as if Elisha's reputation had become a great burden." She smiled, rueful. "Leah was delighted by my decision. By this time she had come to despise the Kanes, though not in public, of course. She, too, had her paranoia and saw plots against her in the most mundane faces and events."

LEAH ORDERS GATHERFORD, her carriage driver, to wait and says that if she does not reappear in half an hour he must come up and retrieve her.

She finds her way down the little alley, up the several stairways. The location has changed yet again and the sign "Pettifew's Ingenuities," though small and discreet, is now of solid brass.

"It was some parade up in Boston, I heard, Mrs. Miller. Or should I say Underhill?" Pettifew queries a short time later.

"Underhill will suffice."

"Yeah, some parade. Thousands strong with marching bands and sky-poppers and a fat lot of children stramming along and dressed in white and singing out their little lungs like some cherubic army. I heard the banners for this spirit organization and that were big enough to read from Heaven's armchairs and that police were needed to keep the scoffers from doing grievous harm."

Leah manages a nod. She did not come to hear Mr. Pettifew's version of Spiritualism's twentieth-anniversary celebrations. She came because Pettifew had written he knew a way to save Spiritualism from gross discredit, and the Fox sisters, too, as follows. She doubts this, but she is hopeful, as always.

"'68 will be my best year yet," Pettifew says. "I'll bet my soul on it." He is perched on a work bench. Time has not bettered the man, though a groomed beard hides his twisted mouth. He wears no visor nor hat, and his head proves a glabrous dome fringed with grey and arrayed with liver spots and crowned with a thin scar.

"Shame about Barnum going on and calling you frauds in that new tell-all book of his, Mrs. Underhill. As if he weren't a raging fraud himself, eh? And your old friend Greeley, well, he hasn't one good item to say about it all these days. He blames Spiritualism for all kinds of ills, like suicide and insanity and dipsomania. And how are your sisters, anyhow?"

He sips noisily at a sarsaparilla. Leah refused the offering of one. Now she is parched. The room is hot and close. These crammed high rooms may not have been aired in years. "My sisters are of no concern to you, sir."

He snickers. "Darned shame Miss Maggie didn't partake of all the celebratory hoopla in Manhattan, though I heard Miss Katie did, and looked as pretty and fey as ever."

"Your point, sir."

"I wasn't invited, mind," he continues, as if he hadn't heard her. "Nope, for all my service the NOS won't even mention my existence. Guess I wouldn't have been fancy-pants enough for the Everett rooms with their gas chandeliers and violins and velvet doo-dads. Not that I mind. I wasn't invited to your wedding neither, come to think of it, and I don't hold a grudge for that. Such is my lot to be ignored. And I've done well by it all, like you . . . Sure you don't want a sarsaparilla? You're looking as if you need one."

"No, I want for nothing. I am pitch-perfect." Leah notices then that Maggie's book, *The Love Life of Dr. Kane*, is displayed on the bookshelf. No doubt Pettifew has touched her sister's name with his perverse, disgusting fingers. Leah shuts her eyes to quell her fury.

"I know what you're thinking," Pettifew says, following her gaze. "Who cares about the love letters of some hero nobody can recollect? The public surely didn't. Not with the war and all them dead and then Lincoln dying. Now that was a grand funeral, put Kane's in the pale . . . Sure you're not wanting a refreshment?"

"Let us not waste our beloved time upon this earth," she says. Where had she heard that phrase? From Chauncey Burr. Yes. And on the last occasion they met.

Pettifew lurches to the bookcase and seizes a faded pamphlet. Shows her the title: *A Report of the Mysterious Noises Heard in the House of Mr. John D. Fox, in Hydesville, Arcadia, Wayne, Authenticated by the Certificates, and Confirmed by the Statements of the Citizens of That Place and Vicinity*, by E.E. Lewis. "One can't find it nowadays," Pettifew says. "Folks have forgotten about the peddler what started it all. Him that had his throat slashed and is buried in the cellar floor."

When he says this, Leah realizes something peculiar: she is afraid. Not merely anxious or startled. When was the last time she felt so? When the pigeons lifted her up? When her father abandoned her? When she realized who Pettifew was? And when was that? The first time she met the man, she must admit, but she left that unpleasant information unacknowledged and sealed in a back drawer of her mind, where she leaves so many things.

Pettifew continues, "They never found him, did they. The peddler? In the cellar?" He thumbs Lewis's pamphlet. "I've read it over and under. All they found was rabbit bones and crockery. No human bones. No corpse in any state of rot. So, what was he about, then? 'I'm buried in the cellar. Poor murdered me.' Maybe he was playing his own practical jape—the ghost, I mean." He scratches at his neck.

Leah's stomach coils up. Her temple begins its staccato throb. Easy to imagine this man, this Pettifew, clawing out of a cellar grave, his slashed throat gaping.

"You ghoul," she whispers.

"Ghoul? 'Cus I make my living from folks having parlour games with the dead? What's that make you, Mrs. Underhill? A ghouless? Hah!"

Leah smoothes the sateen ridges of her dress. Her throat is so dry she is actually tempted by his offering of the sarsaparilla. But no, no.

Recall Persephone. The pomegranate seeds. *Do not partake*, she orders herself, then stands.

But does Mr. Pettifew stand? No. The ill-bred horror sits there and keeps talking. "I was a peddler once, too, though I'll bet you suspect that. I traipsed all through New England, and Arcadia, where your kin still live, ain't that right? I sold infants' toys and patch cloths and silver thimbles and this one special thread. I said it were woven by moon spiders because it were strong as wire and couldn't be seen 'cepting by close scrutiny. The moon spider part was twaddle, sure, but I offer even now, and it sells hot as Hell's pancakes to my privileged clients."

"Your point, sir, or—no, no, I need not hear it. I—"

"And like any peddler what treads the roads I knew damn well what it was like to be accused of all manner of sins and wrong-dealings. Children, they was the worst. And girls, hah. You don't reckon girls can be cruel, but they surely can be, the hoyden bitches."

"Sir! Your language."

"Sorry for that. Sure you ain't thirsty? I's got more than sarsaparilla. I's got Scotch whisky and French claret. I's got the Russian vodka and Barbary rum, the best you can find. What I ain't got is apple cider. I could never abide the taste nor smell of it. As like 'cus children thought apple-chucking at some poor peddler was all swell fun. Happened plenty. I never doubted they woulda stoned me given the chance."

"I fail utterly in seeing how this . . . information is of any assistance to me," Leah says, and grips her reticule. Makes ready, if need be, to use the scissors in the near pocket.

"You will see, Mrs. Underhill. But I's got to tell you that when I first heard about him, that peddler what got murdered and buried, like I said, in your kin's cellar floor, why I groped my throat for a wound in some kind of sympathy. Then I started appreciating the thought of my kind haunting the settled peoples. And when I came back through Arcadia, your business of raising the dead, why it had already become just that, a good business. That's when I saw a niche. Our Fates are knit up, just like I wrote to you at your wedding, recall? I's started small, just like you and your sisters, and I's got competitors now, just like you. But I'm still the best and the richest. I'm the originator. The creator—small c, course—much like yourself."

"Creator? You are a blaspheming, hideous cretin, taking advantage of a modest woman who—"

"Modest? Hah! Now, don't get in a lather. I just want to thank you 'cus I'm a grateful sort and I know what happens to those who ain't. And I want to give you a proper thank you. You sent back the copy of the Blue Book that I gave you for your wedding so I'm guessing it weren't good enough—"

"I was finished with public séances."

"Weren't good enough to have those hard-won listings of séance lovers and their tragedies and habits and heart's-desires. Nor to own intelligence on the dead. But if I could put Spiritualism on the straight path, shut the traps of the naysayers, would that suffice?"

Leah steps back, nearly trips on his brass cane. It is topped with a hound's head she notices, a vulgar embellishment.

Pettifew's manner turns beseeching. "Please, Mrs. Underhill, please, ma'am. Just listen here."

"Why-ever would I listen to you? You, sir, are madder than a March hare."

"I know a resurrection man. We give him his fee and he'll be hush and quick. All's we need is a body. Don't matter who. Any battlefield will yield one up, any old churchyard. Then you put out word that the peddler's ghost is talking again. Says he wants his bones buried proper, with prayers and all that. Folks will dig up the cellar again. And they'll find the bones this time. And then you can say, that it were always true. And then your detractors, your enemies, them naysayers, they'll be sure silenced up. It'll credit Spiritualism. Give it heft again. Make believers. Make my buyers come banging on my door, and heap me with dollars. You too. It'd be of benefit to us both, Mrs. Underhill. What a team we could be, you and me."

"Team? *Team?* The only man worth being a team with was . . ." She doesn't say his name, *Chauncey*, but the thought of him, oddly, gives her courage. She backs away. Turns just as Pettifew thrusts his card in her gloved hand.

"That's his address on the flip side of my card. Those letters. 'R.M.' They stand for resurrection man, 'course. Contact him up when you're ready."

"I could never carry out a deceit of that order," Leah says. She is using her coldest voice, but Pettifew doesn't shiver, as some have been known to do.

"Oh, I doubt that, Mrs. Underhill."

"You, sir, are fortunate my pa is no longer alive. He'd cut your throat for true."

"All right, all right. Just think on it, my proposal."

She can sense him watching her as she threads her way out, her heart athud. Pettifew must live in these wretched rooms, she realizes, because clothing is strewn here and there, as well as crockery and tumblers. Mostly, however, there are the wares of his trade: reaching rods thin as a child's finger and of that metal called aluminum, lead weights to sew into the hems of dresses, shoes with interior tappers and loose shanks, hollow rods to play trumpets from a distance, and gyroscopes to help any item spin. There are magnets of all sizes, phosphorous kept high up in glass jars, reams of tissue paper and pencils of clear wax. There are pots of luminous paint, vials of sympathetic ink, and bolts upon bolts of white shrouding. There are five lanterns with cutaways of faces and human forms, and these hang alongside seven false hands that are coated in silk to approximate the skin's softness in the dark.

Leah reaches the hall by squeezing past two spirit cabinets. They are still being constructed and the tubes and wires snag on her dress.

At last, the door. Leah doesn't turn, but she is certain she can hear Pettifew's dragging gait, his raspy muttery pleas.

Leah clambers into her carriage.

"I was about to come and retrieve you, Mrs. Underhill," Gatherford assures her, and in such a way that he recalls to her that cowardly, gossip-mongering driver who took her out to see the Hydesville house twenty years ago. She looks at him closely. "Gatherford?"

"Yes, ma'am."

"Drive, if you please. To Mother's." She settles back. Soon she will be telling her mother all about Pettifew, his establishment, his horrid proposal. Leah has been confiding completely in Mother these past few years and this confiding always calms her.

Their greater confidence began five years ago, just after the draft riots of '63 when Mother called upon her and, with arms akimbo, said, "Leah. The girls have accused you of directing them like the dancers in one of those tawdry burlesque shows. They have spoken of . . . fraud and—"

"My word, Mother, they were most certainly imbibing," Leah said, and steered the conversation to a Brazilian parrot she had just acquired for her aviary, and who could sing in four languages, including Latin. "And look upon this Chittering grand, Mother. Finer than the Littles of Rochester ever had. It plays in perfect tune, as if delivered from Heaven and not just from England. Do you not sometimes think it miraculous how far we have come from our former poverty and station?"

Her mother claimed that was not the point. The point was deceit and lies. Chicanery. Legerdemain. "They confessed to me, Leah. Yes, they did. Apples. Apples on strings, it was, and then toes snapping on the headboards, and fingers and . . . but you told them it was a lark. Fun. And that money could be made."

"Merciful spirits, you should not take too seriously anything my sisters say. They are so often befuddled from overindulgence—"

"They have stopped all that. Yes, they have."

"Perhaps. But these outrageous claims of theirs cannot explain all that people see and hear. And have these clever scientist fellows ever caught us out? If there was fraud they would have discovered it by now."

"But what of Mr. Burr? Did he not prove—"

"Oh, Chauncey is dead. Or gone. Or both. I never saw him again after the court case. Never. Not once. That man is being chewed at by worms for all I care."

"But the girls said that even you—"

"Certainly at times the spirits do not co-operate as one would like. But sitters demand so much. And then, of course, it is often necessary to add some personal touches. But surely you understood that, Mother dear. Surely."

Her mother surely had not. She had thought her daughters blessed.

"And what does my father say of all this business?" Leah asked. She twiddled her diamond dove broach, a wedding present from Mr. Underhill.

"He said very little, didn't he? Except you might need a bigger box, and with a bigger surprise inside." Her mother let out her tears then. It took a long while for Leah to mollify her.

"Henceforth I promise I will be has honest as I can with you, Mother. I promise."

Leah recalls this conversation, turning it in her mind, probing it for places where she might have put a word wrong. No, she steered it well, as she has steered everything well. *A bigger box? A bigger surprise?* Is that, indeed, what her father had said? She realizes she still has the card Pettifew slipped in her gloved hand. It reads "Pettifews Ingenuities." That is all. She scans the address on the flip side. It is for a wretched neighbourhood of Manhattan. Would she knock on the door and ask cryptically for R.M? It is the kind of intrigue that Dr. Kane would have loved, but not Leah. No.

Leah makes to toss the card out the carriage window. Pauses. She slips it into her reticule, then orders Gatherford to halt at her favourite flower shop. There she purchases her usual bouquet of rustic flowers. Twenty minutes more and she is at the high gates. The rain has been scant and the little stone bench beside her mother's marble gravestone is quite dry. Her mother's grave is smack aside her father's, and Leah supposes that he, too, enjoys Leah's frank chats, her revelatory confessions.

"And can you countenance the impertinence of Pettifew's proposition, Father? The horror of it. Oh, I suppose you could. It would be your kind of trick in the box."

She tips her head, but her father doesn't answer. There is only the song of vesper sparrows, and the mimic calls of crows.

CHAPTER 38.

I woke to a faint, sliding sound. I had nodded off on the ladderback, I allow, and for an uncertain gap of time.

My patient said "Good Morning" (though it was evening) and I searched in my satchel for a bottle. There were a good few, all empty. I came upon my stethoscope and pocket mirror, my books *On the Etiquette of Mourning* and *Ars Moriendi* and my half-worked coverall with its tangled trails of yarn.

On a whim I drew August's letter out of the satchel's side pocket. Out wafted a faint scent. Neroli. Rose oil. I sniffed at it. And then I understood. "You!"

"No need to point. There's no one else here."

"You. You've been snooping in my satchel."

"Sit down, Alvah, you're being rash."

"Rash? Hah! Oh, you and your ways. Ever ferreting information. Stopping at nothing. You've near as admitted it all yourself: employing spies, reading obituaries and gravestones. Ghoulish of you, that's what. Do I look a ninny? A just-born?"

"Nothing like." She patted the bedside. I, in turn, patted the pot of *Mrs. Howe's Neroli and Rose Miracle Hand Cream*. Then I held up August's letter. "Your little hands have been on this."

"I've not a glimmer what you're talking about."

"It smells of the cream. Bitter oranges—neroli and rose oil—"

"Perchance you helped yourself to my handcream. You help yourself to my laudanum, so why not?"

My anger fled me and I apologized for my lapse in professionalism.

"We all have trying days, disastrous days," she said. And then she told me about a day that was trying and disastrous indeed. For her and Leah both.

A SUN-SHOT MORNING IN JUNE OF 1871, and Leah sweeps into her stately dining room and inspects the gleaming silver fish-knives, the silver bone dishes, the salt throne and ice-cream hatchet. Sings:

> "Hi! says the blackbird, sitting on a chair,
> Once I courted a lady fair;
> She proved fickle and turned her back,
> And ever since then I'm dressed in black."

From the aviary, as if in response, comes the muted cacophony of her birds. From the corridor comes the rabble sound of children. The Underhill home on West 37th is often flush with young relations. Leah loves to watch them at their games; she nearly always guesses the winner correctly.

"Good morning, my dovely one," Daniel says as he strolls in. He uses the endearment "dovely" because of her love of birds. He has learned, however, never to use it in public.

"Good morning, yes, Mr. Underhill," Leah says as she sits at her end of the table. The children have already eaten so it is just the two of them, as must happen on occasion.

Daniel counts out the silver-domed platters that Cook has set on the sideboard. "One, two . . . five. That is top!"

"Ship at starboard! *Nil desperandum, nil desperandum*," Vivace calls out from the aviary. He is Leah's favourite talking parrot, and the fourth of that name .

Daniel lifts a silver dome. "Grilled tomatoes! Well, I am twice happy you convinced Cook they're not poisonous. What else—ah, kippers, hung beef, coddled eggs . . ."

Daniel loads his plate, settles at the table's head and snaps open a copy of the *New York Times*. His house-wrap falls open above his nightshirt.

"My dear," Leah says, and gestures upwards. He smiles amiably and adjusts the wrap. He no longer discourages her insistence on ordinary formalities. No longer pulls her onto his lap when they are alone at meals. For this Leah has to thank *Godey's Lady's Book* and its advice on using fine foods to supplant a man's more animal appetites.

On the reverse side of Daniel's paper is a caricature of Horace Greeley. His white whiskers are exaggerated in an unkindly fashion, his expression bewildered as a babe's.

"I have not heard from dear Horace at all since his campaign began," Leah says. "I suppose he is too busy for us now. And yet I was the one who advised him that if he so wanted reform he should run for president himself."

Daniel glances at the caricature. "Ah, you're speaking of Horace . . . Did you say that to him? When?"

"Or words to that effect. In any event, you must vote for him. He is our friend. And it would be nice to have a friend as president."

"He hasn't a dog's chance against Grant," Daniel says mildly and returns to his study of the stock market. He is retired but keeps a hand in things, Leah having allowed him a stipend to invest here and there.

"No, but one must be hopeful, Mr. Underhill."

"Ah, you don't say."

"I do. Indeed, I just did."

An assortment of children tiptoe past the dining room to the courtyard. Nieces, nephews, cousins, but no grandchildren. Do Lizzie's children even know of Leah's existence? Of course they do, Leah tells herself, and if not through ungrateful Lizzie then through chatter and print. People may mock celebrity all they please, but the more you are known, the more you exist. It is a simple equation that anyone can calculate.

Leah adds three sugar chips to her coffee, continues: "Yes, and I am so hopeful that I intend to call upon Katherina and Margaretta . . . today."

Daniel puts the paper down. "Truly? That would be splendid, a hundred times splendid. You must all make up, you know. But why now?"

"I have reports they have sworn off the spirits and for many months now."

"Spirits? That's unfortunate. I miss the—"

"Not *those* spirits. Off of wine and brandy and those endless cocktail concoctions. Indeed, it seems they may at last be cured."

"I see. Well, wouldn't that be tops."

"And as we are paying for their latest apartment let, one of us, at least, should see what they are up to with our money."

"Ah, how is it you know all this?"

"Really, Mr. Underhill, you should have told me."

"You would have insisted we not help them any longer."

"That is because Margaretta is a terrible influence on our Katherina. But if I had known a change of location would be of assistance in their recovery, I would certainly have agreed."

Daniel rubs his brow. "I'm glad, many times glad, that you're not angry. I only wish to do what is best by them. What time do they expect you?"

"They are not *expecting* me. But I shall arrive during the normal calling hours."

"I see. That's capital. Top. Perhaps we should invite them here. It has been two years, my dovely, and—" Daniel looks up at a soft thud. "A spirit?" he whispers hopefully—manifestations rarely happen these days unless privileged guests are about.

"Since when do the spirits sound so?" Leah says, and hurries to the aviary. It is the pride of her house, this aviary, with its array of palms and ferns and rare orchids, with its paths and benches and its hundred-odd birds flitting and roosting and preening and seeming joyful, withal.

She opens the aviary's glass door and nearly treads on the indigo bunting. It lies on the paving stones, its small talons clutching the air. She kneels and holds the bird in her cupped hands.

"Poor mite," says Daniel from behind her.

"He is not dead. He is merely stunned."

"Ah, twice good, then."

"Well, yes, though he should know by now the glass is there."

"Odds are we shan't be back when you return, my dovely," Daniel says that afternoon. He wears a white linen suit on his round frame and a hat of straw. It is just the attire, apparently, for one of these baseball games. He is taking all the children as well as Susie-the-maid and Cook-the-cook, both who got in a huff when Leah resisted their going. She was not being unkind. She just could not imagine why anyone would pay to watch grown men play baseball. She is not alone in this thought. Many reputable people also think it ridiculous, that you might as well pay to watch grown men play tiddlywinks or mumblety-peg.

She calls for Gatherford, then pauses at the curio cabinet. The lily box—stuffed with its select letters and clippings—is safely locked there behind the glass. From there it can easily be viewed by those guests who recall how it saved her reputation after the phosphorous debacle. The lily box is displayed alongside pygmy skulls and giant seashells and two stuffed passenger pigeons, a male and a female. Leah bought the pigeons for her aviary in hopes they would breed. They did not. Worse, they died soon after their arrival. Neither lingered. They simply ceased. No matter. The two did seem drab, a least compared to talking parrots and such. In their flocks of millions, however, the passenger pigeons are the sublime itself. They are a glimpse of the eternal grandeur of existence. Leah has no patience with the claim—put forth by those naturalist sorts—that the pigeons will soon be slaughtered to extinction. *Extinction.* Such an outrageous word, and made common thanks to that Darwin fellow and his incredible theories. The word has the connotation of chances irrevocably gone. But the utter demise of the pigeons is an impossibility. Not even man could destroy such a quantity. Nothing has an utter end—not the pigeons, and certainly not the human soul, which continues on and ever on. It does not cease with the mortal breath, as Chauncey Burr intimated. There is more to existence than the flesh and heart.

Leah has her Phaeton brought round. Gets in stiffly. It is not so much her fifty-seven years, but the new corsets. They thrust a woman forward into action. No more drooping like some hothouse rose in need of rescue. The fashion is all flared-out shoulders and dapper hats and bustles the size of pork barrels. Leah does not favour these trends at all, though she supposes she must stay in fashion.

Trends, yes, and what of these "planchette" boards, as the alphabet boards are now called. They are being machine-made in France and come complete with a triangular token of ivory to glide over the ornate letters and numbers. And books such as *How to Be a Medium* and *How to Raise the Dead* can be purchased at any hawker's stall, as if people have forgotten that spirit raising is a gift from the divine, that it cannot be bought and sold in some manifestation marketplace. Pettifew himself will be advertising to the public next. This is a sardonic thought, though accompanied by a hollow, sinking sensation that Leah cannot quite identify. Would that emotions were alike musical notes, she thinks, as those, of course, she can identify precisely, and in a snap.

The girls live on 44th, twenty-odd blocks from Leah's, but fairly close to Dr. Taylor's Swedish Movement Cure Hospital on 38th. The doctor's wife, Sarah Taylor, has become completely reliant on Katie, and sees her as her only link to their two dead children: Leila and Franklin. It was Sarah Taylor who informed Leah that Daniel was paying for Maggie and Katie's rent, and that both girls have been abstaining for months now. Sarah was particularly delighted at their abstinence. When drunk Katie makes for an unsatisfactory conduit. And when on spree she makes for an absent one. Leah can sympathize. The girls are a trial, but Leah is hopeful there has been a sea change. She is perhaps too hopeful, she knows, and about many things. But what is she to do? Give up? Step back? Allow the Fox sisters a finale without her direction?

The Phaeton halts with spidery elegance. Gatherford never curses his horses nor whips them, which is distasteful and low. He never complains, certainly, when he has to wait. For all this Leah is grateful. She is ever grateful for her wealth and good fortune. Nothing irks her more, in fact, than those who take their good fortune for granted. Or worse, those who toss it on the midden-heap.

"We've arrived, ma'am," Gatherford announces, and settles himself for a nap.

The apartment building is of the new design. The long, windowless corridor is lined with identical doors and identical brass knockers and smells of trapped gas from the wall sconces. In all, the building reminds Leah of a bee's nest, what with its multiple little dwellings, or else a Roman catacomb. How can the girls live like this? she ponders, and checks the number plate on the door. Perhaps she will find them somewhere better to live, an actual house.

She knocks hard. Then harder yet. Hears singing, a discordant organ tune. She checks her pocket watch. Yes, it is the appropriate time for ladies to be home, dressed and waiting should anyone call.

The door flies open. Maggie is without undersleeves or corset. Her dress of bishop's blue, years out of fashion, is patterned with stains. Her hair is dishevelled. Her cheeks flushed apple-red. She gives a staggered, mock curtsy. "The good-goddamn-grief. If it isn't Her Highness, the Tigress, her damned self!"

Leah stares aghast, then sweeps past her. Maggie grabs at the bow on Leah's bustle. "Look at you," Maggie rants. "Rigged out like a ship in a high wind. Flying all the flags in all the damned colours."

"Katherine. Katherina Fox!" Leah calls, frantic. "Where are you? I hope to Providence you are not . . ."

But Katie is. She is drunk as a sailor. Drunk as a fiend. She sways towards Leah and smacks a kiss at her ample cheek, missing completely.

The apartment reeks of brandy and stale wine, of vendor food mouldering in waxed paper. Leah rails at her sisters, scarcely aware of what she is saying. Certainly she scolds them for drinking again. And she may be calling them ungrateful. Or degenerates. Or drunken whores. She throws open the window. ". . . and it stinks like a cesspit in here."

"Do as you please. Is that it?" Maggie screams. "Damn you to hell, Leah! Why do you domineer us so? You've ruined our lives. You knew. We told you everything. And yet you said, 'Oh, but it's true, true, true. The spirits are true. Just don't talk about the practicalities, oh, and for the spirits' sake, don't think!'" Maggie puffs out her cheeks, simpers, "'Oh, he deserved it, my sweetings. I would have done far worse to that heinous peddler. You did not go too far, indeed perhaps you did not go far enough. Such clever, girls! Such improvisation.'"

"Mag," Katie pleads.

"I did not say that," Leah cries, though she had, she realizes, and in those exact words.

Maggie continues her outrageous rants and accusations. "You made us go along, Leah. You horrid awful bitch."

Katie is near hysteria. Leah's mouth is agape.

Maggie wallops it shut. Leah stumbles into a card table, then sprawls on the floor.

Back in her Phaeton, Leah cries torrents, surprising Gatherford, surprising her own self with the force of her tears. Once home she shouts for Daniel, for Susie, for Cook. No answer. The house is empty. She has forgotten about that wretched baseball.

The lily box. It is the one thing that can soothe her. She gropes on top of the curio cabinet for the key, is soon stroking the entwined lilies her dear father carved those years ago. She might even buy a bible for the box one day, and just to please her father, who is surely watching her from Spirit Land or one of its environs.

The sight of the letters is consoling. Many are yellowed with age. At least the medallions are as bright as ever.

Leah is a lady of such admirable qualities . . .

The Fox women are beyond any criticism . . .

I cannot thank Mrs. Fish enough for the solace she has wrought . . .

She pressures the lilies atop the lid just so, opening up the hidden compartment on the lid's thuck underside. Her father's letter is concealed there—which is fitting, seeing as her father was the one who added the hidden compartment for the phosphorous experiment.

Dear Leah, this is an account of my ten years gone . . . The reading eases her sorrow. If only Maggie knew of their father's past, then she would understand. She would forgive all. Or not. Leah stuffs the letter back under the lid.

She trudges upstairs to her private bedroom. Shutters the windows against the sharp June light. Struggles with her dress clasps. Pulls on a lacy bed jacket and ribboned bed cap. Her skin smells of her sisters' alcohol. Her side tooth is loose, surely from Margaretta's wallop. At least she understands why Margaretta takes to her bed after any trial. It is a raft of safety. One can even imagine the bed a cloud, providing the linens are white enough.

Leah is abed for two weeks. She is not always sobbing or sleeping, however. Not always having to look upon Daniel's worried face. She writes letters on a tray. Holds bedside meetings with Charles Livermore—who still bears Katie immense gratitude for raising his wife, Estelle—and with the Taylors. Dr. Taylor agrees with Leah, as does Charles Livermore, as does Horace Greeley, who has graciously takes time off from his presidential campaign to write and advise: *Katherina must be sent to England. In England she will be far from all pernicious influence.* Leah guesses that Maggie is this pernicious influence, not Spiritualism itself, surely. Horace still cares about them, Leah knows, even if he has become chary of their skills as mediums.

"An excellent proposal," Charles Livermore exclaims. "In England our Spiritualists friends will host Katie as the high priestess of the movement that she is. I shall write them straightaway."

"But will she agree?" Dr. Taylor ponders. "She can't abide being parted from Maggie for long."

"We must be persistent," Leah says. "Katherina does not like to make decisions for herself, thus it is important we assist her in that regard. She shall thank us in good time."

The men nod, satisfied. But Sarah Taylor is enraged. "Thank us? Hah! Katie is such an unconscious, thoughtless child that she'll little realize the deprivations her best friends are imposing upon themselves, voluntarily for her sake. She's our sole device of communication, our key to our loved ones in the Other World."

Leah adjusts her ribboned cap, gives her best, most dimpled smile. "Bless the spirits, she is all that, but, Sarah, my dear, I should remind you: Katherina is also *my sister*."

————∞————

CHAPTER 39

Please to Grace Us With Your Presence
on the Occasion of the Joyous Wedding
of

MISS KATHERINE FOX
to
MR. HENRY DIETRICH JENCKEN

St. Marylebone Parish Church, London
9:00 a.m. December 14, 1872

May the God and the Spirits Bless Their Union for Eternity

————∞————

"Very pretty," I said, as my patient put the invitation back into the lily box.

"I didn't attend. Nor Leah. But then, we weren't invited. And England seemed so far off."

"That's because it is, Maggie-duck." I chuckled for a time at this. I had vowed not to drink in front of my patient, which is why I had visited the tavern beforehand, where I had imbided, I allow, more than I intended.

"Katie's first son, Ferdie, he was born in a caul. The midwife said it meant he would be fey. That he would be able to scry the future. Be safe from drowning."

"Hah. That is superstitious balderdash and bullshit, to boot."

"Well, yes, and even Katie took the midwife's predictions with a grain of salt. Still, she wrote that Ferdie smelled just like Heaven's garden and that light just beamed out of his blue eyes. And her husband, Henry, witnessed the babe writing in the air, and in Latin yet. A most singular babe, don't you think?"

"Oh, who doesn't think their babe is some singular perfected thing?"

"There's more. Spectres were often seen about little Ferdie. The nurse swore that little hand-prints appeared on his pillow. Spirit music played when he slept, and so on. Their next son, Henry Junior, was born in '75. He seemed a more ordinary sort of babe, as the second ones generally are."

"I wouldn't know, would I?" I muttered.

ST. MARYLEBONE PARISH CHURCH OF LONDON is near empty this morning but for the Jencken family near the great doors, and but for Maggie, who has come to visit Katie at long last.

Katie sweeps up to her. No more sombre, spinster shades for Katie Fox Jencken. She has returned to the numinous shades she favoured in her youth. Her gown today is of nakara and gold, her hat of the same violet-grey shade as her eyes. She looks quite the gracious and mysterious lady. Particularly aside me, Maggie thinks, though without umbrage. She could still draw admirers if she chose, on this she and Katie have agreed. She still has a good figure. The bishop's blue she favours suits her well.

Maggie runs her fingers over a pew. Near on, Katie's husband, Henry Jencken, cheerfully traipses after Ferdie, aged three, and Henry Junior, aged twenty months. At fifty Henry still has hair of wheat-gold, still moves effortlessly, though he is tall and thickly built. He is a respected and successful barrister; a Spiritualist convert who was thrilled to meet the famed Katie Fox. Henry's mother— once a baroness—apparently left her husband and grown children for her handsome doctor, the man who became Henry's father. Left, that is, position, respect, wealth, reputation. Everything, in truth.

"You see, people do sacrifice lots for love. Everything, even," Katie told Maggie when she first arrived. "Differences in social standing shouldn't matter at all. Neither should family griping and opinion." She didn't mention Elisha's name nor offer criticism of him. But the innuendo? Surely she knew Maggie wouldn't miss it.

"Does your Henry like me?" Maggie now asks.

"He likes you very much, Mag. Everyone does once they've met you. And I'm so glad you're here. And I'm so glad, oh glad, that you're just as cured as I am. It so really helps to confess." As Katie had when Henry was courting her. "I'm a drunkard, Henry," was what she told him. "I drink to oblivion, like a gutter wench."

"I know and it matters not. I love you. I love you. I love you," Henry had replied.

At the incantation of these words, Katie told Maggie, she ceased to be that drunkard. She still craved the drink, yes, but Henry's love and regard she craved the more.

"Well, I just got tired of it all," Maggie owned. "That's why I stopped drinking."

Katie leads Maggie down the church aisle. Tells her all about her wedding. "And here, Mag, there were just mountains of flowers. And there, in the chancel, that's where the knocks came from. Everyone heard them. And the breakfast feast was wondrous. I wish, oh wish, you could have been here. All of Henry's family attended."

Maggie says she'd been too sick, and Katie hastily agrees, neither wanting to remind the other that Maggie-of-the-bad-influence had, in fact, not been invited.

Maggie now listens gravely as Katie boasts of this wedding break-fast, how the table levitated, how the raps sounded, how the son of the Duke of Wellington sent Katie a bottle of costly perfume, how Prince George himself sent her a fan. When Katie speaks of admir-ers among the gentry, of astounding events, she reminds Maggie of Leah, except that Leah's posturing and bragging irks Maggie no end; Katie's she finds endearing. Leah and Katie write to each other, Maggie knows. It is a subject the sisters avoid.

"Ferdie, love, stop that," Katie says of a sudden. Ferdie is stomp-ing on the fish schools of coloured lights that swim on the flooring. The lights are a manifestation of the stained glass windows, but Ferdie doesn't realize this. The lights disappear with the passing sun; Ferdie stares in bewilderment. Maggie laughs. Henry Senior laughs. Katie laughs. Henry Junior, squirming in Katie's arms, screams in fury.

"Ferdie is tall for his age, don't you believe?" Katie asks Maggie, once she has settled Henry.

"I do."

"Such sturdy legs. And doesn't he just favour his father to beat all?"

"He's the same stamp, all right."

"Oh, Henry, don't be a fuss-it," Katie says to still-squirming Henry Junior. She sets him down and he toddles towards his brother. Henry Junior is unsteady on his feet, but he is managing; he will become an ordinary child just like his brother, Ferdie. Katie is insistent about this. And yet she watches him every minute.

"I've been thinking of Mary Greeley," Katie says after a pause. "I could never understand the way she went on about Pickie. I found it all so godawful tiresome. But I understand her now. I'd go stark raving, too, if anything happened to either of my boys . . . Horace went mad, too, they say, I mean after Mary died and then the presi-dential campaign, poor man."

"'The worst-beaten man in history,' that's what the papers called him."

"I hate that he died like that, Mag. All alone and ranting, in some nasty old asylum."

"What did you say? No, no, don't repeat it. Never repeat it."

Katie looks puzzled, as if she has forgotten the peddler's curse, as if her current good fortune is enough of a protection. Maggie, on the other hand, can never forget the words: *You'll die alone and ranting for your lies, you hoyden bitches*. Really, how *could* she forget?

"Never speak like how?" Henry Senior asks jovially from behind them. Ferdie yanks on his coattails.

"We were talking of Horace Greeley, dear, and his . . . assets," Katie says.

Henry shakes his handsome head. "You were speaking of money? Why, darling? You needn't worry about monetary matters any longer. As for Mr. Greeley. Well, I cannot approve of his blighted finances. Those poor daughters of his. A man should ensure a watertight legacy and . . . damn it!" Henry points at Henry Junior, who has gone rigid as a stone saint. He convulses. Spittle flows from his gritted teeth.

Katie rushes over with a shriek. She holds Henry Junior fast while he jerks and bucks. It is over in a moment. He slumps against his mother. Maggie wraps her arms around them both. Henry Senior holds tight to the crying Ferdie. The few parishioners stare. Some mutter protecting prayers. Maggie is tempted to unnerve them further with a loud knock or two. No time for that, mind.

They hurry out to the carriage and off they jolt. Henry Junior drops off into a fast asleep. "He always does after his fits," Katie tells her sister. Ferdie keeps himself occupied by shouting at the fruit-mongers.

Henry Senior leans towards Maggie. "You're so eminently sensible. Advise us. Should we send for a priest? Should there be an exorcism for our little Henry?"

Maggie considers the question. Considers the compliment also: sensible? She might just be, yet. She remembers Katie as a girl, how she would vanish out of herself, her face as blank as Henry Junior's. "No priests. It isn't the spirits or devils, you two, and you know as much." She looks from Henry to Katie. "Your son is afflicted with neuralgic convulsions, just as Katie was. The doctors call it epilepsy these days. The afflicted sometimes hear voices or lose themselves in time . . . I suspect he will grow out of it, as Katie did, I think."

Henry stares at Katie. "But you never told me you had this . . . condition?"

"I told you I was a drunkard, Henry—that seemed enough confessing. Anywise, I've never talked about all that. Neither has Mag." She frowns, exasperated at her sister.

"There's an art to confessing, just as there's an art to dying, " Maggie pronounces. "And like any art, it will surely become easier over time."

The next ten years are wondrously uneventful. Henry Jencken becomes flush with wealth. Katie becomes a vowed teetotaller. Their children grow and thrive. Henry Junior's fits subside in severity and frequency. The only symptom now, Katie writes Maggie, is that from time to time he stares in incomprehension, but then again, who doesn't?

Maggie travels often to England from New York. "Our house is yours, dear Maggie," Henry Senior says. Maggie becomes the most excellent of aunts. Is nothing like Leah in this role. Does not view children as natty accessories to life. Does not delight in their gullibility and indiscriminate affections. She sees them as genuine people, albeit people afflicted with great passion and little understanding. Maggie certainly agrees with Katie that the boys should never be sent to an English boarding school. Agrees they are safest with Katie. Henry does not try to stand against them both. Besides, he would give Katie the sun and the starry firmament if it were in his power.

Katie often begs Maggie to make England her home. And Maggie often considers it. She has made many friends among the Spiritualists in England. Is making a clean start with them. Not a difficult task. The English are more tolerant of eccentricities, Maggie has found, and their investigations into spirit phenomena more respectful. Sir William Crooke himself is conducting many experiments with Katie. From Katie's letters Maggie learns that this Sir William has invented a radiometer that transforms light into matter, has discovered a green element he calls thallium and is now busy proving the existence of "radiant" matter, which is matter in a fourth state independent of corporeal space and human time. "Or *something*," as Katie writes. And yet Sir William cannot explain the knockings, table levitations, glowing orbs and such, other than it must be an undiscovered physic force at work. And he is truly baffled at how Katie can simultaneously answer one question with automatic writing, and another with raps, all while conversing freely. That a woman can do those three things at once is beyond the pale, he apparently told Katie, to her great amusement.

What Maggie likes best about the English, however, is that they have no first-hand sightings of her drinking sprees. Nor will they ever, Maggie has vowed. She and Katie drink only moxie now, that harmless nerve tonic, or sip tea, and with their pinkie fingers crooked. But, no, she will never move to England. America is where Elisha is buried. It is where he is remembered as a heroic leader; where he is, frankly, remembered at all.

And Leah? Paddling through her sixties she is as histrionic and healthy as ever. Styles herself a grand dame of New York. Has money spilling out her heaved-tight corsets. Has an adoring husband. A select few clients who swear by her. Worse, she claims to be writing her memoirs—God help the reading public. Maggie will never read her claptrap. This she has already sworn.

Over luncheon at the Jenckens' one autumn morning of 1881, Maggie mocks Mr. Henry Seybert—a Croesus-rich philanthropist in Philadelphia who pays her handsomely to raise everyone from Newton to the angel Gabriel. In an old man's quivery voice Maggie says, "And I'd like five Old Testament prophets today and three martyred saints. Please do not forget Plato and Homer. And, oh, yes, just a dash of the Holy Spirit. Oh? You're worried that attempting so will damn you to Hell? Come to think, I do wish you'd raise General Benedict Arnold from the fiery pit. I have a question or two for the fiend."

Henry laughs heartily and tucks into a slab of roast beef. His brother Edward, who is visiting for a time, chuckles and wipes his mouth of chutney. Katie laughs also, then, growing serious, says it might be time for Maggie to retire. "I don't like at all the thought of you rapping in boarding houses and for the lowly whom-evers. Please consider again living here with us. Really do this time."

Henry quaffs back a tumbler of ale. "Yes. I should like that and so would the children. Wouldn't you, Henry? Ferdie?" The boys chorus agreement, adding that Mummy doesn't scold them so much when she has Auntie Maggie to play with. The adults all laugh. Even the cook laughs as she sets down Henry Senior's favourite selection of trifle, blood pudding and buttered tarts.

"So, you'll consider it seriously? Moving here?" Katie asks.

"Yes," Maggie says. And this time she is serious. But once back in New York, before she can even pack up her apartment, she receives the dire news: Henry Jencken Senior has dropped dead in his English country home, his heart shutting off like a tap.

Maggie arrives in England that November to find Katie distraught from grief. She does her best to console her. Gently reminds Katie that at least she will spend out her days as a wealthy widow, surrounded by her children and her memories, or so Henry promised should he exit the mortal earth first.

In truth, Henry's financial affairs make Horace Greeley's look like child's arithmetic. The mourning year passes and then four more. And when Henry's finances are untangled at last, it seems there are heavy debts, non-transferable foreign properties, and that Katie will receive two hundred pounds. Not a penny more.

CHAPTER 40.

"You know what Elisha told me once?"

"To *put on your mitten, you silly kitten?*" I laughed at this. My patient did not.

"No, this was about the Hindoos and how they believe that one's soul returns in a different body. If you're good in one life, you get to be rich and happy in another. That's what Elisha said."

"What chalk and nonsense . . . and if you're bad, what then?"

"Then you return in a poor and wretched body, obviously."

"Ah, what did I do?"

"I've not a glimmer."

"With the yarn, I meant." I showed her the cover-all, the lax lines, the uneven ridging. "I suppose I need start all again."

"That would be the practical thing."

"Yes, and I need better light," I added, and turned up the medical lamp. My patient blinked at the bright dance of flame.

"What-ever did you do that for, Katie?" she said, and looked past me.

Katie? I looked to where my patient was looking, which was the vestibule (no Katie-shape was there) and then at the bible box, which was by her side, as it ever was by this time.

15 June, 1885

My Dearest Katherina,

I do hope this letter finds you well. Of course you and my
sweet nephews must stay with us when you return to our
American shores. The boys will view Manhattan with wonder
after being in that darkling isle. Arc lamps have blessed many of
our public spaces and they sparkle sharp as diamonds come
evening. And Edison's illuminating company has been expanding
in leaps and bounds these last three years. Our home was the
first on 37th to be entirely electrified and it is now aglow, top to
bottom, with a sweet, mellow light that never ceases and is
entirely convenient. We also have an "icebox" and can thus
provide a finer table than ever for all our dear friends. But do
not fear such changes, my darling Katherina. It shall be as it
was. Such delightful times we had. Though how terrible your
Mr. Jencken left you in such a state. Next time do ensure that
certain monies are in your own name. Now, do not countenance
that I have turned rights-for-women agitator like our delightful
Amy when I offer such advice. I am practical, that is all.

> Your loving sister,
> Leah

Leah is fanning herself against the August heat when the first scream
comes. She drops the fan. At the second scream she rushes down her
hallway. A crashing alike cymbals hurled. A silence. Leah presses
her ear to the closed door of the second parlour, the one Katie has
taken over for her séances. Hears a muffled commotion. And then:
"Fiddle-dee-damn. Leave, then. Leave! The spirits want you gone."

Leah thrusts open the door, then yanks the chain on the Edison
bulb. Light floods over the séance attendees. They blink owlishly at
the sudden glare. Stare in shock at Katie. Katie ignores them.
Ignores Leah.

"Oh, Henry, darling," Katie cries. "Mother's here. Hush!"

Henry, slight and pale, stands by an upturned chair. He holds his
jaw and whimpers, "It was Ferdie's idea."

Hs brother stifles a laugh. At twelve Ferdie could be mistaken for sixteen. No spirit lights stream from his eyes these days, Leah notes. Only the light of pure mischief.

The sitters rush to leave. A woman jams an old-fashioned bonnet on her silvered hair. "My person has never been so offended!"

"Hah, that I really doubt," Katie says. "Anywise, you need not have kicked my poor Henry."

"Then the brat shouldn't have been under the table."

"He's sickly. It was only in fun."

"Fun? Fun! He grabbed, my, my very . . . oh, I cannot say."

"Your ankle?" Leah offers.

The woman blushes. Her grey-beard husband takes her elbow. "I shall not recommend this establishment to a single soul."

"It is not an 'establishment,' sir," Leah says coldly. "It is *my home.*"

Katie pulls Henry onto her lap as the sitters are ushered out, as Ferdie goes off to terrorize the birds in Leah's aviary. "Here, sweet, would you like your favourite rhyme? Would that be a comfort?"

Henry nods, his thumb in his mouth.

"Sitting in the garden,
In her cloak and hat,
I saw Mother Tabbyskins,
The real old cat!
Very old, very old,
Crumplety and lame;
Teaching kittens how to spit and swear—Was it not a shame?
. . .
Very wrong, very wrong,
Very wrong and bad;
Such a subject for our song
Makes us all too sad.
Old Mother Tabbyskins,
Sticking out her head,
Gave a howl and then a yowl,
Hobbled off to bed.

Very sick, very sick,
Very savage, too . . ."

Leah listens with disapproval. Katie treats Henry as if he were toddling still. And she never allows either boy out of her sight. Will not let them attend public school. Has hired a tutor instead. Does she think merely keeping them in view is what keeps them safe? Certainly she is deaf to Leah's advice on the many ways to keep tabs on children. You can always spy on them, for example, or read their scribbling, or nonchalantly question their friends.

"Such a funny rhyme, don't you think, Henry, darling?" Katie asks. Henry nods.

"Now, I am going to tell you a story, my love, about the Czarina."

"Yes! She was so pretty."

"Not this again," Leah puts in. "It is mere fancy, Henry."

"Hush. It isn't. Henry was there. He remembers everything."

Henry pops his thumb out of his mouth. "Yes. She was beautiful and dressed all in blue silk with diamonds and pearls."

Leah humphs at this. Katie ever insists that she and her boys were whisked off to the court of the Russian Czar not long after Henry's death. As evidence she has a painted egg and a wooden doll that harbours smaller and smaller ones within, but this "evidence" could have been purchased in any Manhattan trinket shop. Katie's stories grow grander at every telling—the Winter Palace hung with chandeliers the size of carriages. People skating on streets of ice as natural as if walking. The gratitude of the court for Katie's assurance that the Czar would not be assassinated like his predecessor. "But do be careful whom you trust" was the spirits' savvy advice.

Leah says, "Mark me, Henry, dear, royalty, which is the mere fortune of birth, should not be confused with reputation, which can only be earned."

Katie whispers to Henry, "That's twaddle-dee-dum. Your Aunt Leah has never been given an audience of royalty. She's jealous, that's all."

"Jealous? Jealous? And what of Mrs. Pierce? The First Lady of our nation? What of all the people of high station and respectability whom I call friend? They make up, well and truly, for one borscht-eating royal of dubious descent. Have you read my memoir? Well, have you, Katherina?"

"*Her* memoir?" Katie says to Henry. "Hah. She may take the credit but it was ghost-written, as everyone knows."

"A ghost wrote it?" Henry asks in faint alarm. He slides from his mother's lap and edges towards the door.

"It's an expression, my darling," Katie says. "People who can't be bothered to put pen to paper will hire someone else to do so, and then swallow up all the credit for themselves."

Leah glares at her sister. Feels that staccato-throb at her temple. Henry makes his escape. Katie tries to follow. Leah grabs her arm. How is it that Katie, little Katherina, has changed so? Motherhood has made her stubborn. Widowhood—of all things—has made her bitter. Her rancour fills the house. Distresses her boys, distresses both Leah and Daniel no end. Leah sniffs discreetly at Katie. Smells no brandy or rum, only that cloying perfume that Katie claims was given her by the Duke of Wellington's son for her wedding to Henry Jencken those fifteen years ago. Well, the bottle must be magicked to last so long, because Katie smells so every day.

"Please, dear sister. It is just that I worry. I worry that you fill Henry's mind with poppycock."

"Well, I'm not going to remind him and Ferdie about the rotting cabbages and the dead peasants in the ditches, am I?"

"You should not have taken the boys. They could have died in that cold."

"I thought you doubted my Russian adventure. Never mind, fiddle-dee-damn, it hardly matters where we are. They're safer with me. They're always safer with me." She shakes off Leah's hand and hurries off, calling for Henry. Calling for Ferdie.

Leah collapses into a tasselled chair. Feels the force of her seventy-two years. Tears drip hotly from her eyes. She has tried and tried. She insisted Katie and the boys stay at her home in hopes of a reconciliation and a return to the fine old days. Indeed, if only Katie would read Leah's memoir, *The Missing Link in Modern Spiritualism*, she would recall the jolly fun they had in their heyday. *The Missing*

Link avoids all those distasteful family squabbles. Avoids all mention of alcohol and accusations. Emphasizes how the world was against the Fox sisters three; but how they continually triumphed with the support of good and worthy people. Tells of the astounding evidence of the spirits: the tables levitating, the objects flying about like the very birds, the pealing bells, the spirit writings, the glowing full-form manifestations, the satisfied clients one and all. Leah sent a copy of her memoir to Katie when she was still in England. She sent one to Maggie also, though she had not spoken to Maggie in years. Surely that was a peace offering to Maggie, if anything was. But not a syllable has come from Maggie in response. And neither has Katie ever mentioned the book. Leah would rather hear their criticism than their silence. Silence is a giant maw, hungering for bad thoughts, and another reason Leah insisted Katie and her boys stay with her and Daniel. The supply of young relatives has been run through. All are grown. As for her daughter, Lizzie . . . Where does she live now? The Catskills, yes, which is still too far to ever visit her own mother, apparently. Thus Leah has only the chatter of her birds and the chewing sound of Daniel's jaws for company.

She dabs expertly at her eyes. Stands with her old vigour. For the next three days she is unfailingly kind to Katie. She refuses to rise to any argument. Does not criticize the boys' presence at séances. She is kindness and understanding itself. This only seems to make Katie more cantankerous.

On the fourth day of Leah's new tack, she wakes to find the boys pottering about the kitchen in their nightshirts and Katie gone. There is an upended bottle in Katie's room and a scrawled note: *Going on home to Rochester.*

CHAPTER 41

I was late arriving this day—the first of March, according to my pocket calendar. I had been out searching for gin and laudanum and had lost my way in the Manhattan streets. Buildings spring up so quickly. The streets and signage change. It is a wonder, to be frank, that anyone gets to anyplace.

Up and up. I was already proclaiming my apologies and thudding down my satchel when I stopped. I could not believe what I saw, by which I mean nothing. The bed was empty. The garret was empty. My patient was gone.

I hollered her name. Twirled about. There was nowhere to hide a mechanical, as I have said, never mind a body. I discovered her, at last, on the far side of her bed and was amazed I had not spied her straightaway. "Oh, Maggie, do come on now."

"She's gone."

"What are you talking about? Oh, never mind," I said, and tucked her in and apologized a good dozen times (I was getting well practised at this apologizing). I gave her the laudanum, my hands ashake.

"And so I went to Rochester," she said, after a time, and told me all about that.

I should mention that she was confusing herself with Katie by this time. An unsurprising thing, considering how entwined they were. Considering how near she was drawing to her mortal end.

THE CHILDREN, dirty and shoeless, rush at Katie as if to push her into the canal. They hoot and catcall as she staggers aside. The world, aside from the rat-children, is fine enough, is green-leafed and sun-warmed. Passersby tut their disapproval. Ah, she is coming into Rochester's Exchange Street. Perhaps she will shop for a hat, one topped with a stuffed bird as is all the rage. Yes, she'll slaughter all of Leah's birds and become a milliner. She could use a change of occupation. She swivels and falls to her knees. The children mimic her and howl with laughter. A boy prods her with a stick. A girl snatches at her shawl. The boy comes at her again, his stick held back like a heathen's spear.

"Cease that! Get thee gone! Wretched, wretched children!" The woman's voice is blade-sharp. The children scatter like pigeons. Are they flying? No. It is only the leaves in the sky above. Someone, perhaps herself, singsongs as she is taken away.

> "'Pray send for a doctor quick,
> Any one will do!'
> Doctor mouse comes creeping,
> Creeping to her bed;
> Lanced her gums and felt her pulse,
> Whispered she was dead.
> Very sly, very sly,
> The real old cat,
> Open kept her weathered eye—
> Mouse! Beware of that!'"

"Katherine? Katie?"

At the cautious utterance of her name Katie looks up to see Amy Post standing afore her in her familiar dark dress with its lace cuffs and collars, her familiar kind expression.

"I'm in your keeping room, Amy," Katie says and with the pride of a child at her lessons. She pats at her badly-pinned hair. Her tartan dress is dirt-streaked and hangs alarmingly at the back, Katie having neglected to wear a bustle. Well, fiddle-de-damn, Amy doesn't wear a bustle either, Katie thinks, and then recalls that Amy is a member of the Society for Rational Dress. But not a member of any Spirit Society. She has not attended sittings for years now, not even when Isaac died. When was that? A decade or more ago? Yes, and that was when Amy said she knew full well that Isaac was in the Glory; that he was with their beloved Matilda and Henry at last and that she, Amy, would be with them all soon enough. Amy said that those who continually seek confirmation of the beyond are alike drunkards continually seeking their next bottle. At this remembrance Katie looks about for brandy, or sherry; surely there is at least sherry in Amy's house.

Machteld, who looks nearly as old as her mistress these days, lumbers in with apple cake and tea. She ignores Katie, as she has for over thirty years now. Katie sips the proferred tea and frowns.

"It's rosehip," Amy explains. "Stimulants of any kind, might not, might not be of benefit for thee, dear."

"Thee, me, three," Katie says, and giggles into her cup.

"When did you arrive, Katherine? How long have you been here?"

"Here? Hah, hah, you mean in Rochester? A day or two or four. I was at the Hotel Brunswick. Oh, the séances were crowded with riff-raffy sorts, but fiddle-dee-dee it's jim-dandy to be back and having jolly times again. I was going to call on you. I was! Oh, but you don't approve of us these days." Katie wags her finger. Amy looks grim. She must be in her eighties, Katie thinks. Who lives so long except the righteous and the good?

Amy sighs. "The policeman was about to arrest thee for public drunkenness, but I dissuaded him and promised to take thee to my home and, for heaven's sake, where are thy senses?"

"I sold them. I lost them. And I just wanted to see the canals. Our pa was a canaller, you know. Ma says he vanished like the earth swallowed him whole, but he were out working the boats. For ten years he was gone. The canals were the best place for a sinning man, I heard. But then the Great Awakening came along and changed everything so."

"I shall telegraph Leah so that she may come for thee."

Katie lurches forward. The tea sloshes on her dress. "Damn,

where's my shawl? Oh, the children. Damn them . . . What did you say about Leah?"

"That I shall telegraph her so that—"

"No, no, no, not her. She can't know. She'll take my boys. She'll use 'em up. She wants everything of mine. She wants to keep me from Mag too. Oh, but I want my Mag, Maggie! Who else has ever loved me for me, me, me, me? Who? But she's planning to go back to England, ain't she? Some rich doctor invited her. She says she'll make pots of money for us both from Dr. Wadsworth, that's the whom-ever's name. That means I'll be mud-stuck with Leah." Katie's voice twangs. Leah's years of grammar training vanish. "Leah's sore afraid of Mag ever since Mag walloped her good, that's why Leah keeps off. She don't love us, Amy."

"She does. She must. And I love thee, dear. And the Lord, Our Saviour, loves thee."

"Does He? And does He say we should be quit of this whole thing? And quick, hah, quite quit quick! Maggie said we gotta."

"Which . . . 'thing'?"

"Spiritualism, 'course. We gotta tell the truth of it to the world, Mag said. I agree. I think I agree or something. Sure I do."

"Mayhap thou need a different cause. A cause is always a goodly thing to keep one from melancholic thoughts. Isaac would have agreed."

"Pish, you were always trying to convince Leah, weren't you? Abolition. Suffragette-ism, or what-ever it's called. Because, oh, wouldn't she be a force for any of your causes."

Amy is quiet, then says coolly, "I shall fix a bed for thee. Thou should bide here, not alone in a hotel and—"

"I'll tell you why she weren't biting," Katie interrupts. "Because that harridan bitch don't wish for women to be considered nothing but stupid and childlike. She likes it that us females are reckoned passive as straw dolls and without guile at all. Didn't that thinking serve us right-dandy, though? Didn't it save us? Mark me, Amy, if we'd been the Fox *brothers* we woulda been rotting in a jail by now. And we woulda mightily deserved it."

Amy folds and unfolds her hands. "Thou deserves a rest, that is all."

———

17 April, 1888

Dearest Kat,

I attained in England yesterday. I couldn't find you before I
left, not in any of your haunts, and not at your apartment,
though I had a nice visit with your Ferdie—who insisted on
cooking me up a fine mess of hash—and with your Henry,
who was all manner of keen when I promised to bring him
back books on the latest continental inventions. By the by, I
told Dr. Wadsworth, and right there at the docks, that
Spiritualism was a fraud. I didn't intend to. It just occurred.
He was unsurprised, though, and admitted that his famed
cure-all Wadsworth Own is naught but laudanum with
bitters. He said that if one asserts with sincere and utter
conviction that something is real and efficacious, then it
becomes so. I do like the man. He was a pugilist once and still
looks like he could bend iron bars. Anywise, I'm going on
with his séances as planned. Peculiar, isn't it? How one can
believe something and not believe it at the same instant. Can't
wait to see you when I get back from England. Stay clear of
Her Fatness.

> Your Loving Sister,
> Mag

"HAVE YOU EVER PLAYED blindman's bluff, Alvah?"

"Certainly, when I was a youngster."

"That's what I was doing. That's why I fell out of the bed,
yesterday—"

"It was just now, not yesterday. It's the same day, duck, as . . .
today."

"I just wanted to try again, that's all. Katie and I played blindman's bluff often at the Hydesville house. Once, when I was the
blinded one, I lost her. I thump-thumped about the room, banging
into furniture, and the place seemed of a sudden so very large and

not my home at all. I tore off the rag, but I could not see Katie. I looked in every nook and corner. And then I felt a swim of air. I whirled and there she was. 'Where have you been?' I cried. 'I've been here all along,' she said."

"Games," I said, a bit asulk. (I was doing my best not to drink and my nerves were fragile threads.) "I do believe you're still at them."

IF ONLY LEAH COULD BELIEVE THAT Katie loves her boys "beyond measure" as she claims. If only she could believe that their welfare is Katie's sole concern. Indeed, if Leah believed any of Katie's claims, even a whit, then she would not be seeking out this god-knows-where office in this god-forsaken neighbourhood of Manhattan, the same neighbourhood, she realizes, as that for R.M, whose address Pettifew wrote on the back on his card. R.M. is likely long gone, of course, which is of no concern to Leah, as his ghoulish skills will, no doubt, never be needed. Resurrection Man is what R.M. stands for—though Grave-Robber, Leah thinks, is a more fitting title.

She pauses and then carries on. Daniel warned her not to go, but Leah was adamant. For Katie's behaviour is in direct odds with her claims. Her poor sons are being left to fend for themselves while she is more and more often out on drinking binges. Oh, Leah has tried and tried, but no amount of cajoling can convince Katie and the boys to return to the Underhill home. "At least let the dear boys stay with us," Leah said. "Daniel and I shall care for them as if they were our own."

Katie's eyes focused for once. "Hah, you've got your own— Lizzie, remember her? And look how that played out. She won't even visit you. In fact I wouldn't wonder if she hated you. No, no, no, the boys won't ever never live with you. You'll twist them up and spit them out."

Twist them? And here Leah was willing to forgive Katie's public drunkenness in Rochester, the account of which had been reported in the *New York Herald*. And didn't the Taylors recently have to drag her out of a miserable saloon? They reported that Katie was despondent because Maggie left for England without saying good-bye in person. That Katie was drinking with a vengeance that put her earlier habits to the pale.

Leah circles round an ash barrel, lifts her bustled skirts out of the various excrements, thinks of how Katie's so-called motherly concern vanishes utterly when she is on a spree. Utterly! She uses her boys as an anchor. That is all they are to her: an anchor to keep herself from total debauchery and all its sluttish potential. She is selfish, selfish, selfish.

A beggar man cups an ear in Leah's direction. "Who's selfish? Me for my poverty and bum leg?"

God and the Spirits help me, Leah thinks as she drops a coin in his hand, the girls have driven me to muttering.

The sign for the SPCA bears the silhouette of a dog cowering from a club-wielding man. Leah mounts the narrow stairs to the office on the third floor. She stops twice to catch her breath. Lately her skirts seem weighed down with bricks, her shoes with lead. Responsibility, she supposes, only now showing its weight. On the office door is another silhouette, this one of a horse staggered in its traces. She sees no images of beaten, neglected children. She was assured, however, that this is the place to come to report such things, has been since a few years back when a SPCA lady came across a naked, half-starved girl wandering a New York slum and brought her back for care. Soon after this the stray children of New York began arriving at the SPCA office in droves.

Leah finds the office at last. It is small as a horse stall and reeks of lister and carbolic. Leah hardly knows where to sit for all the books and animal hair. The window is covered over with a high cabinet that leaks papers. A lone gas light burns on the wall.

The lady hunched behind the desk searches out a form, clears a portion of her desk and dips her pen. She waits without much interest to hear the tale, which will no doubt have similarity to many other tales of woe. Leah has a moment of doubt, then clears her throat: "I am reporting this anonymously. It must be anonymous. Strictly so. I know someone—a woman who is a dipsomaniac of the most extreme kind. She has two young and innocent boys . . ."

"You won't send me to a hospital, Alvah. Please do not. Not even a Quaker one."

She took my hand as she was doing often these days. Her grip was neither too tight nor too loose. I supposed she was practised at hand-holding, having done so in so many dim rooms, with so many strangers. I supposed, too, that she was practised at gleaning information from palms and fingers, and yet I allowed her my hand.

"No. I promised I wouldn't, don't you recall? Ah, never mind."

At that she said, clear as day, and in a voice similar to mine own, "Don't be an addle-pot, duck. Hospitals are only of use during the wars, or for when family are unable to assist, and if it must be a hospital, then a Quaker one is best, they are a goodly lot with a firm belief in practicality."

I gaped, then said her mimicry was a fine trick, though I was peeved. "You are mixing up your memories, making a cocktail of them."

"As is my wont, to be frank," Maggie said, and again in a voice that echoed my own.

She talked of Katie again, and how she was sent to prison. But again she spoke of the experience as if it were somehow her own.

KATIE IS ESCORTED past the blackened ornate pillars, then down through the cell-pocked courtyard, then under the Bridge of Sighs. No pretty bridge where lovers stroll, this, but one over which condemned prisoners walk to the gallows step by quaking step.

"Take her to the Bummer's Hall," the matron says. "I've got plenty on this night." She is rake-thin but she does not appear weak, rather the contrary. Her bones look sharp enough to cleave Katie in twain.

The policeman, one Officer Purdy, pushes back his cap. "She's not drunk is what, though. Not at the moment, like." He is blond and fat and Irish, and at the moment obviously wishing himself in some other occupation.

The matron jabs at the paper. "It says right here that she was arrested for drunkenness and neglect of children."

"The Bummer's Hall will be fine," Katie says, her teeth chattering with cold, with terror of this lady whose appearance reminds her of Amy, but in the cruellest incarnation.

The matron glowers. "Oh, the lady thinks she has a choice, does she? This room or that, as if sashaying herself up to a hotel?"

Katie stutters an answer. Officer Purdy holds up his hand. "You wouldn't want to be in the Bummer's Hall, Mrs. Jencken. There's no private cells, like. Just one room full with drunkards, of the male kind mostly. No place for a lady, that."

"Damn you, Purdy. Here, then." The matron scrabbles at the enormous keys at her waist.

In her cell Katie weeps, and her weeping adds to that of other women in other cells. The sound is one of absolute misery. Surely they must hear it in the Manhattan streets beyond. Ah, no, the dank walls are too thick. Sights and sounds come here to be buried. Not for whimsy is this place was called "the Tombs." Not even the newspapers call it the Halls of Justice, its proper name. Not even the judges and lawyers. It is designed after an Egyptian mausoleum and is haunted by the miasmic air of the swampy land upon which it was built. Odd how Katie has passed the Tombs for many years and never truly noted it. Despite the fact, or perhaps because, it takes up an entire city block. Well, she will certainly notice it henceforth.

A sad-eyed boy sweeps the corridor, his feet shod only in yellow light from the set-down lantern. Another boy walks by holding a chamberpot, and with as much care as a ring bearer at a wedding. The stench as he passes merely adds another layer to those of sweat, rot, vomit. At least Ferdie and Henry escaped incarceration here. Only criminal boys are kept here, and in the same ward as the women prisoners. No, her darling boys are in "juvenile asylum." Officer Purdy assured a sobbing, begging Katie that this asylum is a comfortable place from whence children can be sent to reputable "fostering" families. "It's a grand new system, Mrs. Jencken," Purdy assured her

The mould-coloured light at the high, barred window indicates afternoon. Katie is not to see a judge until the following day. It will all be sorted out then. Yes, it will. She will insist her boys be released to her care. Insist on a newspaper reporter's attention. The name Katie Fox Jencken is still celebrated. Surely. And she will find a way to telegraph Maggie in England. Somehow Maggie will help her. Not Leah. No. This is Leah's damned own doing. It must be. Who else would report that Katie's young men were "neglected children"? Who else would want control of the offspring of the high priestess of Spiritualism, as Katie is still sometimes called? A fostering family? And what "family" would that turn out to be? Katie kicks the stone wall. Curses Leah. Curses her own weaknesses for stimulants. She even curses her beloved Maggie for leaving her so. *I'm staying here a month longer. Dr. Wadsworth's generosity is astounding. We shan't have to worry for a time about money.* Such is what Maggie wrote in her latest missive.

The matron clanks her keys on the bars. "Stop that howling and crying now. It won't make no difference. Shut it, I say!"

Katie bites her palm. Perhaps some brandy will seep from it. There must be enough of the damned stuff in her veins.

They came for her that forenoon. Banged on the apartment door. The neighbours, gluttonous for excitement, ranged behind the officers. Ferdie answered. Katie was at her desk writing a letter. To Maggie in England? Yes, of course, to Maggie. Officer Purdy and his cohort looked puzzled when they realized that Ferdie, this tall, strapping young man, was one of the poor, neglected boys. Henry, too, was a puzzle. Certainly he looked less imposing, but he did not appear ill-fed—ill-mannered, perhaps, given that he looked up from his book and announced he smelled rotting potatoes. The policemen showed the warrant, at which mayhem ensued, what with the boys trying to protect Katie and Katie crying and raging, and the neighbours now turning against the police and protesting the injustice of it all.

Katie thinks of Officer Purdy's broad, anxious face, his muttered apologies as he sat with her in the police wagon, how he said, "You've got the grand luck, you do. You've only got ghosties and ghouls to be dealing with. Me, I've got the damned of this earth traipsing in my precinct."

If it was an attempt at consolation, it scarcely worked.

Katie sits on her hard cot. Imagines Henry as a boy again, his face plumbed against hers, asking for the rhyme again, saying he doesn't give a fig if Auntie Leah hates it.

Old Mother Tabbyskins
Said 'Serves him right!'
Gobbled up mousey doc
With infinite delight.
Very fast, very fast,
Very pleasant, too.
What a pity it can't last.
Send another, do.
Doctor Dog comes running,
Just to see her begs.
Round his neck a comforter,
Trousers on his legs.
. . .
Doctor Dog comes nearer,
Said she must be bled.
I heard Mother Tabbyskins
Screaming in her bed.
Very fast, very fast, scuffling out and in,
Doctor Dog looked full and queer
Where was Tabbyskins?
I will tell the moral
Without any fuss:
Those who lead the young astray
Always suffer thus.

CHAPTER 42

"And how did your Katie escape?" I asked. "Did she slip through the cracks in the walls or floors or what have you? You said she could do such things."

My patient smiled. "You have a sterling memory, Alvah. But no, Katie was released after three days. After it was sorted. She was frantic about the boys. They were staying with Leah and Daniel, Just as Katie predicted. I did what I could from distant England. Thank the good grief for Dr. Wadsworth. I was confiding everything him, though I hadn't known him long. We weren't intimate, no, not in that fashion, but I appreciated that he did not judge me, that he thought it all amusing. Anywise, it was good practice, this honesty, for what came next."

I set down the cover-all. Took up the gin bottle. I was allowing myself only a measured amount per day. Prison. Well. I know prisons. I searched many for August after the war. I did not give up trying to find him.

"I should have looked longer," I muttered, and took up the cover-all again. "I need finish."

"What is that? Finish what now? Not the gin there, you've had sufficient, Alvah."

"Oh, are we switching places? You the caretaker? Me the indigent?" It was a ridiculous question, I realized straightways, being somewhat true. I added, "If you must know, I meant the cover-all."

As I did. August's birthday was the fifth of March. It was marked in the calendar I kept in my satchel. Marked out in indigo ink. "It is imperative I finish it," I further added as I clutched those knitting needles in my fists.

BOYS IN ASYLUM. HEARTSICK. LEAH TO BLAME. NIGHT IN TOMBS. HIDEOUS. MAG PLEASE HELP. KAT

The telegram boy takes one look at Maggie's face and decides against waiting for a tip. She clutches the paper. Damns the sparse, clipped sentences. The unknown is a black hole in Maggie's brain. Better a hysterical letter, scrawled and blotted and lengthy.

She seeks out Dr. Wadsworth. He is rolling pills, his heavy hands deft. Maggie tells him the news, adds, "We must send word back. Immediately. But, God, God, what can I do from England. Nothing!"

God does not answer, but Dr. Wadsworth—who Maggie is starting to believe is the next best thing—has a suggestion.

The telegraph office is cramped and busy. The telegraph operator, his visor hiding his eyes, chooses not to question if the respectable, barrel-chested Dr. Wadsworth is indeed whom he claims to be. Maggie watches the operator's brisk tap-tapping. It is as if he is part of the machinery, and likewise without thought or intent. She reflects on how she has often been called a telegraph, a spirit telegraph, as if she were no more animate than this brass gadgetry. Certainly the tap-tapping bears comparison, as does the vast distance travelled, near instantaneously. What need do people have of magic when man can create such things with his own hands? Maggie wonders. One day such machinery will triumph over superstition. Until then, well, Maggie is forming a plan. Gathering her courage.

In the carriage Dr. Wadsworth claps in triumph. He is enjoying the intrigue. Has no compunctions about drafting the telegram to the New York authorities.

SEND HENRY AND FERDIE JENCKEN HOME AT ONCE TO MRS.
HENRY JENCKEN OF NEW YORK. FUNDS AND DETAILS TO
FOLLOW. BY ORDER. MR EDWARD JENCKEN. BROTHER TO MR
HENRY JENCKEN SENIOR.

Dr. Wadsworth says, "We must follow it with a barrister's letter. I have a friend who will assist us. Not to worry, Mrs. Kane."

"I can't thank you enough."

"As long as the true Uncle Edward does not—"

"He won't. The man is somewhere on the continent. He's not spoken nor written to Kat since her Henry died. He's abandoned her." Maggie leans towards Wadsworth. "Everyone has abandoned her, excepting me. I'm the only one who can save us both. Our souls, that is."

Wadsworth eyes her. "And how shall you do that?"

"Revenge." Maggie thought it would be a difficult utterance, but it is a soft, whispery word. One could easily utter it a hundred times without stumbling.

"I do hope you're not plotting any, any, hmm, bodily harm. I had a time in my life where such actions seemed jolly fun, but the consequences, my dear, they are . . ." Dr. Wadsworth breaks off, his heavy brows raised.

"Not to worry. You can kill without weapons, you know."

"My dear, your nerves are stretched like catgut. Ah, but I have just the thing."

The "thing" is poppy tea mixed with honey and nutmeg. The effect is like that of laudanum—which Wadsworth does not allow Maggie because of the alcohol base—but much stronger. She becomes featherlight. Happiness whirls inside her, like the coloured ribbons round a maypole. Objects—vases, paintings, tables—are all limned with radiance.

Wadsworth and a maid lead her to a bed soft as clouds in which she slumbers on and on until just past midnight, when she wakes with a start. She panics for a clock-tick then recalls that she is in England. *England. That's where I am. At Wadsworth's home. There's hope yet. I'm not alone and ranting. Not yet.*

She walks on her tough, knobby feet to the windows. On the cobbled street a man staggers under the yellow head of a gas light. His shadow stretches and grows monstrous. A mongrel noses at rubbish. Maggie nods to herself, all purpose, then yanks on a grey gown and black cloak. She takes up a pocket-lamp and walks down the corridor, now down the stairs. She is not afraid of waking the household. When she chooses, Maggie can be absence itself. Her sliding feet make no noise. The stairs do not creak at her weight. Not even the cats note her. It is from long practice, from all that disappearing while she let the dead take over her self and soul.

The moon shines out obligingly as she nears a small, squat church. The gates to the graveyard are unlocked. How unlike an American cemetery, she thinks, with its greened expanses around each plot. Here the graves are crammed tight as passengers on a omnibus. She wonders how deep the graves go, how many coffins have been stacked one upon the other over centuries, millennia. Then realizes that in this ancient island country the dead must easily outnumber the living.

She chooses a grave at random: *Hortence Mithelwaith. Beloved Wife. Beloved Mother.* Dead these hundred years. "Speak to me," Maggie whispers. "Please. You must. A token. That's all." Distant sounds of the living stirring in their city. Nothing else.

Maggie moves from grave to grave. The moon has turned a molten silver and she can read the dedications without her pocket-lamp. Here are the veterans of the Napoleonic Wars. There, those who died during the reign of the virgin Queen. There the victims of London's Great Fire. There the victims of Cromwell's terror. Childbirth. Disease. Drowning. Accident. Some of the dead even reached a good age.

She reads the oldest stones by tracing her fingers over the worn indentations. All are silent to her pleas—the wealthy with their tombs, the newly dead with their sharp-carved statuettes, the long-dead infants with their gravestones worn to nubs the size of a hand.

By the time Maggie leaves she is certain at last of what she has always suspected.

———

A week later, Maggie staggers to the railing of the steamer *Italy*. *Trot trot to Brandy. Trot trot to Gin. Better watch out or you might fall in.* She chuckles at her clever rewording. She might be a toddler herself, so unsteady are her steps and so scattered are her thoughts. But she is not going to gin. Nope. She is going to New York, and for revenge.

Voices behind her: "Tsk-tsk." "Oh, my, my." "Disgraceful."

"What of it?" she yells, but at the seagull that bobs in the air before her, as if on a child's string. "The damned letter has been sent."

The seagull caws in agreement. Does Leah have seagulls in her aviary? No, a seagull would be a painful mirror, what with its greed and opportunism, its scavenging ways and, oh, its ability to escape. But Leah won't escape much longer. Maggie and Katie might well go down with her into infamy, but that can't be helped. "We're trussed together, we three!" Maggie yells at the seagull. "Like so much cord-wood, that's what Leah said once. All we need is a raging fire."

Maggie's letter might even now be set to type for the *Herald* newspaper of New York: *I read in your edition of Saturday May 5 an account of the misfortune that has befallen my dear sister Mrs. Katie Fox Jencken. The sad news nearly killed me. My sister's two beautiful boys are her idols. Spiritualism is a curse. God had set his shield against it. I call it a curse, for it is used by heartless persons and vilest miscreants as a cloak for evil doings.* And so forth.

Maggie trembles. She has set in motion something terrible and momentous that cannot be stopped nor slowed. "Have you, now? Really, Maggie Fox, you should be damn accustomed to that sort of thing by now."

She looks around to see who has spoken, then understands that it was her own self.

Before Maggie sent that letter to the *Herald*, she sent a letter to Katie detailing her plans to publicly confess, and asking if Katie agreed. For with Maggie not yet in New York, Katie will have to face the consequences alone. She will have nowhere to hide. In private there will be Leah's wrath. In public there will be a maelstrom. And that is only the beginning of the end. New York's Academy of Music is booked. Maggie will soon be onstage. Will soon be proving to the world, once and for ever-all, that the dead do not return.

Katie's telegram in reply to Maggie's letter read only: DO WHAT IS BEST.

"Damn me, damn me now," Maggie mumbles. Tastes what might be salt spray, or tears. She looks up. The deck is deserted. A flag snaps on a pole. A forgotten book claps its pages. Grey sky and grey deck. And now a man walks briskly towards her.

"Tuttie, pet! Where is the diamond bracelet I gave you? Where are the Honiton undersleeves? And your hair is in a dreadful arrangement. No matter. Christ, but it's cold in that other place. I never cared you were a fraud, you know, for I was much the same."

He is so close Maggie can see the boy-blue of his eyes. Then he is gone. She looks frantic over the rail, as if the deep is where he dwells. "Come back, please, Elisha. You tell them first. You tell them we were wed. Tell them you loved me, *Maggie*. Say my name, you damned prat. You cad."

He doesn't answer. She peers farther over the rail at the waving waves. Calls his name again. The gulls call back as if in mockery. She hikes her petticoats. One leg over. She flinches as the cold metal bites the bare skin between her stockings and pantaloons. He touched her there once. And farther on and farther on. It has been such a long time since she clambered over fences, railings. Was the orchard the last time? Just before she and Katie met the peddler. Yes, back when the world was good. Back when she and Katie were good. How did that encounter lead to millions of people joining hands and asking the dead to rise and speak? It makes no earthly sense.

Both Maggie's legs are over now. She is on the other side of the rail, on the thin ledge over the leaping sea. She clings to the rail behind. A finger slips. Another.

"Ma'am! What in hell!" A thick forearm clamps her waist. A meaty hand grapples at her neck. "Quick now!" "I got her, sir!"

And then a medley of voices as the living rush to claim her.

CHAPTER 43

"Here you are, Maggie-duck, a small gift."

My patient took it with delight. It was *Godfrey's Narrative of the Last Grinnell Expedition in Search of Sir John Franklin 1853–4–5, by W.M.C. Godfrey, One of The Survivors.*

"I sought it out, after your tale of yesterday, the ship, the sea and you seeing Elisha while you were in the grip of alcohol visions." This mention of alcohol reminded me of my gin allotment which, according to my bracelet watch, was as of this instance. The allotment, I allow, had been growing by the day.

"Elisha was as real as you," she said, peeved. The book fell on her lap. She was growing weaker by the hour, I should add.

"Mayhap, but do the dead return just to nag us? It seems unlikely, even for your Elisha, by which I mean it is high-time you laid the man to rest."

"She patted *Godfrey's Narrative.* "And this will help?"

"What? Are you afraid of disobeying your shilly-shally man?"

"Elisha did order me not to read it." She smiled faint. "But then I did return to spirit rapping against his wishes, and this cannot be a worse offense. Go on then, be my dear reader, Alvah June."

The first page showed an etching of the handsome, strong-jawed Godfrey himself. I read aloud to my patient of Elisha's growing paranoia in the long Arctic dark. Of how Godfrey and some others left the ice-locked ship during the first winter and struck for the south. Of their failure and return. Of Elisha's unreasonable hatred for Godfrey. Of how he accused Godfrey of deserting on the occasion when Godfrey was out hunting for them all. How Elisha tried to shoot Godfrey, both men moving at a shuffle because of the cold and scurvy. Godfrey over the ice. Elisha to the gun-stand on the brig. How the shots sludged about Godfrey until he shuffled out of range, and then shuffled another eighty miles more to the Esquimaux settlement and safety. Later Elisha apologized and asked Godfrey to return to *The Advance* and make the journey home with them. Godfrey did so, only to have his reputation destroyed.

"Can you just imagine, duck, trying to run as bullets plume about, but being unable to because of the cold, the scurvy? To be forced to just shuffle, shuffle to safety?"

"Oh, I can imagine that easy as cake."

"As can I, easy as pie." We both thought this no end of amusing.

We came to the book's final page: "*She was a young lady of small stature, rather full of face, brilliant black eyes and eyes of a corresponding hue, and while Dr. Kane looked with mortification and self-blame on his own wavering, it seemed almost equally impossible to take or to renounce the hand of Margaret.*"

"Your name writ out at last," I said.

My patient's smile then was of a different mettle than before, not mischievous, not sly, relieved perhaps. And I admit to pride at offering this succour.

"A shame you did not seek out this Godfrey and make a match of him. The two of you seemed of a piece."

"Other lives as bubbles in a tin tub," she murmured. These were Elisha's words, but her voice, I should mention, was wholly her own.

THERE ARE RUFFLES of applause as Maggie walks slowly onto the stage of New York's Academy of Music this October evening of 1888. A sheaf of papers is in her hand, a red-faced manager at her side. She is not downplaying her fifty-four years. She wears her greying hair drawn severely back, spectacles and an austere dress in her favourite bishop's blue.

The crowd mutters at this unentertaining sight. A man yells, "Where's them lovely girl ghosts, all gauzy draped? That's what we want exposed!" This is such a knee-slapper that the crowd—which is mostly men—takes a while to settle.

Maggie searches out Katie, who, attended by Ferdie, watches from an upper box close on to the stage. Maggie wishes back the supremacy of candles, for in the lime and arc lights Katie's skin appears wax-white, her arched nose a shadowy blade, her eyes puddle-grey. And candlelight would be kinder, also, to the red velvet swagging, which in the lime light appears a noxious, mottled orange.

Katie nods and puts her hand to her heart. Maggie faintly smiles, then adjusts her spectacles and holds the papers before her. Her voice is wooden and she does not look at the crowd as she reads her confession, even when she can barely be heard over the hisses and catcalls from Spiritualism's believers. The cheers from its detractors.

". . . It was forty years ago and we were very mischievous children and we wanted to terrify our dear mother, who was a good woman and easily frightened. At night when we went to bed, we would tie an apple on a string and cause the apple to bump on the floor so that it sounded as steps. Mother did not think us capable of a trick because we were so young. Children, mark me, will always find means to accomplish mischief."

Maggie tells of Leah arriving and taking them off to Rochester. "She knew straightaway. She's always known. Her daughter, Lizzie, helped us at first but then she was wisely quit of the whole thing, as I wish to God Katie and I had been. One has to learn the rapping when one is young—that's why Mr. Chauncey Burr years ago could never make his exposé plausible. And certainly my sister Leah, Mrs. Underhill, could never manage it as we did. And this, among other things, made her jealous and bitter. In time she exhibited us to a lot of spiritual fanatics. She would give us signals to tell us how to answer. She had confederates seek out knowledge of the sitters and she could read a face like a book. In time we could too. In this way she made as much as one hundred fifty dollars a night.

She gave us a measly stipend, and she pocketed the main of our earnings. It was us who began the practice of sitting in the dark around a table, holding hands so that the sitters could not know what went on about them. We called them 'spirit circles' or 'promiscuous circles' because both men and women were there, but everyone calls them séances now."

Then the crowd is treated to the sight of Maggie's knobby, naked feet. She puts them on a low table and waggles them like a child playing in the sand. The manager calls for quiet. There is a rap on the upper proscenium, then on the stage itself, then knocks in the aisle, on the far doors. A number of worthy doctors are called up. They hold Maggie's feet. Declare they can feel the pulsations.

Boos and hisses. Cheers and applause. The crowd seems quite evenly divided. Some people are walking out in a huff. Some are laughing. Some are already exchanging wagered money.

"She's a lying bitch, that one," a man yells.

Maggie staggers back. She knows a moment of utter terror. She visions the crowd transforming into a mob and tearing her to pieces. She visions tarring and feathering, red-hot pokers, the usual lot.

Maggie shudders and brushes at her dress. She gathers her courage, then stalks to the outmost edge of the stage. Her red-faced manager reaches for her, mightily worried. The crowd quiets. Something is not going according to plan. The excitement is palpable.

Maggie drops her papers and glowers at the crowd. Her voice is clear and loud. She no longer speaks as if by rote. "Hear me! All of you! I am the widow of Dr. Elisha Kent Kane, the Arctic explorer, and I swear I would call him to me if it were possible, but there is no such thing as the departed returning to this life. I've tried to do so in every form, and know it cannot be done. I visited a graveyard at the midnight hour. I stood over each grave and called upon the dead to give me some token of their presence. All were silent."

The manager grips her elbow. He mouths apologies to the audience and tries to steer Maggie offstage. She shakes him loose and points at the crowd: "Mark me! The dead do not see us, nor hear us, nor interfere in our worldly affairs. It matters not how we entreat. It matters not how we pray. Our words all fall into the pit.

For the dead do not return. Not any that go up to Heaven! Nor any that go down into Hell!"

She looks to Katie. Katie nods.

Silence from the audience. Cravats are straightened. Hats adjusted. There is a moment of fearful unease. For the living, Maggie well knows, might be terrified of ghosts, ghouls, banshees, doppelgangers; they might be terrified of the rotting dead tottering out of their graves. But that terror is nothing compared to the terror of knowing that the dead dwell across some endless void. Indeed, that the dead might not exist at all.

Katie grips Ferdie tight as he and the red-faced theatre manager force a path through the heckling crowd, Maggie and Katie close behind. Ferdie holds protectively on to them both. The cab waits in a vat of gaslight. They are being jostled on all sides. Maggie is tight-lipped with fear. Her bravado has vanished.

Maggie and Katie stumble against him at the same instant—a small, elderly man in a swank Chesterfield coat. Maggie glimpses a sleek grey beard, a mouth twisted in outrage, a cane topped with a gleaming hound's head.

"I'm sorry, I am," Maggie cries. "We were so young and stupid."

"I'm sorry too. Really, really," Katie echoes.

"Please forgive us!" they say in unison, and clamber into the cab with the manager's blundering assist. When Maggie dares a look behind, she sees this elderly man fronting the crowd. He smiles a contorted smile. Takes two limping steps, and then the cab rattles him from sight.

CHAPTER 44.

"I see that you're all-disgruntled, Alvah," my patient murmured. I was amazed she could see a dust-mote in her deteriorating condition and told her this fact.

"Allow my guess. You've dropped a stitch. Or no, your bracelet watch has stopped again."

I was knitting away, fast as I could (I had nipped at some of her laudanum so my hands were steady enough), and had not dropped a solitary stitch. And the bracelet watch was set as firmly on my wrist as ever.

"Aren't you the fine fisherwoman," I said, then set down the cover-all. "The Medico Society is displeased with me, if you must know. To be more than frank, they are ready to give me the heave-ho and relieve me of my duties, to boot. They say I spend too much time with you. That I am failing in my duties and my reports have been muddled."

"Relieved? Of your duties? I didn't think your sort could be."

"Everyone's game is up and ended, sooner or later."

"Should I tell you how Leah's game ended?"

I picked up the cover-all again, determined now to finish. "Now that I would very much like to hear."

LEAH POLISHES THE SILVER BUTTER PICKS, the ice-cream hatchet, the silver sugar chipper, her thoughts spinning, fiery as a Catherine wheel.

Her new-hired housekeeper—a heavy-faced, insolent creature—tosses the latest editions of the newspapers on the sideboard. The newspapers just miss Leah's bona fide French toile vase, the one that had been her father's. Leah acquired it after he died, and now it sits centred on the sideboard.

The housekeeper trundles off. Leah hesitates, then takes up the newspapers. The reports are gleeful, even savage. There is Margaretta taking the stage at the renowned Academy of Music, waggling her big toes for all to see, cracking and snapping those obscene digits. The dead do not return? Who is Margaretta Fox to say that? Who is she to say that Heaven and Hell are inescapable?

Leah hurls the butter picks and ice-cream hatchet, then any other silverware that comes to hand—the salt throne, the silver fish-knives. Their thudding on the oriental rug sounds alike muffled, staggered steps.

"Mrs. Underhill." Daniel has appeared in the dining room. His face, though calm, is edged with a look Leah has never seen before, nor does she wish to again.

She presses her hand to her chest. Daniel is holding the lily box. He lifts the thick lid, then takes out her supportive letters, her commendations and medallions, and sets them aside with the professional detachment of a banker with a strongbox. Into the silence the birds in Leah's aviary begin their racketing songs, not a comfort this day, only a further enragement because, really, how dare the birds sing when such disaster has befallen her?

"Daniel, dearest. The curio cabinet. The key. It was my private—"

"Oh, I would never dare use your key."

"Then how—"

"I broke the glass," Daniel says. "With a hammer." He pressures the top of the lid, just so, then shows the underside. The interior hatch has opened to reveal the hidden compartment. He does not take out her father's letter, which is jammed in there. At this, at least, Leah is relieved.

"The magic of phosphorous, appearing in a closed box of dirt,"

Daniel announces. "Should I attain one hundred ten years, I will ponder how I could have allowed myself to be fooled by this simple device."

"Mr. Underhill, I shall explain . . ." She rushes to him. She is cumbersome these days what with her flounced skirt trains, what with her girth, and thus she stumbles to her knees. She looks up, and with the same wronged-damsel expression as when she raised her burned hands from the garden dirt, back when Daniel first fell in love with her. Surely he will believe in her now. The man believes in ghosts, for heaven's sake. Why not her avowed words?

"Daniel, it was my father's idea. Truly. Oh, he acted the reformed roustabout, but his heart was never changed, nor reformed nor . . . and he made that box for me, yes, but then, then he tampered with it and insisted I use it for the phosphorous test. He could not bear for my good name to be destroyed . . . Mr. Underhill!"

But Daniel has turned away. Has left Leah to struggle upright on her own. "I have been a good wife to you. I have. Spirits-have-mercy, I know you would have liked a bit of this and that. Shall I try on occasion? Would that help? Would that please you? Daniel? Danny? Come back here this instant."

He pauses but does not turn. "I suggest you visit with your people in Arcadia for a number of weeks, Leah, until this unfortunate business abates." And then he is gone.

Leah presses her hands to her temples. The staccato-beat there threatens to topple her, but it steadies. She steadies. She sweeps up the newspapers. If only she could toss them forthwith into a fire, but the dining room hearth is cold, as are all the hearths—the heat chugs invisibly up through the radiators instead. Candles? Oil lamps? All are stored away. Her electric lights shine bright, too bright, and seem lifeless of a sudden without the burn of flame.

She searches out a lucifer. Stuffs the newspapers into the swept-clean hearth and lights the match. There is a whiff of sulphur, and then the flames consume the etching of Margaret Fox Kane, her toe pointing as if in accusation, straight at Leah.

The dead do not return. Not any that go up to Heaven. Nor any that go down into Hell. So reads the caption for all to see.

Leah sits down heavily on the floor.

———

Four days later and Leah arrives at her brother David's farmstead. From his veranda she surveys the red barns, the stone dry-house, the whitewashed hog pen, the drab oat fields beyond. No more peppermint fields. No more seas of blossoming pink. Peppermint is being grown cheaper elsewhere.

In the near distance are the remains of her father's house. The blackened earth is overlaid with witchgrass and fox grape, the foundation colonized by raccoons and burrowing owls, and the glass shards—from windows, vases, tumblers—are smooth-worn and glint from the burned ruins when the sun draws high.

Leah misses her father mightily these days. Even prays to him for help and guidance. He has yet to answer, the dear stubborn old coot.

Across the foreyard her brother, David, sharpens tools on a lathe. The wheel hums as he works the pedal. A duck waddles by a fence. Cows low to be milked. Odd how David has never wanted more, Leah thinks. Odd how David, like so many others, has only wanted his patch of dirt.

A shriek of childish laughter. Three children race into the yard. The two boys are David's sons. The third, a girl, is a straw-haired tubby thing whom Leah does not recognize. A neighbour, she supposes. Tubby-Girl directs the boys to stand stock. She hauls a tin box out of her pinafore, dumps the contents into the dust. Marbles. Cards. A Jacob's ladder. A knife. The knife is what she wants, for mumblety-peg, as it happens. Leah excelled at the game herself as a girl. Only once did she stab a foot with the thrown knife. Whose foot? David's? She hopes not.

David, as if following her thoughts, calls over to the children, "Finish up, now. The wood needs splitting." His tone is kindly, as if they might have a choice. The boys say, "Yes, sir." David nods and then tests the edge of a spade. Tubby-Girl looks forlorn, her playmates stolen.

David turns back to his pedalling. Pedalling. Pedalling. Yes, that damned peddler, that damned Pettifew, Leah thinks. He died just before Maggie's Music Hall rant. Leah received the news via the NOS. It was said his trusted maid found him alone amid his wares, bottles ranged around him like sentinels. He had taken to ranting, she said, and saw enemies everywhere.

"Davey!" Leah calls. She shadows her tragic eyes. From a distance there is no doubt she would be taken for a much younger woman, what with her ringlets, her tea-gown of floral brocade, her immense straw hat that shields her against the country elements. She calls her brother again. Counts a compound metre of ten as she awaits his response. None comes. Likely because he hasn't heard her over the noise of his lathe.

Has David read Maggie's ridiculous memoir? Surely not. Such damned poppycock and not even written by Maggie, but concocted by one Reuben Davenport. All is "revealed" in the *The Death-Blow to Spiritualism*. Not just the toe trick, but the snapping fingers, the rapping knuckles. And the apples. Ah, yes, the apples. Pounding on the floor in their string cages to mimic ghostly footsteps way back when at the Hydesville house. The book is a diatribe, nothing more. Maggie has revealed only her pettiness, her bitterness, her crazed thoughts, has revealed only her unfathomable hatred for Leah. In *The Death-Blow* Maggie even derides Leah's memoir. She calls *The Missing Link in Modern Spiritualism* "false from title page to finis" and "a book of the flimsiest and most absurd narrative." She then slanders Leah in such variant ways it is risible. Leah is her "damnable" "jealous" sister. Leah is an "evil genius" with "a calculating brain." A "sinister influence" who kept her family "in bondage" and ruled over them with an "iron rod" and with a "mixture or cajolery and terror." She claims Leah is a "blasphemer" with "unholy purposes." She claims that Leah's own daughter, Lizzie, called her "wicked" and that she took Leah to task for "pretending such things." And this brave stand apparently saw poor Lizzie banished. Towards Dr. Kane Leah had nothing but "malignant opposition." Towards Katie she was a "secret persecutor" who sent her to prison and attempted to steal away her beloved children, as if Leah were some hobgoblin alike the ones their mother ever cautioned them about.

Leah paces the veranda. Hah, Maggie failed to mention the way money ran through her and Katie's fingers, the endless shopping for clothes and fripperies. Failed to mention the parties and grand people they met. The attention from the public and print. How both she and Katie's enjoyed all that celebrity just dandy. God and the Spirits, is Maggie's misery her fault? Is her and Katie's drinking her fault? Is the fickleness of that prat Dr. Kane her fault?

No. No. No, Leah decides. Maggie's life has been governed by Maggie's choices. Certainly women are more subject to fortune's wind, but still, Maggie could have charted a different course. Instead she has opted to destroy her entire family along with her own pitiful self. The lying, traitorous slut. Leah will have her shut away, that's what. In a madhouse. The one she took Maggie to visit in Rochester years ago as a warning, for her own good.

Leah presses her hands to her chest. Hums a favourite tune to calm herself. At least she is not all-abandoned. Staunch Spiritualists have rallied to her defense. Have declared that Maggie's feeble raps in the Music Hall denunciation could in no way compare to the power of the knocks at those first séances years ago. Maggie is an erratic, a dipsomaniac, they have insisted, and is being puppeted by evil, greedy managers who have promised her a river of drink in return for the ruination of her family, of Leah.

Can it get worse? It can. The Music Hall denunciation was not enough; the publishing of *Death-Blow* was not enough. No. Leah learned just yesterday that Maggie is touring from town to town, waggling her big toe, telling "all" to all, and with Katie looking on. Yes, Katherina. She is a traitor through and through also. Is being continually led on by Maggie's delusions. Perhaps it had been unwise to have Katie's children taken. But how could Leah have known that Katie would be sent to the Tombs? Or that the juvenile asylum was a wretched institution little better than a prison? She is not as all-seeing as some think.

Chauncey Burr. The name, the image of the man himself, long buried, floats up from the depths. But then Chauncey Burr, her greatest nemesis, is surely the only one who would understand her feelings at this moment, for they must approximate his when the judge ordered him stripped of ten thousand dollars. When he was revealed as a swindler, a humbug, a fraud. I shall write to him, she thinks. We can bury the hatchet. It is not too late. I shall ask for his advice. His help even. He will help me, surely, so long as he hasn't died of apoplexy or been murdered by a fuming compatriot.

Leah gasps. She understands now. Understands wholly. The destruction of Leah's cherished reputation is but one of Maggie's goals. Leah's murder is the other. For *The Death-Blow* in the title of Maggie's book is meant not for Spiritualism, but for Leah.

She collapses onto the deacon's bench. Sobs aloud. Across the foreyard David halts the lathe at last. He walks towards the veranda with some tool in his great hands. He is stooped now but still a man of considerable size. He looks down with misgivings at the steps as if they might not support his weight, then risks them. The stairs hold. He does not sit aside Leah on the deacon's bench; he sits in a rocking chair some paces off.

Leah dabs her eyes. Tries for cheer. Even if David has read Davenport's lies he would not berate her. He never accuses, never gossips, never speaks ill of anyone. Indeed, conversations with David have ever left her grasping for topics.

"Ah, is that a divining rod, Davey? You are seeking out a well?"

He glances at the pronged stick in his hands, points vaguely west. "Water—why, it's ever a problem. William Hyde reckons we can hit an undercurrent over that third drumlin. He's a good man. A fine neighbour. And a far better diviner than I am."

"Is he still . . . is the old Hydesville house still in his possession?"

"William's the son. And, yes, the spook house is his now." David speaks mildly as always, but he does not look at her. Has not much since she arrived. "I keep an eye on it for him. He trusts me, and I do appreciate that. Of course the house is naught but a blight now, a ruination and such. I reckon I'm the only one who goes there. Who wishes to rent a house so haunted, eh?"

She reaches across the gap to hold his hand. "You believe me, Davey, tell me you do."

He spits tobacco over the rail. "There's sure been a hullabaloo since Maggie's confession. The neighbours are calling us blasphemers, just like when the raps first started. And they're saying I knew all along my three sisters were lying. I can't walk about in town without feeling shame. This here, why, it's our home, and all this business, Leah, I confess it has ever been a sorrow to me."

"Surely you cannot doubt me, Davey. Recall when we were children. How we played together. We had such trust then."

"I recall you stealing my molasses sticks and then telling me you were making them sweeter for me. And I recall you saying the pigeons lifted you clear into the sky. Why, I believed that one for years."

"But they did! I swear it. I was abed a fortnight because of it. I had my hair torn out. I was scratched to bits. My arms still bear the marks." She hefts a ruffled sleeve and shows the underside of her forearm, the cross-hatchings there.

He glances down. "They're near gone. The pigeons, I mean. Why, I saw only five this year. I couldn't find the heart to shoot them."

"They shall return and in greater numbers than before. Mark me."

"No, I don't believe they will, Leah. The signs are against it." He stands and trudges down the steps. Looks about his yard. "I'd hate to leave this place, but it might come to that. I've planted crops year to year while you three went away. Watched Pa pine and strive and ever build that darned house so that you'd return. You never did."

"He came to us, in time. He was a help to us—"

"And I've dug more graves than I can count. For neighbours. For kin. You bury enough dead of a place, Leah, and it binds you more than a hundred years' worth of crops. Leaving here, why . . ." He shakes his head, swallows.

She puts her hand on his arm. "You shan't have to leave here, Davey. No. Do not do so."

David proclaims then that he must wash before dinner, that his wife is calling to him, and he must away and help her.

"You are too good."

"We don't see peddlers anymore either," he says by way of reply. "Which is as well. I ever felt pity for the wandering souls."

David takes his leave. Leah watches him cross the foreyard where Tubby girl is closing up her tin box that resembles, yes, a peddler's box. Leah's chest tightens as she thinks of Pettifew, of the awful proposition he made when she visited him those years ago, the proposition to place a body in the cellar of the Hydesville house, and thus give the old story of the peddler credibility. It is an awful plan, yes, but not impossible.

Tubby still loiters in the foreyard. She clutches her tin box now as if it were life and soul, though surely, Leah thinks, she can be convinced to part from it for the right price.

Did not David just say he was the only one who goes to the Hydesville house? And did not her father say he was determined to help his daughters, his Leah, and in any fashion? Did not he inform her that poor Brother Able was buried under a giant oak in a copse of trees near Wayne? That is close to here, Leah realizes, and less of a risk than digging up a cemetery or a church graveyard. And Able's bones would be aged enough. Pettifew gave Leah the address of a resurrection man. Leah has it still, because, Leah must admit, the idea of providing proof for all those naysayers has remained planted in her mind.

Leah recalls her father writing, and surely hinting that Able's resting spot is exactly marked with a slab of whitish stone.

I NEARLY DROPPED MY GIN FLASK. "And was this accomplished? Did the resurrection man dig up the poor boy? Is he now there in the cellar wall? With the tin box?"

"As like he'll be found by bored children one day. Bored children are worse than hobgoblins at causing mischief," Maggie Kane said by way of answer, and as if she knew this better than anyone (which she most certainly did). "You may tell-all, Alvah, once he's found. It would make a sterling story."

"Do I look a scuttle-butt? A back-fence talker? Have I ever babbled out my patient's secrets? No. I carry more secrets, to be frank, than you can imagine. I'm stuffed with them. Drunk with them. Lead-weighted with them."

"Then perhaps the divulging of secrets will be a help to you. It has surely been a help to me, as have you, dear Alvah."

"I may well be in the bone-yard myself by time poor Able is found," I grumbled.

"Now that I very much doubt."

CHAPTER 45.

On this day, Maggie Kane woke and looked at the ceiling with delight. I could not make out what she was saying (her voice was hoarse by then and she slept a great deal), and so set aside my knitting and sat on her bed and leaned close.

"I had a dream, Alvah, a real one." As I have mentioned my patient insisted her dreams were no more than tableaux, by which I mean she claimed they did not hold any narrative sense, nor meaning; nor did they give out prophecy.

I took a nip of my flask. I had another in my coat pocket. My brief attempt at controlling my imbibing had failed. To explain: the blue devils were swarming more than ever. They were clawing at me with their horrid little hands, crossing the rivers of absinthe and gin with ease, and I had decided that an ocean was needed to keep them a bay.

"Pity for you, duck. Dreams can be worse than a plague of locusts. Some are scared to sleep because of them."

She fixed on me her depthless brown eyes, at which I might have blathered recklessly at last. But I did not. I will be clear on this once more. I did not speak of August, nor tell her that I, too, had been dreaming, and it was ever the same dream. It was of me searching and searching the field of Bull Run among skeletons that were whitened by the years, animated by wind, speared through with Aaron's rod, their eye sockets sighted with daises and life-everlastings. In the dream I never found my August. That seemed scarcely fair. A dream should give some consolation.

"What of yours, then, Maggie? Your dream?"

"It is of a cemetery," she said in wonderment.

"DANDY-FINE," Maggie says after listening to Katie's cajolery for a good hour. "I'll come, but I'm only attending to make certain it really is Her Fatness in that coffin. And to make certain she's buried a good six feet down. I suppose a stake through the heart is too much to ask."

"It is," Katie says, and sniffles.

"You can't be crying. Oh, the good grief, Kat, you do recall she sent you to prison. The Tombs? I surely do. It's like I was locked up with you. And she did try to steal your children."

Katie wipes her eyes. "You make her sound so awful and mean. Like some troll or that witch with the candy house."

"Her? No, she got stuffed into an oven. That wasn't Leah's fate, was it?"

Katie reminds Maggie of the grand times the three of them had once. How she and Maggie delighted in Leah's flattery of their skills. How Leah was loyal in her way. And how, really, their lives had been extraordinary because of her.

"Well, yes."

Maggie and Katie arrive dressed in white, like all the other "cele-brants." *Life is but a transition! Happy are the dead!* They are both heavily veiled so as not to be recognized, there being a good few celebrants who consider them traitors to Spiritualism. To Leah. Not to mention to all the living, and all the dead.

They sit at a pew in the back. No other members of the family are in attendance. David wrote that they would hold their own service in Arcadia. Amy, family by association, died a year ago. And Lizzie? Lizzie is in Paris with her husband. Who knows if she even received the telegram announcing Leah's death?

Maggie peers through her veil. The other celebrants become white-shifting forms, their talk disembodied. They have become, indeed, the same old whom-evers.

"Our poor Leah," a scratch-voiced woman says. "I heard that she was terribly afflicted with melancholy this last year. And she constantly imagined hands against her. That insistence of hers that the Hydesville cellar be dug up again, I—"

"Oh, Leah roared and railed at me about that too," interrupts a woman with a singsong voice.

"Was it the peddler again?" asks a woman in a superior tone. "He is giving Lazarus a run for his money."

"Mr. Hyde wasn't having it. He's had ruckus and riot aplenty with that house," puts in Singsong.

"Besides, that cellar has already been dug to China, my dears," says Superior-Tone. "All that will turn up now are relics of Noah's flood."

As which there is chuckling—yes, chuckling at a funeral.

Maggie whispers to Katie, "Leah wanted the cellar dug up again. Why-ever?"

Katie shifts, nearly slides off the pew. "I dunno. She kept saying mayhap they missed something, those years ago. She said they didn't dig up all of the cellar or check, say, the walls. Fuss-it, did you bring a flask?"

"No, we can last, Kat. You had enough brandied coffee this morning."

Scratch-Voice says, "Our Leah was so dreadfully lonely. Daniel was so often away on business or in England for his health."

"Who the devil goes to England for their health?" asks a man, his voice overloud.

"Hush, he's in the front pew, there. He may hear you," warns Singsong.

"He did defend her against her Judas sisters, my dears," says Superior-Tone.

"Indeed, yes, at first," says Scratch-Voice. "But then our Daniel became very quiet."

"But we will surely hear a message from our Leah's spirit soon, I hope." This from a nervous-voiced woman. "Do you think her sisters might . . . ah, no, I suppose not."

"Appalling and atrocious that her sisters haven't come," puts in Singsong.

"Dreadful creatures, indeed, yes," Scratch-Voice says. "And gone to seed. Entirely."

"Did you expect her dashed sisters to come today, ladies?" Overloud Man asks. "After what they did? Their baseless accusations. The deuced musical hall travesty?"

"Leah became such a recluse, didn't she?" Nervous-Voice asks. "Is it true she never received callers? But it's not as if she was being snubbed. I myself was often rather too busy—"

"As was I!" Singsong cries. "I had my own family affairs and business, you see, and—"

"That terrible housekeeper of hers," says Scratch-Voice. "She was the only one our Leah could find who would stay. Apparently her horrid sisters' scandalous accusations are known by the even servant classes."

"Servants are privy to more mysteries than even the finest of mediums, my dears," offers Superior-Tone.

More chuckling.

"Indeed, yes," Scratch-Voice continues. "But it was that horrible housekeeper who broke our Leah's French toile vase and then had the audacity to declare it a fake anywise. Well, you know how Leah was about her things. It put her into such a dreadful rage that she fell instantly to the carpet and—"

"I heard there was no lingering," Nervous-Voice says.

"No. Not a minute, my dears, all reports agree," Superior-Tone says.

"Such a shame and pity," Singsong agrees

"Indeed, yes, a terrible shame," puts in Scratch-Voice. "No beloved family crowding round to hear her last words or watch her last breath escape. Just that terrible housekeeper. How dreadfully terrible to die so unawares."

"Mr. Underhill was there."

"I heard the contrary. That he was out, as always."

"At least our Leah is in joyous Spirit Land now," Scratch-Voice says. "Indeed, I have no doubt whatsoever that our Leah will be extremely joyful now that she is a spirit herself."

"Yes, my dears, and with, you know, all those other spirits for company."

But will those other spirits be joyful and at peace in *her* company? Maggie wonders, and nearly smiles.

After the reverend speaks about Leah's selfless life, her dedication to her husband and family, the injustices heaped upon her, after a long variety of Leah's favourite music is played and sung, the celebrants are left to mill before the funeral procession. Maggie and Katie help themselves to the punch, discreetly lifting their veils.

The cortège draws perplexed onlookers the entire way to the cemetery. But then, what sort of funeral attendees are white-dressed and sing joyful hymns and toss flower petals, as if at a wedding or a May festival? By the time the cortège reaches Brooklyn's Greenwood Cemetery on this cold November day of 1890, Katie is so tired and overcome that she collapses on the broad ivory and cream painted coffin just before it is lowered into the grave. The celebrants murmur in outrage. Who is this disrespectful woman? And who is her companion?

"Forget all them," Maggie whispers to Katie, and gently pulls her off the coffin. "Shush," she adds, because Katie is weeping loudly behind her veil. An odd, hupping sound that could be mistaken for laughter.

CHAPTER 46.

I arrived early on this day. It seemed best I come before my desire for drink overwhelmed my sense of duty. The sun patterned the ceiling, making near-pretty the mottlings there. August's birthday was on the morrow and I had not yet completed the coverall.

"Alvah, I've had the same dream again. Of the same cemetery." My patient tried to sit up, anxious for the telling of it.

"The cemetery where you planted Leah?" I asked, and brought out the medicine and some blancmange. I had little hope she would eat, however; she had scarcely eaten the last week.

"No, no, put that away. Listen, before it vanishes. I am in a war cemetery, not just any, but a military asylum one, the Washington one."

She told her dream in fits and starts while I knitted fast as I could:

She is awander among those endless rows, looking in vain at those identical knee-high lozenges of white marble. But for what? *Unknown. Unknown.* All are a blank. A cipher. And these headstones, they are undulating in their regiment order, and then not undulating, but wading through the grave dirt and over groomed lawns, down declivities, around stands of trees, as if living things intent on some destination. My patient is not troubled by this, nor by the certainty that she is lost. Then in the distance she sees the high, iron gates. That is where I must go, she thinks, and she runs and runs with her skirts held high, and she feels very young, as young as that day with her sister Katie, in the orchard, before they met the peddler. Then, just before the iron gates, she stumbles and falls prone atop a grave. It had been moving like the others, as if to catch up with her. Now everything stops. The sky is the boy-blue of her Elisha's eyes and it is as unreachable, but the grass is soft, the ground surprisingly warm. She lies there, catching her breath. The headstone is blank as all the rest. *Unknown. Unknown.*

"It is the third in from the gate, in the tenth row of that sector. I have had this same dream three times, and each time, Alvah, it is the same headstone."

I set down my knitting and drank a nip, then spooned up some blancmange. "You must eat."

By way of answer she asked for the lily box. I gave it to her. She didn't open it. "Do not forget that this box, and all within, is yours to keep when I pass."

"Eat, you must," I repeated.

"You know that is not practical, Alvah," she said, and with a ghost of her former smile. "You must know that I am done with all that."

ON AN AFTERNOON nearly two years after Leah's funeral, Maggie and Katie walk down 45th Street. Katie's thin shoes are covered with mud and straw. She has lost her coat somewhere. And her hat. She leans heavily on Maggie. They were being stared at. Not that they gave a damn fig. They've been stared at nearly all their lives.

"Come and live with me," Maggie says. "You and the boys."

"Ah, no, Mag. You've reformed. Rah and fiddle-dee-dah!"

This is true. Maggie doesn't go on sprees any longer. Doesn't touch brandy or gin or wine. Instead she drinks her poppy tea and with careful rationing. Keeps her head and thus her few clients, the ones who have low expectations. Because she has returned to rapping, there really being no other way for her to feed herself. They come to her at her apartment, one client at a time. She cannot charge much, granted, not after her labelling her own profession a fraud, but she earns enough money to keep herself from the streets. She always hands the clients her card first.

MARGARET FOX KANE. *Medium.*

I claim not supernatural powers.
My clients can decide for themselves.

The Spiritualist Society, of course, shuns and derides Maggie. They call her a liar for her confessions. An addled sot because of her drinking. They proclaim her words cannot be trusted, not one syllable. Maggie doesn't care. She would no more knock on the door of the Spiritualist Society than on the Gates of Hell.

"You must, Kat. We can be together. We should be together. And I'm not so reformed. I still, well, I don't so much indulge in brandy and such, but I've a lovely tea you must try. Dr. Wadsworth in England gave me the recipe. I do miss the man. But people come and go, excepting me and thee." She smiles. "Do come to my apartment and try it. The tea makes the days pass in coloured dreamy whorl."

Katie halts. Takes both of Maggie's hands. Sways as if wanting a childish game of ring-around-the-rosie. "No, no, no. I'll only drag you into the down and down. You'll take on my habits, and not my nun-like habits, hah! You'll haunt my taverns. Haunts. Hah! As if I'm one of our ghosts. Perhaps I am. Now, don't be a worry-all. You'll always find me, Mag. And I you. Really."

When the knock on Maggie's apartment door comes a day later, she opens it expecting Katie. Her relief and joy are short-lived, however. It is not Katie. It is Daniel Underhill. His kindly eyes are hooded and weary. His cravat badly tied. Pleasantries over, he informs her that Leah's will has finally been sorted.

"She had many assets in her name. And, well, there was complicated accounting in returning those assets to my holdings. But I suppose that you, and Katie, yes, you two, of all people, would know of complicated wills and bequeathments."

"Alas and such, we know very well."

Daniel tries for a smile, but manages something more like a

grimace. "Leah stipulated that you be given this. Discover what you will." He hands her Leah's bible box. "I number myself among the fortunate," he adds enigmatically as he lets himself out.

Maggie places the bible box on the table. Runs her hands over the lilies of the field, the wasp nestled there.

She opens it to find, as she expected, a wealth of letters. From Katie. From her own self. From her mother. From Calvin. From this society and that. From Leah. There are also newspaper clippings galore telling of the Fox sisters' triumphs and tribulations through the years. And a great many reporting on the doings of Chauncey Burr.

"Chauncey, old Chauncey," she murmurs, and takes up the pages that look torn from a journal. A note is pinned to these pages that reads: *You're asking for my damnedo thoughts? Mrs. Foxy Fish Underthehill? Here they are torn out and just for you. A last warning: Don't waste your beloved time on this earth, Leah, I thought that when we met that last time. We are dust-motes in the eye of oblivion.*

Maggie smiles, puts Chauncey aside.

Discover what you will, Daniel had said. Maggie inspects under the strangely thick lid. She taps the inset rectangle that is of a fainter shade. It was obviously added later. Maggie recalls Leah's phosphorous test and runs her hands over the lilies atop the lid. The secret under-compartment reveals itself after some attempts. Inside are a wad of papers. The familiar writing covers both sides, is dense and crabbed but of easy decipherment. Well, Pa, Maggie thinks. Here you are.

She reads of John Fox abandoning his family in Rockland County because of his wife's magic spell. Of him labouring on "Clinton's Big Ditch." Now he is meeting Erastus Bearcup and the crew of the *Morning Star*. Now the pitched battle with the crew of the *Sweet Eleanor G* that left the *Morning Star* men victorious and famed. Now the twin onslaught of Temperance and the Great Awakening and the canallers' temporary victories against it.

Maggie reads even more intently. Brother Able arrives at the weigh-lock in Syracuse and makes a sorry attempt at converting the crew. One by one, John's crewmates fall to the Evangelicals. John stands firm. Ambrose leaves to be again with the Indians. Brother

Able finds John aboard the mud-larked *Morning Star*. Now comes the young man's unfortunate, accidental death by alcohol, and then his return, worm-infested from the grave, his demand that John abstain, that John convert, that John embrace love both mortal and divine and return to his family and be their protector.

Maggie chuckles. Only when she finishes reading her father's account does she notice Leah's bequeathment letter to her and Katie.

Dear Margaretta and Katherina,

One of you asked, years past, if I "just once will say what is really happening." I am mystified as to why such things are of import, but I will tell you this, my dear sisters—Pettifew, the source of all our contrivances, was the selfsame peddler you encountered on the public road by the orchard when you were younger girls. That is my honest belief. Are you solaced to know you did not kill the man, but created a conspirator to our career? He is dead now, of course. He died just before your Music Hall exposé. He was found surrounded by his wares, and a great many bottles. He had been given to ranting, my source in the NOS told me, and he was very much alone.

I admit that I am sorry we three have fallen out and that we are no longer linked as we were. But I have made it right. Pettifew knew the whereabouts of a resurrection man. I knew the whereabouts of likely bones. And if you read the account Pa sent me of his ten years gone (I have no doubt you will find its hiding place) you will know that they must be Brother Able's. Do not worry, Pa would approve. Indeed, it is fitting, yes, because Pa did so want to help me, and his other loved ones, in the end.

Now, what you two girls must put about, as I have been doing, is that the cellar in the Hydesville house must be dug up again. The cellar walls in particular should be investigated. And then we will be vindicated, the Fox sisters three.

Yours till death and after,
Leah

Maggie chuckles. She spends the rest of the afternoon searching for Katie. They will laugh like they haven't in years. The dead, why they return after all. Maggie is not thinking of Able—sitting in the *Morning Star*, worm infested and wrapped in a horsehair blanket shroud. He was formed, as like, out of her father's delirium tremens. No, it is the peddler—Pettifew—that she is thinking on now. He died just before the Music Hall exposé, Leah wrote. But surely she and Katie saw his apparition outside the music hall when they made their way through the heckling crowd. The apparition had that selfsame twisted mouth. He was small and had a limping gait, steadied by a cane that was topped with a hound's head of gold. And he demanded that they apologize, and in the selfsame voice of outrage as he used when Maggie and Katie encountered him by the Hydesville orchard when they were foolish girls. And they did apologize. Better late than never, as they say, and now the wandering soul is all at rest.

Evening draws on, the streets are aglow from the gas lights and electric lamps, and Maggie still hasn't found Katie, not in any of her cocktail taverns. Maggie even ducks into a Turkish smoke parlour or two. She is not worried. Katie always surfaces eventually. She still has her boys to consider, even if they are grown. She still has Maggie. "You'll always find me" was what Katie said.

But now it is two days later, and still no Katie.

"Ma came home last night, then left again this morning," Ferdie says.

Henry adds, "She seemed swell. She said that if we saw you we should tell you not to be a worry-all."

"But I have such news. It's about our pa. And Pettifew. And Leah. Oh, the good grief, I dearly miss Leah."

"Who's Pettifew?" Ferdie asks.

"And what news could matter so much?" Henry asks, but Maggie is already on her way out to search once again.

Katie has been gone now for over a week. Ferdie reports first that she is in Rochester again, then that she is staying with some wealthy Manhattan benefactor.

"I didn't get the details," Ferdie says. "But she'll find her way back. She always does."

A day on and Maggie opens the door to find, not her final client of the day but Ferdie, twisting his hat in his hands as if to strangle it. She does not ask him. She dares not ask him. Asks instead, "How's your brother? How's the weather? Damn, I'm expecting a client. No time to chat. I need all the clients I can get these days. They only pay half of what they once did. Half the price for half the belief in it all. Alas and such, it serves me right after all that silly recanting and the recanting of the recanting."

Ferdie cuts in bluntly. Gives the news: His mother, her Katie, is dead. "I found her in a rented garret. It was nearly empty of furniture. But it was clean," he adds, as if this might ease the telling.

Ah, the wild freedom of being staggering drunk. How Maggie welcomes it after the river-calm of poppy tea. For days she wanders through Katie's haunts, as if to inhabit her last weeks. The few clients she sees soon leave in disgust at her rambling, senseless prophecies. Her limbs have a puffed aspect. Her skin aches at any pressure. Her eyes when she dares the looking glass are tinged with yellow.

By January of '93, Maggie knows what she needs to do. She looks through her cherished possessions—Elisha's white gifts, her books. She reads through Leah's memoir. She kept the copy Leah sent her years ago, but she has never read it—out of stubbornness, she supposes. She reads it now. She laughs and laughs. The events are so enlarged, the forces against the Fox sisters three so easily swatted down, like flies on a sill. It is amusing and sly, not infuriating at all.

She does not consider taking her own books—*The Death-Blow to Spiritualism* and *The Love Life of Dr. Kane*. They are too much her own voice. Katie published nothing, nothing. She cannot be found in books. Still. *You'll always find me* was what she said, and so Maggie must go to her, that much is clear.

Elisha's *Arctic Explorations*, then, is the sole book she takes, because love cannot be shed as easily as mortal flesh. She searches out a garret that is in accordance with Ferdie's description of Katie's last retreat, excepting Maggie's is even higher up, even farther from it all, bare but for a bed and table and that ladderback chair. She pays for two months' rent with her last dollars. She intends to be alone when she dies, just as Katie was.

"But the very next day you arrived, Alvah," my patient said, "and stood there so mysteriously, so insistently in the vestibule, and all haloed by the waning, crackling light of the Edison bulb."

CHAPTER 47

To finish: I did not cry in front of my patients. It was a professional rule. And I wasn't crying. I was merely sniffling hard between swigs from my flask. I had finally finished the cover-all, and it sat bunched in my lap.

"It's his birthday today. It is March fifth," Maggie Kane declared, the way one does a simple truth. Her hands were folded atop the bedclothes. As I have said, she was incapable of cracking a toe joint or anything else by that time.

"Birthday? Whose birthday? What are you—"

"Your son's."

"I've never spoken to you of a son. Nor to anyone. Never!"

But she was not listening, not to me anywise. No. She had the intent look of one straining to hear a far-off tune. She said, "The loss of August is ever with you."

"His name! How did you know it? What trick are you playing now?" I was peeved. No. Outraged. We were both sinners and grievously faulted sorts, from the same kettle of fish as it were, and I hated, to be frank, that she was practising her art on me. I stood up from my little stool. I shouted I didn't believe it. I shouted that she had told me how it was done. It was all a fraud.

I hauled the bedclothes off and pointed to her feet, at which there came a bang so strong the windows shook. It was nothing like the taps she had exhibited for me previously. And she had not moved a joint.

Next came a pat-pattering of raps, alike running steps.

"It's your August. Speak with him. He cannot stay long."

The garret fell very quiet, very still. The far-down din of the streets, the shouts of children, the cries of hawkers, the arguing of the other tenement dwellers. All ceased. The room was empty but for us. And yet. And yet.

"August?" I was rubbery with fear. Breath-stilled with hope. The thuds sounded back straightaway.

I told him how I missed him. I told him I was so very sorry that I did not give him my blessing, sorry that I did not hold vigil nor hear his last words, the words of his true self that would set him right afore the Redeemer. At which there came three loud raps on the side table. I remind you that Maggie Fox Kane had not moved the whole time. Not her feet. Not her hands. Nothing.

She said, "Fetch a paper and pen."

I rummaged frantically in my apron pockets and then my satchel. I couldn't find my little notebook, however, only bottles.

"Never mind, Alvah. Here," Maggie Kane said, and ripped out a picture plate from *Arctic Explorations*. Just like that. As if Elisha's book mattered nothing to her anymore. I have kept the plate, of course. It shows a barren Arctic place called Sanderson's Hope (though I have never discovered who Sanderson was and what hope he found in that dread place).

She wrote rapidly on the plate's blank side. She did not look down as she wrote, but at the garret's three linked windows. When she was done I saw that the script was unintelligible, like a foreigner's script and language.

"What is this? Do I look a linguist? A professor of heathen tongues? Am I—"

"Hush. It's merely backwards. You have a mirror?"

I did. I had my pocket mirror for the gauging of life and breath. I held this mirror to the paper, then nearly dropped them both in astonishment. August's handwriting was in the reflection. The hand was looping and would have seemed careless if it had not run in a straight and purposed line. His writing. Surely so. I would have known it anywhere.

Dearest mother. I was charging the Rebs at Bull Run when a musket-ball stopped me up. Please don't blame poor old Horace Greeley for the debacle at Bull Run. He had no cruel intent and he suffered much for encouraging it. The Quakers at the Washington Hospital were kind. Truly, they're a kind lot. I gave my Last Words to one of them, a lady who looked akin to you. I told her that I was glad to meet my Redeemer. That I was glad to die for the Cause. But glad, too, that I escaped having to kill a fellow man. I told her that I never meant to go off without your blessing.

I know you had some hard years after I vanished. But I don't judge you a whit for losing your sorrow in the remedies of the living. Nor for what you did to Pa. You didn't kill him, by the way, though he's dead just the same. And you should know that we're not judged Above the same way as in the Mortal Sphere. Our hearts are what matters. And yours is the truest and kindest heart a son could want. Yet I beg you: Don't drink spirits any longer. Life should be used for good purpose. And whatever time we have on this blessed earth, why it should be cherished.

The Quakers burned my clothes and identifying papers by mistake because the typhoid was raging. And so I was buried as an Unknown Soldier in Washington's Military Asylum Cemetery. My stone is in the tenth sector, the third from the gate.

> With everlasting love.
> Your son, August

"Your dream! You dreamed of his resting place. The selfsame cemetery," I said, but Maggie Kane was asleep, her breathing very shallow, and I feared then what I had accepted from the very start of our acquaintance.

The succour from this letter was such that, as my August asked, I have not drank spirits since. As for Margaret Fox Kane, she passed to the Glory three days later. She rambled a great deal in her last hours: about Katie, about blue skies and gold warmth, about high-up trees. "But I can see the world from here!" she exclaimed at one point, by which I suppose she meant the Other World.

As I reported in that brief statement eleven years ago, my patient could move neither hand nor foot by this time, and there was no wardrobe, no place to hide, no gadgetry at all. And yet the knocks came again as she departed. This time on the wall, on the ceiling and on the floor. It was as if a hundred joyous spirits had come to meet her. You simply wouldn't believe it.

Alvah June Mellon
December 1904

To tell the story of the Fox Family and the beginnings of the Spiritualist movement I have followed as closely as possible the events as they are known. However, this is a work of fiction and I have freely invented scenes, dialogue, and motivations, and have filled in the blanks in the historical record: namely, whose remains were those found in the cellar of the Hydesville house in 1904, years after all the protagonists were dead? Did the peddler exist at all or was he a pure fabrication of Maggie and Katie? Where did John Fox disappear to for ten years, and what happened during that time to change him from a hard-drinking "sporting" man into a devout believer? And why was this reverend Chauncey Burr so determined to expose the sisters? Lastly, was Mrs. Mellon telling the truth when she declared in her 1893 statement that she heard spirit knockings at Maggie's death? These are the provocative mysteries that provided much of the inspiration for *The Dark*.

For source material I am particularly indebted to the following: *Talking to the Dead: Katie and Maggie Fox and the Rise of Spiritualism* by Barbara Weisberg; *The Reluctant Spiritualist: The Life of Maggie Fox* by Nancy Rubin Stuart; *Exploring Other Worlds: Margaret Fox Kane, Elisha Kent Kane and the Antebellum Cult of Curiousity* by David Chapman; *The Spirit Rappers* by Herbert Jackson; *Time is Kind: The Story of the Unfortunate Fox Family* by Miriam Buckner Pond; *The Epic of New York* by Edward Robb Ellis; and *A Shopkeeper's*

Millennium: Society and Revivals in Rochester, New York, 1825-1837 by Paul E. Johnson.

It should be noted that I have worked into my story many direct quotes taken from memoirs and letters of the protagonists, as well as quotes from newspapers and periodicals of the time. These sources include: *The Love Life of Doctor Kane* by Margaret Fox Kane; *The Missing Link in Modern Spiritualism* by A. Leah Underhill, Revised and Arranged by a Literary Friend; *The Death Blow to Spiritualism* by Rueben Briggs Davenport; *Godfrey's Narrative of the Last Grinnell Arctic Exploring Expedition in Search of Sir John Franklin* by William C. Godfrey; and *Arctic Explorations: The Second Grinnell Expedition in Search of Sir John Franklin 1853, 54, 55* by Elisha Kent Kane.

ACKNOWLEDGEMENTS

I am indebted and endlessly grateful to my agent, Sally Harding, for having faith in me and my work, and to my editor Lynn Henry of Doubleday Canada for her hard work, vision, and insight. I am also grateful to the indefatigable Doubleday Canada team. As well, I give my heartfelt thanks to my first readers Catherine Howe, Alix Noble, Susan Mongar, and Mary-Lou Bertucci for their helpful comments and encouragements, and to Gabriella Heald for her inspired portrait shots.